The SPIRIT

VOLUME -1-

JUNE 2 to DECEMBER 29, 1940

Denny Colt, a young criminologist, believed to have lost his life in a fight against crime, was buried in a state of suspended animation.

He awoke one day in Wildwood Cemetery to carry on his struggle...his true identity known only to Police Commissioner Dolan.

He is feared by criminals of all stripes as the SPIRIT!

DC COMICS

New York, New York

WILL EISNER'S

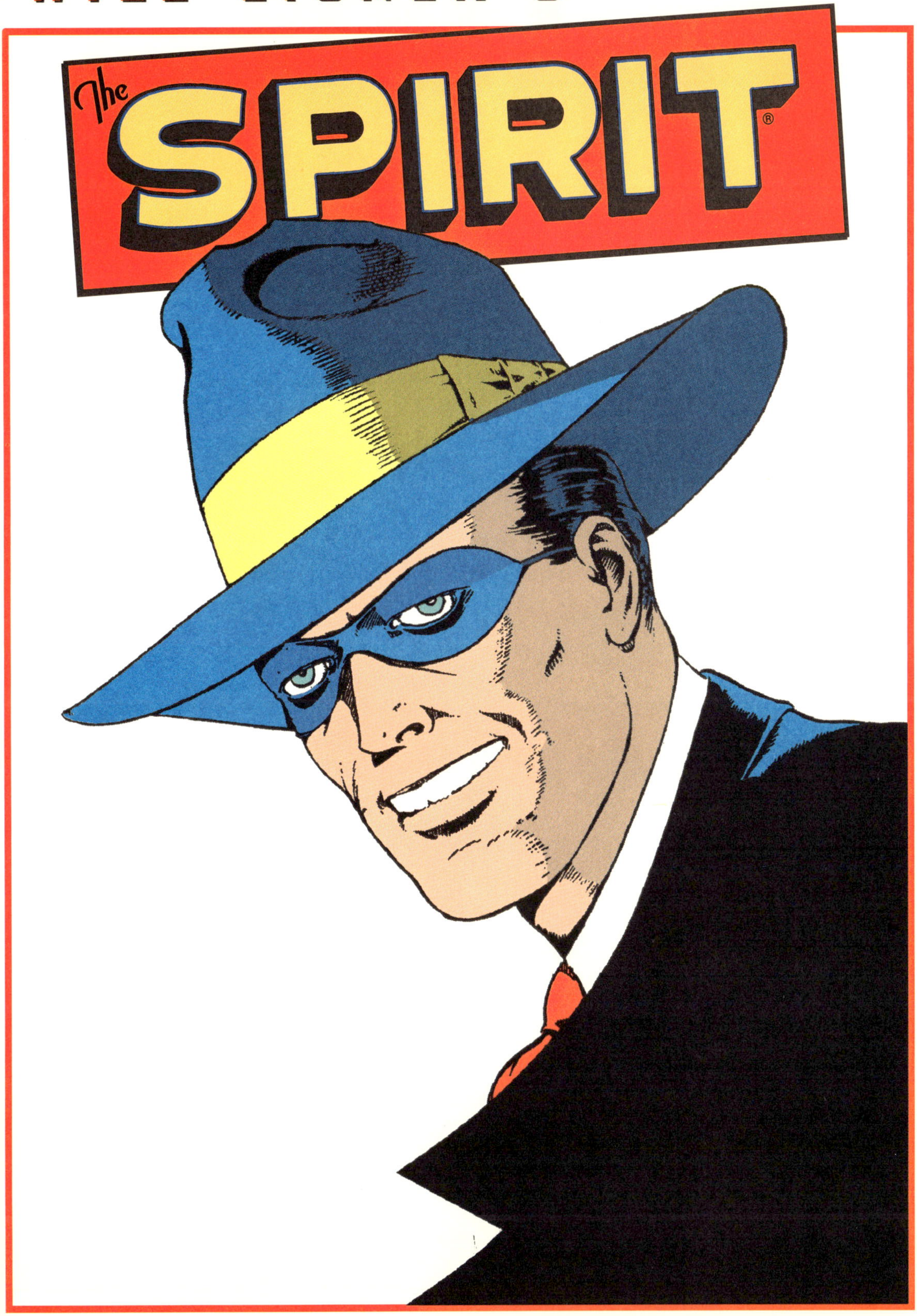
The SPIRIT®

ARCHIVES

DC COMICS

JENETTE KAHN
President & Editor-in-Chief

PAUL LEVITZ
Executive Vice President & Publisher

DALE CRAIN
Editor

MICHAEL WRIGHT
Assistant Editor

GEORG BREWER
Design Director

AMIE BROCKWAY
Art Director

RICHARD BRUNING
VP-Creative Director

PATRICK CALDON
VP-Finance & Operations

DOROTHY CROUCH
VP-Licensed Publishing

TERRI CUNNINGHAM
VP-Managing Editor

JOEL EHRLICH
Senior VP-Advertising & Promotions

ALISON GILL
Exec. Director-Manufacturing

LILLIAN LASERSON
VP & General Counsel

JIM LEE
Editorial Director-WildStorm

JOHN NEE
VP & General Manager-WildStorm

BOB WAYNE
VP-Direct Sales

Cover illustration by
WILL EISNER

Cover color by
DIGITAL CHAMELEON

Art and color reconstruction by
DIGITAL CHAMELEON

Special thanks to
BILL BLACKBEARD
Director of the San Francisco Academy of Comic Art for loan of source material.

Throughout the run of The Spirit, Will Eisner was assisted by several talented individuals, among them John Belfi, Phillip (Tex) Blaisdell, Chris Christiansen, Jack Cole, Martin DeMuth, Jim Dixon, Jules Feiffer, Dick French, Lou Fine, Jerry Grandenetti, Abe Kaenegson, Jack Keller, Robin King, Alex Kotzky, Joe Kubert, Andre LeBlanc, Marilyn Mercer, Klaus Nordling, Ben Oda, Bob Palmer, Don Perlin, Bob Powell, Sam Rosen, Aldo Rubano, Sam Schwartz, John Spranger, Manny Stallman, Manley Wade Wellman, Al Wenzel, Wallace Wood, and Bill Woolfolk. The Author and Publisher wish to thank them for their vital contributions.

WILL EISNER'S THE SPIRIT ARCHIVES VOLUME 1.
Published by DC Comics. Cover, foreword and compilation copyright © 2000 Will Eisner. Introduction copyright © 2000 DC Comics. All Rights Reserved. Originally published as individual weekly comic sections, Copyright 1940. All Rights Reserved.

The SPIRIT, images of Denny Colt, Commissioner Dolan and Ebony are registered trademarks owned by Will Eisner. The stories, characters, and incidents featured in this publication are entirely fictional.

DC Comics, 1700 Broadway, New York, NY 10019. A division of Warner Bros. - A Time Warner Entertainment Company.

Printed and bound in Canada.

ISBN 1-56389-673-7. First Printing.

WILL EISNER'S THE SPIRIT ARCHIVES

volume one

PREFACE *by Will Eisner*.................................... **7**
   The Spirit: How It Came To Be

FOREWORD *by Alan Moore*............................... **11**
   The Pioneering Spirit

INTRODUCTION *by R.C. Harvey*........................ **14**
   The Consummate Comic Book

Strip #	Title	Page Number
1	**THE ORIGIN OF THE SPIRIT**	**21**
	Original publication date: June 2 1940	
2	**THE RETURN OF DR. COBRA**	**28**
	Original publication date: June 9 1940	
3	**THE BLACK QUEEN**	**35**
	Original publication date: June 16 1940	
4	**VOODOO IN MANHATTAN**	**42**
	Original publication date: June 23 1940	
5	**JOHNNY MARSTON**	**49**
	Original publication date: June 30 1940	
6	**THE BLACK QUEEN'S ARMY**	**56**
	Original publication date: July 7 1940	
7	**MR. MIDNIGHT**	**63**
	Original publication date: July 14 1940	
8	**ELDAS THAYER**	**70**
	Original publication date: July 21 1940	
9	**PALYACHI, THE KILLER CLOWN**	**77**
	Original publication date: July 28 1940	
10	**THE DEATH DOLLS**	**84**
	Original publication date: August 4 1940	
11	**THE KIDNAPPING OF DAISY KAY**	**91**
	Original publication date: August 11 1940	
12	**THE MORGER BOYS**	**98**
	Original publication date: August 18 1940	
13	**THE ORPHANS**	**105**
	Original publication date: August 25 1940	
14	**ORANG, THE APE MAN**	**112**
	Original publication date: September 1 1940	
15	**THE RETURN OF ORANG, THE APE THAT IS HUMAN!**	**119**
	Original publication date: September 8 1940	

Strip #	Title	Page Number
16	**EBONY'S X-RAY EYES**	**126**
	Original publication date: September 15 1940	
17	**GANG WARFARE**	**133**
	Original publication date: September 22 1940	
18	**ORIENTAL AGENTS**	**140**
	Original publication date: September 28 1940	
19	**THE MASTERMIND STRIKES!**	**147**
	Original publication date: October 6 1940	
20	**THE SPIRIT! WHO IS HE?**	**154**
	Original publication date: October 13 1940	
21	**OGRE GORAN**	**161**
	Original publication date: October 20 1940	
22	**CONSCRIPTION BILL SIGNED**	**168**
	Original publication date: October 27 1940	
23	**THE MANLY ART OF SELF DEFENSE**	**175**
	Original publication date: November 3 1940	
24	**THE KISS OF DEATH**	**182**
	Original publication date: November 10 1940	
25	**DR. PRINCE VON KALM**	**189**
	Original publication date: November 17 1940	
26	**THE KIDNAPPING OF EBONY**	**196**
	Original publication date: November 24 1940	
27	**THE PROM**	**203**
	Original publication date: December 1 1940	
28	**THE HAUNTED HOUSE**	**210**
	Original publication date: December 8 1940	
29	**SLIM PICKENS**	**217**
	Original publication date: December 15 1940	
30	**THE CHRISTMAS SPIRIT OF 1940: BLACK HENREY AND SIMPLE SIMON**	**224**
	Original publication date: December 22 1940	
31	**THE LEADER**	**231**
	Original publication date: December 29 1940	

THE SPIRIT: HOW IT CAME TO BE

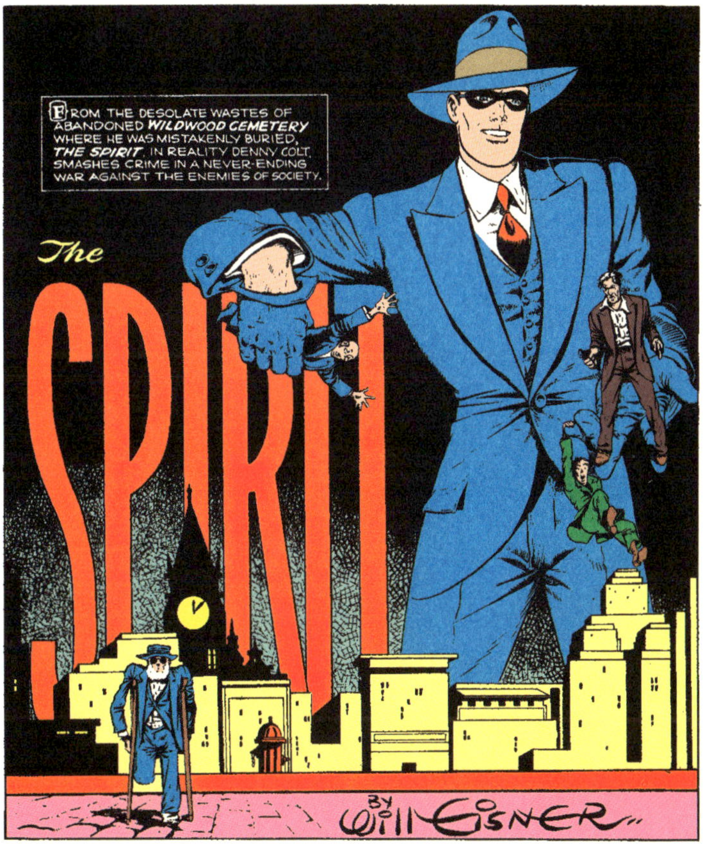
FROM THE DESOLATE WASTES OF ABANDONED WILDWOOD CEMETERY WHERE HE WAS MISTAKENLY BURIED, THE SPIRIT, IN REALITY DENNY COLT, SMASHES CRIME IN A NEVER-ENDING WAR AGAINST THE ENEMIES OF SOCIETY.
The SPIRIT
By Will Eisner

"THE SILK DISTRICT BEAT," 1/12/41.

Sometime in the early fall of 1939 I got a call from Busy Arnold, the owner of QUALITY COMICS. I was at Eisner & Iger, a company that had done some business with him before. I assumed it was his comics magazines he wanted to talk about.

"No" he said. What he had in mind had nothing to with what Eisner & Iger were producing. He wanted to talk to me personally and would I have lunch with him and a man named Henry Martin. The following day I met with them and was surprised by their proposition. They wanted me to personally create the contents of a 16-page "comic magazine" to be nationally syndicated and inserted in Sunday editions of major newspapers—something that had never been done before.

Apparently the Register & Tribune Syndicate of which Martin was Sales Manager had become aware of a growing concern by their client papers over the competition by comic books for their younger readers. Their offer was simple: I would create, write, design and produce the product weekly. They offered a standard syndicate contract which I refused. Instead, I negotiated a partnership agreement which would enable me to own the characters I created. As a compromise the copyright would be in Arnold's name, but when our relationship terminated the property and the ownership of all rights would return to me. I thought at the time that my strength in these negotiations stemmed from their respect for my artistic and creative ability; later I found out that it was really my reputation as a reliable producer that was more important to them. A newspaper feature had to be delivered on time without fail.

I was now faced with a serious choice. I would have to leave Eisner & Iger, which was a successful and profitable production shop creating comic books for various publishers. There was a war coming on, I was 22 years old, and draftable. Besides, the syndicate business was speculative as was the possible fate of any features I created. Even my partner, Jerry Iger, who stood to acquire my half of the company, cautioned me of the risk.

But for me it was an opportunity I had been waiting for. By 1939 I had long been convinced that I was involved with a medium that had real "literary potential." I had decided to spend my life at this, but I was trapped in what to me was a comic-book ghetto where I would be turning out the same sort of formula adventure stories for the same level of reader indefinitely. Newspaper syndication would give me an adult audience and the opportunity to write and draw more sophisticated material. I would be able to realize my long-contained ambition to expand this medium beyond the existing parameters. For a long time I had been sure

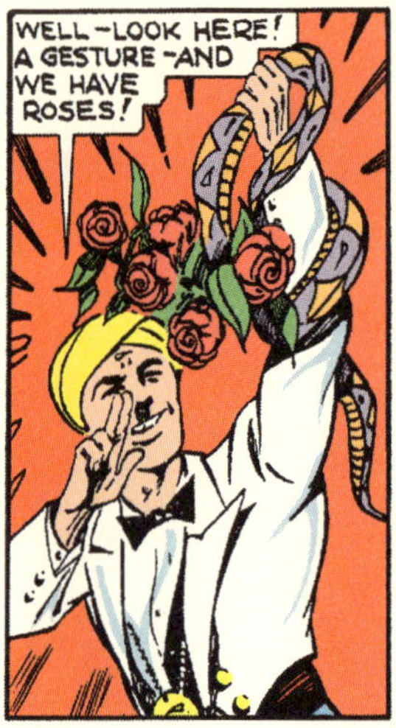
WELL—LOOK HERE! A GESTURE—AND WE HAVE ROSES!

MR. MYSTIC BY BOB POWELL.

that the medium was capable of greater content than had ever been done. Furthermore, under this deal I had enormous creative freedom because no one had attempted anything like this before.

It was worth the gamble.

I sold my shares to Jerry Iger and went right to work. I decided on three features to fill the sixteen-page (later eight-page) section. A detective feature, a costumed heroine and a magician story. The city detective would be the Spirit story, which was seven pages for the first 32 weeks (his real name would be Denny Colt), the costumed girl (Lady Luck) would be four pages and the magician (Mr. Mystic) would be five pages. The design for those was easy and quickly agreed upon. Chuck Mazoujian agreed to do Lady Luck, and Bob Powell would work on Mr. Mystic.

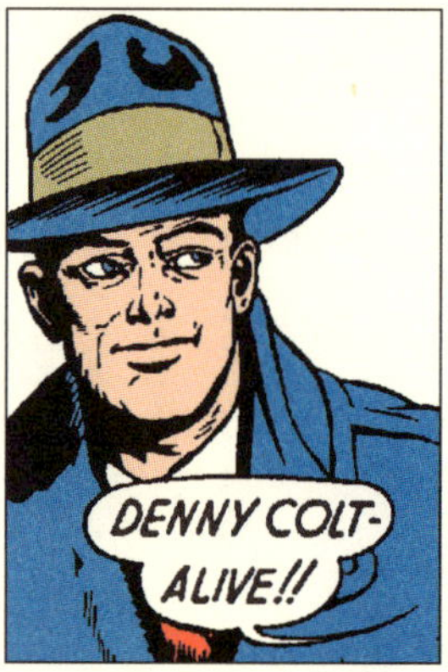
DENNY COLT-ALIVE!!

THE SPIRIT'S FIRST APPEARANCE, SANS MASK. (6/9/40).

LADY LUCK BY CHUCK MAZOUJIAN.

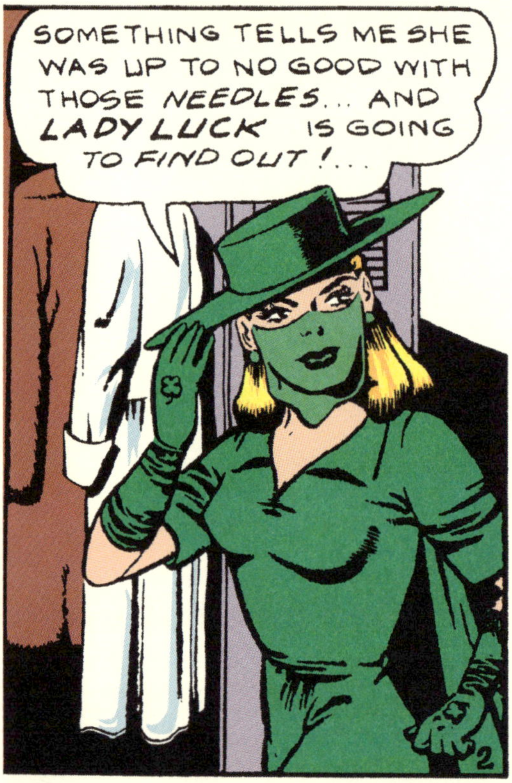
SOMETHING TELLS ME SHE WAS UP TO NO GOOD WITH THOSE NEEDLES... AND LADY LUCK IS GOING TO FIND OUT!...

I would undertake the main story and I began to work on it. It would be built around a crimefighter who had no official affiliation with the police department. He needed to be a free-lance hero because my interest was in producing stories that were not encased by the characteristics of the hero.

The story would be dominant. This needed a hero who was vulnerable and believable. Late one night (it was raining) I got a call from Busy Arnold. I could hear that he was calling from a bar somewhere. He asked me how I was doing. Had I decided on the lead character, for we were getting close to production time? I was working on it at the drawing board as we talked. I described the hero to him as stalwart, clean-cut, intelligent and very athletic. "Does he have a costume?" asked Arnold. "Every comic-book hero, today, has a costume...must have a costume or we can't sell it." I stalled, I drew a mask on him and said: "Yes, Busy, he has a mask and gloves and a blue suit." (Actually, I tried to postpone the costume requirement as long as I could — the Spirit had no mask until the second week, June 9, 1940) Arnold responded with enthusiasm. "Great, go with that," he shouted. I named him Denny Colt, but Arnold insisted on a more heroic name so I called him THE SPIRIT. It was an easy compromise because it left me free to pursue the stories I wanted to write. In January of 1940 I opened a studio in Tudor City where Lou Fine, Bob Powell, and Chuck Mazoujian joined me. The first Spirit story appeared on June 2, 1940 in five Sunday newspapers (it grew to 20 papers nationally at its peak).

Writing and drawing the Spirit on a weekly schedule turned out to be more formidable than I had expected. The delivery deadline was implacable. The standard of quality was more demanding than those of the comic-book market. Producing the kind of story and art to which I was now committed left little room for the kind of compromise or fakery one could get away with in comic magazines. The work load was enormous, but it was a happy time in

WILL EISNER, NICK VISCARDI, AND BOB POWELL IN THE TUDOR CITY STUDIO, 1941.

my career. I was free at last to innovate, experiment and address themes that I never would be able to do in comic books. I was at last writing for grownups.

I had now the chance to draw upon the examples of the men who had influenced me, Milt Caniff and George Herriman. I was also employing what I had learned from years of short story and pulp magazine reading. I could lean on the work of O. Henry, Saki, Ring Lardner and their like. Since no one at the syndicate had any experience with comic books or the use of a complete short story in comics, I was left alone. No one tried to exercise any real editorial control over what I did. Besides, the reader response was good. The Philadelphia Record, a pilot subscriber, reported a 10% increase in circulation when THE SPIRIT section appeared in their Sunday edition.

As fictional characters usually do, THE SPIRIT quickly matured. He was developing a sense of humor. Also, because he was involved in a new story each week, he could appear in (and react) to many more and different situations than if he were in a daily strip. That proved to be true when we attempted a SPIRIT daily strip between 1941 and 1944. It was never as successful as the weekly story. But, above all, he was mortal. That made plotting for him unlimited.

In 1942 I was drafted into the Army.

By then THE SPIRIT had almost tripled its list of subscribers and there was no question about its continuation. While I was in the Army Lou Fine agreed to do the art, and writers like Manley Wade Wellman, Dick French, and a few others wrote scripts. Jack Cole also did some stories. Since I was stationed in Washington, D.C., I could monitor the feature.

In 1945 after my discharge I returned to the Spirit. By then I had matured. I now saw the Spirit as an anti-hero. He was, in my eyes, someone who did not take heroism seriously. Furthermore, he could easily step aside when the story I was telling didn't need him. Many stories were related to and triggered by current events. I was becoming more assertive with innovation. From the very first, the problem of being a freestanding newspaper insert opened a need to deal with the first page. It forced me to devise a solution for having page one function as a cover as well as an introduction or to serve as a reader preparation and mood-setter to the story. This resulted in the "SPLASH PAGE." With this there arose another problem: the Spirit logo. I employed the logo as an integral part of the story setting. This, of course, required that it be different each week. It was an "innovation" fiercely objected to by the

CHIEF WARRANT OFFICER WILL EISNER, 1943.

IT WOULD THOROUGHLY FRIGHTEN YOU GOOD CITIZENS TO REALLY KNOW WHAT THINGS GO ON BENEATH THE SILENCE IN CENTRAL CITY AFTER DARK....FOR INSTANCE.....
BANG!
CLICK
COMMISSIONER DOLAN!! GOOD HEAVENS!! YOU'VE KILLED HIM!!
THE SPIRIT!! WHAT ARE YOU DOING HERE?!!

THE FIRST SPIRIT DAILY, 10/31/41.

sales people at the syndicate for they felt I was depriving them of a promotional gimmick. Newspapers would post titles of comic strips on the sides of their delivery trucks as a circulation builder. Since there was no standard Spirit logo they couldn't do it. I, however, prevailed because I convinced them that readership would fall off if we abandoned the "look" of the Spirit section.

In the years following 1945 I took to experimenting with format as well as story and plot. I did one story entirely in verse, another totally in pantomime, and in one story I indulged in some philosophical moralizing with a story that remained my favorite: GERHARD SCHNOBBLE.

These, for me, were the "very good years" of the Spirit. In 1947 Jules Feiffer joined the shop as a shop assistant and before long began to write many of the stories. He added an intellectual stimulus that enabled me to expand on the "grown-up" focus to which I aspired. The staff grew to include an innovative and brilliant letterer, Abe Kaenegson, and Jerry Grandenetti who came out of an architectural company and provided the feature with sophisticated back grounds that supported the theatrical staging.

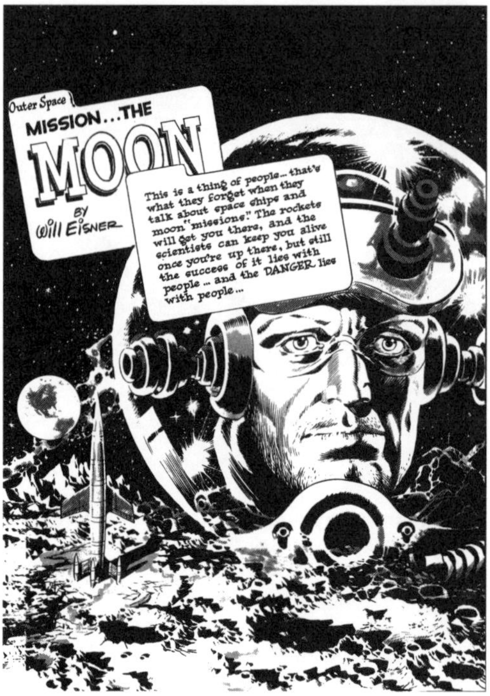
Outer Space
MISSION...THE
MOON
BY
Will Eisner
This is a thing of people... that's what they forget when they talk about space ships and moon "missions." The rockets will get you there, and the scientists can keep you alive once you're up there, but still the success of it lies with people ... and the DANGER lies with people...

"MISSION...THE MOON": LAYOUTS AND SCRIPT BY JULES FEIFFER, ART BY WALLY WOOD, UNDER EISNER'S SUPERVISION. (8/3/57).

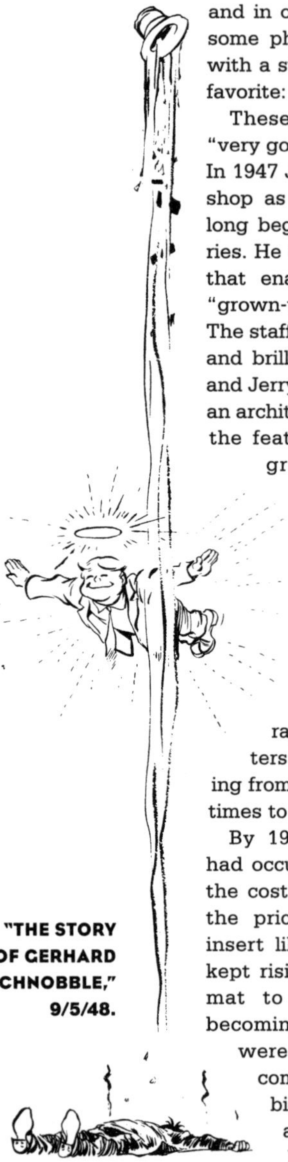

"THE STORY OF GERHARD SCHNOBBLE," 9/5/48.

I now needed to address the current rhythm in American readership, to move from film orientation to a greater realism than one finds on the stage. I also wanted to keep abreast of social humor which was rapidly maturing, with characters like Ebony, who was emerging from simply being a product of the times to a more human persona.

By 1951 many economic changes had occurred in the newspaper field; the cost of newsprint increased, and the price of a 16-page ready-print insert like ours to the client papers kept rising. Even the eight-page format to which we retreated was becoming very costly. Newspapers were reducing the size of their comic strips, which was a harbinger of the fate of continuity adventure newspaper comics. Even a series of Spirit stories by the brilliant Wally Wood did not seem to have much impact.

So in 1952 rather than retreat and try to revive a daily strip, I decided to quit while I was ahead. I was, I admit, pleased by the entreaties of several subscribing papers to continue, but I had other challenging opportunities in comics to pursue. Nevertheless, THE SPIRIT continued in reprint in Europe and America for many years since its cessation.

This Archival edition by DC is monumental and certainly the most rewarding development in THE SPIRIT's publishing history for it will at last consolidate a comprehensive view of its main theme for new and longtime followers. For me this unifying publication is a welcome culmination of my years with THE SPIRIT.

—Will Eisner
Florida 2000

THE PIONEERING SPIRIT

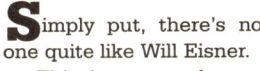

Simply put, there's no one quite like Will Eisner.

This is not to detract from the many other great craftsmen of one persuasion or another that the comics field has been blessed with in the past. No one would deny the sheer physical vitality lent to the field by an artist of Jack Kirby's stature, for example, or dispute the enormous contribution of the extremely literate E.C. line. That said, I find it difficult to argue that Eisner is not the single person most responsible for giving comics their *brains*. I can think of no one who has explored the possibilities of this infant medium so tirelessly and rewardingly, nor anyone who has so successfully managed to evolve a working vocabulary for the parts and functions of the comic strip and the fascinating ways in which its mechanisms can be fitted together.

Whenever you have the occasion to hear either myself or one of the current batch of comic-strip professionals pontificating and theorizing upon the state of the medium, you should bear in mind that, at best, what we're doing is building upon the solid groundwork that Eisner has been laying down for the past forty years. He's THE BOSS, and we know it.

While I could talk for hours about the sheer breadth of innovation that Eisner brought to the medium by his work in THE SPIRIT and his more recent creations such as A CONTRACT WITH GOD or A LIFE FORCE and bore everyone to death with talk about the constant ingenuity of his panel progressions and page layouts, all of this stuff has been done before by commentators far more skilled and incisive than myself and there seems little point in repeating it. Also, I feel that dwelling on the many technical delights that Eisner's work has to offer tends to obscure the poetry and magic that transforms what could be brilliant, but dry, stylistic exercises into something with heart, conviction and effect. I'd rather talk about what his work means to me personally than attempt to reduce the story of Gerhard Schnobble to a simple, technical diagram.

Like many other people in this country, my first exposure to Eisner's work came with the Harvey Comics' reprinting some SPIRIT stories in two chunky, 25-cent color comic books. This was in the mid-60s, and even though the seismic ripples of excitement caused by Lee and Kirby's Marvel renaissance at the beginning of the decade had not quite died away, there was a gradual homogenization of the general comic-book product which, while it can be seen better in retrospect, undoubtedly prefigured the widespread stagnation of the super-hero comics industry that is with us to this day. Back then, in the mid-60s, every month saw another dozen or so Marvel comics coming out and I'd dutifully buy them all, lovingly lapping up each random permutation of assorted super-beings intent on damaging each other with the single-mindedness of a glutton who doesn't know when he's had enough. Into this ceaselessly unwinding fashion parade

OH, WHAT A SITUATION! MR. RAYMOND SEEMS TO BE ON EVERYONE'S KILL-PARADE!
MURDER STALKS OUR HOUSE!
OF COURSE, I COULD ALWAYS KILL MR. RAYMOND!
SAREE, MY POOR CHILD, YOU MAY AS WELL KNOW THAT YOUR STEP-MOTHER IS AN EVIL WOMAN! MARK MY WORDS, SHE'LL MURDER HIM! YOU MUST FOLLOW MY INSTRUCTIONS!
HM, IS THAT SO? ANYTHING ELSE YOU CAN SCRAPE UP ON RAYMOND'S FINANCIAL AFFAIRS FOR ME? HMM...WELL, THAT'LL DO, THANKS!
?
OH, OFFICER, I THINK MY HUSBAND HAS BEEN MURDERED!
FINISHING SCHOOL

"THE SCHOOL FOR GIRLS," 1/19/47.

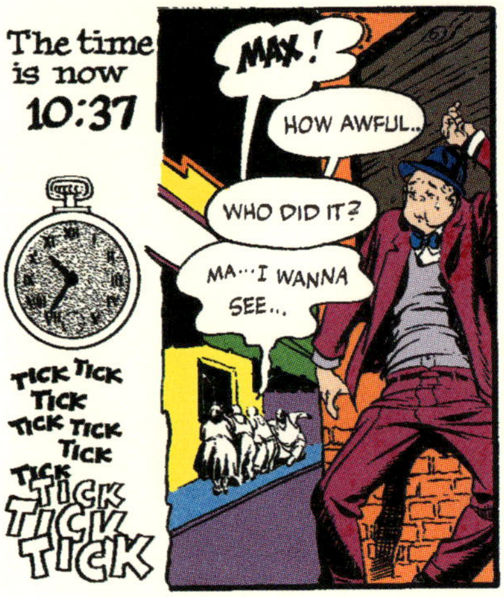
The time is now 10:37
MAX!
HOW AWFUL..
WHO DID IT?
MA··· I WANNA SEE...
TICK TICK
TICK
TICK TICK
TICK
TICK
TICK
TICK
TICK

"TEN MINUTES," 9/11/49.

of costumes, THE SPIRIT's crumpled blue suit came as a breath of fresh air, and the stories, to someone who hadn't realized that there *should* be any point to a story other than which poser the goody uses on the baddie, came as a revelation.

The world of THE SPIRIT was an endlessly inventive American fantasy landscape in which any type of story is likely to occur. It might be the grim tale of Freddy's rapid temptation and punishment in "Ten Minutes," or it might be the ludicrous yet poignant tale of a talking cockroach that dies an unsung hero's death. A convict being shaved for execution shares a grim and bloody conversation with his barber in "The Barber," while in "The Awful Book" a self-righteous comic-book critic falls prey to fears that are entirely within his own imaginings (and, let's face it, it isn't the first time). Within the standard super-hero

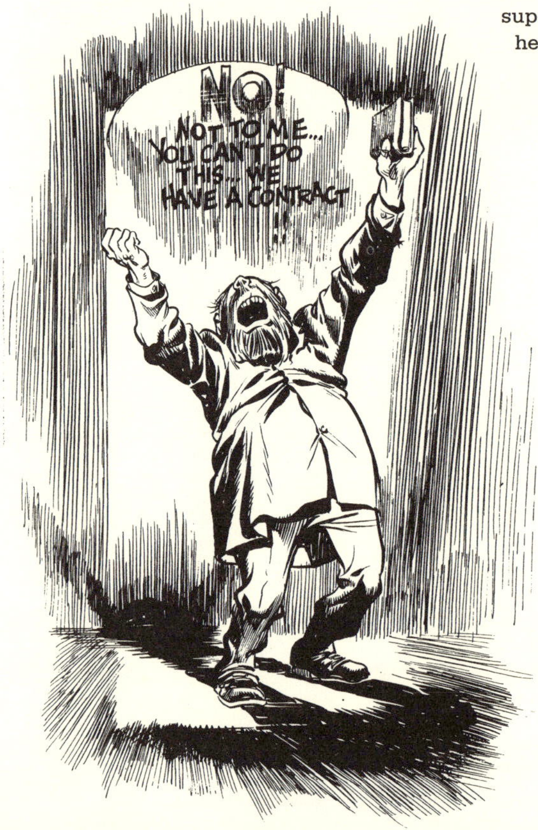
NO!
NOT TO ME... YOU CAN'T DO THIS... WE HAVE A CONTRACT!!

"A CONTRACT WITH GOD," 1978.

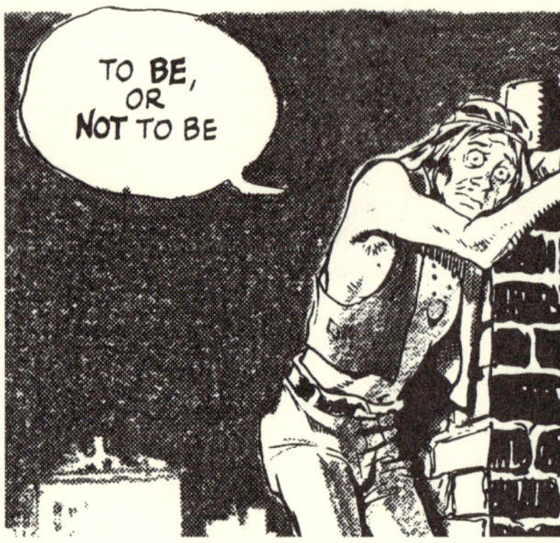
TO BE, OR NOT TO BE

HAMLET.

books that were my staple diet, you were more or less assured of the same sort of story month after month. In the world of THE SPIRIT, however, anything could happen.

From that early conversion, I became an ardent fan of everything that I could find bearing Eisner's signature. I delved into the vast wealth of SPIRIT stories that existed beyond the confines of those two much-thumbed Harvey compilations and came across gems like the tale of Hitler's incognito stroll around the Bronx or flawless pieces of tense storytelling like "The Elevator." I devoured those few interviews or articles that I could find that dealt with Eisner's work in seminal publications like Bill Spicer's *Graphic Story Magazine* or Wally Wood's *Witzend*, and would confess instantly that along with a handful of other luminaries like Alex Toth, Gil Kane, or Harvey Kurtzman, any theory of comics that I've based my work upon has been largely based upon what I could glean from those few available words of wisdom.

If THE SPIRIT were all that Eisner had done, that would in itself be remarkable. The fact that he has continued to produce such a sustained and consistent body of excellent work right up to the present day is nothing short of astonishing, by anyone's standard. From this more recent period, there are several major landmarks, most noticeably Eisner's beautifully observed collection of tenement stories, A CONTRACT WITH GOD. In this intensely involving assortment of stories, Eisner has managed to study the microcosm of a tenement neighborhood and pick out some remarkably human stories for inspection. We have the tale of a street singer busking for money who encounters a failed singer looking for love. We have a study in different kinds of monsters with "The Super," a story concerning a clash between a little girl and the superintendent of her aunt's building. We have the title story itself, a bitter tale of lost faith played out against a background of rumbling urban thunderstorms. Looking at the comic-book racks today, it's still difficult to conceive that anyone might actually want to read a story about human beings, and A CONTRACT WITH GOD still stands as one of the medium's boldest attempts to move comics stories out of their stiflingly adolescent super-hero niche into the richer and wider territories that mainstream literary fiction, motion pictures, and every other medium you care to name has enjoyed since its inception as a matter of course.

Following on this came the stunning LIFE ON ANOTHER PLANET, in which Eisner moved from a collection of finely crafted short stories to a full-blown graphic novel...and by "graphic novel" I mean something actually worthy of the term rather than the pointlessly extended fight scenes that are dignified with that description as a matter of course at the present. In LIFE ON ANOTHER PLANET, Eisner manages to avoid any temptations towards launching himself into science fiction in order to cater to a largely fantasy-dominated market and instead provides us with a touching and sometimes harrowing picture of life upon this planet, in all its variously disposed configurations. At roughly the same time as this magnum opus was presented to us, Eisner kept himself busy by continuing his breathtaking exploration of the art form in his Comic Strip Workshop feature in Kitchen Sink's SPIRIT magazine. This ongoing exploration produced some spellbinding works, most notably his rooftop version of the soliloquy from *Hamlet*, with a single figure dominating the whole comic book "stage" throughout the entire strip and yet still remaining visually gripping.

Add to this recent book COMICS AND SEQUENTIAL ART and the numerous other projects that he's turned his hand to, and you begin to understand the vast contribution that he's made to the art form. He's given us a way to see and to think about comics and has helped to provide an understanding of their workings that we must have if we are to take the medium forward into the future rather than allowing it to stagnate in a backwater of the 1960s. There is no one quite like Will Eisner. There never has been, and on my more pessimistic days I doubt there ever will be.

—Alan Moore
England 1986

I MUST TELL THEM I AM COMING!
BUT HOW, MARCO?
I HAVE A SHORT WAVE RADIO..YES, YES...I WILL SEND A MESSAGE!
?
HELLO.. HELLO EARTH CALLING HELLO
IMAGINE... GOING TO ANOTHER PLANET...A NEW LIFE...A WHOLE NEW LIFE.. YES, YES
I'LL HELP YOU, MARCO! ...I'LL BE RIGHT BACK!
HELLO... EARTH CALLING

"LIFE ON ANOTHER PLANET," 1978.

THE UNKNOWN
THE KNOWN
THREAT
CANDOR

"COMICS AND SEQUENTIAL ART," 1985.

THE CONSUMMATE COMIC BOOK

Yes, the creation of Superman established the comic book as a viable publishing venture. Yes, the subsequent arrival of Batman precipitated a stampede of costumed crime-fighting in four-color splendor. While the content of the new medium was shaped by such creations as these, in Will Eisner's Spirit we have the consummate comic book. In the pages of his Spirit stories, Eisner explored and perfected the very form of the medium. Eisner may not have invented some of the storytelling maneuvers he used, but he made more effective use of these devices because he deployed them for literary purposes—for dramatic effects. And the result of this approach in the long run imparted personality to the characters that peopled his stories, and the stories themselves consequently reflected a humanity more genuine than is usually found in the pulp fiction heroicism that otherwise prevailed in the medium.

Eisner knew very early in his career that the medium of comics was an art form. And as soon as he knew, he nurtured it. No one of Eisner's generation pushed against the envelope of possibilities harder or experimented as thoughtfully or as skillfully over as long a period. And very few of his generation—or of any other—have had as much impact upon the medium as he. Harvey Kurtzman, who was to the postwar generation of comic-book creators what Eisner was to the prewar generation, believed Eisner to be "the greatest" of the early artists in the form. Writing his impressions of the history of comic books, Kurtzman said of Eisner: "It was Eisner, more than anyone else, who developed the multipage booklet story form that became the grammar of the medium." Eisner's influence was first felt when he became the art director of a comic-art production shop in the fall of 1936 while the comic-book industry was still in its infancy, for the most part just reprinting newspaper comic strips.

With partner Jerry Iger, Eisner established the shop to produce comic-strip material for syndication to weekly newspapers and to overseas outlets that were eager to publish American comic strips. Before long, Eisner was recycling this material for publication domestically in the rapidly burgeoning comic-book field, which needed original material to supplement the strip reprints. And it was in reincarnating his weekly strips for this second life that Eisner first explored and discovered the unique potential of the comic-book medium.

The weekly strips had been drawn in Sunday strip format, but since the comic-book pages were of different dimensions than a Sunday newspaper page, the strips had to be revamped for comic-book publication. To this purpose, Eisner cut up the artwork, panel by panel, and created the new pages by pasting up the old panels in modified configurations, often rewriting dialogue and captions to suit the new arrangement and expanding the original pictures to make them fit by adding more drawing to some of the panels. Although it was ostensibly a purely mechanical operation, this task stimulated Eisner's thinking about page layout, leading to the adoption of novel storytelling devices—like the "jump cut" in which the subject seems to

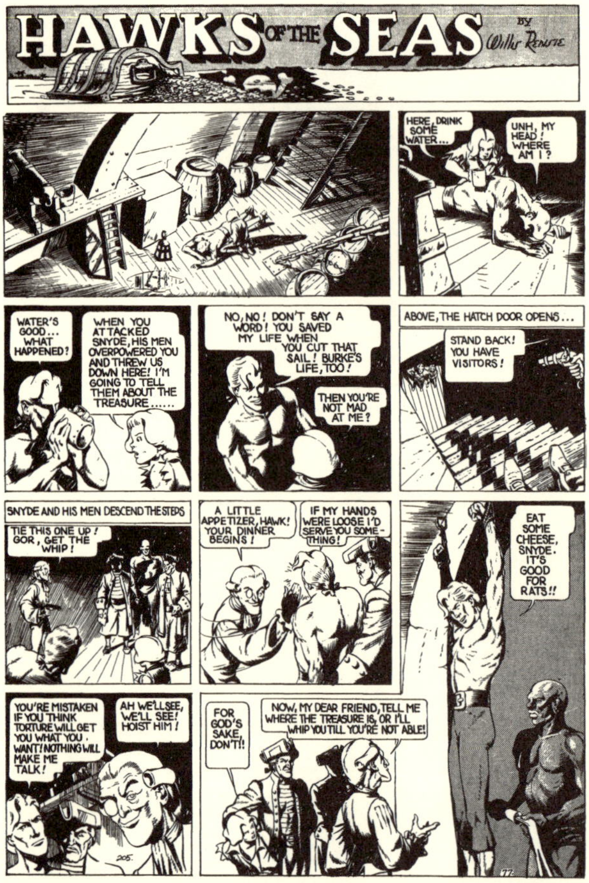
HAWKS OF THE SEAS
BY Willis Rensie
HERE, DRINK SOME WATER...
UNH, MY HEAD! WHERE AM I?
WATER'S GOOD... WHAT HAPPENED?
WHEN YOU ATTACKED SNYDE, HIS MEN OVERPOWERED YOU AND THREW US DOWN HERE! I'M GOING TO TELL THEM ABOUT THE TREASURE......
NO, NO! DON'T SAY A WORD! YOU SAVED MY LIFE WHEN YOU CUT THAT SAIL! BURKE'S LIFE, TOO!
THEN YOU'RE NOT MAD AT ME?
ABOVE, THE HATCH DOOR OPENS...
STAND BACK! YOU HAVE VISITORS!
SNYDE AND HIS MEN DESCEND THE STEPS
TIE THIS ONE UP! GOR, GET THE WHIP!
A LITTLE APPETIZER, HAWK! YOUR DINNER BEGINS!
IF MY HANDS WERE LOOSE I'D SERVE YOU SOME-THING!
EAT SOME CHEESE, SNYDE. IT'S GOOD FOR RATS!!
YOU'RE MISTAKEN IF YOU THINK TORTURE WILL GET YOU WHAT YOU WANT! NOTHING WILL MAKE ME TALK!
AH WE'LL SEE, WE'LL SEE! HOIST HIM!
FOR GOD'S SAKE, DON'T!!
NOW, MY DEAR FRIEND, TELL ME WHERE THE TREASURE IS, OR I'LL WHIP YOU TILL YOU'RE NOT ABLE!

"HAWKS OF THE SEAS."

EISNER MADE THE SPIRIT'S MASK A VIRTUAL SKIN GRAPH.

move rapidly, almost discontinuously, from one activity to another, a result of leaving out a connecting panel because the page wouldn't accommodate as many panels as the strip originally had.

As the Eisner-Iger shop took on more work, the partners hired additional artists and writers. Eventually, the ensemble over which Eisner presided included many of the medium's pacesetters: Jack Kirby, Lou Fine, Bob Kane, Dick Briefer, Chuck Mazoujian, Mort Meskin, Bob Powell, George Tuska, Klaus Nordling, Nick Viscardi, and staff writer Audrey "Toni" Blum. Eisner roughed out stories in nonphoto blue pencil on sheets of illustration board—breaking down the action, designing page layouts, sketching in figures, indicating dialogue. These rough pages he passed on to a writer, who scripted captions and dialogue. Then the page went to the other artists, who finished pencilling and inking and lettering them. At various stages in the production, each page passed under Eisner's eye for approval. When he saw something that didn't meet his standard, he suggested changes.

In supervising their work, the 20-year-old Eisner imposed his own artistic sensibilities. And much of the work produced by the shop bears his imprint. He was enamored of Milton Caniff's use of camera angles in *Terry and the Pirates,* for example, and as he experimented with increasingly extreme viewpoints, the shop's material was riddled with bizarre bird's-eye and worm's-eye shots. The demands of Eisner's assembly line and the challenges of shaping the medium to fit both those demands and his own aesthetic sense absorbed him and satisfied him. And his efforts influenced the future work of all those who pulled the oars in the Eisner-Iger galley, and through them, the storytelling conventions of comic books. Pervasive as Eisner's influence doubtless was by this route, he would leave an even greater mark upon the art form after he left the shop to create one of the great characters in comics, the Spirit.

Elsewhere in these pages, Eisner rehearses the events surrounding the creation of the weekly comic-book newspaper supplement in which the Spirit debuted. It bears emphasizing, however, that Eisner's animating motive was not to create a character like Superman or Dick Tracy: the protagonist he devised was but the hook upon which he would hang stories. Realizing that newspaper readers would enjoy more adult stories than the juvenile readers of comic books, Eisner wanted a framework that would enable him to tell any kind of story he could imagine. He quickly decided upon the detective story as the most adaptable framework.

Eisner's partners in this enterprise expected a costumed character. After all, it was the popularity of Superman and Batman and their ilk that had created the market in newspapers for a weekly comic-book supplement. But Eisner was adamant: "Any kind of costume would have limited the kinds of stories I could do. It would have been an inhibiting factor." Still, he couldn't ignore his partners' wishes entirely. Reluctantly, he put a mask on the Spirit. And, later, he put gloves on his hero.

One of these concessions he turned to advantage. In his treatment of the Spirit's mask, Eisner would establish the uniqueness of his character with trademark precision.

THE SPIRIT'S LOVE INTEREST: ELLEN DOLAN ("THE PROM," 12/1/40).

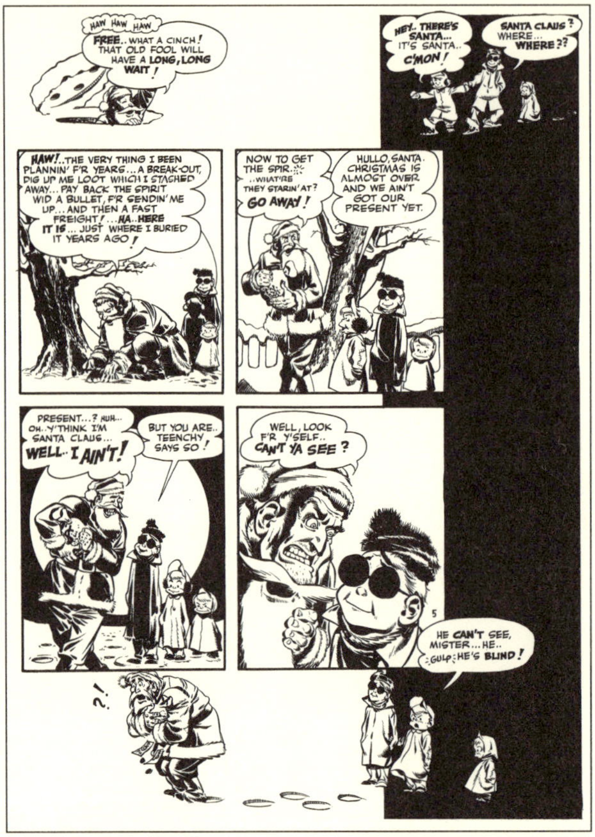
HAW HAW HAW
FREE.. WHAT A CINCH! THAT OLD FOOL WILL HAVE A LONG, LONG WAIT!
HEY.. THERE'S SANTA.. IT'S SANTA.. C'MON!
SANTA CLAUS? WHERE... WHERE??
HAW!..THE VERY THING I BEEN PLANNIN' F'R YEARS... A BREAK-OUT, DIG UP ME LOOT WHICH I STACHED AWAY... PAY BACK THE SPIRIT WID A BULLET, F'R SENDIN' ME UP... AND THEN A FAST FREIGHT!... HA.. HERE IT IS... JUST WHERE I BURIED IT YEARS AGO!
NOW TO GET THE SPIR.. ...WHAT'RE THEY STARIN' AT? GO AWAY!
HULLO, SANTA. CHRISTMAS IS ALMOST OVER AND WE AIN'T GOT OUR PRESENT YET.
PRESENT...? HUH... OH.. Y'THINK I'M SANTA CLAUS... WELL.. I AIN'T!
BUT YOU ARE.. TEENCHY SAYS SO!
WELL, LOOK F'R Y'SELF.. CAN'T YA SEE?
HE CAN'T SEE, MISTER... HE.. GULP HE'S BLIND!
?!

AN EXAMPLE OF EISNER'S CREATIVE PAGE LAYOUTS, FROM "THE CHRISTMAS SPIRIT," 12/19/48.

The bit of blue cloth eventually looked pasted on: it was virtually a skin graft, and the Spirit's features—his eyebrows, the fold of skin under the eye—were as visible through the mask as they would have been without it.

As supporting cast, Eisner conjured up Police Commissioner Eustace P. Dolan—right out of central casting: a gruff, pipe-chomping, jut-jawed Irish cop, given to muttering in his moustache about the many abuses the world and its bureaucracies inflicted upon him but goodhearted under all the bluster and grumping. For a love interest, Eisner gave Dolan a beautiful daughter, Ellen, who, as we shall see anon, falls in love with the Spirit.

On display in the inaugural Spirit story are several of the devices Eisner would employ so distinctively as to make them earmarks of his storytelling style. The pictures are often heavily shadowed and the perspectives unusual. The panels are oddly shaped, sliced into narrow slivers and wedges. The unusual layout was Eisner's reaction to the severe constraint he felt under the seven-page limitation imposed upon his storytelling.

In order to fit into this meager allotment of pages the complexities of the stories he wanted to tell, Eisner used techniques that he had developed while refitting the Eisner-Iger shop Sunday strips to a comic-book format—circular panels, diamond-shaped ones, and diagonals. He had seen storytelling potential in the expedient, and now he began to plumb the possibilities. "I used a flurry of panels to speed up action," he said, "—long odd-shaped panels to show dimension that a standard panel destroyed, characters popping out of panels to add depth. So much to say and so little room to say it in."

Eisner's dilemma was created by his artistic aspirations: in his storytelling, he tried for effect as well as simple narrative. Creating effects takes space. So does narrative clarity. There wasn't much space in seven pages to begin with, and the more complex Eisner's story—the more ambitious his experimental efforts—the more cramped the space became.

One way to conserve space was to cram more narrative freight into some panels than into others in order to create breathing space along the way for other effects. On page two of the first story, for instance, by imposing Dr. Cobra's face over two panels, Eisner was able to give us a close-up that emphasizes the villain's sinister appearance while simultaneously

PAGE 2 OF "THE ORIGIN OF THE SPIRIT," 6/2/40.

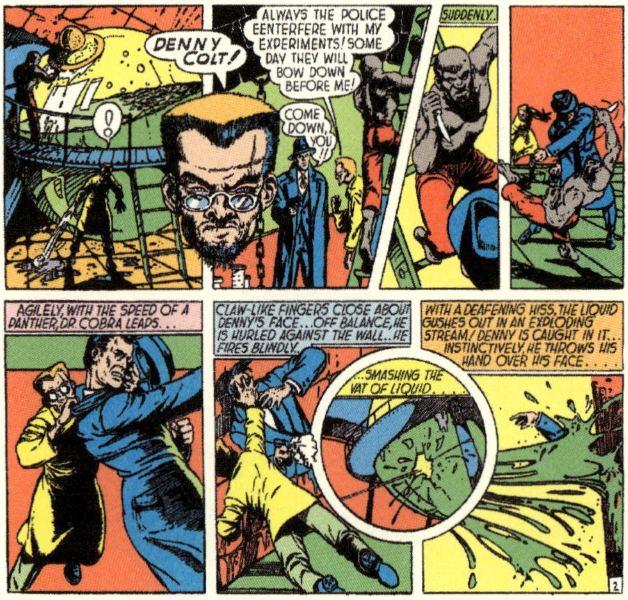
DENNY COLT!
ALWAYS THE POLICE EENTERFERE WITH MY EXPERIMENTS! SOME DAY THEY WILL BOW DOWN BEFORE ME!
COME DOWN, YOU!!
SUDDENLY.
AGILELY, WITH THE SPEED OF A PANTHER, DR. COBRA LEAPS...
CLAW-LIKE FINGERS CLOSE ABOUT DENNY'S FACE... OFF BALANCE, HE IS HURLED AGAINST THE WALL... HE FIRES BLINDLY.
...SMASHING THE VAT OF LIQUID...
WITH A DEAFENING HISS, THE LIQUID GUSHES OUT IN AN EXPLODING STREAM! DENNY IS CAUGHT IN IT... INSTINCTIVELY, HE THROWS HIS HAND OVER HIS FACE...

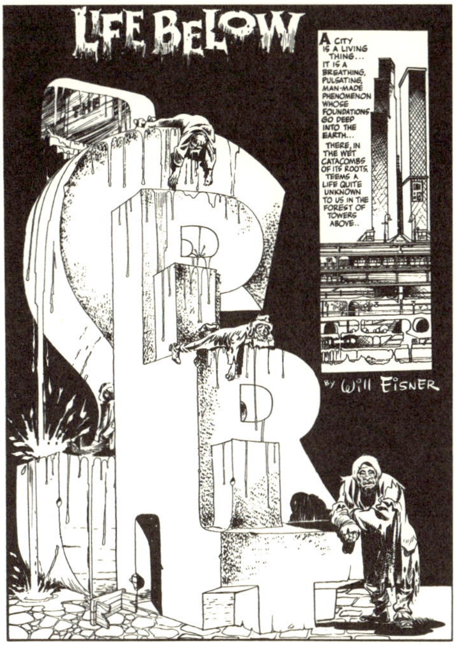
LIFE BELOW
A CITY IS A LIVING THING... IT IS A BREATHING, PULSATING, MAN-MADE PHENOMENON WHOSE FOUNDATIONS GO DEEP INTO THE EARTH...
THERE, IN THE WET CATACOMBS OF ITS ROOTS, TEEMS A LIFE QUITE UNKNOWN TO US IN THE FOREST OF TOWERS ABOVE..
THE SPIRIT
BY WILL EISNER

" LIFE BELOW," ONE OF THE CLASSIC SPLASH PAGES. 2/22/48.

presenting the setting and accouterments of the scientist's laboratory in the panels behind his face. At the same time, the story is advanced by the action depicted in those two panels. In the circular panel in the next tier, Eisner repeats this maneuver, this time striving for additional narrative clarity. By cramming in such visual material as this on the bottom two-thirds of the page, Eisner could lavish two or three panels at the top on purely atmospheric matters, depicting the shadowy crooked narrow alleyway, the entrance through a manhole.

By the sixth outing of the weekly supplement, Eisner's distinctive deployment of the opening page, the "splash page," had begun to surface. He had started using a larger and larger introductory "title" panel as a way of providing the supplement with something akin to a cover, but he eventually realized that the larger imagery would serve another purpose. "The big thing for me in any splash page is to set the mood and form contact with the reader," Eisner said. The reader, prompted by the picture he contemplates for a brief moment, would decide whether the story was a mystery or a fable or a comedy or a tragedy and would assume the appropriate mental posture for encountering the story that followed.

As Eisner became more adept at deploying this aspect of his feature, he made an indelible mark on the art form. Some of his splash pages in later years were such powerful statements of mood and theme that they could stand alone as works of graphic art. We enter a tale about a haunted house by coming through a cobweb-shrouded doorway. For a story that takes place in the sewers of the city, the letters of the title character's name are structured and stacked to represent the architecture of the world beneath the streets. When we meet a treacherous femme fatale named Powder, we see her Circean form first—through a spider's web—in the center of which the Spirit is dangling.

And Eisner had a literary agenda as well as a graphic one. A student of O. Henry and Ambrose Bierce, Eisner knew that a short story was a literary exercise contrived for its ending. But his chief preoccupation was with human personality, the preoccupation of every author of fiction. He frequently treated the Spirit's case in a given week as an excuse to develop an element of general human interest, shifting the spotlight off his hero, sometimes for most of the story (as with the two September stories herein about Orang "the ape that is human," in

" THE NAME IS... POWDER," 1/4/48.

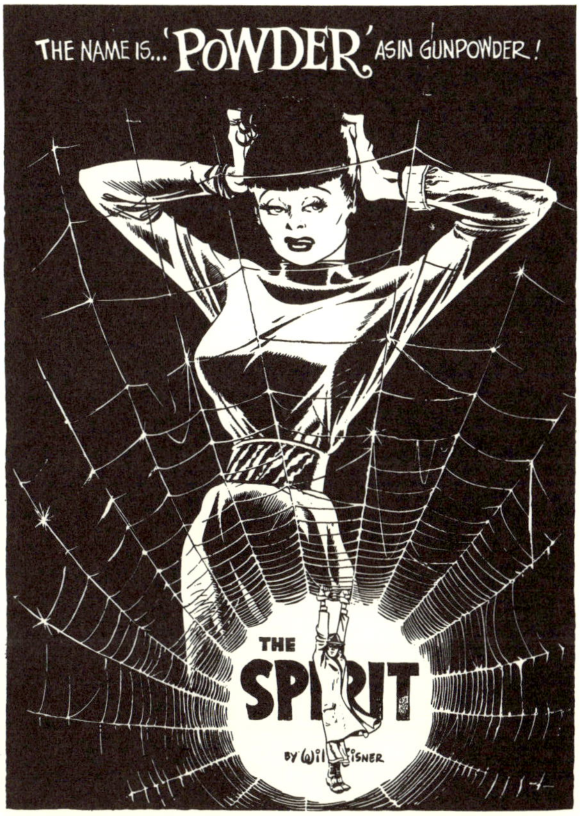
THE NAME IS...'POWDER' AS IN GUNPOWDER!
THE SPIRIT
BY WILL EISNER

which the major effort is to explore the tragic dimensions of Orang's predicament). Time after time, Eisner focused on some ordinary soul, a specimen of common humanity, whom he would confront with some extraordinary event —and then watch to see how the character reacted, how he survived. "I have something of an obsession with this," he admitted, "—with time, with meanings in life, with what motivates people to go on when they're faced with terrible problems, with the idea of a single life being affected by larger events."

MY NAME IS QUADRANT J. STET. I WORK FOR J. PARRISH AND SON, ACCOUNTANTS, AT 14-23 DOCK STREET. I AM A MAN OF REGULAR HABITS. I NEITHER SMOKE NOR GAMBLE... YOU WOULDN'T THINK OF ME AS THE SUBJECT OF AN ADVENTURE STORY.

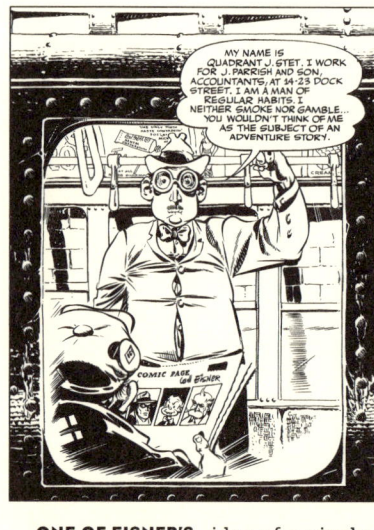

ONE OF EISNER'S ORDINARY PEOPLE. "THE EMBEZZLER," 11/27/49.

By December 1940, all the characteristic Eisner storytelling ingredients were in the mix, and the distinctive Spirit story began appearing regularly. With virtually every appearance, Eisner advanced the art of cartooning, introducing some new attitude or treatment or plot twist that demonstrated what the medium was capable of. And then in the spring of 1941—six months after Pearl Harbor dragged the U.S. into the World War—Eisner was drafted. The Spirit, being a syndicated feature, was continued by other hands during his absence, but when Eisner returned in 1945, he eagerly resumed active control of his experiment.

Both his vision and his graphic style had matured; his sheer technical skill was greater by reason of the additional years of practice he'd accumulated in the Army by producing instructional materials in comic-book format for soldiers. Eisner's postwar graphic style was more confident, his line bolder. His sense of composition was surer: his figures seemed not just to occupy the panels but to fill them. Consequently The Spirit, the end product of vision, style, technical skill and creative passion, ascended to the level of its greatest experimentation and achievement.

In his stories, Eisner continued to peer into the lives and aspirations of ordinary people. And his villains were no more distinguished. As fellow cartoonist Jim Steranko has observed, the Spirit battled "worn-out felons, bowery pickpockets, nickel-and-dime shoplifters, street corner punks, city hall grafters, shabby con men, furtive sneak thieves, stripe-suited pimps, weak-willed winos, sweat-stained stoolies, baggy pants torpedoes and a rogue's gallery of other three-time losers."

The Spirit himself was all too fallible. But he always survived. And in so doing, he embodied an aspect of the theme that pervades Eisner's work—the conviction that the little man, ordinary people in general, can survive the vicissitudes of life and can, perhaps, rise above their apparent limitations, particularly when unexpectedly challenged by an unusual circumstance.

Despite this inherent seriousness of literary purpose, most stories displayed a sense of humor. "I always thought that humor and action weren't mutually exclusive elements and that humor could be used to leaven many scenes," Eisner said. Sometimes he told a story that was outright comedy; sometimes he ran a comic subplot in parallel to the story's serious main event.

The storytelling devices Eisner had introduced before the War he took up again and honed to an acute rhetoric of comic-book storytelling. He lavished particular care upon the splash pages. It was often raining on the splash pages. It rained in sheets; it rained in cascades. Depicting weather, Eisner believed, was one of the few things he could do in the medium that would evoke a predictable response in his readers. Any lonely figure is made forlorn and therefore intriguing if he is standing in the rain.

The splash page for September 19, 1948 incorporates several favorite Eisner devices. It's raining, and it's shrouded black with atmosphere. It's mostly silent—except for evocative sound effects. And there's movement, progression,

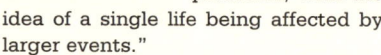

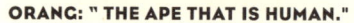

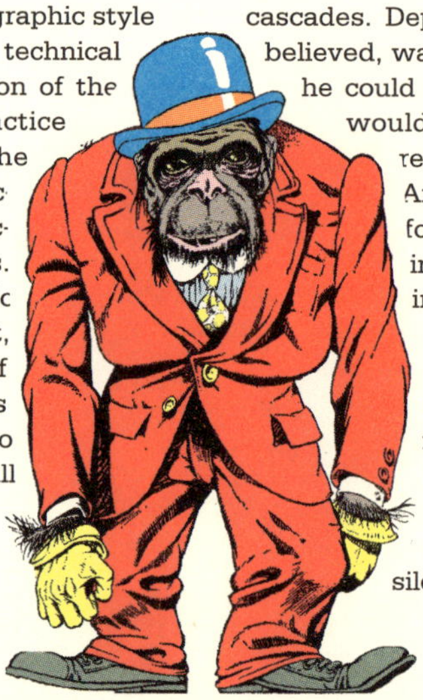

ORANG: "THE APE THAT IS HUMAN."

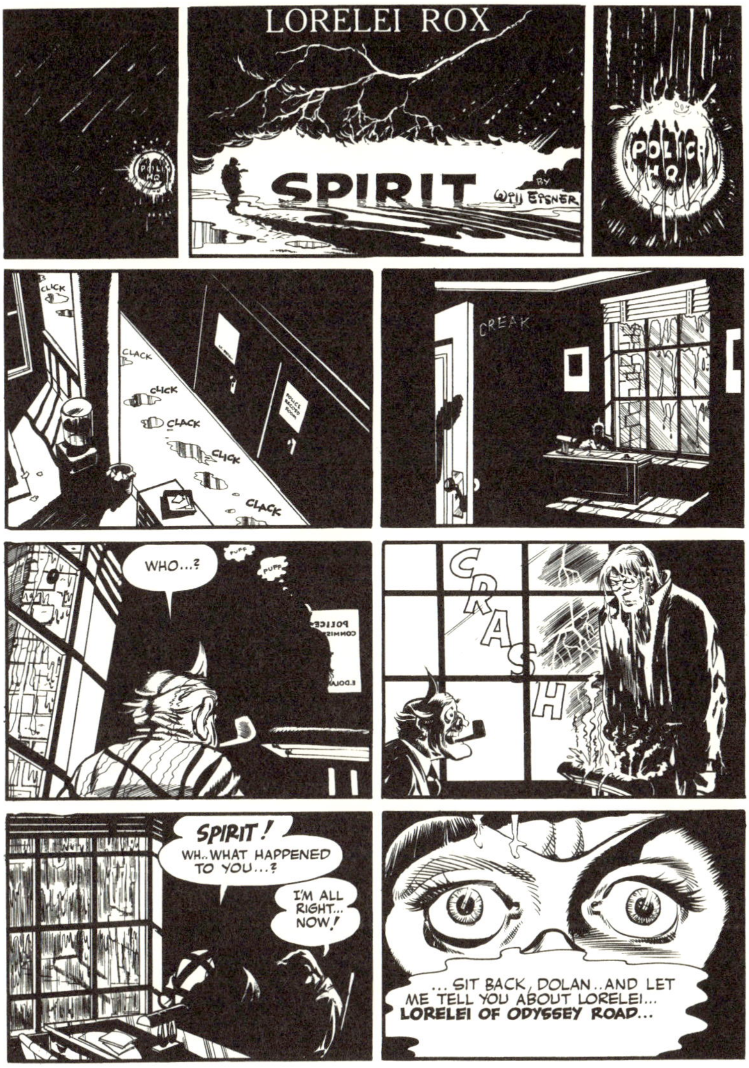
LORELEI ROX
SPIRIT
BY
WILL EISNER
POLICE H.Q.
CLICK
CLACK
CLICK
CLACK
CLICK
CLACK
CREAK
WHO...?
PUFF
PUFF
CRASH
SPIRIT! WH..WHAT HAPPENED TO YOU...?
I'M ALL RIGHT... NOW!
... SIT BACK, DOLAN..AND LET ME TELL YOU ABOUT LORELEI... LORELEI OF ODYSSEY ROAD...

"LORELEI ROX," 9/19/48.

functioning as a sort of prologue. The dark, enveloping cloak of night parts only for light sources—sometimes steady, like the light identifying the police station; sometimes intermittent, like lightning. Punctuating the darkness with instances of light, Eisner tells his story as a series of revealing glimpses. First, we make out a police station in the distance. Then by the flash of a lightning bolt, we see a figure walking in the storm. Since we are closer to the police light in the next panel, we know the figure is approaching the station. Next, he's inside—leaving puddles of water wherever he steps, his heels clicking regardless of the damp. The door to Dolan's office opens with a creak, and we see Dolan, sitting alone in his office, wholly in the dark except for the meager glow from his desk lamp. (We can see the front of his suit coat so we know the desk lamp is alight; further evidence, in panel 7, the water falling from the Spirit sizzles as it strikes the heated metal shade of the lamp.) Dolan can't tell who his visitor is: standing between Dolan and the door, the figure is an anonymous silhouette against the light in the hallway. But when lightning crackles again, Dolan is astonished to find the Spirit before him. The successive moments of illumination are timed by Eisner's silent progression of panels, building suspense until the moment of revelation in panel 7. And then, like a good prologue, one revelation leads to the next, and the Spirit begins to tell his story in the last panel.

The page is a study in visual storytelling. Nothing on this page is haphazard. The objects Eisner elected to show us as well as the moments he chose to reveal those objects were selected with great calculation. Each illuminated detail tells us something that advances the story. Each picture is a successive moment in a progression of moments. The light reveals not only the story but the storyteller: by controlling the light as severely as he does, Eisner demonstrates just how deliberate a craftsman he is. A virtuoso performance, the page sets the mood of mysteriousness and vague alarm for the story to follow by being itself a mystery with a moment of fright.

Each week's story was an opportunity to experiment with treatments and themes. Sometimes Eisner parodied popular radio programs or movies. He often told fables, modern morality dramas. He explored the supernatural, the inexplicable, and he dabbled in science fiction. He played with sound effects and time. He used music—song lyrics—and poetry.

About his tireless experimentation, Kurtzman observed, "Eisner became a virtuoso cartoonist of a kind who had never been seen before in comic

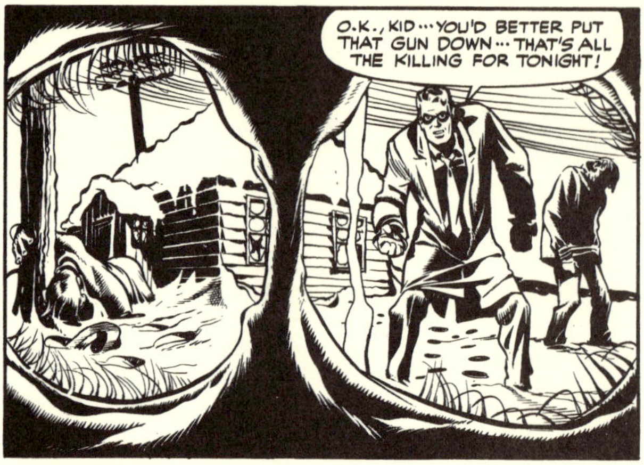
O.K., KID··· YOU'D BETTER PUT THAT GUN DOWN··· THAT'S ALL THE KILLING FOR TONIGHT!

LOOKING THROUGH THE EYES OF "THE KILLER," 12/8/46.

books—or, for that matter, in newspaper strips. He used all the elements of the comic-book page—dialogue, drawing, panel composition, color—with great daring, but never at the cost of narrative clarity."

Eisner's restless creative imagination never left him quite content with what he had done. He was always eager to pursue a new idea to completion. This passion led him finally to abandon his most memorable creation. During these postwar years, even while producing The Spirit, he was actively marketing ideas that he'd developed in the Army for instructional comic books. Eventually, this aspect of his work so consumed his energies that he could not continue doing the syndicated supplement. The decision to give it up was a painful one for Eisner: he had poured into the feature all of his hopes and dreams for the art form for years. "I felt that I was at the epitome of the medium," he once told Jim Steranko, "and that I was helping in the development of a medium in itself. Comics before that were pretty much pictures in sequence, and I was trying to create an art form. It was a continuing laboratory, and I was very lucky because there wasn't anybody who could stop me from doing what I wanted."

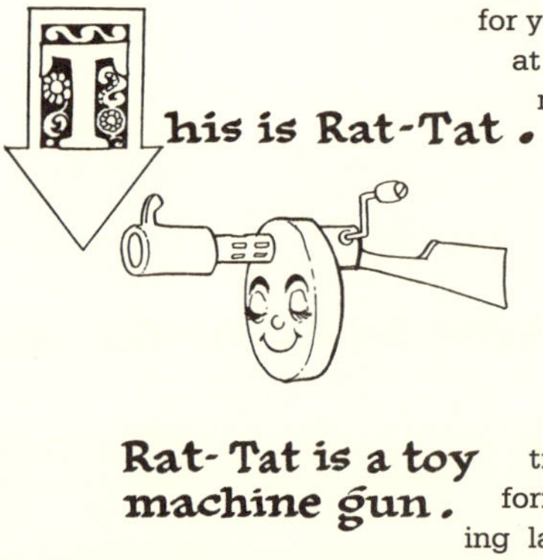
This is Rat-Tat.
Rat-Tat is a toy machine gun.

AN EXAMPLE OF EISNER'S UNCONVENTIONAL STORYTELLING FROM "THE STORY OF RAT-TAT THE TOY MACHINE GUN," 9/4/49.

But there were other creative vistas before him, and he decided at last to move on, discontinuing The Spirit with the story issued on October 5, 1952. But by then, with one virtuoso performance after another, he had amply displayed the artistry in telling stories in the visual-verbal mode, and he had also demonstrated triumphantly the literary validity of the art form.

Eisner would return to comic-book fiction twenty years later to pioneer in yet another use of the form, producing some of the earliest "graphic novels" to deal thoughtfully with mature themes. Successful as he was in this endeavor, for most of us it was still his Spirit creations that had so luminously showed the way during the years that the comic-book form was emerging as something different from newspaper comics. Indeed, Eisner might well be the one who made comic books different from comic strips. And in this library edition of The Spirit, we will have the evidence before us in chronological, developmental, order, page by page by page.

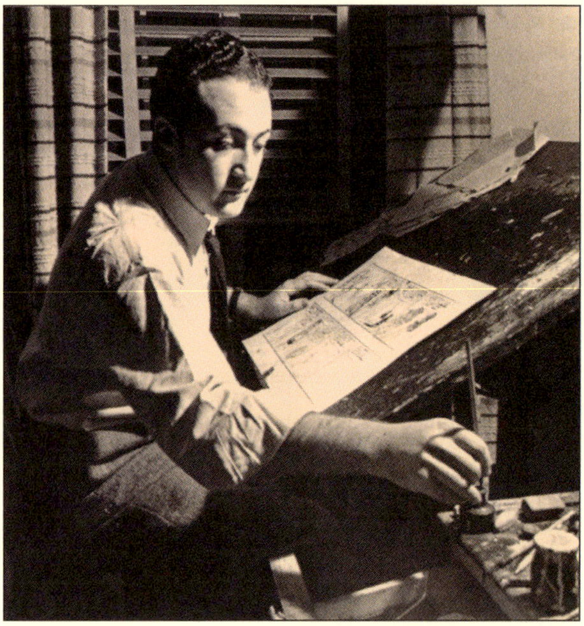

EISNER AT HIS DRAWING TABLE INKING THE SPIRIT DAILIES. 1941.

–R.C. Harvey
Illinois 2000

WEEKLY COMIC BOOK

THE ORIGIN OF THE SPIRIT

3 COMPLETE STORIES

June 2, 1940

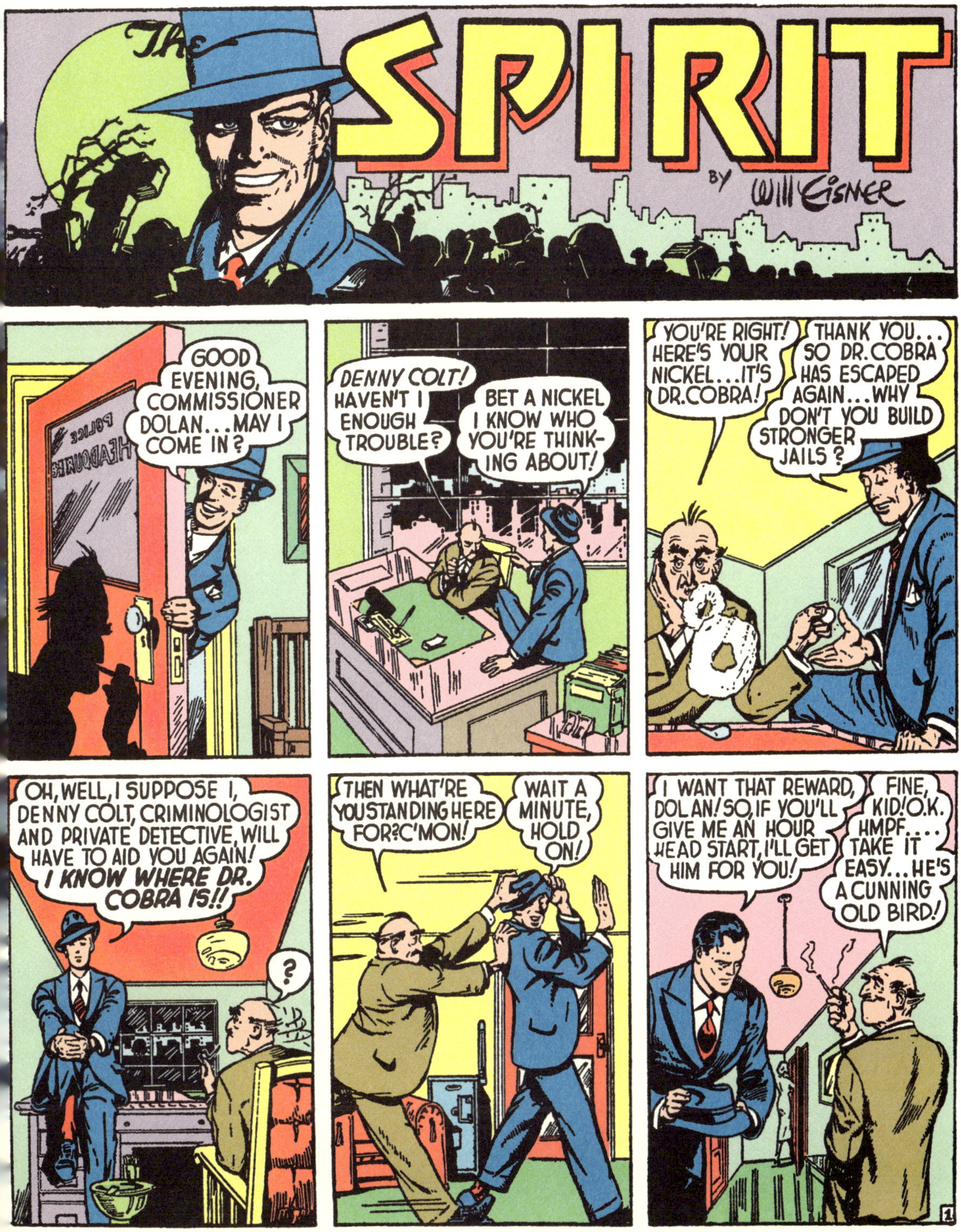
The SPIRIT
BY Will Eisner
GOOD EVENING, COMMISSIONER DOLAN...MAY I COME IN?
DENNY COLT! HAVEN'T I ENOUGH TROUBLE?
BET A NICKEL I KNOW WHO YOU'RE THINKING ABOUT!
YOU'RE RIGHT! HERE'S YOUR NICKEL...IT'S DR.COBRA!
THANK YOU... SO DR.COBRA HAS ESCAPED AGAIN...WHY DON'T YOU BUILD STRONGER JAILS?
OH, WELL, I SUPPOSE I, DENNY COLT, CRIMINOLOGIST AND PRIVATE DETECTIVE, WILL HAVE TO AID YOU AGAIN! I KNOW WHERE DR. COBRA IS!!
?
THEN WHAT'RE YOU STANDING HERE FOR? C'MON!
WAIT A MINUTE, HOLD ON!
I WANT THAT REWARD, DOLAN! SO, IF YOU'LL GIVE ME AN HOUR HEAD START, I'LL GET HIM FOR YOU!
FINE, KID! O.K. HMPF.... TAKE IT EASY... HE'S A CUNNING OLD BIRD!
1

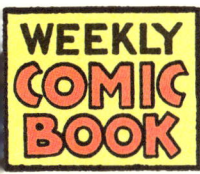

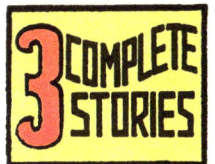

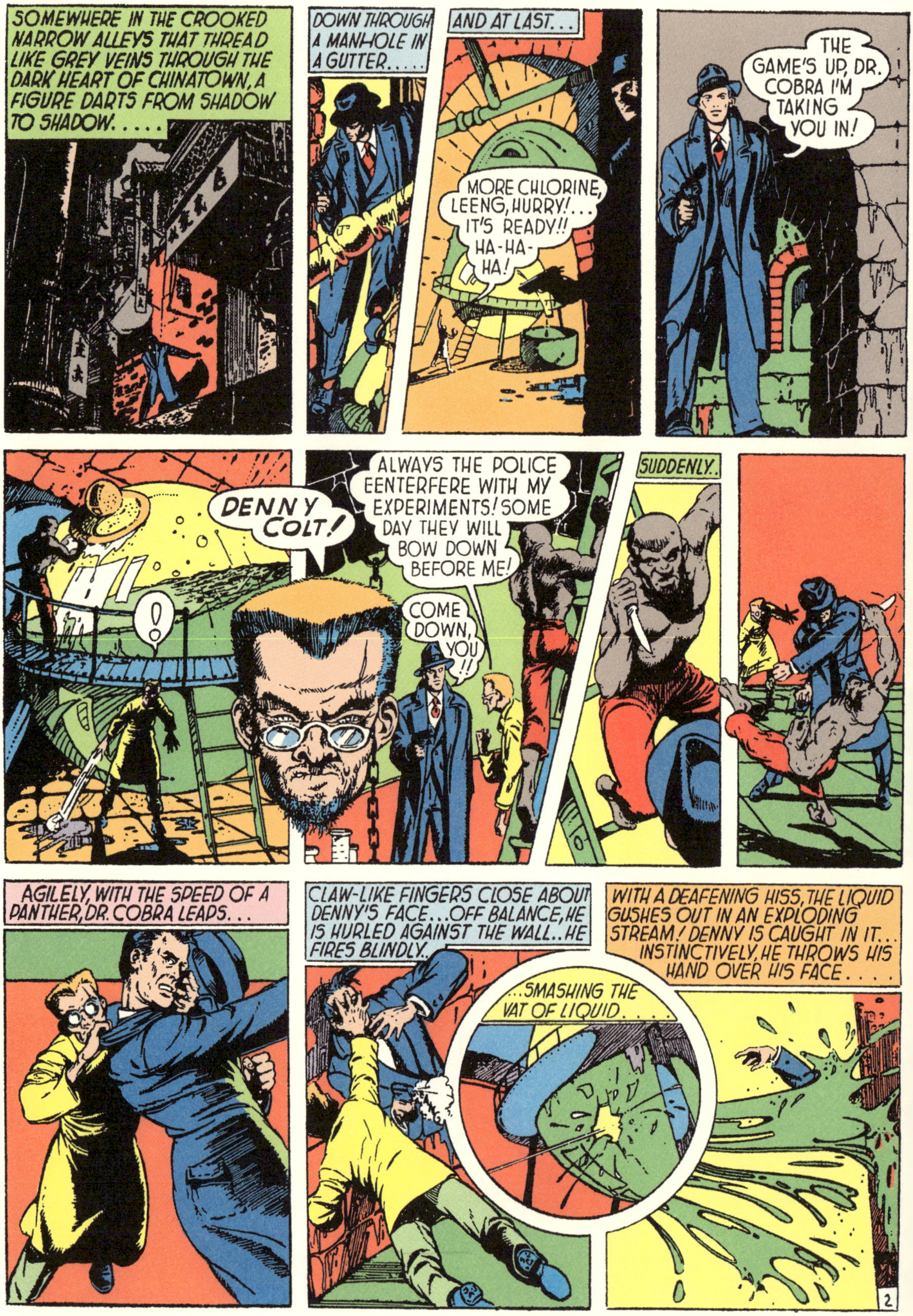
SOMEWHERE IN THE CROOKED NARROW ALLEYS THAT THREAD LIKE GREY VEINS THROUGH THE DARK HEART OF CHINATOWN, A FIGURE DARTS FROM SHADOW TO SHADOW.....
DOWN THROUGH A MANHOLE IN A GUTTER......
AND AT LAST...
MORE CHLORINE, LEENG, HURRY!... IT'S READY!! HA-HA-HA!
THE GAME'S UP, DR. COBRA I'M TAKING YOU IN!
DENNY COLT!
!
ALWAYS THE POLICE EENTERFERE WITH MY EXPERIMENTS! SOME DAY THEY WILL BOW DOWN BEFORE ME!
COME DOWN, YOU !!
SUDDENLY.
AGILELY, WITH THE SPEED OF A PANTHER, DR. COBRA LEAPS...
CLAW-LIKE FINGERS CLOSE ABOUT DENNY'S FACE...OFF BALANCE, HE IS HURLED AGAINST THE WALL.. HE FIRES BLINDLY...
...SMASHING THE VAT OF LIQUID....
WITH A DEAFENING HISS, THE LIQUID GUSHES OUT IN AN EXPLODING STREAM! DENNY IS CAUGHT IN IT... INSTINCTIVELY, HE THROWS HIS HAND OVER HIS FACE....
2

DRENCHED IN THE LIQUID, DENNY SINKS TO THE FLOOR... DR. COBRA DRAGS HIS AIDE OUT THROUGH A SECRET PASSAGE...
AND BEHIND THEM, DIMLY OUTLINED BY THE STRANGE LIGHT CAST BY THE EQUALLY STRANGE CHEMICAL, THE BODY OF DENNY COLT LIES RIGID... UNMOVING!
A FEW MINUTES LATER, A SIREN SHATTERS THE QUIET OF THE NIGHT AS DOLAN AND HIS MEN ARRIVE ON THE SCENE...
HURRY UP, YOU MEN! DENNY MAY BE IN TROUBLE!
THERE'S BEEN A SCRAP! LOOK!! THAT'S DENNY LYING IN THE POOL OF WATER!
DEAD! GET THE CORONER, KELLY!
THIS MAN'S DEAD ALL RIGHT! RIGOR MORTIS HAS ALREADY SET IN! I'D CALL IT HEART FAILURE... NO SERIOUS WOUNDS.
HEART FAILURE DON'T SEEM RIGHT! NO... HE WAS A GREAT KID... I LIKED HIM.
NEXT DAY...
Obituary...
FUNERAL RITES HELD TODAY.
DENNY COLT, CRIMINOLOGIST, KILLED WHILE ATTEMPTING TO CAPTURE A NOTORIOUS MADMAN...
THE FOLLOWING NIGHT, IN A SUBURBAN CEMETERY, A FANTASTIC SIGHT MEETS THE EYE...
AN HOUR LATER, AT POLICE HEADQUARTERS, IN COMMISSIONER DOLAN'S OFFICE...
HEY! HOW'D YOU GET IN?
KEEP YOUR SEAT, COMMISSIONER, AND I'LL DO THE TALKING! DON'T REACH FOR THAT GUN... THAT'S RIGHT, JUST SIT BACK AND LISTEN!
3

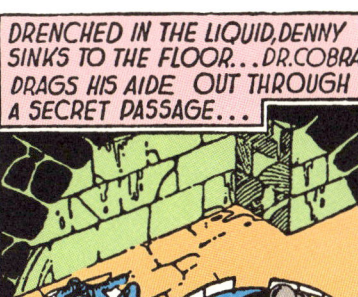

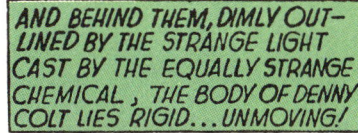

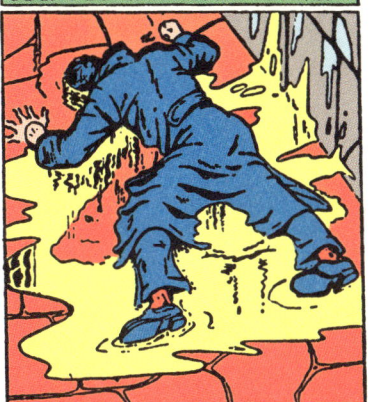

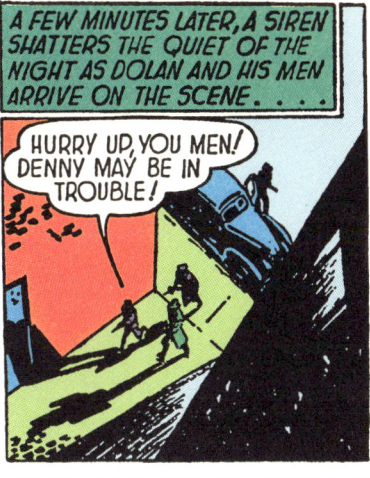

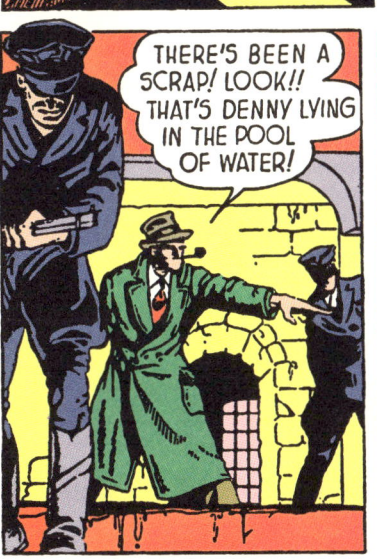

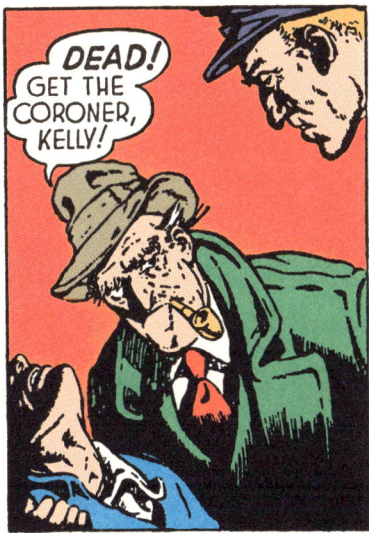

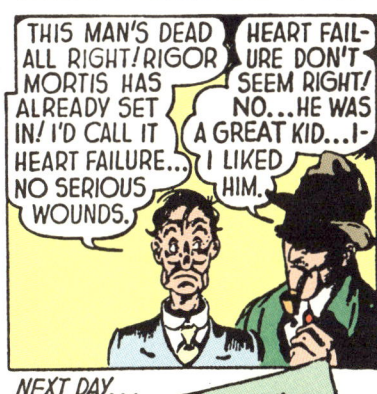

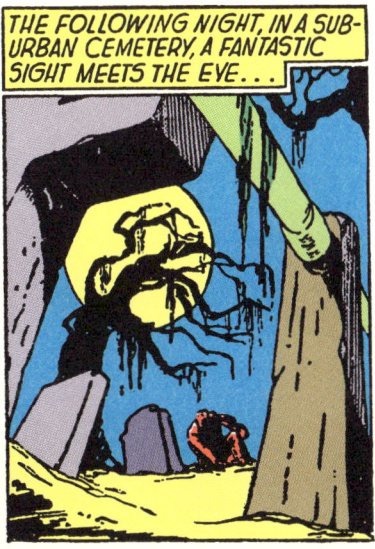

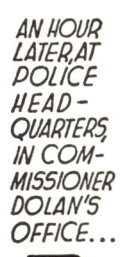

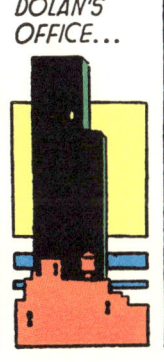

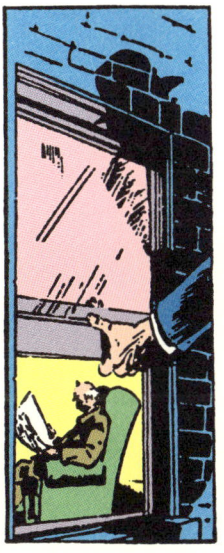

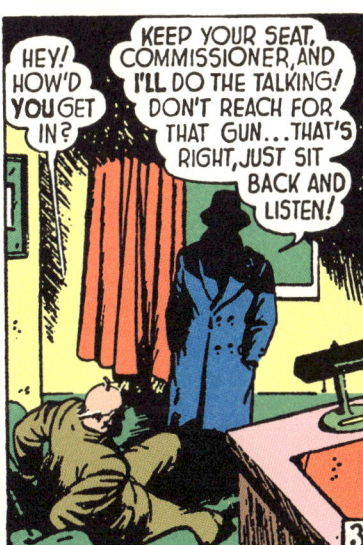

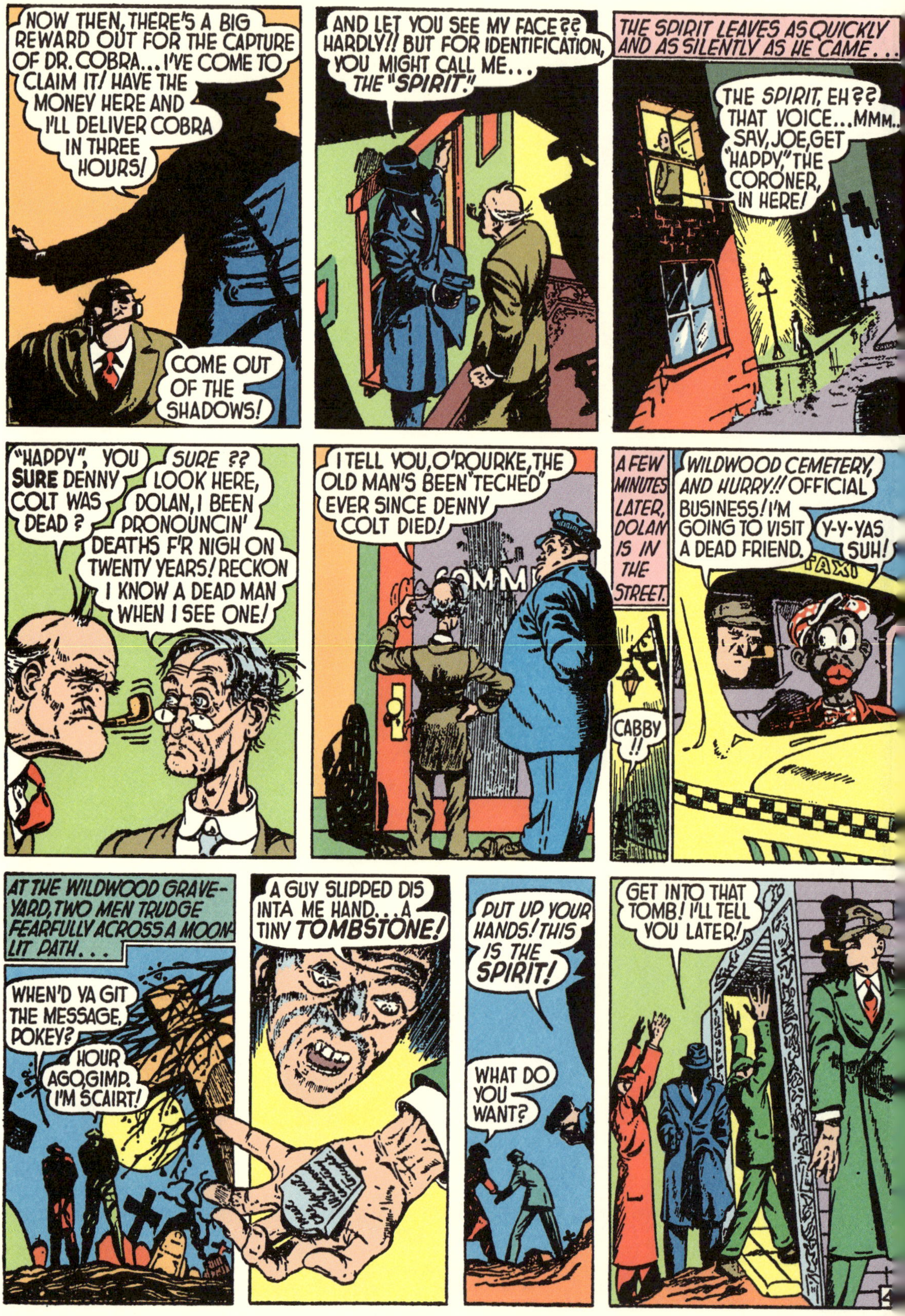
NOW THEN, THERE'S A BIG REWARD OUT FOR THE CAPTURE OF DR. COBRA... I'VE COME TO CLAIM IT! HAVE THE MONEY HERE AND I'LL DELIVER COBRA IN THREE HOURS!
COME OUT OF THE SHADOWS!
AND LET YOU SEE MY FACE?? HARDLY!! BUT FOR IDENTIFICATION, YOU MIGHT CALL ME... THE "SPIRIT."
THE SPIRIT LEAVES AS QUICKLY AND AS SILENTLY AS HE CAME...
THE SPIRIT, EH?? THAT VOICE...MMM.. SAY, JOE, GET "HAPPY," THE CORONER, IN HERE!
"HAPPY", YOU SURE DENNY COLT WAS DEAD?
SURE ?? LOOK HERE, DOLAN, I BEEN PRONOUNCIN' DEATHS F'R NIGH ON TWENTY YEARS! RECKON I KNOW A DEAD MAN WHEN I SEE ONE!
I TELL YOU, O'ROURKE, THE OLD MAN'S BEEN "TECHED" EVER SINCE DENNY COLT DIED!
A FEW MINUTES LATER, DOLAN IS IN THE STREET
CABBY !!
WILDWOOD CEMETERY, AND HURRY!! OFFICIAL BUSINESS! I'M GOING TO VISIT A DEAD FRIEND.
Y-Y-YAS SUH!
TAXI
AT THE WILDWOOD GRAVEYARD, TWO MEN TRUDGE FEARFULLY ACROSS A MOONLIT PATH...
WHEN'D YA GIT THE MESSAGE, POKEY?
HOUR AGO, GIMP. I'M SCAIRT!
A GUY SLIPPED DIS INTA ME HAND... A TINY TOMBSTONE!
PUT UP YOUR HANDS! THIS IS THE SPIRIT!
WHAT DO YOU WANT?
GET INTO THAT TOMB! I'LL TELL YOU LATER!

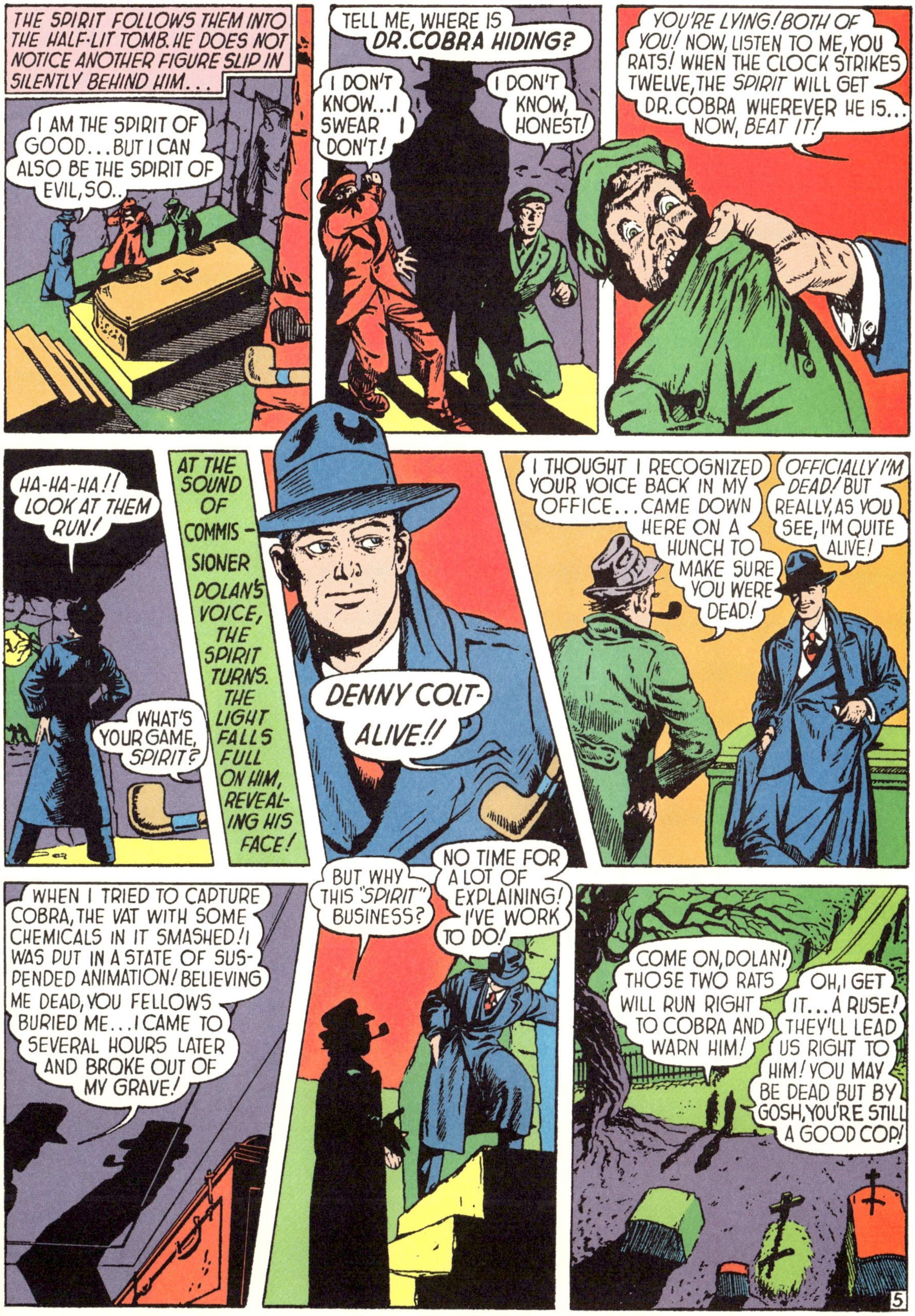
THE SPIRIT FOLLOWS THEM INTO THE HALF-LIT TOMB. HE DOES NOT NOTICE ANOTHER FIGURE SLIP IN SILENTLY BEHIND HIM...
I AM THE SPIRIT OF GOOD... BUT I CAN ALSO BE THE SPIRIT OF EVIL, SO..
TELL ME, WHERE IS DR. COBRA HIDING?
I DON'T KNOW... I SWEAR I DON'T!
I DON'T KNOW, HONEST!
YOU'RE LYING! BOTH OF YOU! NOW, LISTEN TO ME, YOU RATS! WHEN THE CLOCK STRIKES TWELVE, THE SPIRIT WILL GET DR. COBRA WHEREVER HE IS... NOW, BEAT IT!
HA-HA-HA!! LOOK AT THEM RUN!
WHAT'S YOUR GAME, SPIRIT?
AT THE SOUND OF COMMIS-SIONER DOLAN'S VOICE, THE SPIRIT TURNS. THE LIGHT FALLS FULL ON HIM, REVEAL-ING HIS FACE!
DENNY COLT- ALIVE!!
I THOUGHT I RECOGNIZED YOUR VOICE BACK IN MY OFFICE... CAME DOWN HERE ON A HUNCH TO MAKE SURE YOU WERE DEAD!
OFFICIALLY I'M DEAD! BUT REALLY, AS YOU SEE, I'M QUITE ALIVE!
WHEN I TRIED TO CAPTURE COBRA, THE VAT WITH SOME CHEMICALS IN IT SMASHED! I WAS PUT IN A STATE OF SUS-PENDED ANIMATION! BELIEVING ME DEAD, YOU FELLOWS BURIED ME... I CAME TO SEVERAL HOURS LATER AND BROKE OUT OF MY GRAVE!
BUT WHY THIS "SPIRIT" BUSINESS?
NO TIME FOR A LOT OF EXPLAINING! I'VE WORK TO DO!
COME ON, DOLAN! THOSE TWO RATS WILL RUN RIGHT TO COBRA AND WARN HIM!
OH, I GET IT... A RUSE! THEY'LL LEAD US RIGHT TO HIM! YOU MAY BE DEAD BUT BY GOSH, YOU'RE STILL A GOOD COP!
5

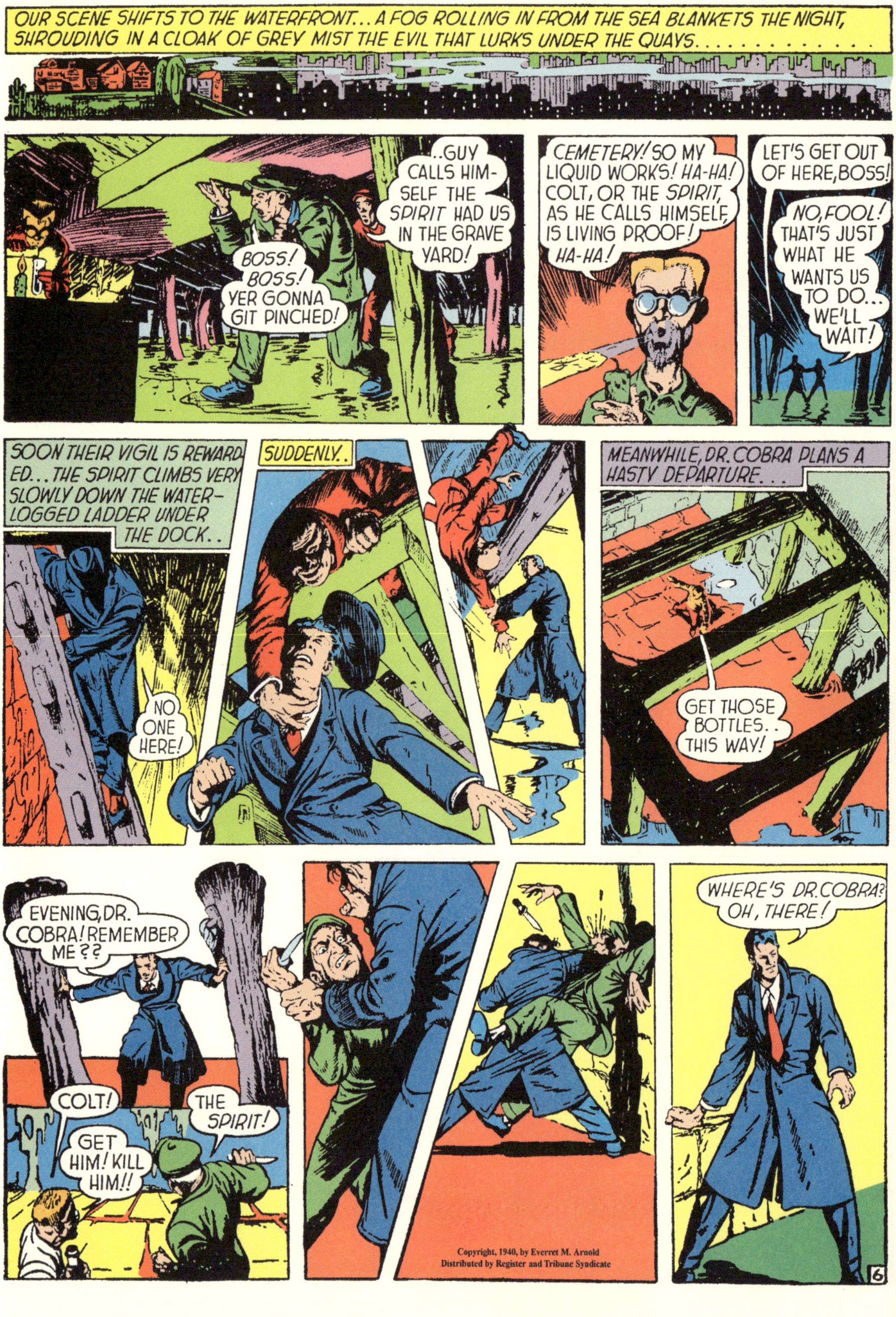
OUR SCENE SHIFTS TO THE WATERFRONT... A FOG ROLLING IN FROM THE SEA BLANKETS THE NIGHT, SHROUDING IN A CLOAK OF GREY MIST THE EVIL THAT LURKS UNDER THE QUAYS............
..GUY CALLS HIMSELF THE SPIRIT HAD US IN THE GRAVE YARD!
BOSS! BOSS! YER GONNA GIT PINCHED!
CEMETERY! SO MY LIQUID WORKS! HA-HA! COLT, OR THE SPIRIT, AS HE CALLS HIMSELF, IS LIVING PROOF! HA-HA!
LET'S GET OUT OF HERE, BOSS!
NO, FOOL! THAT'S JUST WHAT HE WANTS US TO DO... WE'LL WAIT!
SOON THEIR VIGIL IS REWARDED... THE SPIRIT CLIMBS VERY SLOWLY DOWN THE WATER-LOGGED LADDER UNDER THE DOCK..
NO ONE HERE!
SUDDENLY..
MEANWHILE, DR. COBRA PLANS A HASTY DEPARTURE...
GET THOSE BOTTLES.. THIS WAY!
EVENING, DR. COBRA! REMEMBER ME??
COLT!
THE SPIRIT!
GET HIM! KILL HIM!!
WHERE'S DR. COBRA? OH, THERE!
6

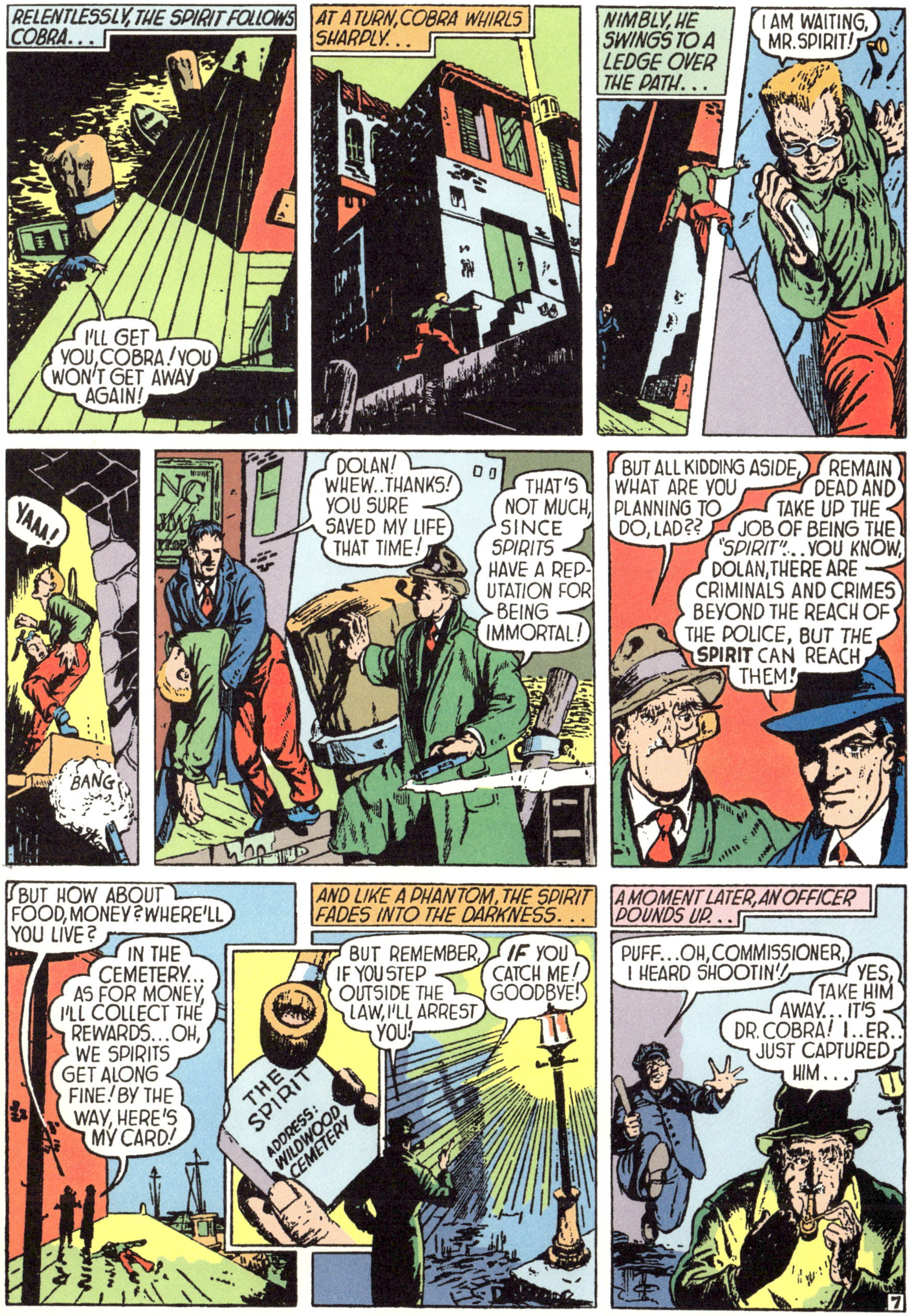
RELENTLESSLY, THE SPIRIT FOLLOWS COBRA...
I'LL GET YOU, COBRA! YOU WON'T GET AWAY AGAIN!
AT A TURN, COBRA WHIRLS SHARPLY...
NIMBLY, HE SWINGS TO A LEDGE OVER THE PATH...
I AM WAITING, MR. SPIRIT!
YAAA!
BANG
DOLAN! WHEW..THANKS! YOU SURE SAVED MY LIFE THAT TIME!
THAT'S NOT MUCH, SINCE SPIRITS HAVE A REPUTATION FOR BEING IMMORTAL!
BUT ALL KIDDING ASIDE, WHAT ARE YOU PLANNING TO DO, LAD??
REMAIN DEAD AND TAKE UP THE JOB OF BEING THE "SPIRIT"... YOU KNOW, DOLAN, THERE ARE CRIMINALS AND CRIMES BEYOND THE REACH OF THE POLICE, BUT THE SPIRIT CAN REACH THEM!
BUT HOW ABOUT FOOD, MONEY? WHERE'LL YOU LIVE?
IN THE CEMETERY... AS FOR MONEY, I'LL COLLECT THE REWARDS... OH, WE SPIRITS GET ALONG FINE! BY THE WAY, HERE'S MY CARD!
THE SPIRIT ADDRESS: WILDWOOD CEMETERY
AND LIKE A PHANTOM, THE SPIRIT FADES INTO THE DARKNESS...
BUT REMEMBER, IF YOU STEP OUTSIDE THE LAW, I'LL ARREST YOU!
IF YOU CATCH ME! GOODBYE!
A MOMENT LATER, AN OFFICER POUNDS UP...
PUFF...OH, COMMISSIONER, I HEARD SHOOTIN'!
YES, TAKE HIM AWAY... IT'S DR. COBRA! I..ER.. JUST CAPTURED HIM...
7

WEEKLY COMIC BOOK

THE RETURN OF DR. COBRA

3 COMPLETE STORIES

June 9, 1940

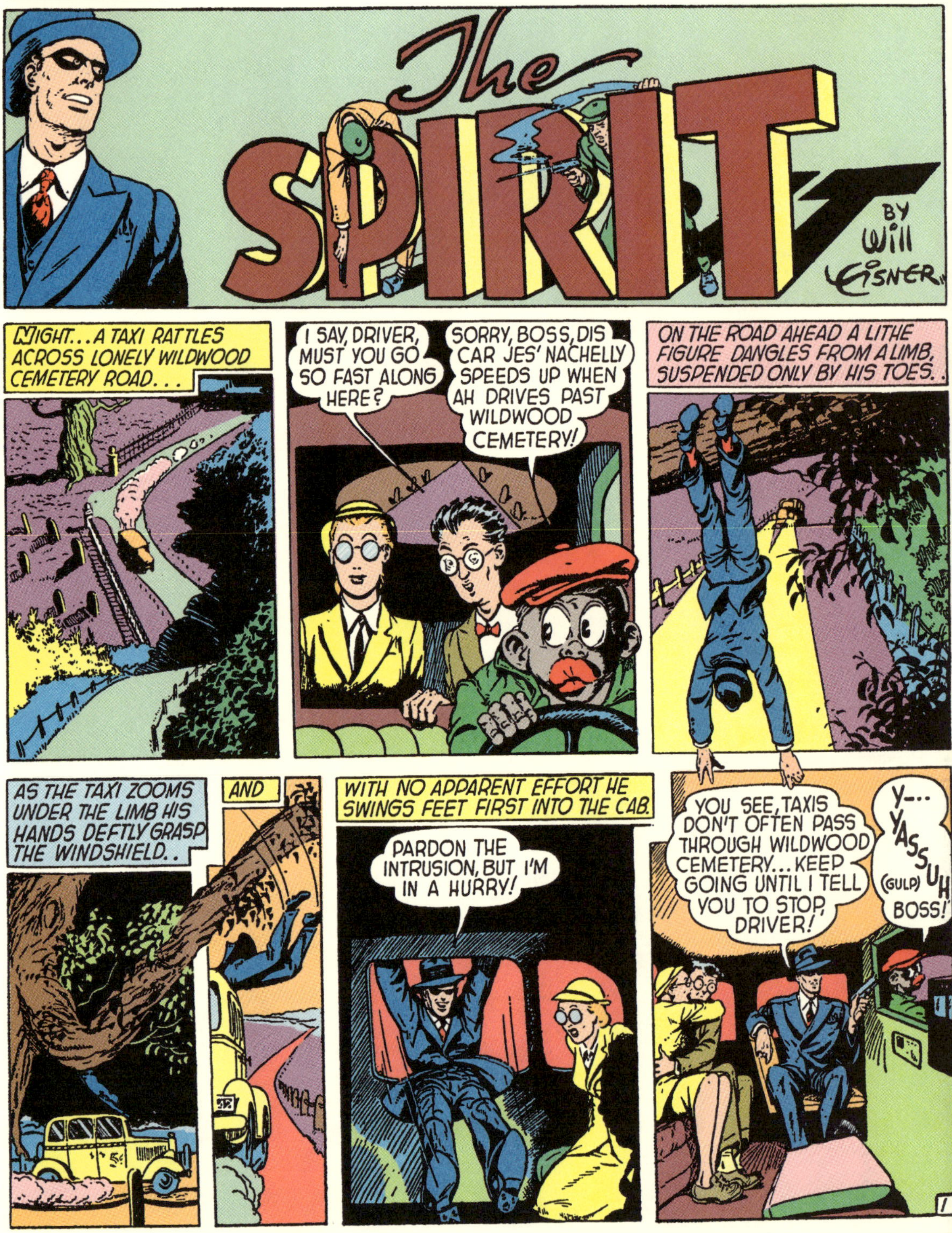

The SPIRIT
BY Will Eisner
NIGHT... A TAXI RATTLES ACROSS LONELY WILDWOOD CEMETERY ROAD...
I SAY, DRIVER, MUST YOU GO SO FAST ALONG HERE?
SORRY, BOSS, DIS CAR JES' NACHELLY SPEEDS UP WHEN AH DRIVES PAST WILDWOOD CEMETERY!
ON THE ROAD AHEAD A LITHE FIGURE DANGLES FROM A LIMB, SUSPENDED ONLY BY HIS TOES.
AS THE TAXI ZOOMS UNDER THE LIMB HIS HANDS DEFTLY GRASP THE WINDSHIELD..
AND
WITH NO APPARENT EFFORT HE SWINGS FEET FIRST INTO THE CAB.
PARDON THE INTRUSION, BUT I'M IN A HURRY!
YOU SEE, TAXIS DON'T OFTEN PASS THROUGH WILDWOOD CEMETERY... KEEP GOING UNTIL I TELL YOU TO STOP, DRIVER!
Y-... YASSUH (GULP) BOSS!
1

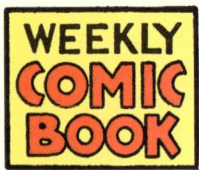

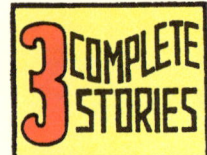

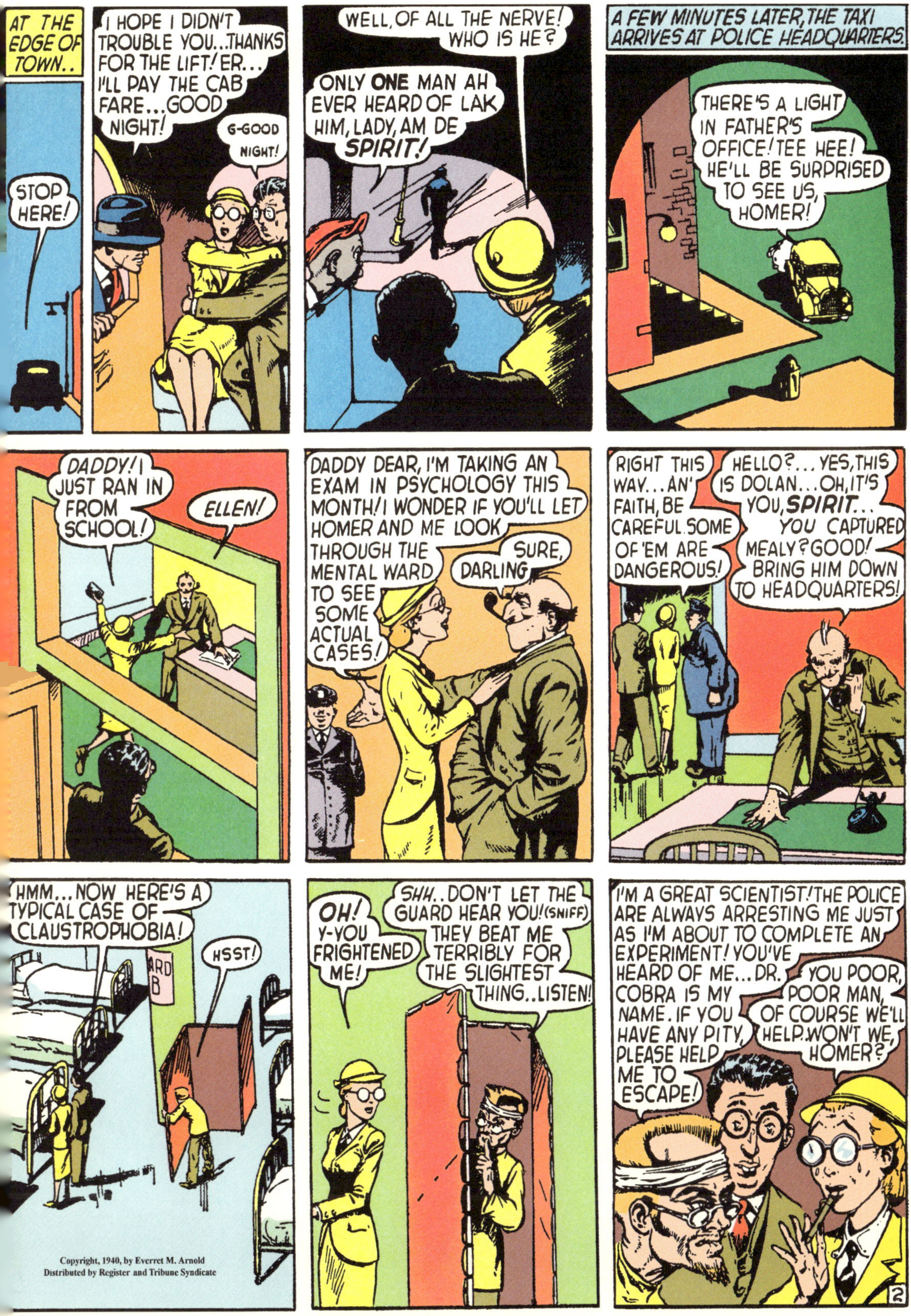
AT THE EDGE OF TOWN..
STOP HERE!
I HOPE I DIDN'T TROUBLE YOU...THANKS FOR THE LIFT! ER... I'LL PAY THE CAB FARE...GOOD NIGHT!
G-GOOD NIGHT!
WELL, OF ALL THE NERVE! WHO IS HE?
ONLY ONE MAN AH EVER HEARD OF LAK HIM, LADY, AM DE SPIRIT!
A FEW MINUTES LATER, THE TAXI ARRIVES AT POLICE HEADQUARTERS.
THERE'S A LIGHT IN FATHER'S OFFICE! TEE HEE! HE'LL BE SURPRISED TO SEE US, HOMER!
DADDY! I JUST RAN IN FROM SCHOOL!
ELLEN!
DADDY DEAR, I'M TAKING AN EXAM IN PSYCHOLOGY THIS MONTH! I WONDER IF YOU'LL LET HOMER AND ME LOOK THROUGH THE MENTAL WARD TO SEE SOME ACTUAL CASES!
SURE, DARLING
RIGHT THIS WAY...AN' FAITH, BE CAREFUL. SOME OF 'EM ARE DANGEROUS!
HELLO?... YES, THIS IS DOLAN...OH, IT'S YOU, SPIRIT... YOU CAPTURED MEALY? GOOD! BRING HIM DOWN TO HEADQUARTERS!
HMM...NOW HERE'S A TYPICAL CASE OF CLAUSTROPHOBIA!
HSST!
OH! Y-YOU FRIGHTENED ME!
SHH..DON'T LET THE GUARD HEAR YOU! (SNIFF) THEY BEAT ME TERRIBLY FOR THE SLIGHTEST THING..LISTEN!
I'M A GREAT SCIENTIST! THE POLICE ARE ALWAYS ARRESTING ME JUST AS I'M ABOUT TO COMPLETE AN EXPERIMENT! YOU'VE HEARD OF ME...DR. COBRA IS MY NAME. IF YOU HAVE ANY PITY, PLEASE HELP ME TO ESCAPE!
YOU POOR, POOR MAN, OF COURSE WE'LL HELP. WON'T WE, HOMER?
2

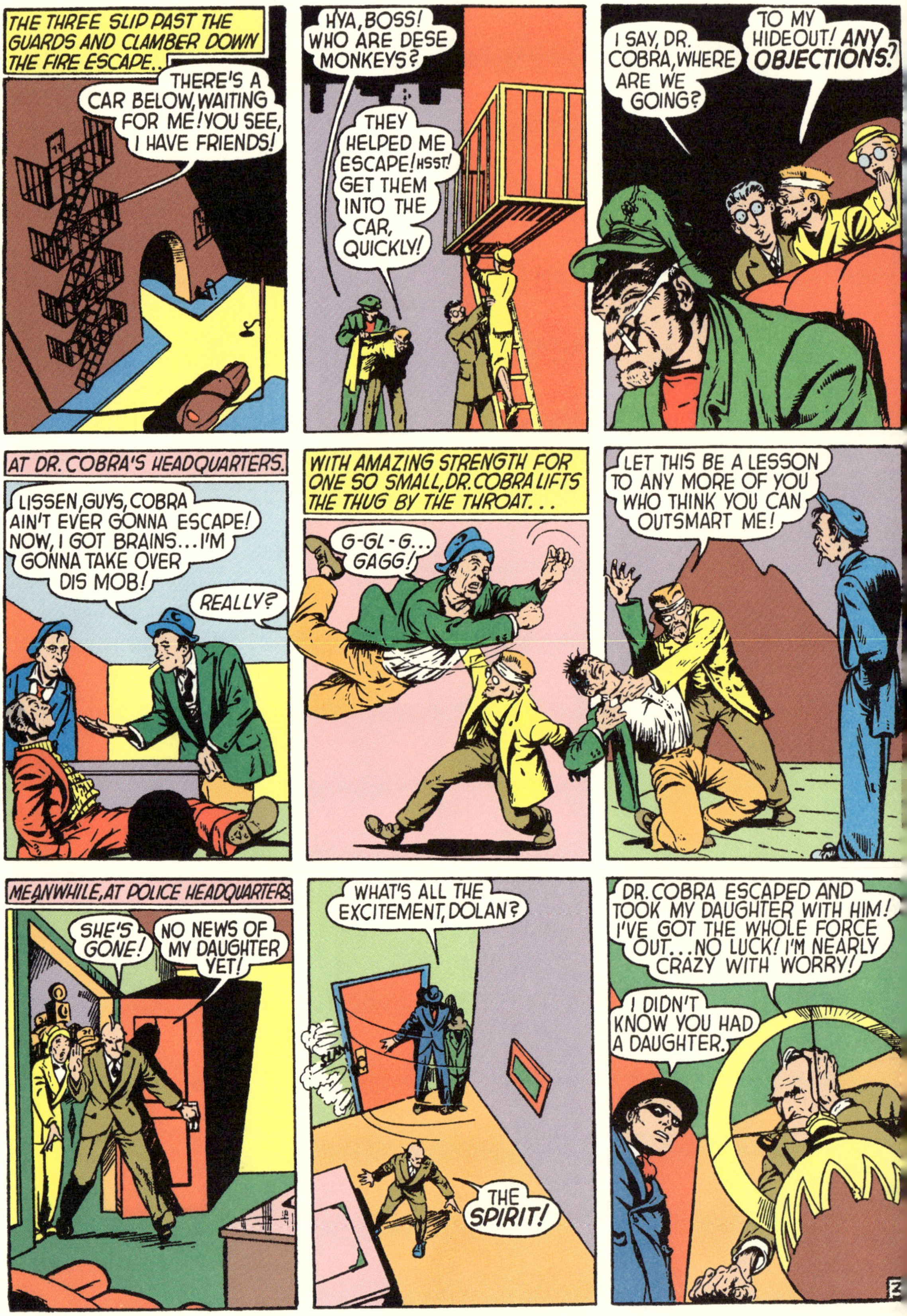

THE THREE SLIP PAST THE GUARDS AND CLAMBER DOWN THE FIRE ESCAPE...
THERE'S A CAR BELOW, WAITING FOR ME! YOU SEE, I HAVE FRIENDS!
HYA, BOSS! WHO ARE DESE MONKEYS?
THEY HELPED ME ESCAPE! HSST! GET THEM INTO THE CAR, QUICKLY!
I SAY, DR. COBRA, WHERE ARE WE GOING?
TO MY HIDEOUT! ANY OBJECTIONS?
AT DR. COBRA'S HEADQUARTERS.
LISSEN, GUYS, COBRA AIN'T EVER GONNA ESCAPE! NOW, I GOT BRAINS... I'M GONNA TAKE OVER DIS MOB!
REALLY?
WITH AMAZING STRENGTH FOR ONE SO SMALL, DR. COBRA LIFTS THE THUG BY THE THROAT...
G-GL-G... GAGG!
LET THIS BE A LESSON TO ANY MORE OF YOU WHO THINK YOU CAN OUTSMART ME!
MEANWHILE, AT POLICE HEADQUARTERS
SHE'S GONE!
NO NEWS OF MY DAUGHTER YET!
WHAT'S ALL THE EXCITEMENT, DOLAN?
THE SPIRIT!
DR. COBRA ESCAPED AND TOOK MY DAUGHTER WITH HIM! I'VE GOT THE WHOLE FORCE OUT... NO LUCK! I'M NEARLY CRAZY WITH WORRY!
I DIDN'T KNOW YOU HAD A DAUGHTER.

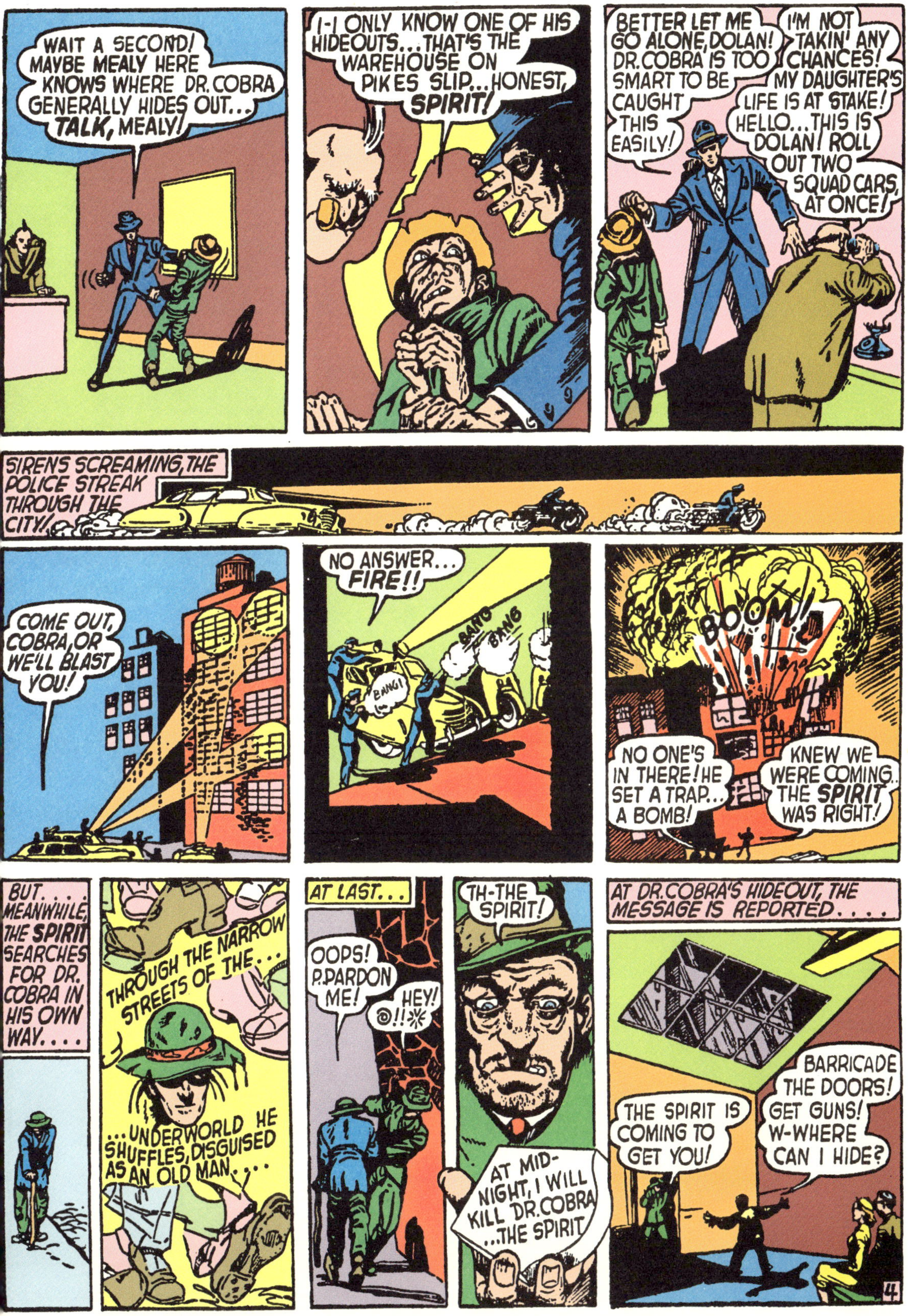
WAIT A SECOND! MAYBE MEALY HERE KNOWS WHERE DR. COBRA GENERALLY HIDES OUT... TALK, MEALY!
I-I ONLY KNOW ONE OF HIS HIDEOUTS... THAT'S THE WAREHOUSE ON PIKES SLIP... HONEST, SPIRIT!
BETTER LET ME GO ALONE, DOLAN! DR. COBRA IS TOO SMART TO BE CAUGHT THIS EASILY!
I'M NOT TAKIN' ANY CHANCES! MY DAUGHTER'S LIFE IS AT STAKE! HELLO... THIS IS DOLAN! ROLL OUT TWO SQUAD CARS, AT ONCE!
SIRENS SCREAMING, THE POLICE STREAK THROUGH THE CITY!
COME OUT, COBRA, OR WE'LL BLAST YOU!
NO ANSWER... FIRE!!
BANG
BANG
BANG!
BOOM!
NO ONE'S IN THERE! HE SET A TRAP... A BOMB!
KNEW WE WERE COMING.. THE SPIRIT WAS RIGHT!
BUT.... MEANWHILE, THE SPIRIT SEARCHES FOR DR. COBRA IN HIS OWN WAY....
THROUGH THE NARROW STREETS OF THE...
...UNDERWORLD HE SHUFFLES, DISGUISED AS AN OLD MAN....
AT LAST...
OOPS! P-PARDON ME!
HEY! @!!*
TH-THE SPIRIT!
AT MID-NIGHT, I WILL KILL DR. COBRA ...THE SPIRIT
AT DR. COBRA'S HIDEOUT, THE MESSAGE IS REPORTED....
THE SPIRIT IS COMING TO GET YOU!
BARRICADE THE DOORS! GET GUNS! W-WHERE CAN I HIDE?
4

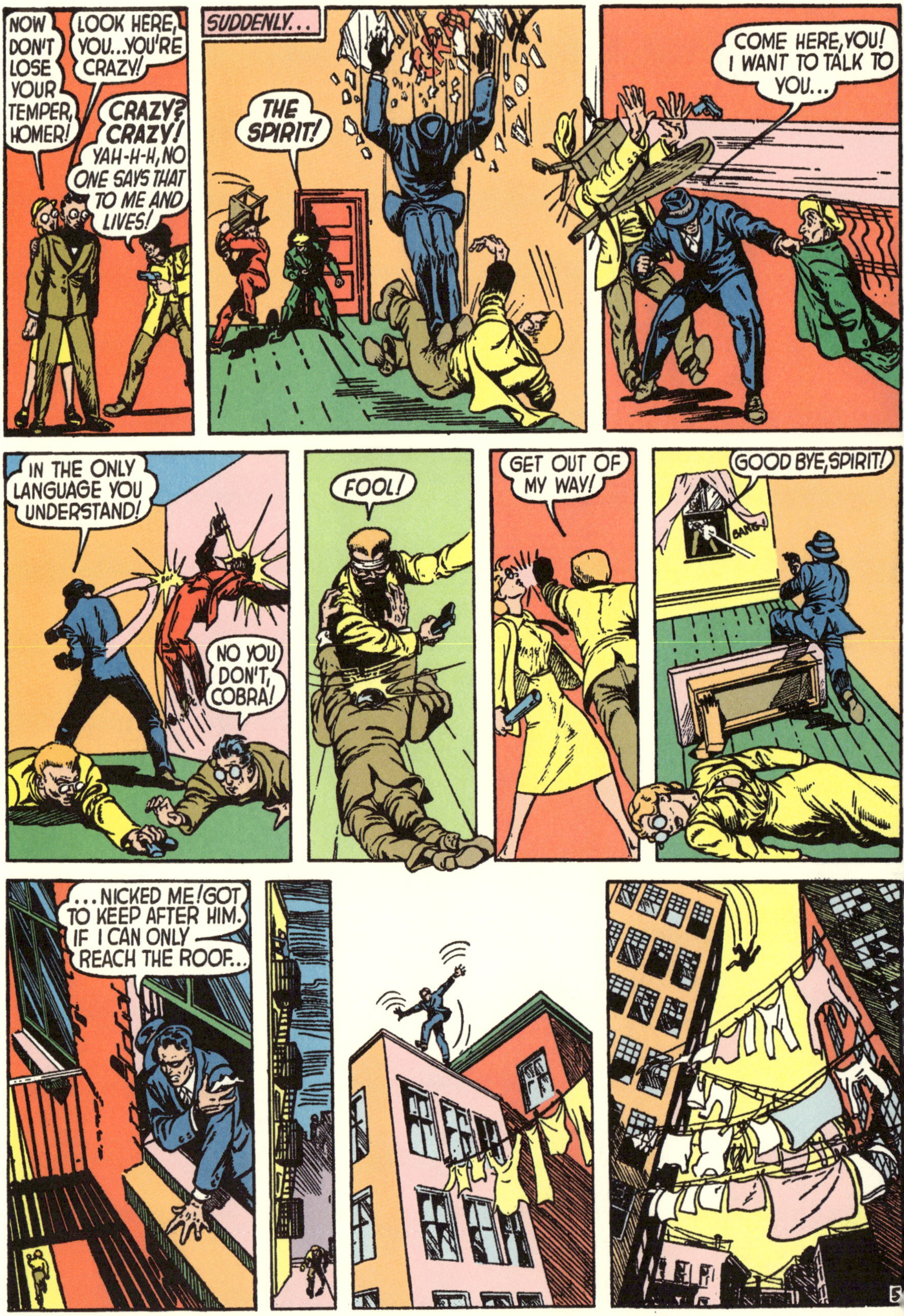
NOW DON'T LOSE YOUR TEMPER, HOMER!
LOOK HERE, YOU...YOU'RE CRAZY!
CRAZY? CRAZY! YAH-H-H, NO ONE SAYS THAT TO ME AND LIVES!
SUDDENLY...
THE SPIRIT!
COME HERE, YOU! I WANT TO TALK TO YOU...
IN THE ONLY LANGUAGE YOU UNDERSTAND!
NO YOU DON'T, COBRA!
FOOL!
GET OUT OF MY WAY!
GOOD BYE, SPIRIT!
...NICKED ME! GOT TO KEEP AFTER HIM. IF I CAN ONLY REACH THE ROOF...
5

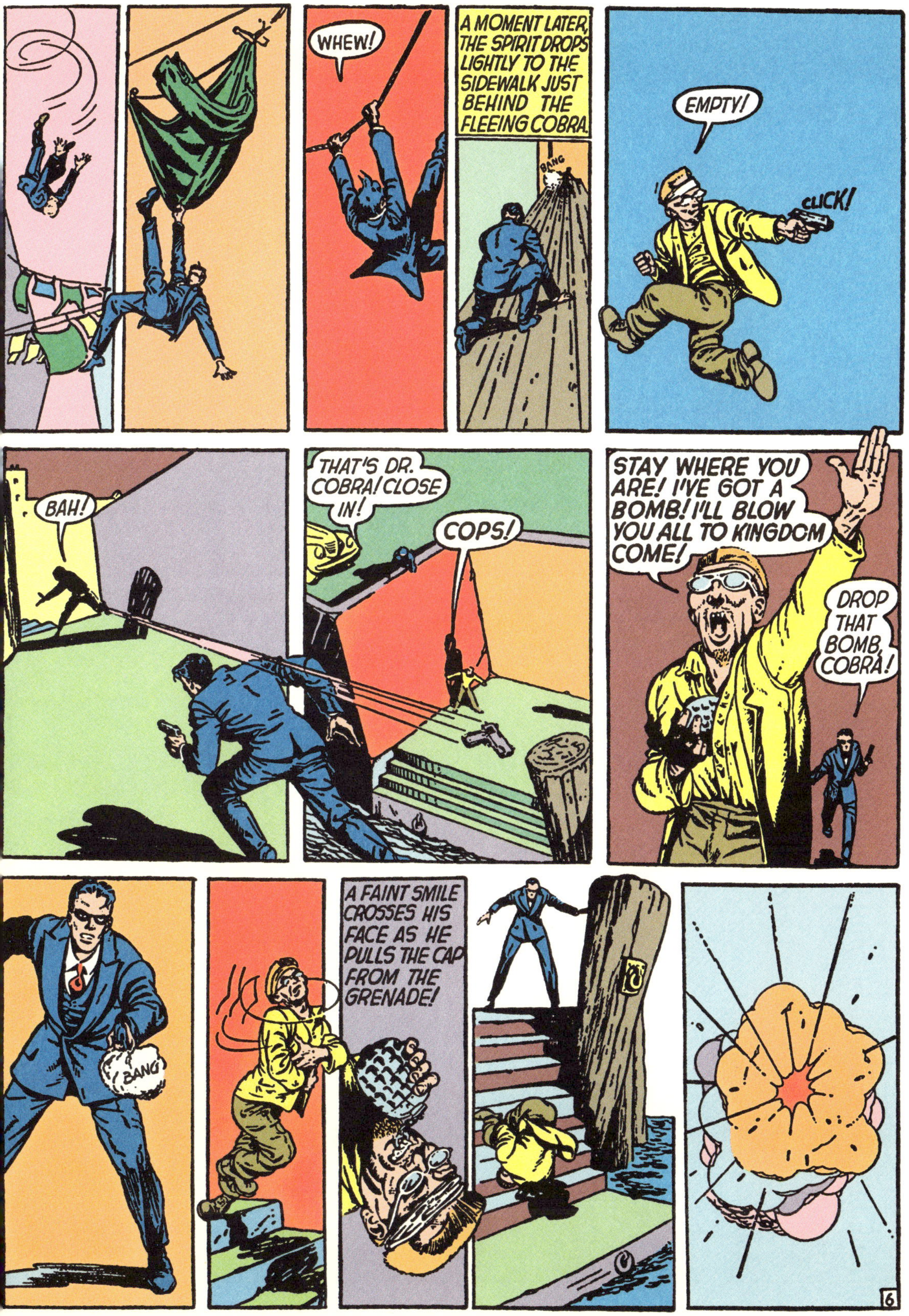
WHEW!
A MOMENT LATER, THE SPIRIT DROPS LIGHTLY TO THE SIDEWALK JUST BEHIND THE FLEEING COBRA.
BANG
EMPTY!
CLICK!
BAH!
THAT'S DR. COBRA! CLOSE IN!
COPS!
STAY WHERE YOU ARE! I'VE GOT A BOMB! I'LL BLOW YOU ALL TO KINGDOM COME!
DROP THAT BOMB, COBRA!
BANG
A FAINT SMILE CROSSES HIS FACE AS HE PULLS THE CAP FROM THE GRENADE!
6

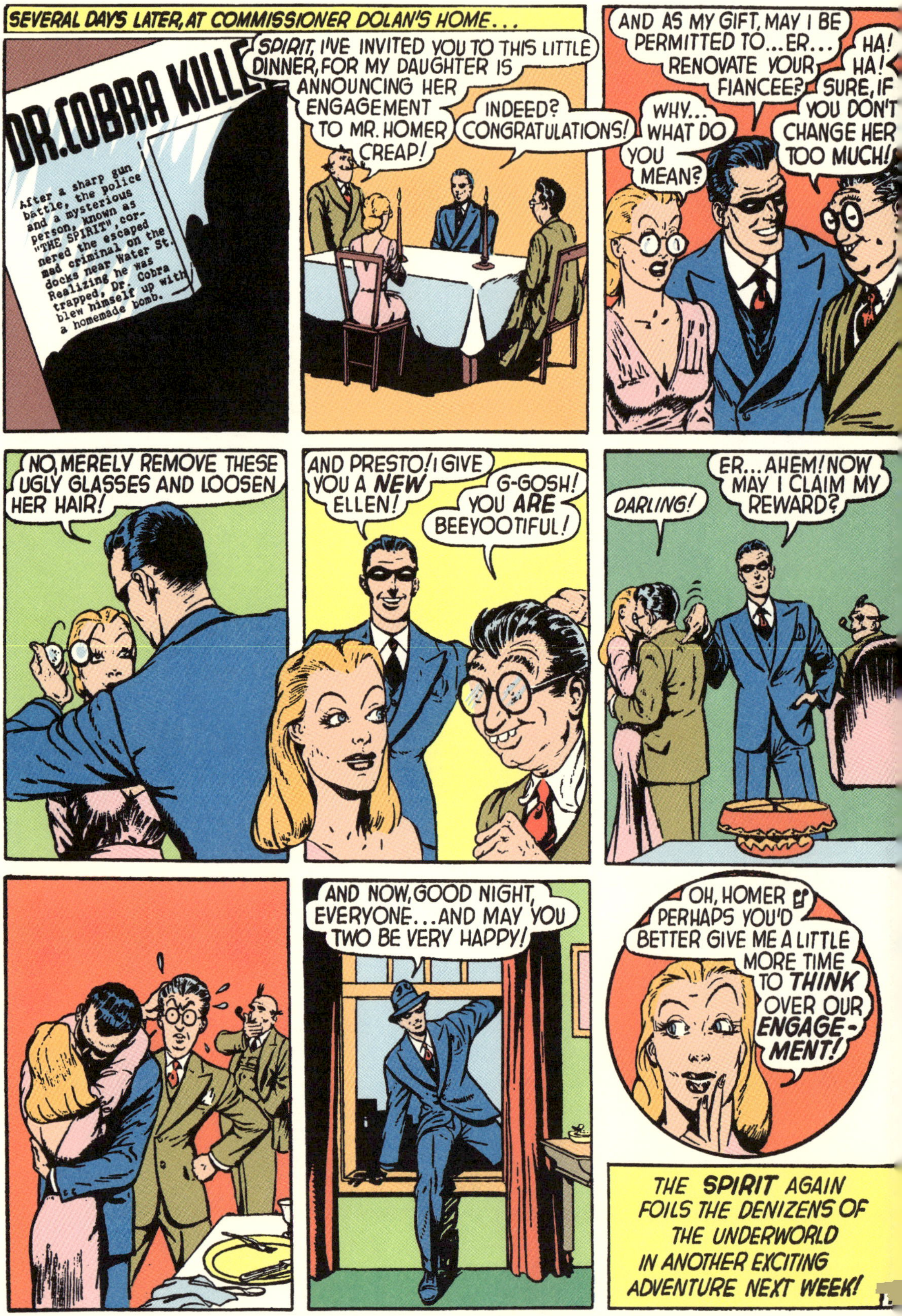
SEVERAL DAYS LATER, AT COMMISSIONER DOLAN'S HOME...
DR.COBRA KILLE
After a sharp gun battle, the police and a mysterious person, known as "THE SPIRIT", cornered the escaped mad criminal on the docks near Water St. Realizing he was trapped, Dr. Cobra blew himself up with a homemade bomb.
SPIRIT, I'VE INVITED YOU TO THIS LITTLE DINNER, FOR MY DAUGHTER IS ANNOUNCING HER ENGAGEMENT TO MR. HOMER CREAP!
INDEED? CONGRATULATIONS!
AND AS MY GIFT, MAY I BE PERMITTED TO...ER... RENOVATE YOUR FIANCEE?
WHY... WHAT DO YOU MEAN?
HA! HA! SURE, IF YOU DON'T CHANGE HER TOO MUCH!
NO, MERELY REMOVE THESE UGLY GLASSES AND LOOSEN HER HAIR!
AND PRESTO! I GIVE YOU A NEW ELLEN!
G-GOSH! YOU ARE BEEYOOTIFUL!
DARLING!
ER...AHEM! NOW MAY I CLAIM MY REWARD?
AND NOW, GOOD NIGHT, EVERYONE...AND MAY YOU TWO BE VERY HAPPY!
OH, HOMER PERHAPS YOU'D BETTER GIVE ME A LITTLE MORE TIME TO THINK OVER OUR ENGAGEMENT!
THE SPIRIT AGAIN FOILS THE DENIZENS OF THE UNDERWORLD IN ANOTHER EXCITING ADVENTURE NEXT WEEK!

WEEKLY COMIC BOOK

THE BLACK QUEEN

3 COMPLETE STORIES

June 16, 1940

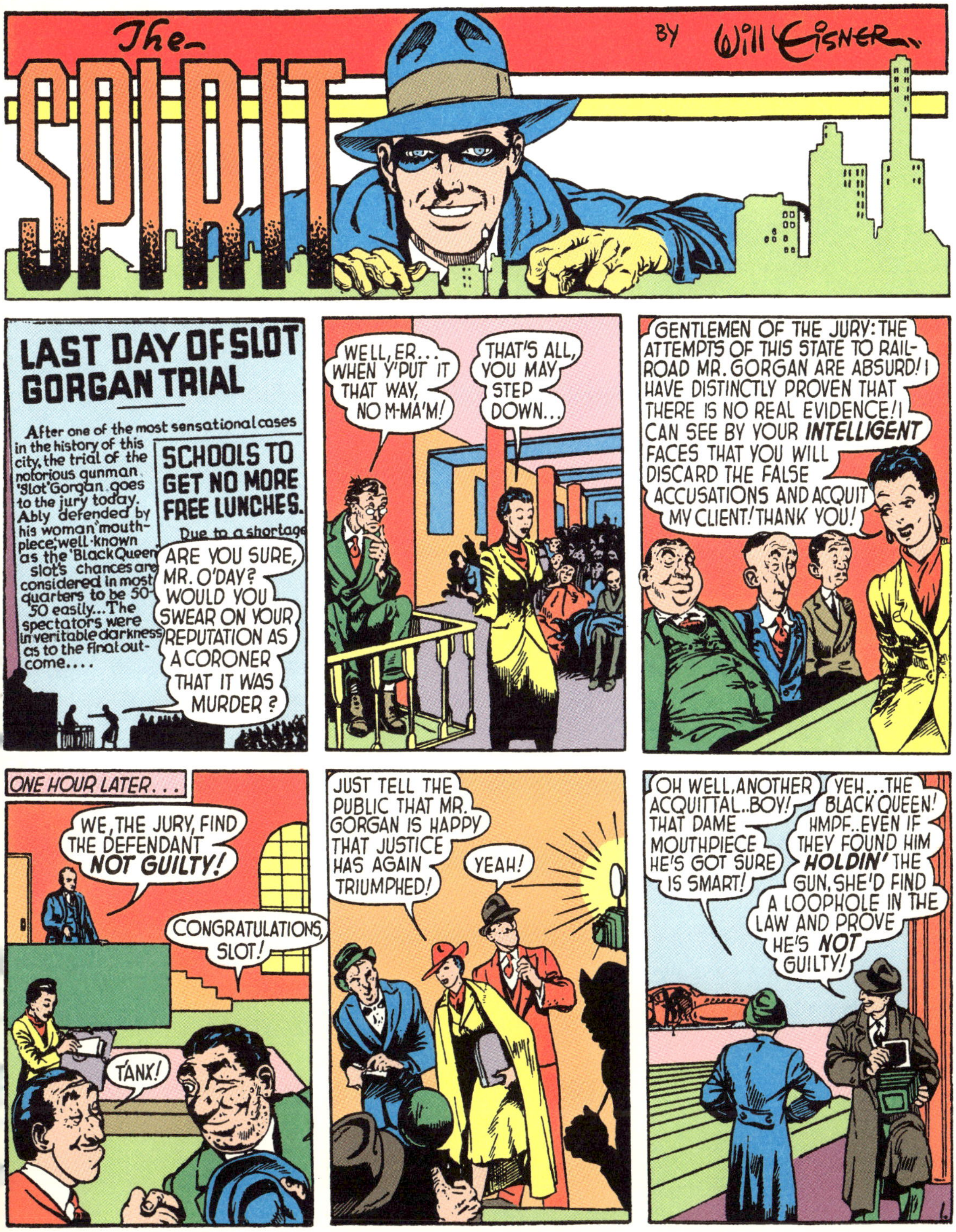

The SPIRIT
BY Will Eisner
LAST DAY OF SLOT GORGAN TRIAL
After one of the most sensational cases in the history of this city, the trial of the notorious gunman 'Slot' Gorgan goes to the jury today. Ably defended by his woman 'mouthpiece,' well-known as the 'Black Queen' slot's chances are considered in most quarters to be 50-50 easily... The spectators were in veritable darkness as to the final outcome....
SCHOOLS TO GET NO MORE FREE LUNCHES.
Due to a shortage
ARE YOU SURE, MR. O'DAY? WOULD YOU SWEAR ON YOUR REPUTATION AS A CORONER THAT IT WAS MURDER?
WELL, ER... WHEN Y'PUT IT THAT WAY, NO M-MA'M!
THAT'S ALL, YOU MAY STEP DOWN...
GENTLEMEN OF THE JURY: THE ATTEMPTS OF THIS STATE TO RAIL-ROAD MR. GORGAN ARE ABSURD! I HAVE DISTINCTLY PROVEN THAT THERE IS NO REAL EVIDENCE! I CAN SEE BY YOUR INTELLIGENT FACES THAT YOU WILL DISCARD THE FALSE ACCUSATIONS AND ACQUIT MY CLIENT! THANK YOU!
ONE HOUR LATER...
WE, THE JURY, FIND THE DEFENDANT NOT GUILTY!
CONGRATULATIONS, SLOT!
T'ANX!
JUST TELL THE PUBLIC THAT MR. GORGAN IS HAPPY THAT JUSTICE HAS AGAIN TRIUMPHED!
YEAH!
OH WELL, ANOTHER ACQUITTAL..BOY! THAT DAME MOUTHPIECE HE'S GOT SURE IS SMART!
YEH... THE BLACK QUEEN! HMPF..EVEN IF THEY FOUND HIM HOLDIN' THE GUN, SHE'D FIND A LOOPHOLE IN THE LAW AND PROVE HE'S NOT GUILTY!

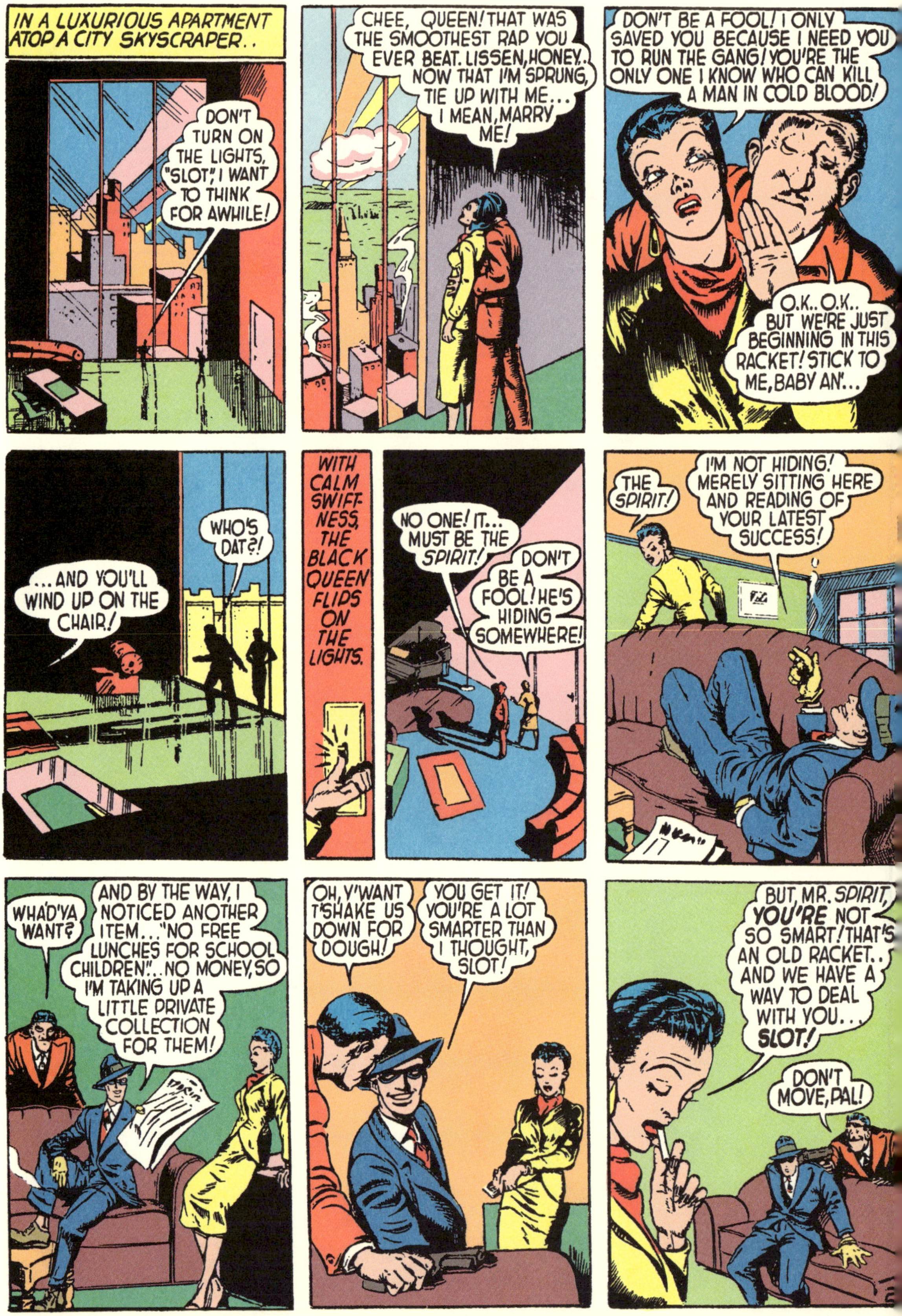
IN A LUXURIOUS APARTMENT ATOP A CITY SKYSCRAPER..
DON'T TURN ON THE LIGHTS, "SLOT," I WANT TO THINK FOR AWHILE!
CHEE, QUEEN! THAT WAS THE SMOOTHEST RAP YOU EVER BEAT. LISSEN, HONEY.. NOW THAT I'M SPRUNG, TIE UP WITH ME... I MEAN, MARRY ME!
DON'T BE A FOOL! I ONLY SAVED YOU BECAUSE I NEED YOU TO RUN THE GANG! YOU'RE THE ONLY ONE I KNOW WHO CAN KILL A MAN IN COLD BLOOD!
O.K.. O.K.. BUT WE'RE JUST BEGINNING IN THIS RACKET! STICK TO ME, BABY AN'...
...AND YOU'LL WIND UP ON THE CHAIR!
WHO'S DAT?!
WITH CALM SWIFTNESS, THE BLACK QUEEN FLIPS ON THE LIGHTS.
NO ONE! IT... MUST BE THE SPIRIT!
DON'T BE A FOOL! HE'S HIDING SOMEWHERE!
THE SPIRIT!
I'M NOT HIDING! MERELY SITTING HERE AND READING OF YOUR LATEST SUCCESS!
WHAD'YA WANT?
AND BY THE WAY, I NOTICED ANOTHER ITEM..."NO FREE LUNCHES FOR SCHOOL CHILDREN"..NO MONEY, SO I'M TAKING UP A LITTLE PRIVATE COLLECTION FOR THEM!
OH, Y'WANT T'SHAKE US DOWN FOR DOUGH!
YOU GET IT! YOU'RE A LOT SMARTER THAN I THOUGHT, SLOT!
BUT MR. SPIRIT, YOU'RE NOT SO SMART! THAT'S AN OLD RACKET.. AND WE HAVE A WAY TO DEAL WITH YOU... SLOT!
DON'T MOVE, PAL!

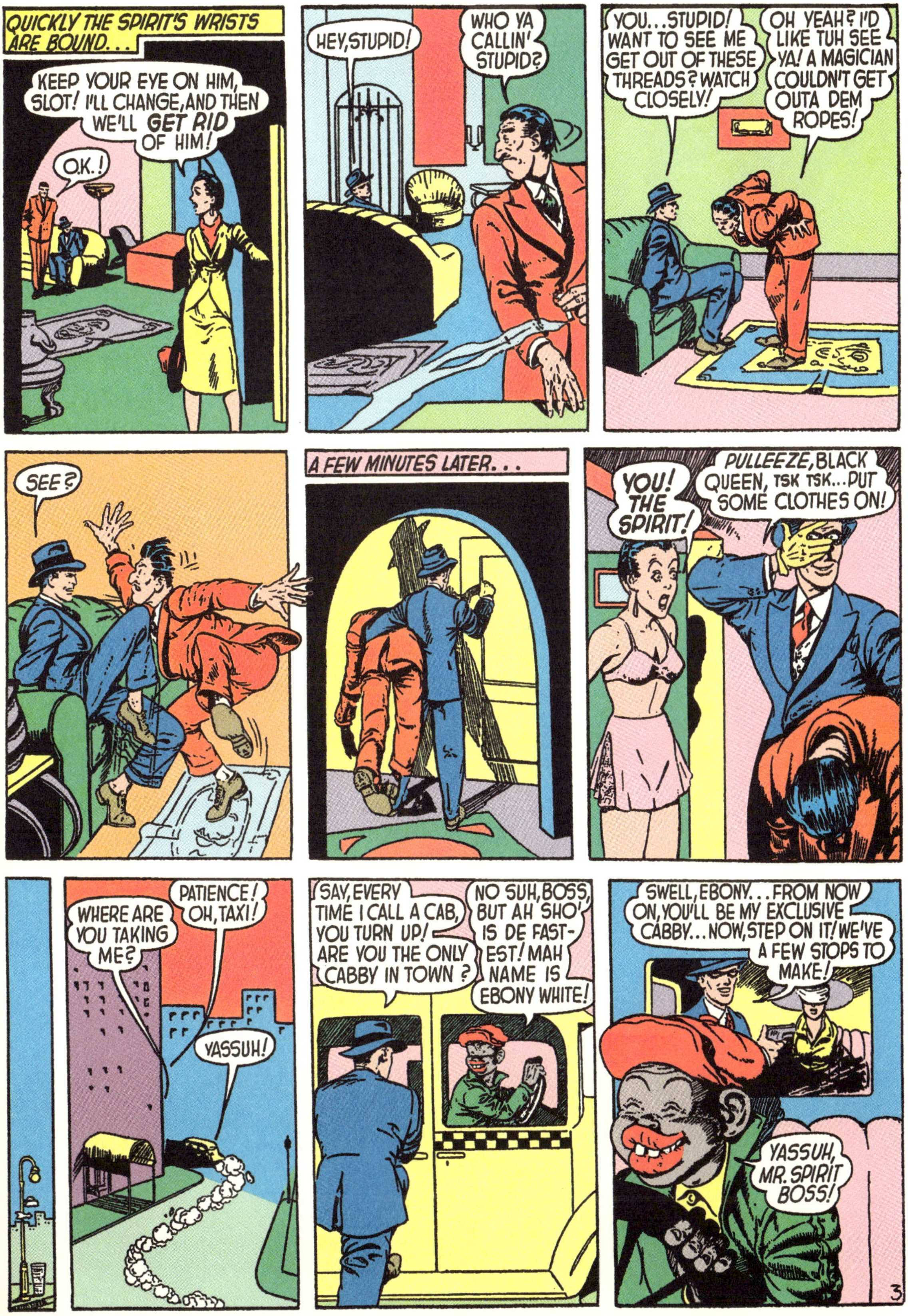

QUICKLY THE SPIRIT'S WRISTS ARE BOUND...
KEEP YOUR EYE ON HIM, SLOT! I'LL CHANGE, AND THEN WE'LL GET RID OF HIM!
O.K.!
HEY, STUPID!
WHO YA CALLIN' STUPID?
YOU...STUPID! WANT TO SEE ME GET OUT OF THESE THREADS? WATCH CLOSELY!
OH YEAH? I'D LIKE TUH SEE YA! A MAGICIAN COULDN'T GET OUTA DEM ROPES!
SEE?
A FEW MINUTES LATER...
YOU! THE SPIRIT!
PULLEEZE, BLACK QUEEN, TSK TSK...PUT SOME CLOTHES ON!
WHERE ARE YOU TAKING ME?
PATIENCE! OH, TAXI!
YASSUH!
SAY, EVERY TIME I CALL A CAB, YOU TURN UP! ARE YOU THE ONLY CABBY IN TOWN?
NO SUH, BOSS, BUT AH SHO' IS DE FASTEST! MAH NAME IS EBONY WHITE!
SWELL, EBONY...FROM NOW ON, YOU'LL BE MY EXCLUSIVE CABBY...NOW, STEP ON IT! WE'VE A FEW STOPS TO MAKE!
YASSUH, MR. SPIRIT BOSS!
3

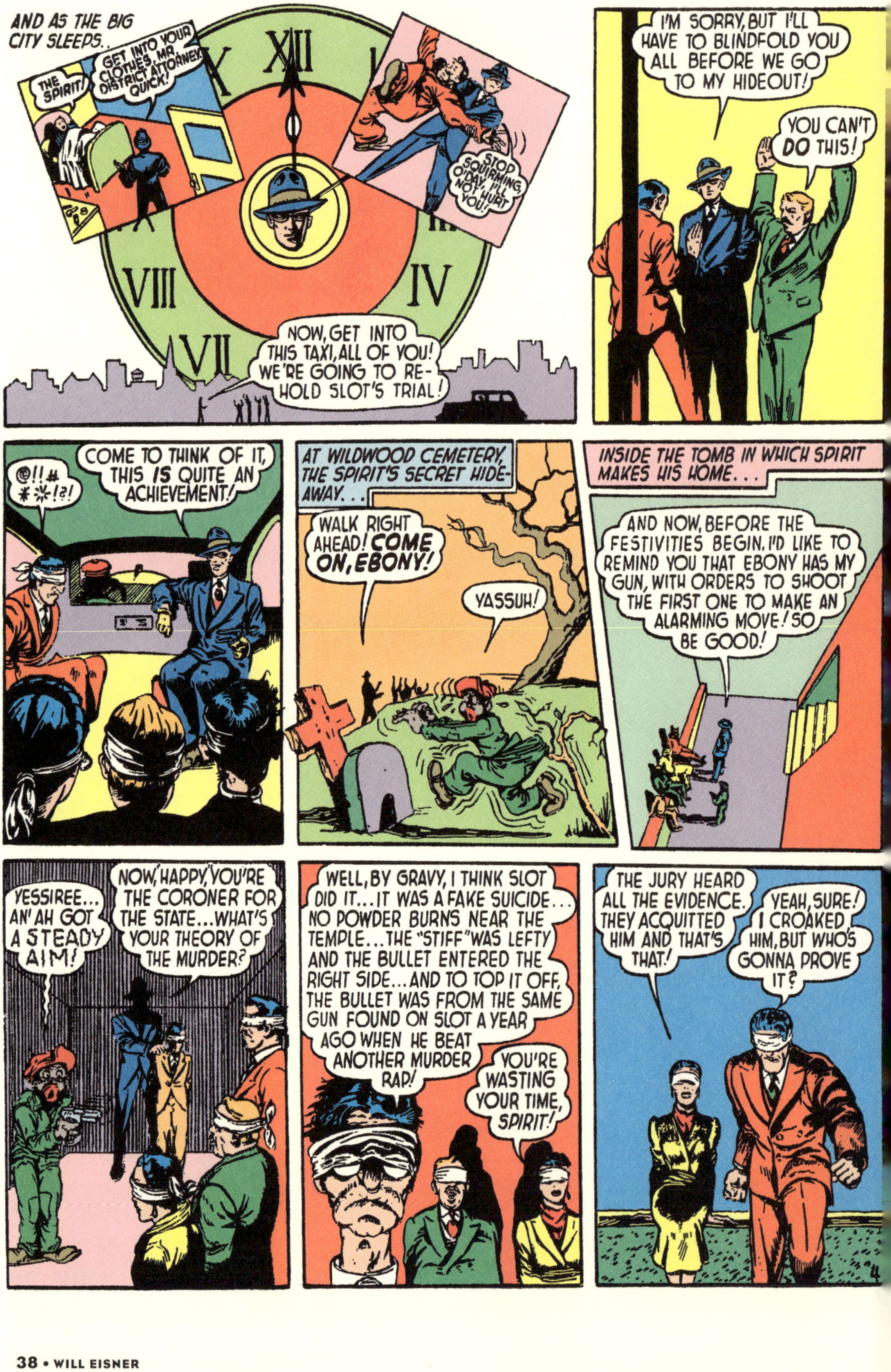

AND AS THE BIG CITY SLEEPS..
THE SPIRIT!
GET INTO YOUR CLOTHES, MR. DISTRICT ATTORNEY. QUICK!
STOP SQUIRMING, O'DAY. I'LL NOT HURT YOU!
NOW, GET INTO THIS TAXI, ALL OF YOU! WE'RE GOING TO RE-HOLD SLOT'S TRIAL!
I'M SORRY, BUT I'LL HAVE TO BLINDFOLD YOU ALL BEFORE WE GO TO MY HIDEOUT!
YOU CAN'T DO THIS!
@!!# *✱!?!
COME TO THINK OF IT, THIS IS QUITE AN ACHIEVEMENT!
AT WILDWOOD CEMETERY, THE SPIRIT'S SECRET HIDE-AWAY...
WALK RIGHT AHEAD! COME ON, EBONY!
YASSUH!
INSIDE THE TOMB IN WHICH SPIRIT MAKES HIS HOME...
AND NOW, BEFORE THE FESTIVITIES BEGIN, I'D LIKE TO REMIND YOU THAT EBONY HAS MY GUN, WITH ORDERS TO SHOOT THE FIRST ONE TO MAKE AN ALARMING MOVE! SO BE GOOD!
NOW, HAPPY, YOU'RE THE CORONER FOR THE STATE...WHAT'S YOUR THEORY OF THE MURDER?
YESSIREE... AN' AH GOT A STEADY AIM!
WELL, BY GRAVY, I THINK SLOT DID IT...IT WAS A FAKE SUICIDE... NO POWDER BURNS NEAR THE TEMPLE...THE "STIFF" WAS LEFTY AND THE BULLET ENTERED THE RIGHT SIDE...AND TO TOP IT OFF, THE BULLET WAS FROM THE SAME GUN FOUND ON SLOT A YEAR AGO WHEN HE BEAT ANOTHER MURDER RAP!
YOU'RE WASTING YOUR TIME, SPIRIT!
THE JURY HEARD ALL THE EVIDENCE. THEY ACQUITTED HIM AND THAT'S THAT!
YEAH, SURE! I CROAKED HIM, BUT WHO'S GONNA PROVE IT?
4

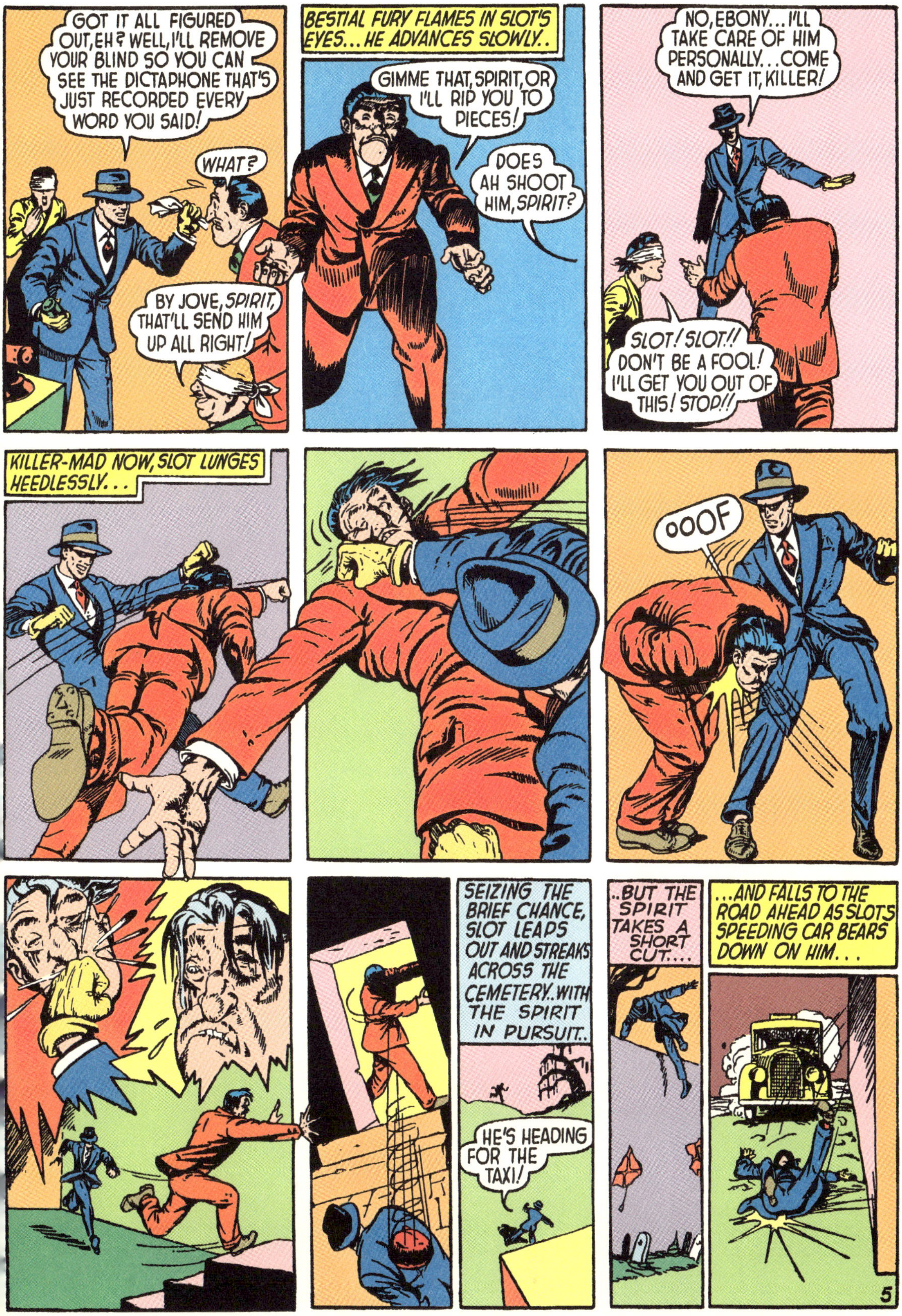
GOT IT ALL FIGURED OUT, EH? WELL, I'LL REMOVE YOUR BLIND SO YOU CAN SEE THE DICTAPHONE THAT'S JUST RECORDED EVERY WORD YOU SAID!
WHAT?
BY JOVE, SPIRIT, THAT'LL SEND HIM UP ALL RIGHT!
BESTIAL FURY FLAMES IN SLOT'S EYES... HE ADVANCES SLOWLY..
GIMME THAT, SPIRIT, OR I'LL RIP YOU TO PIECES!
DOES AH SHOOT HIM, SPIRIT?
NO, EBONY... I'LL TAKE CARE OF HIM PERSONALLY... COME AND GET IT, KILLER!
SLOT! SLOT!! DON'T BE A FOOL! I'LL GET YOU OUT OF THIS! STOP!!
KILLER-MAD NOW, SLOT LUNGES HEEDLESSLY...
OOOF
SEIZING THE BRIEF CHANCE, SLOT LEAPS OUT AND STREAKS ACROSS THE CEMETERY..WITH THE SPIRIT IN PURSUIT..
HE'S HEADING FOR THE TAXI!
..BUT THE SPIRIT TAKES A SHORT CUT....
...AND FALLS TO THE ROAD AHEAD AS SLOT'S SPEEDING CAR BEARS DOWN ON HIM...
5

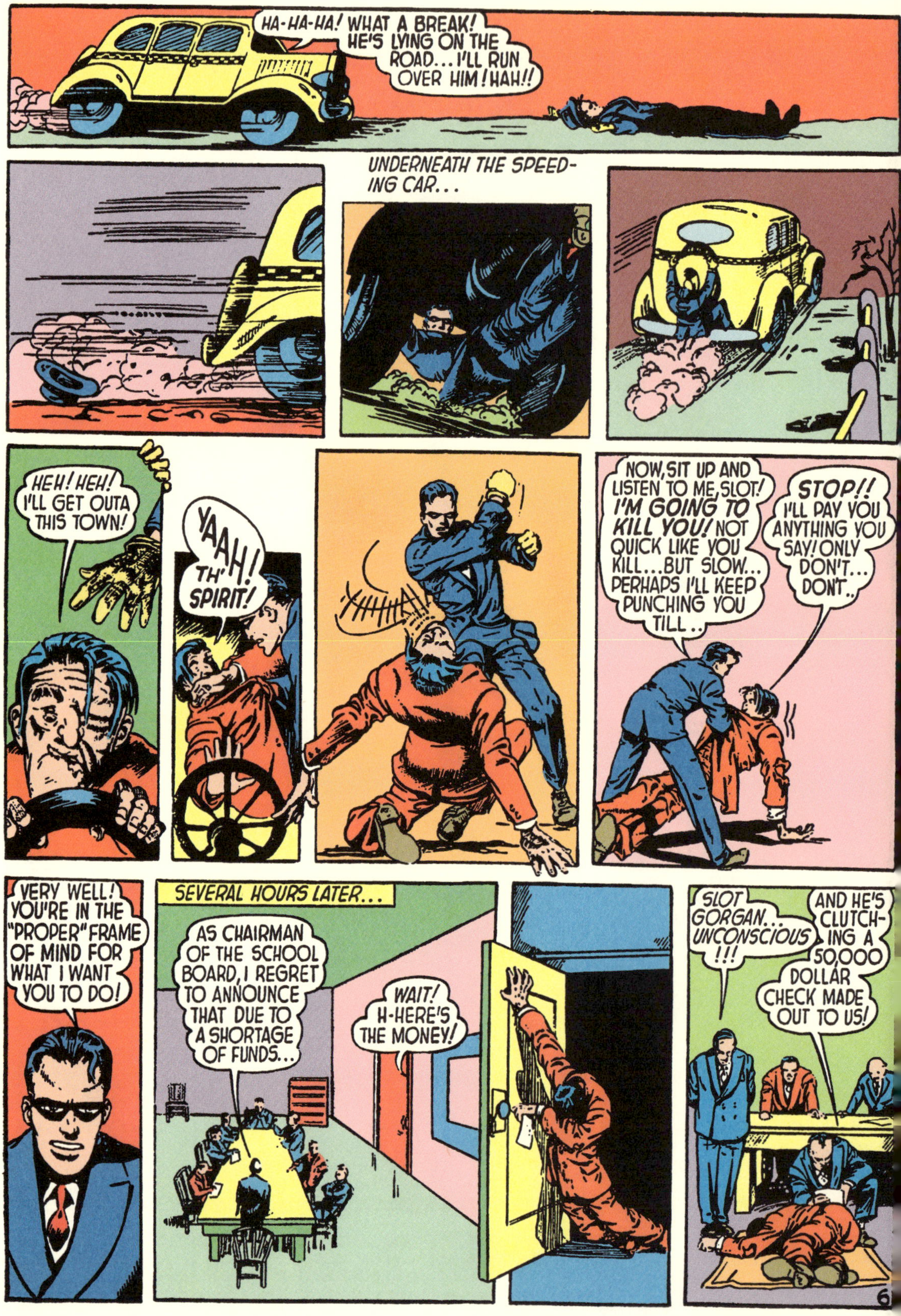
HA-HA-HA! WHAT A BREAK! HE'S LYING ON THE ROAD... I'LL RUN OVER HIM! HAH!!
UNDERNEATH THE SPEEDING CAR...
HEH! HEH! I'LL GET OUTA THIS TOWN!
YAAH! TH' SPIRIT!
NOW, SIT UP AND LISTEN TO ME, SLOT! I'M GOING TO KILL YOU! NOT QUICK LIKE YOU KILL... BUT SLOW... PERHAPS I'LL KEEP PUNCHING YOU TILL..
STOP!! I'LL PAY YOU ANYTHING YOU SAY! ONLY DON'T... DON'T..
VERY WELL! YOU'RE IN THE "PROPER" FRAME OF MIND FOR WHAT I WANT YOU TO DO!
SEVERAL HOURS LATER...
AS CHAIRMAN OF THE SCHOOL BOARD, I REGRET TO ANNOUNCE THAT DUE TO A SHORTAGE OF FUNDS...
WAIT! H-HERE'S THE MONEY!
SLOT GORGAN... UNCONSCIOUS!!!
AND HE'S CLUTCHING A 50,000 DOLLAR CHECK MADE OUT TO US!
6

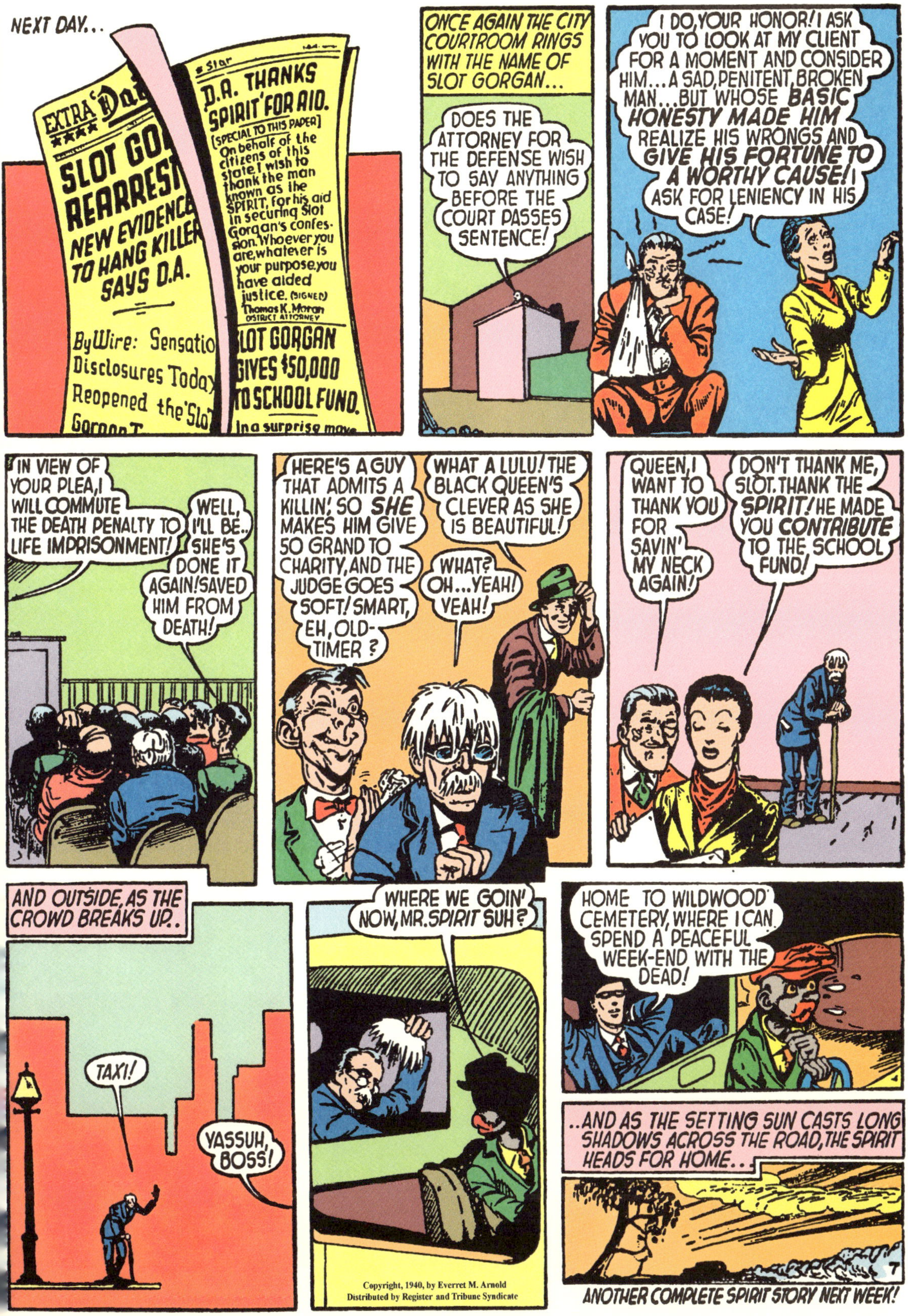
NEXT DAY...
EXTRA Daily
SLOT GO
REARREST
NEW EVIDENCE TO HANG KILLER SAYS D.A.
By Wire: Sensatio Disclosures Today Reopened the 'Slot Gorgan T
Star
D.A. THANKS SPIRIT FOR AID.
[SPECIAL TO THIS PAPER] On behalf of the citizens of this state I wish to thank the man known as the SPIRIT, for his aid in securing Slot Gorgan's confession. Whoever you are, whatever is your purpose, you have aided justice. (SIGNED) Thomas K. Moran DISTRICT ATTORNEY
SLOT GORGAN GIVES $50,000 TO SCHOOL FUND.
In a surprise move
ONCE AGAIN THE CITY COURTROOM RINGS WITH THE NAME OF SLOT GORGAN...
DOES THE ATTORNEY FOR THE DEFENSE WISH TO SAY ANYTHING BEFORE THE COURT PASSES SENTENCE!
I DO, YOUR HONOR! I ASK YOU TO LOOK AT MY CLIENT FOR A MOMENT AND CONSIDER HIM... A SAD, PENITENT, BROKEN MAN... BUT WHOSE BASIC HONESTY MADE HIM REALIZE HIS WRONGS AND GIVE HIS FORTUNE TO A WORTHY CAUSE! I ASK FOR LENIENCY IN HIS CASE!
IN VIEW OF YOUR PLEA, I WILL COMMUTE THE DEATH PENALTY TO LIFE IMPRISONMENT!
WELL, I'LL BE.. SHE'S DONE IT AGAIN! SAVED HIM FROM DEATH!
HERE'S A GUY THAT ADMITS A KILLIN', SO SHE MAKES HIM GIVE 50 GRAND TO CHARITY, AND THE JUDGE GOES SOFT! SMART, EH, OLD-TIMER?
WHAT A LULU! THE BLACK QUEEN'S CLEVER AS SHE IS BEAUTIFUL!
WHAT? OH... YEAH! YEAH!
QUEEN, I WANT TO THANK YOU FOR SAVIN' MY NECK AGAIN!
DON'T THANK ME, SLOT. THANK THE SPIRIT! HE MADE YOU CONTRIBUTE TO THE SCHOOL FUND!
AND OUTSIDE, AS THE CROWD BREAKS UP..
TAXI!
YASSUH, BOSS!
WHERE WE GOIN' NOW, MR. SPIRIT SUH?
HOME TO WILDWOOD CEMETERY, WHERE I CAN SPEND A PEACEFUL WEEK-END WITH THE DEAD!
..AND AS THE SETTING SUN CASTS LONG SHADOWS ACROSS THE ROAD, THE SPIRIT HEADS FOR HOME..
7
ANOTHER COMPLETE SPIRIT STORY NEXT WEEK!

WEEKLY COMIC BOOK

VOODOO IN MANHATTAN

3 COMPLETE STORIES

June 23, 1940

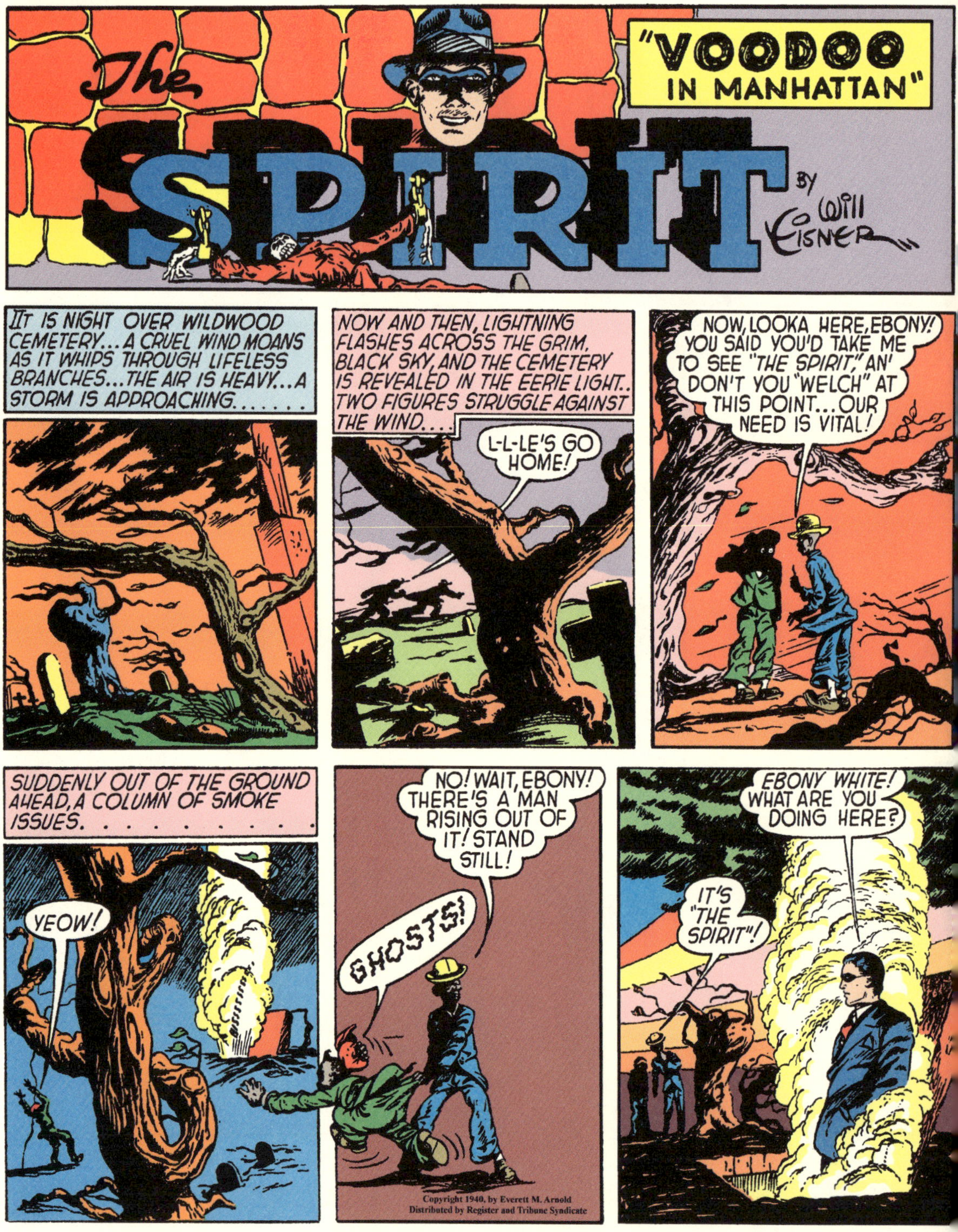
The SPIRIT
"VOODOO IN MANHATTAN"
BY Will Eisner
IT IS NIGHT OVER WILDWOOD CEMETERY... A CRUEL WIND MOANS AS IT WHIPS THROUGH LIFELESS BRANCHES...THE AIR IS HEAVY...A STORM IS APPROACHING......
NOW AND THEN, LIGHTNING FLASHES ACROSS THE GRIM, BLACK SKY, AND THE CEMETERY IS REVEALED IN THE EERIE LIGHT.. TWO FIGURES STRUGGLE AGAINST THE WIND....
L-L-LE'S GO HOME!
NOW, LOOKA HERE, EBONY! YOU SAID YOU'D TAKE ME TO SEE "THE SPIRIT," AN' DON'T YOU "WELCH" AT THIS POINT...OUR NEED IS VITAL!
SUDDENLY OUT OF THE GROUND AHEAD, A COLUMN OF SMOKE ISSUES. . . . .
YEOW!
NO! WAIT, EBONY! THERE'S A MAN RISING OUT OF IT! STAND STILL!
GHOSTS!
Copyright 1940, by Everett M. Arnold
Distributed by Register and Tribune Syndicate
EBONY WHITE! WHAT ARE YOU DOING HERE?
IT'S "THE SPIRIT"!

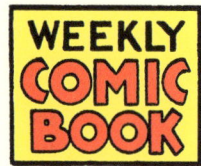

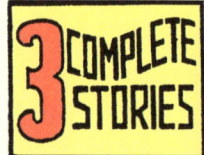

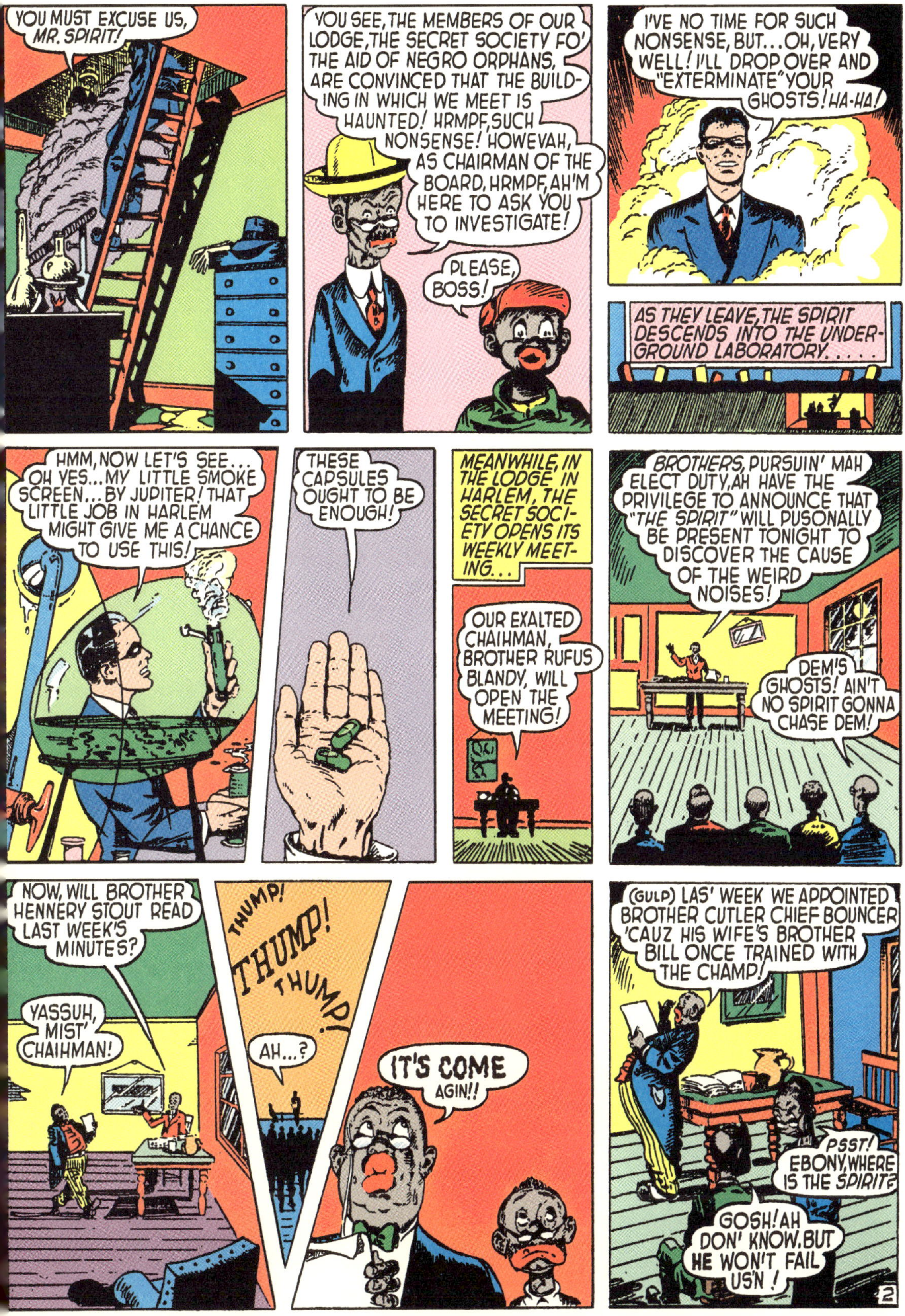
YOU MUST EXCUSE US, MR. SPIRIT!
YOU SEE, THE MEMBERS OF OUR LODGE, THE SECRET SOCIETY FO' THE AID OF NEGRO ORPHANS, ARE CONVINCED THAT THE BUILDING IN WHICH WE MEET IS HAUNTED! HRMPF, SUCH NONSENSE! HOWEVAH, AS CHAIRMAN OF THE BOARD, HRMPF, AH'M HERE TO ASK YOU TO INVESTIGATE!
PLEASE, BOSS!
I'VE NO TIME FOR SUCH NONSENSE, BUT...OH, VERY WELL! I'LL DROP OVER AND "EXTERMINATE" YOUR GHOSTS! HA-HA!
AS THEY LEAVE, THE SPIRIT DESCENDS INTO THE UNDERGROUND LABORATORY....
HMM, NOW LET'S SEE... OH YES... MY LITTLE SMOKE SCREEN... BY JUPITER! THAT LITTLE JOB IN HARLEM MIGHT GIVE ME A CHANCE TO USE THIS!
THESE CAPSULES OUGHT TO BE ENOUGH!
MEANWHILE, IN THE LODGE IN HARLEM, THE SECRET SOCIETY OPENS ITS WEEKLY MEETING...
OUR EXALTED CHAIHMAN, BROTHER RUFUS BLANDY, WILL OPEN THE MEETING!
BROTHERS, PURSUIN' MAH ELECT DUTY, AH HAVE THE PRIVILEGE TO ANNOUNCE THAT "THE SPIRIT" WILL PUSONALLY BE PRESENT TONIGHT TO DISCOVER THE CAUSE OF THE WEIRD NOISES!
DEM'S GHOSTS! AIN'T NO SPIRIT GONNA CHASE DEM!
NOW, WILL BROTHER HENNERY STOUT READ LAST WEEK'S MINUTES?
YASSUH, MIST' CHAIHMAN!
THUMP! THUMP! THUMP!
AH...?
IT'S COME AGIN!!
(GULP) LAS' WEEK WE APPOINTED BROTHER CUTLER CHIEF BOUNCER 'CAUZ HIS WIFE'S BROTHER BILL ONCE TRAINED WITH THE CHAMP!
PSST! EBONY, WHERE IS THE SPIRIT?
GOSH! AH DON' KNOW, BUT HE WON'T FAIL US'N!
2

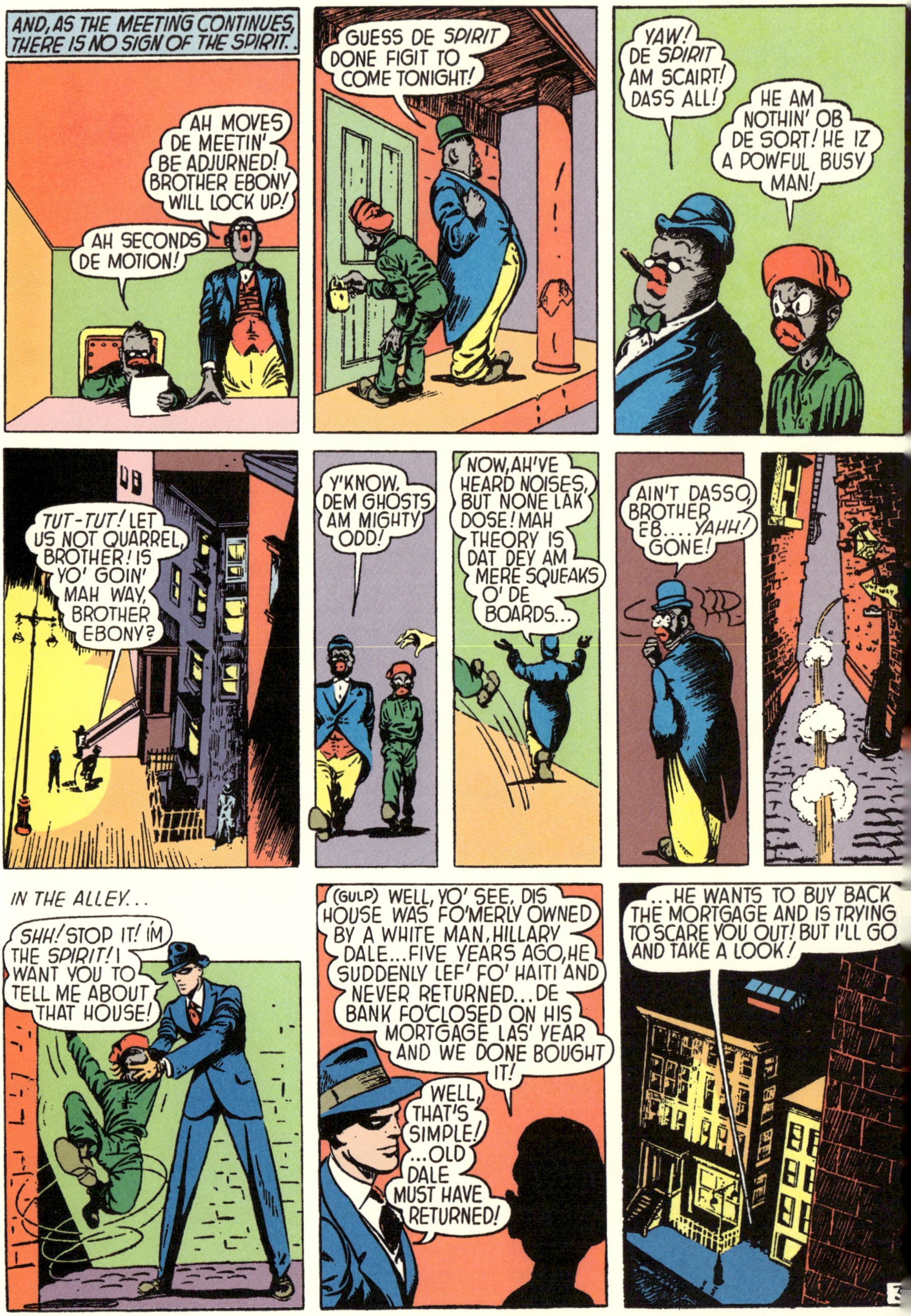

AND, AS THE MEETING CONTINUES, THERE IS NO SIGN OF THE SPIRIT...
AH MOVES DE MEETIN' BE ADJURNED! BROTHER EBONY WILL LOCK UP!
AH SECONDS DE MOTION!
GUESS DE SPIRIT DONE FIGIT TO COME TONIGHT!
YAW! DE SPIRIT AM SCAIRT! DASS ALL!
HE AM NOTHIN' OB DE SORT! HE IZ A POWFUL BUSY MAN!
TUT-TUT! LET US NOT QUARREL, BROTHER! IS YO' GOIN' MAH WAY, BROTHER EBONY?
Y'KNOW, DEM GHOSTS AM MIGHTY ODD!
NOW, AH'VE HEARD NOISES, BUT NONE LAK DOSE! MAH THEORY IS DAT DEY AM MERE SQUEAKS O' DE BOARDS...
AIN'T DASSO, BROTHER EB.... YAHH! GONE!
IN THE ALLEY...
SHH! STOP IT! I'M THE SPIRIT! I WANT YOU TO TELL ME ABOUT THAT HOUSE!
(GULP) WELL, YO' SEE, DIS HOUSE WAS FO'MERLY OWNED BY A WHITE MAN, HILLARY DALE... FIVE YEARS AGO, HE SUDDENLY LEF' FO' HAITI AND NEVER RETURNED... DE BANK FO'CLOSED ON HIS MORTGAGE LAS' YEAR AND WE DONE BOUGHT IT!
WELL, THAT'S SIMPLE! ...OLD DALE MUST HAVE RETURNED!
...HE WANTS TO BUY BACK THE MORTGAGE AND IS TRYING TO SCARE YOU OUT! BUT I'LL GO AND TAKE A LOOK!

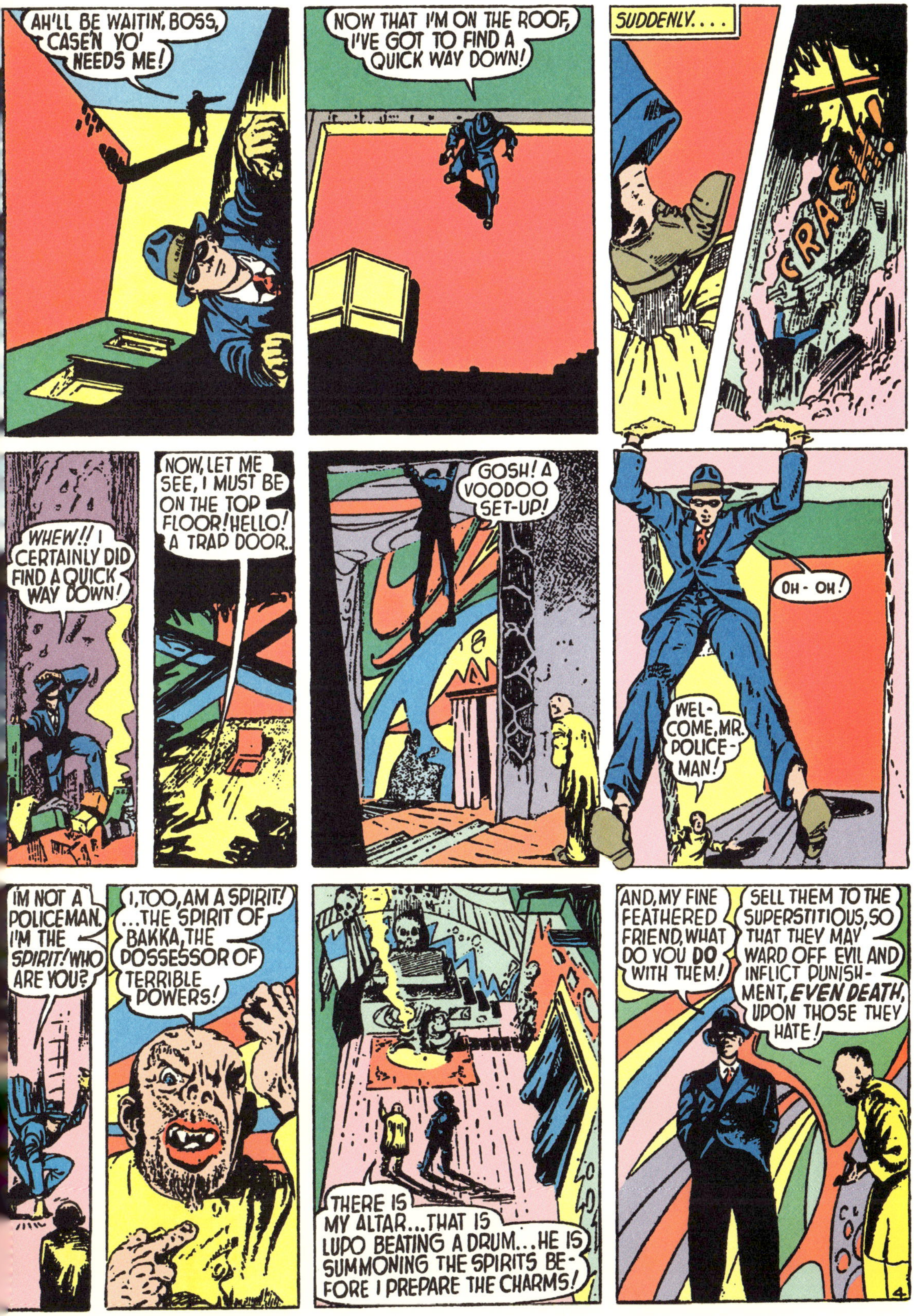
AH'LL BE WAITIN', BOSS, CASE'N YO' NEEDS ME!
NOW THAT I'M ON THE ROOF, I'VE GOT TO FIND A QUICK WAY DOWN!
SUDDENLY....
CRASH!
WHEW!! I CERTAINLY DID FIND A QUICK WAY DOWN!
NOW, LET ME SEE, I MUST BE ON THE TOP FLOOR! HELLO! A TRAP DOOR..
GOSH! A VOODOO SET-UP!
OH - OH!
WEL-COME, MR. POLICE-MAN!
I'M NOT A POLICEMAN. I'M THE SPIRIT! WHO ARE YOU?
I, TOO, AM A SPIRIT! ...THE SPIRIT OF BAKKA, THE POSSESSOR OF TERRIBLE POWERS!
THERE IS MY ALTAR...THAT IS LUPO BEATING A DRUM...HE IS SUMMONING THE SPIRITS BEFORE I PREPARE THE CHARMS!
AND, MY FINE FEATHERED FRIEND, WHAT DO YOU DO WITH THEM!
SELL THEM TO THE SUPERSTITIOUS, SO THAT THEY MAY WARD OFF EVIL AND INFLICT PUNISHMENT, EVEN DEATH, UPON THOSE THEY HATE!

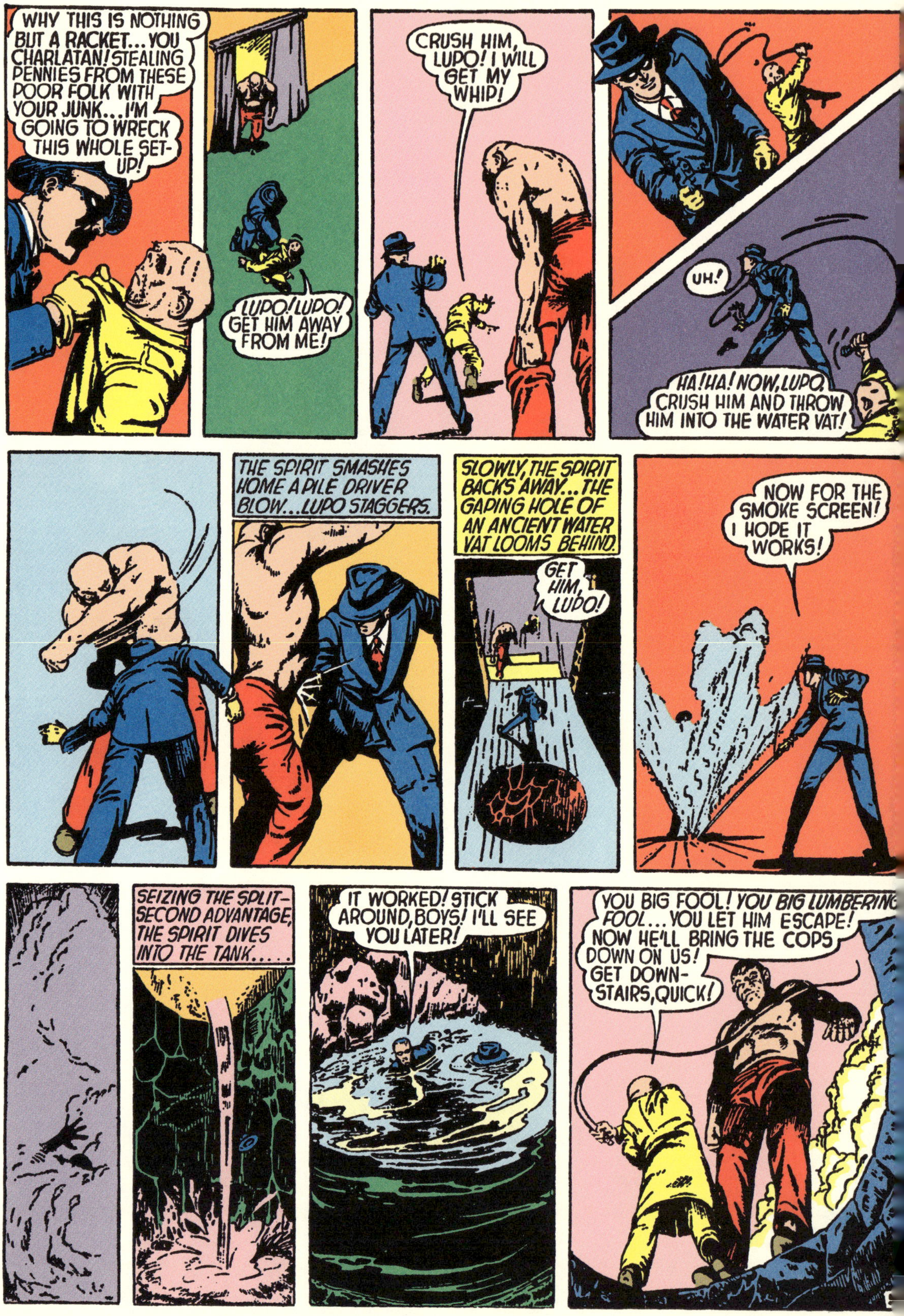

WHY THIS IS NOTHING BUT A RACKET...YOU CHARLATAN! STEALING PENNIES FROM THESE POOR FOLK WITH YOUR JUNK...I'M GOING TO WRECK THIS WHOLE SET-UP!
LUPO! LUPO! GET HIM AWAY FROM ME!
CRUSH HIM, LUPO! I WILL GET MY WHIP!
UH!
HA! HA! NOW, LUPO, CRUSH HIM AND THROW HIM INTO THE WATER VAT!
THE SPIRIT SMASHES HOME A PILE DRIVER BLOW...LUPO STAGGERS.
SLOWLY, THE SPIRIT BACKS AWAY...THE GAPING HOLE OF AN ANCIENT WATER VAT LOOMS BEHIND.
GET HIM, LUPO!
NOW FOR THE SMOKE SCREEN! I HOPE IT WORKS!
SEIZING THE SPLIT-SECOND ADVANTAGE, THE SPIRIT DIVES INTO THE TANK....
IT WORKED! STICK AROUND, BOYS! I'LL SEE YOU LATER!
YOU BIG FOOL! YOU BIG LUMBERING FOOL...YOU LET HIM ESCAPE! NOW HE'LL BRING THE COPS DOWN ON US! GET DOWN-STAIRS, QUICK!

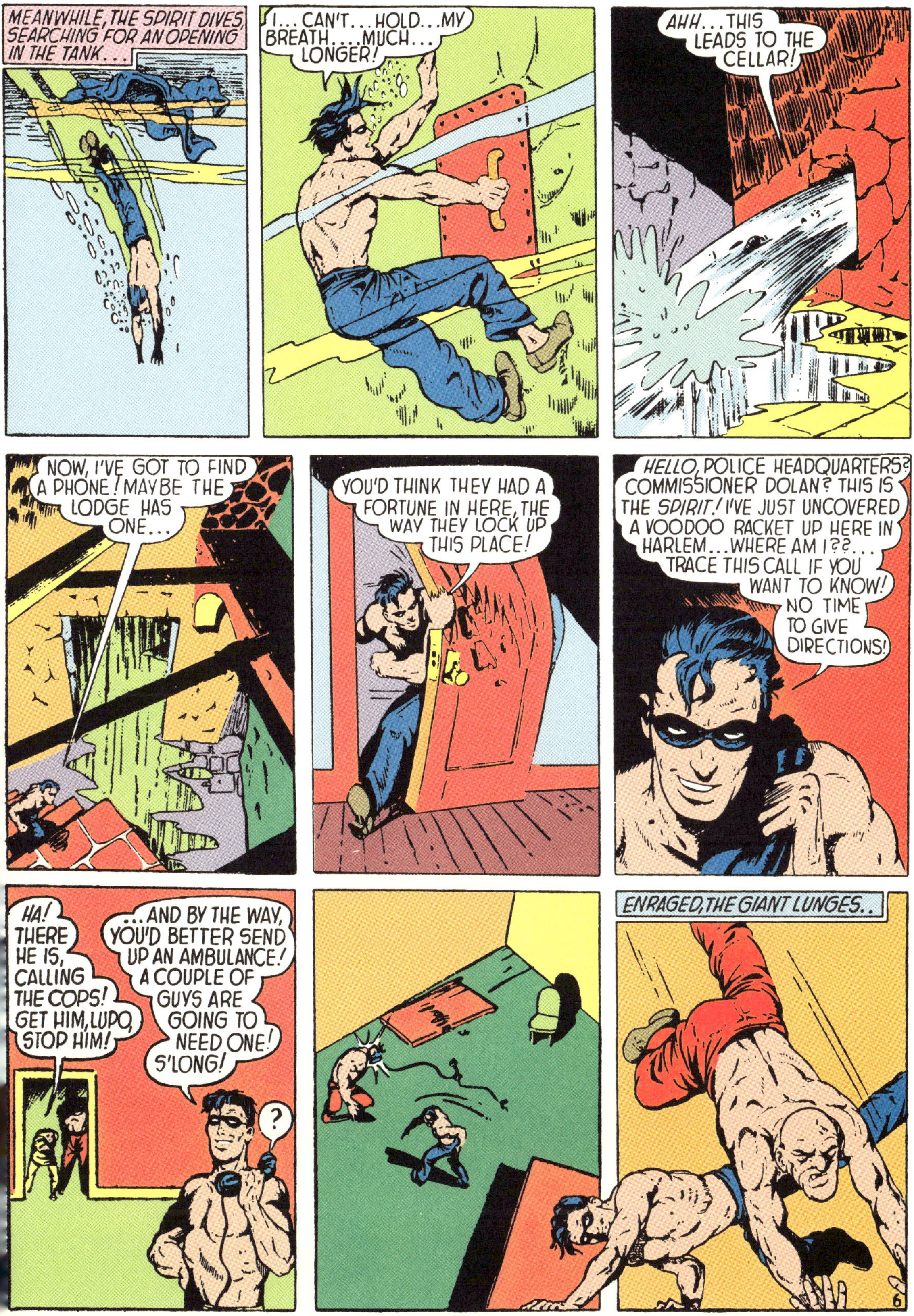

MEANWHILE, THE SPIRIT DIVES, SEARCHING FOR AN OPENING IN THE TANK...
I... CAN'T... HOLD... MY BREATH.... MUCH... LONGER!
AHH... THIS LEADS TO THE CELLAR!
NOW, I'VE GOT TO FIND A PHONE! MAYBE THE LODGE HAS ONE...
YOU'D THINK THEY HAD A FORTUNE IN HERE, THE WAY THEY LOCK UP THIS PLACE!
HELLO, POLICE HEADQUARTERS? COMMISSIONER DOLAN? THIS IS THE SPIRIT! I'VE JUST UNCOVERED A VOODOO RACKET UP HERE IN HARLEM... WHERE AM I??... TRACE THIS CALL IF YOU WANT TO KNOW!
NO TIME TO GIVE DIRECTIONS!
HA! THERE HE IS, CALLING THE COPS! GET HIM, LUPO, STOP HIM!
...AND BY THE WAY, YOU'D BETTER SEND UP AN AMBULANCE! A COUPLE OF GUYS ARE GOING TO NEED ONE! S'LONG!
?
ENRAGED, THE GIANT LUNGES..
6

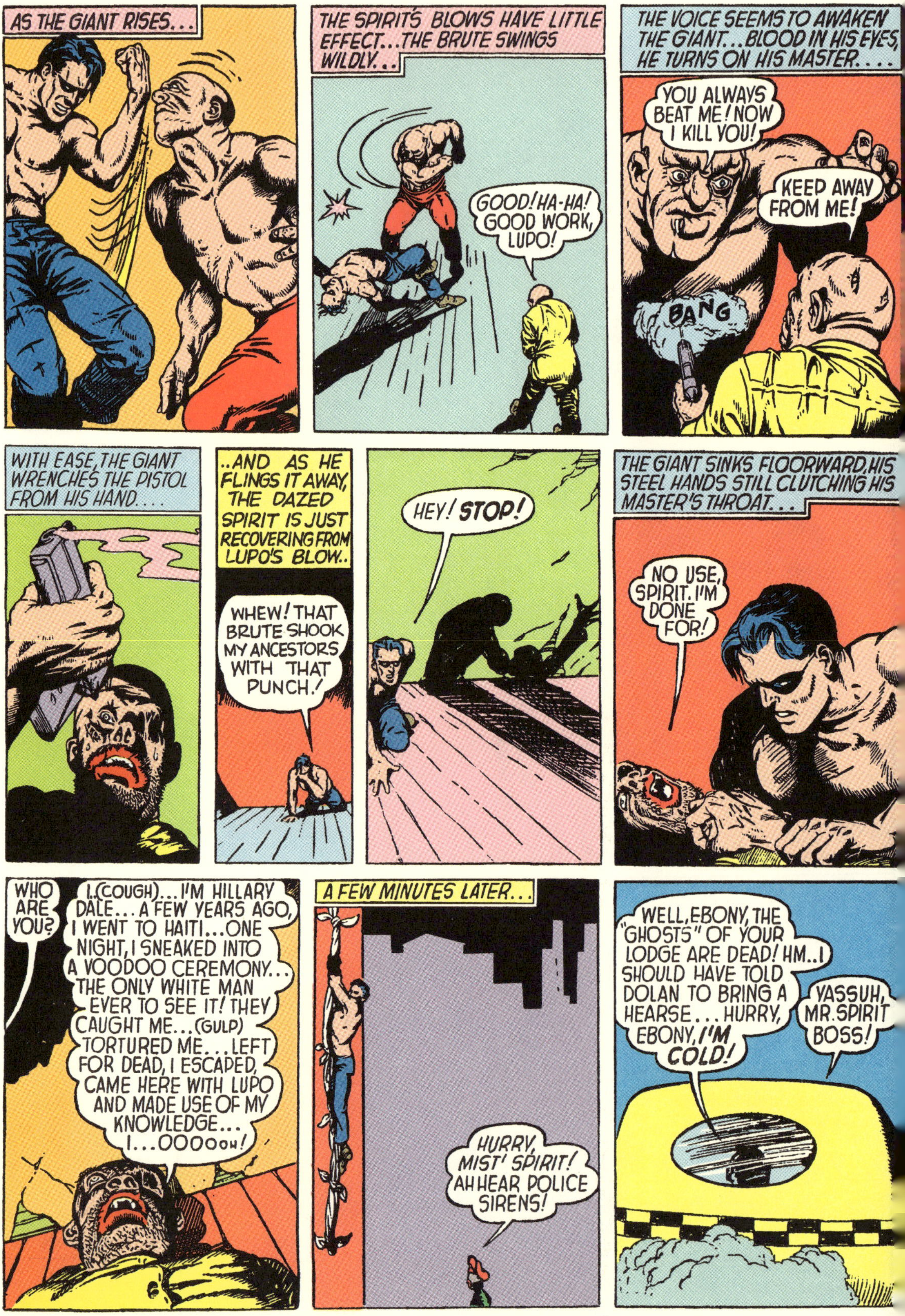

AS THE GIANT RISES...
THE SPIRIT'S BLOWS HAVE LITTLE EFFECT...THE BRUTE SWINGS WILDLY...
GOOD! HA-HA! GOOD WORK, LUPO!
THE VOICE SEEMS TO AWAKEN THE GIANT...BLOOD IN HIS EYES, HE TURNS ON HIS MASTER....
YOU ALWAYS BEAT ME! NOW I KILL YOU!
KEEP AWAY FROM ME!
BANG
WITH EASE, THE GIANT WRENCHES THE PISTOL FROM HIS HAND....
..AND AS HE FLINGS IT AWAY, THE DAZED SPIRIT IS JUST RECOVERING FROM LUPO'S BLOW..
WHEW! THAT BRUTE SHOOK MY ANCESTORS WITH THAT PUNCH!
HEY! STOP!
THE GIANT SINKS FLOORWARD, HIS STEEL HANDS STILL CLUTCHING HIS MASTER'S THROAT...
NO USE, SPIRIT. I'M DONE FOR!
WHO ARE YOU?
I..(COUGH)...I'M HILLARY DALE... A FEW YEARS AGO, I WENT TO HAITI...ONE NIGHT, I SNEAKED INTO A VOODOO CEREMONY... THE ONLY WHITE MAN EVER TO SEE IT! THEY CAUGHT ME...(GULP) TORTURED ME...LEFT FOR DEAD, I ESCAPED, CAME HERE WITH LUPO AND MADE USE OF MY KNOWLEDGE... I...OOOOoh!
A FEW MINUTES LATER...
HURRY, MIST' SPIRIT! AH HEAR POLICE SIRENS!
WELL, EBONY, THE "GHOSTS" OF YOUR LODGE ARE DEAD! HM..I SHOULD HAVE TOLD DOLAN TO BRING A HEARSE...HURRY, EBONY, I'M COLD!
YASSUH, MR. SPIRIT BOSS!

JOHNNY MARSTON

June 30, 1940

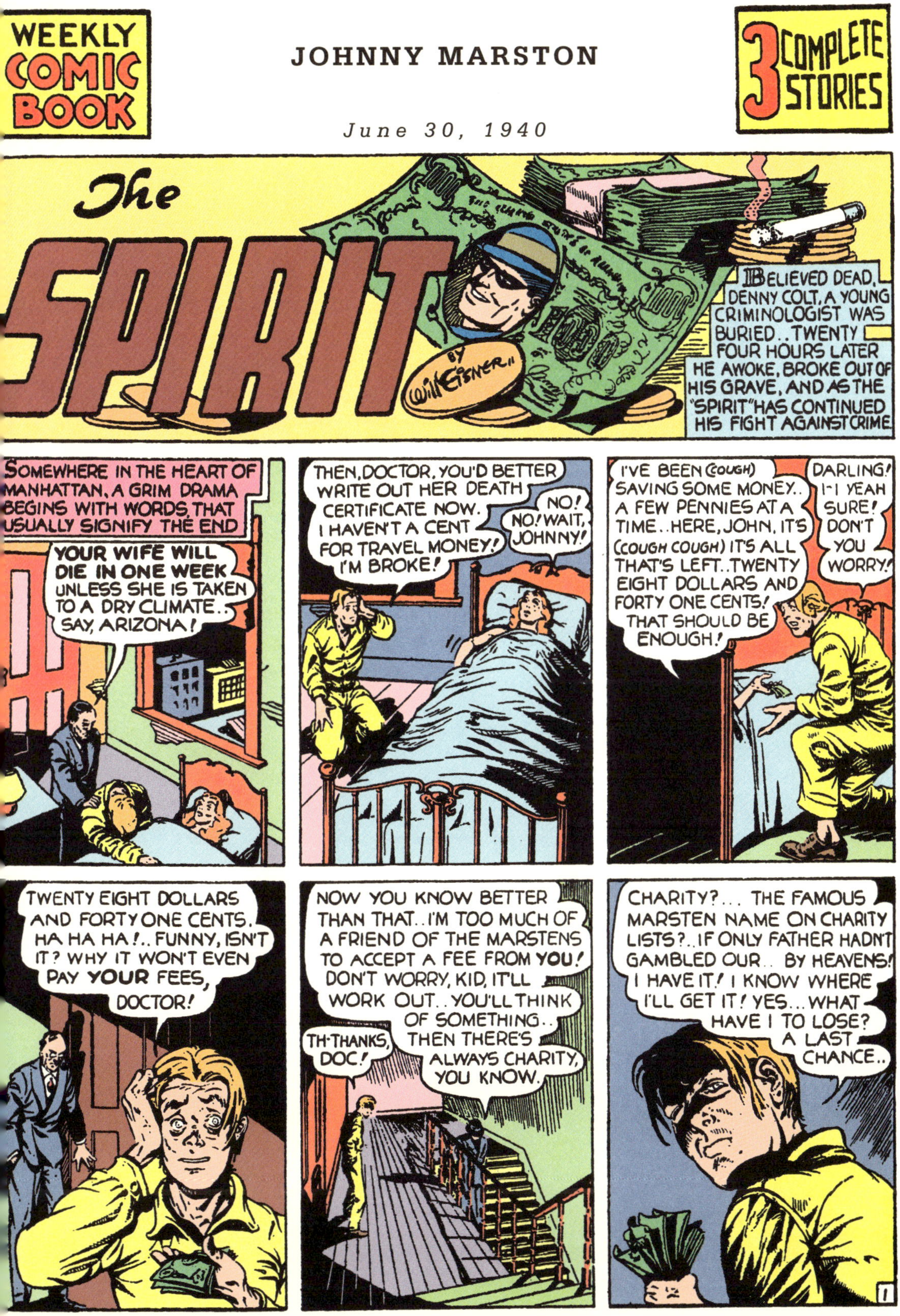
WEEKLY COMIC BOOK
3 COMPLETE STORIES
The SPIRIT
BY Will Eisner
BELIEVED DEAD, DENNY COLT, A YOUNG CRIMINOLOGIST WAS BURIED.. TWENTY FOUR HOURS LATER HE AWOKE, BROKE OUT OF HIS GRAVE, AND AS THE "SPIRIT" HAS CONTINUED HIS FIGHT AGAINST CRIME
SOMEWHERE IN THE HEART OF MANHATTAN, A GRIM DRAMA BEGINS WITH WORDS THAT USUALLY SIGNIFY THE END
YOUR WIFE WILL DIE IN ONE WEEK UNLESS SHE IS TAKEN TO A DRY CLIMATE.. SAY, ARIZONA!
THEN, DOCTOR, YOU'D BETTER WRITE OUT HER DEATH CERTIFICATE NOW. I HAVEN'T A CENT FOR TRAVEL MONEY! I'M BROKE!
NO! NO! WAIT, JOHNNY!
I'VE BEEN (COUGH) SAVING SOME MONEY.. A FEW PENNIES AT A TIME.. HERE, JOHN, IT'S (COUGH COUGH) IT'S ALL THAT'S LEFT.. TWENTY EIGHT DOLLARS AND FORTY ONE CENTS! THAT SHOULD BE ENOUGH!
DARLING! I-I YEAH SURE! DON'T YOU WORRY!
TWENTY EIGHT DOLLARS AND FORTY ONE CENTS. HA HA HA!.. FUNNY, ISN'T IT? WHY IT WON'T EVEN PAY YOUR FEES, DOCTOR!
NOW YOU KNOW BETTER THAN THAT.. I'M TOO MUCH OF A FRIEND OF THE MARSTENS TO ACCEPT A FEE FROM YOU! DON'T WORRY, KID, IT'LL WORK OUT.. YOU'LL THINK OF SOMETHING.. THEN THERE'S ALWAYS CHARITY, YOU KNOW.
TH-THANKS, DOC!
CHARITY?... THE FAMOUS MARSTEN NAME ON CHARITY LISTS?.. IF ONLY FATHER HADN'T GAMBLED OUR.. BY HEAVENS! I HAVE IT! I KNOW WHERE I'LL GET IT! YES... WHAT HAVE I TO LOSE? A LAST CHANCE..
1

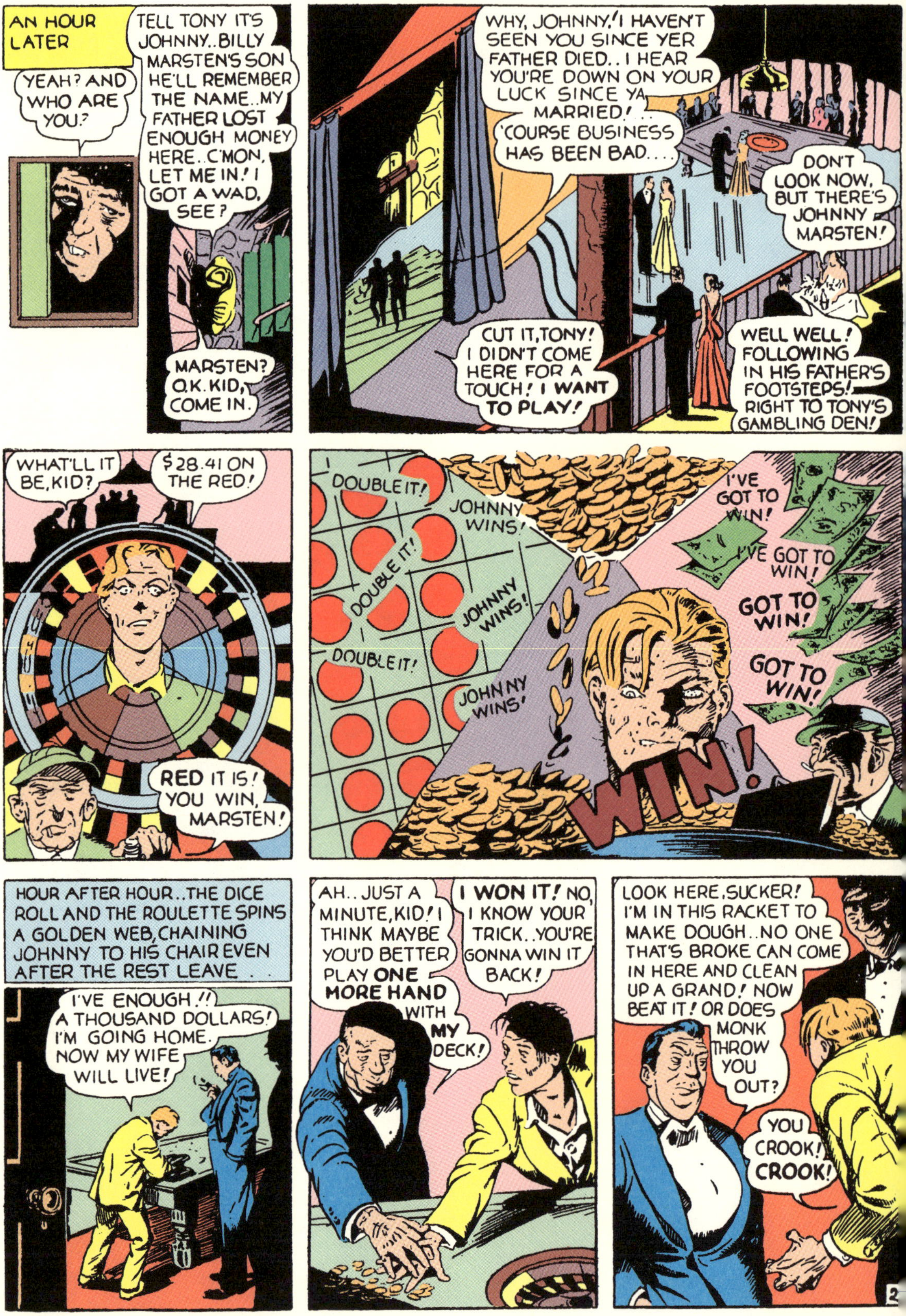
AN HOUR LATER
YEAH? AND WHO ARE YOU?
TELL TONY IT'S JOHNNY..BILLY MARSTEN'S SON HE'LL REMEMBER THE NAME..MY FATHER LOST ENOUGH MONEY HERE..C'MON, LET ME IN! I GOT A WAD, SEE?
MARSTEN? O.K. KID, COME IN.
WHY, JOHNNY, I HAVEN'T SEEN YOU SINCE YER FATHER DIED.. I HEAR YOU'RE DOWN ON YOUR LUCK SINCE YA MARRIED!.. 'COURSE BUSINESS HAS BEEN BAD....
CUT IT, TONY! I DIDN'T COME HERE FOR A TOUCH! I WANT TO PLAY!
DON'T LOOK NOW, BUT THERE'S JOHNNY MARSTEN!
WELL WELL! FOLLOWING IN HIS FATHER'S FOOTSTEPS! RIGHT TO TONY'S GAMBLING DEN!
WHAT'LL IT BE, KID?
$28.41 ON THE RED!
RED IT IS! YOU WIN, MARSTEN!
DOUBLE IT!
JOHNNY WINS!
DOUBLE IT!
JOHNNY WINS!
DOUBLE IT!
JOHNNY WINS!
I'VE GOT TO WIN!
I'VE GOT TO WIN!
GOT TO WIN!
GOT TO WIN!
WIN!
HOUR AFTER HOUR..THE DICE ROLL AND THE ROULETTE SPINS A GOLDEN WEB, CHAINING JOHNNY TO HIS CHAIR EVEN AFTER THE REST LEAVE . .
I'VE ENOUGH!! A THOUSAND DOLLARS! I'M GOING HOME. NOW MY WIFE WILL LIVE!
AH.. JUST A MINUTE, KID! I THINK MAYBE YOU'D BETTER PLAY ONE MORE HAND WITH MY DECK!
I WON IT! NO, I KNOW YOUR TRICK..YOU'RE GONNA WIN IT BACK!
LOOK HERE, SUCKER! I'M IN THIS RACKET TO MAKE DOUGH..NO ONE THAT'S BROKE CAN COME IN HERE AND CLEAN UP A GRAND! NOW BEAT IT! OR DOES MONK THROW YOU OUT?
YOU CROOK! CROOK!
2

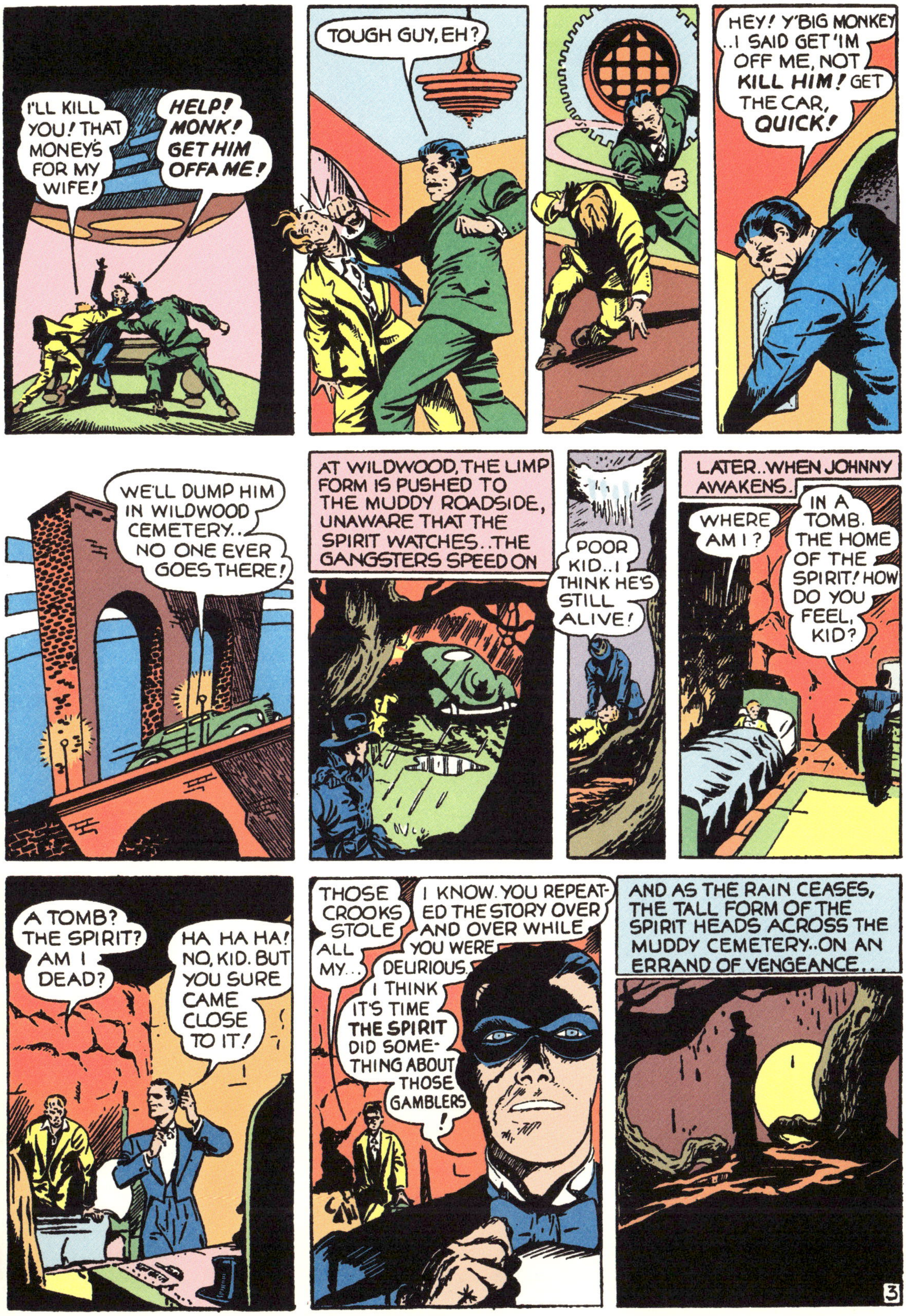
I'LL KILL YOU! THAT MONEY'S FOR MY WIFE!
HELP! MONK! GET HIM OFFA ME!
TOUGH GUY, EH?
HEY! Y'BIG MONKEY ..I SAID GET 'IM OFF ME, NOT KILL HIM! GET THE CAR, QUICK!
WE'LL DUMP HIM IN WILDWOOD CEMETERY.. NO ONE EVER GOES THERE!
AT WILDWOOD, THE LIMP FORM IS PUSHED TO THE MUDDY ROADSIDE, UNAWARE THAT THE SPIRIT WATCHES..THE GANGSTERS SPEED ON
POOR KID..I THINK HE'S STILL ALIVE!
LATER..WHEN JOHNNY AWAKENS.
WHERE AM I?
IN A TOMB. THE HOME OF THE SPIRIT! HOW DO YOU FEEL, KID?
A TOMB? THE SPIRIT? AM I DEAD?
HA HA HA! NO, KID. BUT YOU SURE CAME CLOSE TO IT!
THOSE CROOKS STOLE ALL MY...
I KNOW. YOU REPEATED THE STORY OVER AND OVER WHILE YOU WERE DELIRIOUS. I THINK IT'S TIME THE SPIRIT DID SOMETHING ABOUT THOSE GAMBLERS!
AND AS THE RAIN CEASES, THE TALL FORM OF THE SPIRIT HEADS ACROSS THE MUDDY CEMETERY..ON AN ERRAND OF VENGEANCE...
3

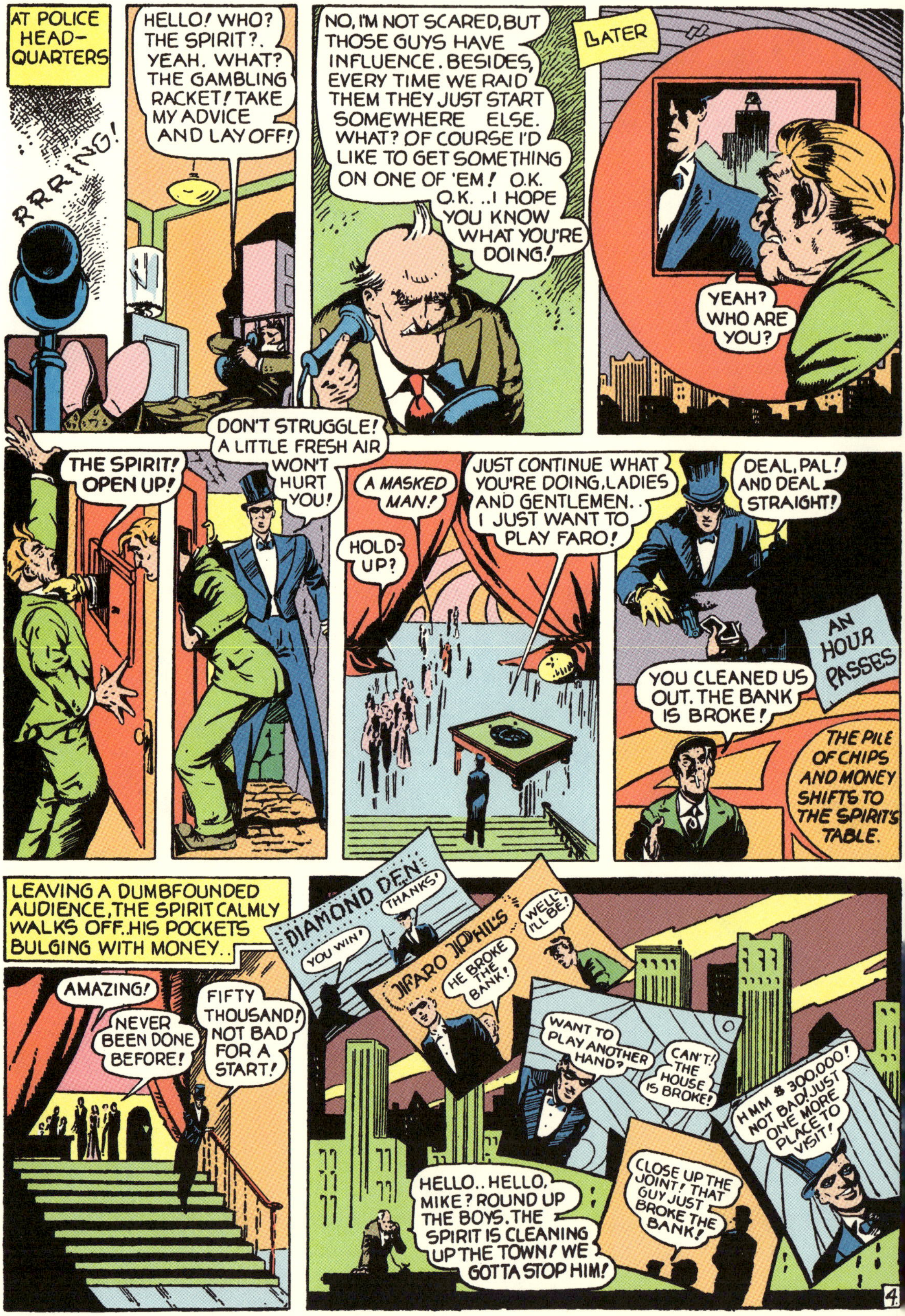
AT POLICE HEAD-QUARTERS
RRRING!
HELLO! WHO? THE SPIRIT?. YEAH. WHAT? THE GAMBLING RACKET! TAKE MY ADVICE AND LAY OFF!
NO, I'M NOT SCARED, BUT THOSE GUYS HAVE INFLUENCE. BESIDES, EVERY TIME WE RAID THEM THEY JUST START SOMEWHERE ELSE. WHAT? OF COURSE I'D LIKE TO GET SOMETHING ON ONE OF 'EM! O.K. O.K. ..I HOPE YOU KNOW WHAT YOU'RE DOING!
LATER
YEAH? WHO ARE YOU?
THE SPIRIT! OPEN UP!
DON'T STRUGGLE! A LITTLE FRESH AIR WON'T HURT YOU!
A MASKED MAN!
HOLD-UP?
JUST CONTINUE WHAT YOU'RE DOING, LADIES AND GENTLEMEN.. I JUST WANT TO PLAY FARO!
DEAL, PAL! AND DEAL STRAIGHT!
AN HOUR PASSES
YOU CLEANED US OUT. THE BANK IS BROKE!
THE PILE OF CHIPS AND MONEY SHIFTS TO THE SPIRIT'S TABLE.
LEAVING A DUMBFOUNDED AUDIENCE, THE SPIRIT CALMLY WALKS OFF..HIS POCKETS BULGING WITH MONEY..
AMAZING!
NEVER BEEN DONE BEFORE!
FIFTY THOUSAND! NOT BAD FOR A START!
DIAMOND DEN
YOU WIN!
THANKS!
FARO PHIL'S
HE BROKE THE BANK!
WELL-I'LL BE!
WANT TO PLAY ANOTHER HAND?
CAN'T! THE HOUSE IS BROKE!
HMM $300,000! NOT BAD! JUST ONE MORE PLACE TO VISIT!
CLOSE UP THE JOINT! THAT GUY JUST BROKE THE BANK!
HELLO.. HELLO. MIKE? ROUND UP THE BOYS. THE SPIRIT IS CLEANING UP THE TOWN! WE GOTTA STOP HIM!
4

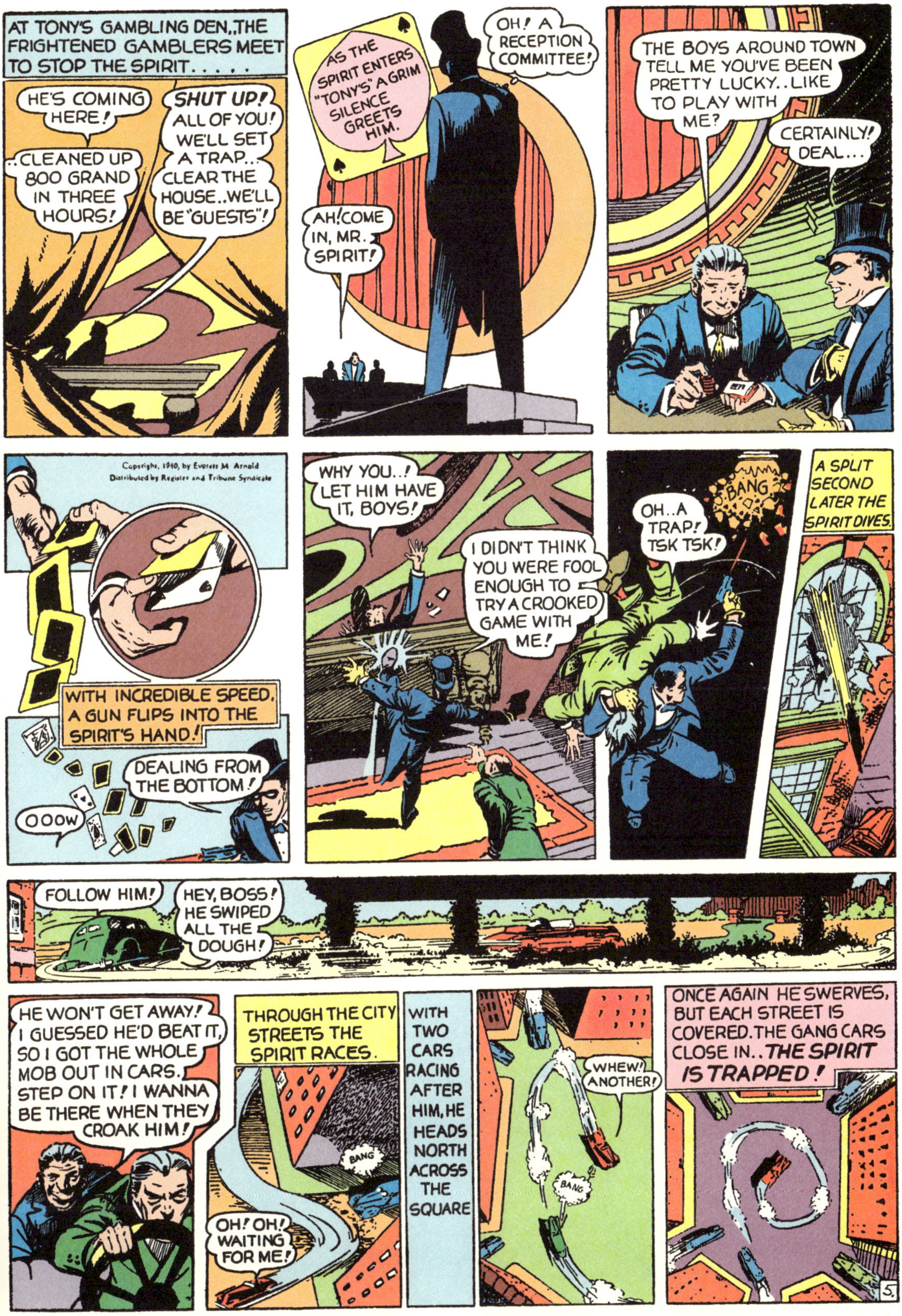
AT TONY'S GAMBLING DEN,.THE FRIGHTENED GAMBLERS MEET TO STOP THE SPIRIT. . . . .
HE'S COMING HERE!
..CLEANED UP 800 GRAND IN THREE HOURS!
SHUT UP! ALL OF YOU! WE'LL SET A TRAP.. CLEAR THE HOUSE..WE'LL BE "GUESTS"!
AS THE SPIRIT ENTERS "TONY'S" A GRIM SILENCE GREETS HIM.
OH! A RECEPTION COMMITTEE!
AH! COME IN, MR. SPIRIT!
THE BOYS AROUND TOWN TELL ME YOU'VE BEEN PRETTY LUCKY..LIKE TO PLAY WITH ME?
CERTAINLY! DEAL...
Copyright, 1940, by Everett M. Arnold
Distributed by Register and Tribune Syndicate
WITH INCREDIBLE SPEED, A GUN FLIPS INTO THE SPIRIT'S HAND!
DEALING FROM THE BOTTOM!
OOOW
WHY YOU..! LET HIM HAVE IT, BOYS!
I DIDN'T THINK YOU WERE FOOL ENOUGH TO TRY A CROOKED GAME WITH ME!
BANG
OH..A TRAP! TSK TSK!
A SPLIT SECOND LATER THE SPIRIT DIVES.
FOLLOW HIM!
HEY, BOSS! HE SWIPED ALL THE DOUGH!
HE WON'T GET AWAY! I GUESSED HE'D BEAT IT, SO I GOT THE WHOLE MOB OUT IN CARS. STEP ON IT! I WANNA BE THERE WHEN THEY CROAK HIM!
THROUGH THE CITY STREETS THE SPIRIT RACES.
BANG
OH! OH! WAITING FOR ME!
WITH TWO CARS RACING AFTER HIM, HE HEADS NORTH ACROSS THE SQUARE
WHEW! ANOTHER!
BANG
ONCE AGAIN HE SWERVES, BUT EACH STREET IS COVERED. THE GANG CARS CLOSE IN.. THE SPIRIT IS TRAPPED!
5.

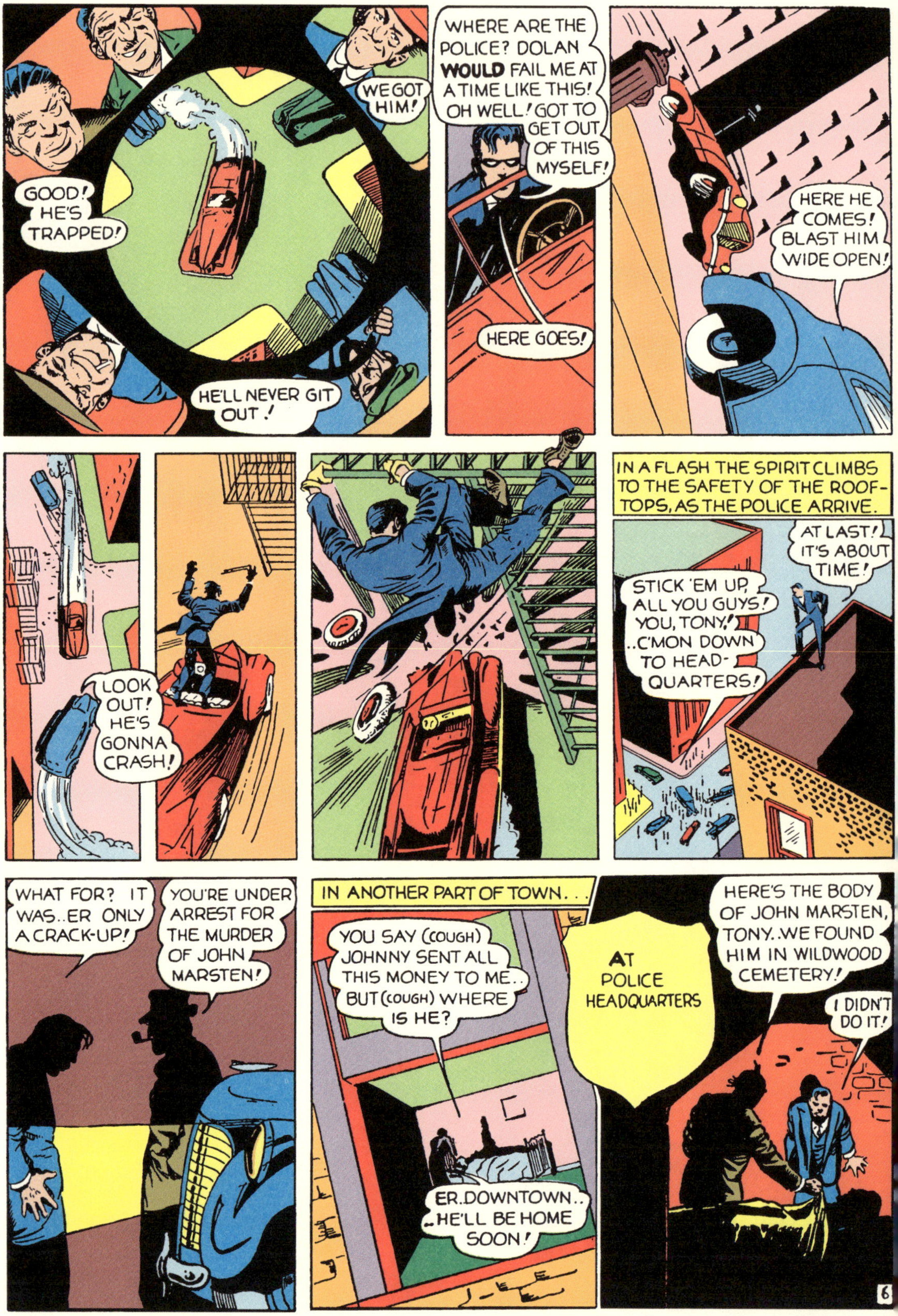
GOOD! HE'S TRAPPED!
WE GOT HIM!
HE'LL NEVER GIT OUT!
WHERE ARE THE POLICE? DOLAN WOULD FAIL ME AT A TIME LIKE THIS! OH WELL! GOT TO GET OUT OF THIS MYSELF!
HERE GOES!
HERE HE COMES! BLAST HIM WIDE OPEN!
LOOK OUT! HE'S GONNA CRASH!
IN A FLASH THE SPIRIT CLIMBS TO THE SAFETY OF THE ROOF-TOPS, AS THE POLICE ARRIVE.
AT LAST! IT'S ABOUT TIME!
STICK 'EM UP, ALL YOU GUYS! YOU, TONY! ..C'MON DOWN TO HEAD-QUARTERS!
WHAT FOR? IT WAS..ER ONLY A CRACK-UP!
YOU'RE UNDER ARREST FOR THE MURDER OF JOHN MARSTEN!
IN ANOTHER PART OF TOWN. . .
YOU SAY (COUGH) JOHNNY SENT ALL THIS MONEY TO ME.. BUT (COUGH) WHERE IS HE?
ER..DOWNTOWN.. ..HE'LL BE HOME SOON!
AT POLICE HEADQUARTERS
HERE'S THE BODY OF JOHN MARSTEN, TONY..WE FOUND HIM IN WILDWOOD CEMETERY!
I DIDN'T DO IT!
6

..BEFORE HE DIED, HE WROTE OUT THIS STATEMENT... SAYING THAT YOU AND MONK BEAT HIM UP AND DROPPED HIM IN WILDWOOD ..'COURSE MONK WAS KILLED IN THE AUTO CRASH, SO...
MONK'S DEAD?! HE DID IT! MONK ...I TRIED TO STOP HIM..BUT MONK WAS ALWAYS A KILLER! I-I ADMIT I ROBBED HIM..
O.K. LET MONK IN!
I HEARD YA! YOU SQUEALIN' RAT! COMMISSIONER, I'LL TELL THE WHOLE STORY NOW!
MONK'S ALIVE?!
NOW THAT THEY'VE SIGNED THEIR CONFESSION, I GUESS I'D BETTER GET HOME TO MY WIFE!
MARSTEN!
ALIVE!
THOSE TWO WILL GET A NICE STRETCH FOR INTENDED MURDER! GOOD LUCK, KID..AND REMEMBER, KEEP AWAY FROM GAMBLING, EVEN WHEN YOU'RE IN A JAM!
SEVERAL DAYS LATER, LONG AFTER SUNDOWN, A MAILMAN PACES NERVOUSLY BEFORE WILDWOOD CEMETERY.
WELL, I'LL BE..
THE ONLY ADDRESS ON THIS LETTER IS, THE SPIRIT, WILDWOOD CEMETERY!
..MUST BE A JOKE, OR..
GONE!
Dear Spirit: I will never be able to thank you enough for saving my wife's life. Thats just what you did when you helped me get that money. I am keeping only a little of the money, the rest is going to charity. I expect a job soon and the doctors here say that my wife has an even chance. God Bless you. John Marsten Arizona
FOLLOW THE ADVENTURES OF THE SPIRIT.......

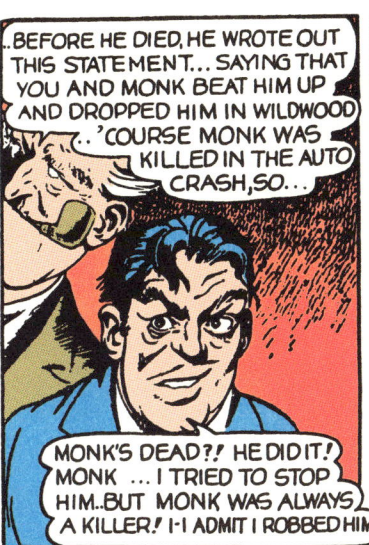

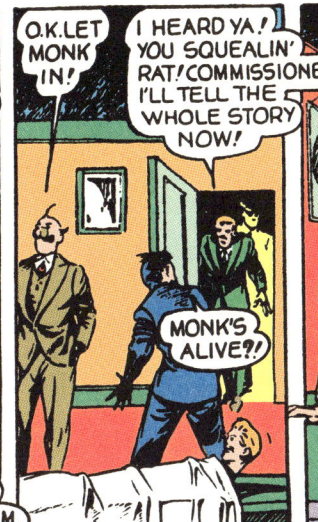

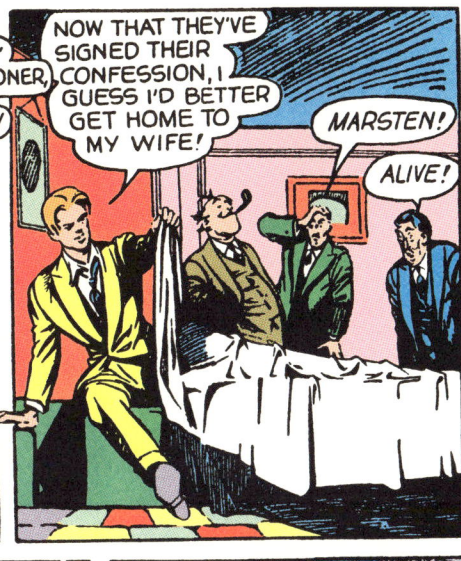

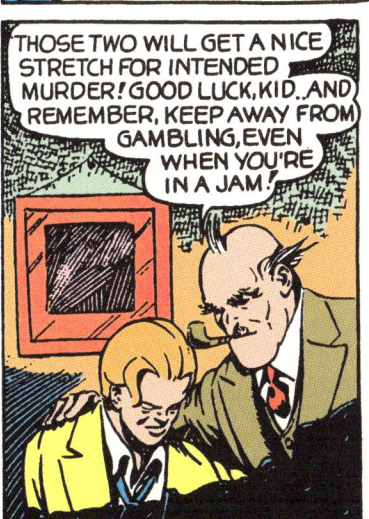

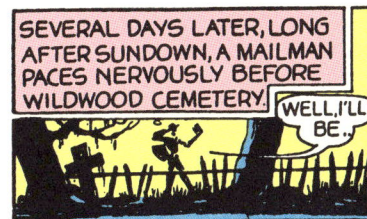

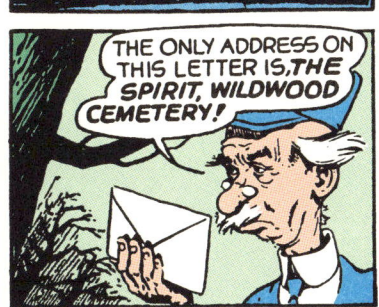

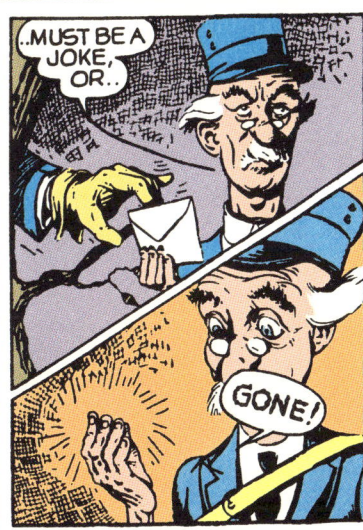

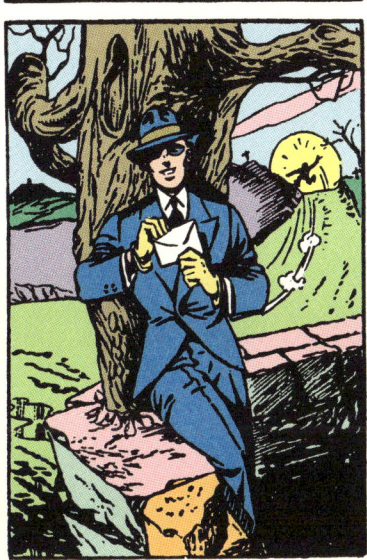

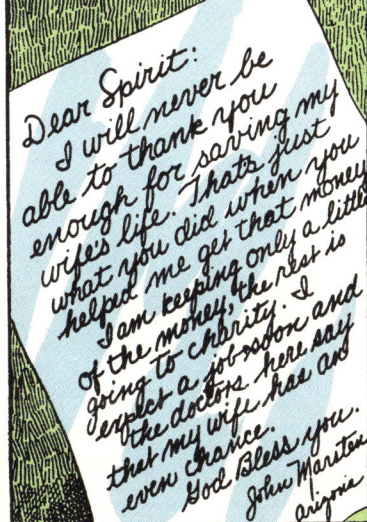

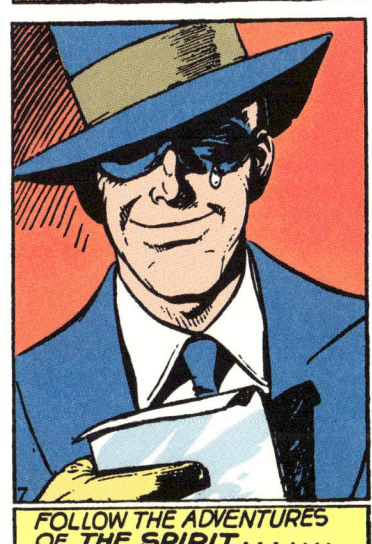

THE BLACK QUEEN'S ARMY

July 7, 1940

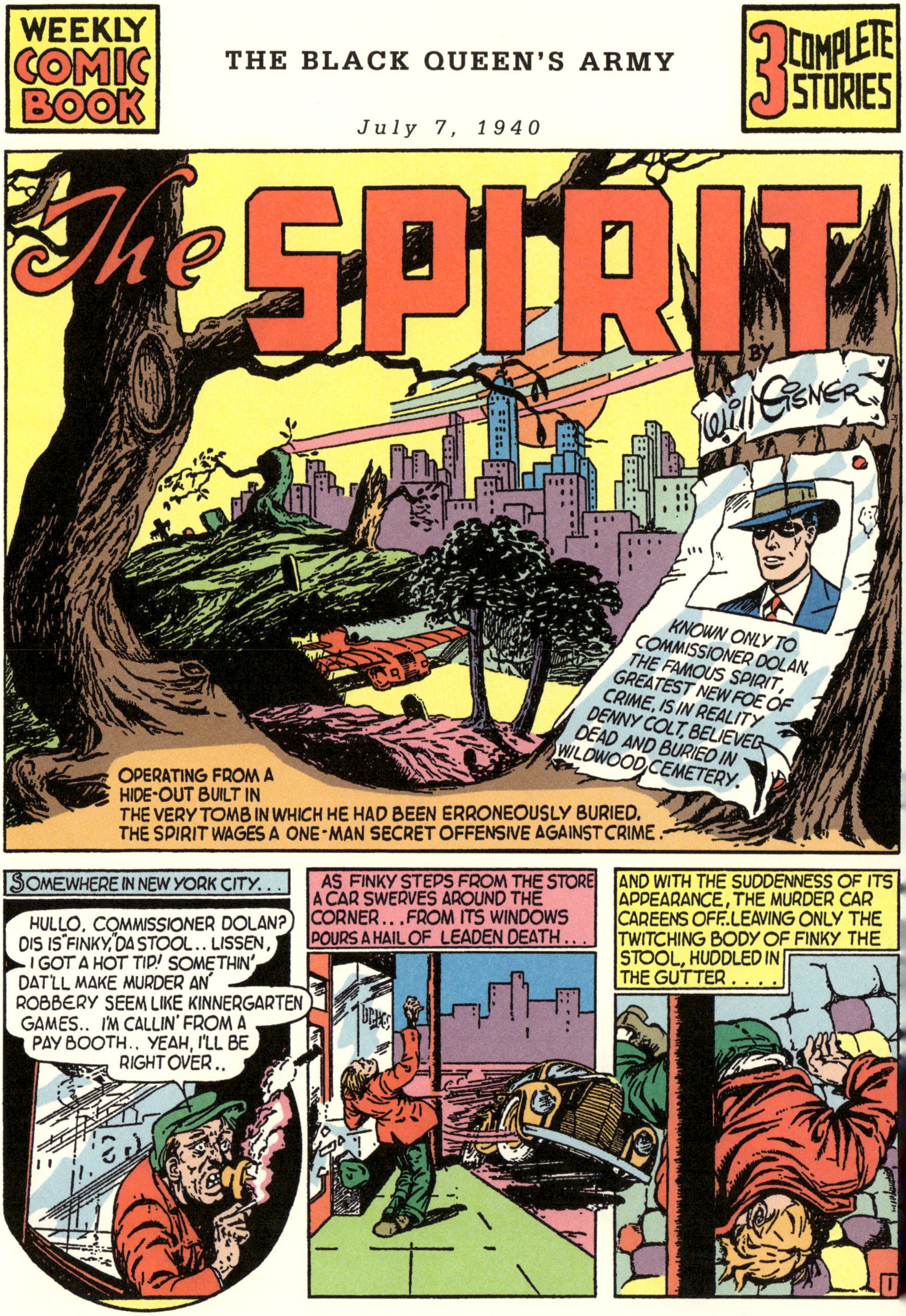
WEEKLY COMIC BOOK
3 COMPLETE STORIES
The SPIRIT
BY Will Eisner
KNOWN ONLY TO COMMISSIONER DOLAN, THE FAMOUS SPIRIT, GREATEST NEW FOE OF CRIME, IS IN REALITY DENNY COLT, BELIEVED DEAD AND BURIED IN WILDWOOD CEMETERY.
OPERATING FROM A HIDE-OUT BUILT IN THE VERY TOMB IN WHICH HE HAD BEEN ERRONEOUSLY BURIED. THE SPIRIT WAGES A ONE-MAN SECRET OFFENSIVE AGAINST CRIME.
SOMEWHERE IN NEW YORK CITY...
HULLO, COMMISSIONER DOLAN? DIS IS "FINKY," DA STOOL.. LISSEN, I GOT A HOT TIP! SOMETHIN' DAT'LL MAKE MURDER AN' ROBBERY SEEM LIKE KINNERGARTEN GAMES.. I'M CALLIN' FROM A PAY BOOTH.. YEAH, I'LL BE RIGHT OVER..
AS FINKY STEPS FROM THE STORE A CAR SWERVES AROUND THE CORNER...FROM ITS WINDOWS POURS A HAIL OF LEADEN DEATH...
AND WITH THE SUDDENNESS OF ITS APPEARANCE, THE MURDER CAR CAREENS OFF..LEAVING ONLY THE TWITCHING BODY OF FINKY THE STOOL, HUDDLED IN THE GUTTER....

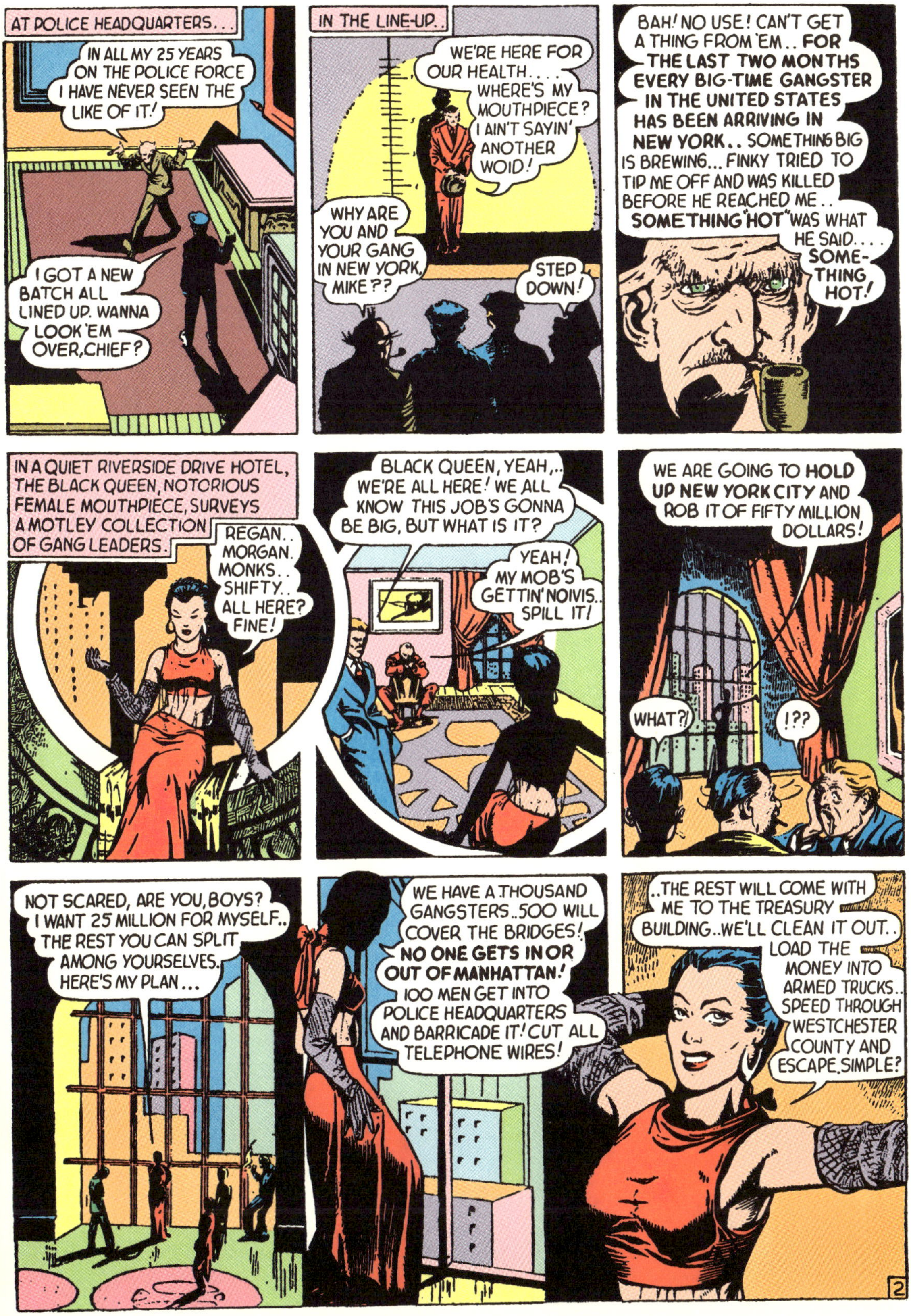

AT POLICE HEADQUARTERS...
IN ALL MY 25 YEARS ON THE POLICE FORCE I HAVE NEVER SEEN THE LIKE OF IT!
I GOT A NEW BATCH ALL LINED UP. WANNA LOOK 'EM OVER, CHIEF?
IN THE LINE-UP..
WE'RE HERE FOR OUR HEALTH.... WHERE'S MY MOUTHPIECE? I AIN'T SAYIN' ANOTHER WOID!
WHY ARE YOU AND YOUR GANG IN NEW YORK, MIKE??
STEP DOWN!
BAH! NO USE! CAN'T GET A THING FROM 'EM.. FOR THE LAST TWO MONTHS EVERY BIG-TIME GANGSTER IN THE UNITED STATES HAS BEEN ARRIVING IN NEW YORK.. SOMETHING BIG IS BREWING... FINKY TRIED TO TIP ME OFF AND WAS KILLED BEFORE HE REACHED ME.. SOMETHING "HOT" WAS WHAT HE SAID.... SOMETHING HOT!
IN A QUIET RIVERSIDE DRIVE HOTEL, THE BLACK QUEEN, NOTORIOUS FEMALE MOUTHPIECE, SURVEYS A MOTLEY COLLECTION OF GANG LEADERS.
REGAN.. MORGAN. MONKS.. SHIFTY.. ALL HERE? FINE!
BLACK QUEEN, YEAH,.. WE'RE ALL HERE! WE ALL KNOW THIS JOB'S GONNA BE BIG, BUT WHAT IS IT?
YEAH! MY MOB'S GETTIN' NOIVIS.. SPILL IT!
WE ARE GOING TO HOLD UP NEW YORK CITY AND ROB IT OF FIFTY MILLION DOLLARS!
WHAT?!
!??
NOT SCARED, ARE YOU, BOYS? I WANT 25 MILLION FOR MYSELF.. THE REST YOU CAN SPLIT AMONG YOURSELVES. HERE'S MY PLAN...
WE HAVE A THOUSAND GANGSTERS..500 WILL COVER THE BRIDGES! NO ONE GETS IN OR OUT OF MANHATTAN! 100 MEN GET INTO POLICE HEADQUARTERS AND BARRICADE IT! CUT ALL TELEPHONE WIRES!
..THE REST WILL COME WITH ME TO THE TREASURY BUILDING..WE'LL CLEAN IT OUT.. LOAD THE MONEY INTO ARMED TRUCKS.. SPEED THROUGH WESTCHESTER COUNTY AND ESCAPE. SIMPLE?
2

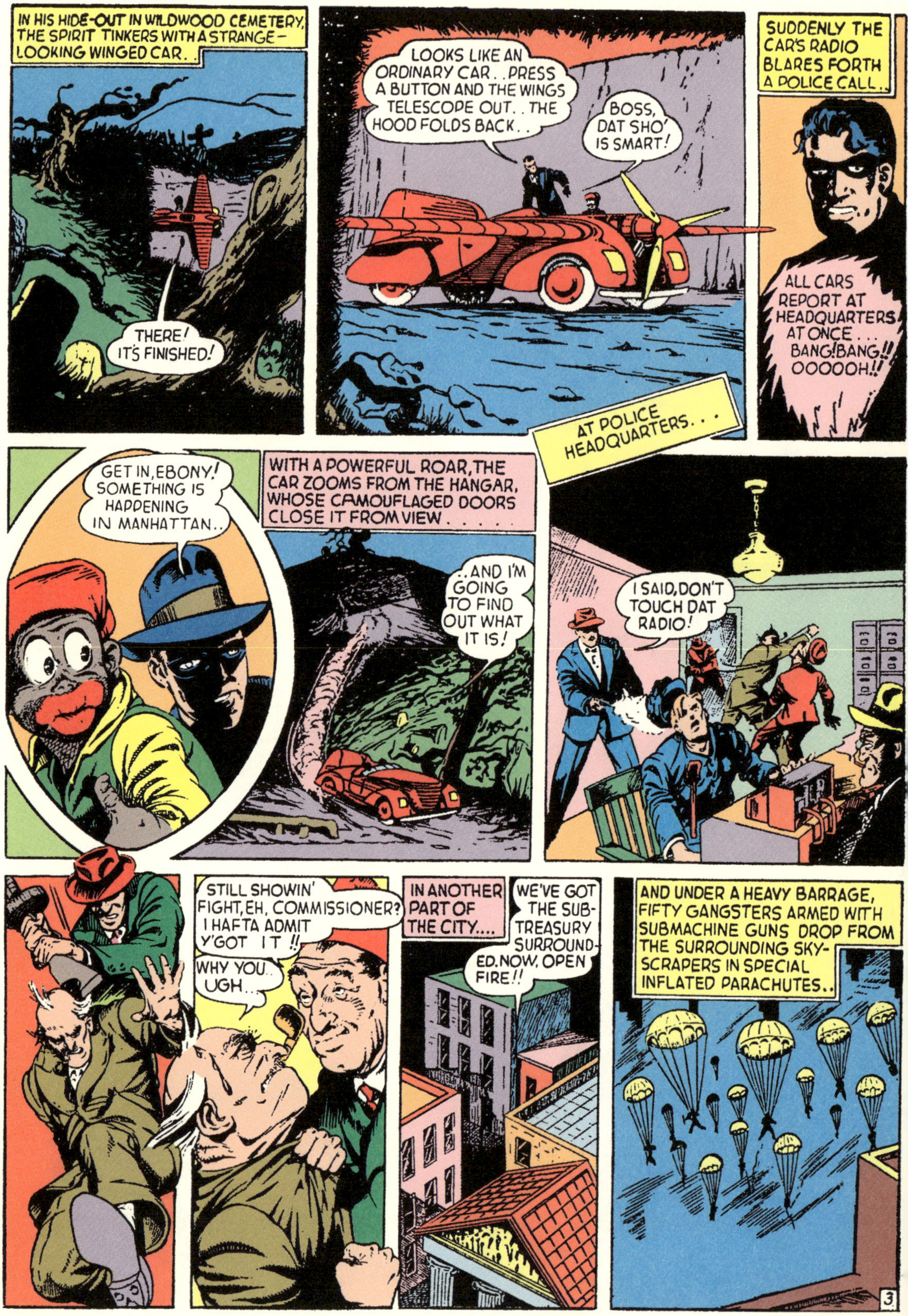
IN HIS HIDE-OUT IN WILDWOOD CEMETERY, THE SPIRIT TINKERS WITH A STRANGE-LOOKING WINGED CAR.
THERE! IT'S FINISHED!
LOOKS LIKE AN ORDINARY CAR.. PRESS A BUTTON AND THE WINGS TELESCOPE OUT.. THE HOOD FOLDS BACK..
BOSS, DAT SHO' IS SMART!
SUDDENLY THE CAR'S RADIO BLARES FORTH A POLICE CALL..
ALL CARS REPORT AT HEADQUARTERS AT ONCE... BANG! BANG!! OOOOOH!!
GET IN, EBONY! SOMETHING IS HAPPENING IN MANHATTAN..
WITH A POWERFUL ROAR, THE CAR ZOOMS FROM THE HANGAR, WHOSE CAMOUFLAGED DOORS CLOSE IT FROM VIEW....
..AND I'M GOING TO FIND OUT WHAT IT IS!
AT POLICE HEADQUARTERS...
I SAID, DON'T TOUCH DAT RADIO!
STILL SHOWIN' FIGHT, EH, COMMISSIONER? I HAFTA ADMIT Y'GOT IT!!
WHY YOU.. UGH..
IN ANOTHER PART OF THE CITY....
WE'VE GOT THE SUB-TREASURY SURROUND-ED. NOW, OPEN FIRE!!
AND UNDER A HEAVY BARRAGE, FIFTY GANGSTERS ARMED WITH SUBMACHINE GUNS DROP FROM THE SURROUNDING SKY-SCRAPERS IN SPECIAL INFLATED PARACHUTES..
3

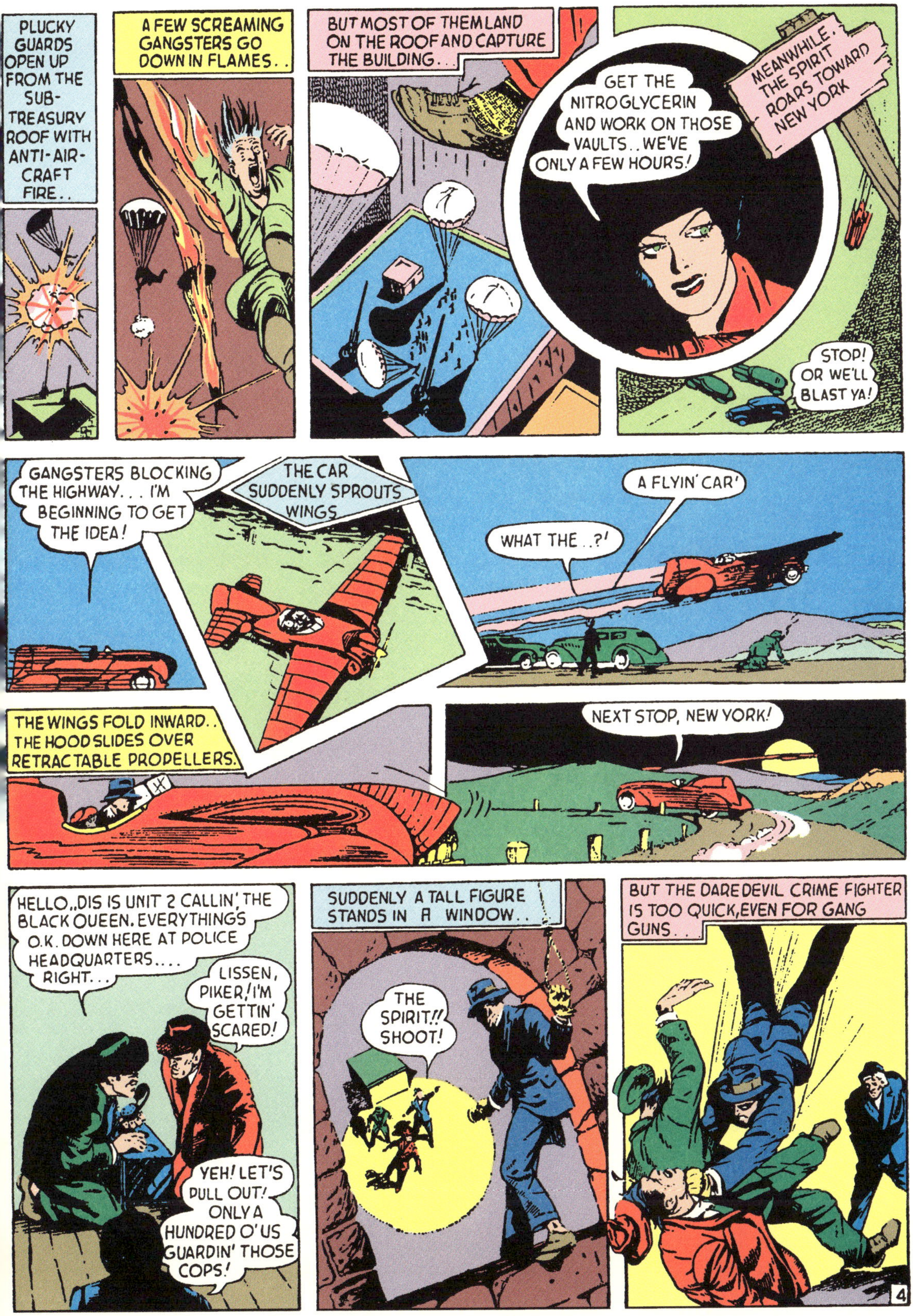
PLUCKY GUARDS OPEN UP FROM THE SUB-TREASURY ROOF WITH ANTI-AIR-CRAFT FIRE..
A FEW SCREAMING GANGSTERS GO DOWN IN FLAMES..
BUT MOST OF THEM LAND ON THE ROOF AND CAPTURE THE BUILDING..
MEANWHILE, THE SPIRIT ROARS TOWARD NEW YORK
GET THE NITROGLYCERIN AND WORK ON THOSE VAULTS..WE'VE ONLY A FEW HOURS!
STOP! OR WE'LL BLAST YA!
GANGSTERS BLOCKING THE HIGHWAY... I'M BEGINNING TO GET THE IDEA!
THE CAR SUDDENLY SPROUTS WINGS
A FLYIN' CAR!
WHAT THE ..?!
THE WINGS FOLD INWARD.. THE HOOD SLIDES OVER RETRACTABLE PROPELLERS.
NEXT STOP, NEW YORK!
HELLO..DIS IS UNIT 2 CALLIN' THE BLACK QUEEN. EVERYTHING'S O.K. DOWN HERE AT POLICE HEADQUARTERS.... RIGHT...
LISSEN, PIKER! I'M GETTIN' SCARED!
YEH! LET'S PULL OUT! ONLY A HUNDRED O' US GUARDIN' THOSE COPS!
SUDDENLY A TALL FIGURE STANDS IN A WINDOW..
THE SPIRIT!! SHOOT!
BUT THE DAREDEVIL CRIME FIGHTER IS TOO QUICK, EVEN FOR GANG GUNS..
4

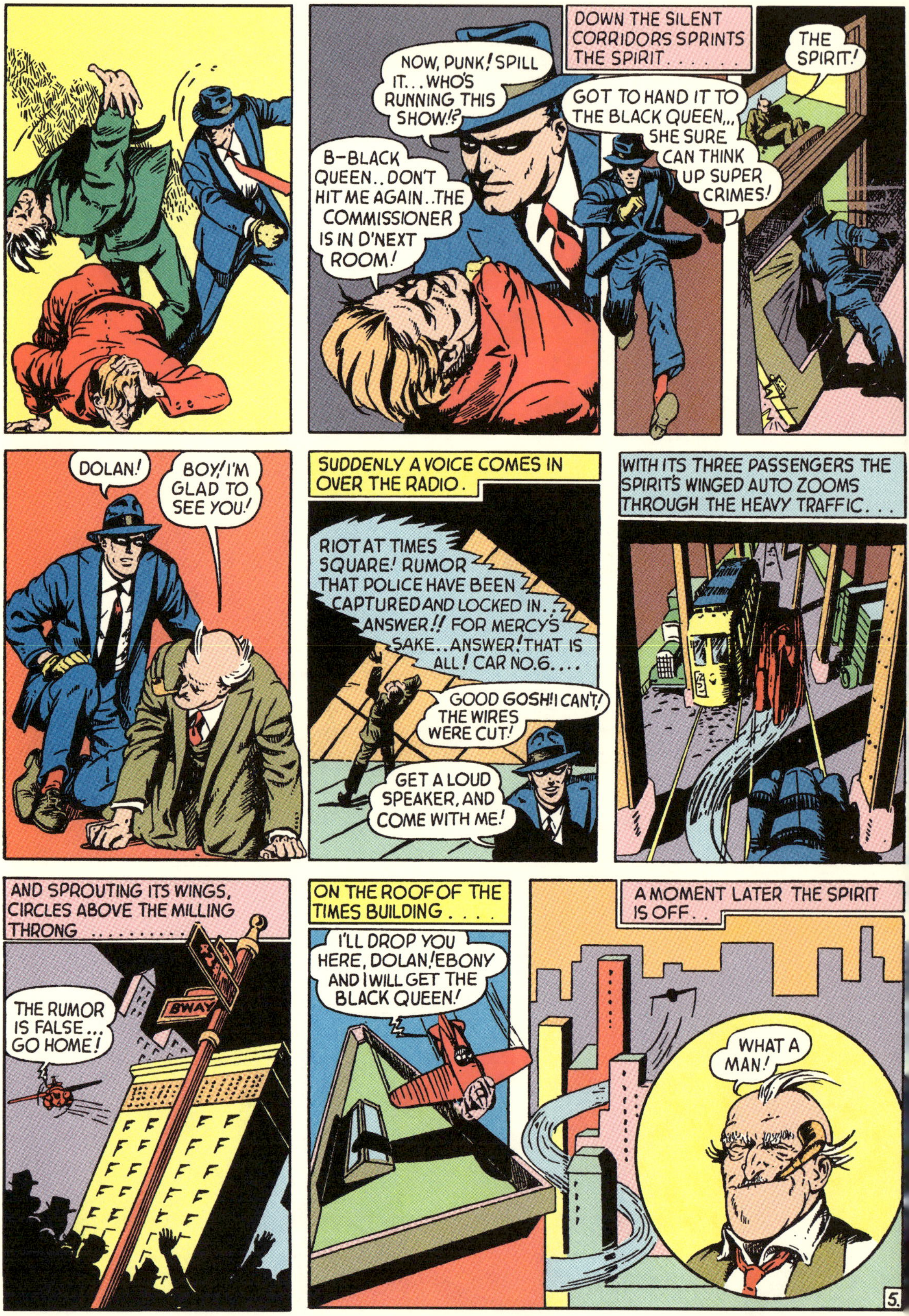

NOW, PUNK! SPILL IT... WHO'S RUNNING THIS SHOW!?
B-BLACK QUEEN.. DON'T HIT ME AGAIN..THE COMMISSIONER IS IN D'NEXT ROOM!
DOWN THE SILENT CORRIDORS SPRINTS THE SPIRIT......
GOT TO HAND IT TO THE BLACK QUEEN,.. SHE SURE CAN THINK UP SUPER CRIMES!
THE SPIRIT!
DOLAN!
BOY! I'M GLAD TO SEE YOU!
SUDDENLY A VOICE COMES IN OVER THE RADIO.
RIOT AT TIMES SQUARE! RUMOR THAT POLICE HAVE BEEN CAPTURED AND LOCKED IN.. ANSWER!! FOR MERCY'S SAKE..ANSWER! THAT IS ALL! CAR NO.6....
GOOD GOSH! I CAN'T! THE WIRES WERE CUT!
GET A LOUD SPEAKER, AND COME WITH ME!
WITH ITS THREE PASSENGERS THE SPIRIT'S WINGED AUTO ZOOMS THROUGH THE HEAVY TRAFFIC...
AND SPROUTING ITS WINGS, CIRCLES ABOVE THE MILLING THRONG ....
42
BWAY
THE RUMOR IS FALSE... GO HOME!
ON THE ROOF OF THE TIMES BUILDING....
I'LL DROP YOU HERE, DOLAN! EBONY AND I WILL GET THE BLACK QUEEN!
A MOMENT LATER THE SPIRIT IS OFF..
WHAT A MAN!
5.

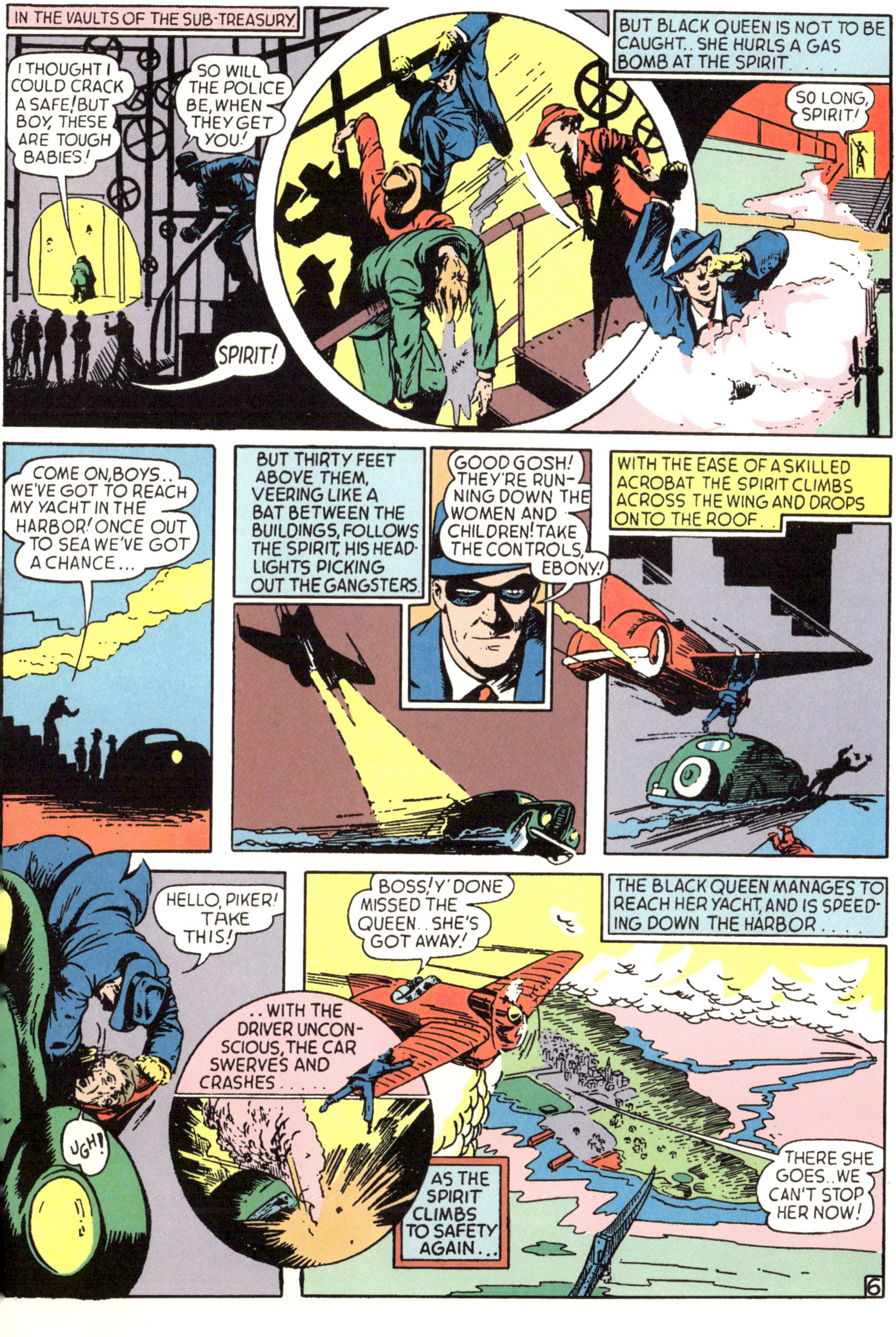
IN THE VAULTS OF THE SUB-TREASURY
I THOUGHT I COULD CRACK A SAFE! BUT BOY, THESE ARE TOUGH BABIES!
SO WILL THE POLICE BE, WHEN THEY GET YOU!
SPIRIT!
BUT BLACK QUEEN IS NOT TO BE CAUGHT.. SHE HURLS A GAS BOMB AT THE SPIRIT . . .
SO LONG, SPIRIT!
COME ON, BOYS.. WE'VE GOT TO REACH MY YACHT IN THE HARBOR! ONCE OUT TO SEA WE'VE GOT A CHANCE...
BUT THIRTY FEET ABOVE THEM, VEERING LIKE A BAT BETWEEN THE BUILDINGS, FOLLOWS THE SPIRIT, HIS HEAD-LIGHTS PICKING OUT THE GANGSTERS.
GOOD GOSH! THEY'RE RUN-NING DOWN THE WOMEN AND CHILDREN! TAKE THE CONTROLS, EBONY!
WITH THE EASE OF A SKILLED ACROBAT THE SPIRIT CLIMBS ACROSS THE WING AND DROPS ONTO THE ROOF . .
HELLO, PIKER! TAKE THIS!
UGH!
..WITH THE DRIVER UNCON-SCIOUS, THE CAR SWERVES AND CRASHES . . . .
BOSS! Y' DONE MISSED THE QUEEN.. SHE'S GOT AWAY!
THE BLACK QUEEN MANAGES TO REACH HER YACHT, AND IS SPEED-ING DOWN THE HARBOR . . .
AS THE SPIRIT CLIMBS TO SAFETY AGAIN..
THERE SHE GOES..WE CAN'T STOP HER NOW!
6

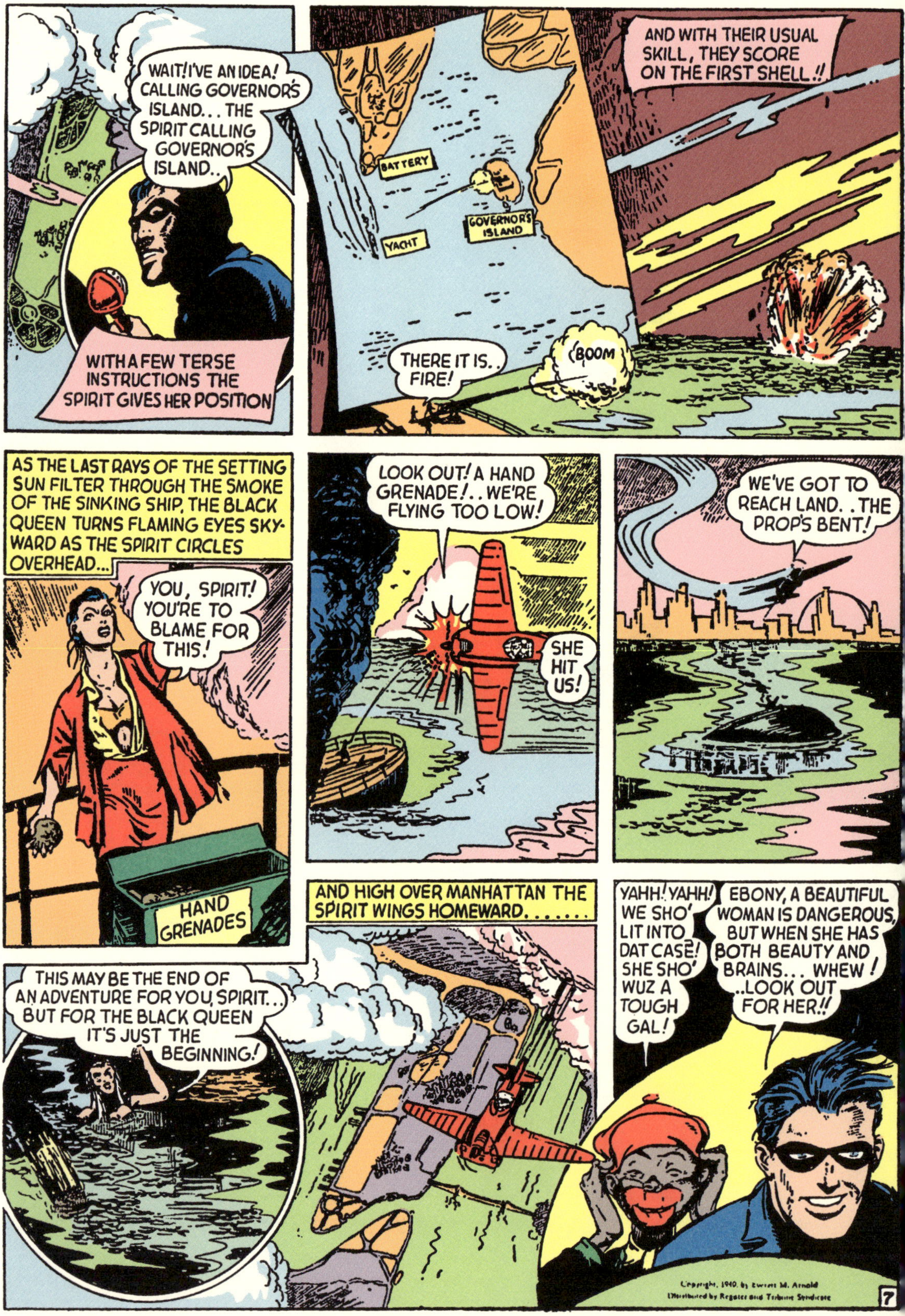
WAIT! I'VE AN IDEA! CALLING GOVERNOR'S ISLAND... THE SPIRIT CALLING GOVERNOR'S ISLAND..
WITH A FEW TERSE INSTRUCTIONS THE SPIRIT GIVES HER POSITION
AND WITH THEIR USUAL SKILL, THEY SCORE ON THE FIRST SHELL.!!
BATTERY
GOVERNOR'S ISLAND
YACHT
THERE IT IS.. FIRE!
BOOM
AS THE LAST RAYS OF THE SETTING SUN FILTER THROUGH THE SMOKE OF THE SINKING SHIP, THE BLACK QUEEN TURNS FLAMING EYES SKYWARD AS THE SPIRIT CIRCLES OVERHEAD...
YOU, SPIRIT! YOU'RE TO BLAME FOR THIS!
HAND GRENADES
LOOK OUT! A HAND GRENADE!.. WE'RE FLYING TOO LOW!
SHE HIT US!
WE'VE GOT TO REACH LAND.. THE PROP'S BENT!
THIS MAY BE THE END OF AN ADVENTURE FOR YOU, SPIRIT... BUT FOR THE BLACK QUEEN IT'S JUST THE BEGINNING!
AND HIGH OVER MANHATTAN THE SPIRIT WINGS HOMEWARD......
YAHH! YAHH! WE SHO' LIT INTO DAT CASE! SHE SHO' WUZ A TOUGH GAL!
EBONY, A BEAUTIFUL WOMAN IS DANGEROUS, BUT WHEN SHE HAS BOTH BEAUTY AND BRAINS... WHEW! ..LOOK OUT FOR HER!!
Copyright, 1940, by Everett M. Arnold
Distributed by Register and Tribune Syndicate
7

WEEKLY COMIC BOOK

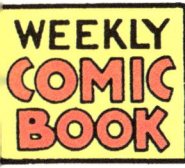

MR. MIDNIGHT

July 14, 1940

3 COMPLETE STORIES

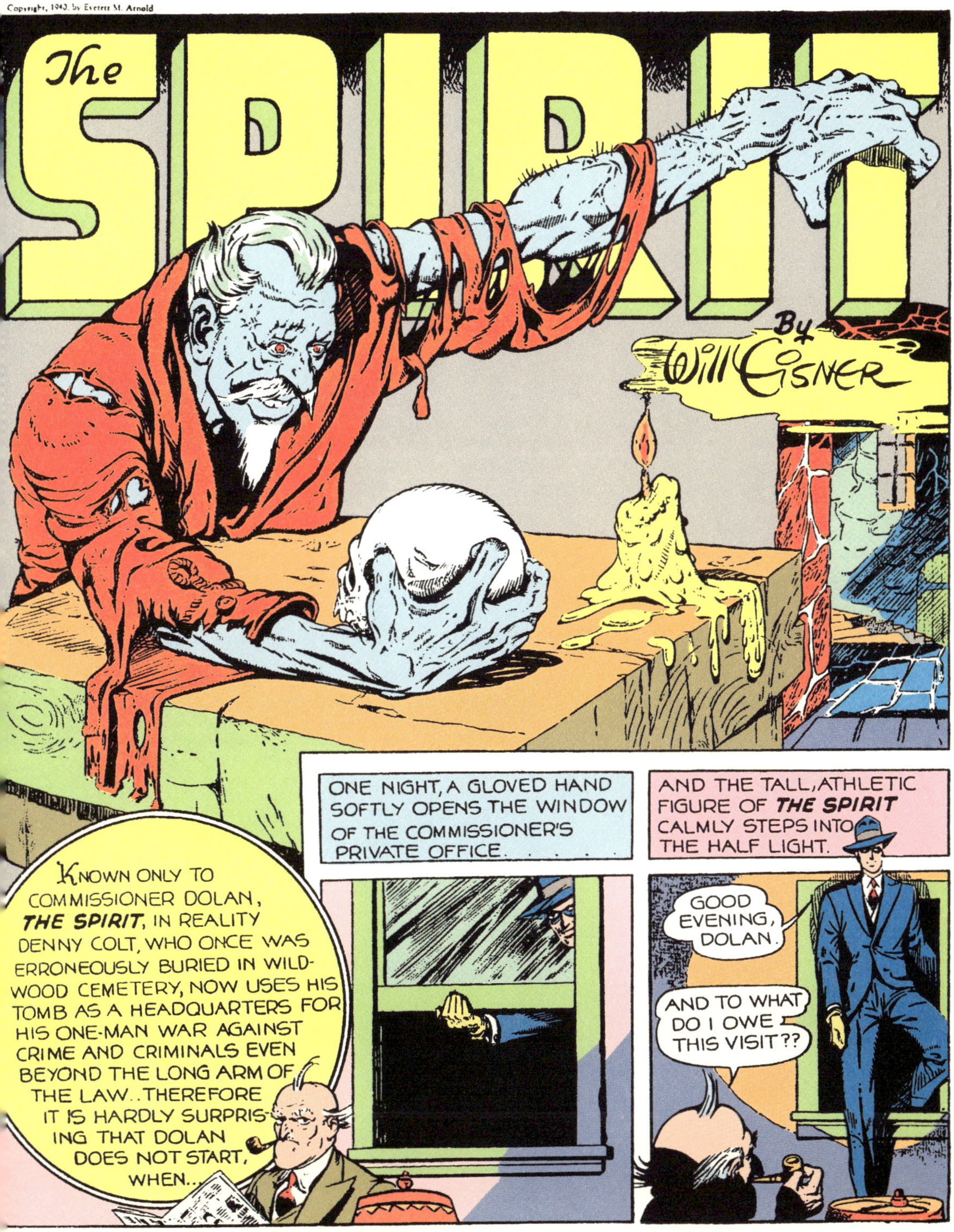

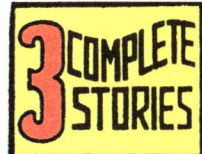

The SPIRIT
By Will Eisner
KNOWN ONLY TO COMMISSIONER DOLAN, THE SPIRIT, IN REALITY DENNY COLT, WHO ONCE WAS ERRONEOUSLY BURIED IN WILDWOOD CEMETERY, NOW USES HIS TOMB AS A HEADQUARTERS FOR HIS ONE-MAN WAR AGAINST CRIME AND CRIMINALS EVEN BEYOND THE LONG ARM OF THE LAW..THEREFORE IT IS HARDLY SURPRISING THAT DOLAN DOES NOT START, WHEN...
ONE NIGHT, A GLOVED HAND SOFTLY OPENS THE WINDOW OF THE COMMISSIONER'S PRIVATE OFFICE. . . .
AND THE TALL, ATHLETIC FIGURE OF THE SPIRIT CALMLY STEPS INTO THE HALF LIGHT.
GOOD EVENING, DOLAN.
AND TO WHAT DO I OWE THIS VISIT??

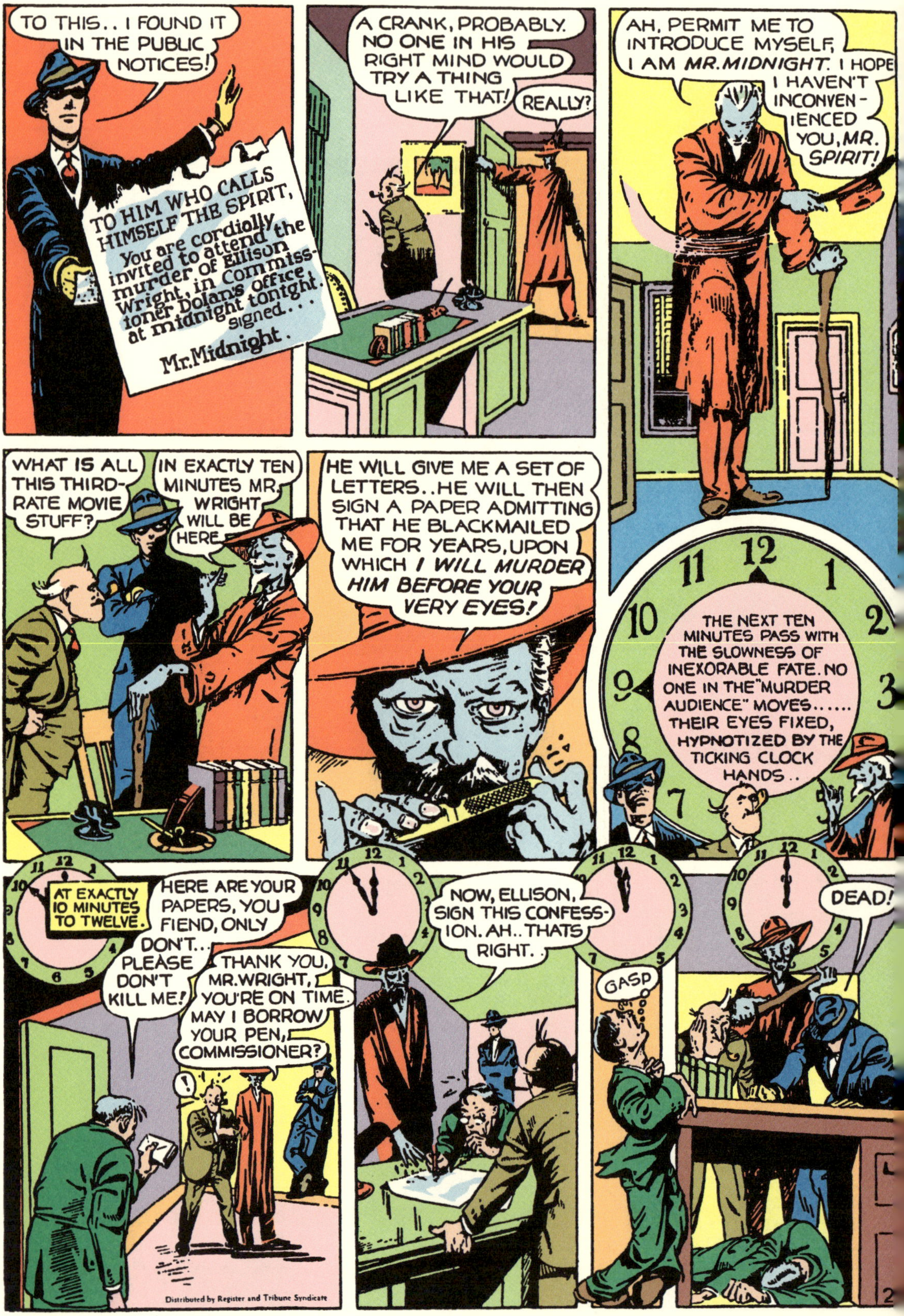
TO THIS.. I FOUND IT IN THE PUBLIC NOTICES!
TO HIM WHO CALLS HIMSELF THE SPIRIT, You are cordially invited to attend the murder of Ellison Wright, in Commiss-ioner Dolan's office at midnight tonight. signed... Mr. Midnight.
A CRANK, PROBABLY. NO ONE IN HIS RIGHT MIND WOULD TRY A THING LIKE THAT!
REALLY?
AH, PERMIT ME TO INTRODUCE MYSELF, I AM MR. MIDNIGHT. I HOPE I HAVEN'T INCONVEN-IENCED YOU, MR. SPIRIT!
WHAT IS ALL THIS THIRD-RATE MOVIE STUFF?
IN EXACTLY TEN MINUTES MR. WRIGHT WILL BE HERE.
HE WILL GIVE ME A SET OF LETTERS..HE WILL THEN SIGN A PAPER ADMITTING THAT HE BLACKMAILED ME FOR YEARS, UPON WHICH I WILL MURDER HIM BEFORE YOUR VERY EYES!
THE NEXT TEN MINUTES PASS WITH THE SLOWNESS OF INEXORABLE FATE. NO ONE IN THE "MURDER AUDIENCE" MOVES...... THEIR EYES FIXED, HYPNOTIZED BY THE TICKING CLOCK HANDS..
AT EXACTLY 10 MINUTES TO TWELVE.
HERE ARE YOUR PAPERS, YOU FIEND, ONLY DON'T.. PLEASE DON'T KILL ME!
THANK YOU, MR. WRIGHT, YOU'RE ON TIME. MAY I BORROW YOUR PEN, COMMISSIONER?
!
Distributed by Register and Tribune Syndicate
NOW, ELLISON, SIGN THIS CONFESS-ION. AH.. THATS RIGHT..
GASP
DEAD!
2

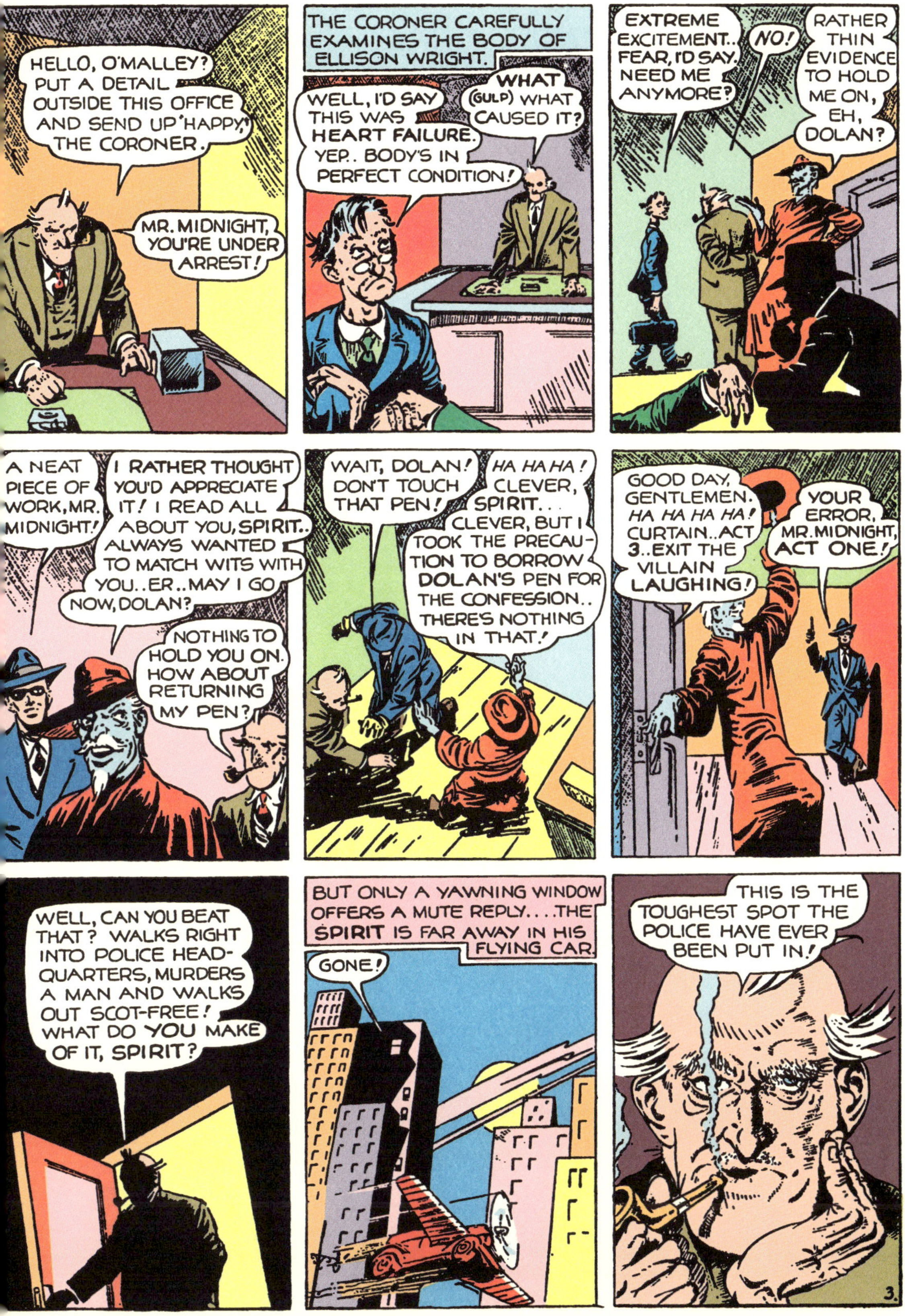
HELLO, O'MALLEY? PUT A DETAIL OUTSIDE THIS OFFICE AND SEND UP 'HAPPY' THE CORONER.
MR. MIDNIGHT, YOU'RE UNDER ARREST!
THE CORONER CAREFULLY EXAMINES THE BODY OF ELLISON WRIGHT.
WELL, I'D SAY THIS WAS HEART FAILURE. YEP.. BODY'S IN PERFECT CONDITION!
WHAT (GULP) WHAT CAUSED IT?
EXTREME EXCITEMENT.. FEAR, I'D SAY. NEED ME ANYMORE?
NO!
RATHER THIN EVIDENCE TO HOLD ME ON, EH, DOLAN?
A NEAT PIECE OF WORK, MR. MIDNIGHT!
I RATHER THOUGHT YOU'D APPRECIATE IT! I READ ALL ABOUT YOU, SPIRIT.. ALWAYS WANTED TO MATCH WITS WITH YOU..ER..MAY I GO NOW, DOLAN?
NOTHING TO HOLD YOU ON. HOW ABOUT RETURNING MY PEN?
WAIT, DOLAN! DON'T TOUCH THAT PEN!
HA HA HA! CLEVER, SPIRIT... CLEVER, BUT I TOOK THE PRECAUTION TO BORROW DOLAN'S PEN FOR THE CONFESSION.. THERE'S NOTHING IN THAT!
GOOD DAY, GENTLEMEN. HA HA HA HA! CURTAIN..ACT 3..EXIT THE VILLAIN LAUGHING!
YOUR ERROR, MR. MIDNIGHT, ACT ONE!
WELL, CAN YOU BEAT THAT? WALKS RIGHT INTO POLICE HEADQUARTERS, MURDERS A MAN AND WALKS OUT SCOT-FREE! WHAT DO YOU MAKE OF IT, SPIRIT?
BUT ONLY A YAWNING WINDOW OFFERS A MUTE REPLY.... THE SPIRIT IS FAR AWAY IN HIS FLYING CAR.
GONE!
THIS IS THE TOUGHEST SPOT THE POLICE HAVE EVER BEEN PUT IN!
3.

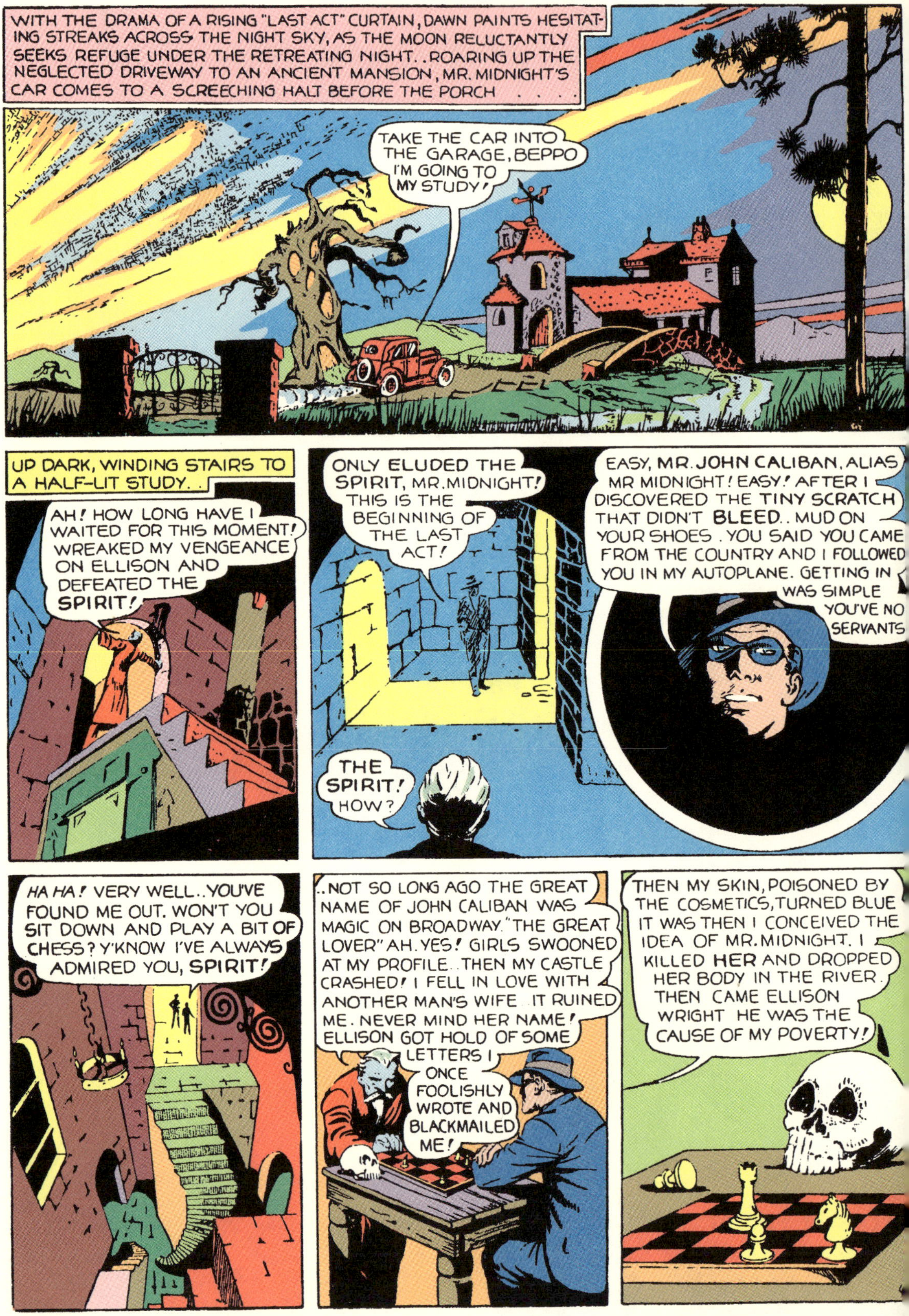
WITH THE DRAMA OF A RISING "LAST ACT" CURTAIN, DAWN PAINTS HESITATING STREAKS ACROSS THE NIGHT SKY, AS THE MOON RELUCTANTLY SEEKS REFUGE UNDER THE RETREATING NIGHT. . ROARING UP THE NEGLECTED DRIVEWAY TO AN ANCIENT MANSION, MR. MIDNIGHT'S CAR COMES TO A SCREECHING HALT BEFORE THE PORCH . . . .
TAKE THE CAR INTO THE GARAGE, BEPPO I'M GOING TO MY STUDY!
UP DARK, WINDING STAIRS TO A HALF-LIT STUDY. .
AH! HOW LONG HAVE I WAITED FOR THIS MOMENT! WREAKED MY VENGEANCE ON ELLISON AND DEFEATED THE SPIRIT!
ONLY ELUDED THE SPIRIT, MR. MIDNIGHT! THIS IS THE BEGINNING OF THE LAST ACT!
THE SPIRIT! HOW?
EASY, MR. JOHN CALIBAN, ALIAS MR MIDNIGHT! EASY! AFTER I DISCOVERED THE TINY SCRATCH THAT DIDN'T BLEED. . MUD ON YOUR SHOES . YOU SAID YOU CAME FROM THE COUNTRY AND I FOLLOWED YOU IN MY AUTOPLANE. GETTING IN WAS SIMPLE YOU'VE NO SERVANTS
HA HA! VERY WELL. . YOU'VE FOUND ME OUT. WON'T YOU SIT DOWN AND PLAY A BIT OF CHESS? Y'KNOW I'VE ALWAYS ADMIRED YOU, SPIRIT!
. . NOT SO LONG AGO THE GREAT NAME OF JOHN CALIBAN WAS MAGIC ON BROADWAY. "THE GREAT LOVER" AH. YES! GIRLS SWOONED AT MY PROFILE. . THEN MY CASTLE CRASHED! I FELL IN LOVE WITH ANOTHER MAN'S WIFE . IT RUINED ME. NEVER MIND HER NAME! ELLISON GOT HOLD OF SOME LETTERS I ONCE FOOLISHLY WROTE AND BLACKMAILED ME!
THEN MY SKIN, POISONED BY THE COSMETICS, TURNED BLUE IT WAS THEN I CONCEIVED THE IDEA OF MR. MIDNIGHT. I KILLED HER AND DROPPED HER BODY IN THE RIVER. THEN CAME ELLISON WRIGHT HE WAS THE CAUSE OF MY POVERTY!

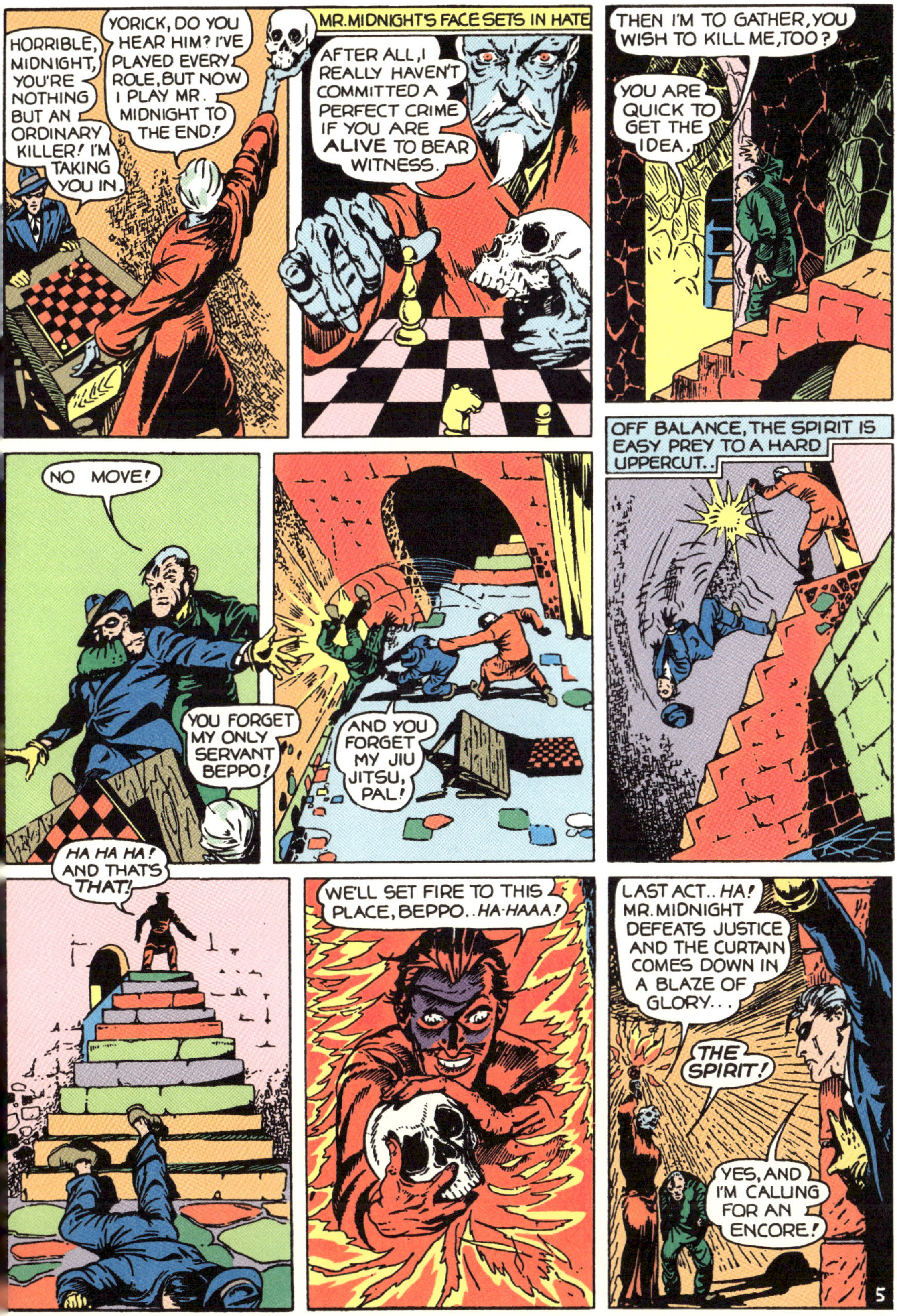
HORRIBLE, MIDNIGHT, YOU'RE NOTHING BUT AN ORDINARY KILLER! I'M TAKING YOU IN.
YORICK, DO YOU HEAR HIM? I'VE PLAYED EVERY ROLE, BUT NOW I PLAY MR. MIDNIGHT TO THE END!
MR. MIDNIGHT'S FACE SETS IN HATE
AFTER ALL, I REALLY HAVEN'T COMMITTED A PERFECT CRIME IF YOU ARE ALIVE TO BEAR WITNESS.
THEN I'M TO GATHER, YOU WISH TO KILL ME, TOO?
YOU ARE QUICK TO GET THE IDEA.
NO MOVE!
YOU FORGET MY ONLY SERVANT BEPPO!
AND YOU FORGET MY JIU JITSU, PAL!
OFF BALANCE, THE SPIRIT IS EASY PREY TO A HARD UPPERCUT..
HA HA HA! AND THAT'S THAT!
WE'LL SET FIRE TO THIS PLACE, BEPPO.. HA-HAAA!
LAST ACT.. HA! MR. MIDNIGHT DEFEATS JUSTICE AND THE CURTAIN COMES DOWN IN A BLAZE OF GLORY...
THE SPIRIT!
YES, AND I'M CALLING FOR AN ENCORE!
5

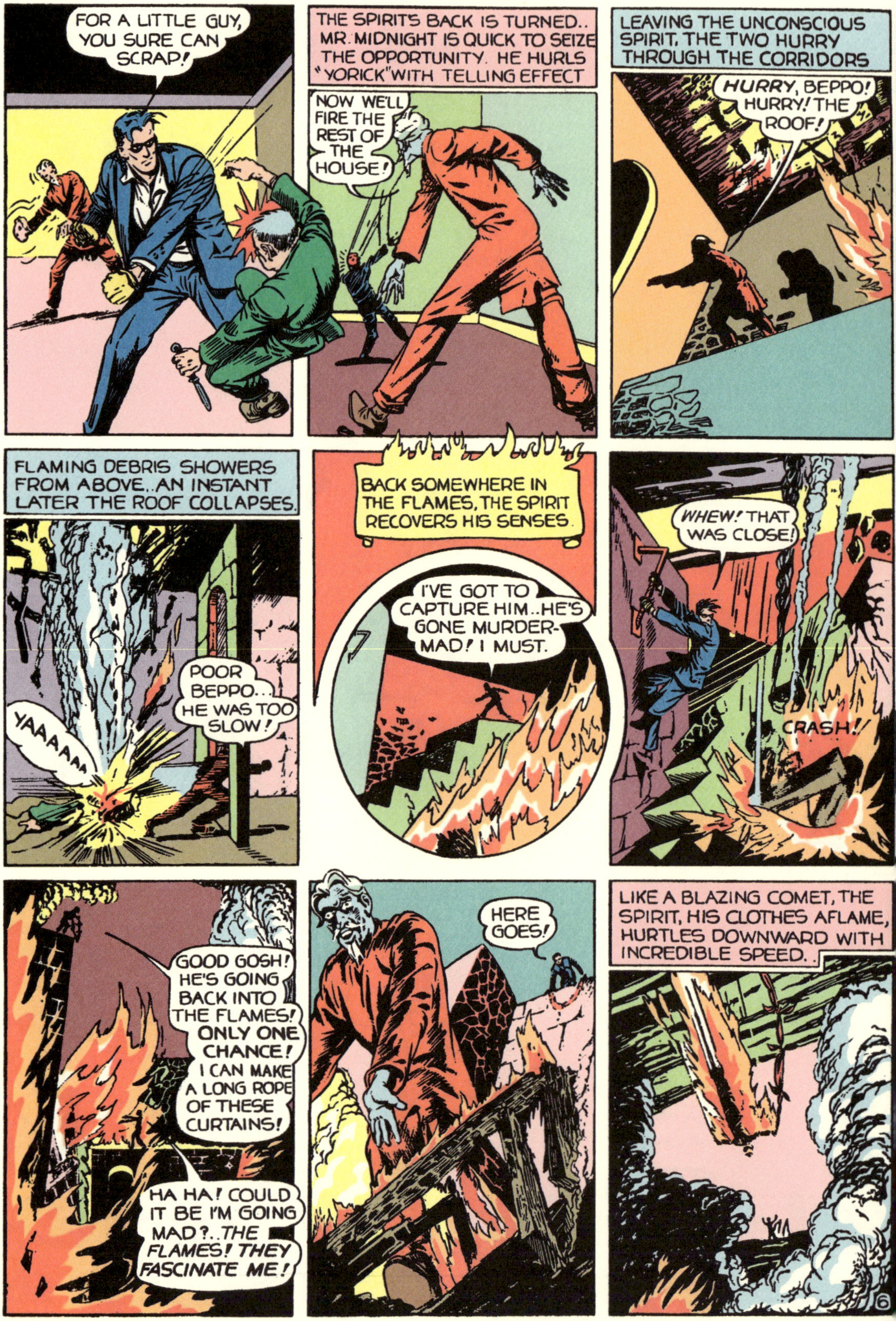
FOR A LITTLE GUY, YOU SURE CAN SCRAP!
THE SPIRIT'S BACK IS TURNED.. MR. MIDNIGHT IS QUICK TO SEIZE THE OPPORTUNITY. HE HURLS "YORICK" WITH TELLING EFFECT
NOW WE'LL FIRE THE REST OF THE HOUSE!
LEAVING THE UNCONSCIOUS SPIRIT, THE TWO HURRY THROUGH THE CORRIDORS
HURRY, BEPPO! HURRY! THE ROOF!
FLAMING DEBRIS SHOWERS FROM ABOVE..AN INSTANT LATER THE ROOF COLLAPSES.
YAAAAAA
POOR BEPPO... HE WAS TOO SLOW!
BACK SOMEWHERE IN THE FLAMES, THE SPIRIT RECOVERS HIS SENSES.
I'VE GOT TO CAPTURE HIM..HE'S GONE MURDER-MAD! I MUST.
WHEW! THAT WAS CLOSE!
CRASH!
GOOD GOSH! HE'S GOING BACK INTO THE FLAMES! ONLY ONE CHANCE! I CAN MAKE A LONG ROPE OF THESE CURTAINS!
HA HA! COULD IT BE I'M GOING MAD?..THE FLAMES! THEY FASCINATE ME!
HERE GOES!
LIKE A BLAZING COMET, THE SPIRIT, HIS CLOTHES AFLAME, HURTLES DOWNWARD WITH INCREDIBLE SPEED.
6

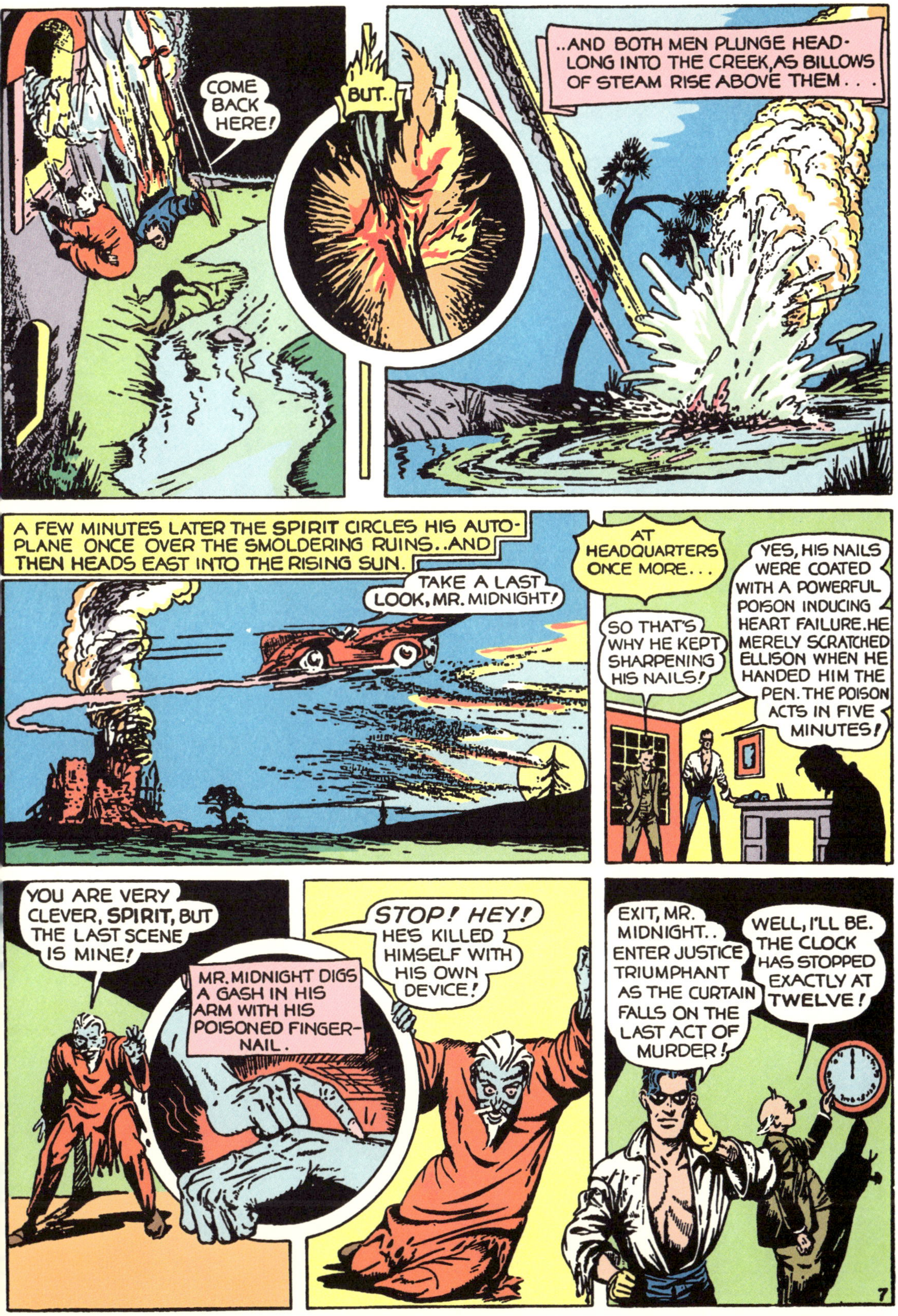
COME BACK HERE!
BUT..
..AND BOTH MEN PLUNGE HEAD-LONG INTO THE CREEK, AS BILLOWS OF STEAM RISE ABOVE THEM . . .
A FEW MINUTES LATER THE SPIRIT CIRCLES HIS AUTO-PLANE ONCE OVER THE SMOLDERING RUINS..AND THEN HEADS EAST INTO THE RISING SUN.
TAKE A LAST LOOK, MR. MIDNIGHT!
AT HEADQUARTERS ONCE MORE . . .
SO THAT'S WHY HE KEPT SHARPENING HIS NAILS!
YES, HIS NAILS WERE COATED WITH A POWERFUL POISON INDUCING HEART FAILURE. HE MERELY SCRATCHED ELLISON WHEN HE HANDED HIM THE PEN. THE POISON ACTS IN FIVE MINUTES!
YOU ARE VERY CLEVER, SPIRIT, BUT THE LAST SCENE IS MINE!
MR. MIDNIGHT DIGS A GASH IN HIS ARM WITH HIS POISONED FINGER-NAIL.
STOP! HEY! HE'S KILLED HIMSELF WITH HIS OWN DEVICE!
EXIT, MR. MIDNIGHT.. ENTER JUSTICE TRIUMPHANT AS THE CURTAIN FALLS ON THE LAST ACT OF MURDER!
WELL, I'LL BE. THE CLOCK HAS STOPPED EXACTLY AT TWELVE!
7

ELDAS THAYER

July 21, 1940

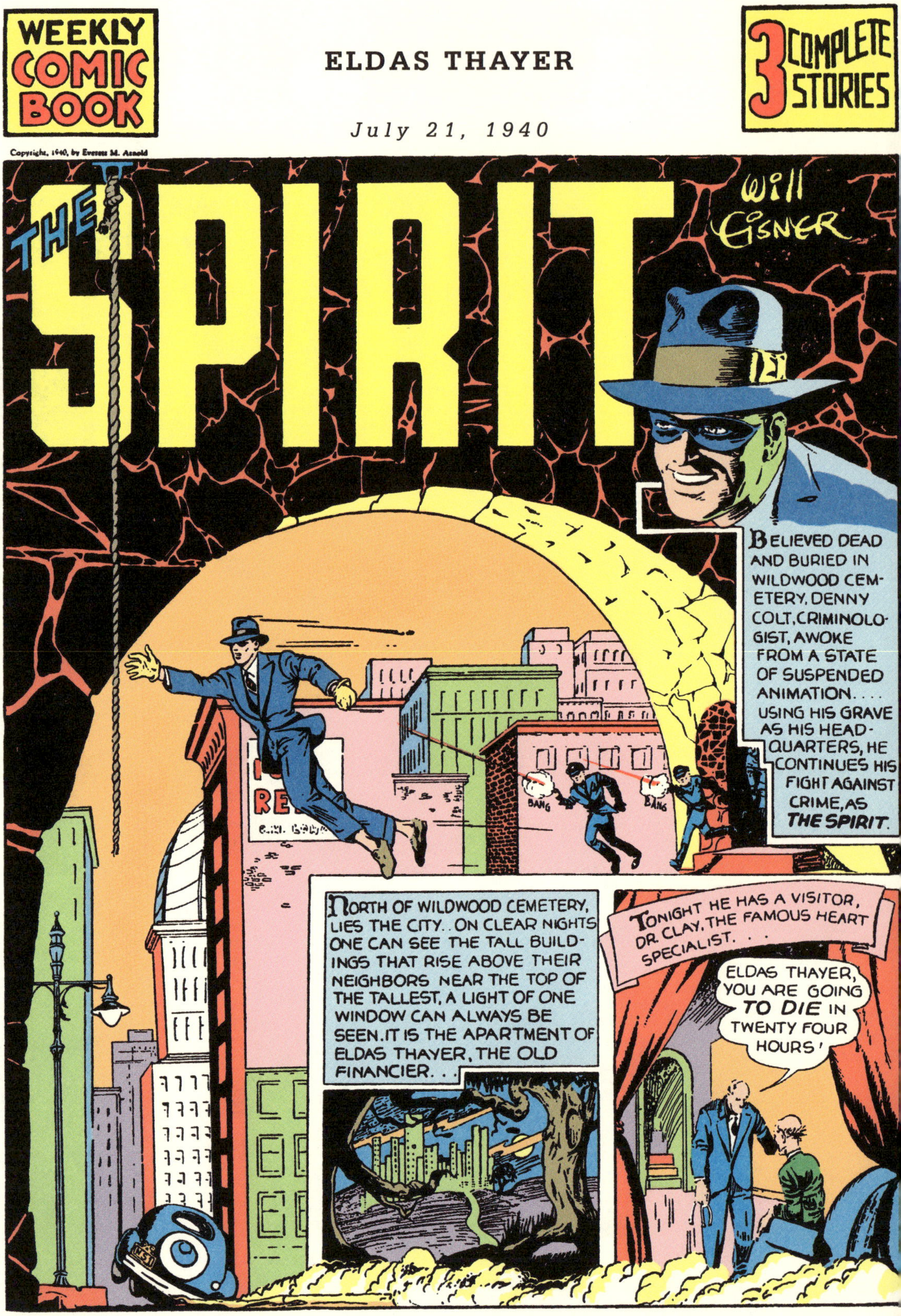
WEEKLY COMIC BOOK
3 COMPLETE STORIES
Copyright, 1940, by Everett M. Arnold
THE SPIRIT
Will Eisner
BELIEVED DEAD AND BURIED IN WILDWOOD CEMETERY, DENNY COLT, CRIMINOLOGIST, AWOKE FROM A STATE OF SUSPENDED ANIMATION.... USING HIS GRAVE AS HIS HEADQUARTERS, HE CONTINUES HIS FIGHT AGAINST CRIME, AS THE SPIRIT.
BANG
BANG
NORTH OF WILDWOOD CEMETERY, LIES THE CITY.. ON CLEAR NIGHTS ONE CAN SEE THE TALL BUILDINGS THAT RISE ABOVE THEIR NEIGHBORS NEAR THE TOP OF THE TALLEST, A LIGHT OF ONE WINDOW CAN ALWAYS BE SEEN. IT IS THE APARTMENT OF ELDAS THAYER, THE OLD FINANCIER...
TONIGHT HE HAS A VISITOR, DR. CLAY, THE FAMOUS HEART SPECIALIST...
ELDAS THAYER, YOU ARE GOING TO DIE IN TWENTY FOUR HOURS!

GET OUT, YOU QUACK! GET OUT! GET OUT!
I'M SORRY, ELDAS. IT'S YOUR HEART AND YOUR CONFOUNDED TEMPER! NO WONDER EVERY-ONE HATES YOU! GOOD-BYE!
AS THE DOCTOR LEAVES, A TALL FIGURE DETACHES HIMSELF FROM THE SHADOWS...
TH'.. THE SPIRIT!
WHAT DO YOU WANT OF ME? I TOLD YOU BEFORE I'LL NEVER GIVE THAT NIECE OF MINE A CENT! LET HER DIE LIKE ME! BAH!
THAYER, IF THAT POOR GIRL DIES, YOU'LL BE A MURDERER!.. GIVE HER THAT OPERATION MONEY. YOU'RE GOING TO DIE ANYWAY! BE HUMAN!
NO! AND THAT'S FINAL!
VERY WELL, THEN GOODBYE, AND I HOPE IN YOUR LAST HOURS, YOUR CONSCIENCE GIVES YOU NO PEACE! YOU OLD SKINFLINT! I'D LIKE TO WRING YOUR NECK!
ALONE, ELDAS THAYER MUSES... HIS COMING DEATH SHAKES HIM..
WRING MY NECK, WOULD HE!? HE'S BRAVE AND STRONG, BUT I CAN FIGHT TOO!. IN A WAY THAT'LL HURT HIM.. SO LIVING WILL BE A BURDEN... YES! I HAVE A WAY!.. HA HA HA! HA HA!
EVERY MOVEMENT AN EFFORT, THE OLD MAN PAINFULLY, BUT CAREFULLY, SETS A MACABRE SCENE.
HEAVY KNIFE
CHANDELIER
LIGHT CORD TO FIXTURE
WHEN.. HEH HEH! WHEN I PULL THIS CORD, THE CHANDELIER MOVES AWAY AND THE KNIFE DROPS IN MY BACK..
WHAT DOES IT MATTER IF I DIE NOW, OR IN TWENTY FOUR HOURS I'LL BE ABLE TO AVENGE MYSELF ON THE SPIRIT.. HE REPRESENTS GOOD, AND I, EVIL.. HA HA!
THE CORD IS PULLED!
YAAA GASP!
AND WHEN THE POLICE ARRIVE..
WHO KNIFED YOU?
THE SPIRIT.. HE KILLED ME!
OOOH
HE'S DONE FOR!
AT HEADQUARTERS, IN COMMISSIONER DOLAN'S OFFICE.
I CAN'T BELIEVE IT! NO.. IT'S IMPOSSIBLE! NOT MURDER! THE SPIRIT IS NOT A KILLER!
THE OLD-TIMER SAID SO. THE WORD OF A DYING MAN.. AND WITNESSED TOO! GUESS WE'D BETTER SEND OUT AN ALARM!

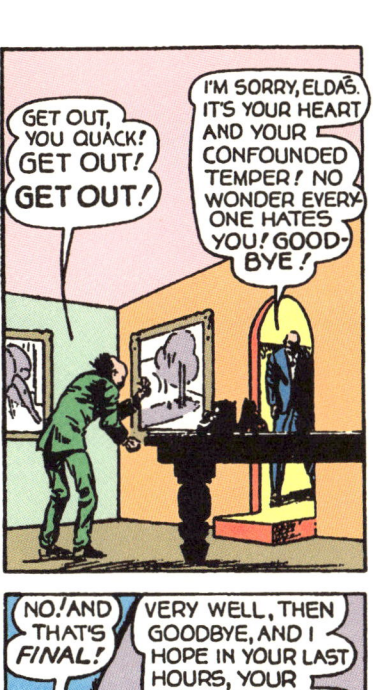

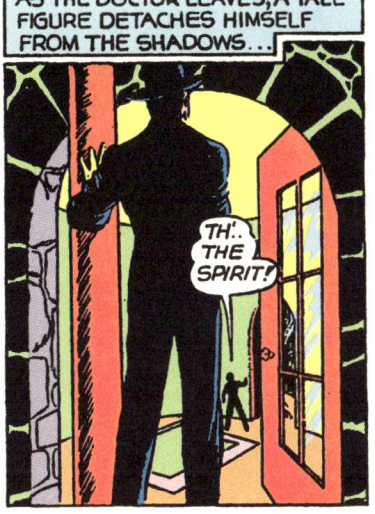

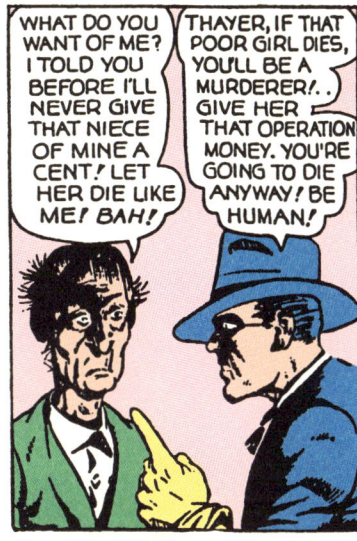

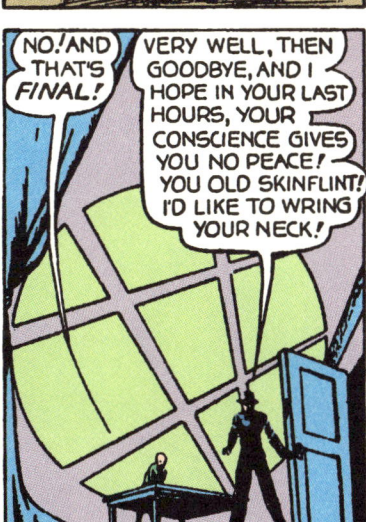

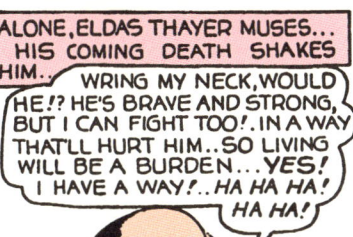

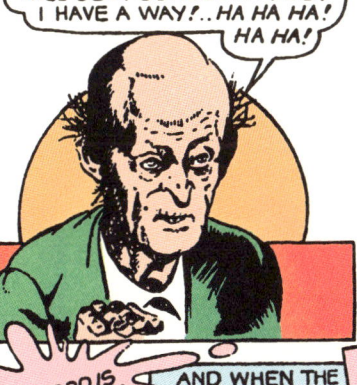

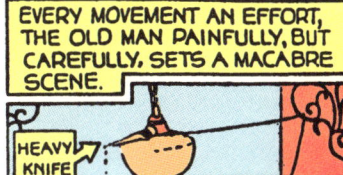

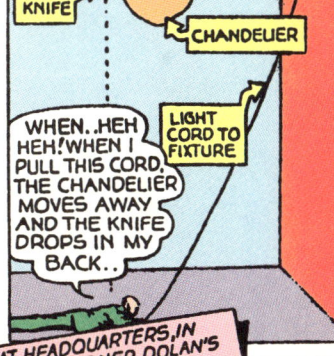

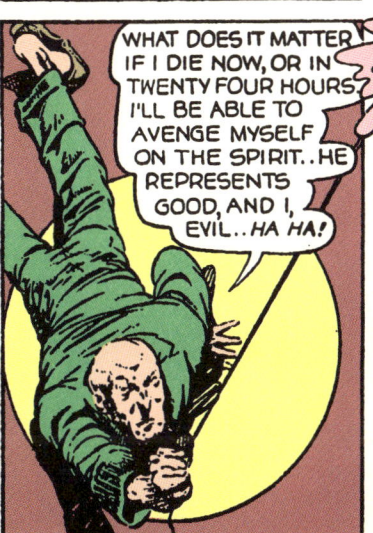

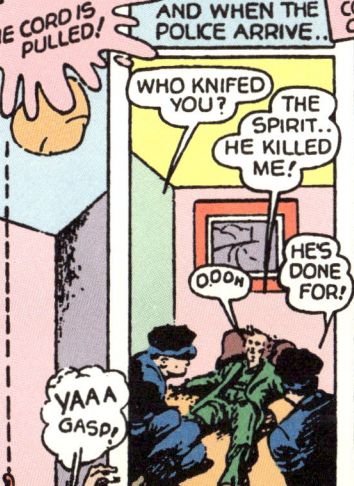

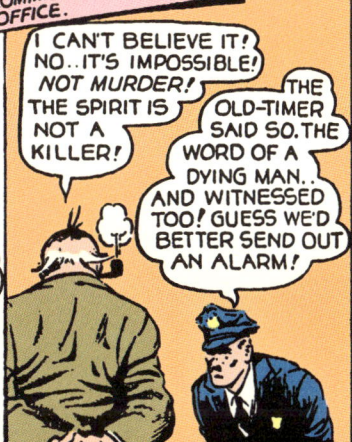

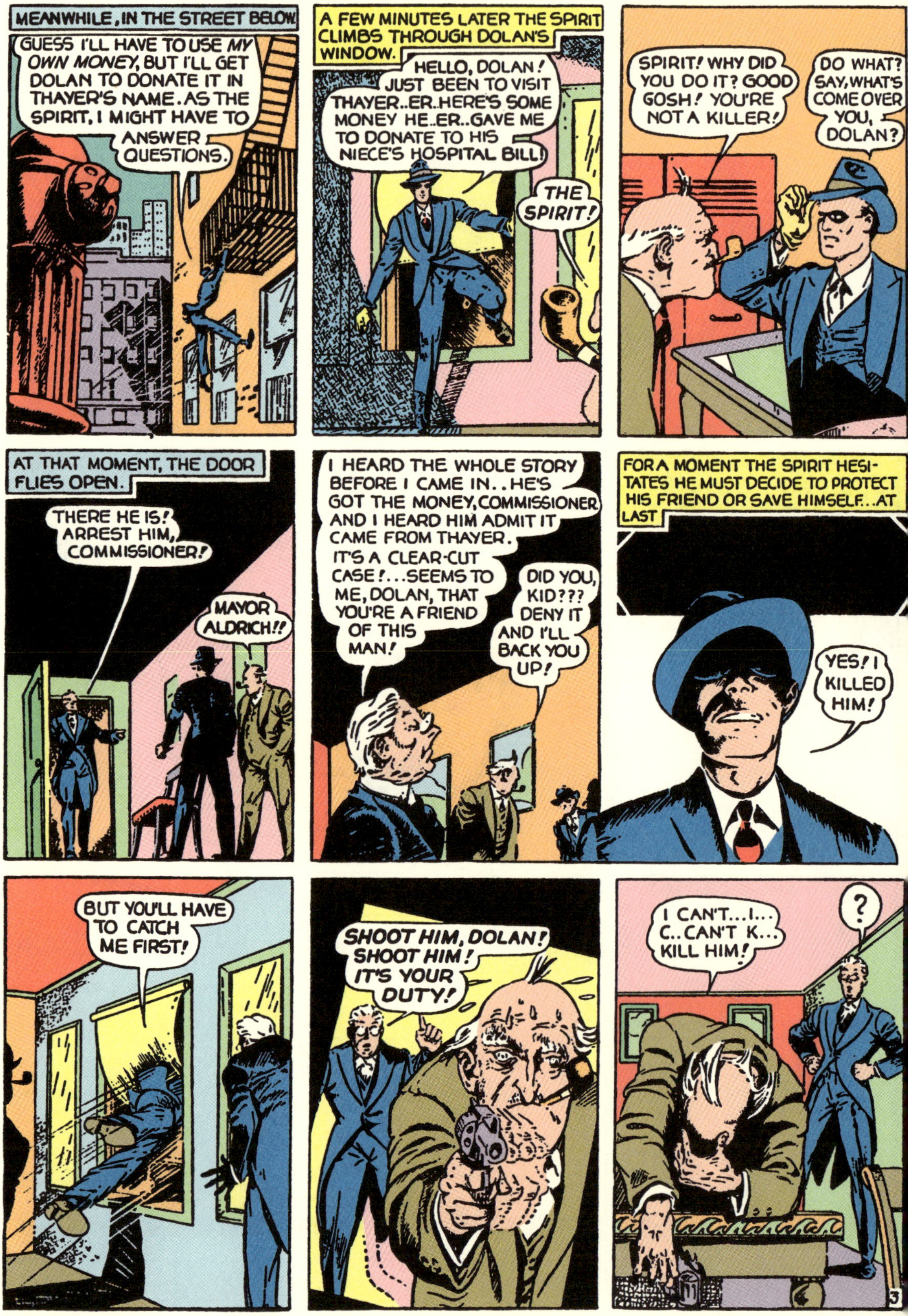
MEANWHILE, IN THE STREET BELOW
GUESS I'LL HAVE TO USE *MY OWN MONEY*, BUT I'LL GET DOLAN TO DONATE IT IN THAYER'S NAME. AS THE SPIRIT, I MIGHT HAVE TO ANSWER QUESTIONS.
A FEW MINUTES LATER THE SPIRIT CLIMBS THROUGH DOLAN'S WINDOW.
HELLO, DOLAN! JUST BEEN TO VISIT THAYER..ER..HERE'S SOME MONEY HE..ER..GAVE ME TO DONATE TO HIS NIECE'S HOSPITAL BILL!
THE SPIRIT!
SPIRIT! WHY DID YOU DO IT? GOOD GOSH! YOU'RE NOT A KILLER!
DO WHAT? SAY, WHAT'S COME OVER YOU, DOLAN?
AT THAT MOMENT, THE DOOR FLIES OPEN.
THERE HE IS! ARREST HIM, COMMISSIONER!
MAYOR ALDRICH!!
I HEARD THE WHOLE STORY BEFORE I CAME IN.. HE'S GOT THE MONEY, COMMISSIONER AND I HEARD HIM ADMIT IT CAME FROM THAYER.
IT'S A CLEAR-CUT CASE!...SEEMS TO ME, DOLAN, THAT YOU'RE A FRIEND OF THIS MAN!
DID YOU, KID??? DENY IT AND I'LL BACK YOU UP!
FOR A MOMENT THE SPIRIT HESITATES HE MUST DECIDE TO PROTECT HIS FRIEND OR SAVE HIMSELF...AT LAST
YES! I KILLED HIM!
BUT YOU'LL HAVE TO CATCH ME FIRST!
SHOOT HIM, DOLAN! SHOOT HIM! IT'S YOUR DUTY!
I CAN'T...I... C..CAN'T K... KILL HIM!
?
3

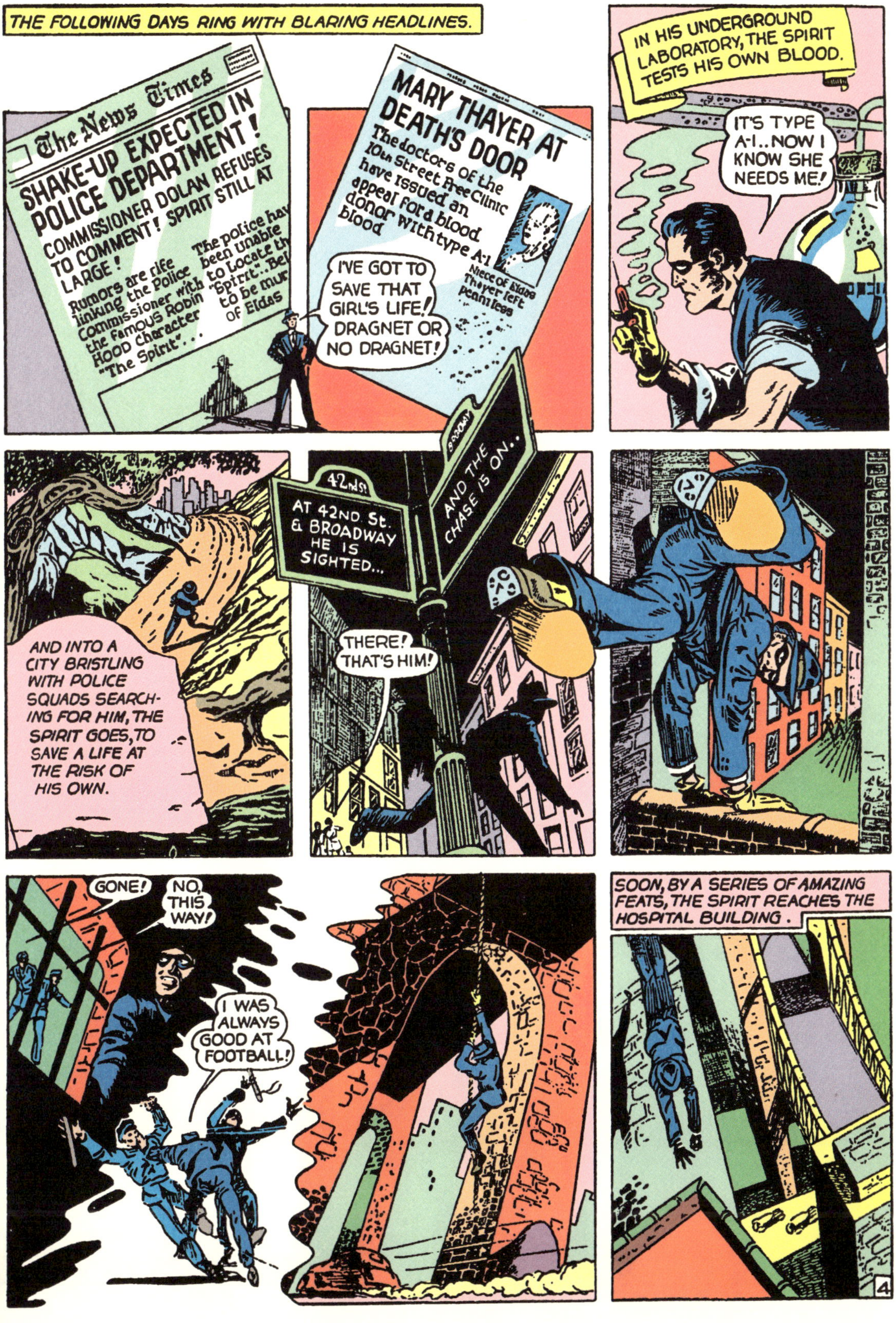
THE FOLLOWING DAYS RING WITH BLARING HEADLINES.
The News Times
SHAKE-UP EXPECTED IN POLICE DEPARTMENT!
COMMISSIONER DOLAN REFUSES TO COMMENT! SPIRIT STILL AT LARGE!
Rumors are rife linking the Police Commissioner with the famous Robin Hood character "The Spirit"...
The police hav been unable to Locate th "Spirit". Bel to be mur of Eldas
MARY THAYER AT DEATH'S DOOR
The doctors of the 10th Street Free Clinic have issued an appeal for a blood donor with type A-1 blood
Niece of Eldas Thayer left penniless
I'VE GOT TO SAVE THAT GIRL'S LIFE! DRAGNET OR NO DRAGNET!
IN HIS UNDERGROUND LABORATORY, THE SPIRIT TESTS HIS OWN BLOOD.
IT'S TYPE A-1..NOW I KNOW SHE NEEDS ME!
AND INTO A CITY BRISTLING WITH POLICE SQUADS SEARCHING FOR HIM, THE SPIRIT GOES, TO SAVE A LIFE AT THE RISK OF HIS OWN.
42nd St.
AT 42ND. St. & BROADWAY HE IS SIGHTED...
AND THE CHASE IS ON..
THERE! THAT'S HIM!
GONE!
NO, THIS WAY!
I WAS ALWAYS GOOD AT FOOTBALL!
SOON, BY A SERIES OF AMAZING FEATS, THE SPIRIT REACHES THE HOSPITAL BUILDING.
4

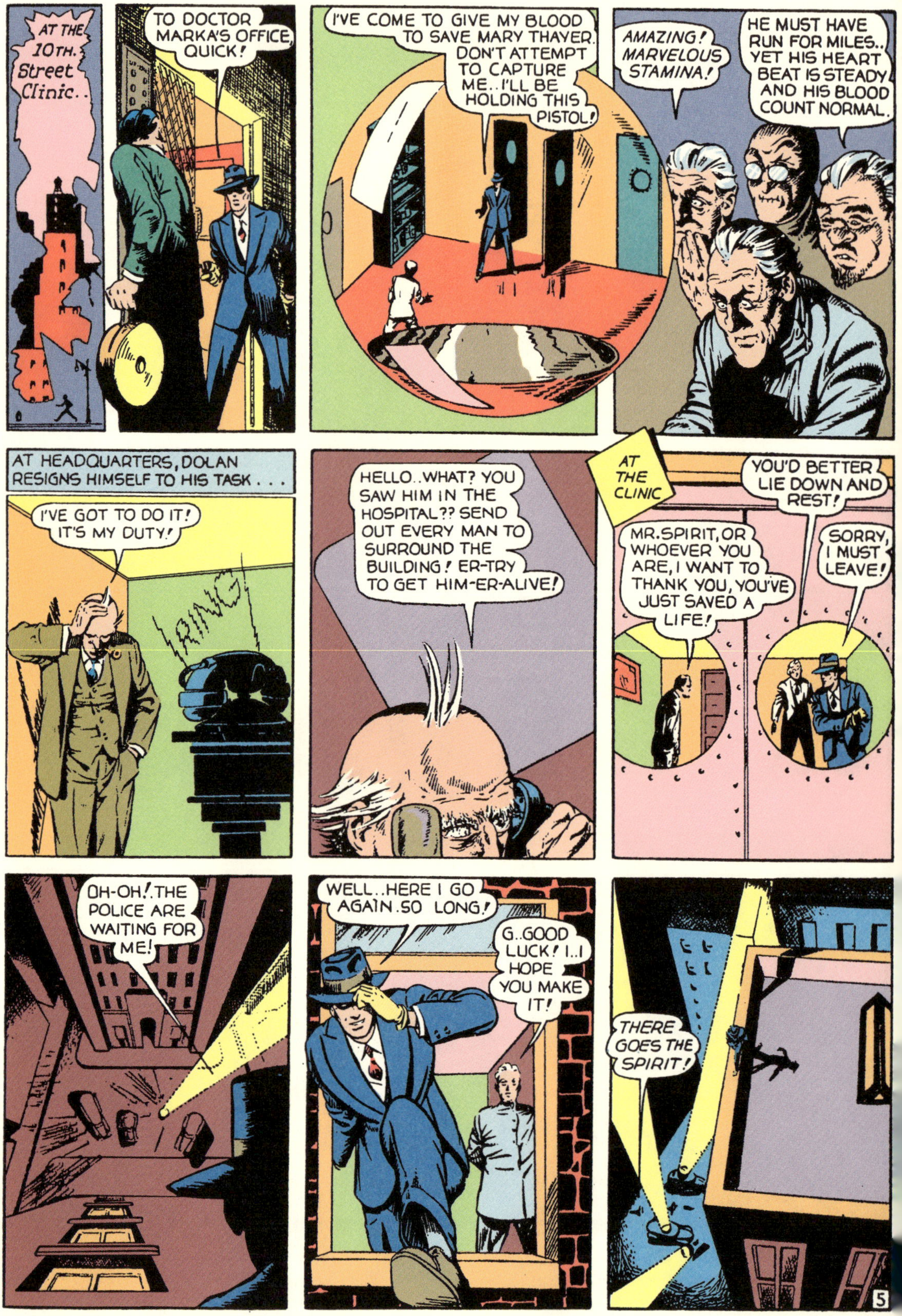
AT THE 10TH. Street Clinic..
TO DOCTOR MARKA'S OFFICE, QUICK!
I'VE COME TO GIVE MY BLOOD TO SAVE MARY THAYER. DON'T ATTEMPT TO CAPTURE ME..I'LL BE HOLDING THIS PISTOL!
AMAZING! MARVELOUS STAMINA!
HE MUST HAVE RUN FOR MILES.. YET HIS HEART BEAT IS STEADY AND HIS BLOOD COUNT NORMAL.
AT HEADQUARTERS, DOLAN RESIGNS HIMSELF TO HIS TASK . . .
I'VE GOT TO DO IT! IT'S MY DUTY!
RING!
HELLO..WHAT? YOU SAW HIM IN THE HOSPITAL?? SEND OUT EVERY MAN TO SURROUND THE BUILDING! ER-TRY TO GET HIM-ER-ALIVE!
AT THE CLINIC
YOU'D BETTER LIE DOWN AND REST!
MR. SPIRIT, OR WHOEVER YOU ARE, I WANT TO THANK YOU, YOU'VE JUST SAVED A LIFE!
SORRY, I MUST LEAVE!
OH-OH! THE POLICE ARE WAITING FOR ME!
WELL..HERE I GO AGAIN. SO LONG!
G..GOOD LUCK! I..I HOPE YOU MAKE IT!
THERE GOES THE SPIRIT!
5

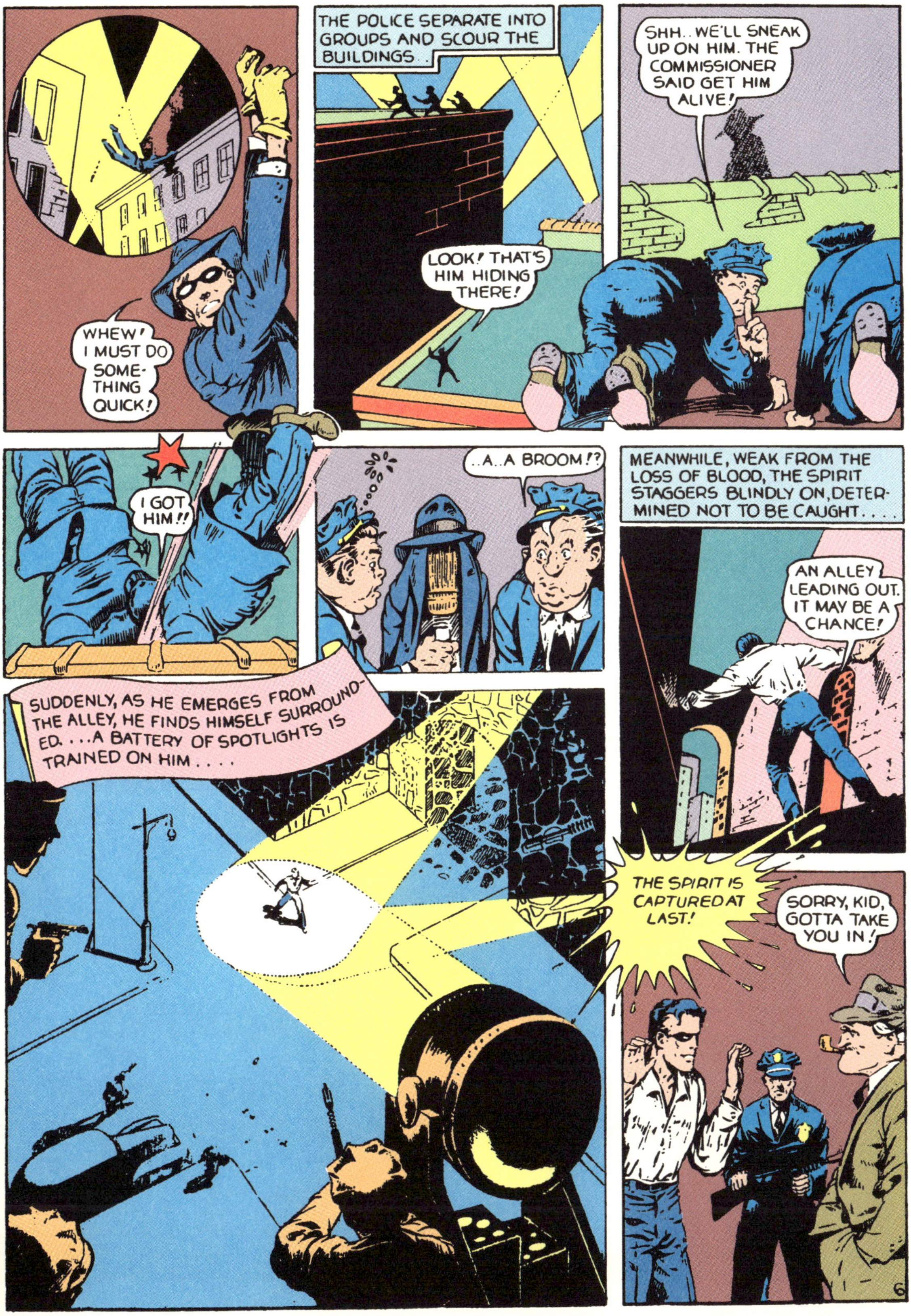
WHEW! I MUST DO SOME-THING QUICK!
THE POLICE SEPARATE INTO GROUPS AND SCOUR THE BUILDINGS.
LOOK! THAT'S HIM HIDING THERE!
SHH.. WE'LL SNEAK UP ON HIM. THE COMMISSIONER SAID GET HIM ALIVE!
I GOT HIM!!
..A..A BROOM!?
MEANWHILE, WEAK FROM THE LOSS OF BLOOD, THE SPIRIT STAGGERS BLINDLY ON, DETER-MINED NOT TO BE CAUGHT....
AN ALLEY! LEADING OUT. IT MAY BE A CHANCE!
SUDDENLY, AS HE EMERGES FROM THE ALLEY, HE FINDS HIMSELF SURROUND-ED....A BATTERY OF SPOTLIGHTS IS TRAINED ON HIM....
THE SPIRIT IS CAPTURED AT LAST!
SORRY, KID, GOTTA TAKE YOU IN!
6

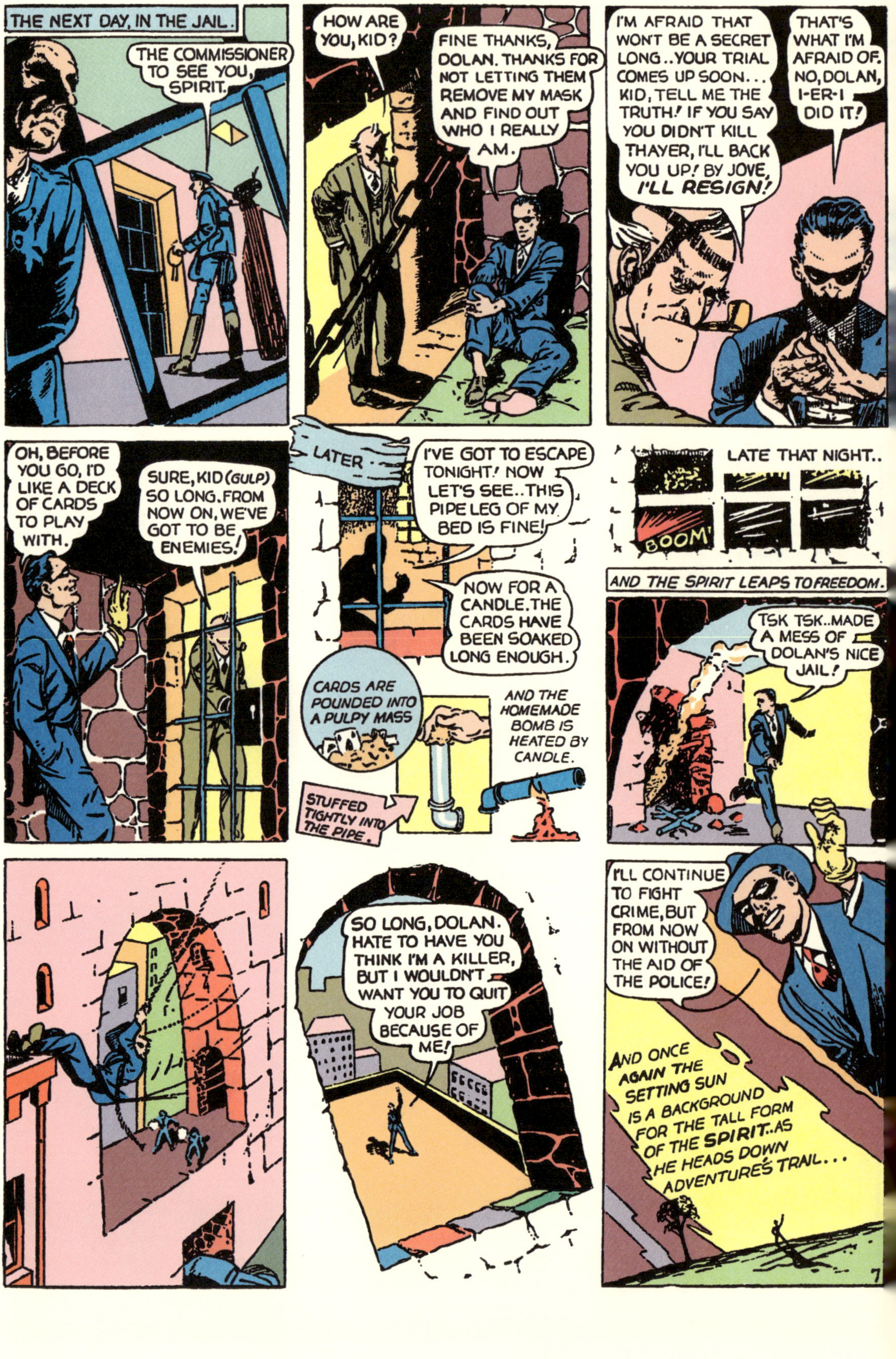
THE NEXT DAY, IN THE JAIL.
THE COMMISSIONER TO SEE YOU, SPIRIT.
HOW ARE YOU, KID?
FINE THANKS, DOLAN. THANKS FOR NOT LETTING THEM REMOVE MY MASK AND FIND OUT WHO I REALLY AM.
I'M AFRAID THAT WON'T BE A SECRET LONG..YOUR TRIAL COMES UP SOON... KID, TELL ME THE TRUTH! IF YOU SAY YOU DIDN'T KILL THAYER, I'LL BACK YOU UP! BY JOVE, I'LL RESIGN!
THAT'S WHAT I'M AFRAID OF. NO, DOLAN, I-ER-I DID IT!
OH, BEFORE YOU GO, I'D LIKE A DECK OF CARDS TO PLAY WITH.
SURE, KID (GULP) SO LONG. FROM NOW ON, WE'VE GOT TO BE ENEMIES!
LATER
I'VE GOT TO ESCAPE TONIGHT! NOW LET'S SEE..THIS PIPE LEG OF MY BED IS FINE!
NOW FOR A CANDLE. THE CARDS HAVE BEEN SOAKED LONG ENOUGH.
CARDS ARE POUNDED INTO A PULPY MASS
STUFFED TIGHTLY INTO THE PIPE.
AND THE HOMEMADE BOMB IS HEATED BY CANDLE.
LATE THAT NIGHT..
BOOM!
AND THE SPIRIT LEAPS TO FREEDOM.
TSK TSK..MADE A MESS OF DOLAN'S NICE JAIL!
SO LONG, DOLAN. HATE TO HAVE YOU THINK I'M A KILLER, BUT I WOULDN'T WANT YOU TO QUIT YOUR JOB BECAUSE OF ME!
I'LL CONTINUE TO FIGHT CRIME, BUT FROM NOW ON WITHOUT THE AID OF THE POLICE!
AND ONCE AGAIN THE SETTING SUN IS A BACKGROUND FOR THE TALL FORM OF THE SPIRIT..AS HE HEADS DOWN ADVENTURE'S TRAIL...
7

COMIC BOOK SECTION

PALYACHI, THE KILLER CLOWN

July 28, 1940

3 COMPLETE STORIES

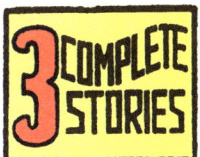

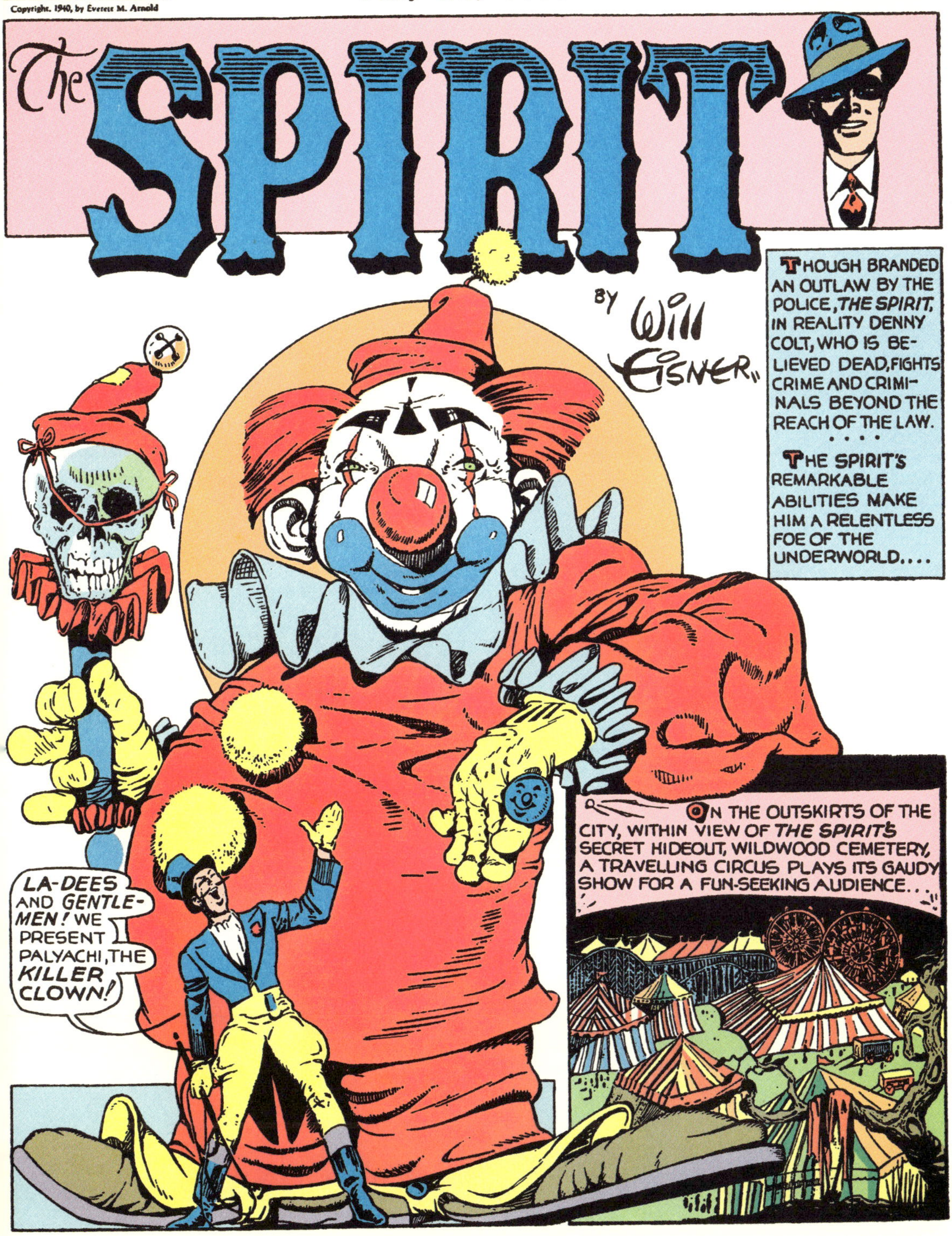
The SPIRIT
BY WILL EISNER
THOUGH BRANDED AN OUTLAW BY THE POLICE, THE SPIRIT, IN REALITY DENNY COLT, WHO IS BELIEVED DEAD, FIGHTS CRIME AND CRIMINALS BEYOND THE REACH OF THE LAW. . . . .
THE SPIRIT'S REMARKABLE ABILITIES MAKE HIM A RELENTLESS FOE OF THE UNDERWORLD. . . .
ON THE OUTSKIRTS OF THE CITY, WITHIN VIEW OF THE SPIRIT'S SECRET HIDEOUT, WILDWOOD CEMETERY, A TRAVELLING CIRCUS PLAYS ITS GAUDY SHOW FOR A FUN-SEEKING AUDIENCE. . .
LA-DEES AND GENTLEMEN! WE PRESENT PALYACHI, THE KILLER CLOWN!

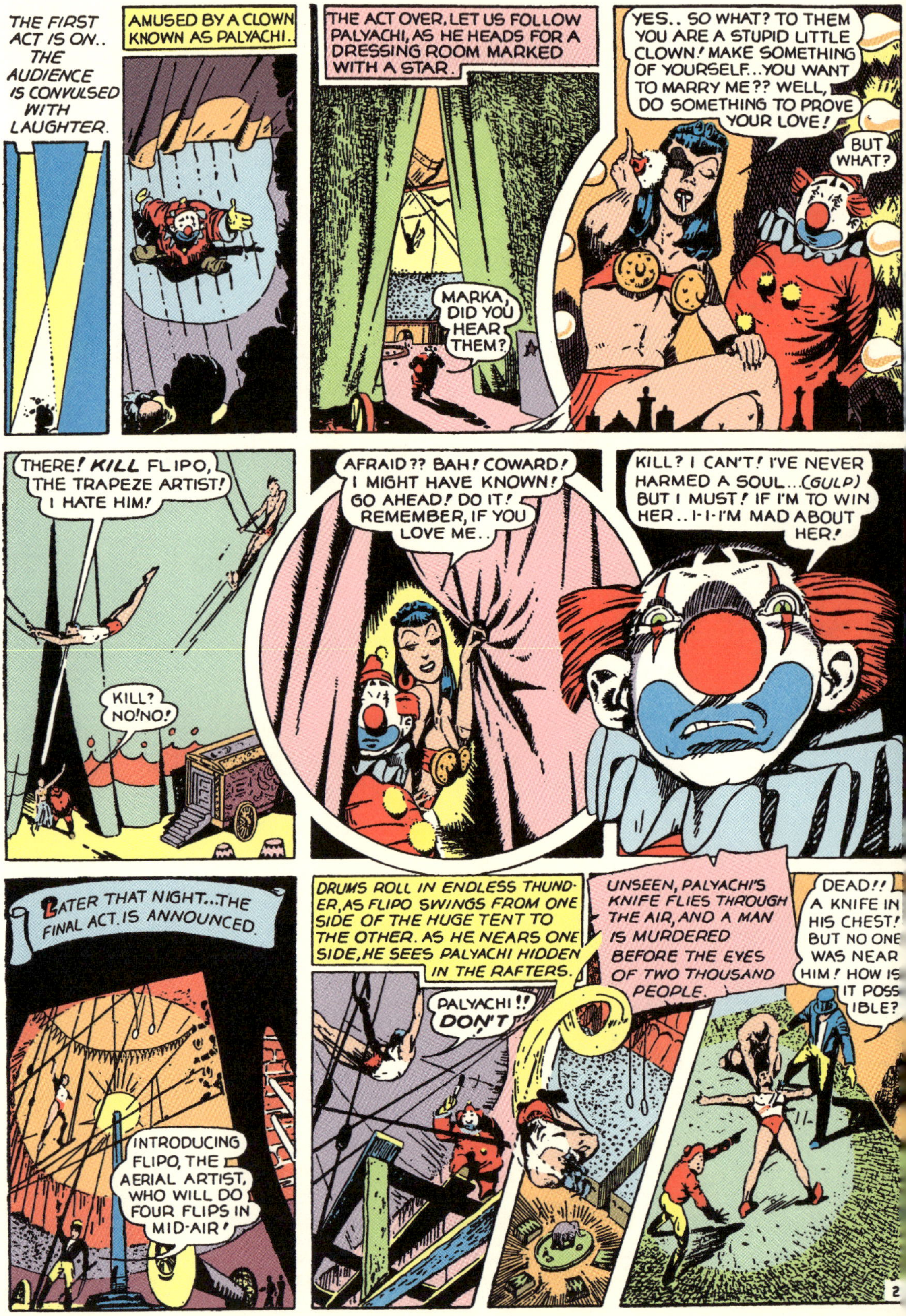

THE FIRST ACT IS ON.. THE AUDIENCE IS CONVULSED WITH LAUGHTER.
AMUSED BY A CLOWN KNOWN AS PALYACHI.
THE ACT OVER, LET US FOLLOW PALYACHI, AS HE HEADS FOR A DRESSING ROOM MARKED WITH A STAR.
MARKA, DID YOU HEAR THEM?
YES.. SO WHAT? TO THEM YOU ARE A STUPID LITTLE CLOWN! MAKE SOMETHING OF YOURSELF...YOU WANT TO MARRY ME?? WELL, DO SOMETHING TO PROVE YOUR LOVE!
BUT WHAT?
THERE! KILL FLIPO, THE TRAPEZE ARTIST! I HATE HIM!
KILL? NO!NO!
AFRAID?? BAH! COWARD! I MIGHT HAVE KNOWN! GO AHEAD! DO IT! REMEMBER, IF YOU LOVE ME..
KILL? I CAN'T! I'VE NEVER HARMED A SOUL...(GULP) BUT I MUST! IF I'M TO WIN HER.. I-I-I'M MAD ABOUT HER!
LATER THAT NIGHT...THE FINAL ACT IS ANNOUNCED.
INTRODUCING FLIPO, THE AERIAL ARTIST, WHO WILL DO FOUR FLIPS IN MID-AIR!
DRUMS ROLL IN ENDLESS THUNDER, AS FLIPO SWINGS FROM ONE SIDE OF THE HUGE TENT TO THE OTHER. AS HE NEARS ONE SIDE, HE SEES PALYACHI HIDDEN IN THE RAFTERS.
PALYACHI!! DON'T
UNSEEN, PALYACHI'S KNIFE FLIES THROUGH THE AIR, AND A MAN IS MURDERED BEFORE THE EYES OF TWO THOUSAND PEOPLE.
DEAD!! A KNIFE IN HIS CHEST! BUT NO ONE WAS NEAR HIM! HOW IS IT POSSIBLE?
2

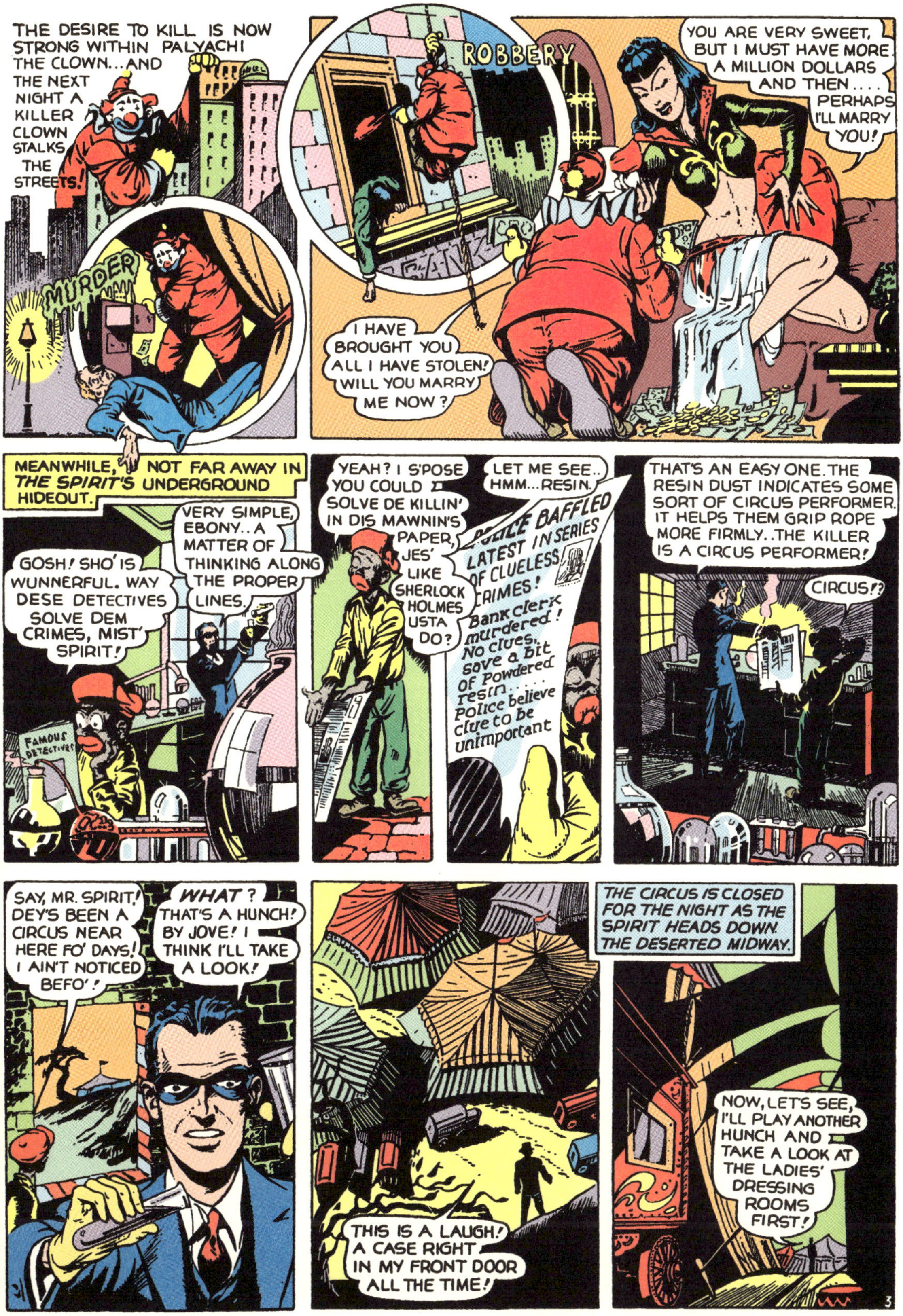
THE DESIRE TO KILL IS NOW STRONG WITHIN PALYACHI THE CLOWN...AND THE NEXT NIGHT A KILLER CLOWN STALKS THE STREETS!
MURDER
ROBBERY
YOU ARE VERY SWEET, BUT I MUST HAVE MORE. A MILLION DOLLARS AND THEN.... PERHAPS I'LL MARRY YOU!
I HAVE BROUGHT YOU ALL I HAVE STOLEN! WILL YOU MARRY ME NOW?
MEANWHILE, NOT FAR AWAY IN THE SPIRIT'S UNDERGROUND HIDEOUT.
GOSH! SHO'IS WUNNERFUL. WAY DESE DETECTIVES SOLVE DEM CRIMES, MIST' SPIRIT!
VERY SIMPLE, EBONY.. A MATTER OF THINKING ALONG THE PROPER LINES.
FAMOUS DETECTIVES
YEAH? I S'POSE YOU COULD SOLVE DE KILLIN' IN DIS MAWNIN'S PAPER, JES' LIKE SHERLOCK HOLMES USTA DO?
LET ME SEE.. HMM...RESIN.
POLICE BAFFLED LATEST IN SERIES OF CLUELESS CRIMES! Bank clerk murdered! No clues, save a bit of powdered resin..... Police believe clue to be unimportant
THAT'S AN EASY ONE. THE RESIN DUST INDICATES SOME SORT OF CIRCUS PERFORMER. IT HELPS THEM GRIP ROPE MORE FIRMLY..THE KILLER IS A CIRCUS PERFORMER!
CIRCUS!?
SAY, MR. SPIRIT! DEY'S BEEN A CIRCUS NEAR HERE FO' DAYS! I AIN'T NOTICED BEFO'!
WHAT? THAT'S A HUNCH! BY JOVE! I THINK I'LL TAKE A LOOK!
THIS IS A LAUGH! A CASE RIGHT IN MY FRONT DOOR ALL THE TIME!
THE CIRCUS IS CLOSED FOR THE NIGHT AS THE SPIRIT HEADS DOWN THE DESERTED MIDWAY.
NOW, LET'S SEE, I'LL PLAY ANOTHER HUNCH AND TAKE A LOOK AT THE LADIES' DRESSING ROOMS FIRST!
3

THIS MUST BE THE STAR'S ROOM.. HOLY SMOKE! JEWELRY AND MONEY! ODD FOR A CIRCUS PERFORMER TO BE SO WEALTHY!
NEED ANY HELP, COPPER?
AH CORRECTION. I AM NOT A POLICEMAN..I AM THE SPIRIT!
OH...I'VE HEARD OF YOU!
QUITE AN INTERESTING COLLECTION OF JEWELRY YOU HAVE! I'LL WAGER THEY ALL FIT THE DESCRIPTION OF THOSE STOLEN LAST NIGHT.. COME CLEAN!
WELL. YES..THEY ARE! SO WHAT?
I DIDN'T DO IT, BUT I'LL MAKE A DEAL WITH YOU. I'M ANXIOUS TO GET RID OF PALYACHI ANYHOW!
SO I'LL TELL YOU WHO DID IT..TURN HIM OVER TO THE COPS AND THEN YOU AND I CAN GO INTO PARTNERSHIP..YOU'RE PRETTY CLEVER..AND HANDSOME TOO.
WHO?
PALYACHI, THE CLOWN DID IT!
THAT'S ALL I WANT TO KNOW.. HEY! SOMEONE'S BEEN LISTENING IN! WHY, IT'S A CLOWN! ONE SIDE!
STREAKING IN PURSUIT, THE SPIRIT GAINS RAPIDLY ON THE CLOWN.
BUT ABOVE
OH! SO THERE YOU ARE! LOST YOU FOR A MOMENT!
LIKE A TRAINED ACROBAT, THE SPIRIT SEIZES A TRAPEZE AND DEFTLY SWINGS IN PURSUIT. . . . .
YOU'RE PLAYING ON MY HOME GROUNDS, SPIRIT! YOU'RE AS GOOD AS FINISHED!
AN INSTANT LATER THE TWO CLASH IN MID-AIR!
4

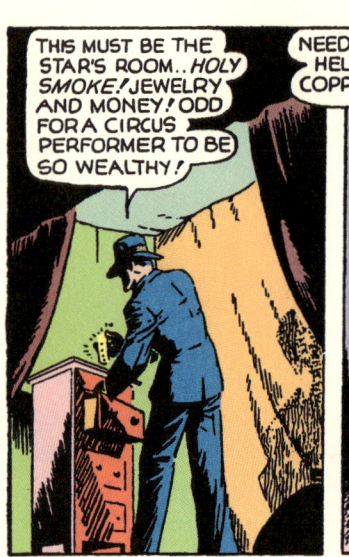

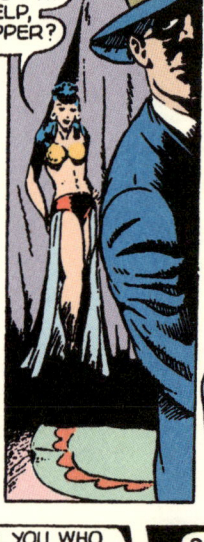

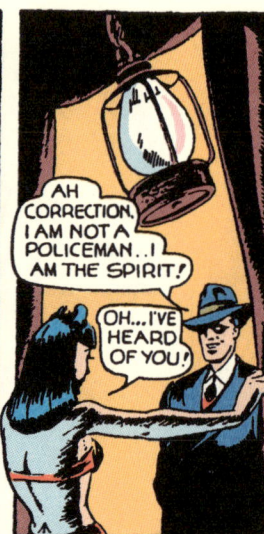

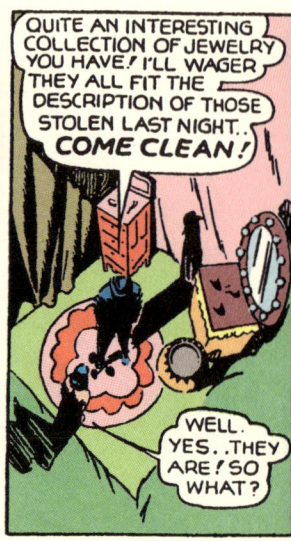

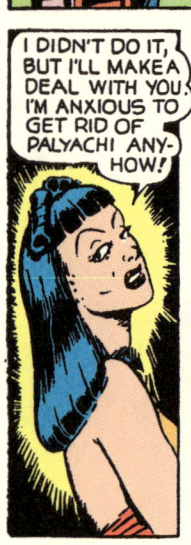

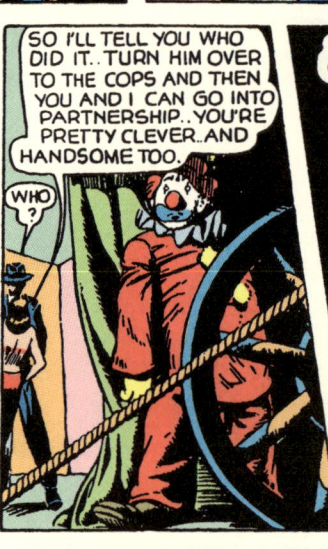

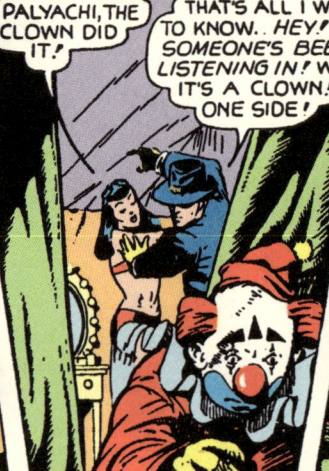

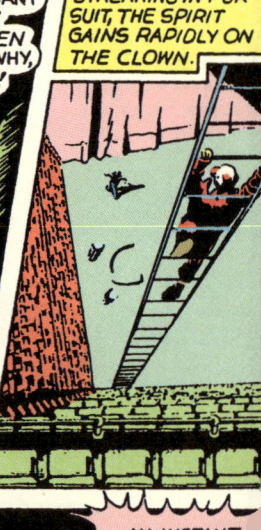

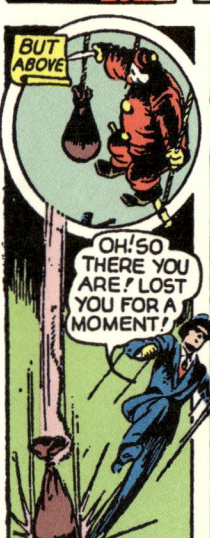

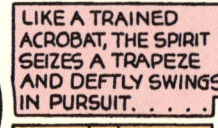

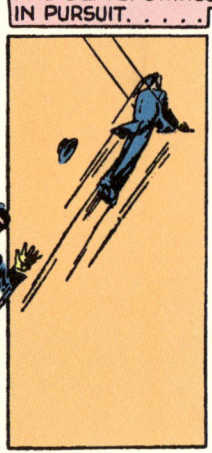

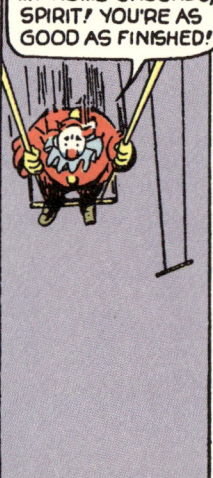

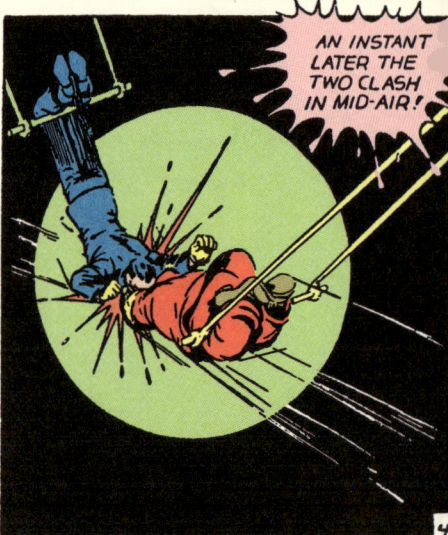

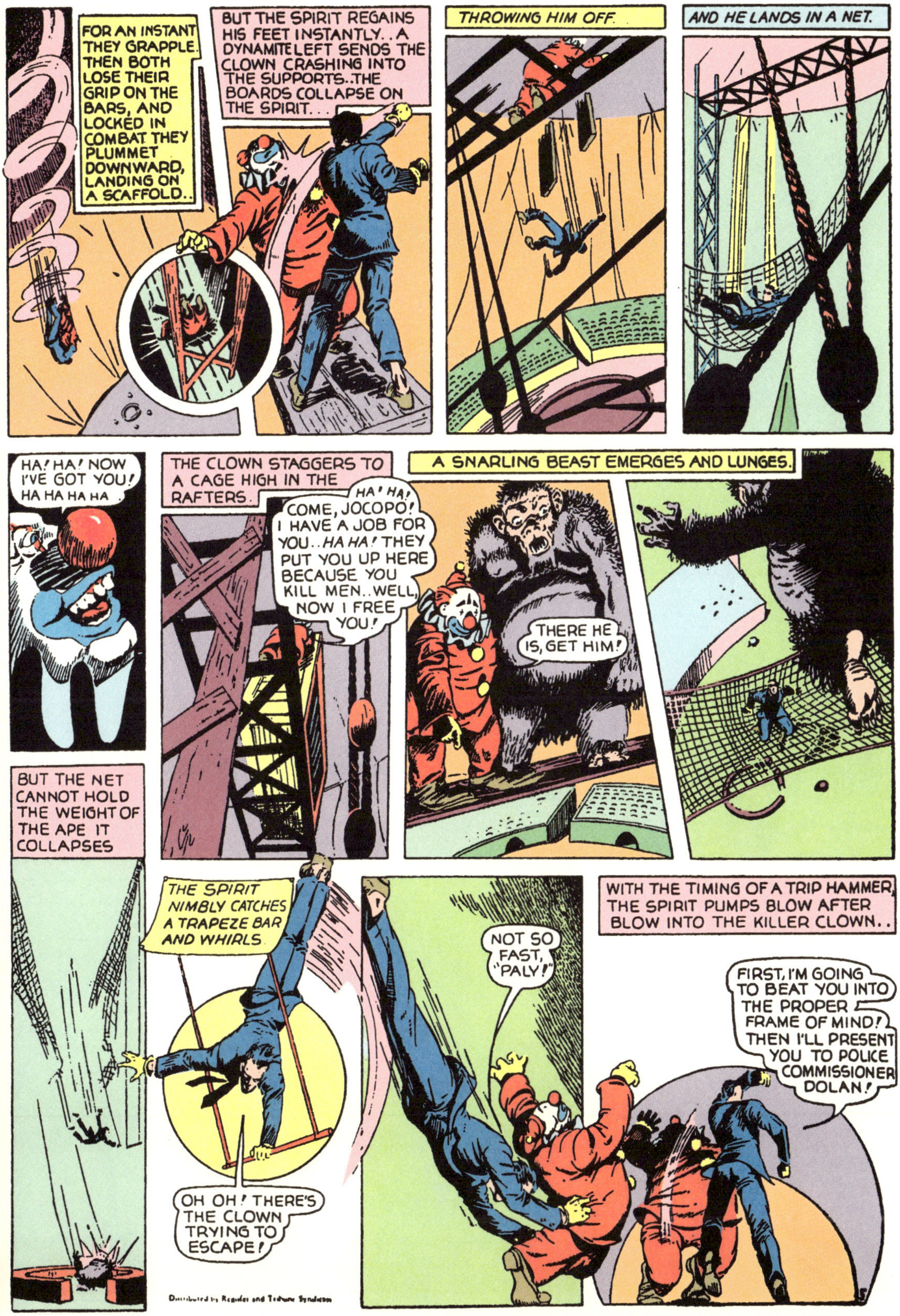
FOR AN INSTANT THEY GRAPPLE. THEN BOTH LOSE THEIR GRIP ON THE BARS, AND LOCKED IN COMBAT THEY PLUMMET DOWNWARD, LANDING ON A SCAFFOLD..
BUT THE SPIRIT REGAINS HIS FEET INSTANTLY.. A DYNAMITE LEFT SENDS THE CLOWN CRASHING INTO THE SUPPORTS..THE BOARDS COLLAPSE ON THE SPIRIT...
THROWING HIM OFF.
AND HE LANDS IN A NET.
HA! HA! NOW I'VE GOT YOU! HA HA HA HA
THE CLOWN STAGGERS TO A CAGE HIGH IN THE RAFTERS.
HA! HA! COME, JOCOPO! I HAVE A JOB FOR YOU..HA HA! THEY PUT YOU UP HERE BECAUSE YOU KILL MEN..WELL, NOW I FREE YOU!
A SNARLING BEAST EMERGES AND LUNGES.
THERE HE IS, GET HIM!
BUT THE NET CANNOT HOLD THE WEIGHT OF THE APE IT COLLAPSES
THE SPIRIT NIMBLY CATCHES A TRAPEZE BAR AND WHIRLS
OH OH! THERE'S THE CLOWN TRYING TO ESCAPE!
NOT SO FAST, "PALY!"
WITH THE TIMING OF A TRIP HAMMER, THE SPIRIT PUMPS BLOW AFTER BLOW INTO THE KILLER CLOWN..
FIRST, I'M GOING TO BEAT YOU INTO THE PROPER FRAME OF MIND! THEN I'LL PRESENT YOU TO POLICE COMMISSIONER DOLAN!

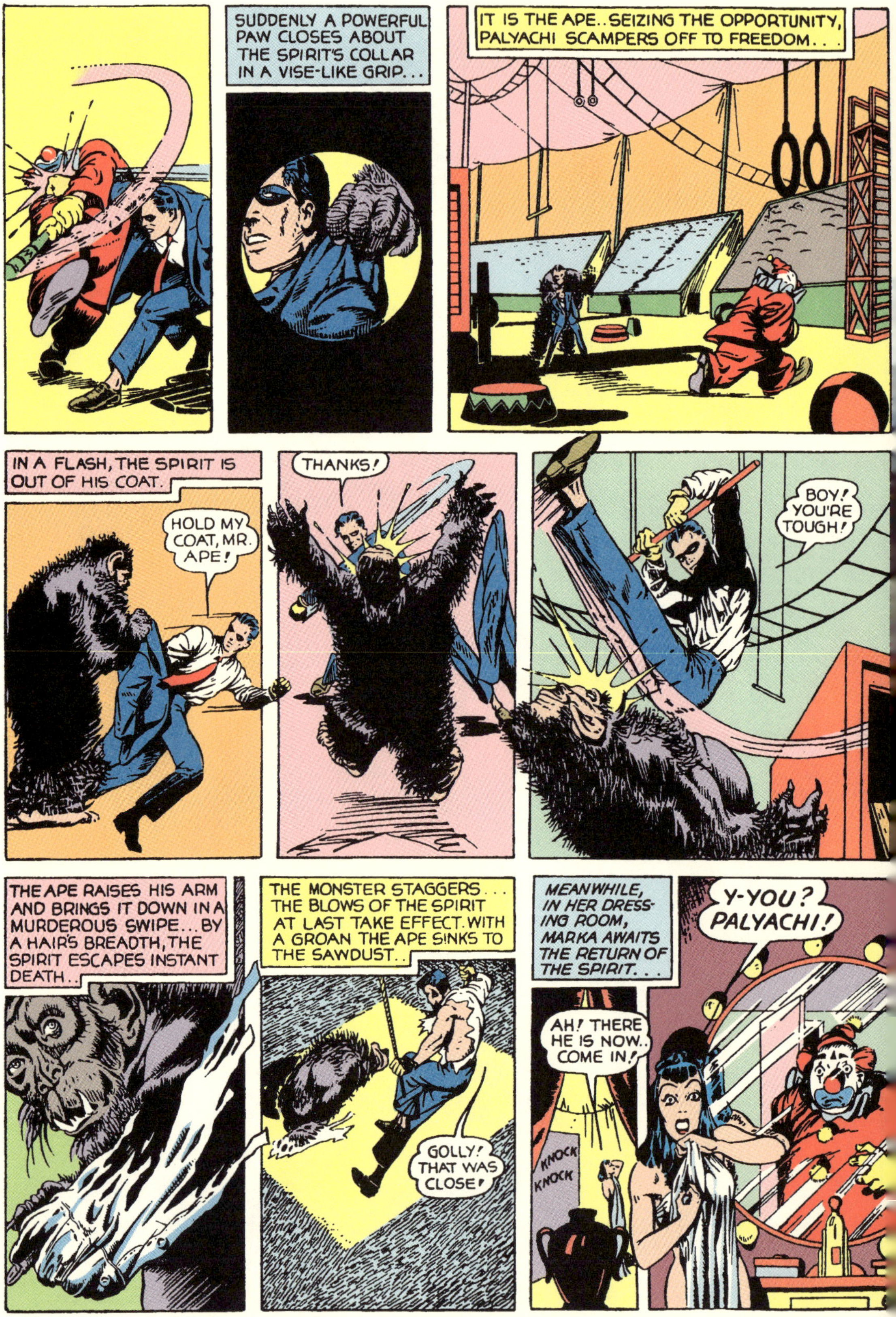
SUDDENLY A POWERFUL PAW CLOSES ABOUT THE SPIRIT'S COLLAR IN A VISE-LIKE GRIP...
IT IS THE APE.. SEIZING THE OPPORTUNITY, PALYACHI SCAMPERS OFF TO FREEDOM...
IN A FLASH, THE SPIRIT IS OUT OF HIS COAT.
HOLD MY COAT, MR. APE!
THANKS!
BOY! YOU'RE TOUGH!
THE APE RAISES HIS ARM AND BRINGS IT DOWN IN A MURDEROUS SWIPE... BY A HAIR'S BREADTH, THE SPIRIT ESCAPES INSTANT DEATH..
THE MONSTER STAGGERS... THE BLOWS OF THE SPIRIT AT LAST TAKE EFFECT. WITH A GROAN THE APE SINKS TO THE SAWDUST..
GOLLY! THAT WAS CLOSE!
MEANWHILE, IN HER DRESSING ROOM, MARKA AWAITS THE RETURN OF THE SPIRIT...
AH! THERE HE IS NOW.. COME IN!
KNOCK KNOCK
Y-YOU? PALYACHI!

NO NO NO! (GULP) LISTEN TO ME.. I DIDN'T MEAN TO SQUEAL ON YOU.. I LOVE YOU! HEH HEH.. I'LL MARRY YOU! DO YOU HEAR?
SUDDENLY THE PLEADING IS CUT SHORT.. A HORRIBLE SILENCE IS PUNCTUATED BY AN AWFUL GASP..
THEN AFTER A MOMENT, THE LITTLE MAD CLOWN LIFTS HIS FACE IN A LAUGHTER SO BLOOD-CURDLING THAT IT MAKES THE SPIRIT FREEZE IN HORROR.
THE SPIRIT LEAPS TO A NEARBY TELEPHONE.
HELLO, DOLAN? THIS IS THE SPIRIT! IF YOU COME DOWN TO THE CIRCUS, YOU'LL FIND THE KILLER YOU'VE BEEN LOOKING FOR!
AND NOW YOU'D BETTER TELL ME THE WHOLE STORY!
MEANWHILE, COMMISSIONER DOLAN ARRIVES WITH A SQUAD OF POLICE.
SURROUND THE PLACE! NO! LOOK.. THERE GOES THE SPIRIT! NAB HIM!
WITH THE ENTIRE SQUAD AT HIS HEELS, THE SPIRIT ROUNDS A CORNER.
A MOMENT LATER..
I KILLED HER! HA-HA-HA!
YOU'LL GET THE CHAIR FOR THIS!
WAIT, DOLAN!
WHERE ARE MY MEN?
OFF ON A LITTLE SPRINT.. SHE IS THE REAL KILLER! SHE WAS THE RING-MASTER, AND THE CLOWN BUT A FREAK OF HER DESIGN IN A CIRCUS OF MURDER!
...AND AS ANOTHER PEAL OF MAD LAUGHTER SHAKES THE CLOWN, THE SPIRIT VANISHES INTO THE MIST...
7

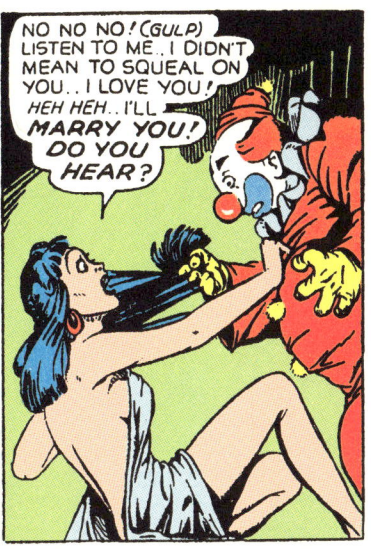

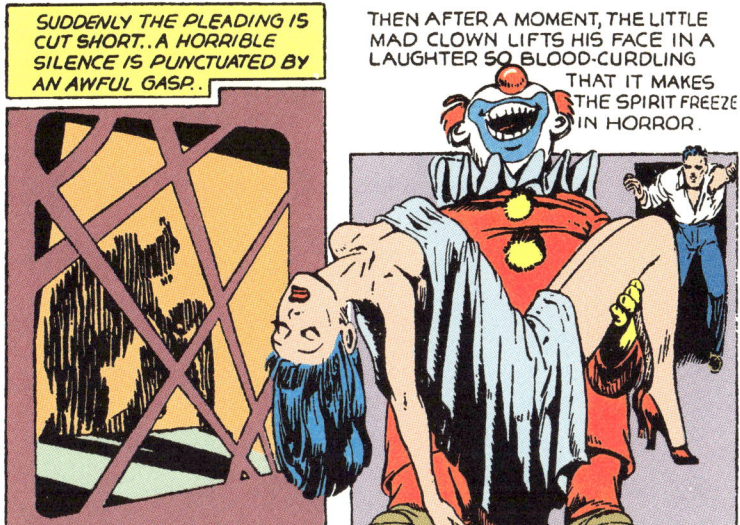

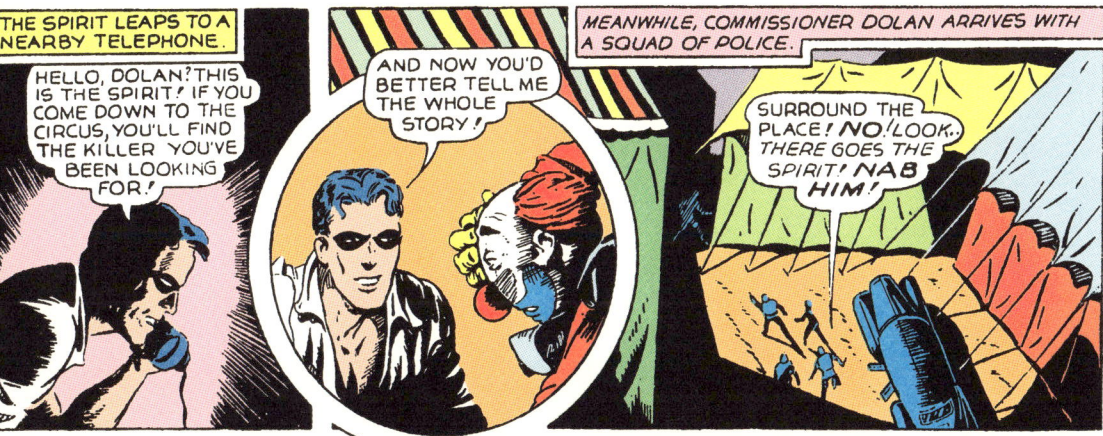

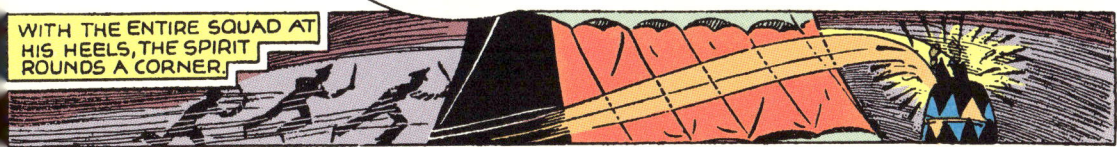

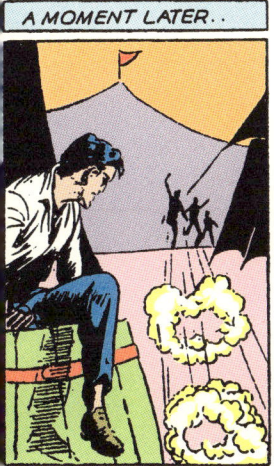

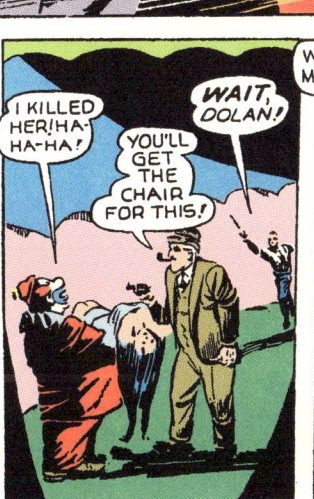

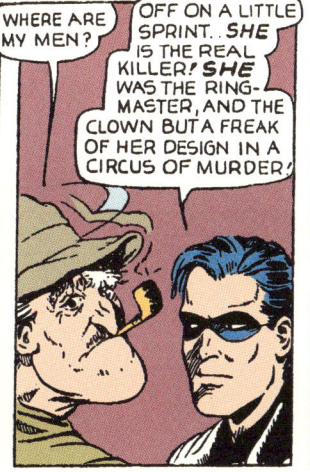

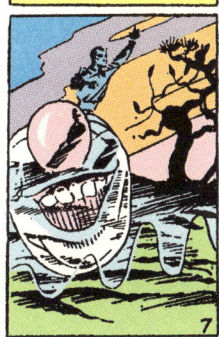

THE DEATH DOLLS

August 4, 1940

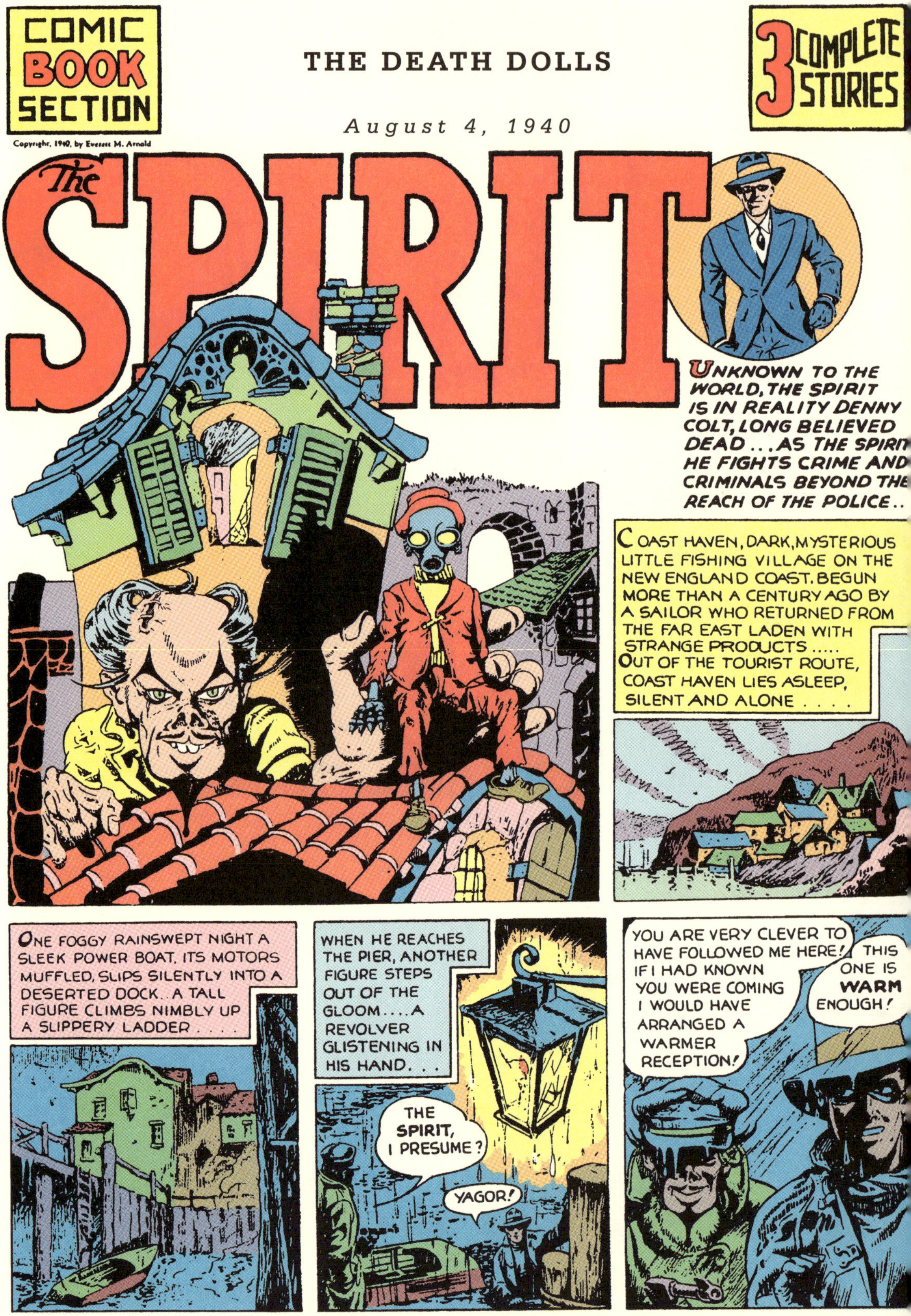

COMIC BOOK SECTION
Copyright, 1940, by Everett M. Arnold
3 COMPLETE STORIES
The SPIRIT
UNKNOWN TO THE WORLD, THE SPIRIT IS IN REALITY DENNY COLT, LONG BELIEVED DEAD . . . AS THE SPIRIT HE FIGHTS CRIME AND CRIMINALS BEYOND THE REACH OF THE POLICE . .
COAST HAVEN, DARK, MYSTERIOUS LITTLE FISHING VILLAGE ON THE NEW ENGLAND COAST. BEGUN MORE THAN A CENTURY AGO BY A SAILOR WHO RETURNED FROM THE FAR EAST LADEN WITH STRANGE PRODUCTS ..... OUT OF THE TOURIST ROUTE, COAST HAVEN LIES ASLEEP, SILENT AND ALONE . . .
ONE FOGGY RAINSWEPT NIGHT A SLEEK POWER BOAT, ITS MOTORS MUFFLED, SLIPS SILENTLY INTO A DESERTED DOCK.. A TALL FIGURE CLIMBS NIMBLY UP A SLIPPERY LADDER . . .
WHEN HE REACHES THE PIER, ANOTHER FIGURE STEPS OUT OF THE GLOOM . . . . A REVOLVER GLISTENING IN HIS HAND. . .
THE SPIRIT, I PRESUME?
YAGOR!
YOU ARE VERY CLEVER TO HAVE FOLLOWED ME HERE! IF I HAD KNOWN YOU WERE COMING I WOULD HAVE ARRANGED A WARMER RECEPTION!
THIS ONE IS WARM ENOUGH!

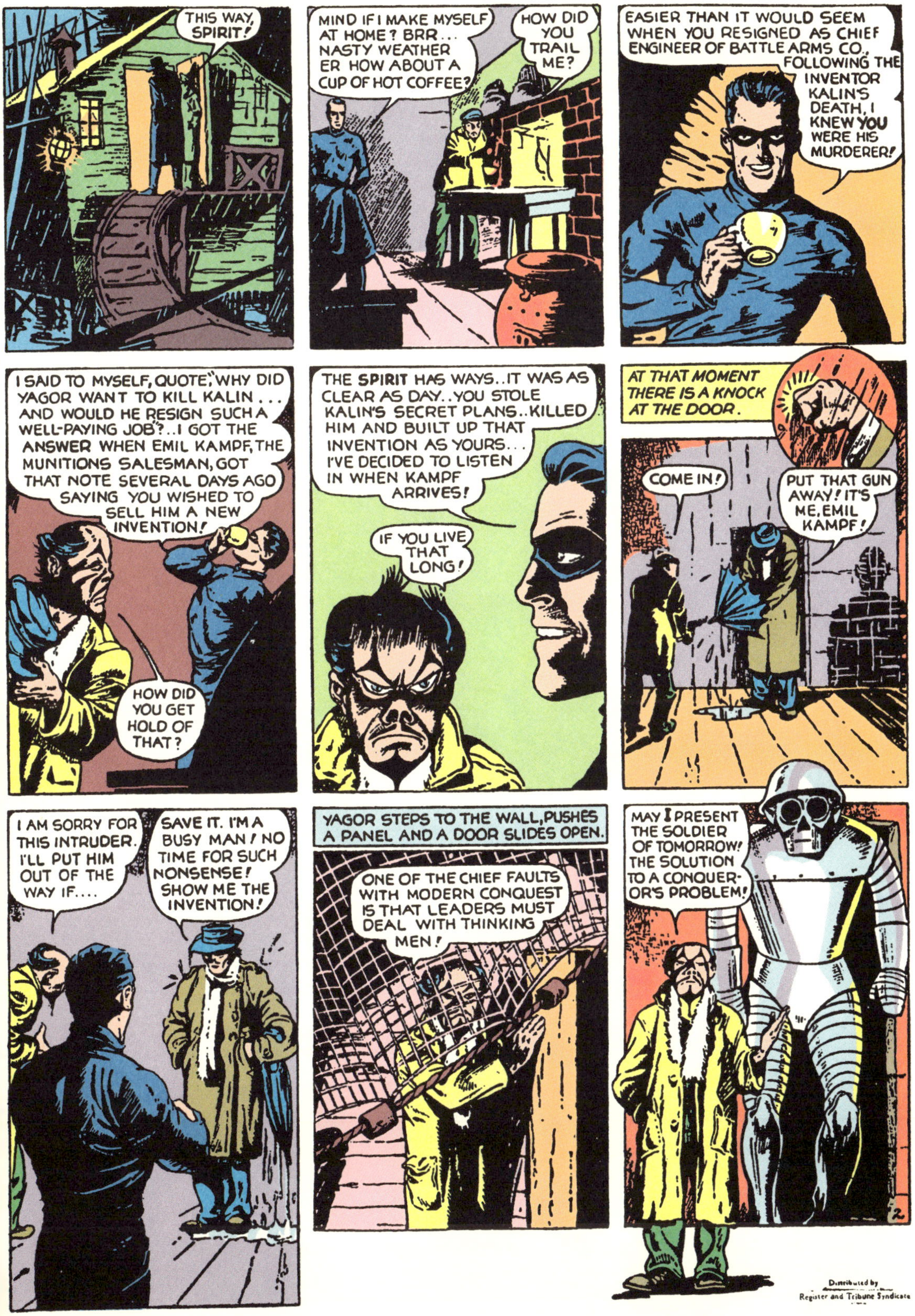
THIS WAY, SPIRIT!
MIND IF I MAKE MYSELF AT HOME? BRR... NASTY WEATHER ER HOW ABOUT A CUP OF HOT COFFEE?
HOW DID YOU TRAIL ME?
EASIER THAN IT WOULD SEEM WHEN YOU RESIGNED AS CHIEF ENGINEER OF BATTLE ARMS CO., FOLLOWING THE INVENTOR KALIN'S DEATH, I KNEW YOU WERE HIS MURDERER!
I SAID TO MYSELF, QUOTE, "WHY DID YAGOR WANT TO KILL KALIN... AND WOULD HE RESIGN SUCH A WELL-PAYING JOB"?...I GOT THE ANSWER WHEN EMIL KAMPF, THE MUNITIONS SALESMAN, GOT THAT NOTE SEVERAL DAYS AGO SAYING YOU WISHED TO SELL HIM A NEW INVENTION!
HOW DID YOU GET HOLD OF THAT?
THE SPIRIT HAS WAYS..IT WAS AS CLEAR AS DAY..YOU STOLE KALIN'S SECRET PLANS..KILLED HIM AND BUILT UP THAT INVENTION AS YOURS... I'VE DECIDED TO LISTEN IN WHEN KAMPF ARRIVES!
IF YOU LIVE THAT LONG!
AT THAT MOMENT THERE IS A KNOCK AT THE DOOR.
COME IN!
PUT THAT GUN AWAY! IT'S ME, EMIL KAMPF!
I AM SORRY FOR THIS INTRUDER. I'LL PUT HIM OUT OF THE WAY IF....
SAVE IT. I'M A BUSY MAN! NO TIME FOR SUCH NONSENSE! SHOW ME THE INVENTION!
YAGOR STEPS TO THE WALL, PUSHES A PANEL AND A DOOR SLIDES OPEN.
ONE OF THE CHIEF FAULTS WITH MODERN CONQUEST IS THAT LEADERS MUST DEAL WITH THINKING MEN!
MAY I PRESENT THE SOLDIER OF TOMORROW! THE SOLUTION TO A CONQUEROR'S PROBLEM!
2
Distributed by Register and Tribune Syndicate

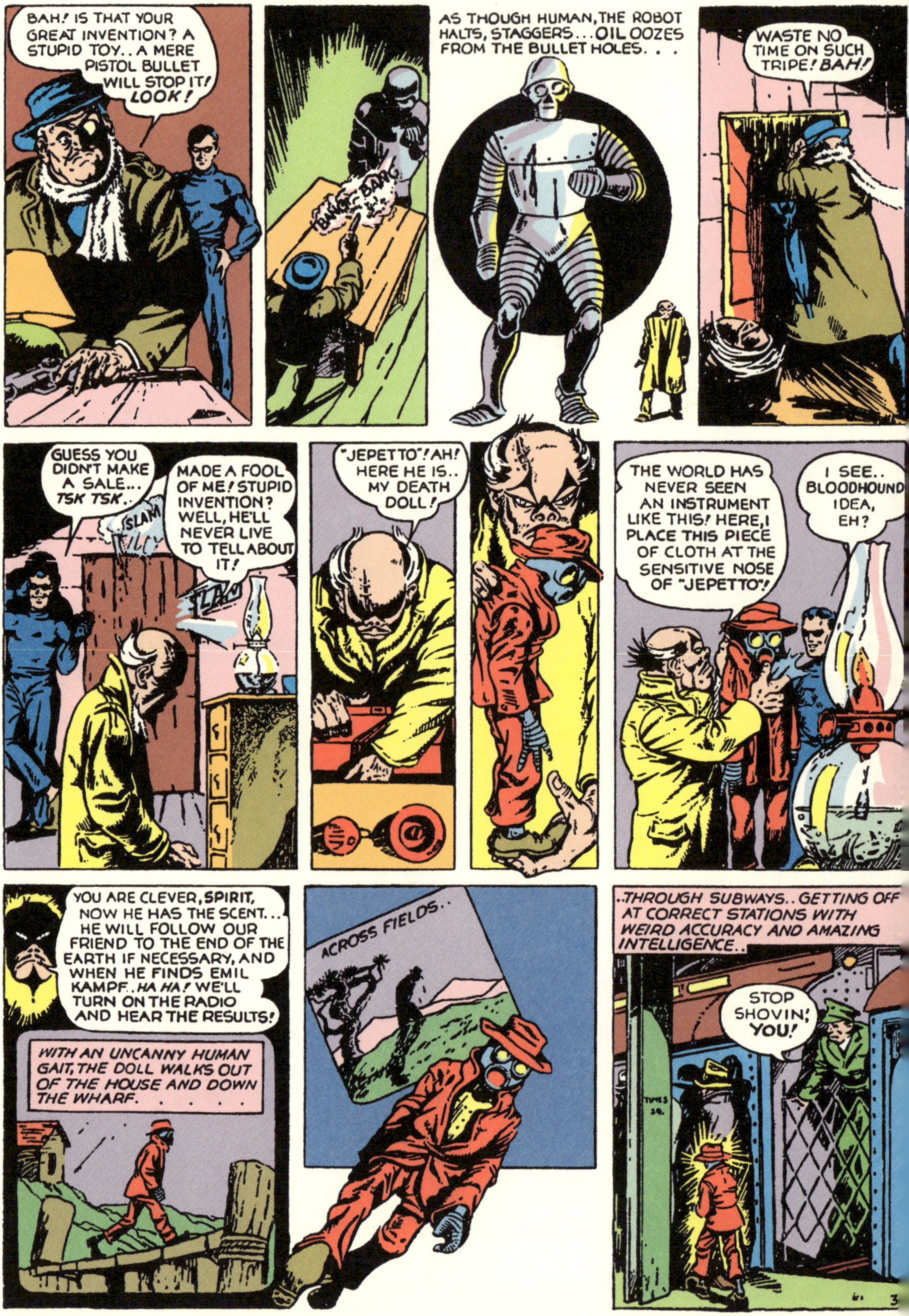

BAH! IS THAT YOUR GREAT INVENTION? A STUPID TOY.. A MERE PISTOL BULLET WILL STOP IT! LOOK!
BANG BANG
AS THOUGH HUMAN, THE ROBOT HALTS, STAGGERS... OIL OOZES FROM THE BULLET HOLES. . .
WASTE NO TIME ON SUCH TRIPE! BAH!
GUESS YOU DIDN'T MAKE A SALE... TSK TSK..
SLAM
MADE A FOOL OF ME! STUPID INVENTION? WELL, HE'LL NEVER LIVE TO TELL ABOUT IT!
SLAM
"JEPETTO"! AH! HERE HE IS.. MY DEATH DOLL!
THE WORLD HAS NEVER SEEN AN INSTRUMENT LIKE THIS! HERE, I PLACE THIS PIECE OF CLOTH AT THE SENSITIVE NOSE OF "JEPETTO"!
I SEE.. BLOODHOUND IDEA, EH?
YOU ARE CLEVER, SPIRIT, NOW HE HAS THE SCENT... HE WILL FOLLOW OUR FRIEND TO THE END OF THE EARTH IF NECESSARY, AND WHEN HE FINDS EMIL KAMPF.. HA HA! WE'LL TURN ON THE RADIO AND HEAR THE RESULTS!
WITH AN UNCANNY HUMAN GAIT, THE DOLL WALKS OUT OF THE HOUSE AND DOWN THE WHARF. . . . .
ACROSS FIELDS..
..THROUGH SUBWAYS.. GETTING OFF AT CORRECT STATIONS WITH WEIRD ACCURACY AND AMAZING INTELLIGENCE..
STOP SHOVIN'! YOU!

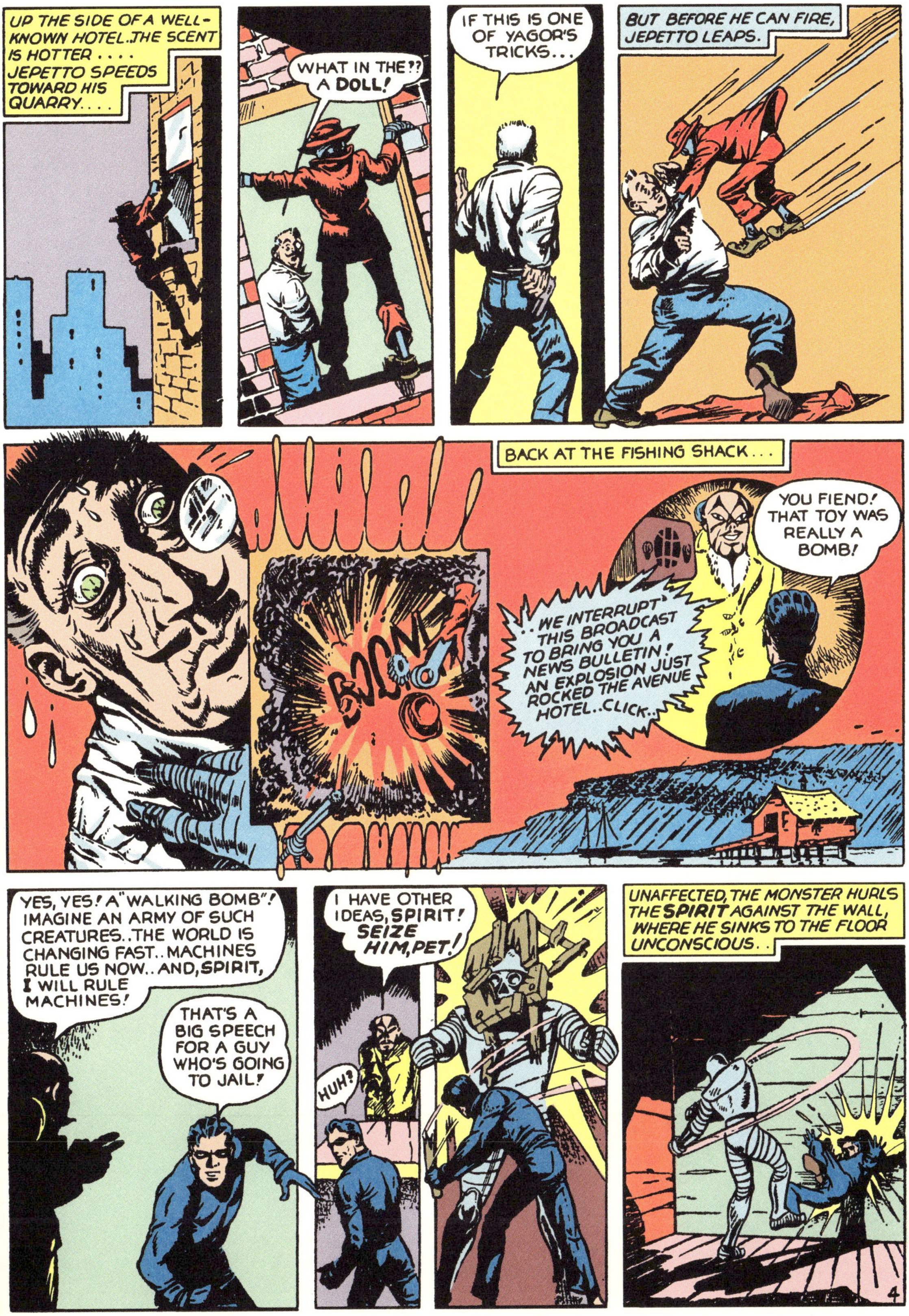

UP THE SIDE OF A WELL-KNOWN HOTEL..THE SCENT IS HOTTER.... JEPETTO SPEEDS TOWARD HIS QUARRY....
WHAT IN THE?? A DOLL!
IF THIS IS ONE OF YAGOR'S TRICKS...
BUT BEFORE HE CAN FIRE, JEPETTO LEAPS.
BACK AT THE FISHING SHACK...
BOOM
YOU FIEND! THAT TOY WAS REALLY A BOMB!
..WE INTERRUPT THIS BROADCAST TO BRING YOU A NEWS BULLETIN! AN EXPLOSION JUST ROCKED THE AVENUE HOTEL..CLICK..
YES, YES! A "WALKING BOMB"! IMAGINE AN ARMY OF SUCH CREATURES..THE WORLD IS CHANGING FAST..MACHINES RULE US NOW..AND, SPIRIT, I WILL RULE MACHINES!
THAT'S A BIG SPEECH FOR A GUY WHO'S GOING TO JAIL!
I HAVE OTHER IDEAS, SPIRIT! SEIZE HIM, PET!
HUH?
UNAFFECTED, THE MONSTER HURLS THE SPIRIT AGAINST THE WALL, WHERE HE SINKS TO THE FLOOR UNCONSCIOUS..
4

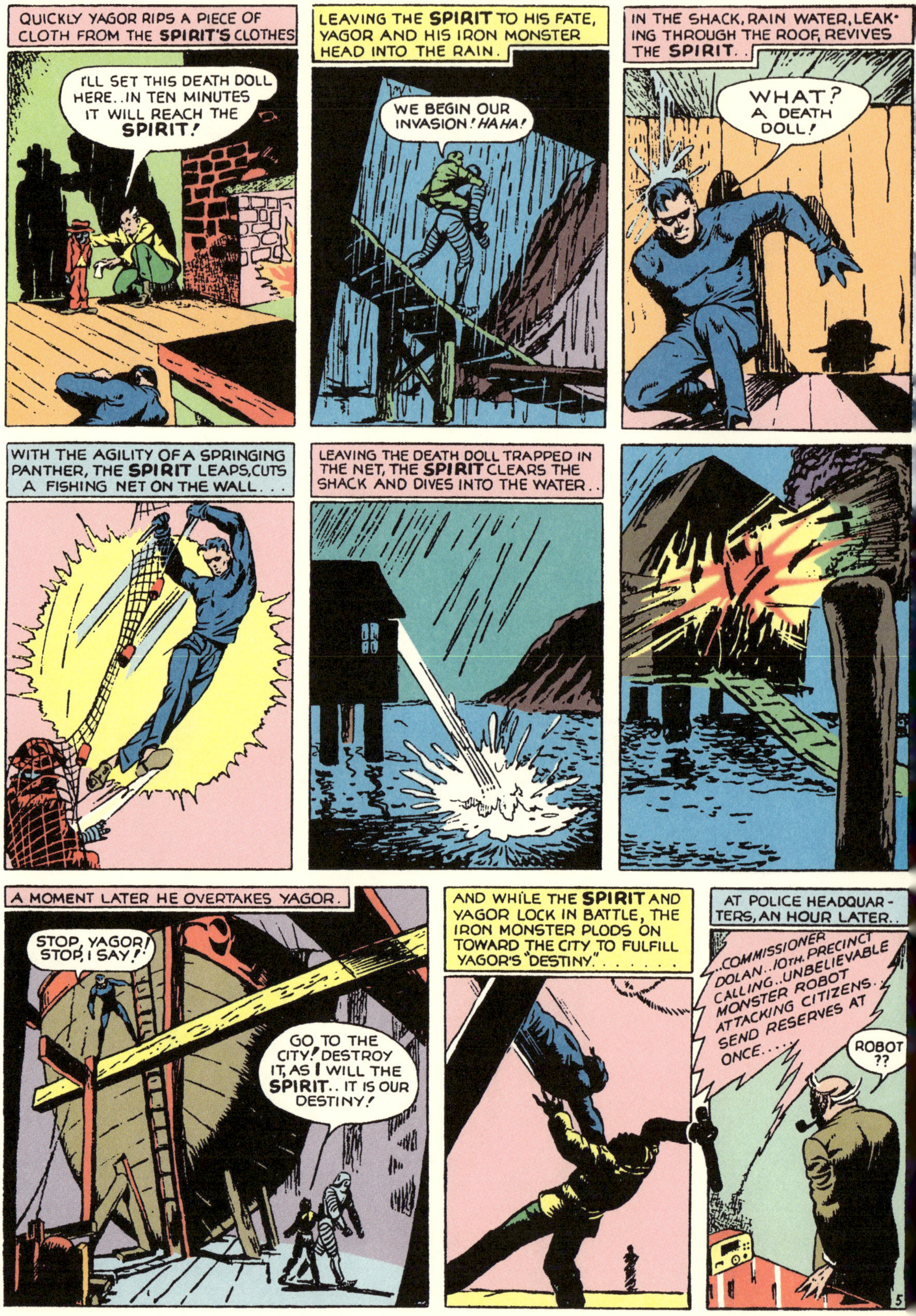
QUICKLY YAGOR RIPS A PIECE OF CLOTH FROM THE SPIRIT'S CLOTHES
I'LL SET THIS DEATH DOLL HERE..IN TEN MINUTES IT WILL REACH THE SPIRIT!
LEAVING THE SPIRIT TO HIS FATE, YAGOR AND HIS IRON MONSTER HEAD INTO THE RAIN.
WE BEGIN OUR INVASION! HAHA!
IN THE SHACK, RAIN WATER, LEAKING THROUGH THE ROOF, REVIVES THE SPIRIT..
WHAT? A DEATH DOLL!
WITH THE AGILITY OF A SPRINGING PANTHER, THE SPIRIT LEAPS, CUTS A FISHING NET ON THE WALL...
LEAVING THE DEATH DOLL TRAPPED IN THE NET, THE SPIRIT CLEARS THE SHACK AND DIVES INTO THE WATER..
A MOMENT LATER HE OVERTAKES YAGOR.
STOP, YAGOR! STOP, I SAY!
GO TO THE CITY! DESTROY IT, AS I WILL THE SPIRIT.. IT IS OUR DESTINY!
AND WHILE THE SPIRIT AND YAGOR LOCK IN BATTLE, THE IRON MONSTER PLODS ON TOWARD THE CITY TO FULFILL YAGOR'S "DESTINY."......
AT POLICE HEADQUARTERS, AN HOUR LATER..
..COMMISSIONER DOLAN..10TH PRECINCT CALLING..UNBELIEVABLE MONSTER ROBOT ATTACKING CITIZENS.. SEND RESERVES AT ONCE.....
ROBOT ??
5

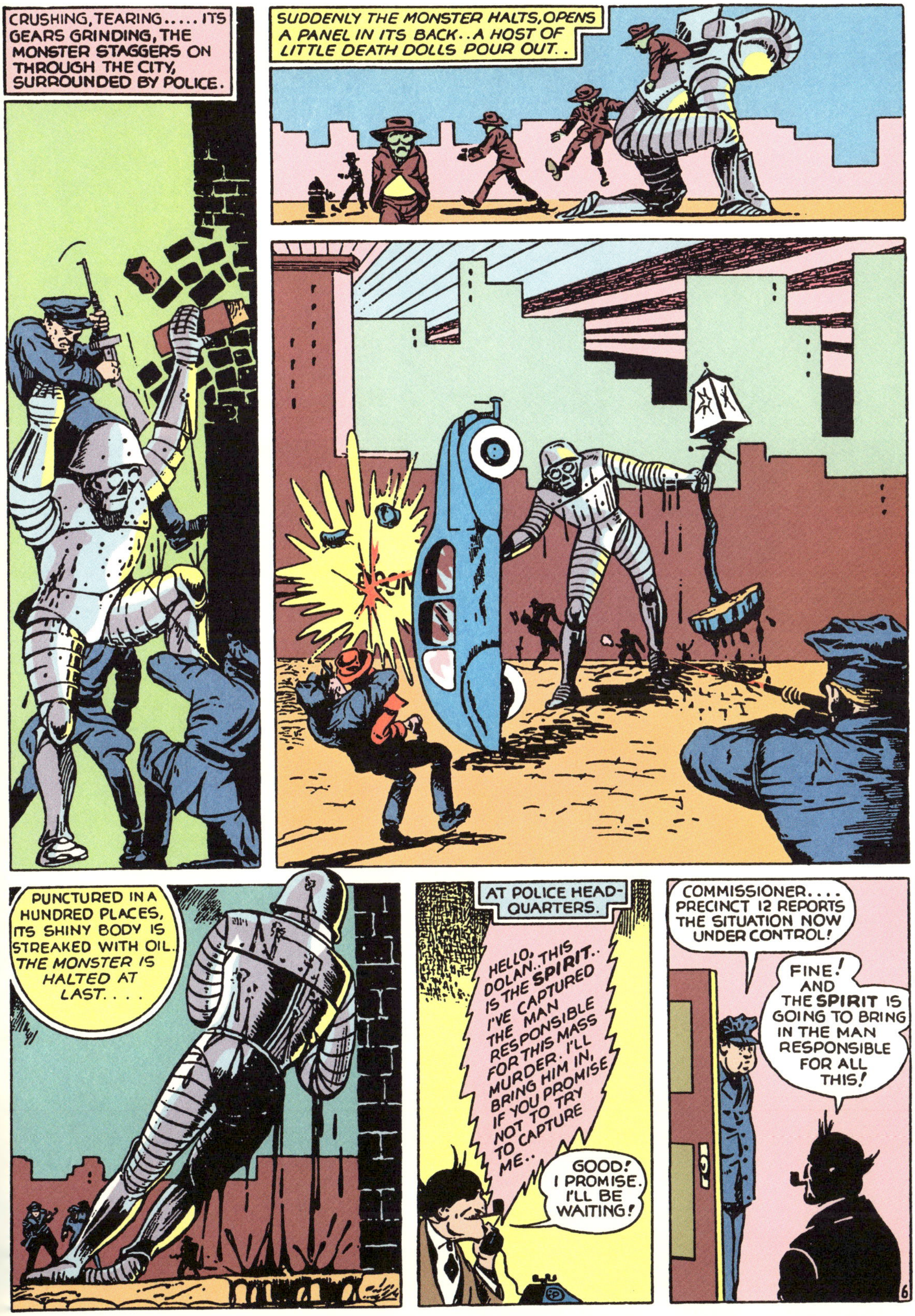

CRUSHING, TEARING..... ITS GEARS GRINDING, THE MONSTER STAGGERS ON THROUGH THE CITY, SURROUNDED BY POLICE.
SUDDENLY THE MONSTER HALTS, OPENS A PANEL IN ITS BACK.. A HOST OF LITTLE DEATH DOLLS POUR OUT..
PUNCTURED IN A HUNDRED PLACES, ITS SHINY BODY IS STREAKED WITH OIL.. THE MONSTER IS HALTED AT LAST....
AT POLICE HEAD-QUARTERS.
HELLO, DOLAN.. THIS IS THE SPIRIT.. I'VE CAPTURED THE MAN RESPONSIBLE FOR THIS MASS MURDER. I'LL BRING HIM IN, IF YOU PROMISE NOT TO TRY TO CAPTURE ME..
GOOD! I PROMISE. I'LL BE WAITING!
COMMISSIONER.... PRECINCT 12 REPORTS THE SITUATION NOW UNDER CONTROL!
FINE! AND THE SPIRIT IS GOING TO BRING IN THE MAN RESPONSIBLE FOR ALL THIS!
6

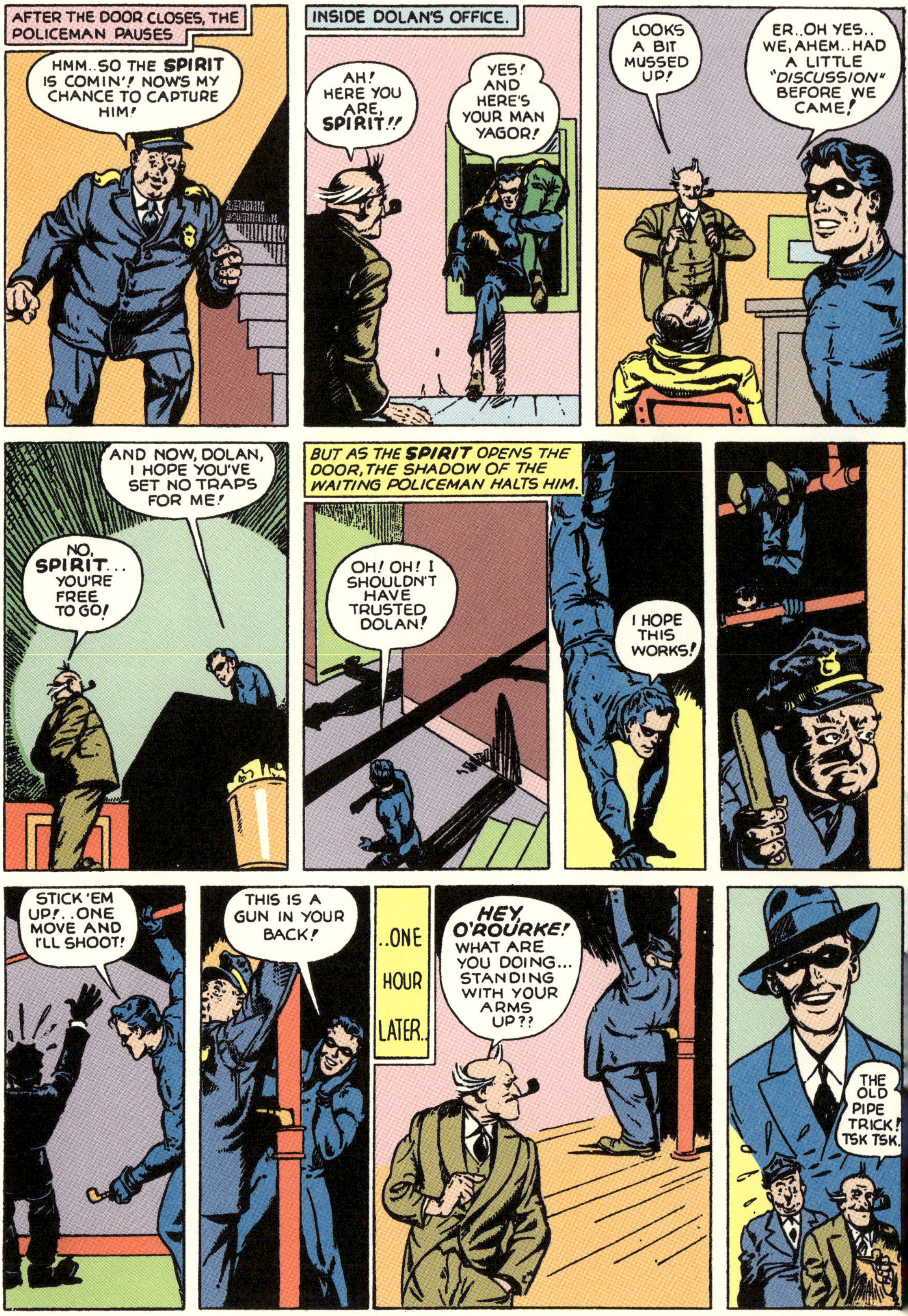
AFTER THE DOOR CLOSES, THE POLICEMAN PAUSES
HMM..SO THE SPIRIT IS COMIN'! NOW'S MY CHANCE TO CAPTURE HIM!
INSIDE DOLAN'S OFFICE.
AH! HERE YOU ARE, SPIRIT!!
YES! AND HERE'S YOUR MAN YAGOR!
LOOKS A BIT MUSSED UP!
ER..OH YES.. WE, AHEM..HAD A LITTLE "DISCUSSION" BEFORE WE CAME!
AND NOW, DOLAN, I HOPE YOU'VE SET NO TRAPS FOR ME!
NO, SPIRIT... YOU'RE FREE TO GO!
BUT AS THE SPIRIT OPENS THE DOOR, THE SHADOW OF THE WAITING POLICEMAN HALTS HIM.
OH! OH! I SHOULDN'T HAVE TRUSTED DOLAN!
I HOPE THIS WORKS!
STICK 'EM UP!..ONE MOVE AND I'LL SHOOT!
THIS IS A GUN IN YOUR BACK!
..ONE HOUR LATER..
HEY, O'ROURKE! WHAT ARE YOU DOING... STANDING WITH YOUR ARMS UP??
THE OLD PIPE TRICK! TSK TSK.

THE KIDNAPPING OF DAISY KAY

August 11, 1940

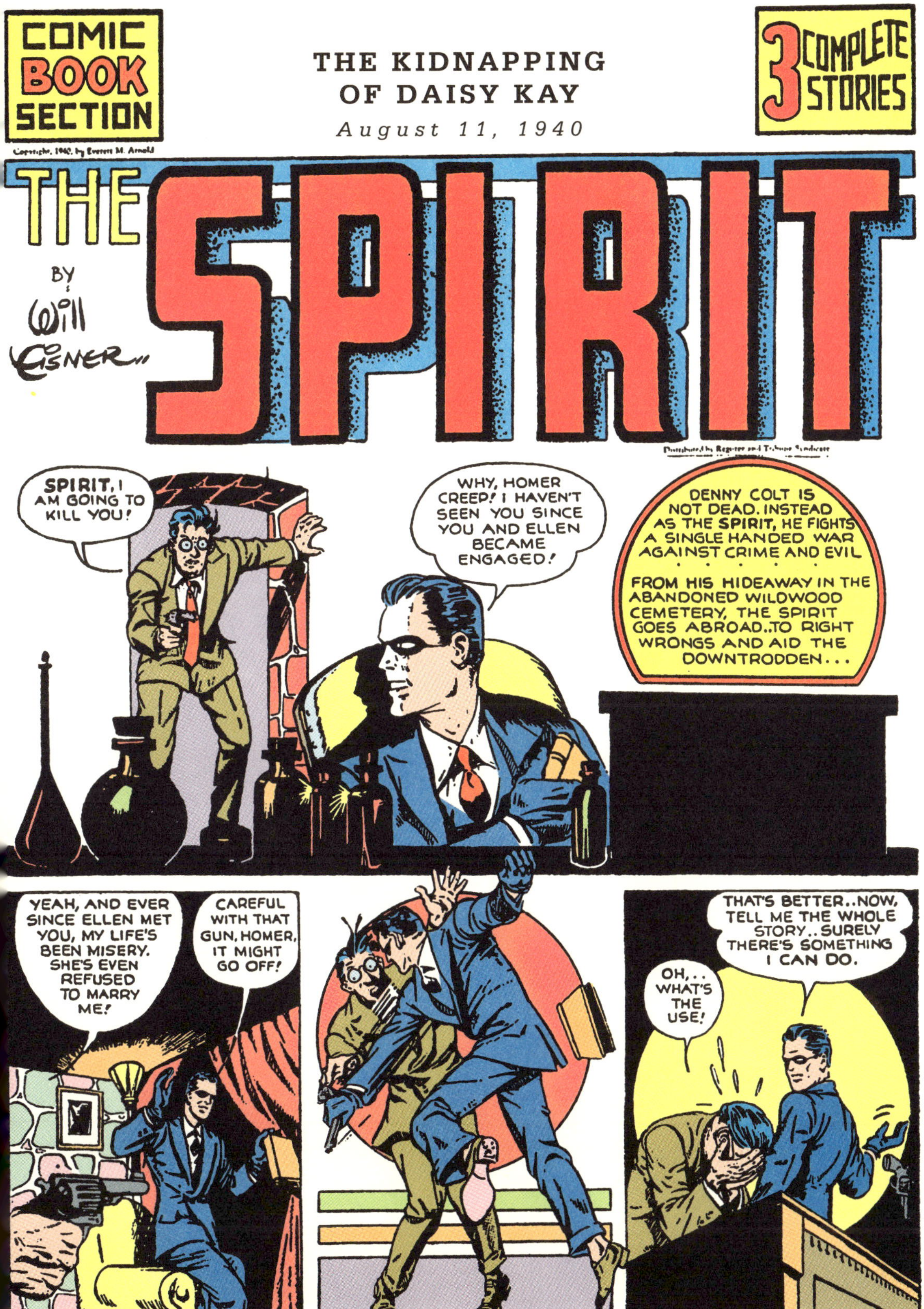

COMIC BOOK SECTION
3 COMPLETE STORIES
Copyright, 1940, by Everett M. Arnold
THE SPIRIT
BY Will Eisner
SPIRIT, I AM GOING TO KILL YOU!
WHY, HOMER CREEP! I HAVEN'T SEEN YOU SINCE YOU AND ELLEN BECAME ENGAGED!
DENNY COLT IS NOT DEAD. INSTEAD AS THE SPIRIT, HE FIGHTS A SINGLE HANDED WAR AGAINST CRIME AND EVIL . . . . .
FROM HIS HIDEAWAY IN THE ABANDONED WILDWOOD CEMETERY, THE SPIRIT GOES ABROAD..TO RIGHT WRONGS AND AID THE DOWNTRODDEN...
YEAH, AND EVER SINCE ELLEN MET YOU, MY LIFE'S BEEN MISERY. SHE'S EVEN REFUSED TO MARRY ME!
CAREFUL WITH THAT GUN, HOMER, IT MIGHT GO OFF!
THAT'S BETTER..NOW, TELL ME THE WHOLE STORY.. SURELY THERE'S SOMETHING I CAN DO.
OH,.. WHAT'S THE USE!

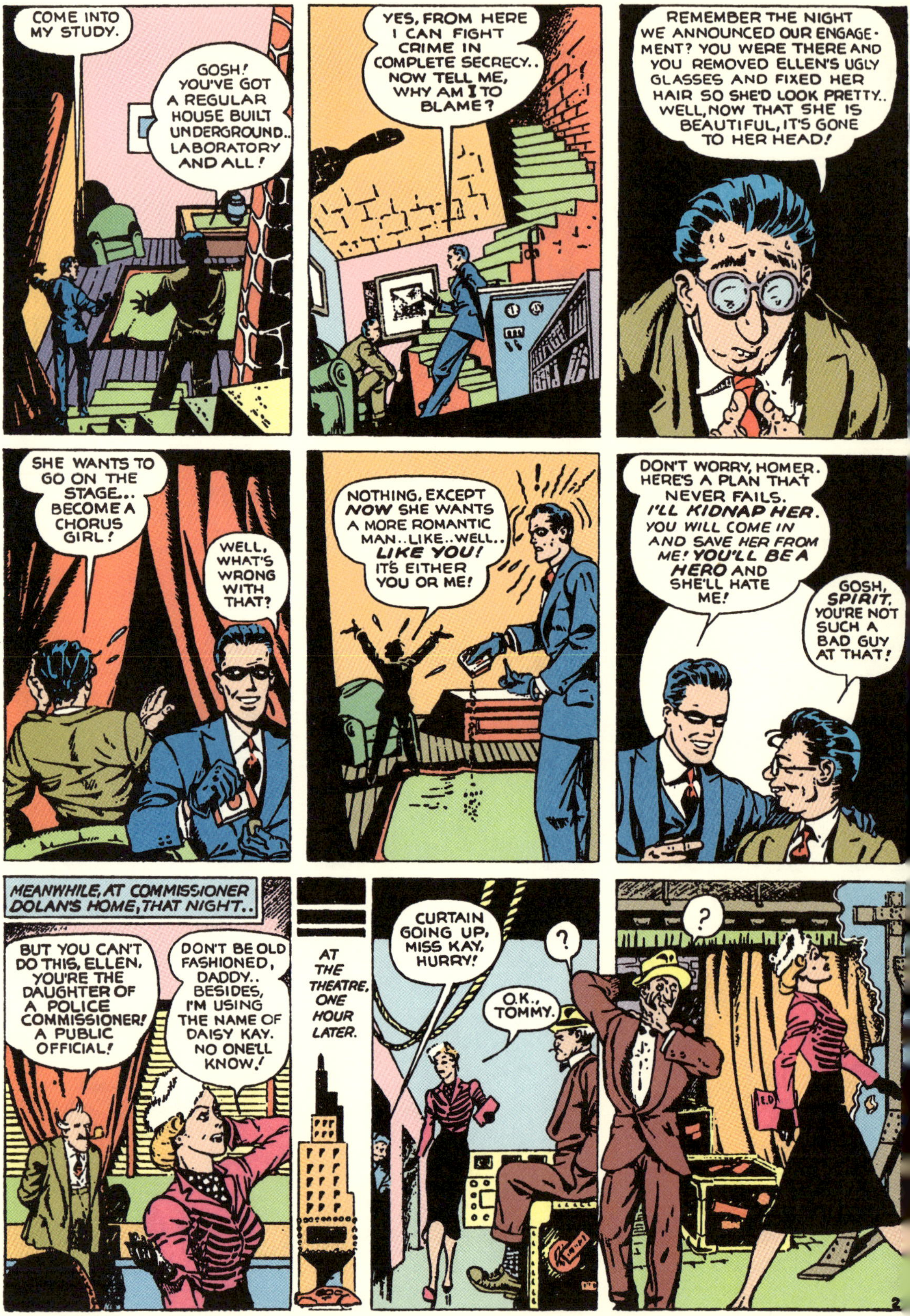
COME INTO MY STUDY.
GOSH! YOU'VE GOT A REGULAR HOUSE BUILT UNDERGROUND.. LABORATORY AND ALL!
YES, FROM HERE I CAN FIGHT CRIME IN COMPLETE SECRECY.. NOW TELL ME, WHY AM I TO BLAME?
REMEMBER THE NIGHT WE ANNOUNCED OUR ENGAGE-MENT? YOU WERE THERE AND YOU REMOVED ELLEN'S UGLY GLASSES AND FIXED HER HAIR SO SHE'D LOOK PRETTY.. WELL, NOW THAT SHE IS BEAUTIFUL, IT'S GONE TO HER HEAD!
SHE WANTS TO GO ON THE STAGE... BECOME A CHORUS GIRL!
WELL, WHAT'S WRONG WITH THAT?
NOTHING, EXCEPT NOW SHE WANTS A MORE ROMANTIC MAN..LIKE..WELL.. LIKE YOU! IT'S EITHER YOU OR ME!
DON'T WORRY, HOMER. HERE'S A PLAN THAT NEVER FAILS. I'LL KIDNAP HER. YOU WILL COME IN AND SAVE HER FROM ME! YOU'LL BE A HERO AND SHE'LL HATE ME!
GOSH, SPIRIT, YOU'RE NOT SUCH A BAD GUY AT THAT!
MEANWHILE, AT COMMISSIONER DOLAN'S HOME, THAT NIGHT..
BUT YOU CAN'T DO THIS, ELLEN, YOU'RE THE DAUGHTER OF A POLICE COMMISSIONER! A PUBLIC OFFICIAL!
DON'T BE OLD FASHIONED, DADDY.. BESIDES, I'M USING THE NAME OF DAISY KAY. NO ONE'LL KNOW!
AT THE THEATRE, ONE HOUR LATER.
CURTAIN GOING UP, MISS KAY, HURRY!
O.K., TOMMY.
?
?
2

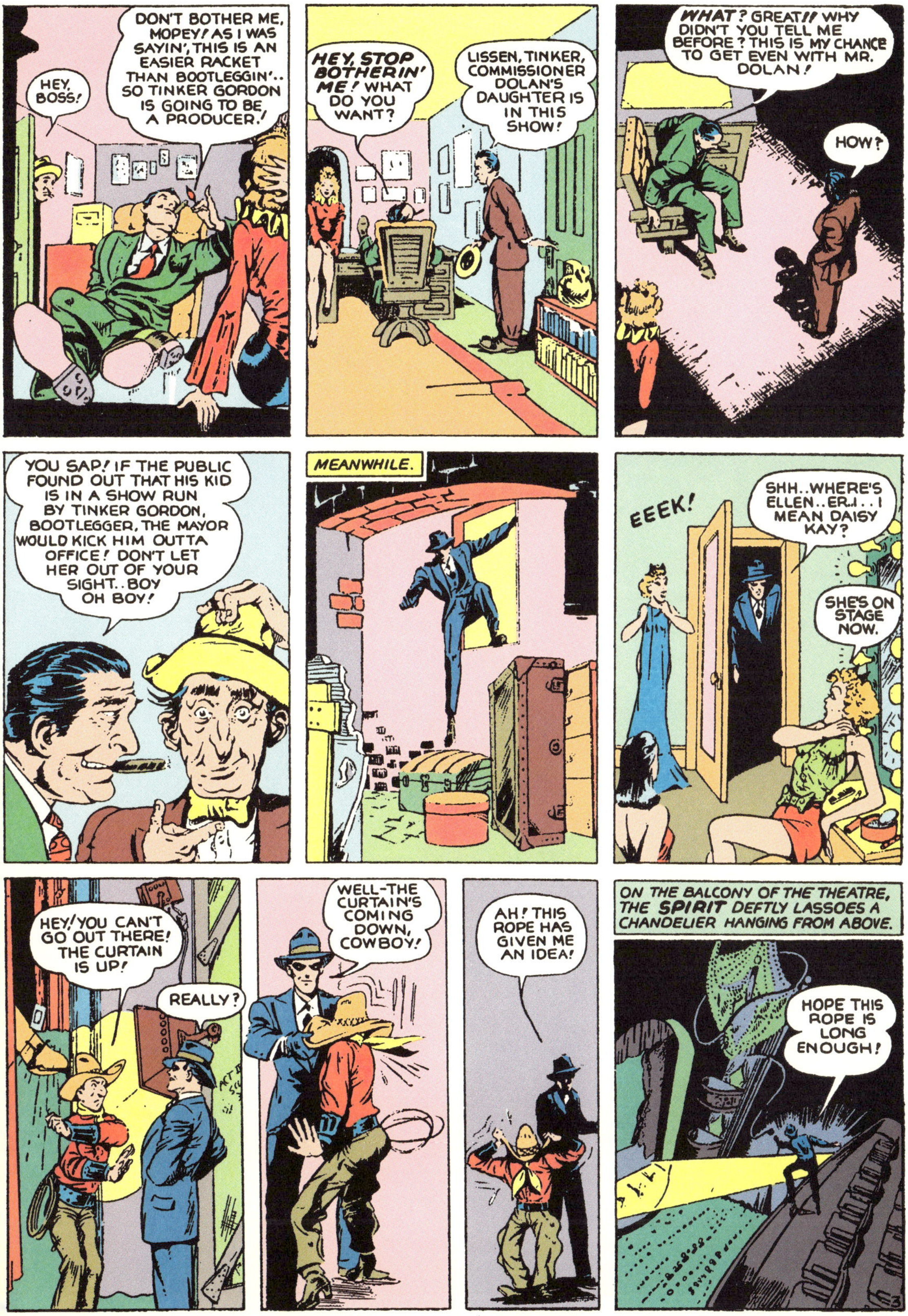
HEY, BOSS!
DON'T BOTHER ME, MOPEY! AS I WAS SAYIN', THIS IS AN EASIER RACKET THAN BOOTLEGGIN'.. SO TINKER GORDON IS GOING TO BE A PRODUCER!
HEY, STOP BOTHERIN' ME! WHAT DO YOU WANT?
LISSEN, TINKER, COMMISSIONER DOLAN'S DAUGHTER IS IN THIS SHOW!
WHAT? GREAT!! WHY DIDN'T YOU TELL ME BEFORE? THIS IS MY CHANCE TO GET EVEN WITH MR. DOLAN!
HOW?
YOU SAP! IF THE PUBLIC FOUND OUT THAT HIS KID IS IN A SHOW RUN BY TINKER GORDON, BOOTLEGGER, THE MAYOR WOULD KICK HIM OUTTA OFFICE! DON'T LET HER OUT OF YOUR SIGHT.. BOY OH BOY!
MEANWHILE.
EEEK!
SHH.. WHERE'S ELLEN.. ER.I.. I MEAN DAISY KAY?
SHE'S ON STAGE NOW.
HEY! YOU CAN'T GO OUT THERE! THE CURTAIN IS UP!
REALLY?
WELL-THE CURTAIN'S COMING DOWN, COWBOY!
AH! THIS ROPE HAS GIVEN ME AN IDEA!
ON THE BALCONY OF THE THEATRE, THE SPIRIT DEFTLY LASSOES A CHANDELIER HANGING FROM ABOVE.
HOPE THIS ROPE IS LONG ENOUGH!
3

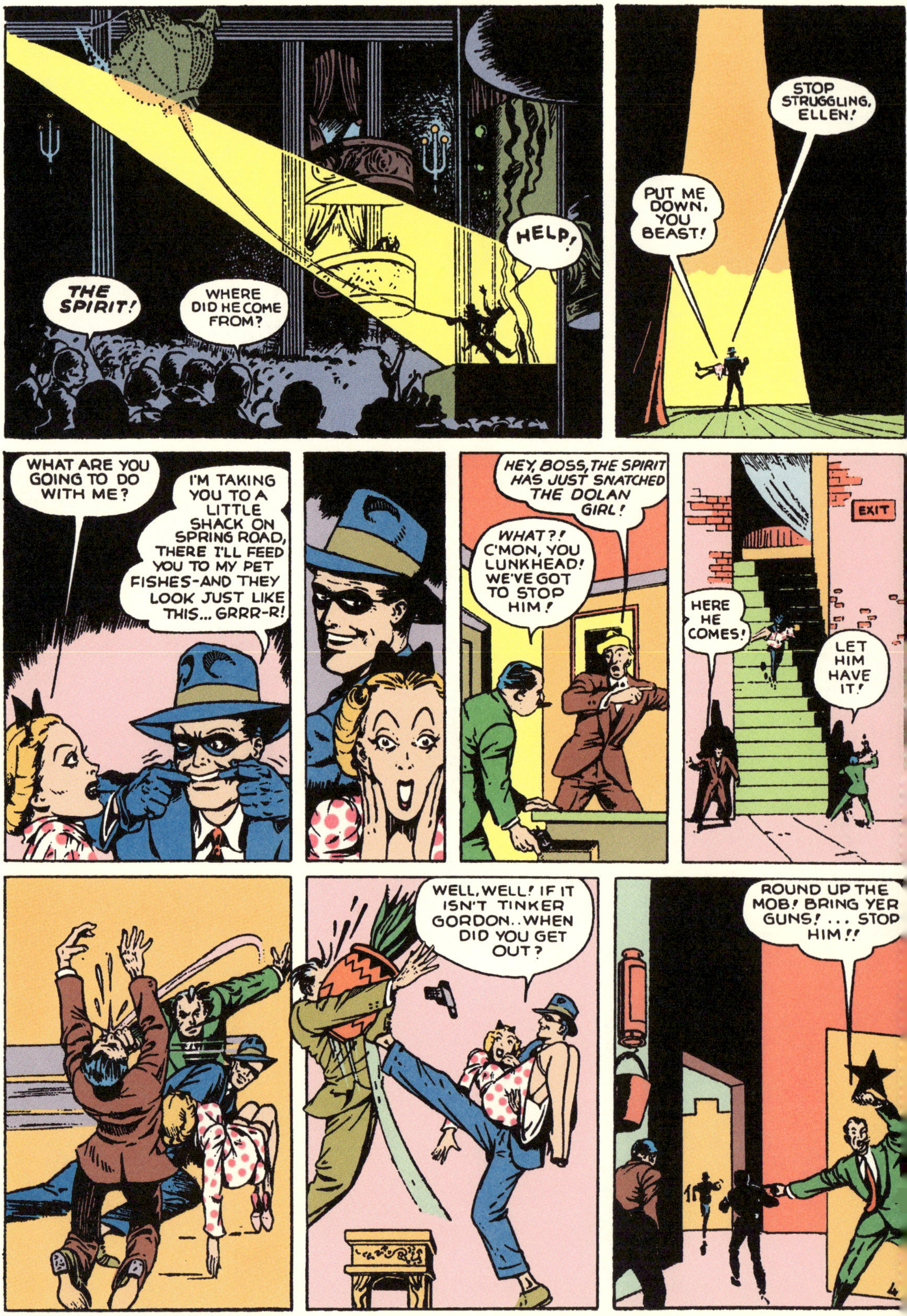
HELP!
THE SPIRIT!
WHERE DID HE COME FROM?
STOP STRUGGLING, ELLEN!
PUT ME DOWN, YOU BEAST!
WHAT ARE YOU GOING TO DO WITH ME?
I'M TAKING YOU TO A LITTLE SHACK ON SPRING ROAD, THERE I'LL FEED YOU TO MY PET FISHES-AND THEY LOOK JUST LIKE THIS... GRRR-R!
HEY, BOSS, THE SPIRIT HAS JUST SNATCHED THE DOLAN GIRL!
WHAT?! C'MON, YOU LUNKHEAD! WE'VE GOT TO STOP HIM!
EXIT
HERE HE COMES!
LET HIM HAVE IT!
WELL, WELL! IF IT ISN'T TINKER GORDON.. WHEN DID YOU GET OUT?
ROUND UP THE MOB! BRING YER GUNS! ... STOP HIM!!

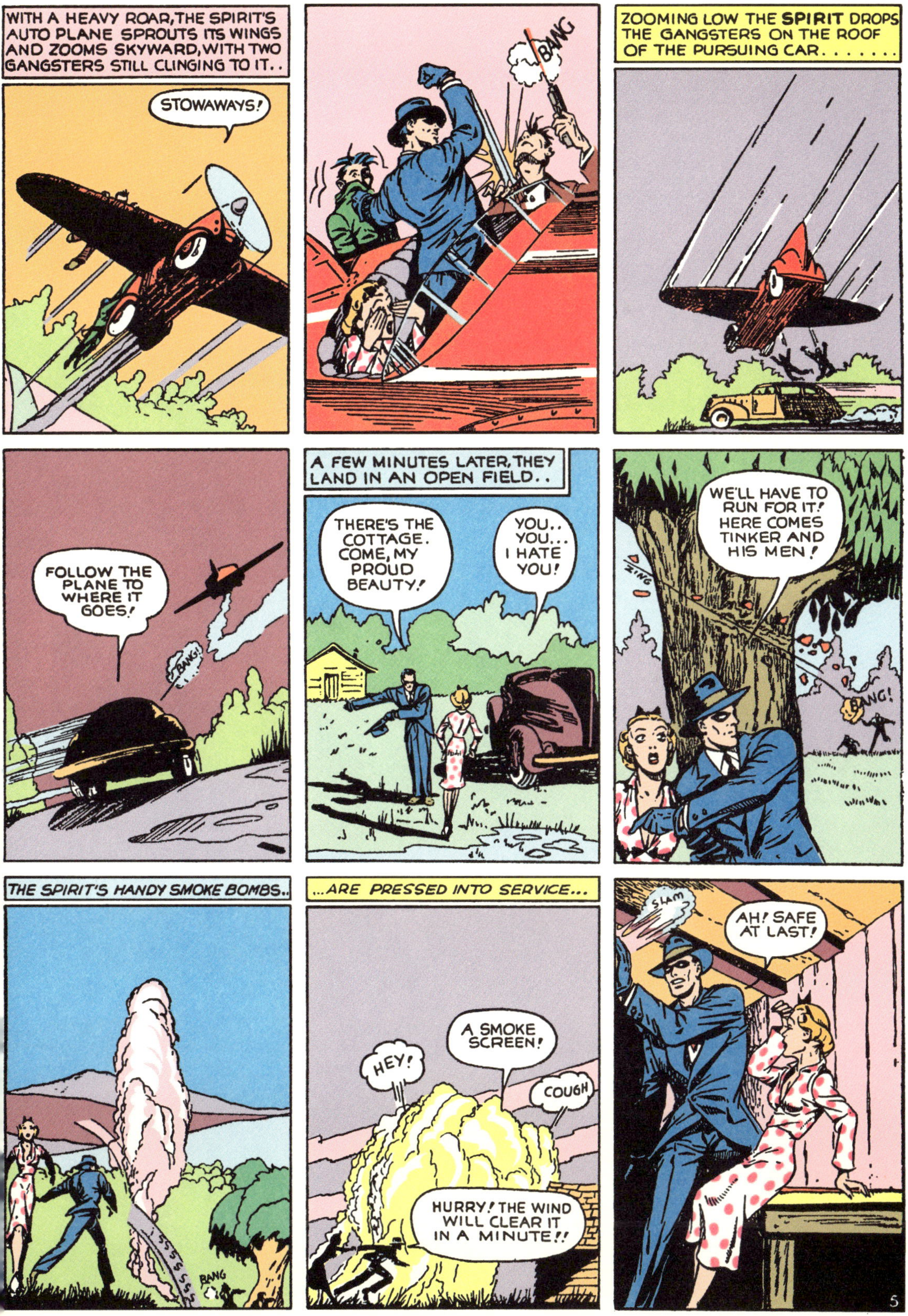
WITH A HEAVY ROAR, THE SPIRIT'S AUTO PLANE SPROUTS ITS WINGS AND ZOOMS SKYWARD, WITH TWO GANGSTERS STILL CLINGING TO IT..
STOWAWAYS!
BANG
ZOOMING LOW THE SPIRIT DROPS THE GANGSTERS ON THE ROOF OF THE PURSUING CAR.......
FOLLOW THE PLANE TO WHERE IT GOES!
BANG!
A FEW MINUTES LATER, THEY LAND IN AN OPEN FIELD..
THERE'S THE COTTAGE. COME, MY PROUD BEAUTY!
YOU.. YOU... I HATE YOU!
WE'LL HAVE TO RUN FOR IT! HERE COMES TINKER AND HIS MEN!
ZING
BANG!
THE SPIRIT'S HANDY SMOKE BOMBS..
BANG
...ARE PRESSED INTO SERVICE...
HEY!
A SMOKE SCREEN!
COUGH
HURRY! THE WIND WILL CLEAR IT IN A MINUTE!!
SLAM
AH! SAFE AT LAST!
5

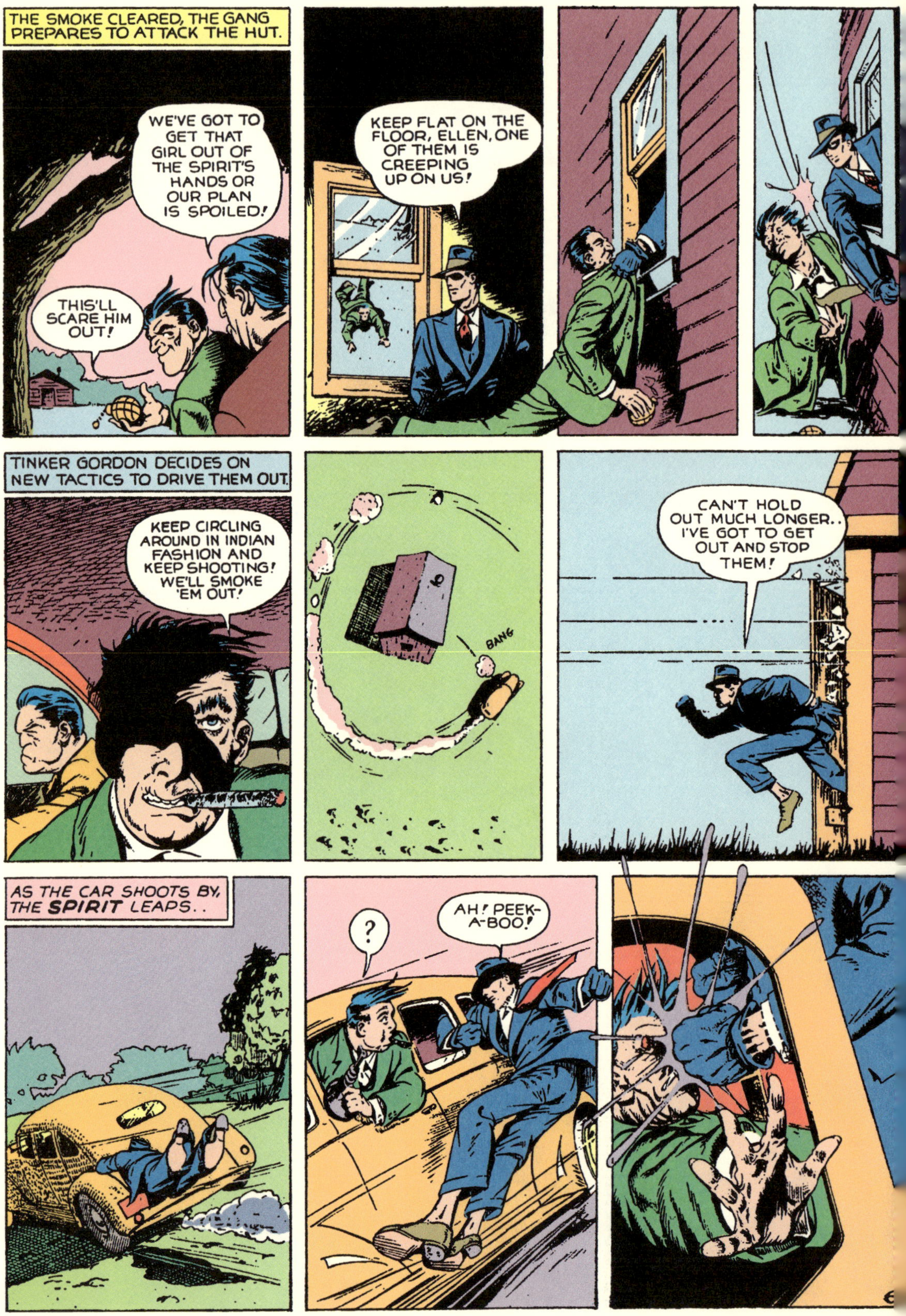
THE SMOKE CLEARED, THE GANG PREPARES TO ATTACK THE HUT.
WE'VE GOT TO GET THAT GIRL OUT OF THE SPIRIT'S HANDS OR OUR PLAN IS SPOILED!
THIS'LL SCARE HIM OUT!
KEEP FLAT ON THE FLOOR, ELLEN, ONE OF THEM IS CREEPING UP ON US!
TINKER GORDON DECIDES ON NEW TACTICS TO DRIVE THEM OUT.
KEEP CIRCLING AROUND IN INDIAN FASHION AND KEEP SHOOTING! WE'LL SMOKE 'EM OUT!
BANG
CAN'T HOLD OUT MUCH LONGER.. I'VE GOT TO GET OUT AND STOP THEM!
AS THE CAR SHOOTS BY, THE SPIRIT LEAPS..
?
AH! PEEK-A-BOO!

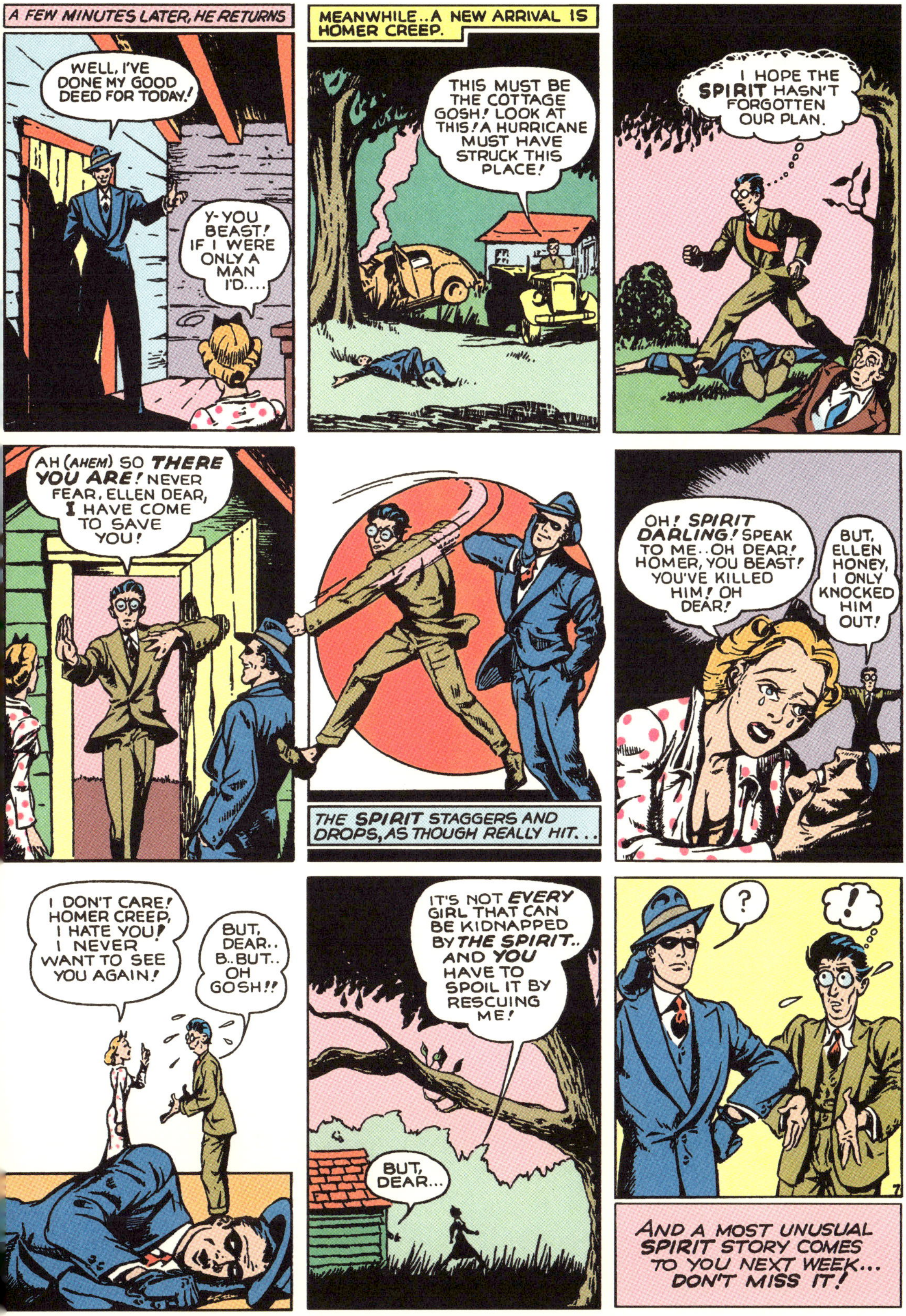

A FEW MINUTES LATER, HE RETURNS
WELL, I'VE DONE MY GOOD DEED FOR TODAY!
Y-YOU BEAST! IF I WERE ONLY A MAN I'D....
MEANWHILE.. A NEW ARRIVAL IS HOMER CREEP.
THIS MUST BE THE COTTAGE GOSH! LOOK AT THIS! A HURRICANE MUST HAVE STRUCK THIS PLACE!
I HOPE THE SPIRIT HASN'T FORGOTTEN OUR PLAN.
AH (AHEM) SO THERE YOU ARE! NEVER FEAR, ELLEN DEAR, I HAVE COME TO SAVE YOU!
THE SPIRIT STAGGERS AND DROPS, AS THOUGH REALLY HIT...
OH! SPIRIT DARLING! SPEAK TO ME.. OH DEAR! HOMER, YOU BEAST! YOU'VE KILLED HIM! OH DEAR!
BUT, ELLEN HONEY, I ONLY KNOCKED HIM OUT!
I DON'T CARE! HOMER CREEP, I HATE YOU! I NEVER WANT TO SEE YOU AGAIN!
BUT, DEAR.. B..BUT.. OH GOSH!!
IT'S NOT EVERY GIRL THAT CAN BE KIDNAPPED BY THE SPIRIT.. AND YOU HAVE TO SPOIL IT BY RESCUING ME!
BUT, DEAR...
?
!
7
AND A MOST UNUSUAL SPIRIT STORY COMES TO YOU NEXT WEEK... DON'T MISS IT!

THE MORGER BOYS

August 18, 1940

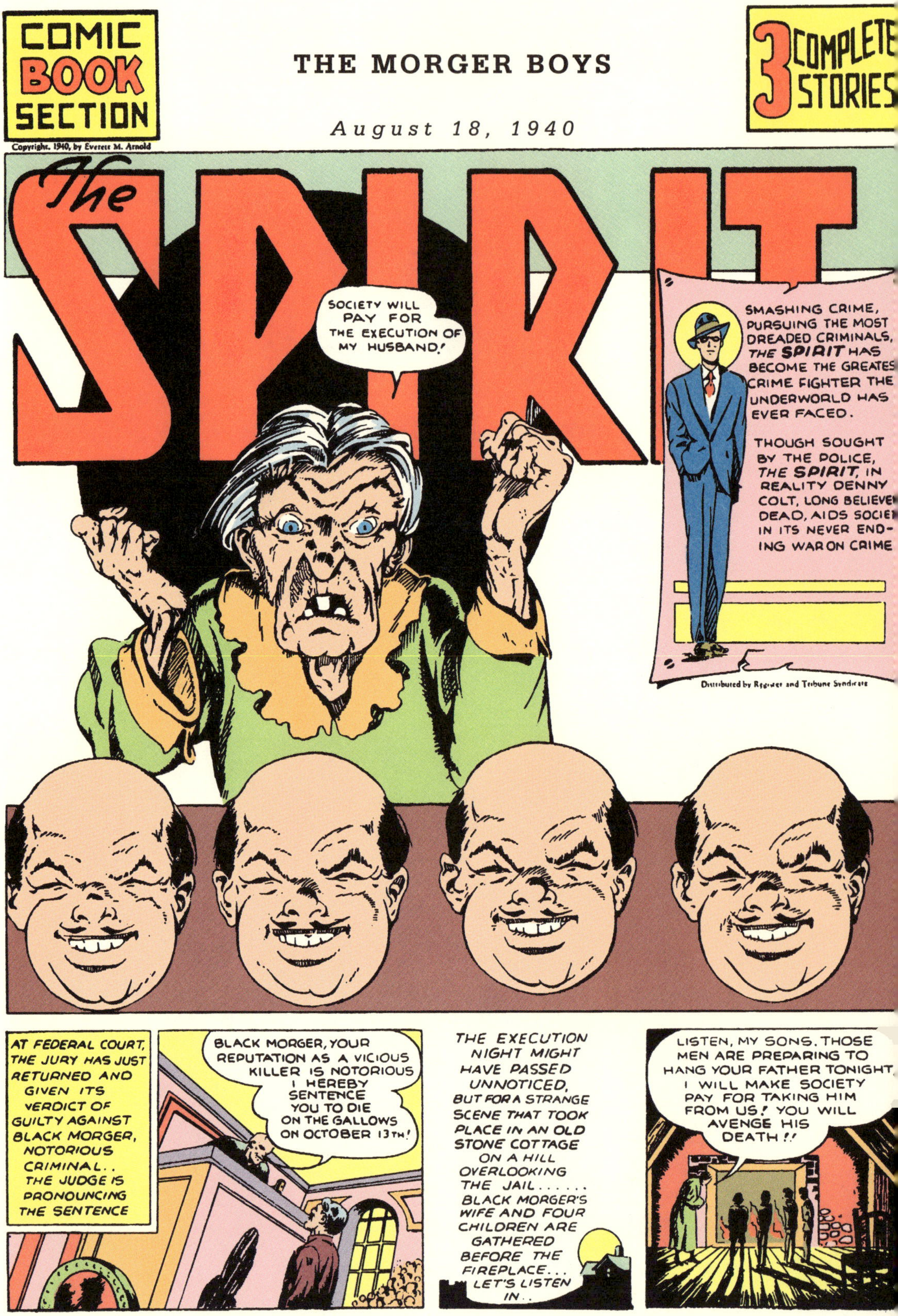

COMIC BOOK SECTION
Copyright, 1940, by Everett M. Arnold
3 COMPLETE STORIES
The SPIRIT
SOCIETY WILL PAY FOR THE EXECUTION OF MY HUSBAND!
SMASHING CRIME, PURSUING THE MOST DREADED CRIMINALS, THE SPIRIT HAS BECOME THE GREATES CRIME FIGHTER THE UNDERWORLD HAS EVER FACED.
THOUGH SOUGHT BY THE POLICE, THE SPIRIT, IN REALITY DENNY COLT, LONG BELIEVE DEAD, AIDS SOCIE IN ITS NEVER ENDING WAR ON CRIME
Distributed by Register and Tribune Syndicate
AT FEDERAL COURT, THE JURY HAS JUST RETURNED AND GIVEN ITS VERDICT OF GUILTY AGAINST BLACK MORGER, NOTORIOUS CRIMINAL.. THE JUDGE IS PRONOUNCING THE SENTENCE
BLACK MORGER, YOUR REPUTATION AS A VICIOUS KILLER IS NOTORIOUS I HEREBY SENTENCE YOU TO DIE ON THE GALLOWS ON OCTOBER 13TH!
THE EXECUTION NIGHT MIGHT HAVE PASSED UNNOTICED, BUT FOR A STRANGE SCENE THAT TOOK PLACE IN AN OLD STONE COTTAGE ON A HILL OVERLOOKING THE JAIL..... BLACK MORGER'S WIFE AND FOUR CHILDREN ARE GATHERED BEFORE THE FIREPLACE... LET'S LISTEN IN..
LISTEN, MY SONS. THOSE MEN ARE PREPARING TO HANG YOUR FATHER TONIGHT. I WILL MAKE SOCIETY PAY FOR TAKING HIM FROM US! YOU WILL AVENGE HIS DEATH!!

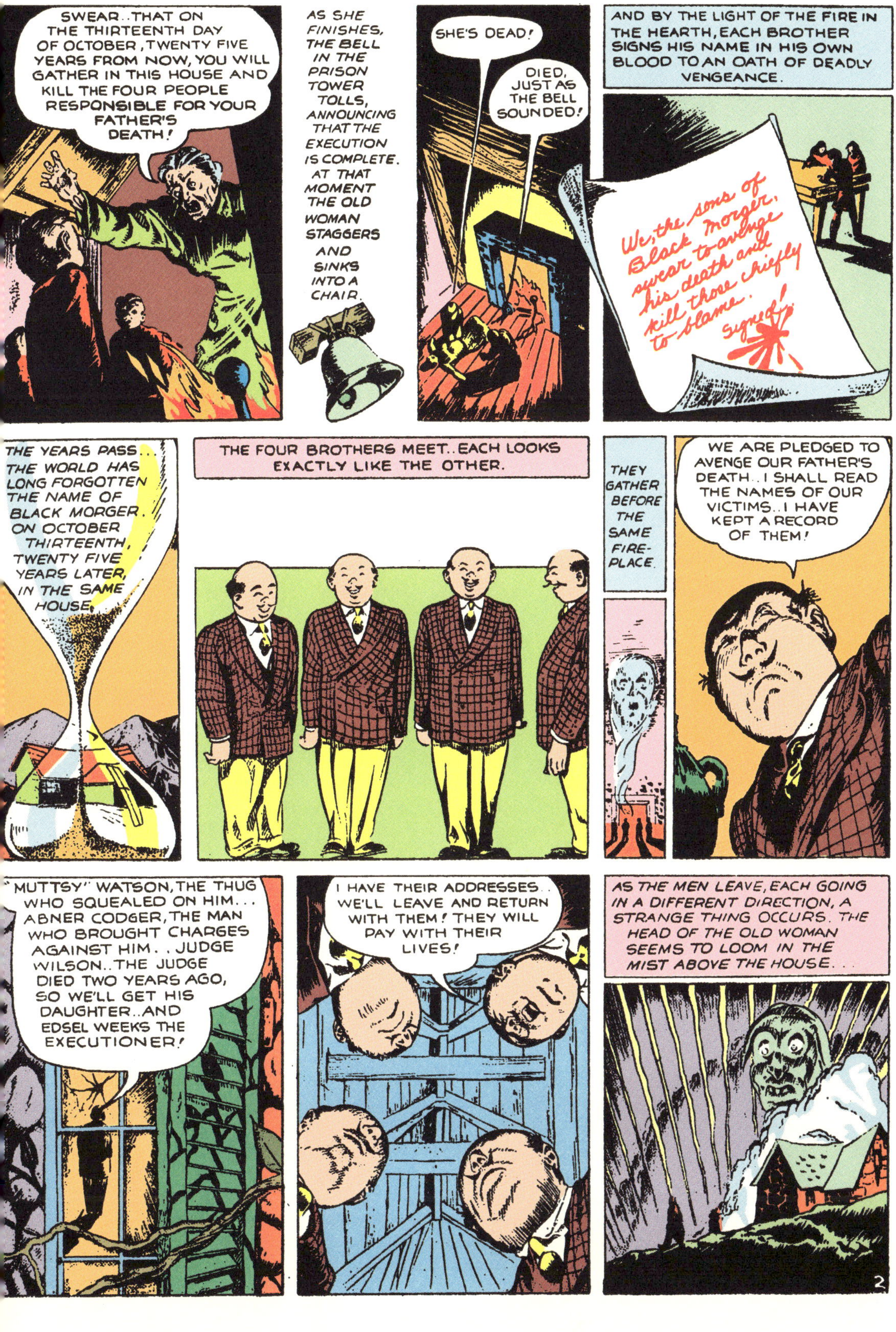

SWEAR..THAT ON THE THIRTEENTH DAY OF OCTOBER, TWENTY FIVE YEARS FROM NOW, YOU WILL GATHER IN THIS HOUSE AND KILL THE FOUR PEOPLE RESPONSIBLE FOR YOUR FATHER'S DEATH!
AS SHE FINISHES, THE BELL IN THE PRISON TOWER TOLLS, ANNOUNCING THAT THE EXECUTION IS COMPLETE. AT THAT MOMENT THE OLD WOMAN STAGGERS AND SINKS INTO A CHAIR.
SHE'S DEAD!
DIED, JUST AS THE BELL SOUNDED!
AND BY THE LIGHT OF THE FIRE IN THE HEARTH, EACH BROTHER SIGNS HIS NAME IN HIS OWN BLOOD TO AN OATH OF DEADLY VENGEANCE.
We, the sons of Black Morger, swear to avenge his death and kill those chiefly to blame.
Signed!
THE YEARS PASS.. THE WORLD HAS LONG FORGOTTEN THE NAME OF BLACK MORGER. ON OCTOBER THIRTEENTH, TWENTY FIVE YEARS LATER, IN THE SAME HOUSE..
THE FOUR BROTHERS MEET..EACH LOOKS EXACTLY LIKE THE OTHER.
THEY GATHER BEFORE THE SAME FIRE-PLACE.
WE ARE PLEDGED TO AVENGE OUR FATHER'S DEATH..I SHALL READ THE NAMES OF OUR VICTIMS..I HAVE KEPT A RECORD OF THEM!
"MUTTSY" WATSON, THE THUG WHO SQUEALED ON HIM... ABNER CODGER, THE MAN WHO BROUGHT CHARGES AGAINST HIM.. JUDGE WILSON..THE JUDGE DIED TWO YEARS AGO, SO WE'LL GET HIS DAUGHTER..AND EDSEL WEEKS THE EXECUTIONER!
I HAVE THEIR ADDRESSES.. WE'LL LEAVE AND RETURN WITH THEM! THEY WILL PAY WITH THEIR LIVES!
AS THE MEN LEAVE, EACH GOING IN A DIFFERENT DIRECTION, A STRANGE THING OCCURS. THE HEAD OF THE OLD WOMAN SEEMS TO LOOM IN THE MIST ABOVE THE HOUSE...
2

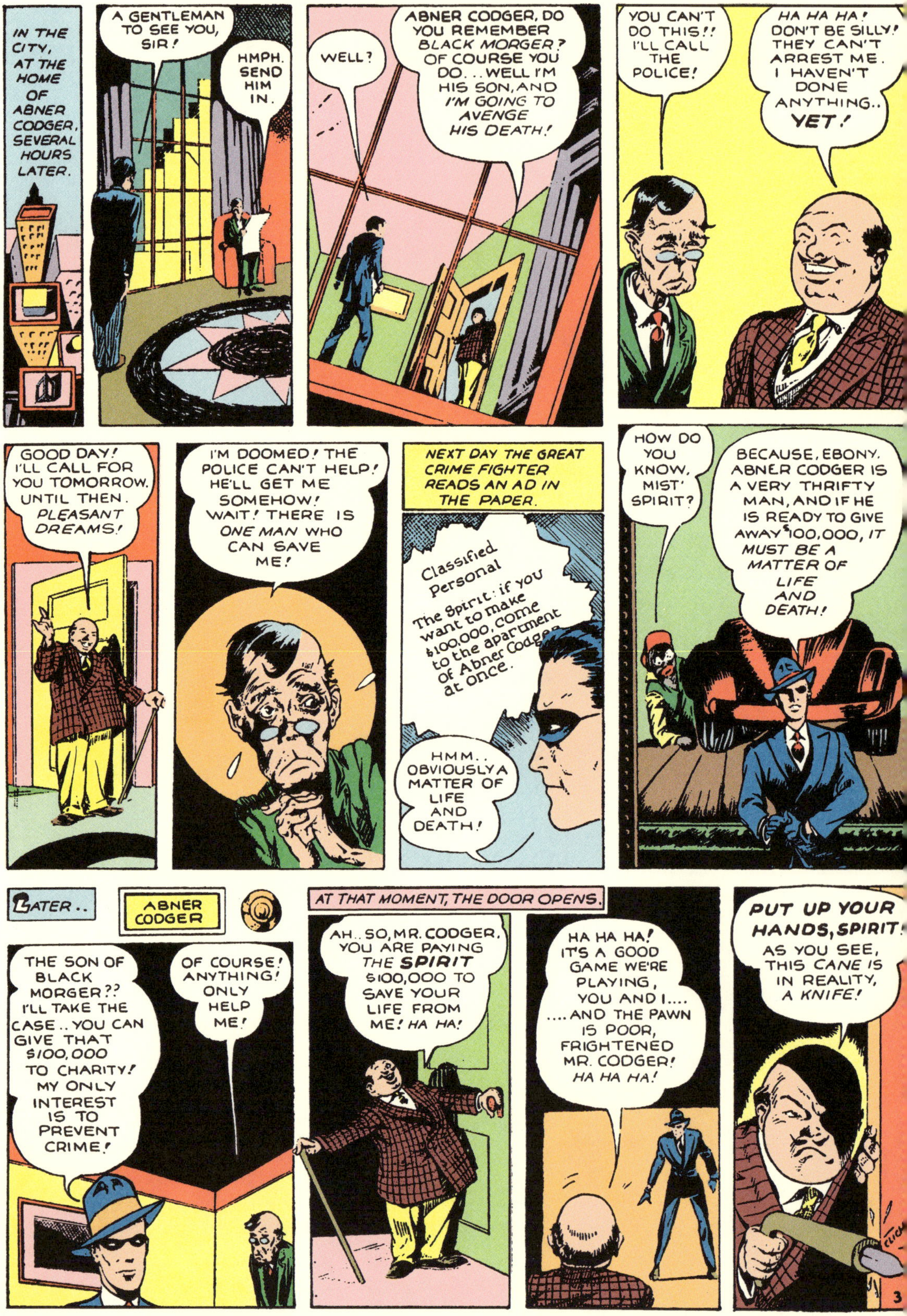
IN THE CITY, AT THE HOME OF ABNER CODGER, SEVERAL HOURS LATER.
A GENTLEMAN TO SEE YOU, SIR!
HMPH. SEND HIM IN.
WELL?
ABNER CODGER, DO YOU REMEMBER BLACK MORGER? OF COURSE YOU DO... WELL I'M HIS SON, AND I'M GOING TO AVENGE HIS DEATH!
YOU CAN'T DO THIS!! I'LL CALL THE POLICE!
HA HA HA! DON'T BE SILLY! THEY CAN'T ARREST ME. I HAVEN'T DONE ANYTHING.. YET!
GOOD DAY! I'LL CALL FOR YOU TOMORROW. UNTIL THEN. PLEASANT DREAMS!
I'M DOOMED! THE POLICE CAN'T HELP! HE'LL GET ME SOMEHOW! WAIT! THERE IS ONE MAN WHO CAN SAVE ME!
NEXT DAY THE GREAT CRIME FIGHTER READS AN AD IN THE PAPER.
Classified Personal
The Spirit: if you want to make $100,000, come to the apartment of Abner Codger at once.
HMM.. OBVIOUSLY A MATTER OF LIFE AND DEATH!
HOW DO YOU KNOW, MIST' SPIRIT?
BECAUSE, EBONY, ABNER CODGER IS A VERY THRIFTY MAN, AND IF HE IS READY TO GIVE AWAY $100,000, IT MUST BE A MATTER OF LIFE AND DEATH!
LATER..
ABNER CODGER
THE SON OF BLACK MORGER?? I'LL TAKE THE CASE.. YOU CAN GIVE THAT $100,000 TO CHARITY! MY ONLY INTEREST IS TO PREVENT CRIME!
OF COURSE! ANYTHING! ONLY HELP ME!
AT THAT MOMENT, THE DOOR OPENS.
AH.. SO, MR. CODGER, YOU ARE PAYING THE SPIRIT $100,000 TO SAVE YOUR LIFE FROM ME! HA HA!
HA HA HA! IT'S A GOOD GAME WE'RE PLAYING, YOU AND I.... ....AND THE PAWN IS POOR, FRIGHTENED MR. CODGER! HA HA HA!
PUT UP YOUR HANDS, SPIRIT! AS YOU SEE, THIS CANE IS IN REALITY, A KNIFE!
CLICK
3

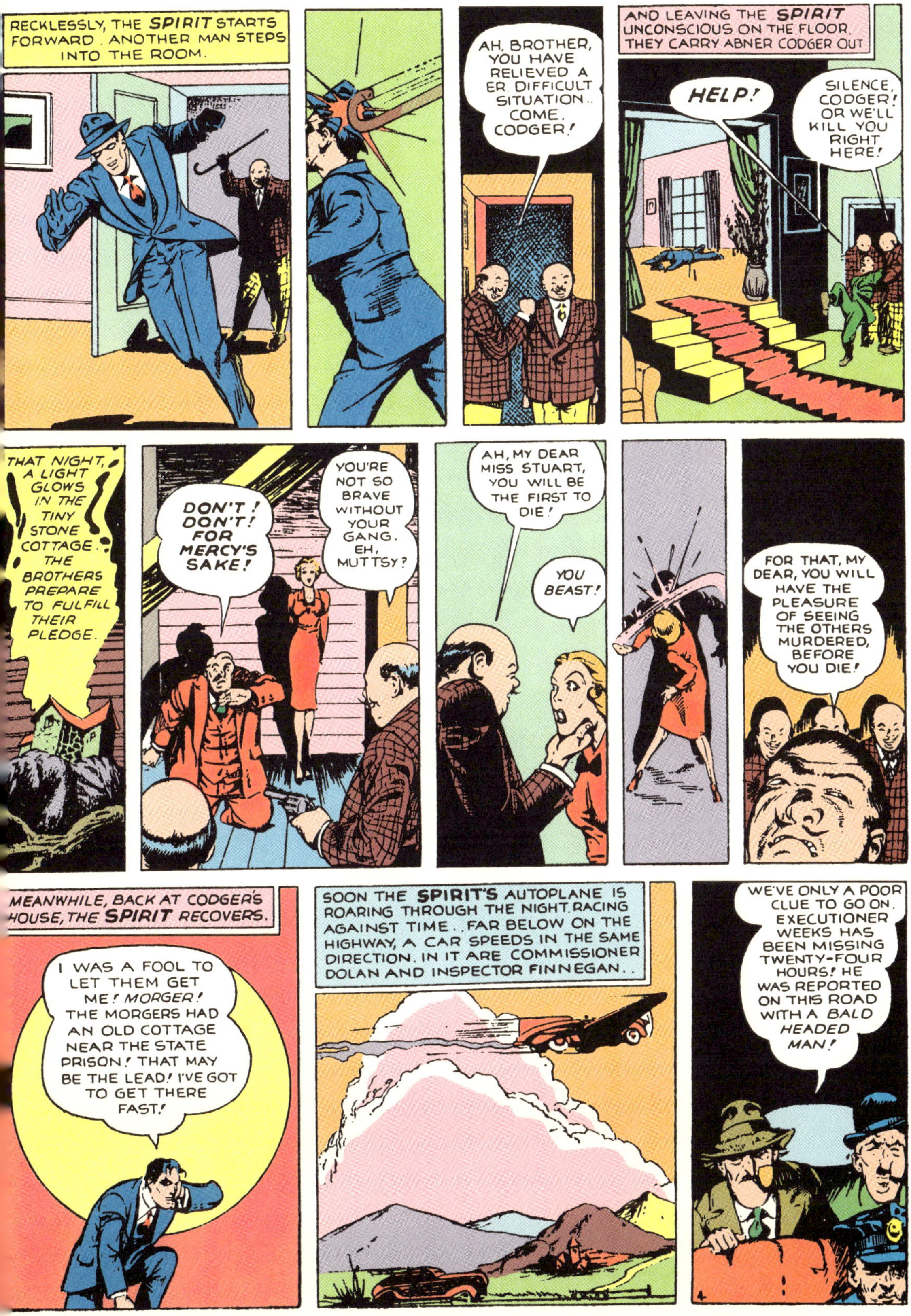
RECKLESSLY, THE SPIRIT STARTS FORWARD. ANOTHER MAN STEPS INTO THE ROOM.
AH, BROTHER, YOU HAVE RELIEVED A ER. DIFFICULT SITUATION.. COME, CODGER!
AND LEAVING THE SPIRIT UNCONSCIOUS ON THE FLOOR, THEY CARRY ABNER CODGER OUT
HELP!
SILENCE, CODGER! OR WE'LL KILL YOU RIGHT HERE!
THAT NIGHT, A LIGHT GLOWS IN THE TINY STONE COTTAGE. THE BROTHERS PREPARE TO FULFILL THEIR PLEDGE.
DON'T! DON'T! FOR MERCY'S SAKE!
YOU'RE NOT SO BRAVE WITHOUT YOUR GANG, EH, MUTTSY?
AH, MY DEAR MISS STUART, YOU WILL BE THE FIRST TO DIE!
YOU BEAST!
FOR THAT, MY DEAR, YOU WILL HAVE THE PLEASURE OF SEEING THE OTHERS MURDERED, BEFORE YOU DIE!
MEANWHILE, BACK AT CODGER'S HOUSE, THE SPIRIT RECOVERS.
I WAS A FOOL TO LET THEM GET ME! MORGER! THE MORGERS HAD AN OLD COTTAGE NEAR THE STATE PRISON! THAT MAY BE THE LEAD! I'VE GOT TO GET THERE FAST!
SOON THE SPIRIT'S AUTOPLANE IS ROARING THROUGH THE NIGHT, RACING AGAINST TIME.. FAR BELOW ON THE HIGHWAY, A CAR SPEEDS IN THE SAME DIRECTION. IN IT ARE COMMISSIONER DOLAN AND INSPECTOR FINNEGAN..
WE'VE ONLY A POOR CLUE TO GO ON. EXECUTIONER WEEKS HAS BEEN MISSING TWENTY-FOUR HOURS! HE WAS REPORTED ON THIS ROAD WITH A BALD HEADED MAN!

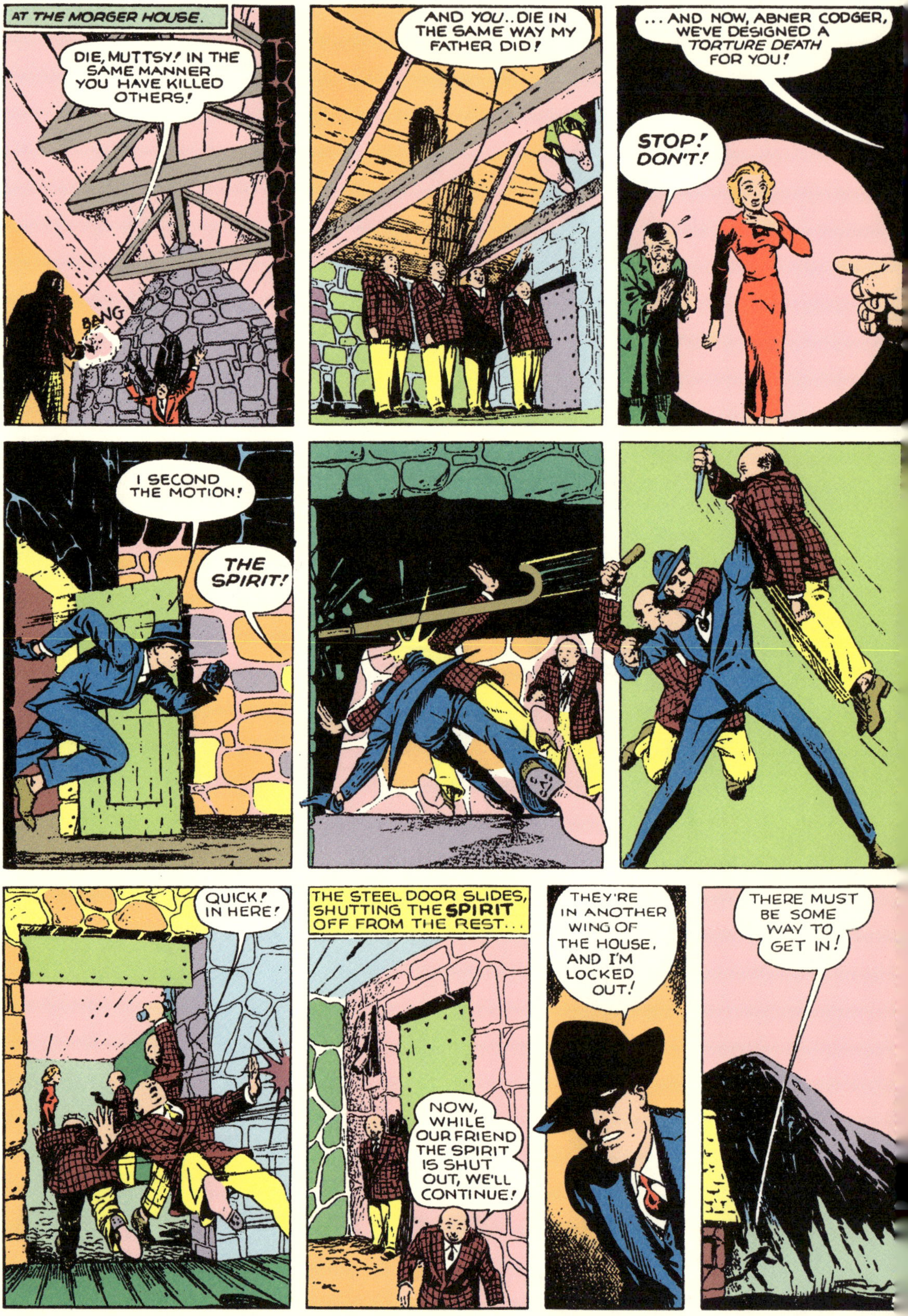
AT THE MORGER HOUSE.
DIE, MUTTSY! IN THE SAME MANNER YOU HAVE KILLED OTHERS!
BANG
AND YOU..DIE IN THE SAME WAY MY FATHER DID!
... AND NOW, ABNER CODGER, WE'VE DESIGNED A TORTURE DEATH FOR YOU!
STOP! DON'T!
I SECOND THE MOTION!
THE SPIRIT!
QUICK! IN HERE!
THE STEEL DOOR SLIDES, SHUTTING THE SPIRIT OFF FROM THE REST...
NOW, WHILE OUR FRIEND THE SPIRIT IS SHUT OUT, WE'LL CONTINUE!
THEY'RE IN ANOTHER WING OF THE HOUSE, AND I'M LOCKED OUT!
THERE MUST BE SOME WAY TO GET IN!

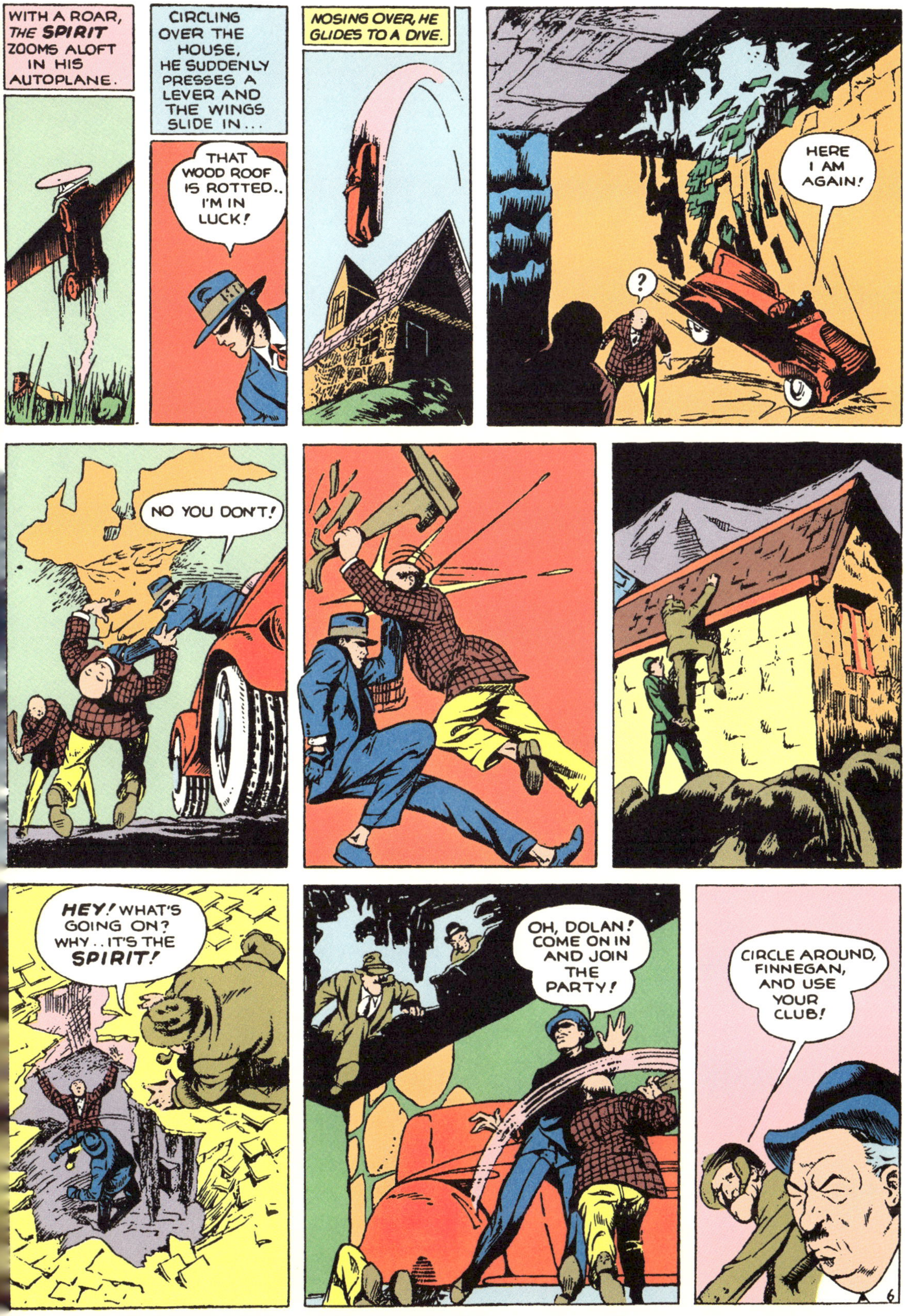
WITH A ROAR, THE SPIRIT ZOOMS ALOFT IN HIS AUTOPLANE.
CIRCLING OVER THE HOUSE, HE SUDDENLY PRESSES A LEVER AND THE WINGS SLIDE IN...
THAT WOOD ROOF IS ROTTED.. I'M IN LUCK!
NOSING OVER, HE GLIDES TO A DIVE.
?
HERE I AM AGAIN!
NO YOU DON'T!
HEY! WHAT'S GOING ON? WHY..IT'S THE SPIRIT!
OH, DOLAN! COME ON IN AND JOIN THE PARTY!
CIRCLE AROUND, FINNEGAN, AND USE YOUR CLUB!
6

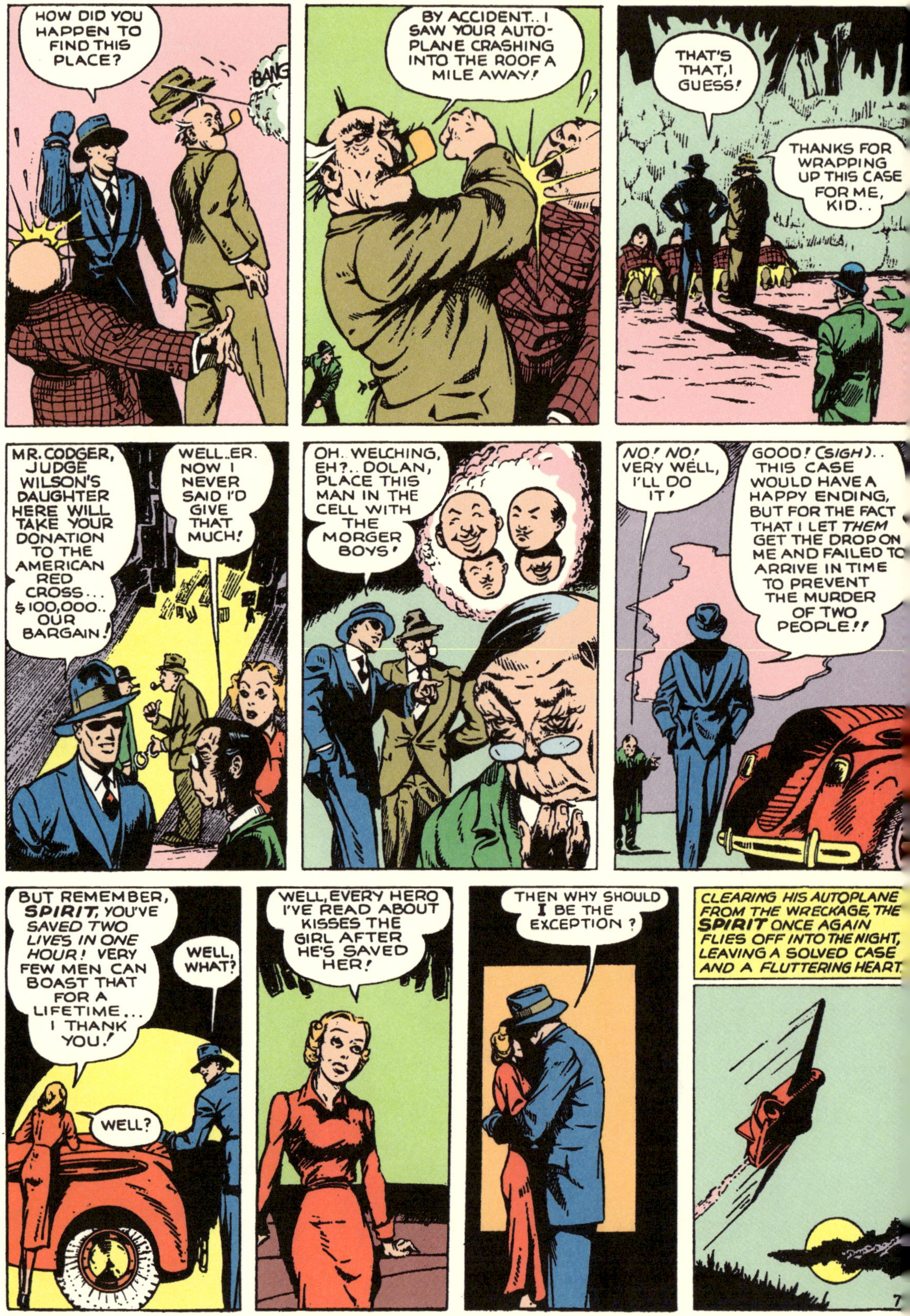
HOW DID YOU HAPPEN TO FIND THIS PLACE?
BANG
BY ACCIDENT.. I SAW YOUR AUTO-PLANE CRASHING INTO THE ROOF A MILE AWAY!
THAT'S THAT, I GUESS!
THANKS FOR WRAPPING UP THIS CASE FOR ME, KID..
MR. CODGER, JUDGE WILSON'S DAUGHTER HERE WILL TAKE YOUR DONATION TO THE AMERICAN RED CROSS... $100,000.. OUR BARGAIN!
WELL..ER. NOW I NEVER SAID I'D GIVE THAT MUCH!
OH.. WELCHING, EH?.. DOLAN, PLACE THIS MAN IN THE CELL WITH THE MORGER BOYS!
NO! NO! VERY WELL, I'LL DO IT!
GOOD! (SIGH).. THIS CASE WOULD HAVE A HAPPY ENDING, BUT FOR THE FACT THAT I LET THEM GET THE DROP ON ME AND FAILED TO ARRIVE IN TIME TO PREVENT THE MURDER OF TWO PEOPLE!!
BUT REMEMBER, SPIRIT, YOU'VE SAVED TWO LIVES IN ONE HOUR! VERY FEW MEN CAN BOAST THAT FOR A LIFETIME... I THANK YOU!
WELL, WHAT?
WELL?
WELL, EVERY HERO I'VE READ ABOUT KISSES THE GIRL AFTER HE'S SAVED HER!
THEN WHY SHOULD I BE THE EXCEPTION ?
CLEARING HIS AUTOPLANE FROM THE WRECKAGE, THE SPIRIT ONCE AGAIN FLIES OFF INTO THE NIGHT, LEAVING A SOLVED CASE AND A FLUTTERING HEART.
7

THE ORPHANS

August 25, 1940

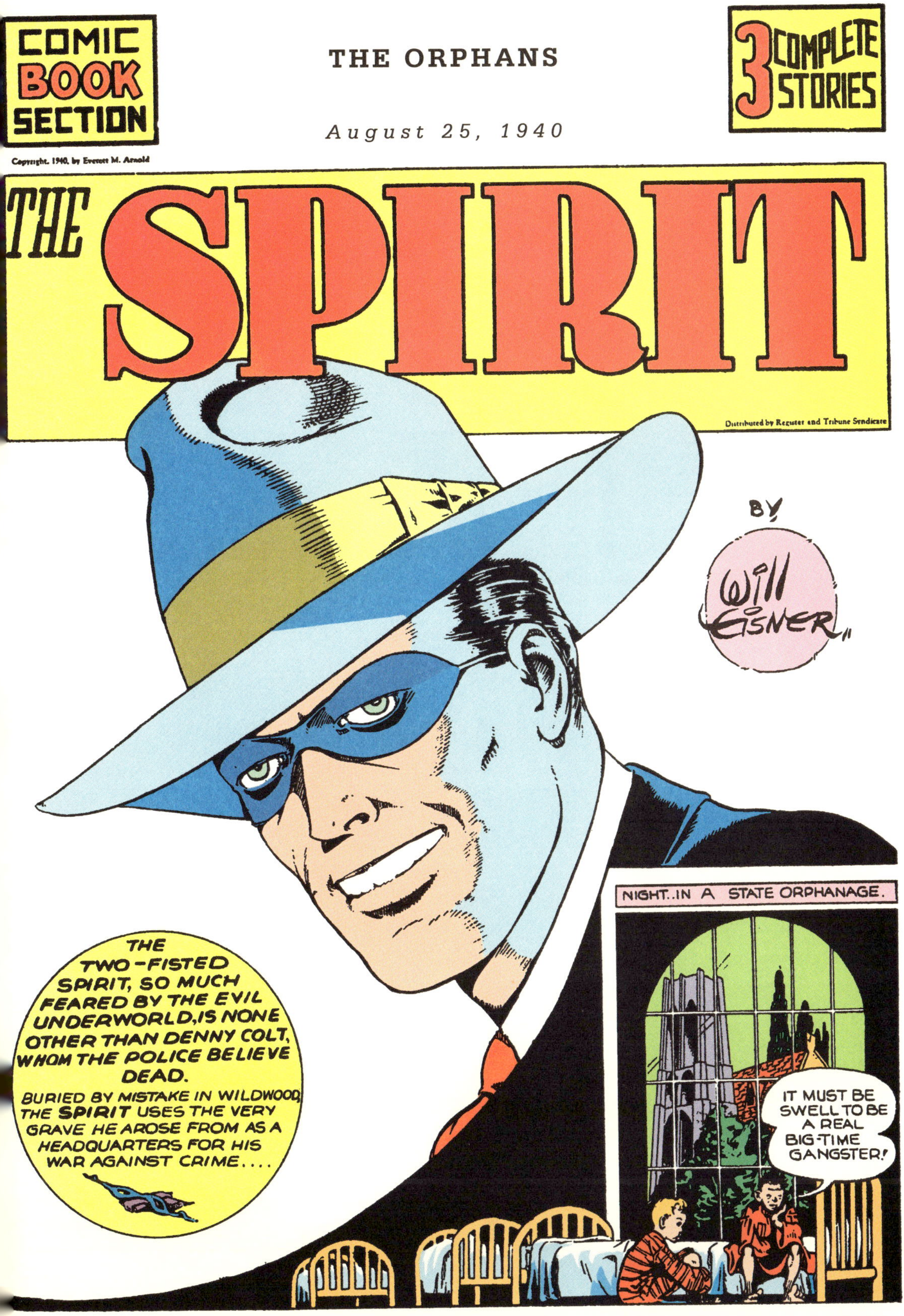

COMIC BOOK SECTION
Copyright, 1940, by Everett M. Arnold
3 COMPLETE STORIES
THE SPIRIT
Distributed by Register and Tribune Syndicate
BY Will Eisner
THE TWO-FISTED SPIRIT, SO MUCH FEARED BY THE EVIL UNDERWORLD, IS NONE OTHER THAN DENNY COLT, WHOM THE POLICE BELIEVE DEAD.
BURIED BY MISTAKE IN WILDWOOD, THE SPIRIT USES THE VERY GRAVE HE AROSE FROM AS A HEADQUARTERS FOR HIS WAR AGAINST CRIME....
NIGHT..IN A STATE ORPHANAGE.
IT MUST BE SWELL TO BE A REAL BIG-TIME GANGSTER!

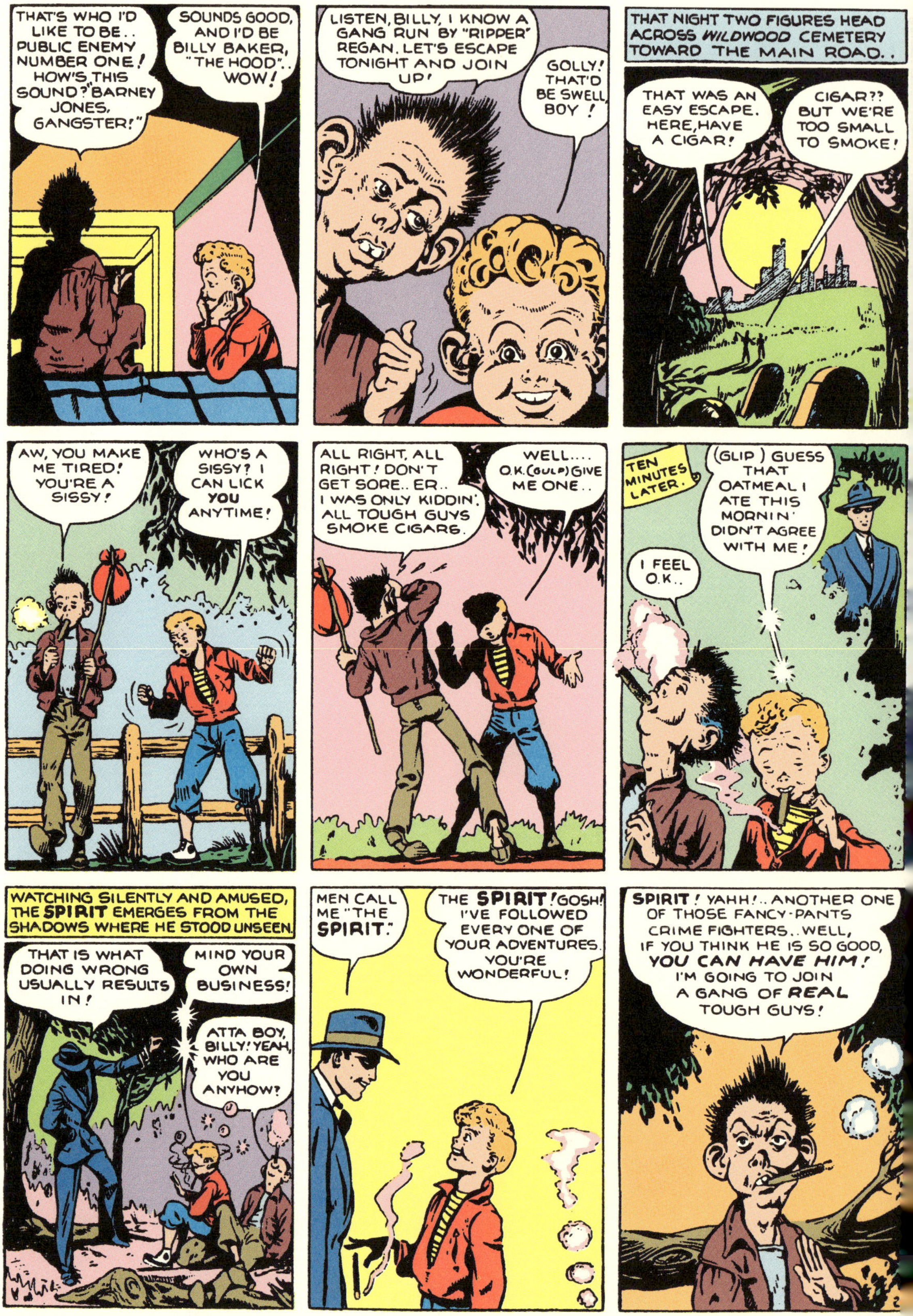
THAT'S WHO I'D LIKE TO BE.. PUBLIC ENEMY NUMBER ONE! HOW'S THIS SOUND? "BARNEY JONES, GANGSTER!"
SOUNDS GOOD, AND I'D BE BILLY BAKER, "THE HOOD".. WOW!
LISTEN, BILLY, I KNOW A GANG RUN BY "RIPPER" REGAN. LET'S ESCAPE TONIGHT AND JOIN UP!
GOLLY! THAT'D BE SWELL, BOY!
THAT NIGHT TWO FIGURES HEAD ACROSS WILDWOOD CEMETERY TOWARD THE MAIN ROAD..
THAT WAS AN EASY ESCAPE. HERE, HAVE A CIGAR!
CIGAR?? BUT WE'RE TOO SMALL TO SMOKE!
AW, YOU MAKE ME TIRED! YOU'RE A SISSY!
WHO'S A SISSY? I CAN LICK YOU ANYTIME!
ALL RIGHT, ALL RIGHT! DON'T GET SORE.. ER.. I WAS ONLY KIDDIN'. ALL TOUGH GUYS SMOKE CIGARS.
WELL.... O.K. (GULP) GIVE ME ONE..
TEN MINUTES LATER.
(GLIP) GUESS THAT OATMEAL I ATE THIS MORNIN' DIDN'T AGREE WITH ME!
I FEEL O.K..
WATCHING SILENTLY AND AMUSED, THE SPIRIT EMERGES FROM THE SHADOWS WHERE HE STOOD UNSEEN.
THAT IS WHAT DOING WRONG USUALLY RESULTS IN!
MIND YOUR OWN BUSINESS!
ATTA BOY, BILLY! YEAH, WHO ARE YOU ANYHOW?
MEN CALL ME "THE SPIRIT."
THE SPIRIT! GOSH! I'VE FOLLOWED EVERY ONE OF YOUR ADVENTURES. YOU'RE WONDERFUL!
SPIRIT! YAHH!.. ANOTHER ONE OF THOSE FANCY-PANTS CRIME FIGHTERS.. WELL, IF YOU THINK HE IS SO GOOD, YOU CAN HAVE HIM! I'M GOING TO JOIN A GANG OF REAL TOUGH GUYS!

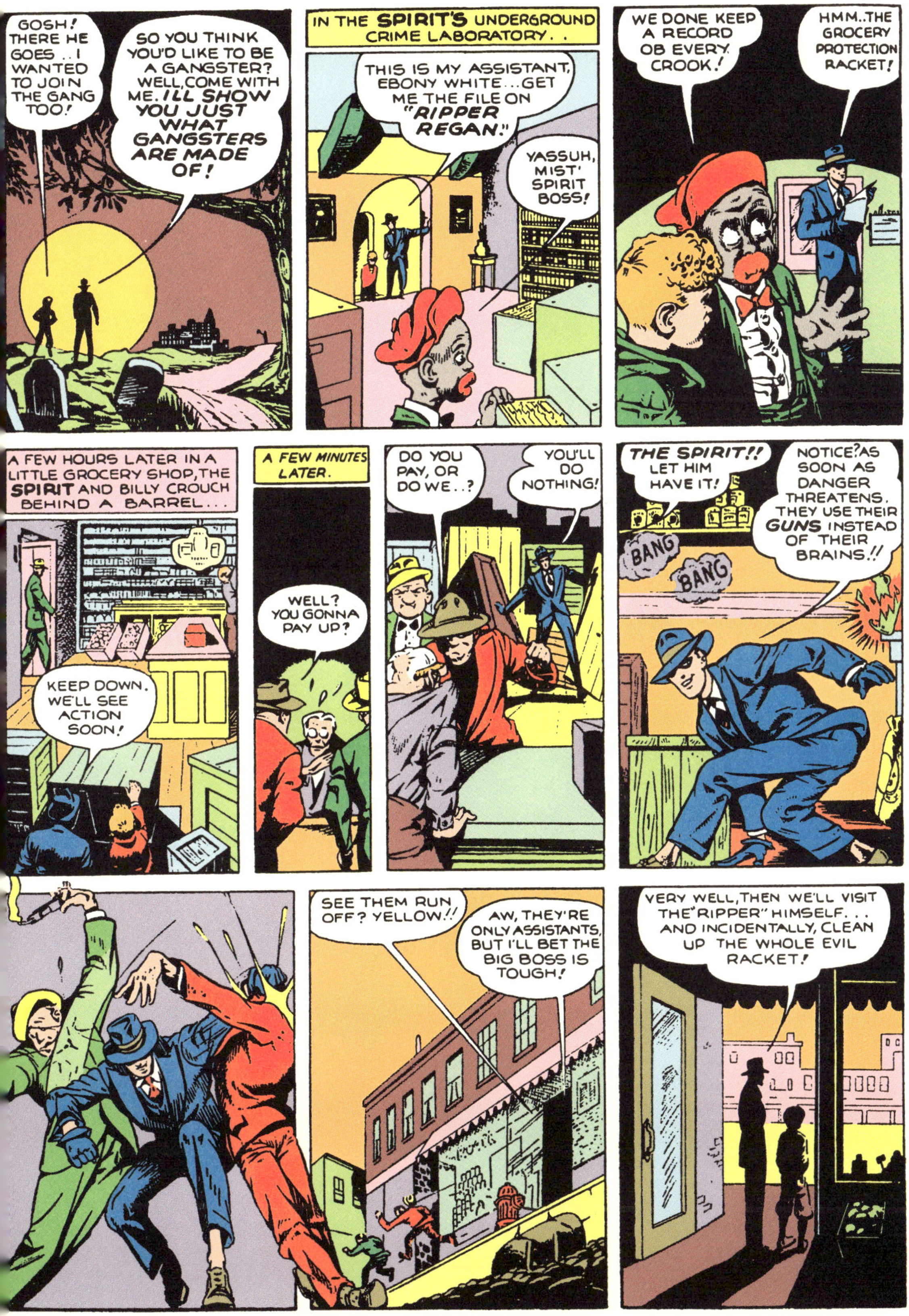
GOSH! THERE HE GOES.. I WANTED TO JOIN THE GANG TOO!
SO YOU THINK YOU'D LIKE TO BE A GANGSTER? WELL, COME WITH ME. I'LL SHOW YOU JUST WHAT GANGSTERS ARE MADE OF!
IN THE SPIRIT'S UNDERGROUND CRIME LABORATORY..
THIS IS MY ASSISTANT, EBONY WHITE... GET ME THE FILE ON "RIPPER REGAN."
YASSUH, MIST' SPIRIT BOSS!
WE DONE KEEP A RECORD OB EVERY CROOK!
HMM..THE GROCERY PROTECTION RACKET!
A FEW HOURS LATER IN A LITTLE GROCERY SHOP, THE SPIRIT AND BILLY CROUCH BEHIND A BARREL...
KEEP DOWN. WE'LL SEE ACTION SOON!
A FEW MINUTES LATER.
WELL? YOU GONNA PAY UP?
DO YOU PAY, OR DO WE..?
YOU'LL DO NOTHING!
THE SPIRIT!! LET HIM HAVE IT!
NOTICE? AS SOON AS DANGER THREATENS, THEY USE THEIR GUNS INSTEAD OF THEIR BRAINS!!
BANG
BANG
SEE THEM RUN OFF? YELLOW!!
AW, THEY'RE ONLY ASSISTANTS, BUT I'LL BET THE BIG BOSS IS TOUGH!
VERY WELL, THEN WE'LL VISIT THE "RIPPER" HIMSELF... AND INCIDENTALLY, CLEAN UP THE WHOLE EVIL RACKET!

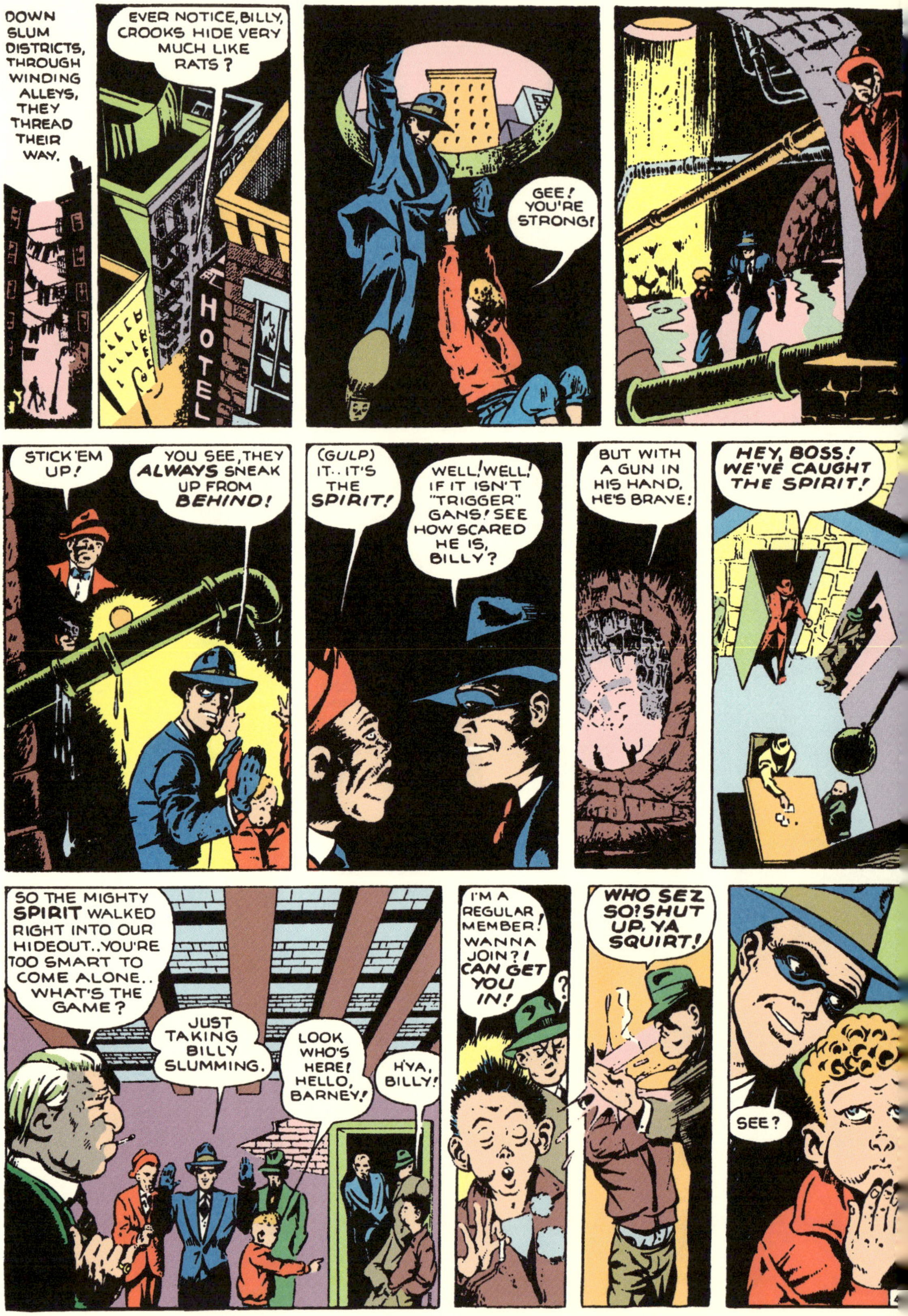
DOWN SLUM DISTRICTS, THROUGH WINDING ALLEYS, THEY THREAD THEIR WAY.
EVER NOTICE, BILLY, CROOKS HIDE VERY MUCH LIKE RATS ?
HOTEL
GEE! YOU'RE STRONG!
STICK 'EM UP!
YOU SEE, THEY ALWAYS SNEAK UP FROM BEHIND!
(GULP) IT.. IT'S THE SPIRIT!
WELL! WELL! IF IT ISN'T "TRIGGER" GANS! SEE HOW SCARED HE IS, BILLY?
BUT WITH A GUN IN HIS HAND, HE'S BRAVE!
HEY, BOSS! WE'VE CAUGHT THE SPIRIT!
SO THE MIGHTY SPIRIT WALKED RIGHT INTO OUR HIDEOUT..YOU'RE TOO SMART TO COME ALONE.. WHAT'S THE GAME?
JUST TAKING BILLY SLUMMING.
LOOK WHO'S HERE! HELLO, BARNEY!
H'YA, BILLY!
I'M A REGULAR MEMBER! WANNA JOIN? I CAN GET YOU IN!
?
WHO SEZ SO! SHUT UP, YA SQUIRT!
SEE?

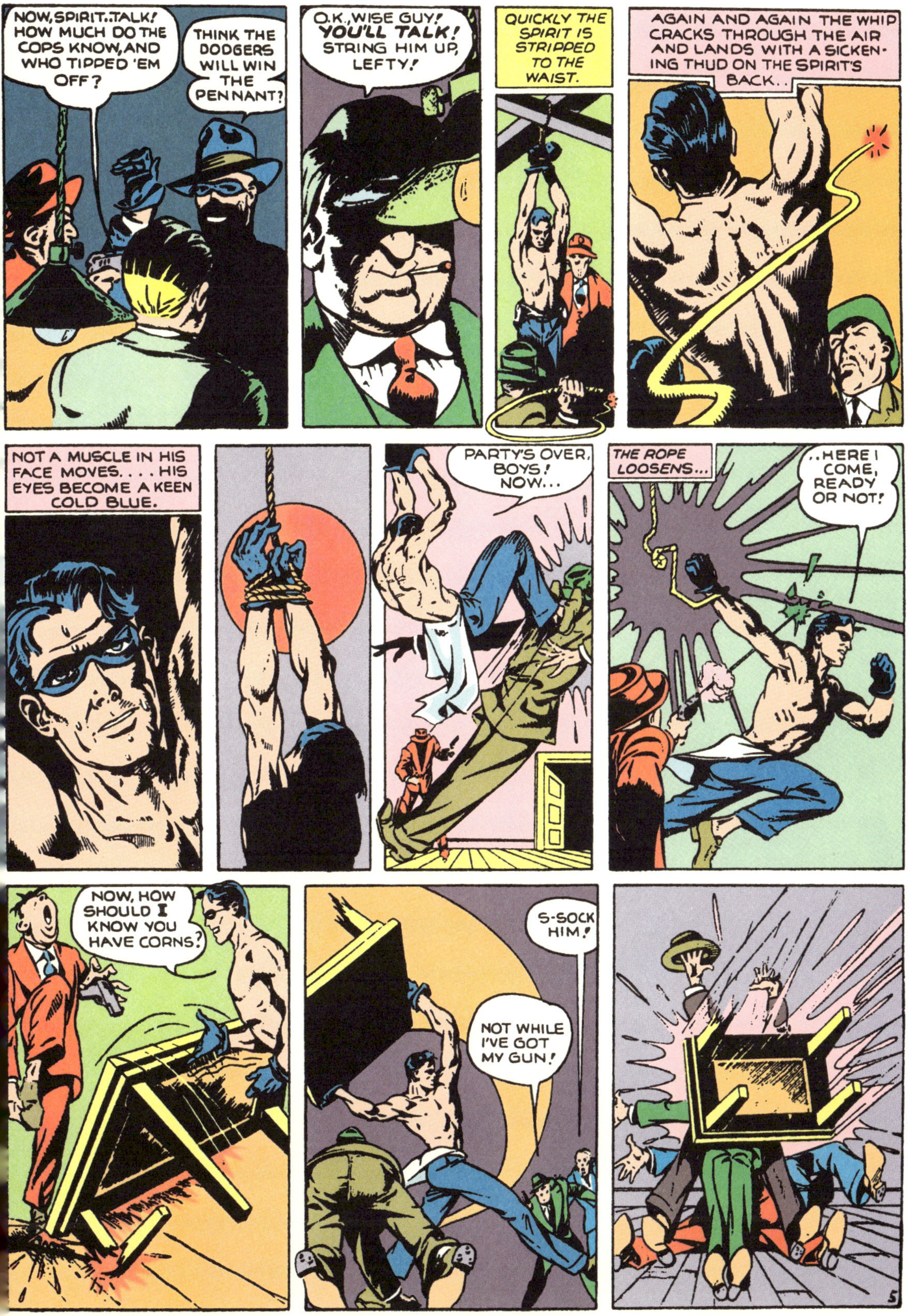

NOW, SPIRIT..TALK! HOW MUCH DO THE COPS KNOW, AND WHO TIPPED 'EM OFF?
THINK THE DODGERS WILL WIN THE PENNANT?
O.K., WISE GUY! YOU'LL TALK! STRING HIM UP, LEFTY!
QUICKLY THE SPIRIT IS STRIPPED TO THE WAIST.
AGAIN AND AGAIN THE WHIP CRACKS THROUGH THE AIR AND LANDS WITH A SICKENING THUD ON THE SPIRIT'S BACK..
NOT A MUSCLE IN HIS FACE MOVES.... HIS EYES BECOME A KEEN COLD BLUE.
PARTY'S OVER, BOYS! NOW...
THE ROPE LOOSENS...
..HERE I COME, READY OR NOT!
NOW, HOW SHOULD I KNOW YOU HAVE CORNS?
S-SOCK HIM!
NOT WHILE I'VE GOT MY GUN!
5

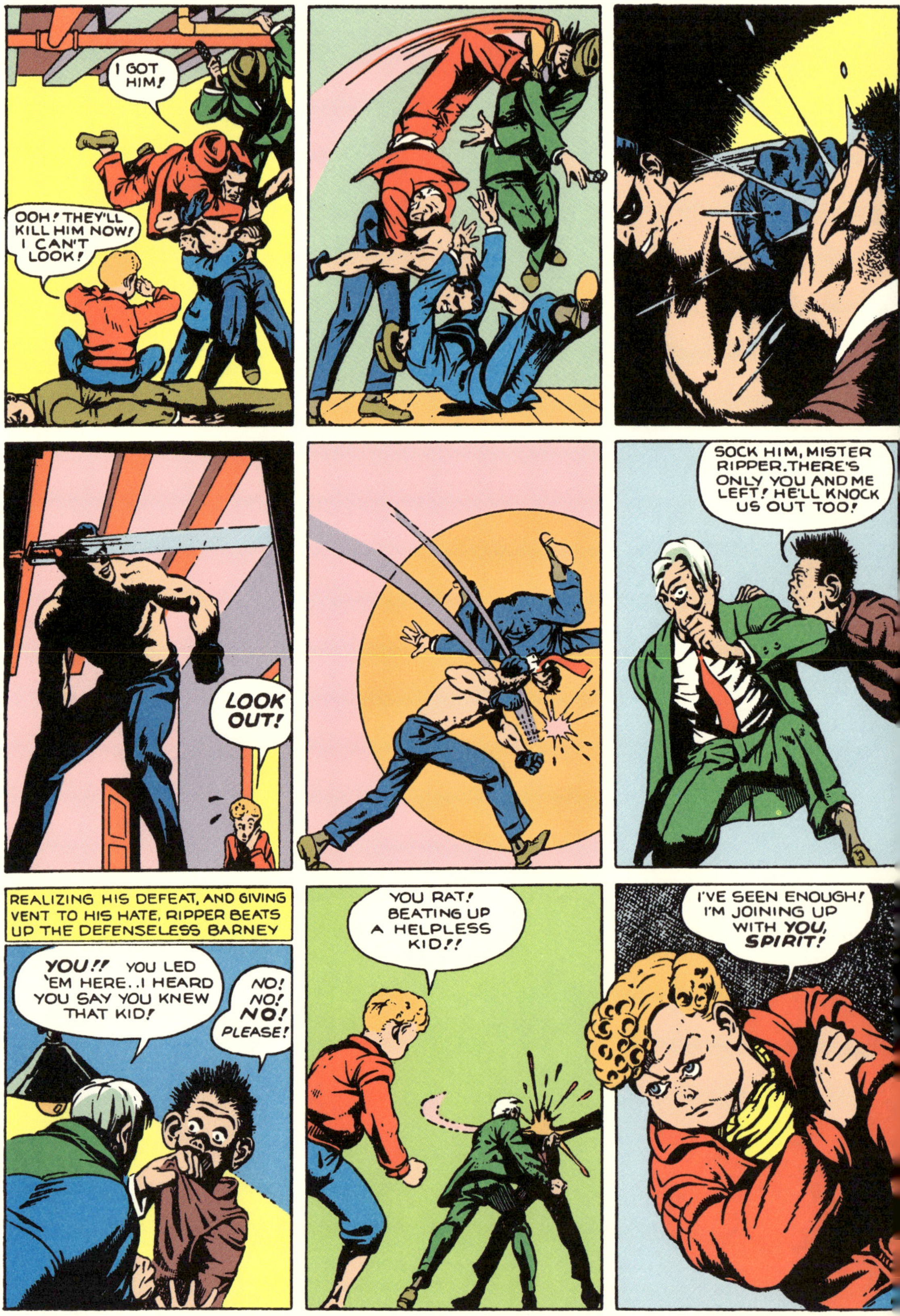
I GOT HIM!
OOH! THEY'LL KILL HIM NOW! I CAN'T LOOK!
LOOK OUT!
SOCK HIM, MISTER RIPPER. THERE'S ONLY YOU AND ME LEFT! HE'LL KNOCK US OUT TOO!
REALIZING HIS DEFEAT, AND GIVING VENT TO HIS HATE, RIPPER BEATS UP THE DEFENSELESS BARNEY
YOU!! YOU LED 'EM HERE..I HEARD YOU SAY YOU KNEW THAT KID!
NO! NO! NO! PLEASE!
YOU RAT! BEATING UP A HELPLESS KID!!
I'VE SEEN ENOUGH! I'M JOINING UP WITH YOU, SPIRIT!

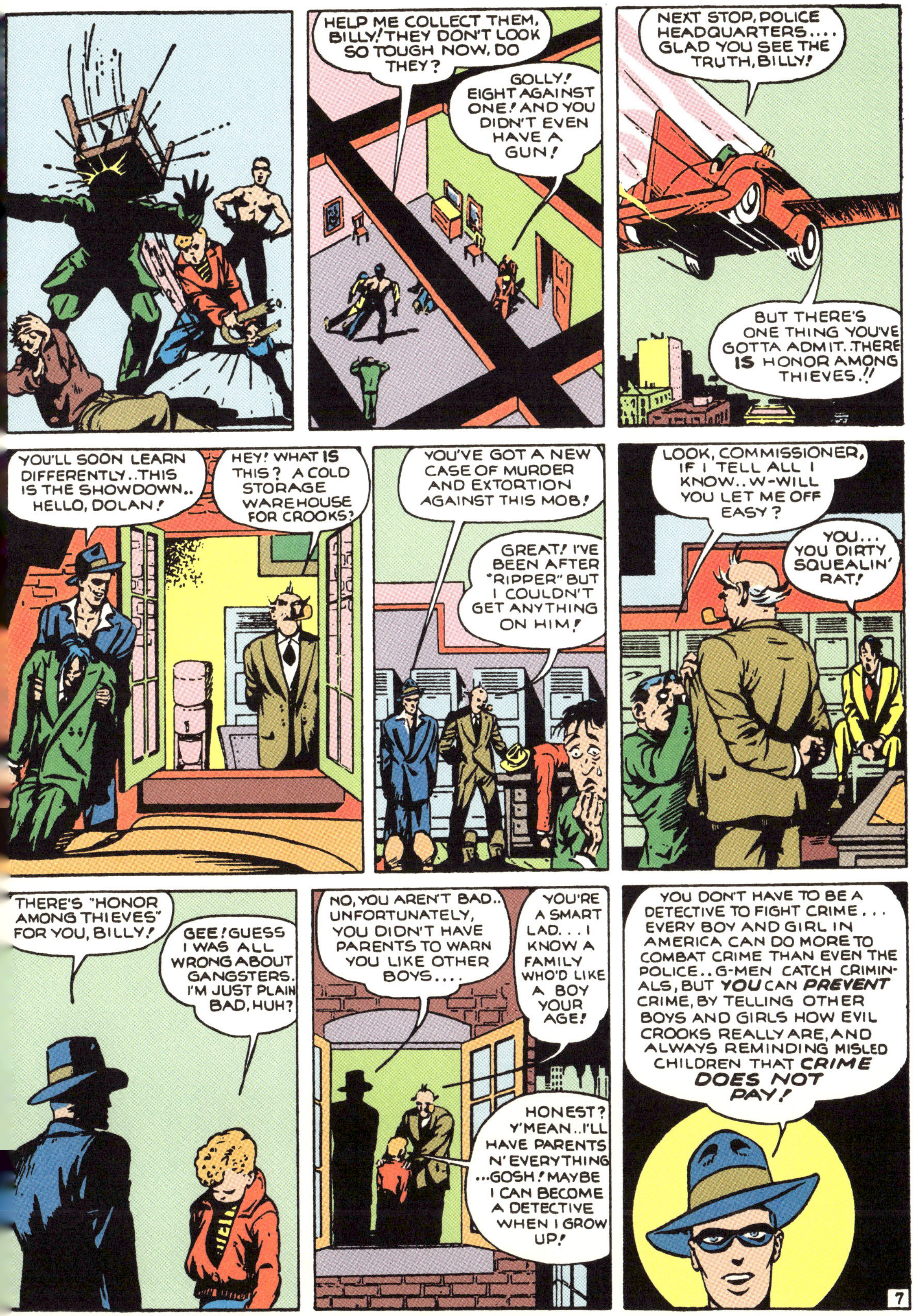
HELP ME COLLECT THEM, BILLY! THEY DON'T LOOK SO TOUGH NOW, DO THEY?
GOLLY! EIGHT AGAINST ONE! AND YOU DIDN'T EVEN HAVE A GUN!
NEXT STOP, POLICE HEADQUARTERS.... GLAD YOU SEE THE TRUTH, BILLY!
BUT THERE'S ONE THING YOU'VE GOTTA ADMIT..THERE IS HONOR AMONG THIEVES.!!
YOU'LL SOON LEARN DIFFERENTLY..THIS IS THE SHOWDOWN.. HELLO, DOLAN!
HEY! WHAT IS THIS? A COLD STORAGE WAREHOUSE FOR CROOKS?
YOU'VE GOT A NEW CASE OF MURDER AND EXTORTION AGAINST THIS MOB!
GREAT! I'VE BEEN AFTER "RIPPER" BUT I COULDN'T GET ANYTHING ON HIM!
LOOK, COMMISSIONER, IF I TELL ALL I KNOW..W-WILL YOU LET ME OFF EASY?
YOU... YOU DIRTY SQUEALIN' RAT!
THERE'S "HONOR AMONG THIEVES" FOR YOU, BILLY!
GEE! GUESS I WAS ALL WRONG ABOUT GANGSTERS. I'M JUST PLAIN BAD, HUH?
NO, YOU AREN'T BAD.. UNFORTUNATELY, YOU DIDN'T HAVE PARENTS TO WARN YOU LIKE OTHER BOYS....
YOU'RE A SMART LAD... I KNOW A FAMILY WHO'D LIKE A BOY YOUR AGE!
HONEST? Y'MEAN..I'LL HAVE PARENTS N' EVERYTHING ...GOSH! MAYBE I CAN BECOME A DETECTIVE WHEN I GROW UP!
YOU DON'T HAVE TO BE A DETECTIVE TO FIGHT CRIME... EVERY BOY AND GIRL IN AMERICA CAN DO MORE TO COMBAT CRIME THAN EVEN THE POLICE.. G-MEN CATCH CRIMINALS, BUT YOU CAN PREVENT CRIME, BY TELLING OTHER BOYS AND GIRLS HOW EVIL CROOKS REALLY ARE, AND ALWAYS REMINDING MISLED CHILDREN THAT CRIME DOES NOT PAY!
7

ORANG, THE APE MAN

September 1, 1940

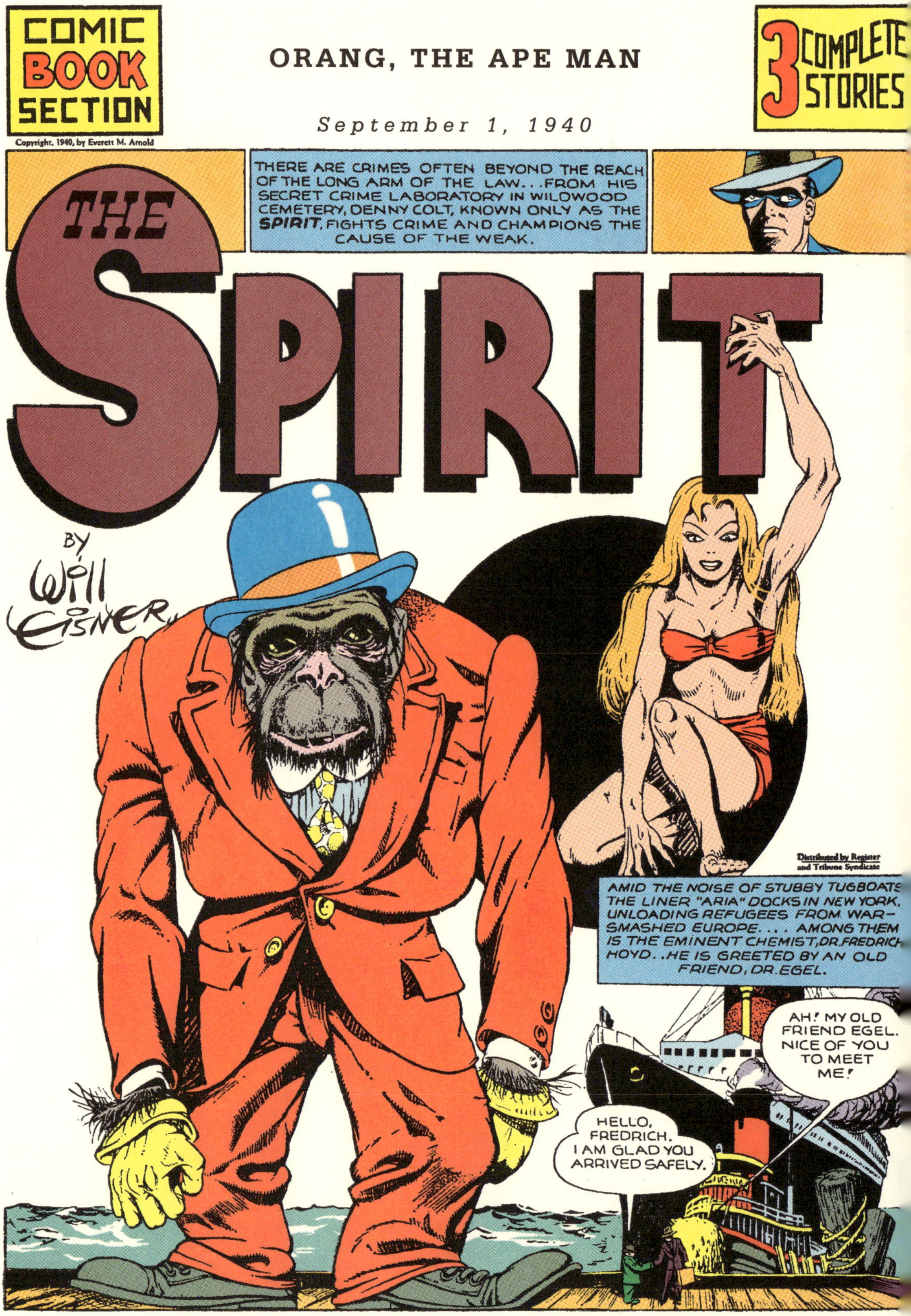

COMIC BOOK SECTION
Copyright, 1940, by Everett M. Arnold
3 COMPLETE STORIES
THERE ARE CRIMES OFTEN BEYOND THE REACH OF THE LONG ARM OF THE LAW...FROM HIS SECRET CRIME LABORATORY IN WILDWOOD CEMETERY, DENNY COLT, KNOWN ONLY AS THE SPIRIT, FIGHTS CRIME AND CHAMPIONS THE CAUSE OF THE WEAK.
THE SPIRIT
BY WILL EISNER
Distributed by Register and Tribune Syndicate
AMID THE NOISE OF STUBBY TUGBOATS THE LINER "ARIA" DOCKS IN NEW YORK, UNLOADING REFUGEES FROM WAR-SMASHED EUROPE.... AMONG THEM IS THE EMINENT CHEMIST, DR. FREDRICH HOYD..HE IS GREETED BY AN OLD FRIEND, DR. EGEL.
AH! MY OLD FRIEND EGEL. NICE OF YOU TO MEET ME!
HELLO, FREDRICH. I AM GLAD YOU ARRIVED SAFELY.

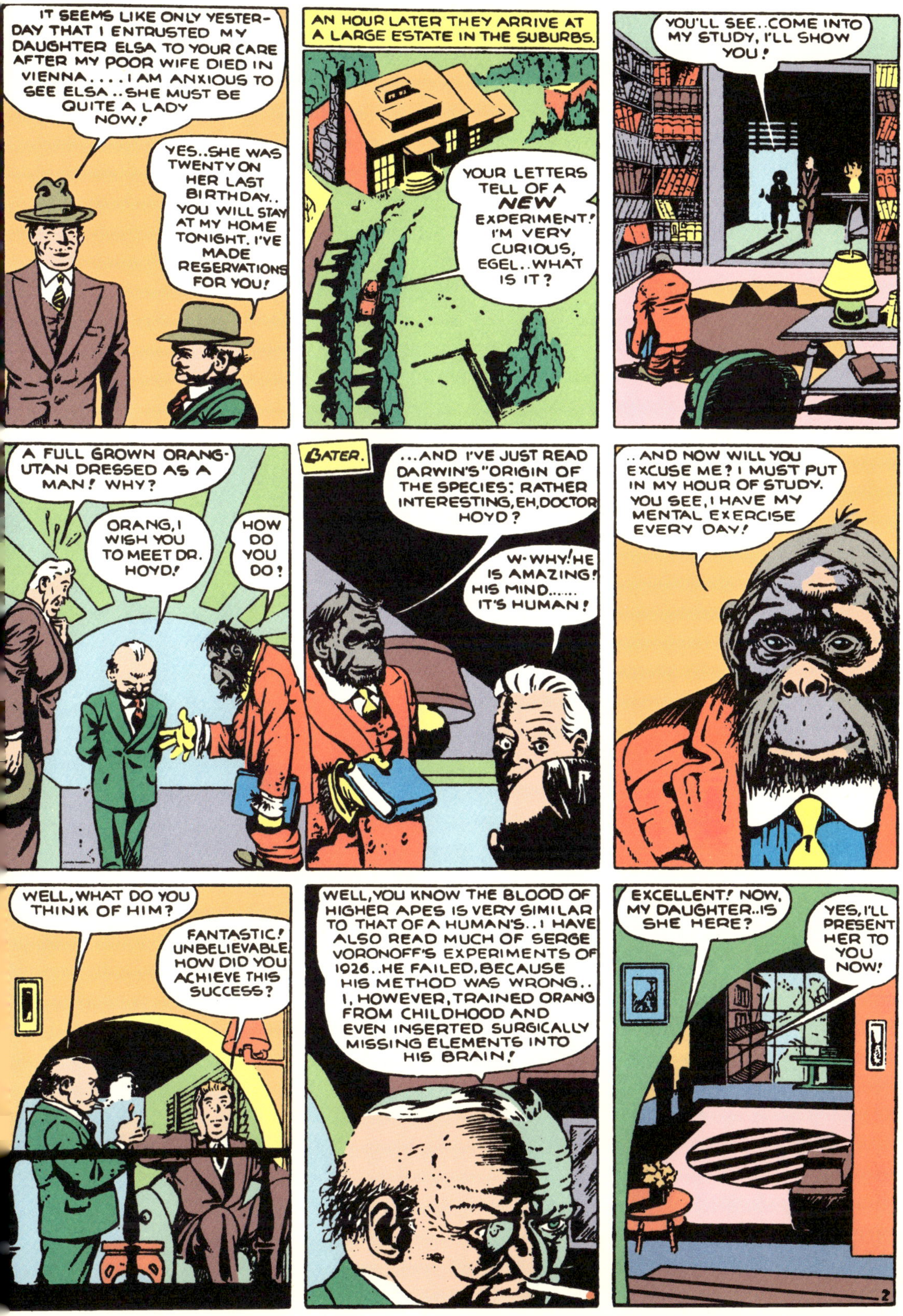
IT SEEMS LIKE ONLY YESTERDAY THAT I ENTRUSTED MY DAUGHTER ELSA TO YOUR CARE AFTER MY POOR WIFE DIED IN VIENNA.... I AM ANXIOUS TO SEE ELSA.. SHE MUST BE QUITE A LADY NOW!
YES..SHE WAS TWENTY ON HER LAST BIRTHDAY.. YOU WILL STAY AT MY HOME TONIGHT. I'VE MADE RESERVATIONS FOR YOU!
AN HOUR LATER THEY ARRIVE AT A LARGE ESTATE IN THE SUBURBS.
YOUR LETTERS TELL OF A NEW EXPERIMENT! I'M VERY CURIOUS, EGEL.. WHAT IS IT?
YOU'LL SEE..COME INTO MY STUDY, I'LL SHOW YOU!
A FULL GROWN ORANG-UTAN DRESSED AS A MAN! WHY?
ORANG, I WISH YOU TO MEET DR. HOYD!
HOW DO YOU DO!
LATER.
...AND I'VE JUST READ DARWIN'S "ORIGIN OF THE SPECIES: RATHER INTERESTING, EH, DOCTOR HOYD?
W-WHY! HE IS AMAZING! HIS MIND...... IT'S HUMAN!
..AND NOW WILL YOU EXCUSE ME? I MUST PUT IN MY HOUR OF STUDY. YOU SEE, I HAVE MY MENTAL EXERCISE EVERY DAY!
WELL, WHAT DO YOU THINK OF HIM?
FANTASTIC! UNBELIEVABLE. HOW DID YOU ACHIEVE THIS SUCCESS?
WELL, YOU KNOW THE BLOOD OF HIGHER APES IS VERY SIMILAR TO THAT OF A HUMAN'S.. I HAVE ALSO READ MUCH OF SERGE VORONOFF'S EXPERIMENTS OF 1926..HE FAILED, BECAUSE HIS METHOD WAS WRONG.. I, HOWEVER, TRAINED ORANG FROM CHILDHOOD AND EVEN INSERTED SURGICALLY MISSING ELEMENTS INTO HIS BRAIN!
EXCELLENT! NOW, MY DAUGHTER..IS SHE HERE?
YES, I'LL PRESENT HER TO YOU NOW!
2

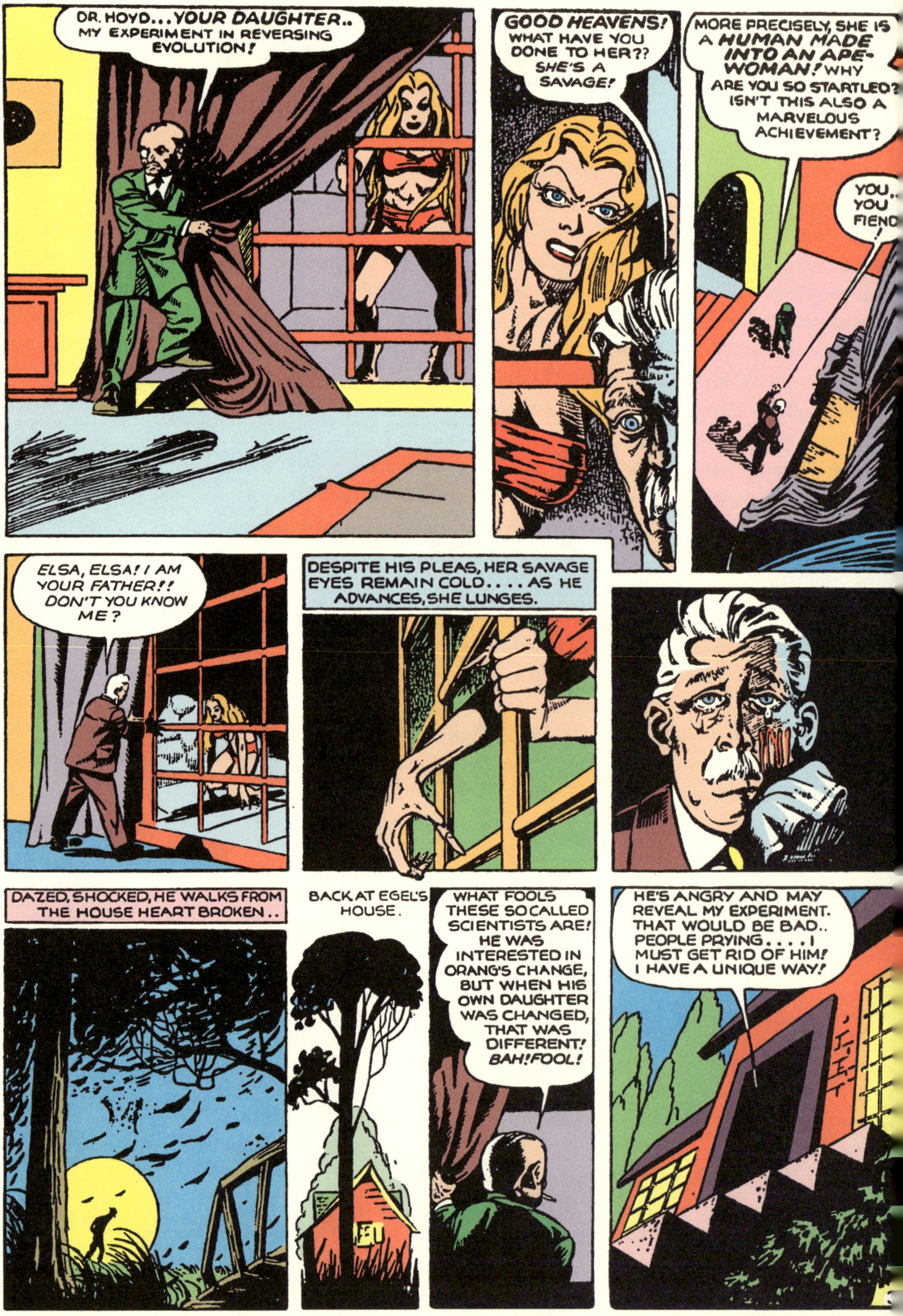

DR. HOYD...YOUR DAUGHTER.. MY EXPERIMENT IN REVERSING EVOLUTION!
GOOD HEAVENS! WHAT HAVE YOU DONE TO HER?? SHE'S A SAVAGE!
MORE PRECISELY, SHE IS A HUMAN MADE INTO AN APE-WOMAN! WHY ARE YOU SO STARTLED? ISN'T THIS ALSO A MARVELOUS ACHIEVEMENT?
YOU.. YOU FIEND!
ELSA, ELSA! I AM YOUR FATHER!! DON'T YOU KNOW ME?
DESPITE HIS PLEAS, HER SAVAGE EYES REMAIN COLD.... AS HE ADVANCES, SHE LUNGES.
DAZED, SHOCKED, HE WALKS FROM THE HOUSE HEART BROKEN..
BACK AT EGEL'S HOUSE.
WHAT FOOLS THESE SO CALLED SCIENTISTS ARE! HE WAS INTERESTED IN ORANG'S CHANGE, BUT WHEN HIS OWN DAUGHTER WAS CHANGED, THAT WAS DIFFERENT! BAH! FOOL!
HE'S ANGRY AND MAY REVEAL MY EXPERIMENT. THAT WOULD BE BAD.. PEOPLE PRYING.... I MUST GET RID OF HIM! I HAVE A UNIQUE WAY!

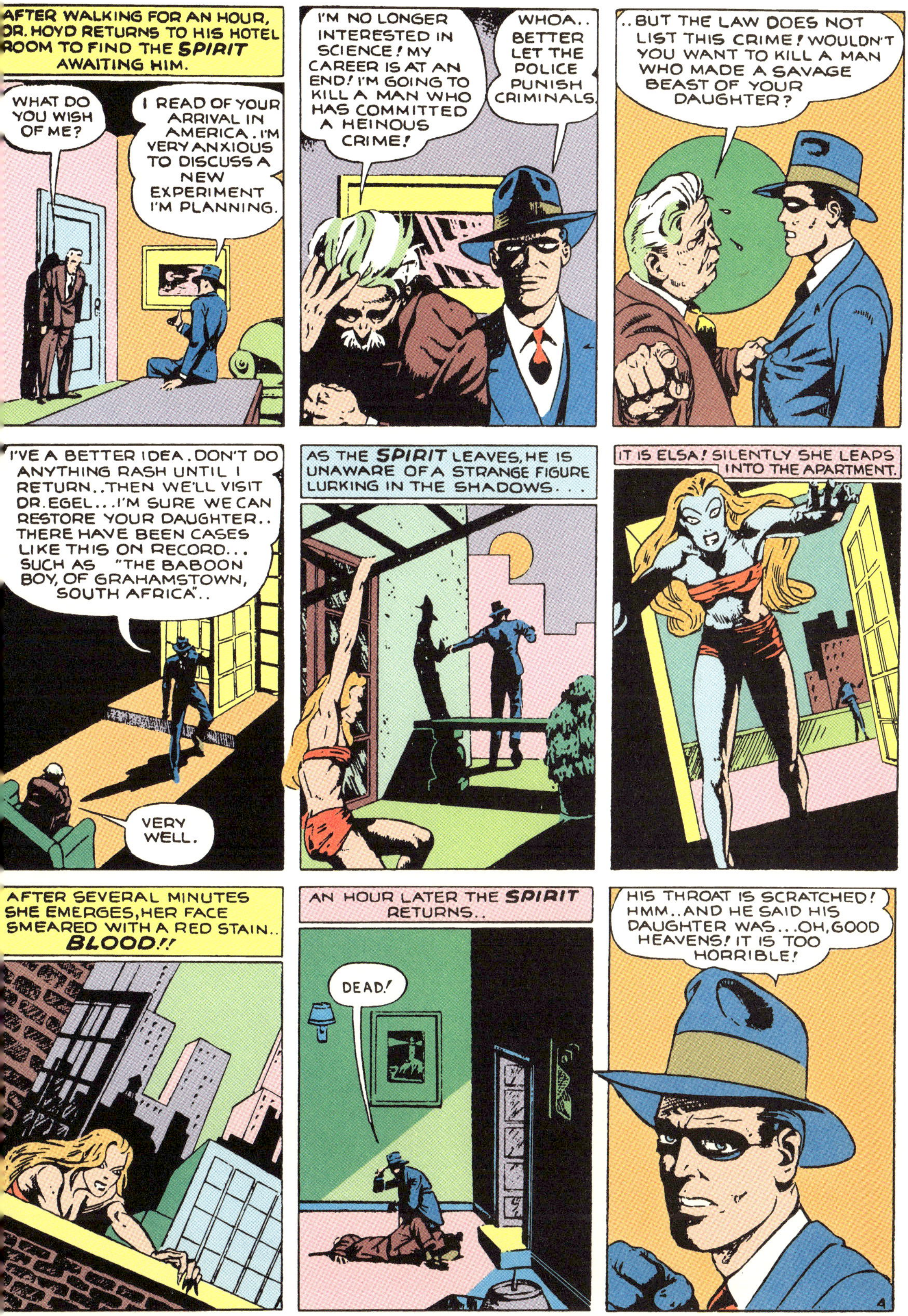
AFTER WALKING FOR AN HOUR, DR. HOYD RETURNS TO HIS HOTEL ROOM TO FIND THE SPIRIT AWAITING HIM.
WHAT DO YOU WISH OF ME?
I READ OF YOUR ARRIVAL IN AMERICA. I'M VERY ANXIOUS TO DISCUSS A NEW EXPERIMENT I'M PLANNING.
I'M NO LONGER INTERESTED IN SCIENCE! MY CAREER IS AT AN END! I'M GOING TO KILL A MAN WHO HAS COMMITTED A HEINOUS CRIME!
WHOA.. BETTER LET THE POLICE PUNISH CRIMINALS.
..BUT THE LAW DOES NOT LIST THIS CRIME! WOULDN'T YOU WANT TO KILL A MAN WHO MADE A SAVAGE BEAST OF YOUR DAUGHTER?
I'VE A BETTER IDEA. DON'T DO ANYTHING RASH UNTIL I RETURN..THEN WE'LL VISIT DR. EGEL...I'M SURE WE CAN RESTORE YOUR DAUGHTER.. THERE HAVE BEEN CASES LIKE THIS ON RECORD... SUCH AS "THE BABOON BOY, OF GRAHAMSTOWN, SOUTH AFRICA"..
VERY WELL.
AS THE SPIRIT LEAVES, HE IS UNAWARE OF A STRANGE FIGURE LURKING IN THE SHADOWS...
IT IS ELSA! SILENTLY SHE LEAPS INTO THE APARTMENT.
AFTER SEVERAL MINUTES SHE EMERGES, HER FACE SMEARED WITH A RED STAIN.. BLOOD!!
AN HOUR LATER THE SPIRIT RETURNS..
DEAD!
HIS THROAT IS SCRATCHED! HMM..AND HE SAID HIS DAUGHTER WAS...OH, GOOD HEAVENS! IT IS TOO HORRIBLE!
4

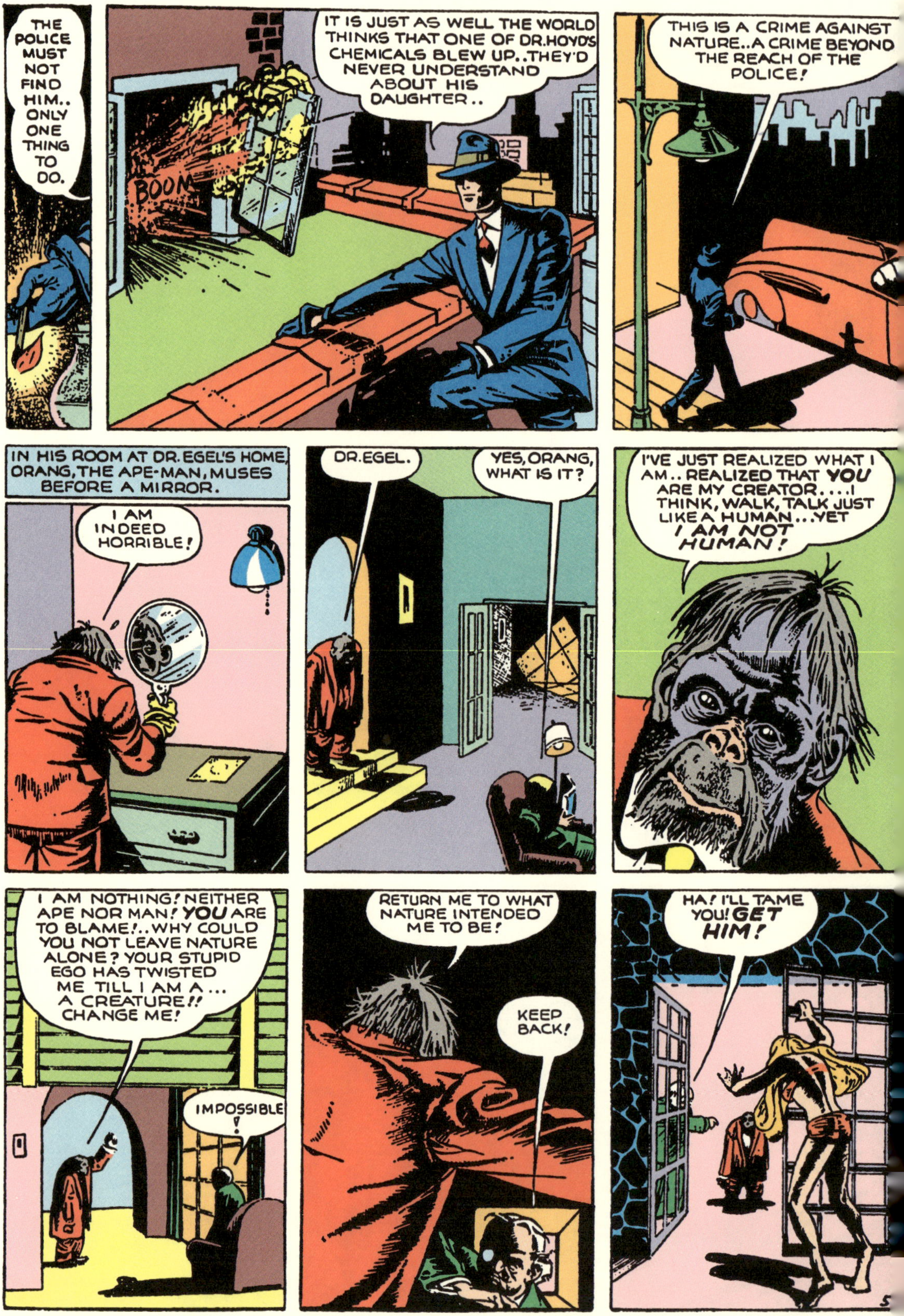
THE POLICE MUST NOT FIND HIM.. ONLY ONE THING TO DO.
BOOM
IT IS JUST AS WELL THE WORLD THINKS THAT ONE OF DR.HOYD'S CHEMICALS BLEW UP..THEY'D NEVER UNDERSTAND ABOUT HIS DAUGHTER..
THIS IS A CRIME AGAINST NATURE..A CRIME BEYOND THE REACH OF THE POLICE!
IN HIS ROOM AT DR.EGEL'S HOME, ORANG, THE APE-MAN, MUSES BEFORE A MIRROR.
I AM INDEED HORRIBLE!
DR.EGEL.
YES, ORANG, WHAT IS IT?
I'VE JUST REALIZED WHAT I AM.. REALIZED THAT YOU ARE MY CREATOR....I THINK, WALK, TALK JUST LIKE A HUMAN...YET I AM NOT HUMAN!
I AM NOTHING! NEITHER APE NOR MAN! YOU ARE TO BLAME!..WHY COULD YOU NOT LEAVE NATURE ALONE? YOUR STUPID EGO HAS TWISTED ME TILL I AM A... A CREATURE!! CHANGE ME!
IMPOSSIBLE!
RETURN ME TO WHAT NATURE INTENDED ME TO BE!
KEEP BACK!
HA! I'LL TAME YOU! GET HIM!
5

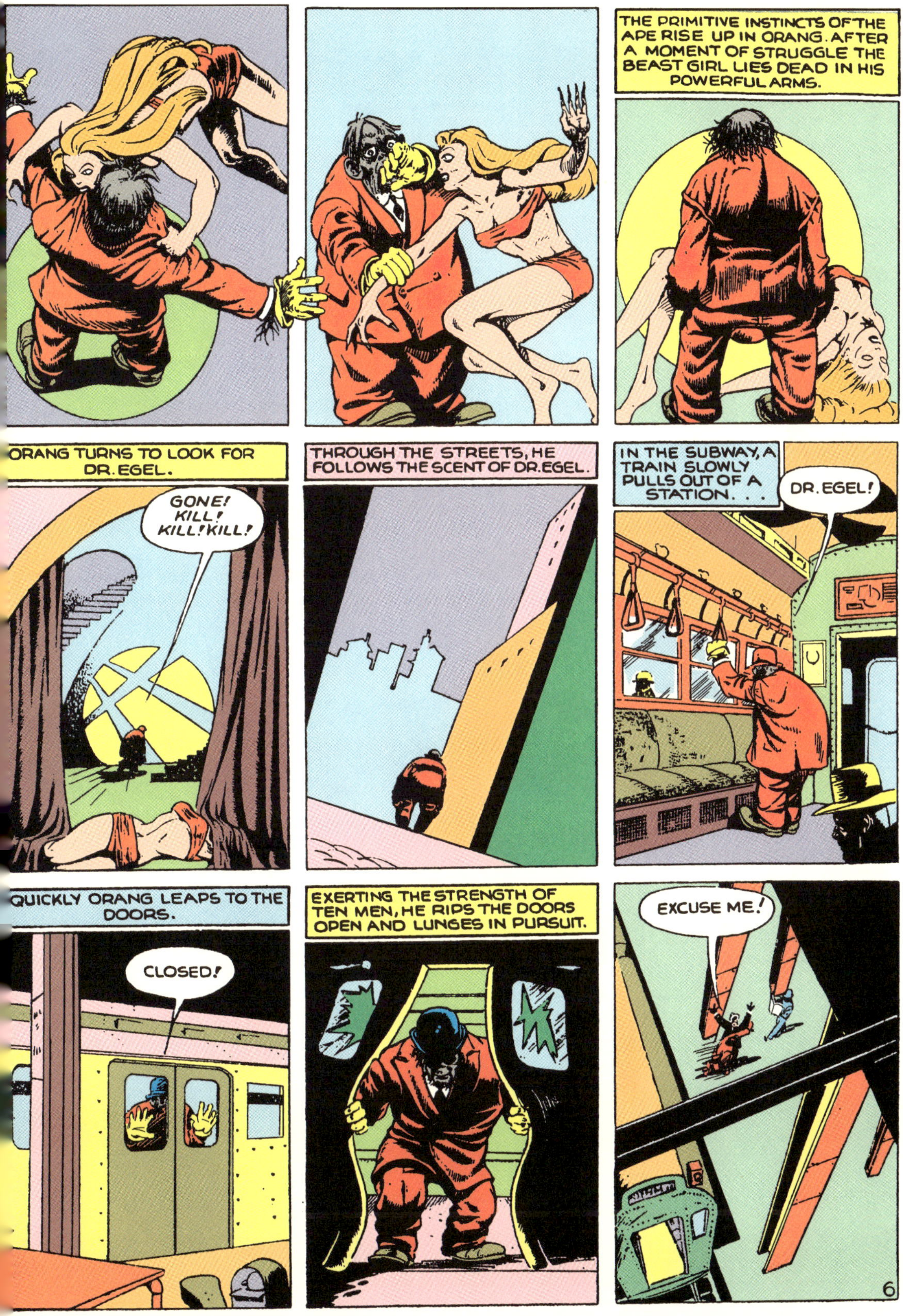
THE PRIMITIVE INSTINCTS OF THE APE RISE UP IN ORANG. AFTER A MOMENT OF STRUGGLE THE BEAST GIRL LIES DEAD IN HIS POWERFUL ARMS.
ORANG TURNS TO LOOK FOR DR. EGEL.
GONE! KILL! KILL! KILL!
THROUGH THE STREETS, HE FOLLOWS THE SCENT OF DR. EGEL.
IN THE SUBWAY, A TRAIN SLOWLY PULLS OUT OF A STATION. . .
DR. EGEL!
QUICKLY ORANG LEAPS TO THE DOORS.
CLOSED!
EXERTING THE STRENGTH OF TEN MEN, HE RIPS THE DOORS OPEN AND LUNGES IN PURSUIT.
EXCUSE ME!
6

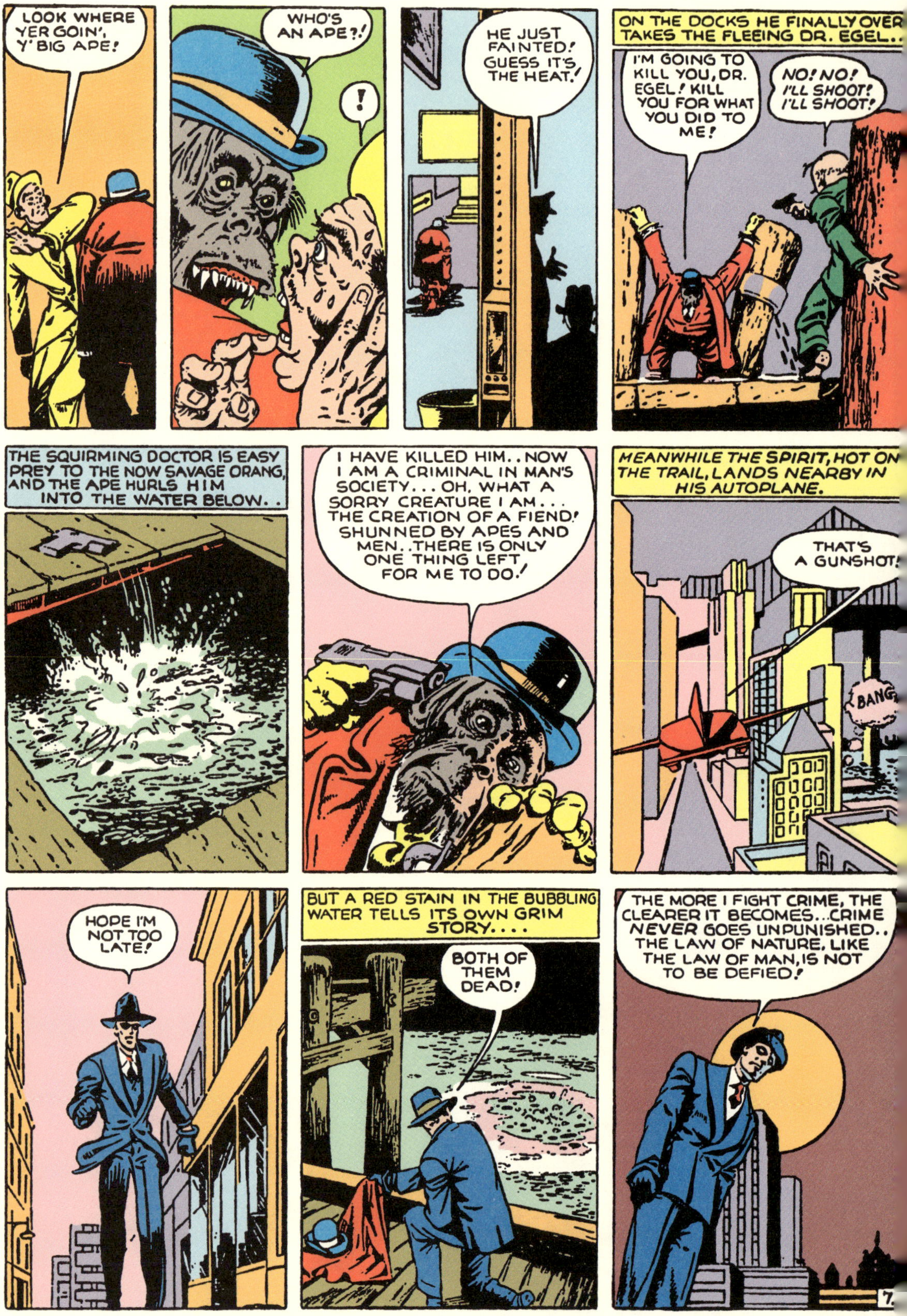
LOOK WHERE YER GOIN', Y' BIG APE!
WHO'S AN APE?!
!
HE JUST FAINTED! GUESS IT'S THE HEAT!
ON THE DOCKS HE FINALLY OVERTAKES THE FLEEING DR. EGEL..
I'M GOING TO KILL YOU, DR. EGEL! KILL YOU FOR WHAT YOU DID TO ME!
NO! NO! I'LL SHOOT! I'LL SHOOT!
THE SQUIRMING DOCTOR IS EASY PREY TO THE NOW SAVAGE ORANG, AND THE APE HURLS HIM INTO THE WATER BELOW..
I HAVE KILLED HIM..NOW I AM A CRIMINAL IN MAN'S SOCIETY... OH, WHAT A SORRY CREATURE I AM... THE CREATION OF A FIEND! SHUNNED BY APES AND MEN..THERE IS ONLY ONE THING LEFT FOR ME TO DO!
MEANWHILE THE SPIRIT, HOT ON THE TRAIL, LANDS NEARBY IN HIS AUTOPLANE.
THAT'S A GUNSHOT!
BANG
HOPE I'M NOT TOO LATE!
BUT A RED STAIN IN THE BUBBLING WATER TELLS ITS OWN GRIM STORY....
BOTH OF THEM DEAD!
THE MORE I FIGHT CRIME, THE CLEARER IT BECOMES...CRIME NEVER GOES UNPUNISHED.. THE LAW OF NATURE, LIKE THE LAW OF MAN, IS NOT TO BE DEFIED!
7

COMIC BOOK SECTION
Copyright, 1940, by Everett M. Arnold

THE RETURN OF ORANG, THE APE THAT IS HUMAN

September 8, 1940

3 COMPLETE STORIES

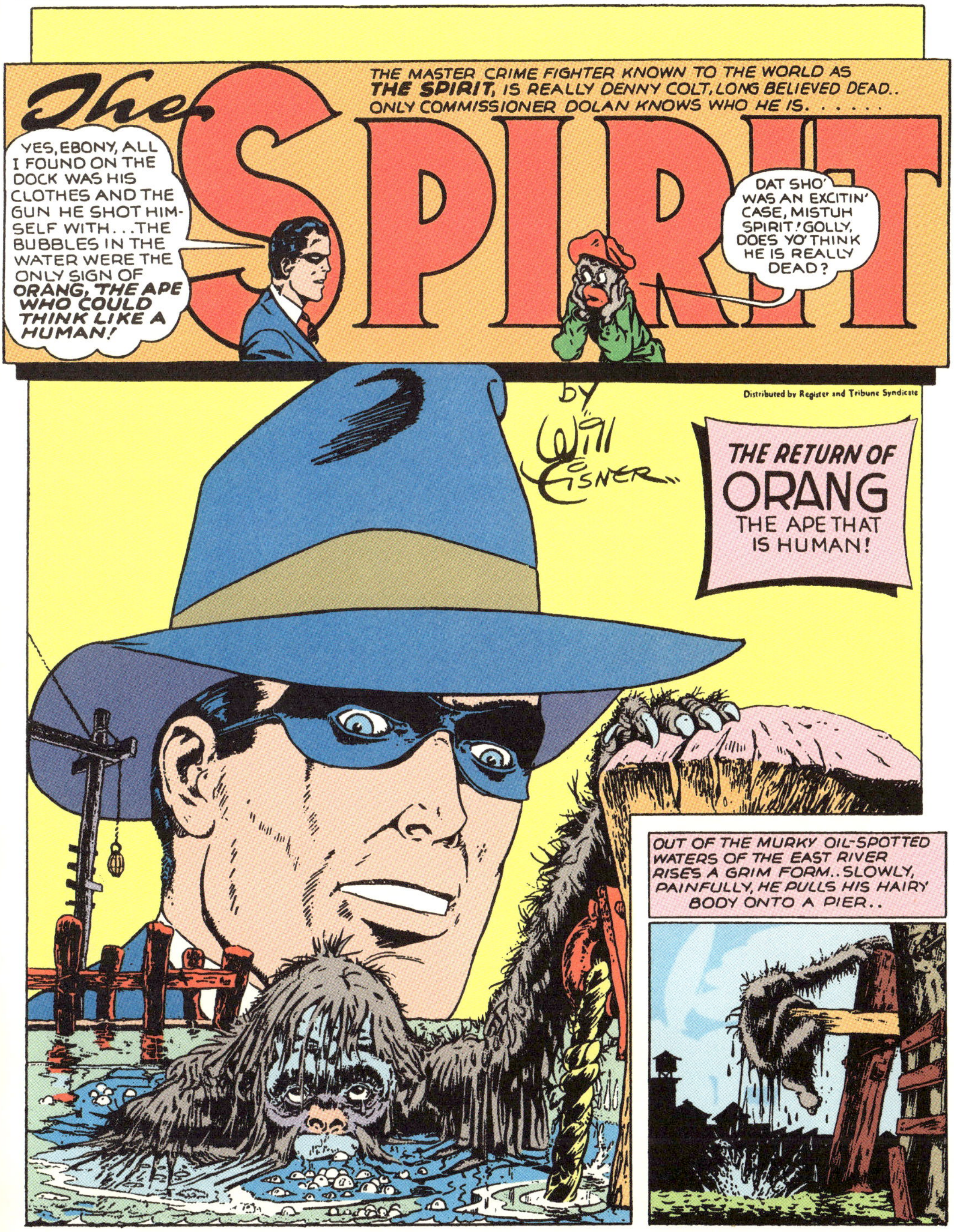
The SPIRIT
THE MASTER CRIME FIGHTER KNOWN TO THE WORLD AS THE SPIRIT, IS REALLY DENNY COLT, LONG BELIEVED DEAD.. ONLY COMMISSIONER DOLAN KNOWS WHO HE IS. . . . .
YES, EBONY, ALL I FOUND ON THE DOCK WAS HIS CLOTHES AND THE GUN HE SHOT HIMSELF WITH. . . THE BUBBLES IN THE WATER WERE THE ONLY SIGN OF ORANG, THE APE WHO COULD THINK LIKE A HUMAN!
DAT SHO' WAS AN EXCITIN' CASE, MISTUH SPIRIT! GOLLY, DOES YO' THINK HE IS REALLY DEAD?
Distributed by Register and Tribune Syndicate
by Will Eisner
THE RETURN OF ORANG THE APE THAT IS HUMAN!
OUT OF THE MURKY OIL-SPOTTED WATERS OF THE EAST RIVER RISES A GRIM FORM.. SLOWLY, PAINFULLY, HE PULLS HIS HAIRY BODY ONTO A PIER..

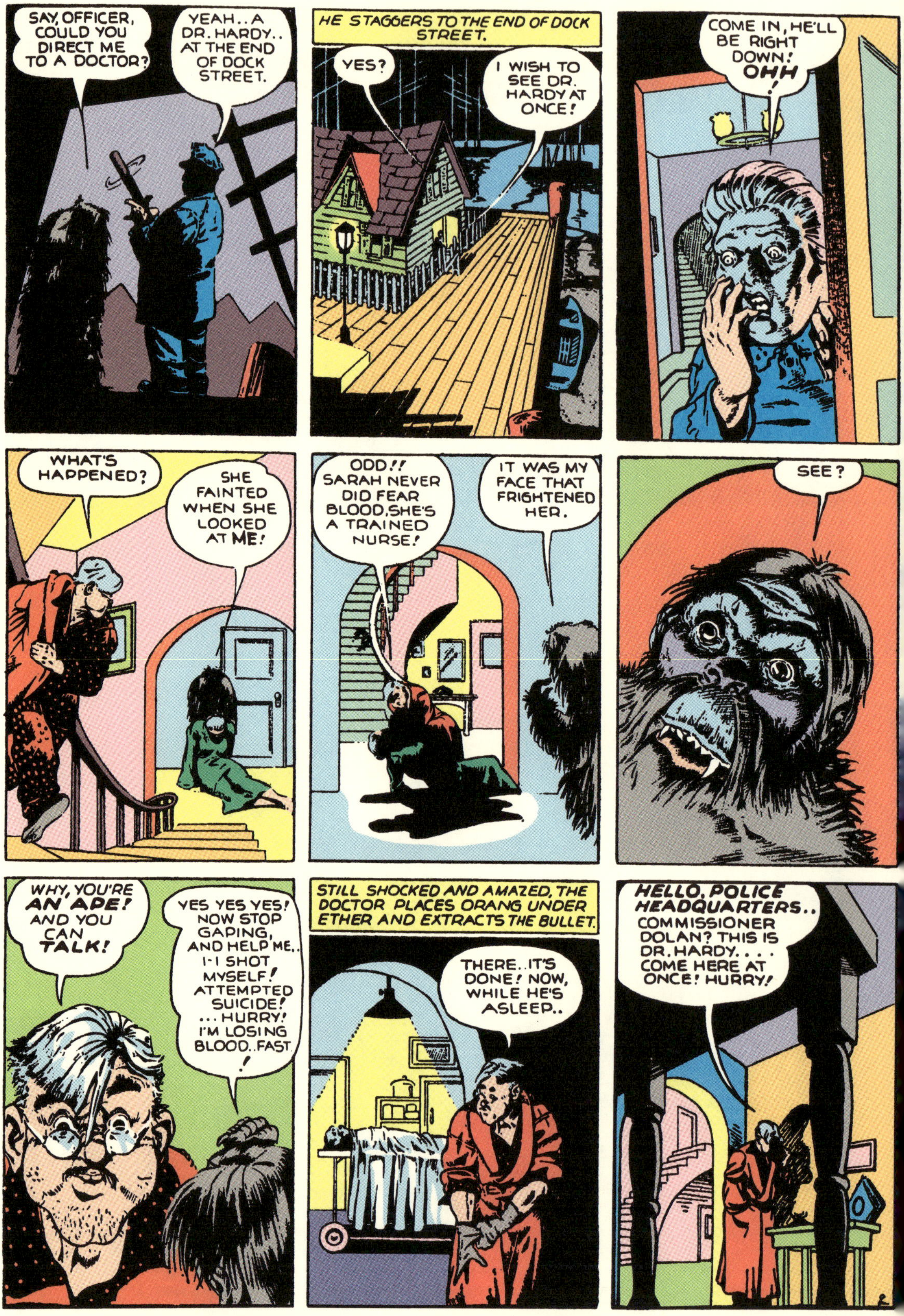
SAY, OFFICER, COULD YOU DIRECT ME TO A DOCTOR?
YEAH..A DR. HARDY.. AT THE END OF DOCK STREET.
HE STAGGERS TO THE END OF DOCK STREET.
YES?
I WISH TO SEE DR. HARDY AT ONCE!
COME IN, HE'LL BE RIGHT DOWN! OHH!
WHAT'S HAPPENED?
SHE FAINTED WHEN SHE LOOKED AT ME!
ODD!! SARAH NEVER DID FEAR BLOOD, SHE'S A TRAINED NURSE!
IT WAS MY FACE THAT FRIGHTENED HER.
SEE?
WHY, YOU'RE AN APE! AND YOU CAN TALK!
YES YES YES! NOW STOP GAPING, AND HELP ME.. I-I SHOT MYSELF! ATTEMPTED SUICIDE! ...HURRY! I'M LOSING BLOOD..FAST!
STILL SHOCKED AND AMAZED, THE DOCTOR PLACES ORANG UNDER ETHER AND EXTRACTS THE BULLET.
THERE..IT'S DONE! NOW, WHILE HE'S ASLEEP..
HELLO, POLICE HEADQUARTERS.. COMMISSIONER DOLAN? THIS IS DR. HARDY.... COME HERE AT ONCE! HURRY!

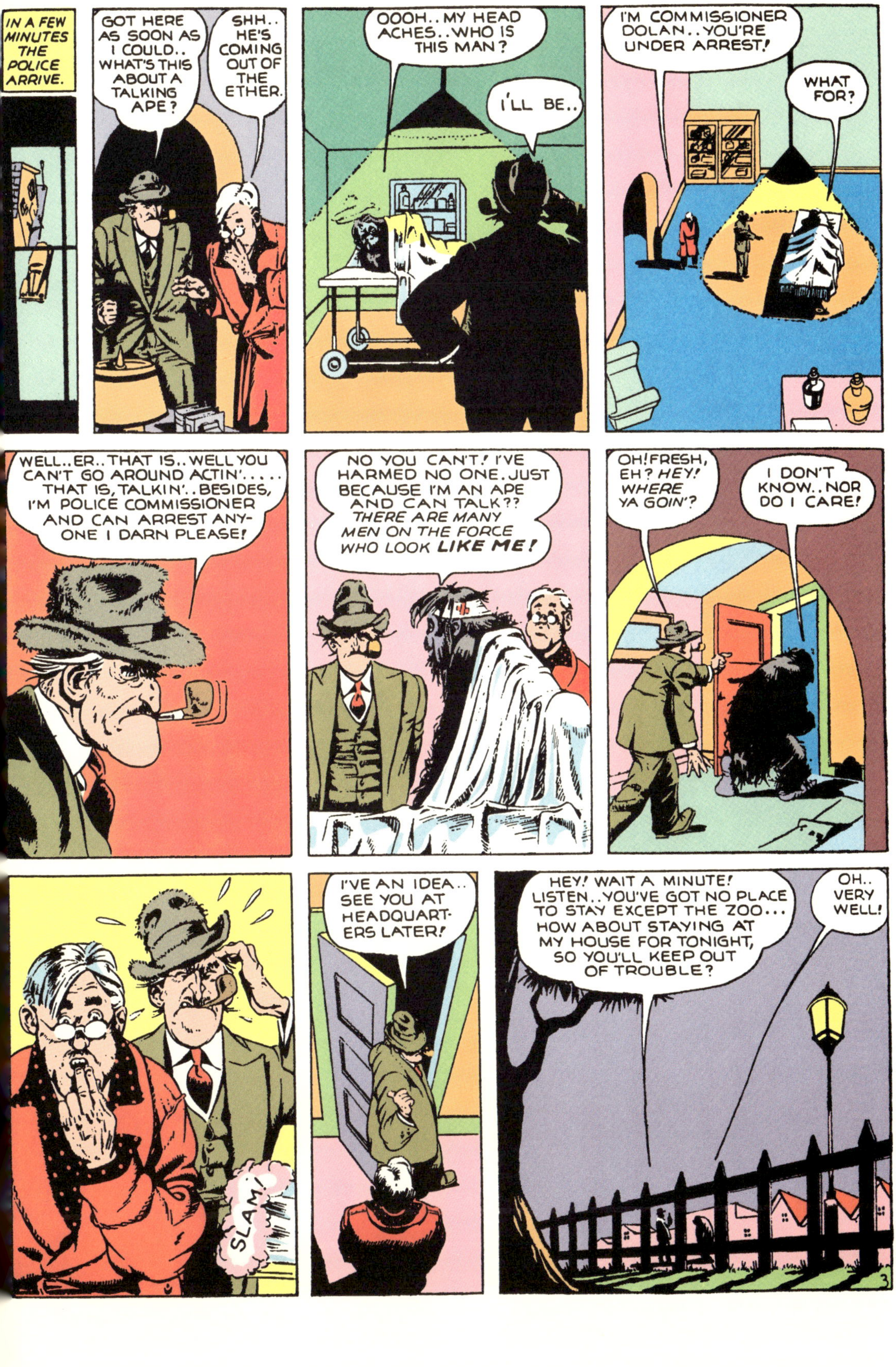
IN A FEW MINUTES THE POLICE ARRIVE.
GOT HERE AS SOON AS I COULD.. WHAT'S THIS ABOUT A TALKING APE?
SHH.. HE'S COMING OUT OF THE ETHER.
OOOH.. MY HEAD ACHES.. WHO IS THIS MAN?
I'LL BE..
I'M COMMISSIONER DOLAN.. YOU'RE UNDER ARREST!
WHAT FOR?
WELL..ER..THAT IS..WELL YOU CAN'T GO AROUND ACTIN'..... THAT IS, TALKIN'.. BESIDES, I'M POLICE COMMISSIONER AND CAN ARREST ANY-ONE I DARN PLEASE!
NO YOU CAN'T! I'VE HARMED NO ONE. JUST BECAUSE I'M AN APE AND CAN TALK?? THERE ARE MANY MEN ON THE FORCE WHO LOOK LIKE ME!
OH! FRESH, EH? HEY! WHERE YA GOIN'?
I DON'T KNOW.. NOR DO I CARE!
SLAM!
I'VE AN IDEA.. SEE YOU AT HEADQUART-ERS LATER!
HEY! WAIT A MINUTE! LISTEN.. YOU'VE GOT NO PLACE TO STAY EXCEPT THE ZOO... HOW ABOUT STAYING AT MY HOUSE FOR TONIGHT, SO YOU'LL KEEP OUT OF TROUBLE?
OH.. VERY WELL!
3

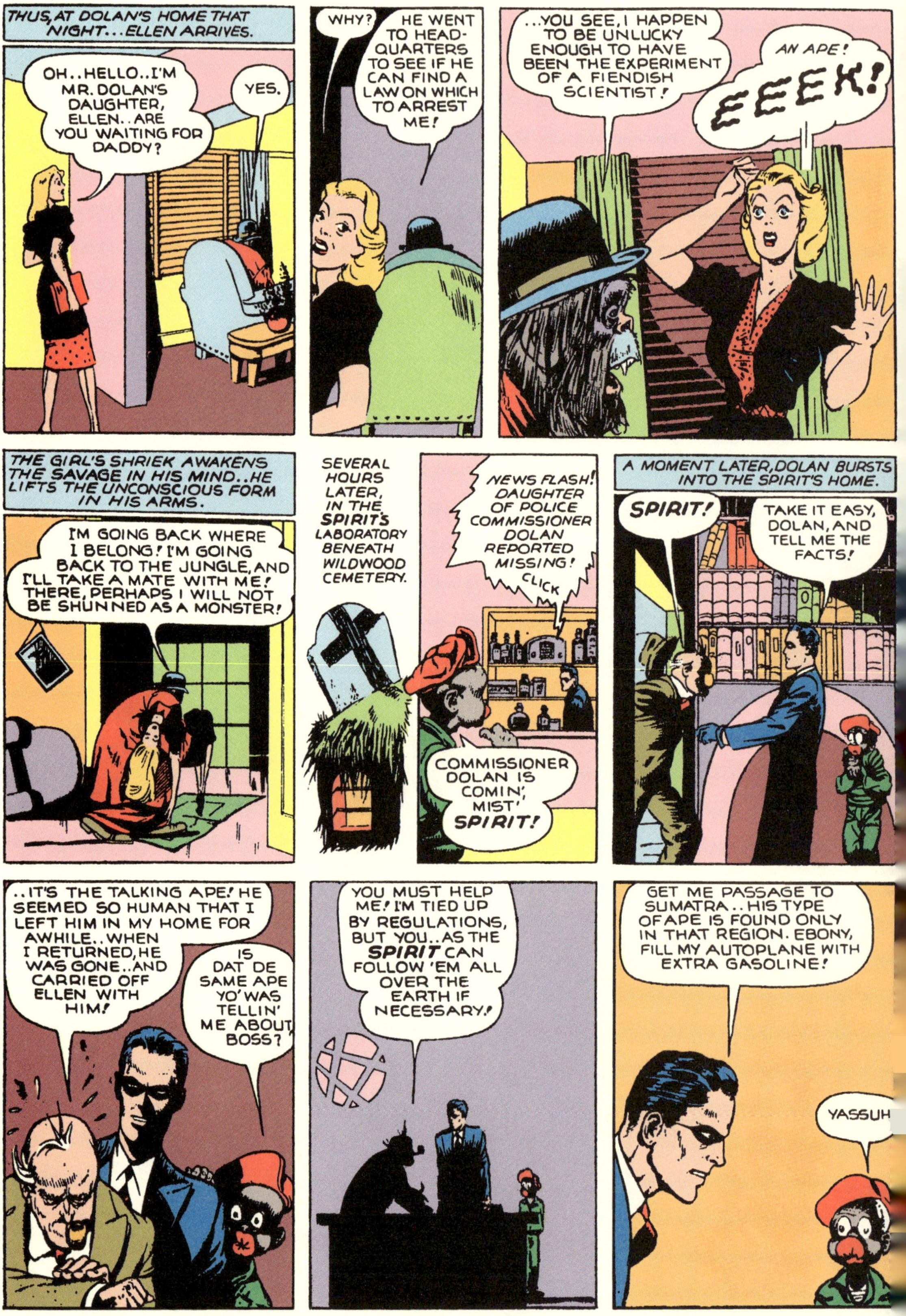
THUS, AT DOLAN'S HOME THAT NIGHT... ELLEN ARRIVES.
OH..HELLO..I'M MR. DOLAN'S DAUGHTER, ELLEN..ARE YOU WAITING FOR DADDY?
YES.
WHY?
HE WENT TO HEAD-QUARTERS TO SEE IF HE CAN FIND A LAW ON WHICH TO ARREST ME!
...YOU SEE, I HAPPEN TO BE UNLUCKY ENOUGH TO HAVE BEEN THE EXPERIMENT OF A FIENDISH SCIENTIST!
AN APE!
EEEK!
THE GIRL'S SHRIEK AWAKENS THE SAVAGE IN HIS MIND..HE LIFTS THE UNCONSCIOUS FORM IN HIS ARMS.
I'M GOING BACK WHERE I BELONG! I'M GOING BACK TO THE JUNGLE, AND I'LL TAKE A MATE WITH ME! THERE, PERHAPS I WILL NOT BE SHUNNED AS A MONSTER!
SEVERAL HOURS LATER, IN THE SPIRIT'S LABORATORY BENEATH WILDWOOD CEMETERY.
NEWS FLASH! DAUGHTER OF POLICE COMMISSIONER DOLAN REPORTED MISSING!
CLICK
COMMISSIONER DOLAN IS COMIN', MIST' SPIRIT!
A MOMENT LATER, DOLAN BURSTS INTO THE SPIRIT'S HOME.
SPIRIT!
TAKE IT EASY, DOLAN, AND TELL ME THE FACTS!
..IT'S THE TALKING APE! HE SEEMED SO HUMAN THAT I LEFT HIM IN MY HOME FOR AWHILE..WHEN I RETURNED, HE WAS GONE..AND CARRIED OFF ELLEN WITH HIM!
IS DAT DE SAME APE YO' WAS TELLIN' ME ABOUT, BOSS?
YOU MUST HELP ME! I'M TIED UP BY REGULATIONS, BUT YOU..AS THE SPIRIT CAN FOLLOW 'EM ALL OVER THE EARTH IF NECESSARY!
GET ME PASSAGE TO SUMATRA..HIS TYPE OF APE IS FOUND ONLY IN THAT REGION. EBONY, FILL MY AUTOPLANE WITH EXTRA GASOLINE!
YASSUH

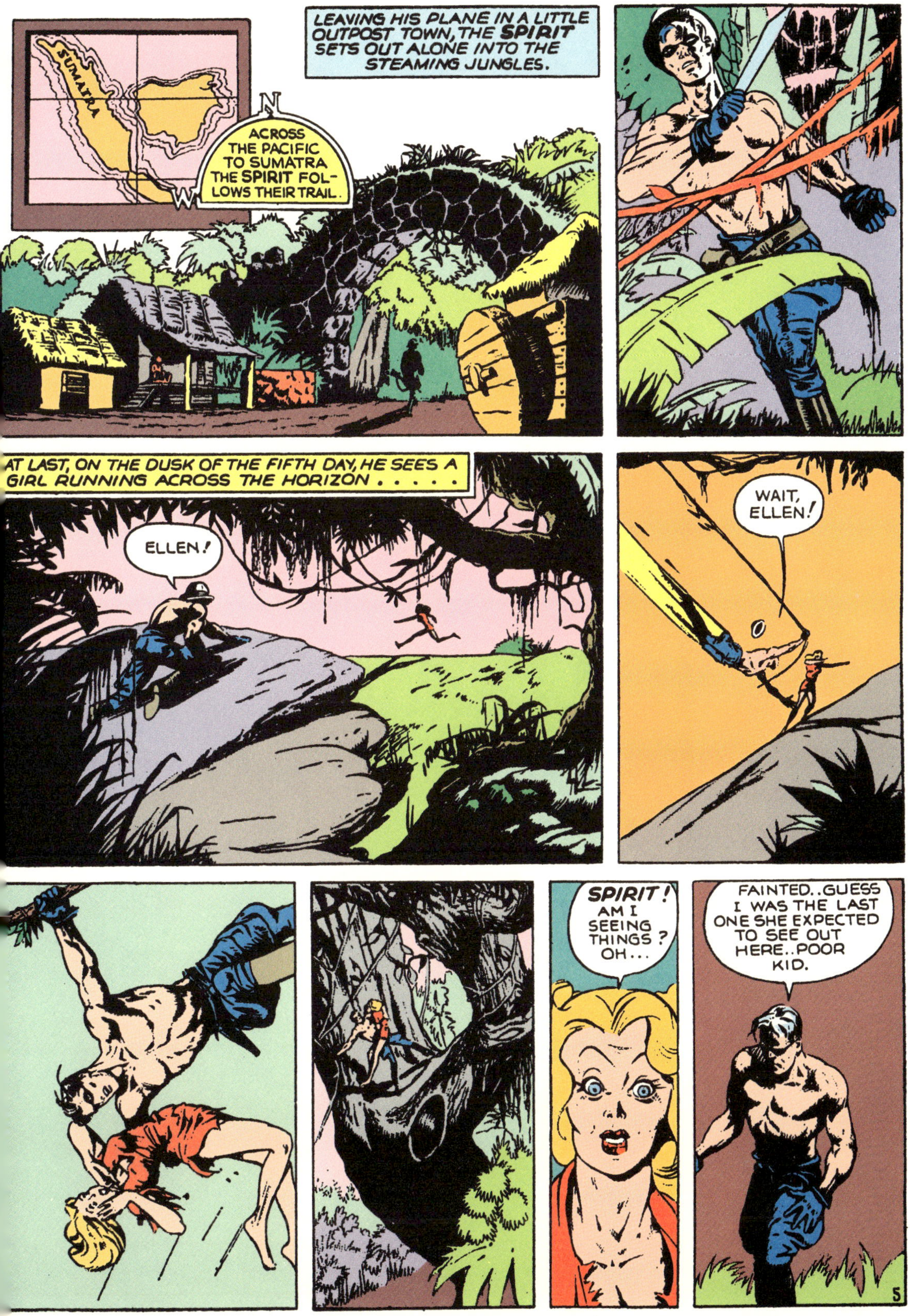
ACROSS THE PACIFIC TO SUMATRA THE SPIRIT FOL-LOWS THEIR TRAIL.
SUMATRA
N
W
LEAVING HIS PLANE IN A LITTLE OUTPOST TOWN, THE SPIRIT SETS OUT ALONE INTO THE STEAMING JUNGLES.
AT LAST, ON THE DUSK OF THE FIFTH DAY, HE SEES A GIRL RUNNING ACROSS THE HORIZON . . . . .
ELLEN!
WAIT, ELLEN!
SPIRIT! AM I SEEING THINGS? OH...
FAINTED..GUESS I WAS THE LAST ONE SHE EXPECTED TO SEE OUT HERE..POOR KID.
5

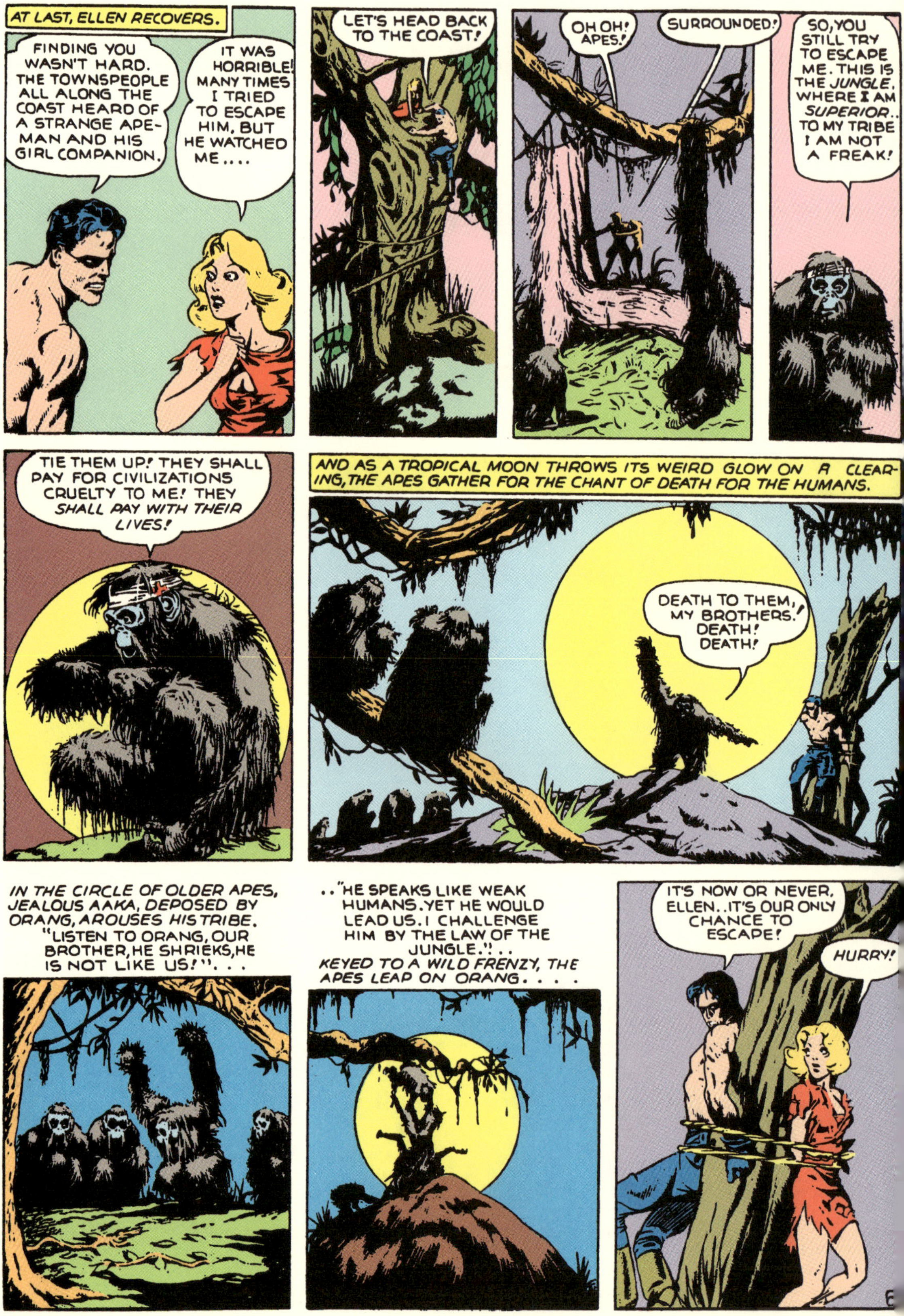

AT LAST, ELLEN RECOVERS.
FINDING YOU WASN'T HARD. THE TOWNSPEOPLE ALL ALONG THE COAST HEARD OF A STRANGE APE-MAN AND HIS GIRL COMPANION.
IT WAS HORRIBLE! MANY TIMES I TRIED TO ESCAPE HIM, BUT HE WATCHED ME....
LET'S HEAD BACK TO THE COAST!
OH OH! APES!
SURROUNDED!
SO, YOU STILL TRY TO ESCAPE ME. THIS IS THE *JUNGLE*, WHERE I AM *SUPERIOR*.. TO MY TRIBE I AM NOT A FREAK!
TIE THEM UP! THEY SHALL PAY FOR CIVILIZATIONS CRUELTY TO ME! THEY *SHALL PAY WITH THEIR LIVES!*
AND AS A TROPICAL MOON THROWS ITS WEIRD GLOW ON A CLEARING, THE APES GATHER FOR THE CHANT OF DEATH FOR THE HUMANS.
DEATH TO THEM, MY BROTHERS! DEATH! DEATH!
IN THE CIRCLE OF OLDER APES, JEALOUS AAKA, DEPOSED BY ORANG, AROUSES HIS TRIBE. "LISTEN TO ORANG, OUR BROTHER, HE SHRIEKS, HE IS NOT LIKE US!"...
.."HE SPEAKS LIKE WEAK HUMANS. YET HE WOULD LEAD US. I CHALLENGE HIM BY THE LAW OF THE JUNGLE."!..
KEYED TO A WILD FRENZY, THE APES LEAP ON ORANG....
IT'S NOW OR NEVER, ELLEN..IT'S OUR ONLY CHANCE TO ESCAPE!
HURRY!

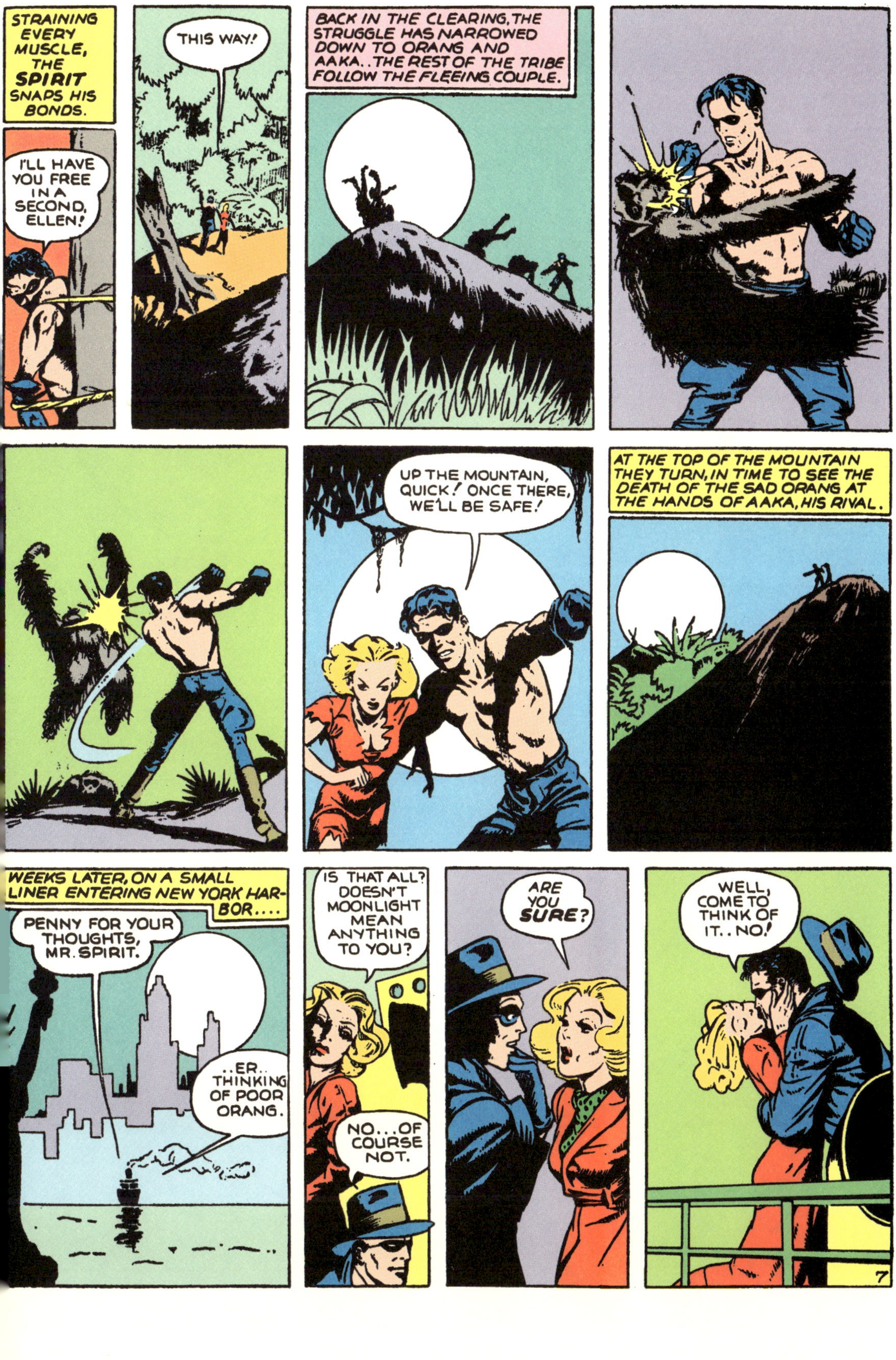
STRAINING EVERY MUSCLE, THE SPIRIT SNAPS HIS BONDS.
I'LL HAVE YOU FREE IN A SECOND, ELLEN!
THIS WAY!
BACK IN THE CLEARING, THE STRUGGLE HAS NARROWED DOWN TO ORANG AND AAKA.. THE REST OF THE TRIBE FOLLOW THE FLEEING COUPLE.
UP THE MOUNTAIN, QUICK! ONCE THERE, WE'LL BE SAFE!
AT THE TOP OF THE MOUNTAIN THEY TURN, IN TIME TO SEE THE DEATH OF THE SAD ORANG AT THE HANDS OF AAKA, HIS RIVAL.
WEEKS LATER, ON A SMALL LINER ENTERING NEW YORK HARBOR....
PENNY FOR YOUR THOUGHTS, MR. SPIRIT.
..ER.. THINKING OF POOR ORANG.
IS THAT ALL? DOESN'T MOONLIGHT MEAN ANYTHING TO YOU?
NO...OF COURSE NOT.
ARE YOU SURE?
WELL, COME TO THINK OF IT.. NO!
7

EBONY'S X-RAY EYES

September 15, 1940

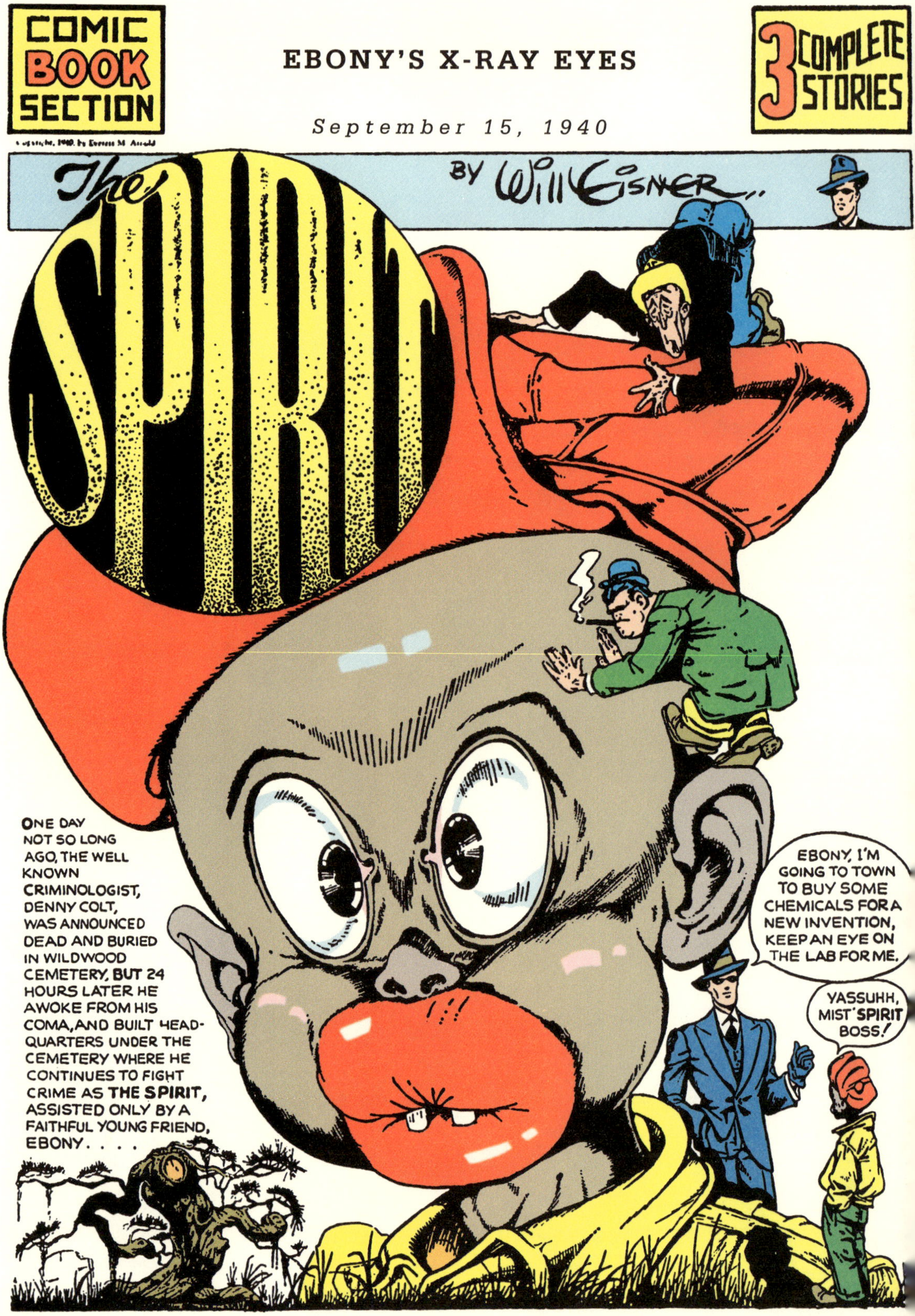

COMIC BOOK SECTION
3 COMPLETE STORIES
The SPIRIT
BY Will Eisner
ONE DAY NOT SO LONG AGO, THE WELL KNOWN CRIMINOLOGIST, DENNY COLT, WAS ANNOUNCED DEAD AND BURIED IN WILDWOOD CEMETERY, BUT 24 HOURS LATER HE AWOKE FROM HIS COMA, AND BUILT HEAD-QUARTERS UNDER THE CEMETERY WHERE HE CONTINUES TO FIGHT CRIME AS THE SPIRIT, ASSISTED ONLY BY A FAITHFUL YOUNG FRIEND, EBONY . . . .
EBONY, I'M GOING TO TOWN TO BUY SOME CHEMICALS FOR A NEW INVENTION, KEEP AN EYE ON THE LAB FOR ME.
YASSUHH, MIST' SPIRIT BOSS!

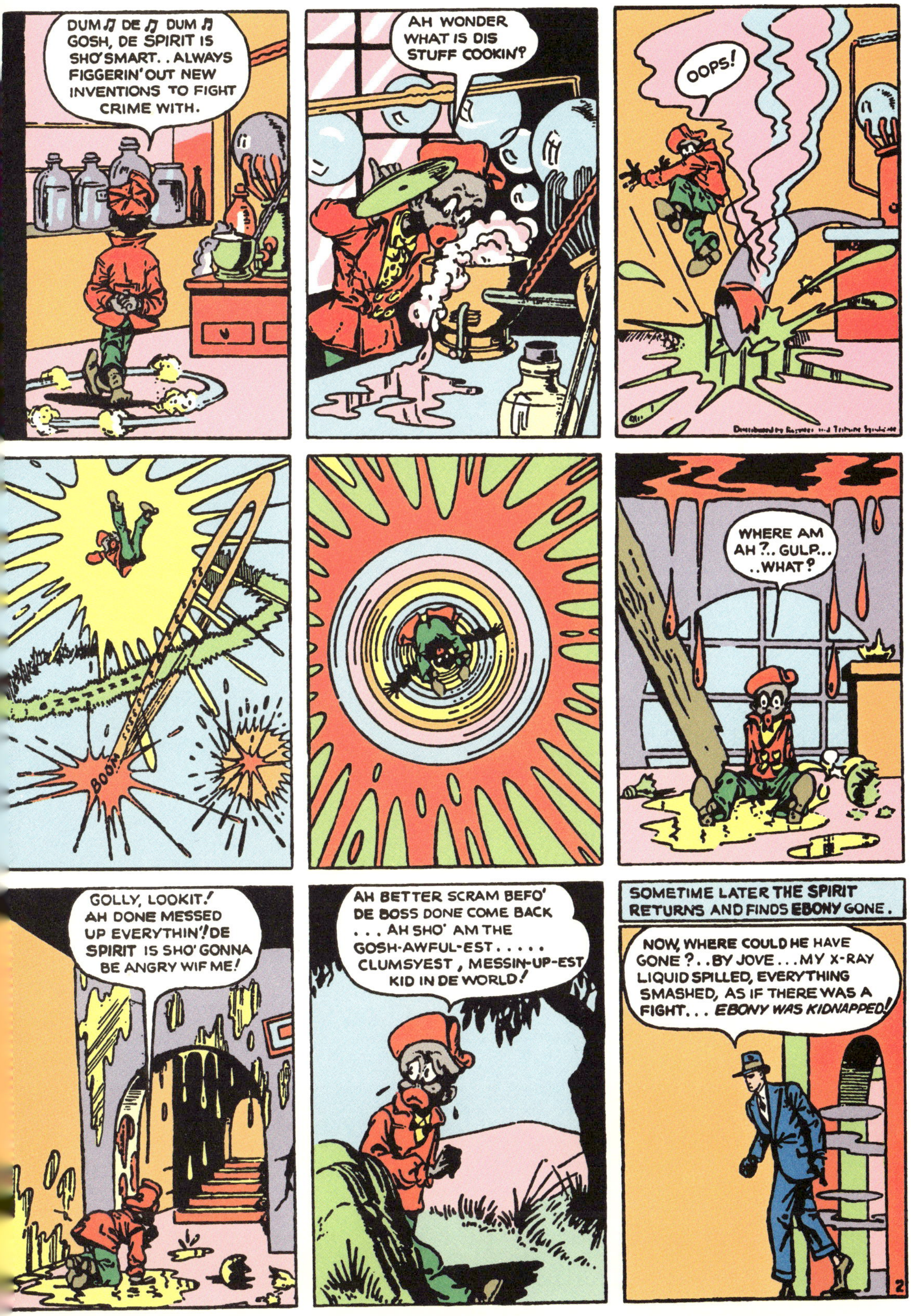
DUM ♫ DE ♫ DUM ♫ GOSH, DE SPIRIT IS SHO' SMART. . ALWAYS FIGGERIN' OUT NEW INVENTIONS TO FIGHT CRIME WITH.
AH WONDER WHAT IS DIS STUFF COOKIN'?
OOPS!
BOOM
WHERE AM AH ?.. GULP... ..WHAT?
GOLLY, LOOKIT! AH DONE MESSED UP EVERYTHIN'! DE SPIRIT IS SHO' GONNA BE ANGRY WIF ME!
AH BETTER SCRAM BEFO' DE BOSS DONE COME BACK . . . AH SHO' AM THE GOSH-AWFUL-EST . . . . . CLUMSYEST , MESSIN-UP-EST KID IN DE WORLD!
SOMETIME LATER THE SPIRIT RETURNS AND FINDS EBONY GONE.
NOW, WHERE COULD HE HAVE GONE ?. . BY JOVE . . . MY X-RAY LIQUID SPILLED, EVERYTHING SMASHED, AS IF THERE WAS A FIGHT. . . EBONY WAS KIDNAPPED!
2

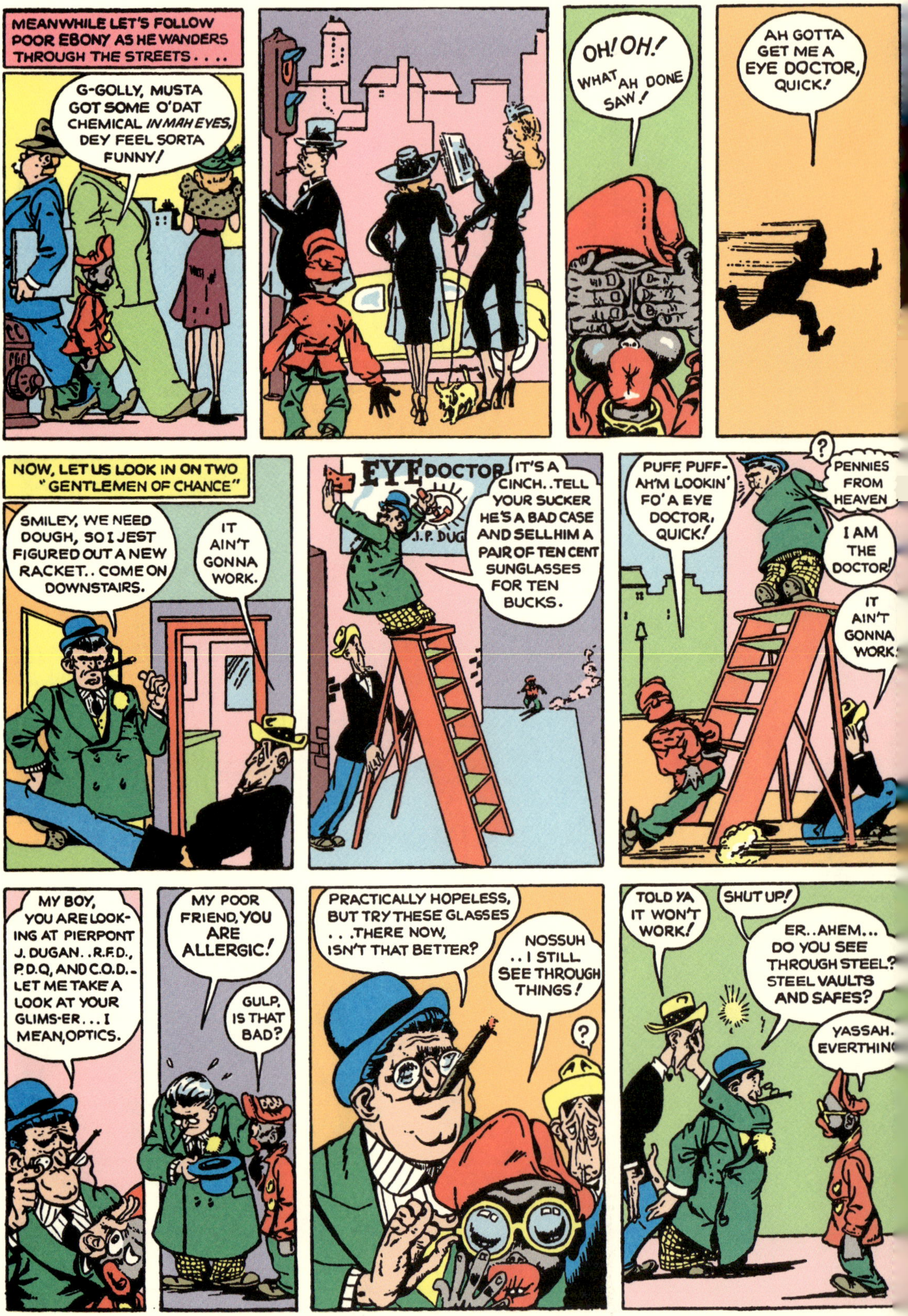
MEANWHILE LET'S FOLLOW POOR EBONY AS HE WANDERS THROUGH THE STREETS....
G-GOLLY, MUSTA GOT SOME O'DAT CHEMICAL *IN MAH EYES*, DEY FEEL SORTA FUNNY!
OH! OH! WHAT AH DONE SAW!
AH GOTTA GET ME A EYE DOCTOR, QUICK!
NOW, LET US LOOK IN ON TWO "GENTLEMEN OF CHANCE"
SMILEY, WE NEED DOUGH, SO I JEST FIGURED OUT A NEW RACKET.. COME ON DOWNSTAIRS.
IT AIN'T GONNA WORK.
EYE DOCTOR
J.P. DUG
IT'S A CINCH.. TELL YOUR SUCKER HE'S A BAD CASE AND SELL HIM A PAIR OF TEN CENT SUNGLASSES FOR TEN BUCKS.
PUFF, PUFF- AH'M LOOKIN' FO' A EYE DOCTOR, QUICK!
?
PENNIES FROM HEAVEN
I AM THE DOCTOR!
IT AIN'T GONNA WORK!
MY BOY, YOU ARE LOOKING AT PIERPONT J. DUGAN.. R.F.D., P.D.Q. AND C.O.D.- LET ME TAKE A LOOK AT YOUR GLIMS-ER... I MEAN, OPTICS.
MY POOR FRIEND, YOU ARE ALLERGIC!
GULP, IS THAT BAD?
PRACTICALLY HOPELESS, BUT TRY THESE GLASSES ... THERE NOW, ISN'T THAT BETTER?
NOSSUH .. I STILL SEE THROUGH THINGS!
?
TOLD YA IT WON'T WORK!
SHUT UP!
ER.. AHEM... DO YOU SEE THROUGH STEEL? STEEL VAULTS AND SAFES?
YASSAH. EVERTHIN

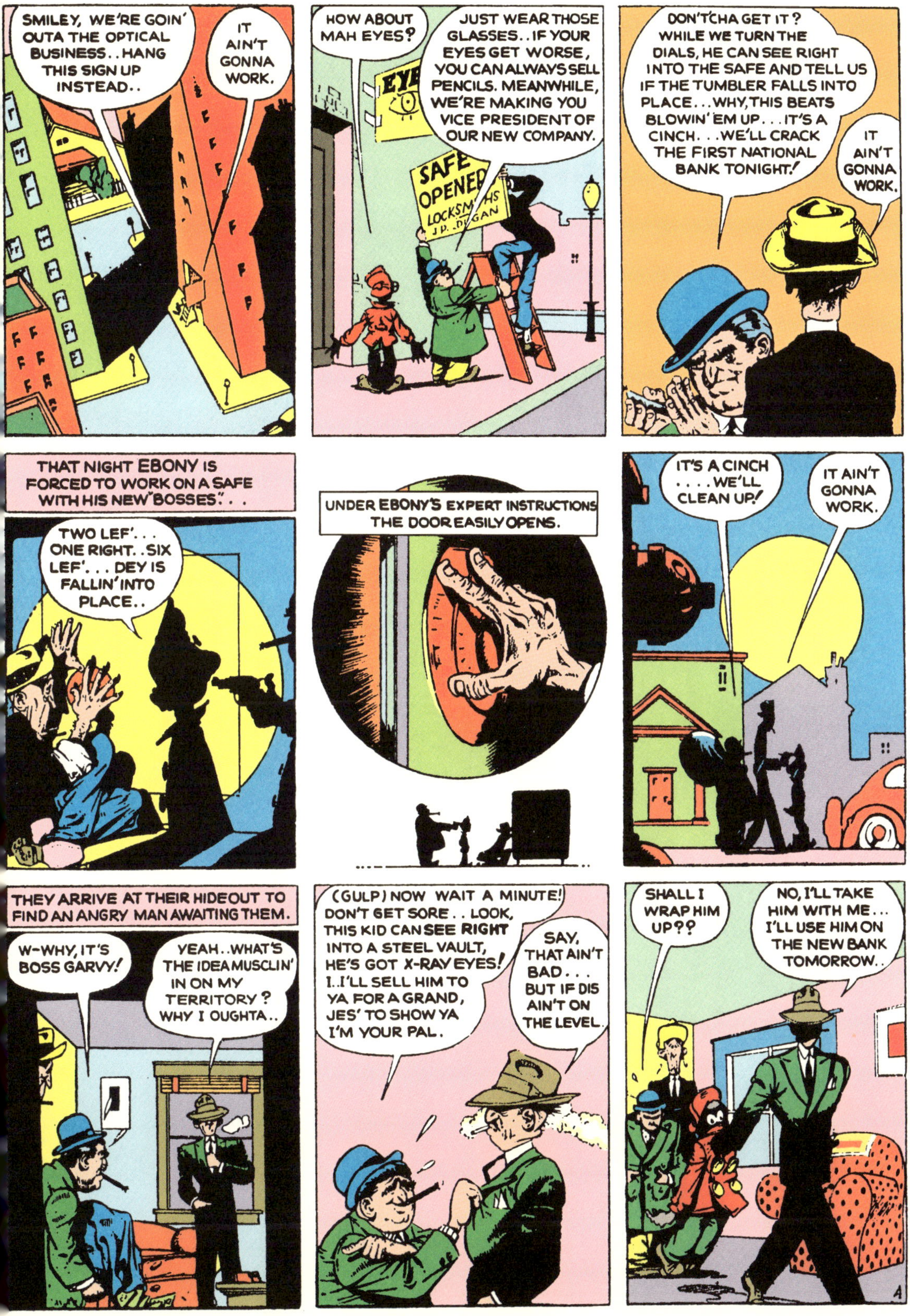
SMILEY, WE'RE GOIN' OUTA THE OPTICAL BUSINESS..HANG THIS SIGN UP INSTEAD..
IT AIN'T GONNA WORK.
HOW ABOUT MAH EYES?
JUST WEAR THOSE GLASSES..IF YOUR EYES GET WORSE, YOU CAN ALWAYS SELL PENCILS. MEANWHILE, WE'RE MAKING YOU VICE PRESIDENT OF OUR NEW COMPANY.
SAFE OPENER
DON'T'CHA GET IT? WHILE WE TURN THE DIALS, HE CAN SEE RIGHT INTO THE SAFE AND TELL US IF THE TUMBLER FALLS INTO PLACE...WHY, THIS BEATS BLOWIN' 'EM UP...IT'S A CINCH...WE'LL CRACK THE FIRST NATIONAL BANK TONIGHT!
IT AIN'T GONNA WORK.
THAT NIGHT EBONY IS FORCED TO WORK ON A SAFE WITH HIS NEW "BOSSES"..
TWO LEF'... ONE RIGHT..SIX LEF'...DEY IS FALLIN' INTO PLACE..
UNDER EBONY'S EXPERT INSTRUCTIONS THE DOOR EASILY OPENS.
IT'S A CINCH ....WE'LL CLEAN UP!
IT AIN'T GONNA WORK.
THEY ARRIVE AT THEIR HIDEOUT TO FIND AN ANGRY MAN AWAITING THEM.
W-WHY, IT'S BOSS GARVY!
YEAH..WHAT'S THE IDEA MUSCLIN' IN ON MY TERRITORY? WHY I OUGHTA..
(GULP) NOW WAIT A MINUTE! DON'T GET SORE..LOOK, THIS KID CAN SEE RIGHT INTO A STEEL VAULT, HE'S GOT X-RAY EYES! I..I'LL SELL HIM TO YA FOR A GRAND, JES' TO SHOW YA I'M YOUR PAL.
SAY, THAT AIN'T BAD... BUT IF DIS AIN'T ON THE LEVEL.
SHALL I WRAP HIM UP??
NO, I'LL TAKE HIM WITH ME... I'LL USE HIM ON THE NEW BANK TOMORROW..

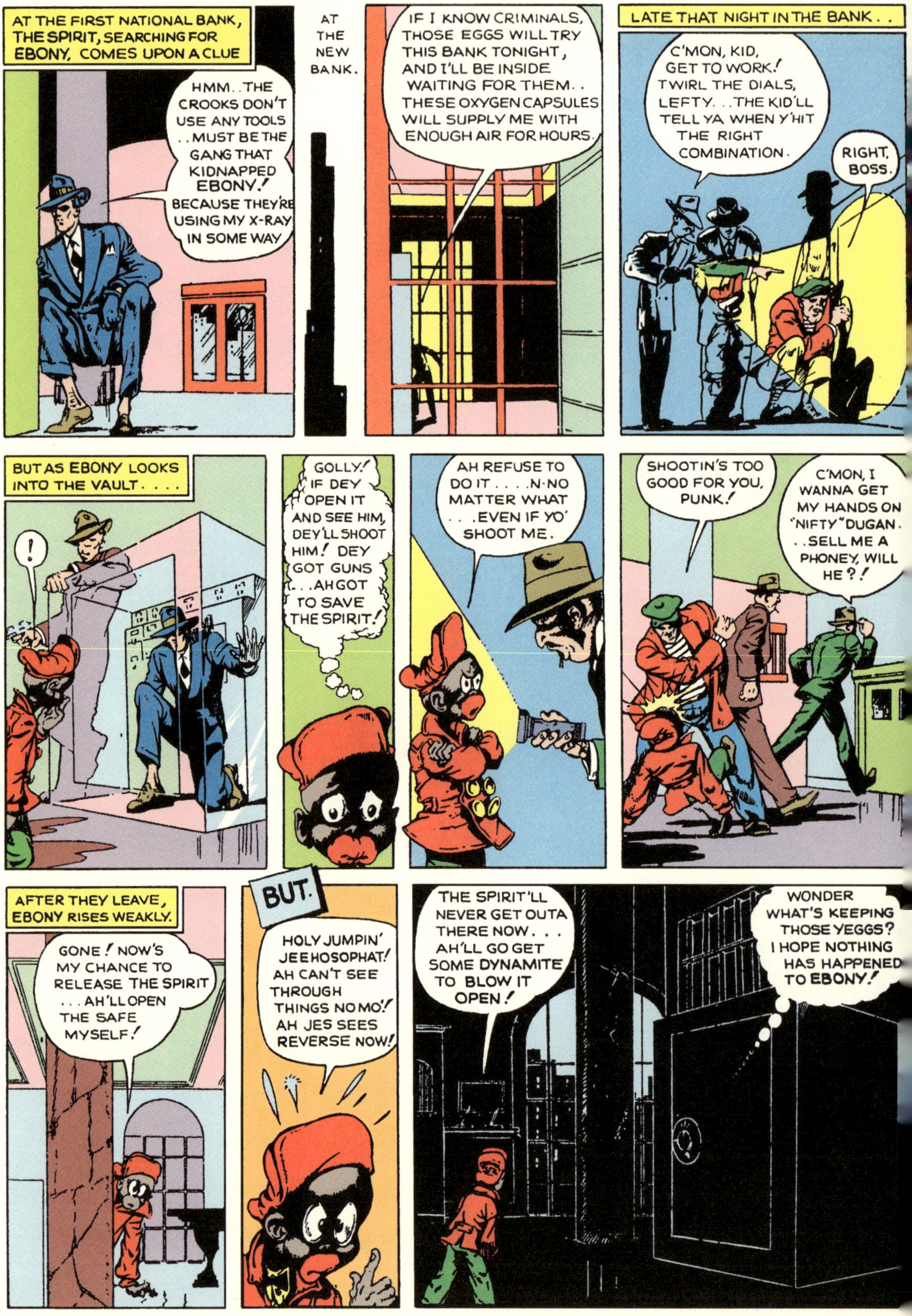
AT THE FIRST NATIONAL BANK, THE SPIRIT, SEARCHING FOR EBONY, COMES UPON A CLUE
HMM..THE CROOKS DON'T USE ANY TOOLS ..MUST BE THE GANG THAT KIDNAPPED EBONY! BECAUSE THEY'RE USING MY X-RAY IN SOME WAY
AT THE NEW BANK.
IF I KNOW CRIMINALS, THOSE EGGS WILL TRY THIS BANK TONIGHT, AND I'LL BE INSIDE WAITING FOR THEM.. THESE OXYGEN CAPSULES WILL SUPPLY ME WITH ENOUGH AIR FOR HOURS.
LATE THAT NIGHT IN THE BANK..
C'MON, KID, GET TO WORK! TWIRL THE DIALS, LEFTY...THE KID'LL TELL YA WHEN Y'HIT THE RIGHT COMBINATION.
RIGHT, BOSS.
BUT AS EBONY LOOKS INTO THE VAULT....
!
GOLLY! IF DEY OPEN IT AND SEE HIM, DEY'LL SHOOT HIM! DEY GOT GUNS ...AH GOT TO SAVE THE SPIRIT!
AH REFUSE TO DO IT....N-NO MATTER WHAT ...EVEN IF YO' SHOOT ME.
SHOOTIN'S TOO GOOD FOR YOU, PUNK!
C'MON, I WANNA GET MY HANDS ON "NIFTY" DUGAN. ..SELL ME A PHONEY, WILL HE?!
AFTER THEY LEAVE, EBONY RISES WEAKLY.
GONE! NOW'S MY CHANCE TO RELEASE THE SPIRIT ...AH'LL OPEN THE SAFE MYSELF!
BUT.
HOLY JUMPIN' JEEHOSOPHAT! AH CAN'T SEE THROUGH THINGS NO MO'! AH JES SEES REVERSE NOW!
THE SPIRIT'LL NEVER GET OUTA THERE NOW... AH'LL GO GET SOME DYNAMITE TO BLOW IT OPEN!
WONDER WHAT'S KEEPING THOSE YEGGS? I HOPE NOTHING HAS HAPPENED TO EBONY!

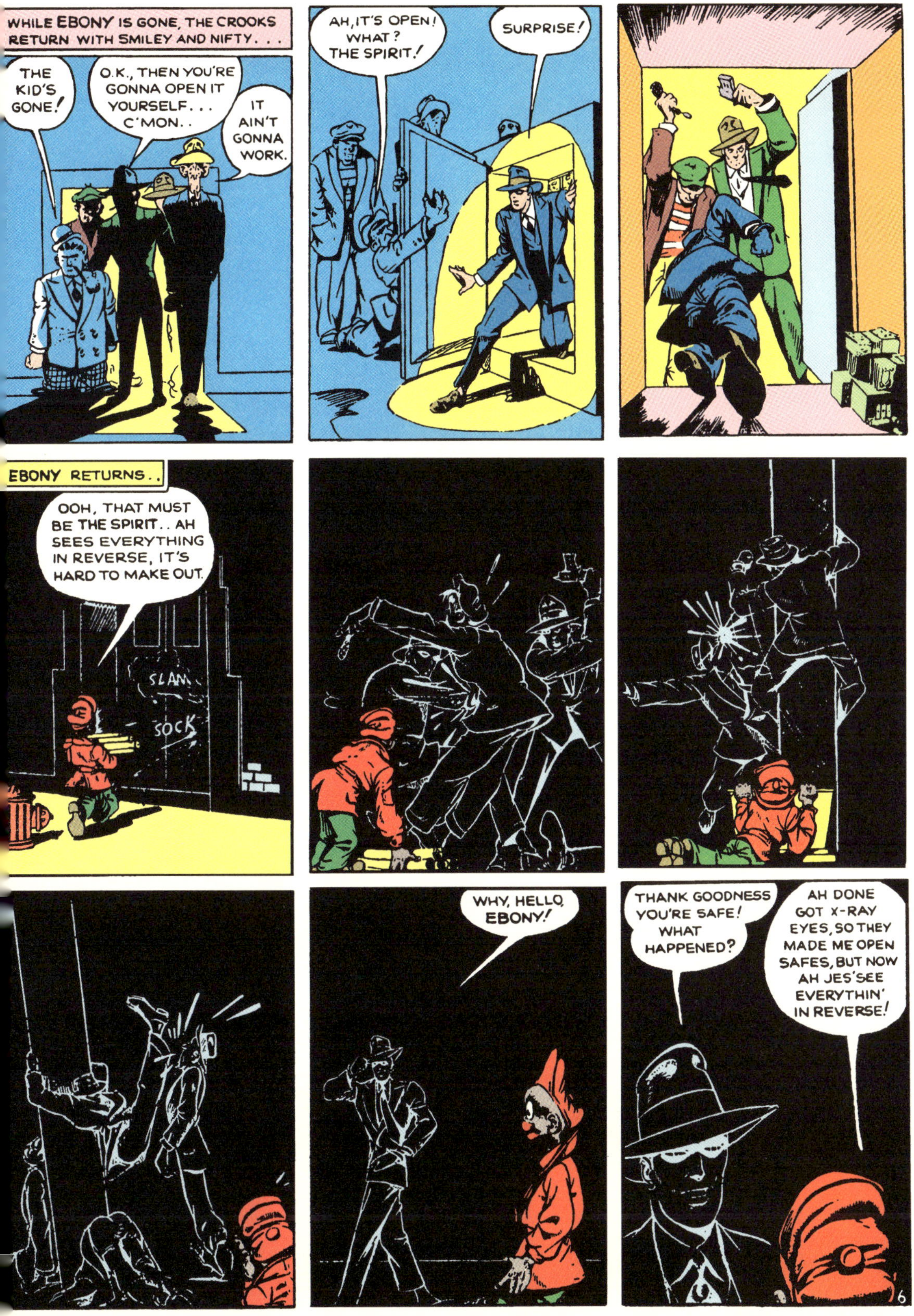
WHILE EBONY IS GONE, THE CROOKS RETURN WITH SMILEY AND NIFTY. . .
THE KID'S GONE!
O.K., THEN YOU'RE GONNA OPEN IT YOURSELF. . . C'MON. .
IT AIN'T GONNA WORK.
AH, IT'S OPEN! WHAT? THE SPIRIT!
SURPRISE!
EBONY RETURNS. .
OOH, THAT MUST BE THE SPIRIT. . AH SEES EVERYTHING IN REVERSE, IT'S HARD TO MAKE OUT.
SLAM
SOCK
WHY, HELLO EBONY!
THANK GOODNESS YOU'RE SAFE! WHAT HAPPENED?
AH DONE GOT X-RAY EYES, SO THEY MADE ME OPEN SAFES, BUT NOW AH JES'SEE EVERYTHIN' IN REVERSE!
6

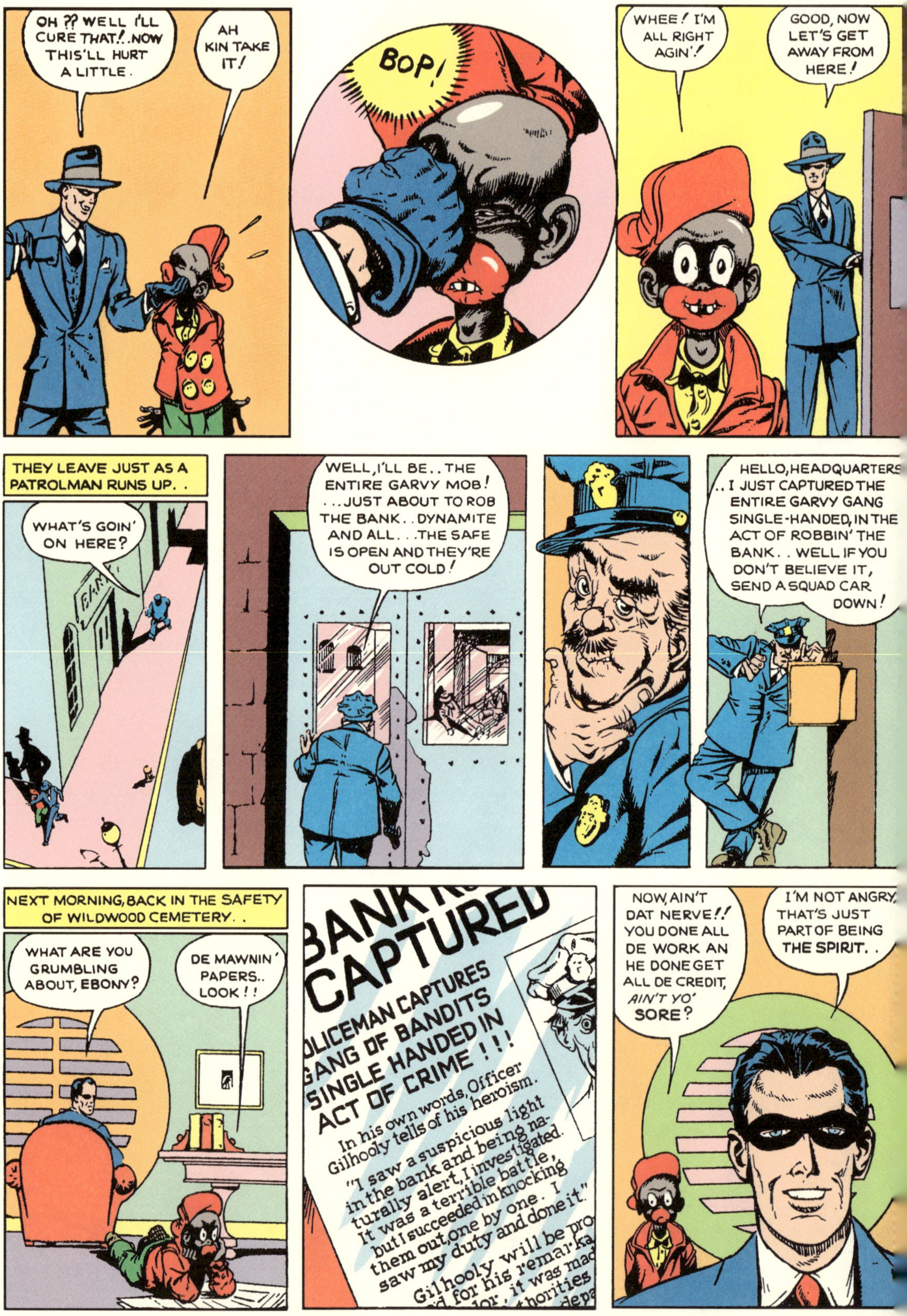
OH ?? WELL I'LL CURE THAT!..NOW THIS'LL HURT A LITTLE.
AH KIN TAKE IT!
BOP!
WHEE! I'M ALL RIGHT AGIN'!
GOOD, NOW LET'S GET AWAY FROM HERE!
THEY LEAVE JUST AS A PATROLMAN RUNS UP..
WHAT'S GOIN' ON HERE?
WELL, I'LL BE.. THE ENTIRE GARVY MOB! ...JUST ABOUT TO ROB THE BANK.. DYNAMITE AND ALL...THE SAFE IS OPEN AND THEY'RE OUT COLD!
HELLO, HEADQUARTERS.. I JUST CAPTURED THE ENTIRE GARVY GANG SINGLE-HANDED, IN THE ACT OF ROBBIN' THE BANK.. WELL IF YOU DON'T BELIEVE IT, SEND A SQUAD CAR DOWN!
NEXT MORNING, BACK IN THE SAFETY OF WILDWOOD CEMETERY..
WHAT ARE YOU GRUMBLING ABOUT, EBONY?
DE MAWNIN' PAPERS.. LOOK!!
CAPTURED
OLICEMAN CAPTURES
GANG OF BANDITS
SINGLE HANDED IN
ACT OF CRIME!!!
In his own words, Officer Gilhooly tells of his heroism.
"I saw a suspicious light in the bank and being na-turally alert, I investigated. It was a terrible battle, but I succeeded in knocking them out, one by one. I saw my duty and done it."
NOW, AIN'T DAT NERVE!! YOU DONE ALL DE WORK AN HE DONE GET ALL DE CREDIT, AIN'T YO' SORE?
I'M NOT ANGRY, THAT'S JUST PART OF BEING THE SPIRIT..

GANG WARFARE

September 22, 1940

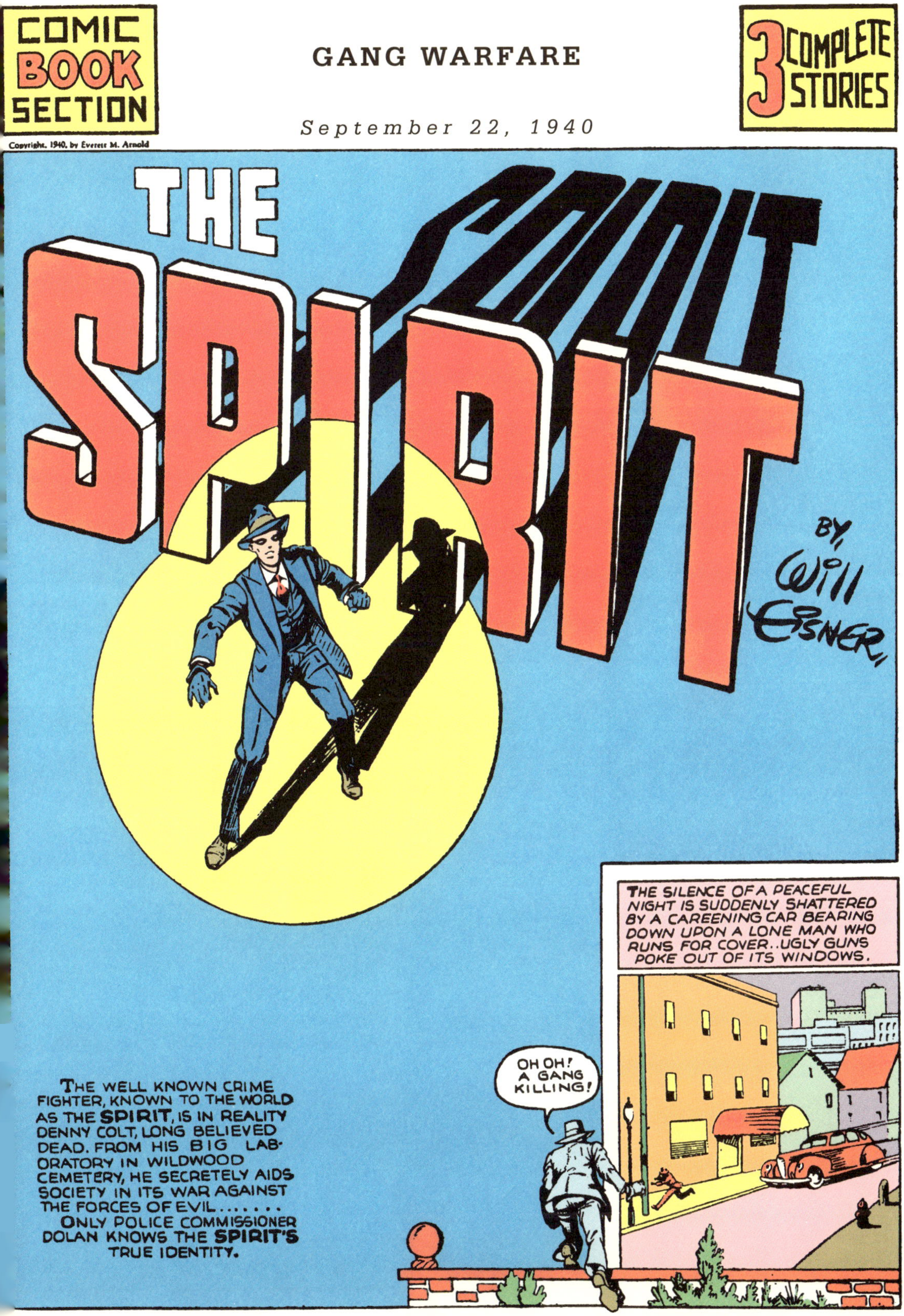

COMIC BOOK SECTION
Copyright, 1940, by Everett M. Arnold
3 COMPLETE STORIES
THE SPIRIT
BY, Will Eisner
THE SILENCE OF A PEACEFUL NIGHT IS SUDDENLY SHATTERED BY A CAREENING CAR BEARING DOWN UPON A LONE MAN WHO RUNS FOR COVER..UGLY GUNS POKE OUT OF ITS WINDOWS.
OH OH! A GANG KILLING!
THE WELL KNOWN CRIME FIGHTER, KNOWN TO THE WORLD AS THE SPIRIT, IS IN REALITY DENNY COLT, LONG BELIEVED DEAD. FROM HIS BIG LABORATORY IN WILDWOOD CEMETERY, HE SECRETELY AIDS SOCIETY IN ITS WAR AGAINST THE FORCES OF EVIL.......
ONLY POLICE COMMISSIONER DOLAN KNOWS THE SPIRIT'S TRUE IDENTITY.

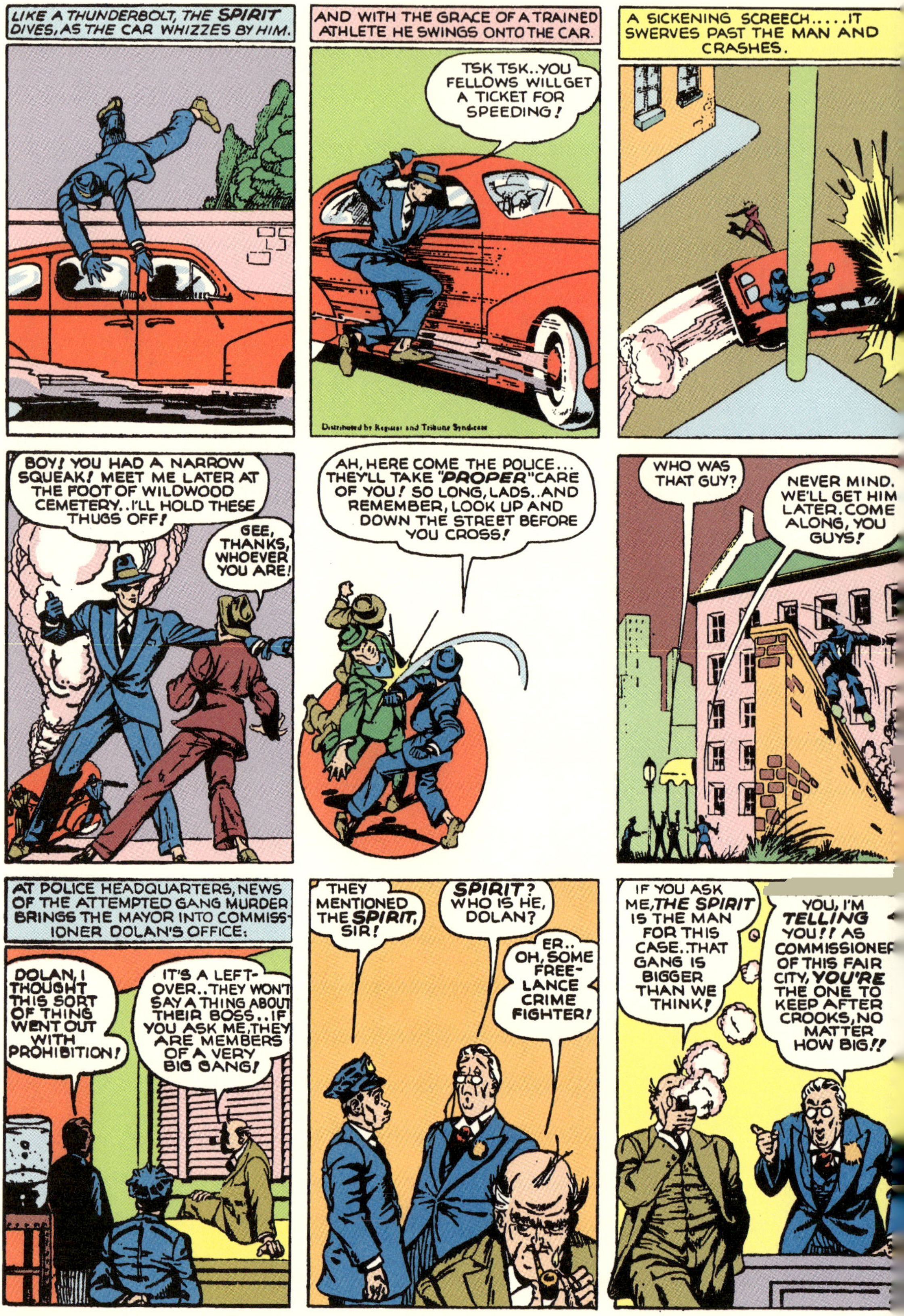

LIKE A THUNDERBOLT, THE SPIRIT DIVES, AS THE CAR WHIZZES BY HIM.
AND WITH THE GRACE OF A TRAINED ATHLETE HE SWINGS ONTO THE CAR.
TSK TSK..YOU FELLOWS WILL GET A TICKET FOR SPEEDING!
Distributed by Register and Tribune Syndicate
A SICKENING SCREECH.....IT SWERVES PAST THE MAN AND CRASHES.
BOY! YOU HAD A NARROW SQUEAK! MEET ME LATER AT THE FOOT OF WILDWOOD CEMETERY..I'LL HOLD THESE THUGS OFF!
GEE, THANKS, WHOEVER YOU ARE!
AH, HERE COME THE POLICE... THEY'LL TAKE "PROPER" CARE OF YOU! SO LONG, LADS..AND REMEMBER, LOOK UP AND DOWN THE STREET BEFORE YOU CROSS!
WHO WAS THAT GUY?
NEVER MIND. WE'LL GET HIM LATER. COME ALONG, YOU GUYS!
AT POLICE HEADQUARTERS, NEWS OF THE ATTEMPTED GANG MURDER BRINGS THE MAYOR INTO COMMISSIONER DOLAN'S OFFICE:
DOLAN, I THOUGHT THIS SORT OF THING WENT OUT WITH PROHIBITION!
IT'S A LEFT-OVER..THEY WON'T SAY A THING ABOUT THEIR BOSS..IF YOU ASK ME, THEY ARE MEMBERS OF A VERY BIG GANG!
THEY MENTIONED THE SPIRIT, SIR!
SPIRIT? WHO IS HE, DOLAN?
ER.. OH, SOME FREE-LANCE CRIME FIGHTER!
IF YOU ASK ME, THE SPIRIT IS THE MAN FOR THIS CASE..THAT GANG IS BIGGER THAN WE THINK!
YOU, I'M TELLING YOU!! AS COMMISSIONE OF THIS FAIR CITY, YOU'RE THE ONE TO KEEP AFTER CROOKS, NO MATTER HOW BIG!!

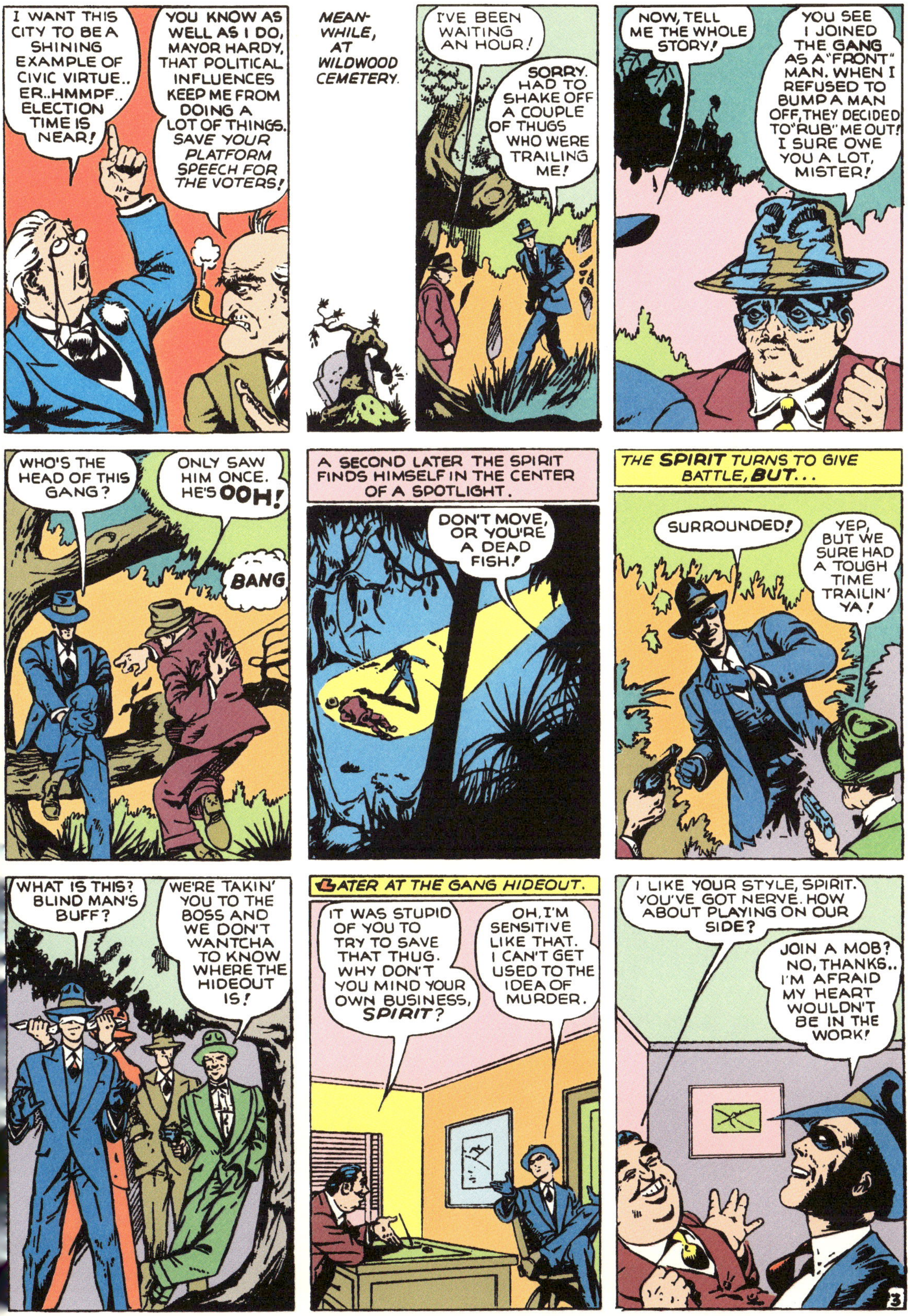
I WANT THIS CITY TO BE A SHINING EXAMPLE OF CIVIC VIRTUE.. ER..HMMPF.. ELECTION TIME IS NEAR!
YOU KNOW AS WELL AS I DO, MAYOR HARDY, THAT POLITICAL INFLUENCES KEEP ME FROM DOING A LOT OF THINGS. SAVE YOUR PLATFORM SPEECH FOR THE VOTERS!
MEAN-WHILE, AT WILDWOOD CEMETERY.
I'VE BEEN WAITING AN HOUR!
SORRY. HAD TO SHAKE OFF A COUPLE OF THUGS WHO WERE TRAILING ME!
NOW, TELL ME THE WHOLE STORY!
YOU SEE I JOINED THE GANG AS A "FRONT" MAN. WHEN I REFUSED TO BUMP A MAN OFF, THEY DECIDED TO "RUB" ME OUT! I SURE OWE YOU A LOT, MISTER!
WHO'S THE HEAD OF THIS GANG?
ONLY SAW HIM ONCE. HE'S OOH!
BANG
A SECOND LATER THE SPIRIT FINDS HIMSELF IN THE CENTER OF A SPOTLIGHT.
DON'T MOVE, OR YOU'RE A DEAD FISH!
THE SPIRIT TURNS TO GIVE BATTLE, BUT...
SURROUNDED!
YEP, BUT WE SURE HAD A TOUGH TIME TRAILIN' YA!
WHAT IS THIS? BLIND MAN'S BUFF?
WE'RE TAKIN' YOU TO THE BOSS AND WE DON'T WANTCHA TO KNOW WHERE THE HIDEOUT IS!
LATER AT THE GANG HIDEOUT.
IT WAS STUPID OF YOU TO TRY TO SAVE THAT THUG. WHY DON'T YOU MIND YOUR OWN BUSINESS, SPIRIT?
OH, I'M SENSITIVE LIKE THAT. I CAN'T GET USED TO THE IDEA OF MURDER.
I LIKE YOUR STYLE, SPIRIT. YOU'VE GOT NERVE. HOW ABOUT PLAYING ON OUR SIDE?
JOIN A MOB? NO, THANKS.. I'M AFRAID MY HEART WOULDN'T BE IN THE WORK!
3

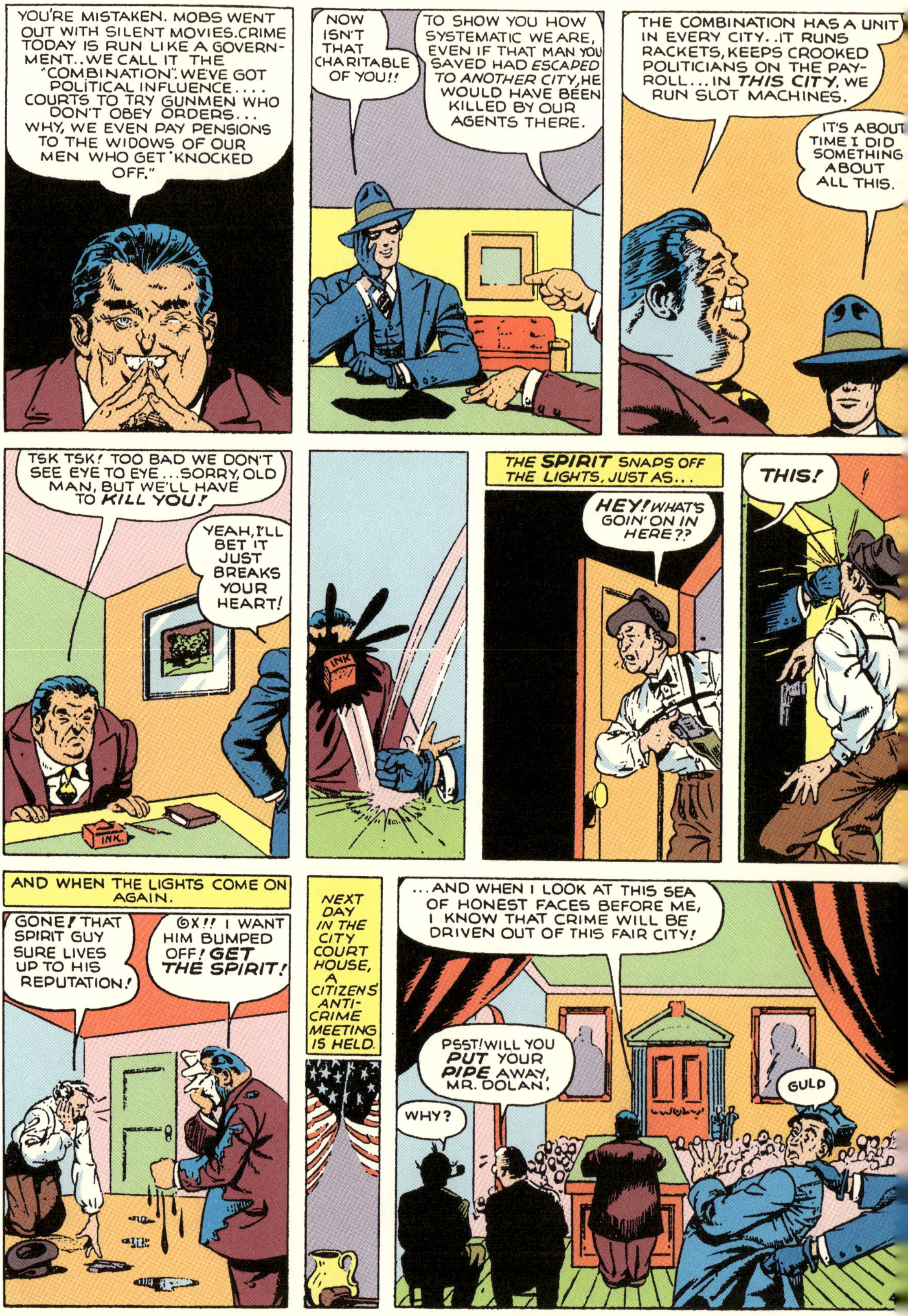
YOU'RE MISTAKEN. MOBS WENT OUT WITH SILENT MOVIES. CRIME TODAY IS RUN LIKE A GOVERNMENT.. WE CALL IT THE "COMBINATION". WE'VE GOT POLITICAL INFLUENCE.... COURTS TO TRY GUNMEN WHO DON'T OBEY ORDERS... WHY, WE EVEN PAY PENSIONS TO THE WIDOWS OF OUR MEN WHO GET "KNOCKED OFF."
NOW ISN'T THAT CHARITABLE OF YOU!!
TO SHOW YOU HOW SYSTEMATIC WE ARE, EVEN IF THAT MAN YOU SAVED HAD ESCAPED TO ANOTHER CITY, HE WOULD HAVE BEEN KILLED BY OUR AGENTS THERE.
THE COMBINATION HAS A UNIT IN EVERY CITY. .IT RUNS RACKETS, KEEPS CROOKED POLITICIANS ON THE PAYROLL... IN THIS CITY, WE RUN SLOT MACHINES.
IT'S ABOUT TIME I DID SOMETHING ABOUT ALL THIS.
TSK TSK! TOO BAD WE DON'T SEE EYE TO EYE... SORRY, OLD MAN, BUT WE'LL HAVE TO KILL YOU!
YEAH, I'LL BET IT JUST BREAKS YOUR HEART!
INK
THE SPIRIT SNAPS OFF THE LIGHTS, JUST AS...
HEY! WHAT'S GOIN' ON IN HERE??
THIS!
AND WHEN THE LIGHTS COME ON AGAIN.
GONE! THAT SPIRIT GUY SURE LIVES UP TO HIS REPUTATION!
@X!! I WANT HIM BUMPED OFF! GET THE SPIRIT!
NEXT DAY IN THE CITY COURT HOUSE, A CITIZENS' ANTI-CRIME MEETING IS HELD.
...AND WHEN I LOOK AT THIS SEA OF HONEST FACES BEFORE ME, I KNOW THAT CRIME WILL BE DRIVEN OUT OF THIS FAIR CITY!
PSST! WILL YOU PUT YOUR PIPE AWAY, MR. DOLAN.
WHY?
GULP

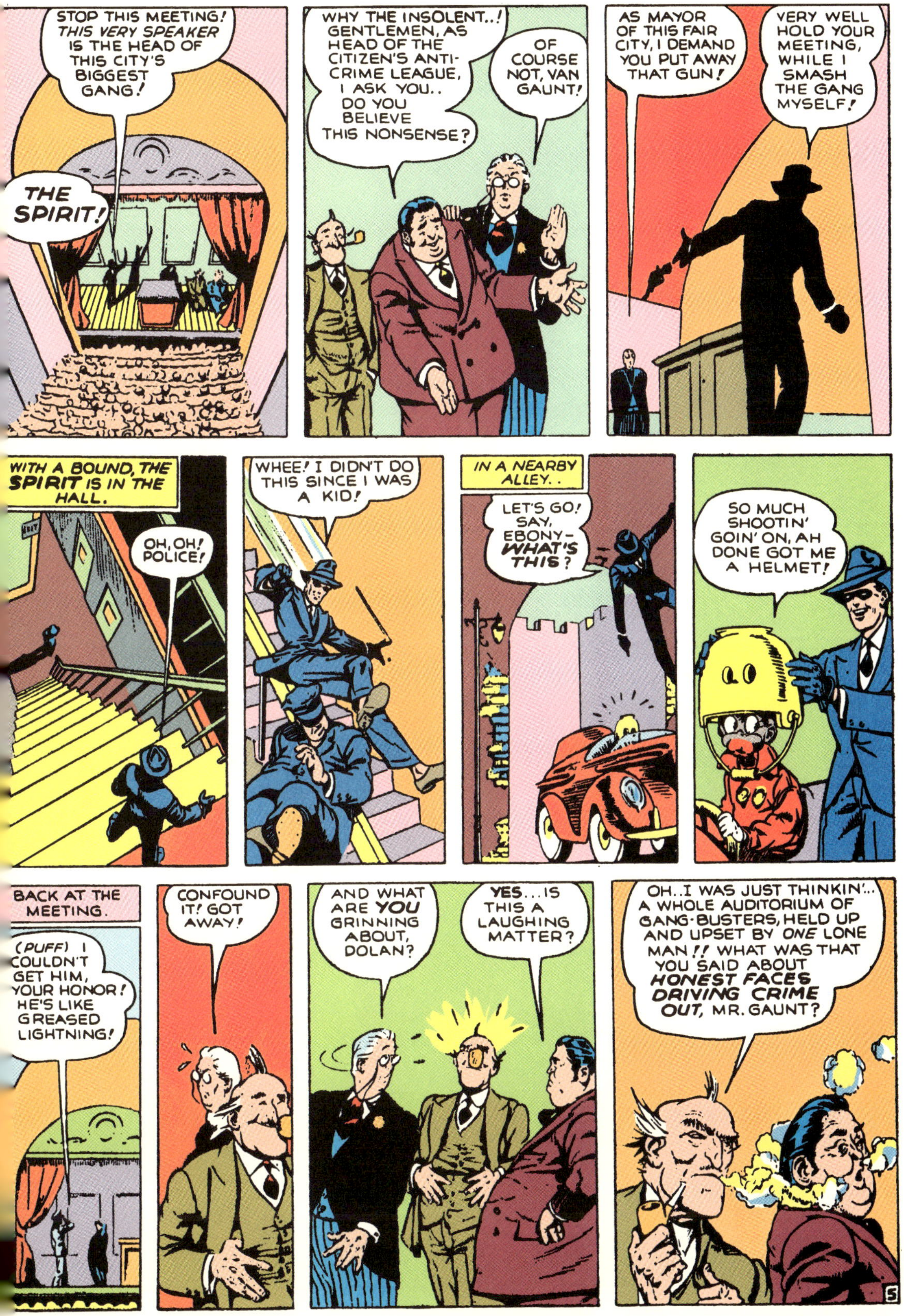

STOP THIS MEETING! THIS VERY SPEAKER IS THE HEAD OF THIS CITY'S BIGGEST GANG!
THE SPIRIT!
WHY THE INSOLENT..! GENTLEMEN, AS HEAD OF THE CITIZEN'S ANTI-CRIME LEAGUE, I ASK YOU.. DO YOU BELIEVE THIS NONSENSE?
OF COURSE NOT, VAN GAUNT!
AS MAYOR OF THIS FAIR CITY, I DEMAND YOU PUT AWAY THAT GUN!
VERY WELL HOLD YOUR MEETING, WHILE I SMASH THE GANG MYSELF!
WITH A BOUND, THE SPIRIT IS IN THE HALL.
OH, OH! POLICE!
WHEE! I DIDN'T DO THIS SINCE I WAS A KID!
IN A NEARBY ALLEY..
LET'S GO! SAY, EBONY- WHAT'S THIS?
SO MUCH SHOOTIN' GOIN' ON, AH DONE GOT ME A HELMET!
BACK AT THE MEETING.
(PUFF) I COULDN'T GET HIM, YOUR HONOR! HE'S LIKE GREASED LIGHTNING!
CONFOUND IT! GOT AWAY!
AND WHAT ARE YOU GRINNING ABOUT, DOLAN?
YES...IS THIS A LAUGHING MATTER?
OH..I WAS JUST THINKIN'.. A WHOLE AUDITORIUM OF GANG-BUSTERS, HELD UP AND UPSET BY ONE LONE MAN!! WHAT WAS THAT YOU SAID ABOUT HONEST FACES DRIVING CRIME OUT, MR. GAUNT?
5

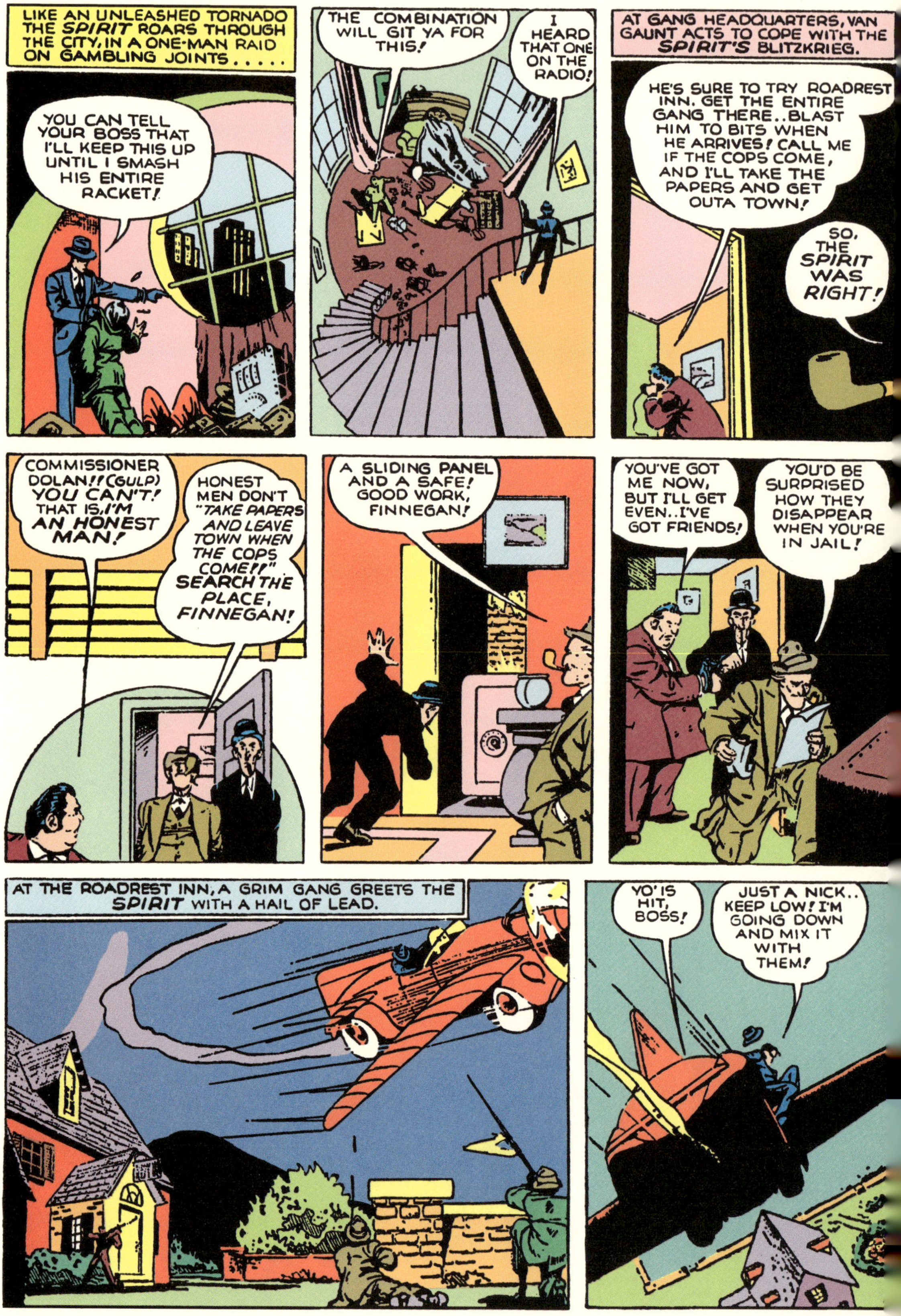
LIKE AN UNLEASHED TORNADO THE SPIRIT ROARS THROUGH THE CITY, IN A ONE-MAN RAID ON GAMBLING JOINTS.....
YOU CAN TELL YOUR BOSS THAT I'LL KEEP THIS UP UNTIL I SMASH HIS ENTIRE RACKET!
THE COMBINATION WILL GIT YA FOR THIS!
I HEARD THAT ONE ON THE RADIO!
AT GANG HEADQUARTERS, VAN GAUNT ACTS TO COPE WITH THE SPIRIT'S BLITZKRIEG.
HE'S SURE TO TRY ROADREST INN. GET THE ENTIRE GANG THERE..BLAST HIM TO BITS WHEN HE ARRIVES! CALL ME IF THE COPS COME, AND I'LL TAKE THE PAPERS AND GET OUTA TOWN!
SO, THE SPIRIT WAS RIGHT!
COMMISSIONER DOLAN!! (GULP) YOU CAN'T! THAT IS, I'M AN HONEST MAN!
HONEST MEN DON'T "TAKE PAPERS AND LEAVE TOWN WHEN THE COPS COME!!" SEARCH THE PLACE, FINNEGAN!
A SLIDING PANEL AND A SAFE! GOOD WORK, FINNEGAN!
YOU'VE GOT ME NOW, BUT I'LL GET EVEN..I'VE GOT FRIENDS!
YOU'D BE SURPRISED HOW THEY DISAPPEAR WHEN YOU'RE IN JAIL!
AT THE ROADREST INN, A GRIM GANG GREETS THE SPIRIT WITH A HAIL OF LEAD.
YO' IS HIT, BOSS!
JUST A NICK.. KEEP LOW! I'M GOING DOWN AND MIX IT WITH THEM!

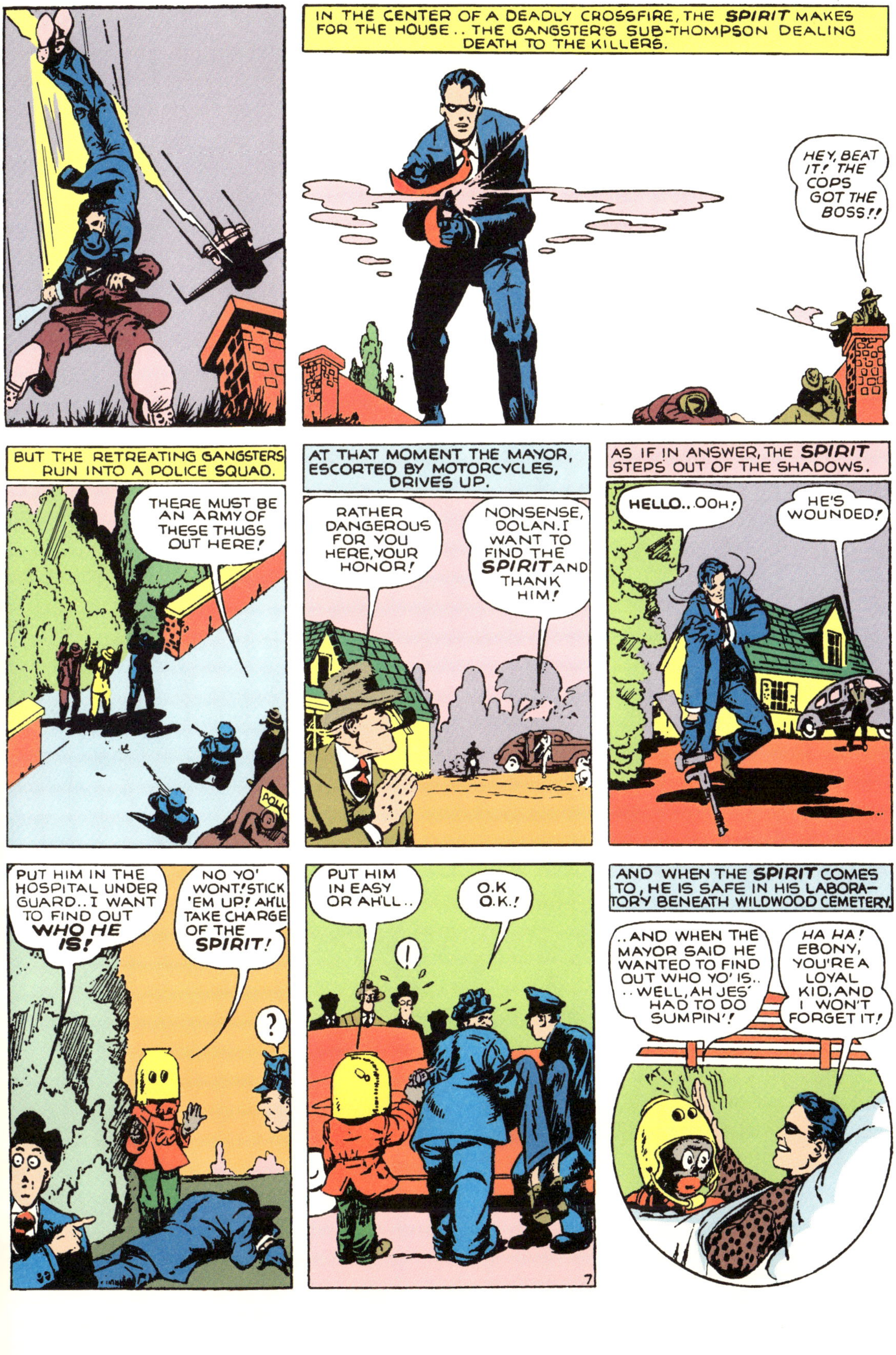

IN THE CENTER OF A DEADLY CROSSFIRE, THE SPIRIT MAKES FOR THE HOUSE.. THE GANGSTER'S SUB-THOMPSON DEALING DEATH TO THE KILLERS.
HEY, BEAT IT! THE COPS GOT THE BOSS!!
BUT THE RETREATING GANGSTERS RUN INTO A POLICE SQUAD.
THERE MUST BE AN ARMY OF THESE THUGS OUT HERE!
AT THAT MOMENT THE MAYOR, ESCORTED BY MOTORCYCLES, DRIVES UP.
RATHER DANGEROUS FOR YOU HERE, YOUR HONOR!
NONSENSE, DOLAN. I WANT TO FIND THE SPIRIT AND THANK HIM!
AS IF IN ANSWER, THE SPIRIT STEPS OUT OF THE SHADOWS.
HELLO.. OOH!
HE'S WOUNDED!
PUT HIM IN THE HOSPITAL UNDER GUARD.. I WANT TO FIND OUT WHO HE IS!
NO YO' WONT! STICK 'EM UP! AH'LL TAKE CHARGE OF THE SPIRIT!
?
PUT HIM IN EASY OR AH'LL..
O.K O.K.!
!
AND WHEN THE SPIRIT COMES TO, HE IS SAFE IN HIS LABORATORY BENEATH WILDWOOD CEMETERY.
..AND WHEN THE MAYOR SAID HE WANTED TO FIND OUT WHO YO' IS.. ..WELL, AH JES' HAD TO DO SUMPIN'!
HA HA! EBONY, YOU'RE A LOYAL KID, AND I WON'T FORGET IT!
PAT! PAT!
7

ORIENTAL AGENTS

September 28, 1940

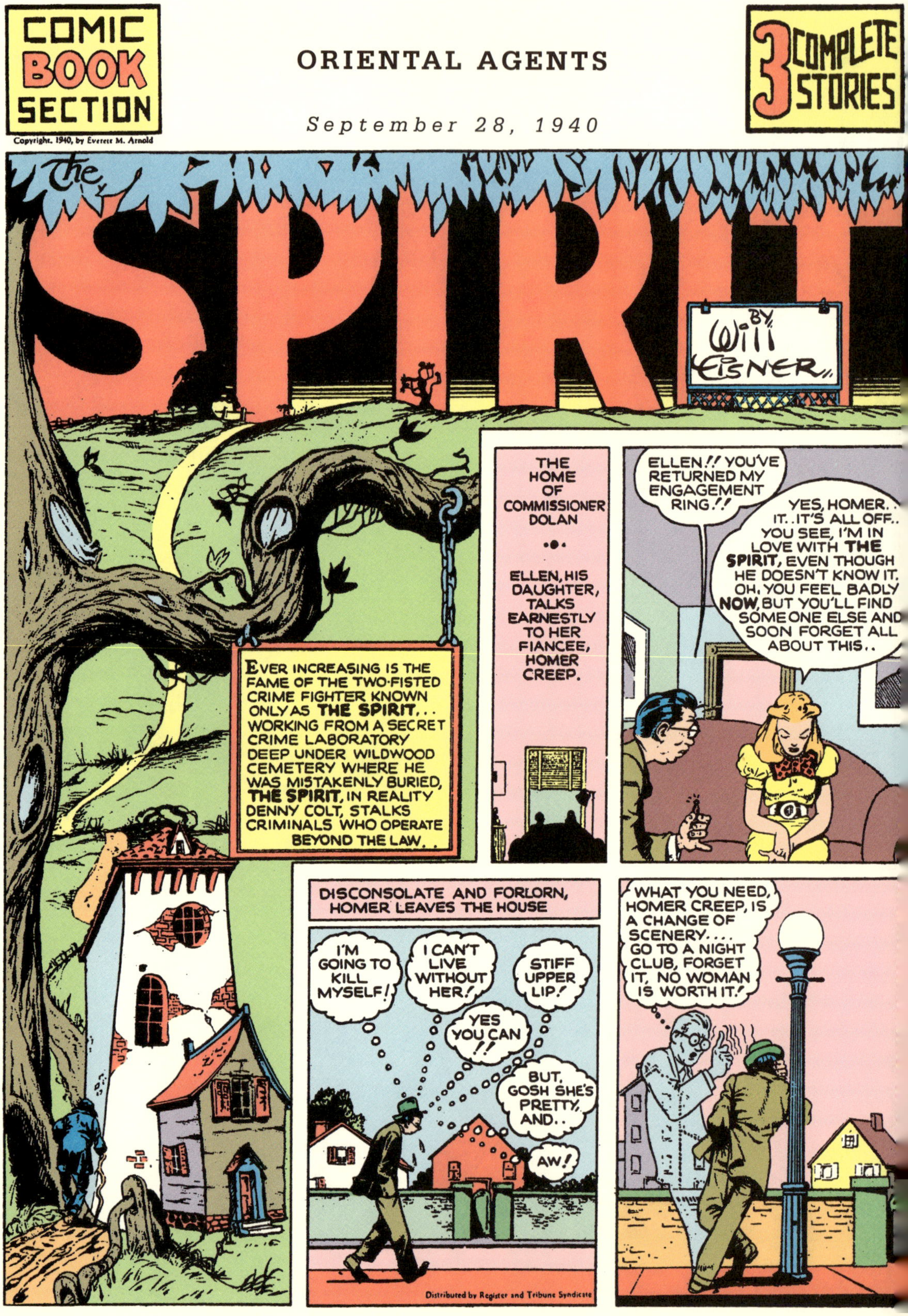
COMIC BOOK SECTION
Copyright, 1940, by Everett M. Arnold
3 COMPLETE STORIES
The SPIRIT
BY Will Eisner
EVER INCREASING IS THE FAME OF THE TWO-FISTED CRIME FIGHTER KNOWN ONLY AS THE SPIRIT... WORKING FROM A SECRET CRIME LABORATORY DEEP UNDER WILDWOOD CEMETERY WHERE HE WAS MISTAKENLY BURIED, THE SPIRIT, IN REALITY DENNY COLT, STALKS CRIMINALS WHO OPERATE BEYOND THE LAW..
THE HOME OF COMMISSIONER DOLAN
ELLEN, HIS DAUGHTER, TALKS EARNESTLY TO HER FIANCEE, HOMER CREEP.
ELLEN!! YOU'VE RETURNED MY ENGAGEMENT RING!!
YES, HOMER.. IT..IT'S ALL OFF.. YOU SEE, I'M IN LOVE WITH THE SPIRIT, EVEN THOUGH HE DOESN'T KNOW IT. OH, YOU FEEL BADLY NOW, BUT YOU'LL FIND SOME ONE ELSE AND SOON FORGET ALL ABOUT THIS..
DISCONSOLATE AND FORLORN, HOMER LEAVES THE HOUSE
I'M GOING TO KILL MYSELF!
I CAN'T LIVE WITHOUT HER!
STIFF UPPER LIP!
YES YOU CAN!!
BUT, GOSH SHE'S PRETTY, AND..
AW!
Distributed by Register and Tribune Syndicate
WHAT YOU NEED, HOMER CREEP, IS A CHANGE OF SCENERY.... GO TO A NIGHT CLUB, FORGET IT, NO WOMAN IS WORTH IT!

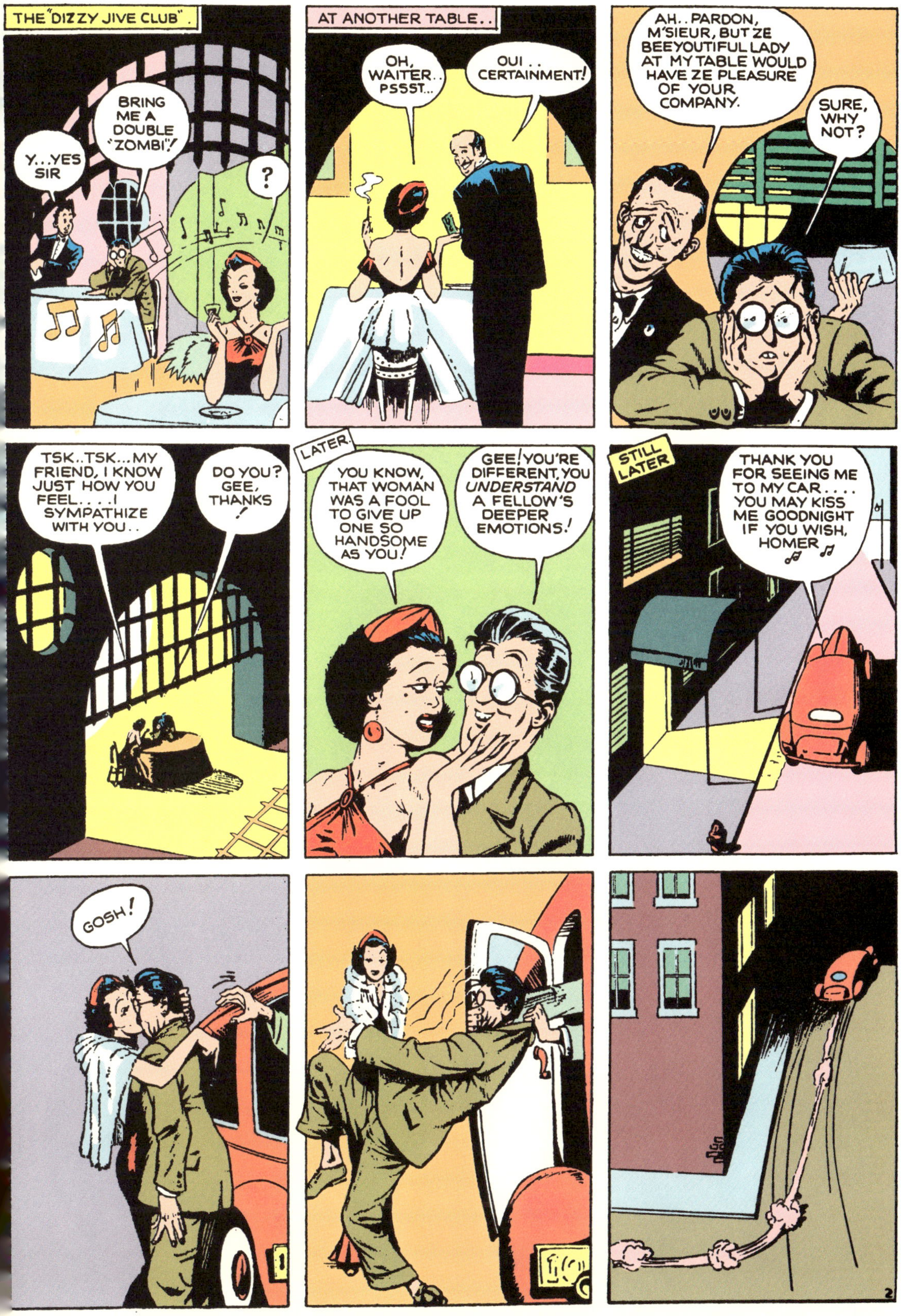
THE "DIZZY JIVE CLUB".
BRING ME A DOUBLE "ZOMBI"!
Y...YES SIR
?
AT ANOTHER TABLE..
OH, WAITER.. PSSST...
OUI.. CERTAINMENT!
AH.. PARDON, M'SIEUR, BUT ZE BEEYOUTIFUL LADY AT MY TABLE WOULD HAVE ZE PLEASURE OF YOUR COMPANY.
SURE, WHY NOT?
TSK..TSK...MY FRIEND, I KNOW JUST HOW YOU FEEL....I SYMPATHIZE WITH YOU..
DO YOU? GEE, THANKS!
LATER
YOU KNOW, THAT WOMAN WAS A FOOL TO GIVE UP ONE SO HANDSOME AS YOU!
GEE! YOU'RE DIFFERENT, YOU *UNDERSTAND* A FELLOW'S DEEPER EMOTIONS!
STILL LATER
THANK YOU FOR SEEING ME TO MY CAR.... YOU MAY KISS ME GOODNIGHT IF YOU WISH, HOMER
GOSH!
2

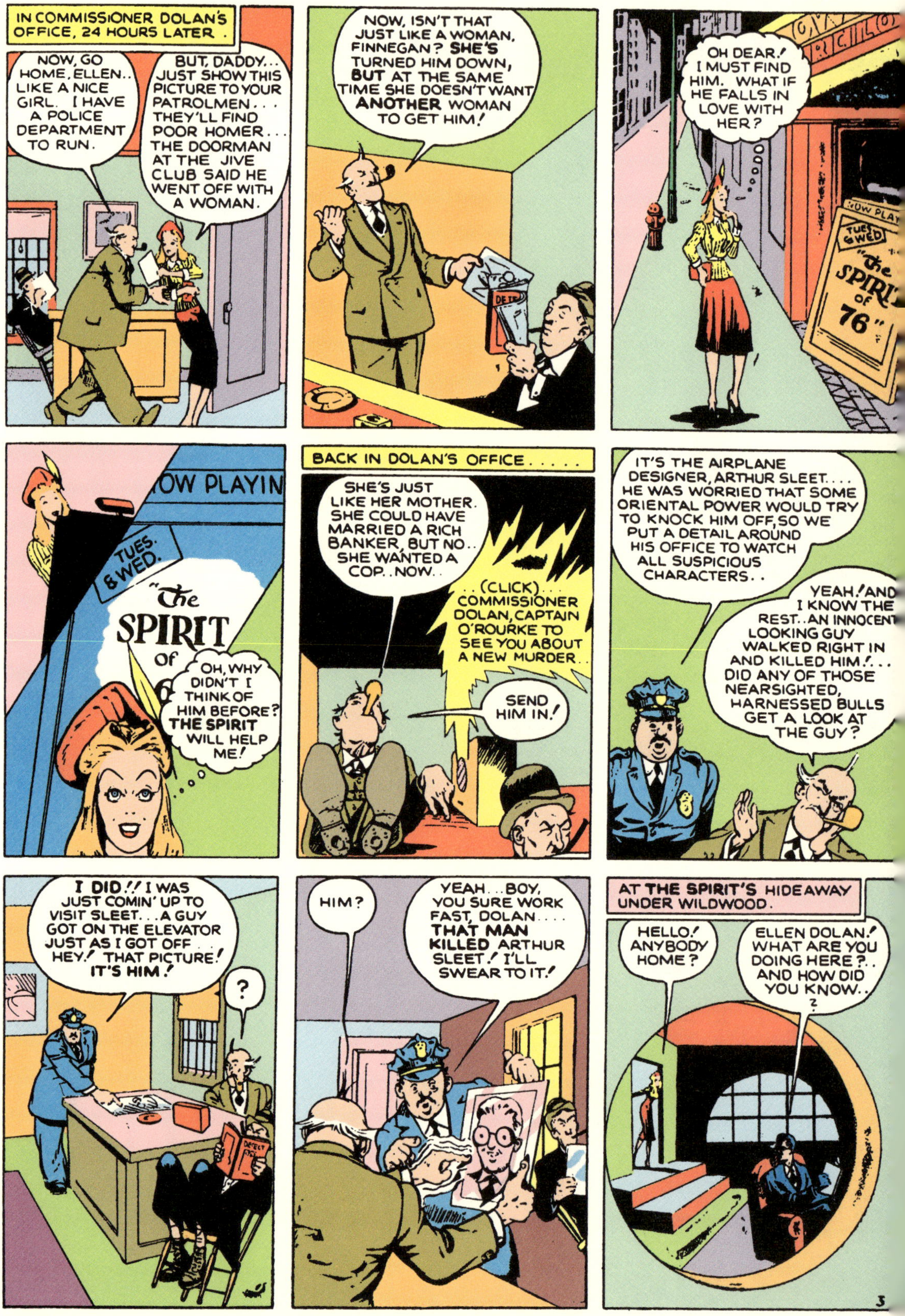

IN COMMISSIONER DOLAN'S OFFICE, 24 HOURS LATER.
NOW, GO HOME, ELLEN.. LIKE A NICE GIRL. I HAVE A POLICE DEPARTMENT TO RUN.
BUT, DADDY... JUST SHOW THIS PICTURE TO YOUR PATROLMEN... THEY'LL FIND POOR HOMER... THE DOORMAN AT THE JIVE CLUB SAID HE WENT OFF WITH A WOMAN.
NOW, ISN'T THAT JUST LIKE A WOMAN, FINNEGAN? SHE'S TURNED HIM DOWN, BUT AT THE SAME TIME SHE DOESN'T WANT ANOTHER WOMAN TO GET HIM!
OH DEAR! I MUST FIND HIM. WHAT IF HE FALLS IN LOVE WITH HER?
TUES & WED
"The SPIRIT of 76"
NOW PLAYIN
TUES. & WED.
"The SPIRIT of
OH, WHY DIDN'T I THINK OF HIM BEFORE? THE SPIRIT WILL HELP ME!
BACK IN DOLAN'S OFFICE.....
SHE'S JUST LIKE HER MOTHER. SHE COULD HAVE MARRIED A RICH BANKER, BUT NO.. SHE WANTED A COP..NOW..
..(CLICK)... COMMISSIONER DOLAN, CAPTAIN O'ROURKE TO SEE YOU ABOUT A NEW MURDER...
SEND HIM IN!
IT'S THE AIRPLANE DESIGNER, ARTHUR SLEET.... HE WAS WORRIED THAT SOME ORIENTAL POWER WOULD TRY TO KNOCK HIM OFF, SO WE PUT A DETAIL AROUND HIS OFFICE TO WATCH ALL SUSPICIOUS CHARACTERS..
YEAH! AND I KNOW THE REST..AN INNOCENT LOOKING GUY WALKED RIGHT IN AND KILLED HIM!... DID ANY OF THOSE NEARSIGHTED, HARNESSED BULLS GET A LOOK AT THE GUY?
I DID!! I WAS JUST COMIN' UP TO VISIT SLEET...A GUY GOT ON THE ELEVATOR JUST AS I GOT OFF.. HEY! THAT PICTURE! IT'S HIM!
?
HIM?
YEAH...BOY, YOU SURE WORK FAST, DOLAN.... THAT MAN KILLED ARTHUR SLEET! I'LL SWEAR TO IT!
AT THE SPIRIT'S HIDEAWAY UNDER WILDWOOD.
HELLO! ANYBODY HOME?
ELLEN DOLAN! WHAT ARE YOU DOING HERE?.. AND HOW DID YOU KNOW..?
3

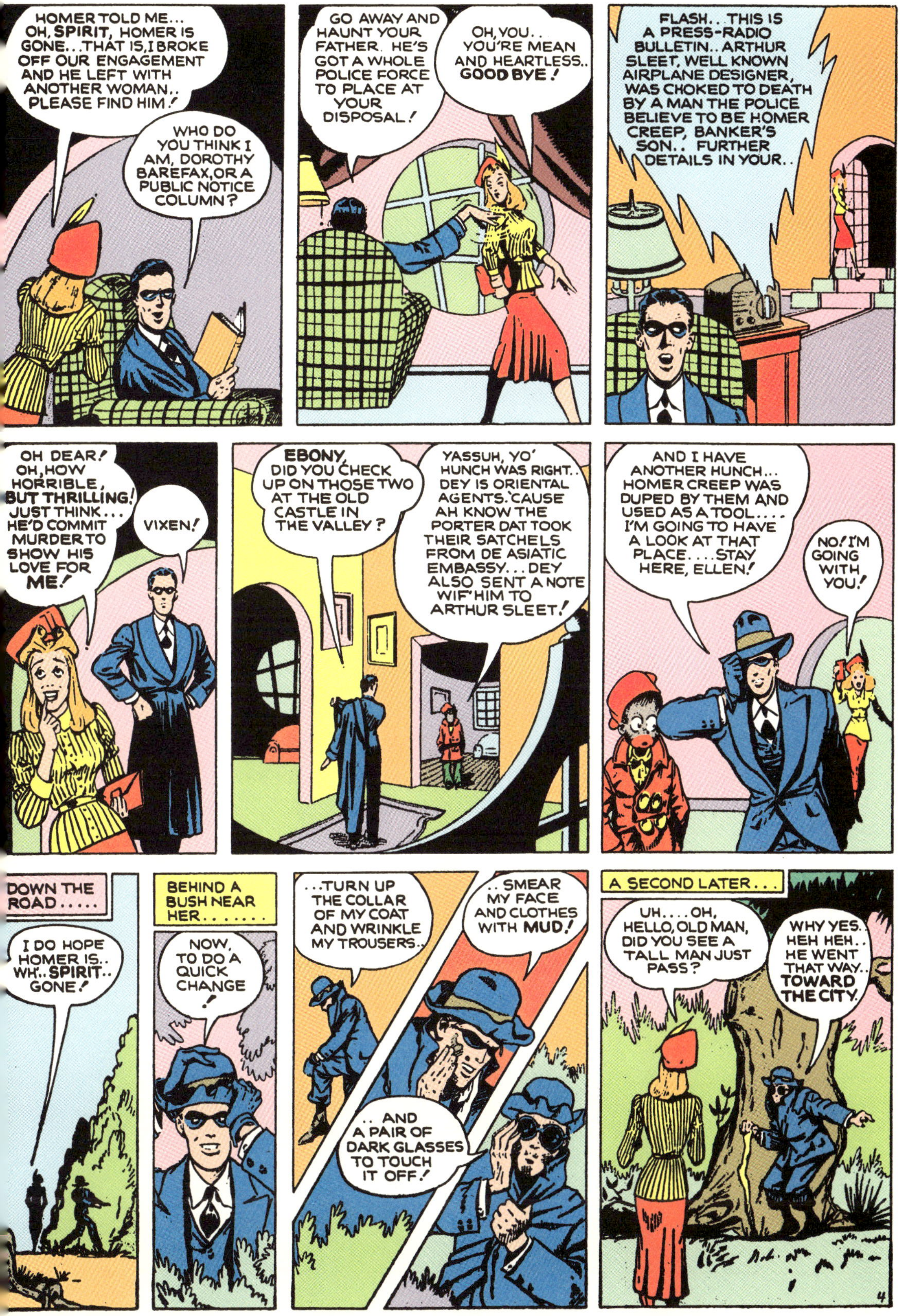

HOMER TOLD ME... OH, SPIRIT, HOMER IS GONE... THAT IS, I BROKE OFF OUR ENGAGEMENT AND HE LEFT WITH ANOTHER WOMAN.. PLEASE FIND HIM!
WHO DO YOU THINK I AM, DOROTHY BAREFAX, OR A PUBLIC NOTICE COLUMN?
GO AWAY AND HAUNT YOUR FATHER. HE'S GOT A WHOLE POLICE FORCE TO PLACE AT YOUR DISPOSAL!
OH, YOU.. YOU'RE MEAN AND HEARTLESS.. GOOD BYE!
FLASH.. THIS IS A PRESS-RADIO BULLETIN.. ARTHUR SLEET, WELL KNOWN AIRPLANE DESIGNER, WAS CHOKED TO DEATH BY A MAN THE POLICE BELIEVE TO BE HOMER CREEP, BANKER'S SON.. FURTHER DETAILS IN YOUR..
OH DEAR! OH, HOW HORRIBLE, BUT THRILLING! JUST THINK... HE'D COMMIT MURDER TO SHOW HIS LOVE FOR ME!
VIXEN!
EBONY, DID YOU CHECK UP ON THOSE TWO AT THE OLD CASTLE IN THE VALLEY?
YASSUH, YO' HUNCH WAS RIGHT.. DEY IS ORIENTAL AGENTS. 'CAUSE AH KNOW THE PORTER DAT TOOK THEIR SATCHELS FROM DE ASIATIC EMBASSY... DEY ALSO SENT A NOTE WIF HIM TO ARTHUR SLEET!
AND I HAVE ANOTHER HUNCH... HOMER CREEP WAS DUPED BY THEM AND USED AS A TOOL.... I'M GOING TO HAVE A LOOK AT THAT PLACE.... STAY HERE, ELLEN!
NO! I'M GOING WITH YOU!
DOWN THE ROAD.....
I DO HOPE HOMER IS.. WH'.. SPIRIT.. GONE!
BEHIND A BUSH NEAR HER......
NOW, TO DO A QUICK CHANGE!
...TURN UP THE COLLAR OF MY COAT AND WRINKLE MY TROUSERS..
..SMEAR MY FACE AND CLOTHES WITH MUD!
..AND A PAIR OF DARK GLASSES TO TOUCH IT OFF!
A SECOND LATER...
UH.... OH, HELLO, OLD MAN, DID YOU SEE A TALL MAN JUST PASS?
WHY YES. HEH HEH.. HE WENT THAT WAY.. TOWARD THE CITY.
4

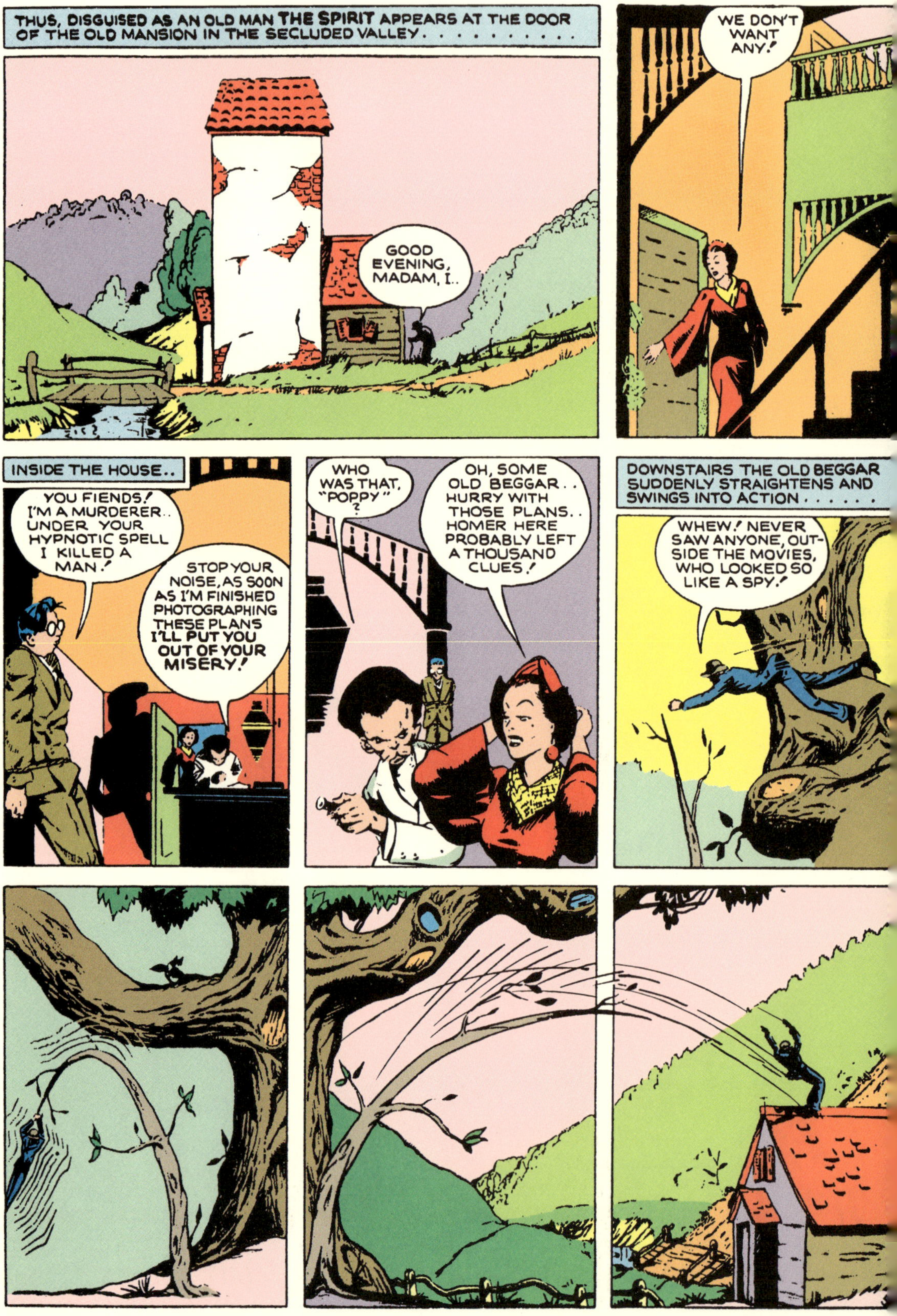
THUS, DISGUISED AS AN OLD MAN THE SPIRIT APPEARS AT THE DOOR OF THE OLD MANSION IN THE SECLUDED VALLEY. . . . .
GOOD EVENING, MADAM, I..
WE DON'T WANT ANY!
INSIDE THE HOUSE..
YOU FIENDS! I'M A MURDERER.. UNDER YOUR HYPNOTIC SPELL I KILLED A MAN!
STOP YOUR NOISE, AS SOON AS I'M FINISHED PHOTOGRAPHING THESE PLANS I'LL PUT YOU OUT OF YOUR MISERY!
WHO WAS THAT, "POPPY"?
OH, SOME OLD BEGGAR.. HURRY WITH THOSE PLANS.. HOMER HERE PROBABLY LEFT A THOUSAND CLUES!
DOWNSTAIRS THE OLD BEGGAR SUDDENLY STRAIGHTENS AND SWINGS INTO ACTION . . . . .
WHEW! NEVER SAW ANYONE, OUTSIDE THE MOVIES, WHO LOOKED SO LIKE A SPY!

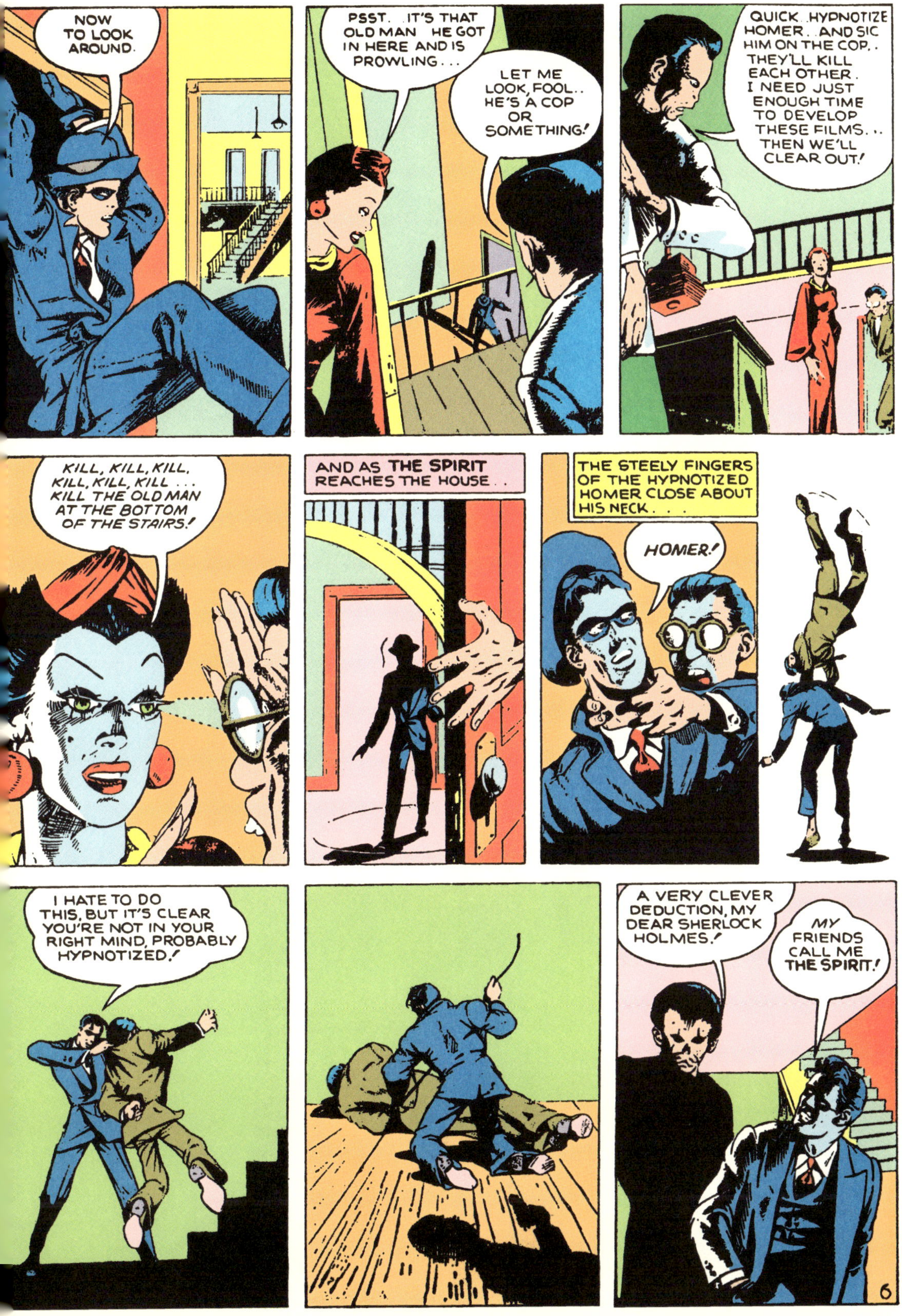
NOW TO LOOK AROUND.
PSST.. IT'S THAT OLD MAN.. HE GOT IN HERE AND IS PROWLING...
LET ME LOOK, FOOL.. HE'S A COP OR SOMETHING!
QUICK..HYPNOTIZE HOMER..AND SIC HIM ON THE COP.. THEY'LL KILL EACH OTHER. I NEED JUST ENOUGH TIME TO DEVELOP THESE FILMS... THEN WE'LL CLEAR OUT!
KILL, KILL, KILL, KILL, KILL, KILL... KILL THE OLD MAN AT THE BOTTOM OF THE STAIRS!
AND AS THE SPIRIT REACHES THE HOUSE..
THE STEELY FINGERS OF THE HYPNOTIZED HOMER CLOSE ABOUT HIS NECK...
HOMER!
I HATE TO DO THIS, BUT IT'S CLEAR YOU'RE NOT IN YOUR RIGHT MIND, PROBABLY HYPNOTIZED!
A VERY CLEVER DEDUCTION, MY DEAR SHERLOCK HOLMES!
MY FRIENDS CALL ME THE SPIRIT!
6

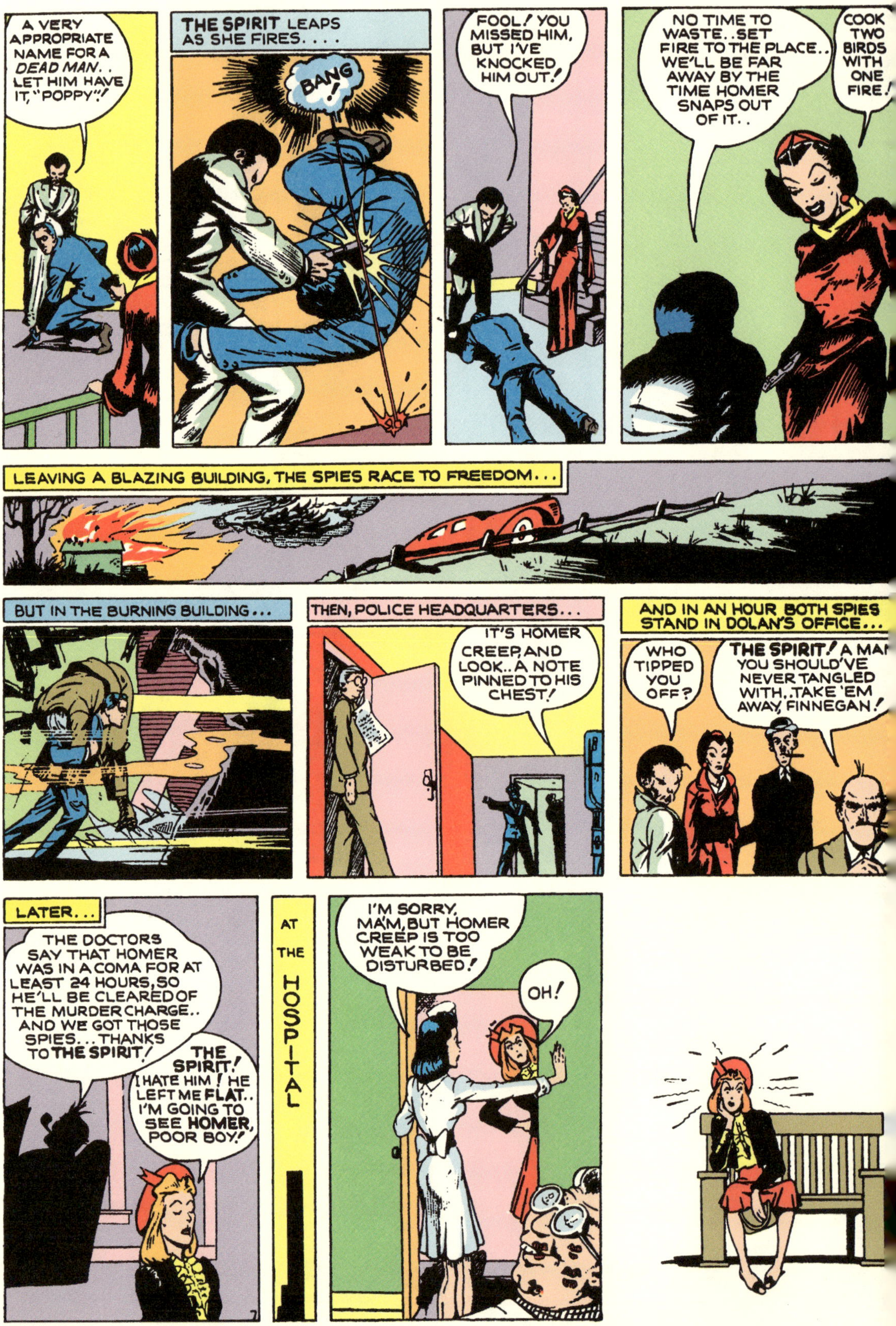
A VERY APPROPRIATE NAME FOR A DEAD MAN.. LET HIM HAVE IT, "POPPY"!
THE SPIRIT LEAPS AS SHE FIRES. . . .
BANG!
FOOL! YOU MISSED HIM, BUT I'VE KNOCKED HIM OUT!
NO TIME TO WASTE..SET FIRE TO THE PLACE.. WE'LL BE FAR AWAY BY THE TIME HOMER SNAPS OUT OF IT..
COOK TWO BIRDS WITH ONE FIRE!
LEAVING A BLAZING BUILDING, THE SPIES RACE TO FREEDOM...
BUT IN THE BURNING BUILDING...
THEN, POLICE HEADQUARTERS...
IT'S HOMER CREEP, AND LOOK..A NOTE PINNED TO HIS CHEST!
AND IN AN HOUR BOTH SPIES STAND IN DOLAN'S OFFICE...
WHO TIPPED YOU OFF?
THE SPIRIT! A MAN YOU SHOULD'VE NEVER TANGLED WITH..TAKE 'EM AWAY, FINNEGAN!
LATER...
THE DOCTORS SAY THAT HOMER WAS IN A COMA FOR AT LEAST 24 HOURS, SO HE'LL BE CLEARED OF THE MURDER CHARGE.. AND WE GOT THOSE SPIES... THANKS TO THE SPIRIT!
THE SPIRIT! I HATE HIM! HE LEFT ME FLAT.. I'M GOING TO SEE HOMER, POOR BOY!
AT THE HOSPITAL
I'M SORRY, MA'M, BUT HOMER CREEP IS TOO WEAK TO BE DISTURBED!
OH!

COMIC BOOK SECTION

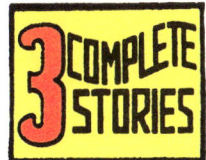

THE MASTERMIND STRIKES

3 COMPLETE STORIES

October 6, 1940

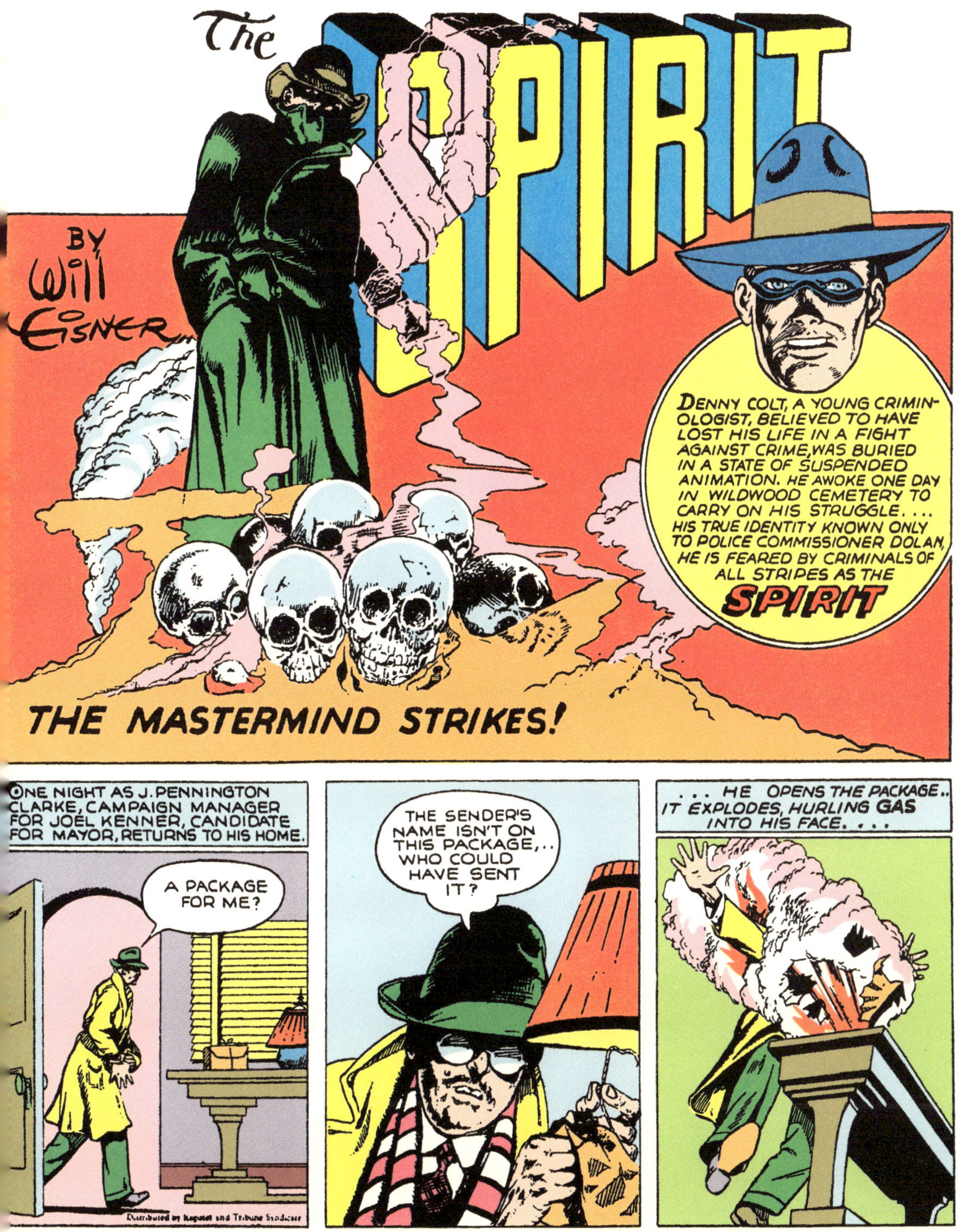
The SPIRIT
BY Will Eisner
DENNY COLT, A YOUNG CRIMINOLOGIST, BELIEVED TO HAVE LOST HIS LIFE IN A FIGHT AGAINST CRIME, WAS BURIED IN A STATE OF SUSPENDED ANIMATION. HE AWOKE ONE DAY IN WILDWOOD CEMETERY TO CARRY ON HIS STRUGGLE. . . . HIS TRUE IDENTITY KNOWN ONLY TO POLICE COMMISSIONER DOLAN, HE IS FEARED BY CRIMINALS OF ALL STRIPES AS THE SPIRIT
THE MASTERMIND STRIKES!
ONE NIGHT AS J. PENNINGTON CLARKE, CAMPAIGN MANAGER FOR JOEL KENNER, CANDIDATE FOR MAYOR, RETURNS TO HIS HOME.
A PACKAGE FOR ME?
Distributed by Register and Tribune Syndicate
THE SENDER'S NAME ISN'T ON THIS PACKAGE,.. WHO COULD HAVE SENT IT?
. . . HE OPENS THE PACKAGE.. IT EXPLODES, HURLING GAS INTO HIS FACE. . . .

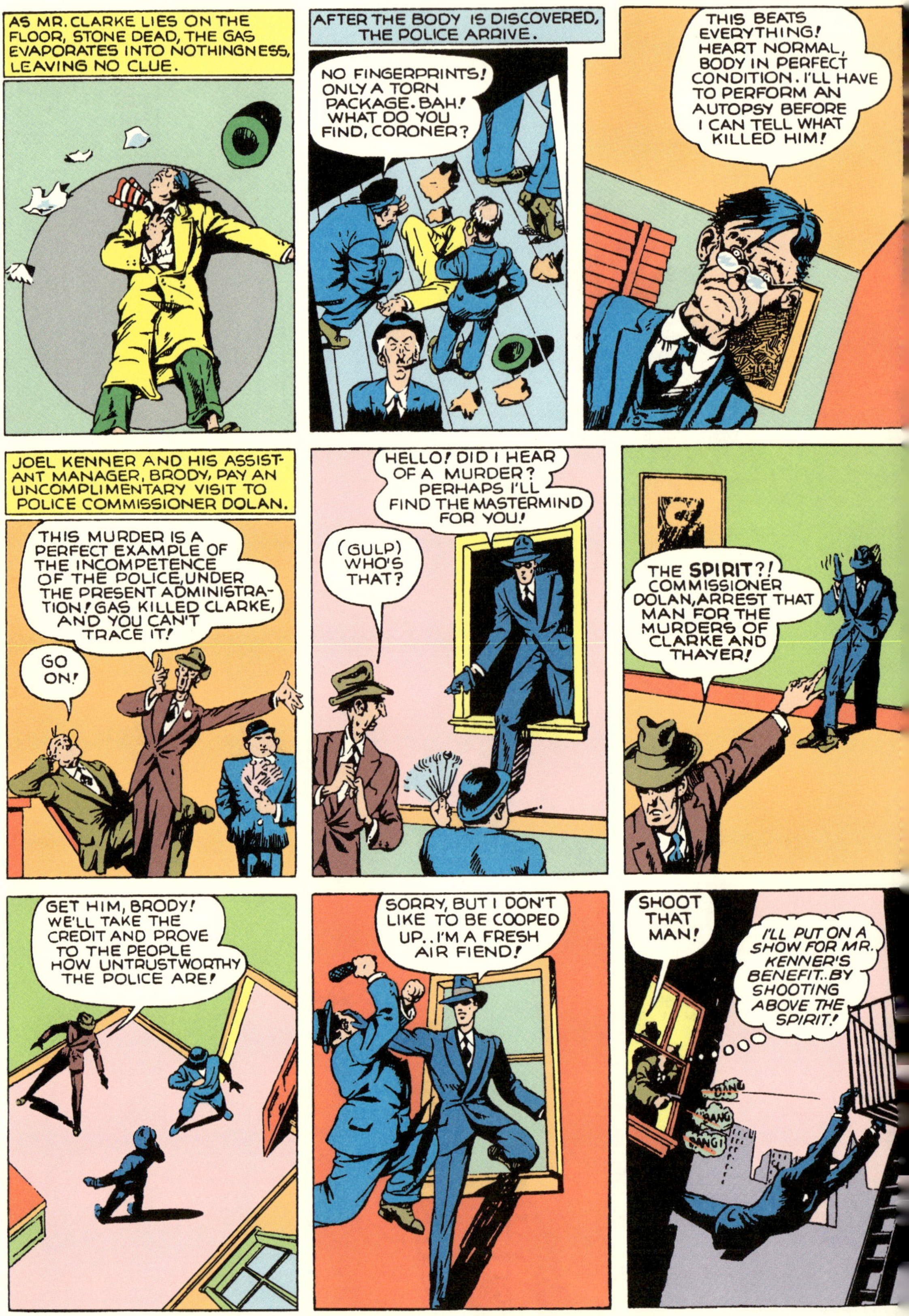
AS MR. CLARKE LIES ON THE FLOOR, STONE DEAD, THE GAS EVAPORATES INTO NOTHINGNESS, LEAVING NO CLUE.
AFTER THE BODY IS DISCOVERED, THE POLICE ARRIVE.
NO FINGERPRINTS! ONLY A TORN PACKAGE. BAH! WHAT DO YOU FIND, CORONER?
THIS BEATS EVERYTHING! HEART NORMAL, BODY IN PERFECT CONDITION. I'LL HAVE TO PERFORM AN AUTOPSY BEFORE I CAN TELL WHAT KILLED HIM!
JOEL KENNER AND HIS ASSISTANT MANAGER, BRODY, PAY AN UNCOMPLIMENTARY VISIT TO POLICE COMMISSIONER DOLAN.
THIS MURDER IS A PERFECT EXAMPLE OF THE INCOMPETENCE OF THE POLICE, UNDER THE PRESENT ADMINISTRATION! GAS KILLED CLARKE, AND YOU CAN'T TRACE IT!
GO ON!
HELLO! DID I HEAR OF A MURDER? PERHAPS I'LL FIND THE MASTERMIND FOR YOU!
(GULP) WHO'S THAT?
THE SPIRIT?! COMMISSIONER DOLAN, ARREST THAT MAN FOR THE MURDERS OF CLARKE AND THAYER!
GET HIM, BRODY! WE'LL TAKE THE CREDIT AND PROVE TO THE PEOPLE HOW UNTRUSTWORTHY THE POLICE ARE!
SORRY, BUT I DON'T LIKE TO BE COOPED UP.. I'M A FRESH AIR FIEND!
SHOOT THAT MAN!
I'LL PUT ON A SHOW FOR MR. KENNER'S BENEFIT.. BY SHOOTING ABOVE THE SPIRIT!

HOODWINKED! IT'S AN OUTRAGE! I'LL MAKE TROUBLE FOR YOU!
THAT SEEMS TO BE YOUR HOBBY!
LATER, A MYSTERIOUS MAN, "THE MASTERMIND," DOPES BRODY'S CAR.. WHO IS HE??
SCORE ONE, CLARKE! A PERFECT CRIME.... NOW, BRODY..HE'LL BE SURPRISED! HEH, HEH, HEH!
UNAWARE OF IMPENDING DOOM, BRODY STARTS HIS CAR. . . .
WHAT A FOOL ERRAND KENNER'S SENDING ME ON AT THIS TIME OF NIGHT!
ROCKET CHEMICALS HURL THE CAR TO DESTRUCTION.
THE CHEMICALS DISINTEGRATE, LEAVING NO CLUE AT ALL..
THE POLICE ARE BAFFLED. . . . .
FIRST, CLARKE, NOW BRODY! THIS MASTERMIND BUSINESS IS GETTING MY GOAT!
KENNER MAKES CAPITAL OF THE CRIME..
THE MAYOR AND THE POLICE ARE HIDING FACTS! IT'S THE SPIRIT WHO MURDERED BRODY AND CLARKE! WHY? BECAUSE HE OWES THE MAYOR AND DOLAN PROTECTION!
IF I'M ELECTED, I'LL DISCHARGE DOLAN!
THE SPIRIT LISTENS GRIMLY. . . .
I'LL TAKE THAT AS A PERSONAL CHALLENGE!

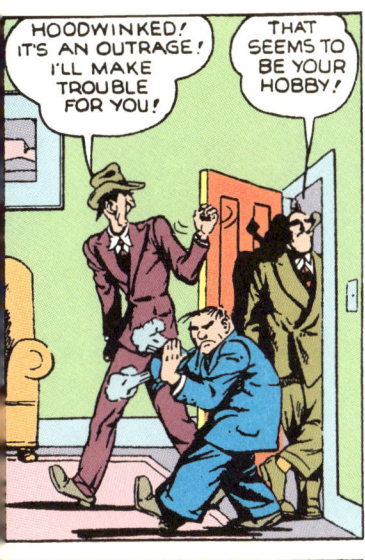

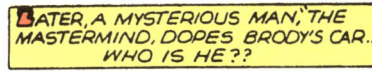

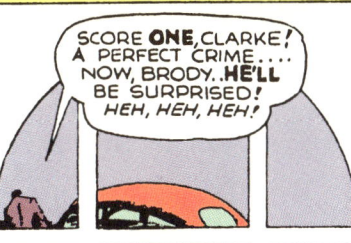

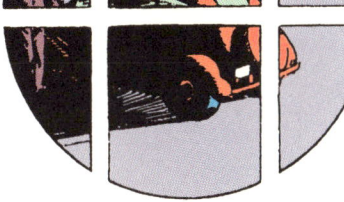

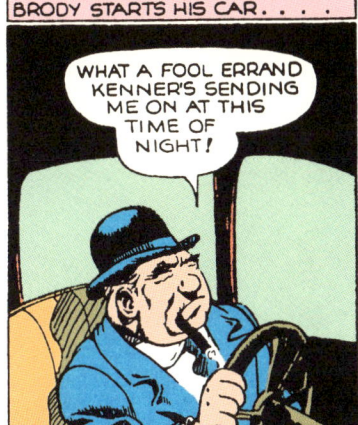

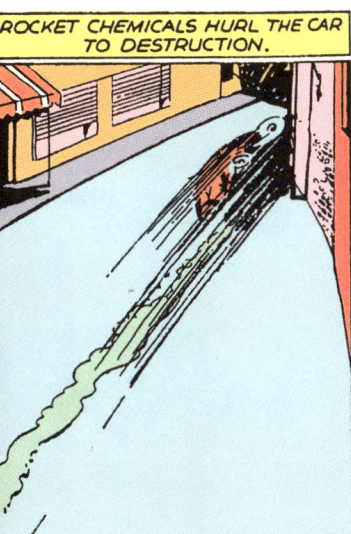

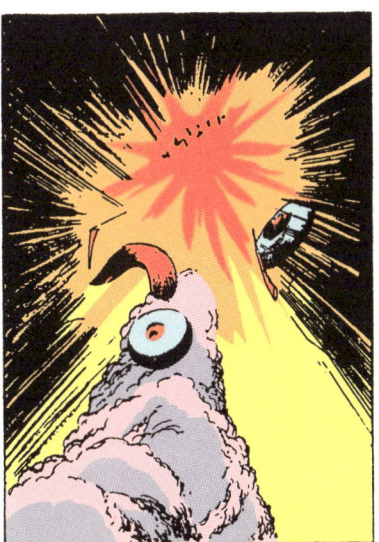

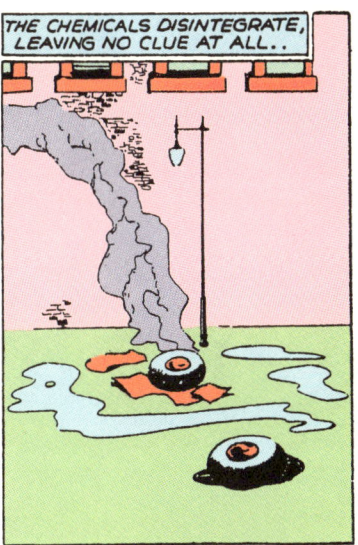

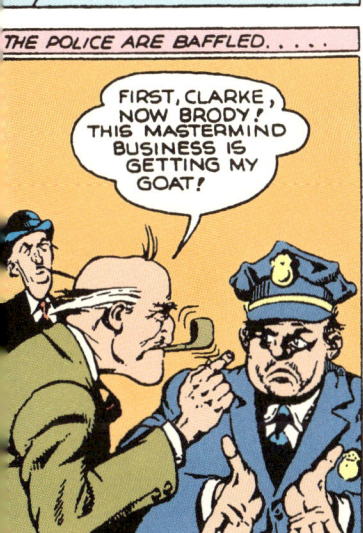

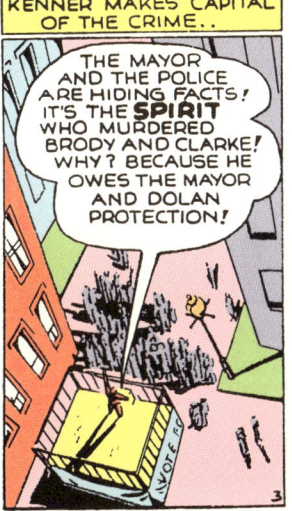

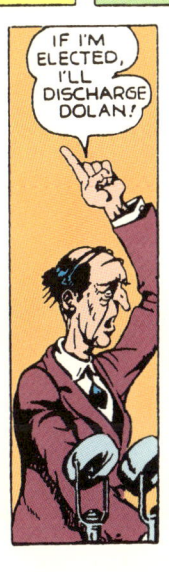

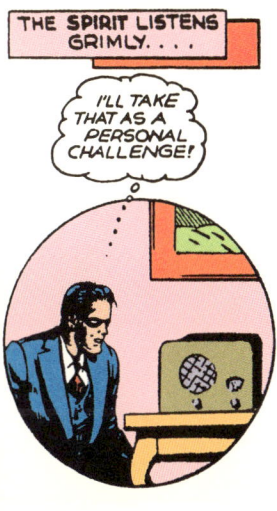

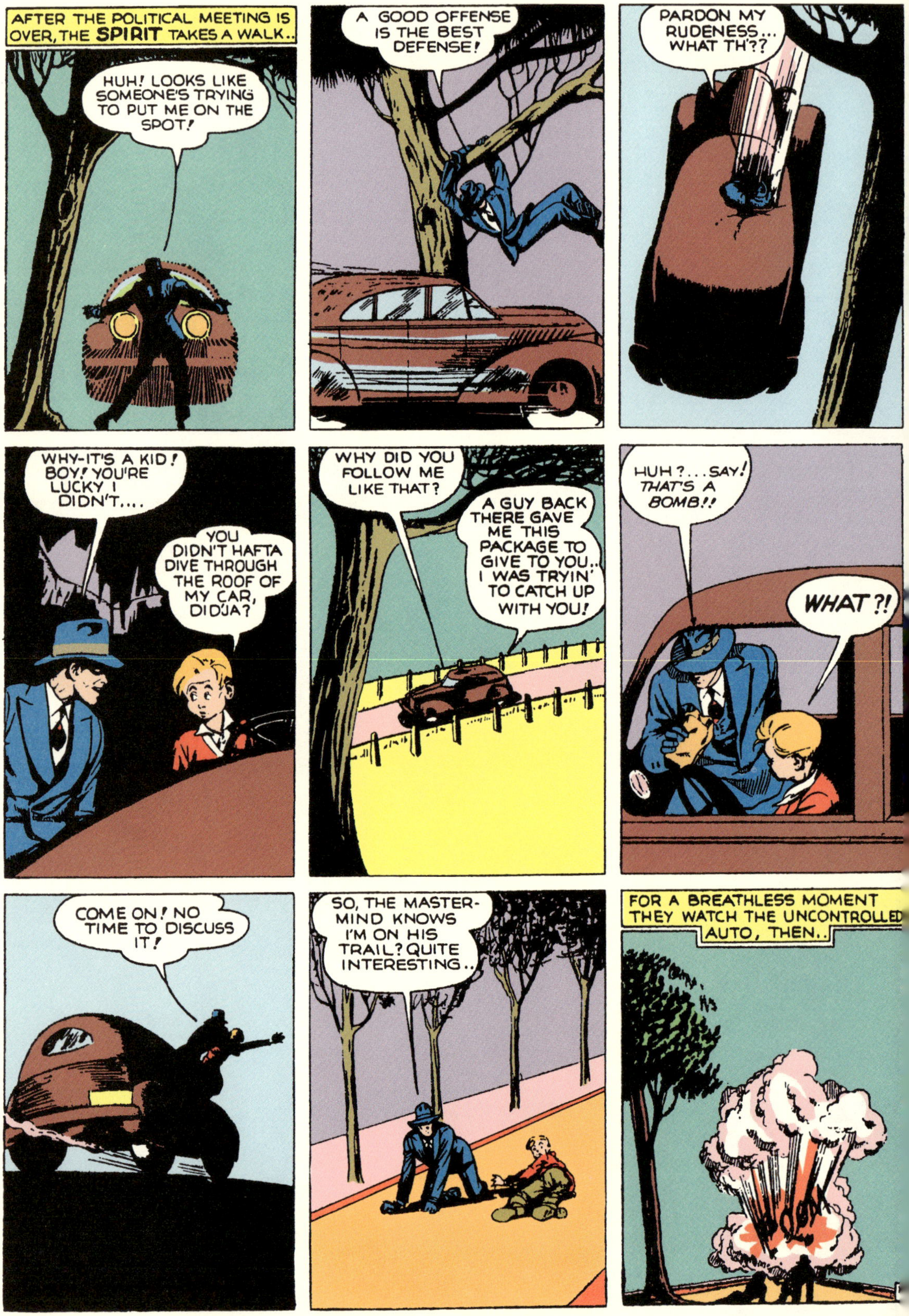
AFTER THE POLITICAL MEETING IS OVER, THE SPIRIT TAKES A WALK..
HUH! LOOKS LIKE SOMEONE'S TRYING TO PUT ME ON THE SPOT!
A GOOD OFFENSE IS THE BEST DEFENSE!
PARDON MY RUDENESS... WHAT TH'??
WHY-IT'S A KID! BOY! YOU'RE LUCKY I DIDN'T....
YOU DIDN'T HAFTA DIVE THROUGH THE ROOF OF MY CAR, DIDJA?
WHY DID YOU FOLLOW ME LIKE THAT?
A GUY BACK THERE GAVE ME THIS PACKAGE TO GIVE TO YOU.. I WAS TRYIN' TO CATCH UP WITH YOU!
HUH?... SAY! THAT'S A BOMB!!
WHAT?!
COME ON! NO TIME TO DISCUSS IT!
SO, THE MASTER-MIND KNOWS I'M ON HIS TRAIL? QUITE INTERESTING..
FOR A BREATHLESS MOMENT THEY WATCH THE UNCONTROLLED AUTO, THEN..

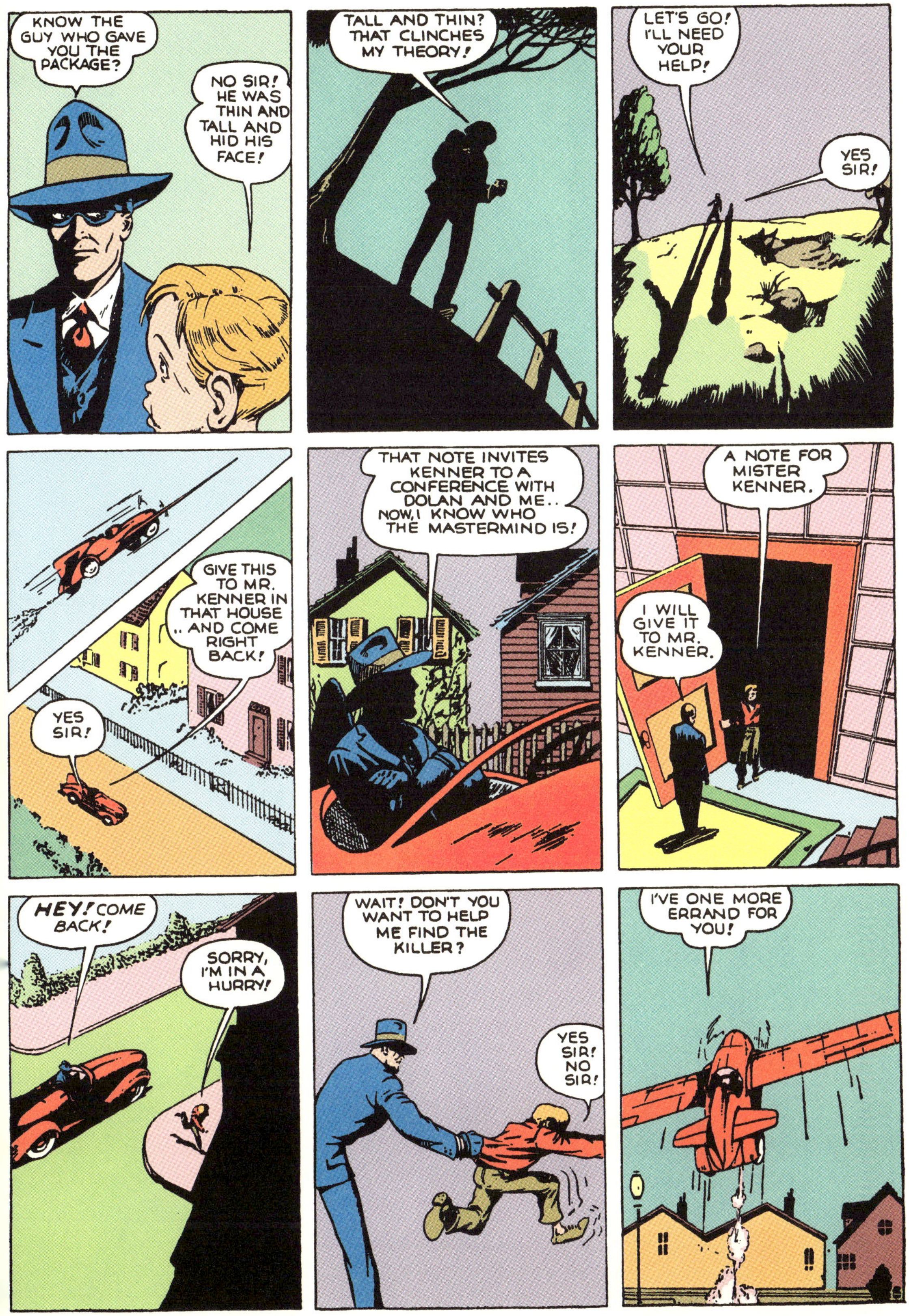
KNOW THE GUY WHO GAVE YOU THE PACKAGE?
NO SIR! HE WAS THIN AND TALL AND HID HIS FACE!
TALL AND THIN? THAT CLINCHES MY THEORY!
LET'S GO! I'LL NEED YOUR HELP!
YES SIR!
GIVE THIS TO MR. KENNER IN THAT HOUSE .. AND COME RIGHT BACK!
YES SIR!
THAT NOTE INVITES KENNER TO A CONFERENCE WITH DOLAN AND ME.. NOW, I KNOW WHO THE MASTERMIND IS!
A NOTE FOR MISTER KENNER.
I WILL GIVE IT TO MR. KENNER.
HEY! COME BACK!
SORRY, I'M IN A HURRY!
WAIT! DON'T YOU WANT TO HELP ME FIND THE KILLER?
YES SIR! NO SIR!
I'VE ONE MORE ERRAND FOR YOU!

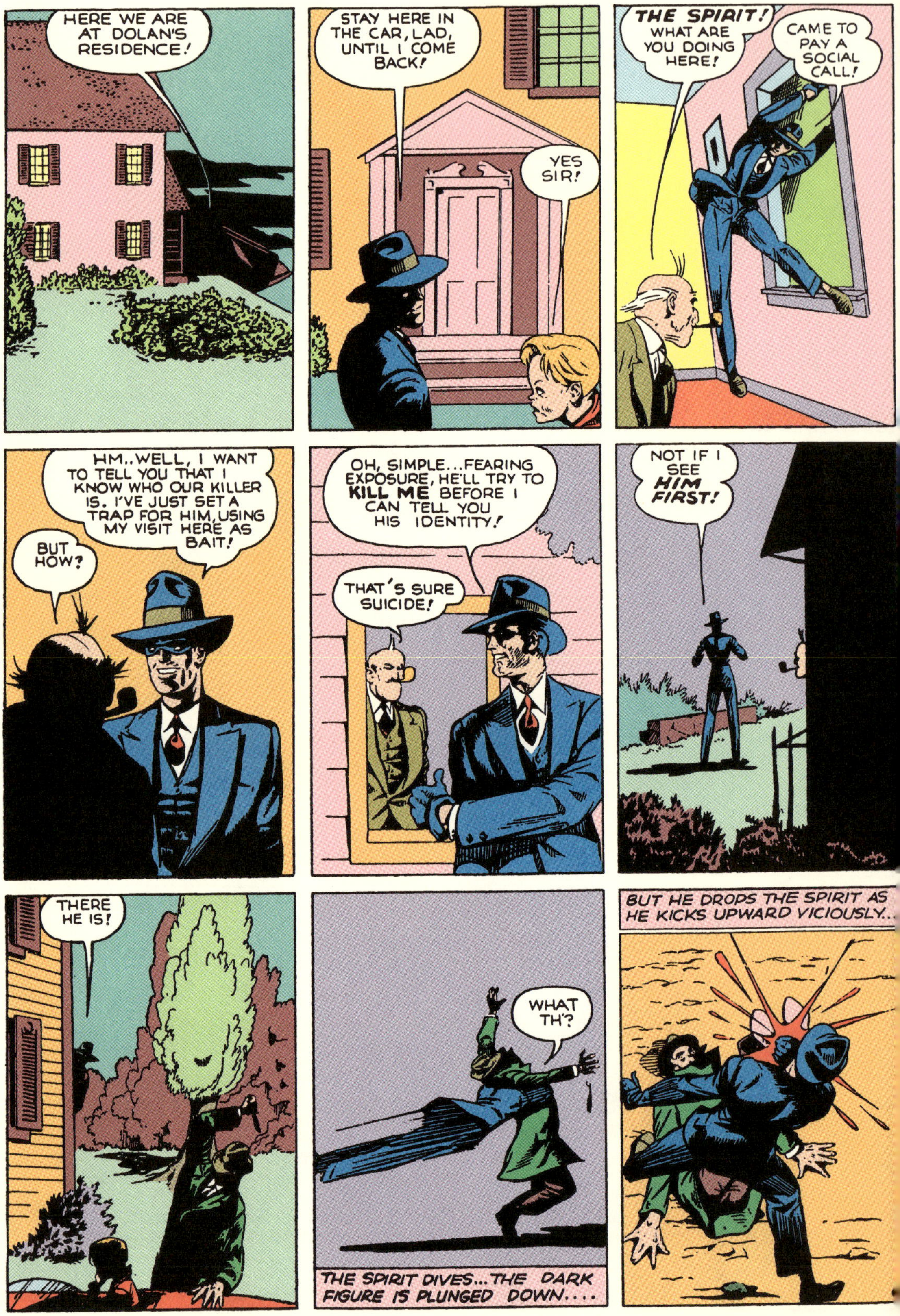
HERE WE ARE AT DOLAN'S RESIDENCE!
STAY HERE IN THE CAR, LAD, UNTIL I COME BACK!
YES SIR!
THE SPIRIT! WHAT ARE YOU DOING HERE!
CAME TO PAY A SOCIAL CALL!
HM..WELL, I WANT TO TELL YOU THAT I KNOW WHO OUR KILLER IS. I'VE JUST SET A TRAP FOR HIM, USING MY VISIT HERE AS BAIT!
BUT HOW?
OH, SIMPLE...FEARING EXPOSURE, HE'LL TRY TO KILL ME BEFORE I CAN TELL YOU HIS IDENTITY!
THAT'S SURE SUICIDE!
NOT IF I SEE HIM FIRST!
THERE HE IS!
WHAT TH'?
THE SPIRIT DIVES...THE DARK FIGURE IS PLUNGED DOWN....
BUT HE DROPS THE SPIRIT AS HE KICKS UPWARD VICIOUSLY..

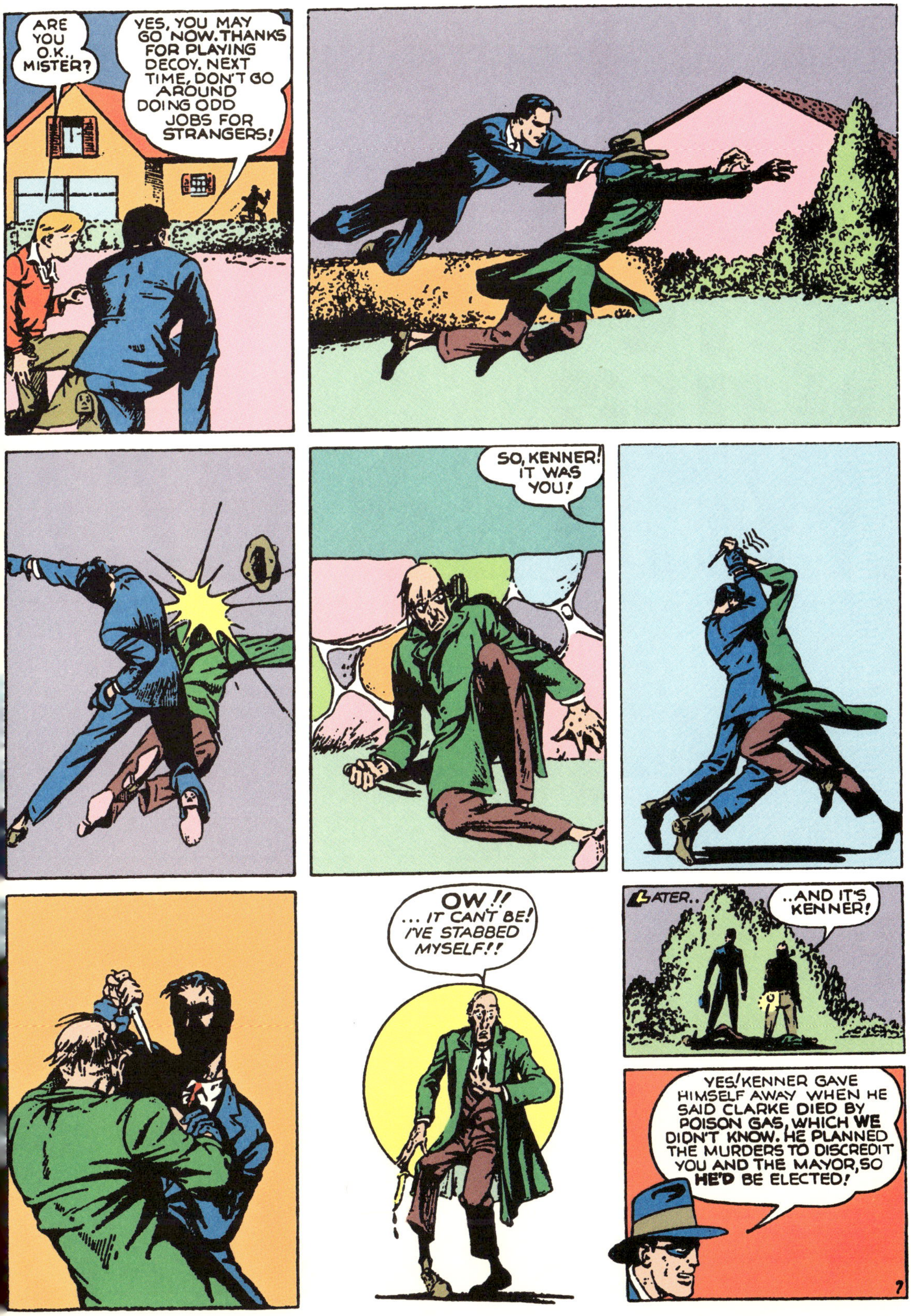
ARE YOU O.K., MISTER?
YES, YOU MAY GO NOW. THANKS FOR PLAYING DECOY. NEXT TIME, DON'T GO AROUND DOING ODD JOBS FOR STRANGERS!
SO, KENNER! IT WAS YOU!
OW!! ... IT CAN'T BE! I'VE STABBED MYSELF!!
LATER..
..AND IT'S KENNER!
YES! KENNER GAVE HIMSELF AWAY WHEN HE SAID CLARKE DIED BY POISON GAS, WHICH WE DIDN'T KNOW. HE PLANNED THE MURDERS TO DISCREDIT YOU AND THE MAYOR, SO HE'D BE ELECTED!
7

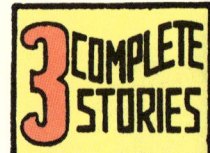

COMIC BOOK SECTION

THE SPIRIT! WHO IS HE?

3 COMPLETE STORIES

October 13, 1940

THE SPIRIT! WHO IS HE?

Daily Press launches campaign to discover identity of mysterious crime fighter. "Are you society's friend or foe?" asks editor Robert E. Grit.

Ever since his mysterious aid in the capture of Dr. Cobra, an escaped mad killer, the mystery man, known only as The Spirit, has secretly helped the police in many ways.

According to information collected by our reporters stationed at Police Headquarters, the solutions of most of the major crimes in our city were due to the efforts of The Spirit.

It was The Spirit who really smashed Tony Morgan's gambling chain. The fantastic attempt by this country's big gang leaders to rob the Sub-Treasury was frustrated by The Spirit. From reliable sources we learn that Yagor, the fiendish creator of the huge robot that ran amuck in our city not long ago, was believed to have been captured and placed in the hands of the police by The Spirit. The four Morger boys had the name of The Spirit on their lips before they were executed by the State.

On one hand he is obviously aiding society, yet on the other this mystery man is accused of causing the death of Eldas Thayer, a respected citizen, and is branded an outlaw by the Police.

What is the explanation? Who is The Spirit?

His description, offered by persons who have seen him, is: over six feet tall, wears a blue mask and blue suit. Any information leading to the identity of The Spirit will be appreciated and kept confidential. All correspondence should be addressed to the editor.

MAYOR AND CIVIC LEADERS APPROVE OF PRESS CAMPAIGN

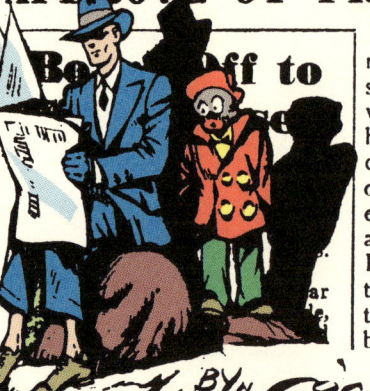

In a letter addressed to this newspaper today, the Mayor, speaking for himself and the various civic societies, said that he approved highly of this new campaign to learn the identity of The Spirit. "His frequent escapes," he added, "have made a laughing stock of the Police Force and The Spirit's continued exploits lowers the prestige of our law enforcement bodies."

BY WILL EISNER

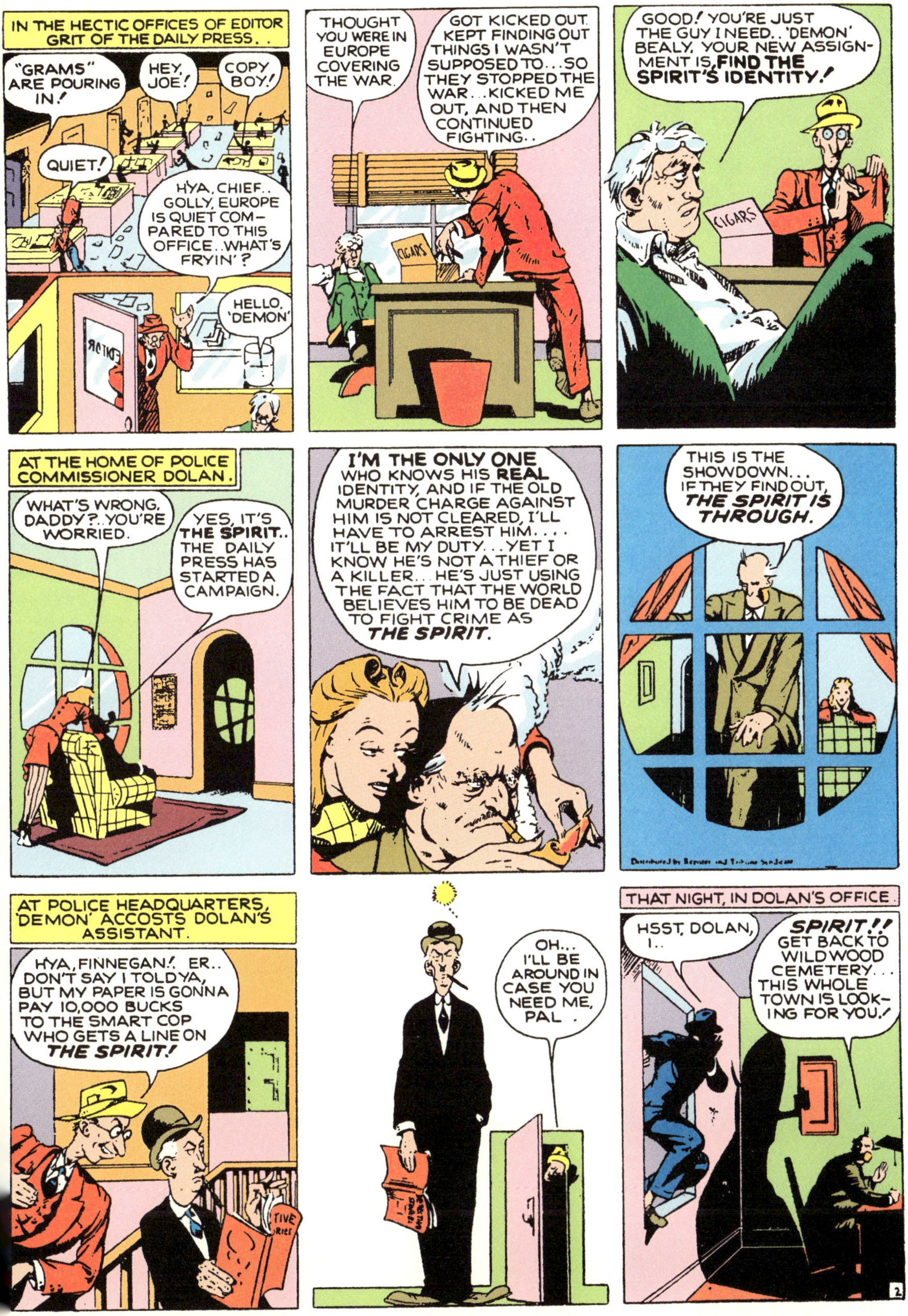
IN THE HECTIC OFFICES OF EDITOR GRIT OF THE DAILY PRESS. .
"GRAMS" ARE POURING IN!
HEY, JOE!
COPY BOY!
QUIET!
HYA, CHIEF.. GOLLY, EUROPE IS QUIET COMPARED TO THIS OFFICE..WHAT'S FRYIN'?
HELLO, 'DEMON'
THOUGHT YOU WERE IN EUROPE COVERING THE WAR.
GOT KICKED OUT. KEPT FINDING OUT THINGS I WASN'T SUPPOSED TO...SO THEY STOPPED THE WAR...KICKED ME OUT, AND THEN CONTINUED FIGHTING..
CIGARS
GOOD! YOU'RE JUST THE GUY I NEED.. 'DEMON' BEALY, YOUR NEW ASSIGNMENT IS, FIND THE SPIRIT'S IDENTITY!
CIGARS
AT THE HOME OF POLICE COMMISSIONER DOLAN.
WHAT'S WRONG, DADDY?..YOU'RE WORRIED.
YES, IT'S THE SPIRIT.. THE DAILY PRESS HAS STARTED A CAMPAIGN.
I'M THE ONLY ONE WHO KNOWS HIS REAL IDENTITY, AND IF THE OLD MURDER CHARGE AGAINST HIM IS NOT CLEARED, I'LL HAVE TO ARREST HIM.... IT'LL BE MY DUTY...YET I KNOW HE'S NOT A THIEF OR A KILLER... HE'S JUST USING THE FACT THAT THE WORLD BELIEVES HIM TO BE DEAD TO FIGHT CRIME AS THE SPIRIT.
THIS IS THE SHOWDOWN... IF THEY FIND OUT, THE SPIRIT IS THROUGH.
AT POLICE HEADQUARTERS, 'DEMON' ACCOSTS DOLAN'S ASSISTANT.
HYA, FINNEGAN! ER.. DON'T SAY I TOLD YA, BUT MY PAPER IS GONNA PAY 10,000 BUCKS TO THE SMART COP WHO GETS A LINE ON THE SPIRIT!
OH... I'LL BE AROUND IN CASE YOU NEED ME, PAL.
THAT NIGHT, IN DOLAN'S OFFICE.
HSST, DOLAN, I..
SPIRIT!! GET BACK TO WILDWOOD CEMETERY... THIS WHOLE TOWN IS LOOKING FOR YOU!
2

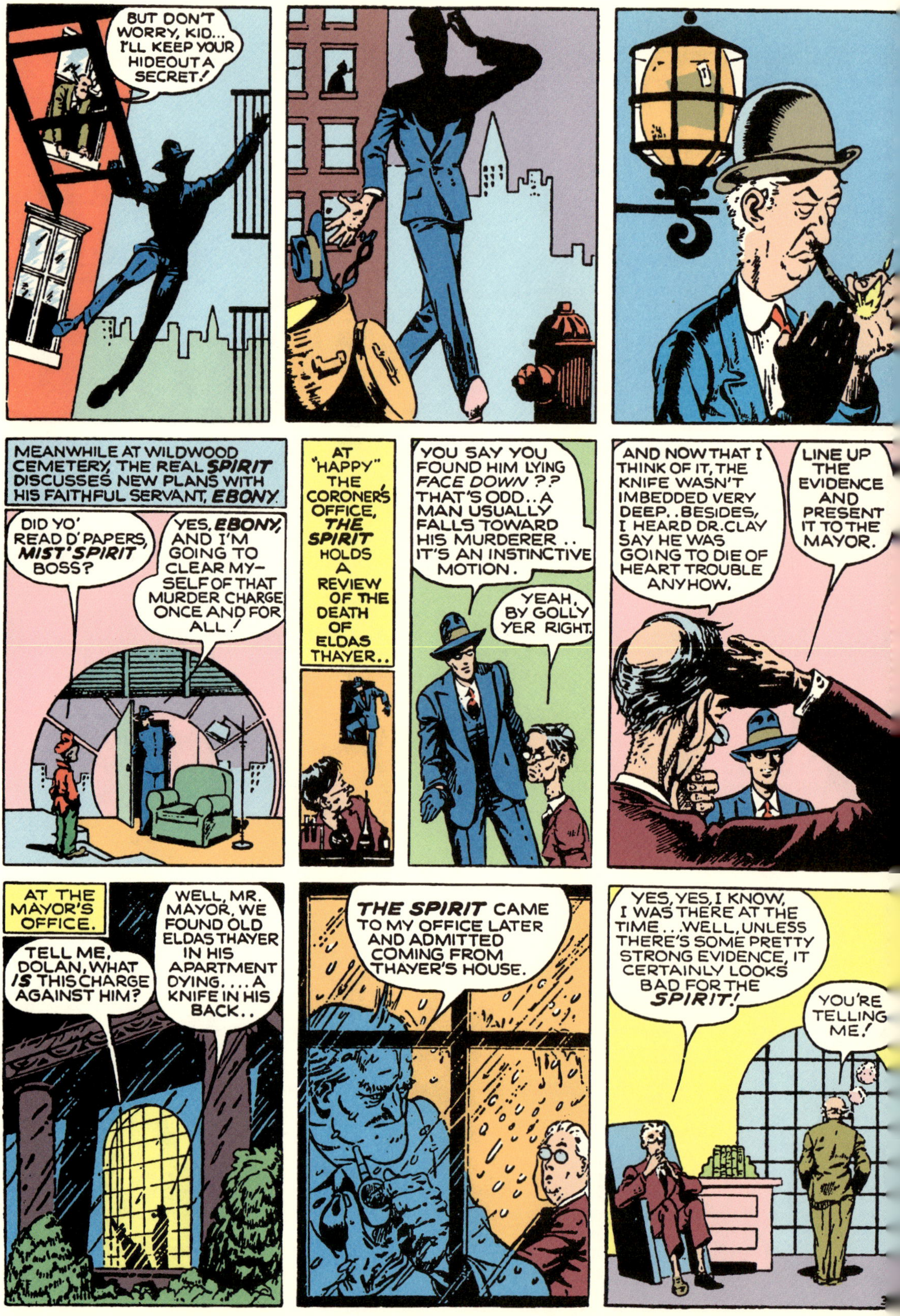

BUT DON'T WORRY, KID... I'LL KEEP YOUR HIDEOUT A SECRET!
MEANWHILE AT WILDWOOD CEMETERY, THE REAL SPIRIT DISCUSSES NEW PLANS WITH HIS FAITHFUL SERVANT, EBONY.
DID YO' READ D' PAPERS, MIST' SPIRIT BOSS?
YES, EBONY, AND I'M GOING TO CLEAR MYSELF OF THAT MURDER CHARGE ONCE AND FOR ALL!
AT "HAPPY" THE CORONER'S OFFICE, THE SPIRIT HOLDS A REVIEW OF THE DEATH OF ELDAS THAYER..
YOU SAY YOU FOUND HIM LYING FACE DOWN ?? THAT'S ODD.. A MAN USUALLY FALLS TOWARD HIS MURDERER.. IT'S AN INSTINCTIVE MOTION.
YEAH, BY GOLLY YER RIGHT.
AND NOW THAT I THINK OF IT, THE KNIFE WASN'T IMBEDDED VERY DEEP.. BESIDES, I HEARD DR. CLAY SAY HE WAS GOING TO DIE OF HEART TROUBLE ANYHOW.
LINE UP THE EVIDENCE AND PRESENT IT TO THE MAYOR.
AT THE MAYOR'S OFFICE.
TELL ME, DOLAN, WHAT IS THIS CHARGE AGAINST HIM?
WELL, MR. MAYOR, WE FOUND OLD ELDAS THAYER IN HIS APARTMENT DYING.... A KNIFE IN HIS BACK..
THE SPIRIT CAME TO MY OFFICE LATER AND ADMITTED COMING FROM THAYER'S HOUSE.
YES, YES, I KNOW, I WAS THERE AT THE TIME... WELL, UNLESS THERE'S SOME PRETTY STRONG EVIDENCE, IT CERTAINLY LOOKS BAD FOR THE SPIRIT!
YOU'RE TELLING ME!

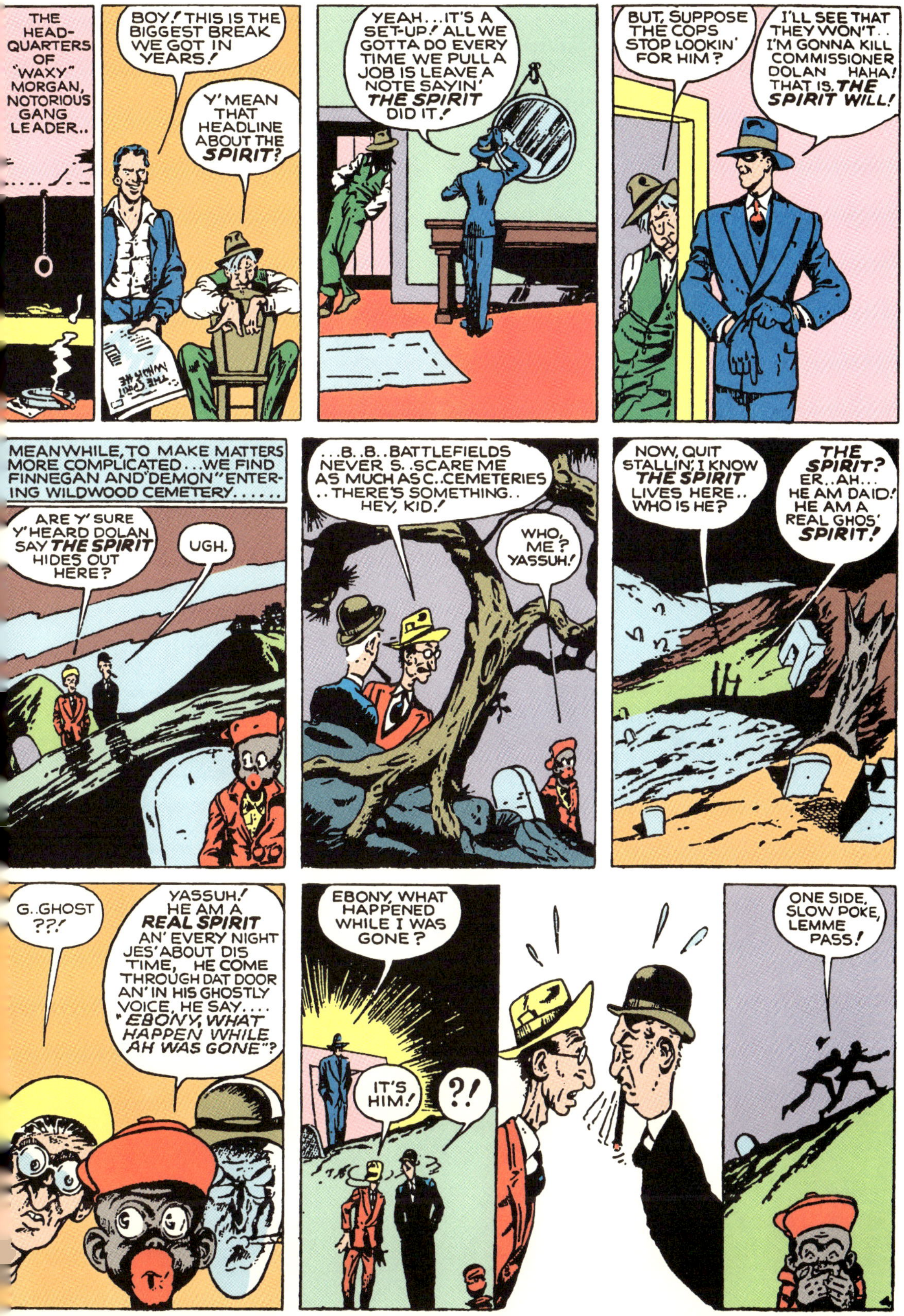
THE HEAD-QUARTERS OF "WAXY" MORGAN, NOTORIOUS GANG LEADER..
BOY! THIS IS THE BIGGEST BREAK WE GOT IN YEARS!
Y'MEAN THAT HEADLINE ABOUT THE SPIRIT?
YEAH...IT'S A SET-UP! ALL WE GOTTA DO EVERY TIME WE PULL A JOB IS LEAVE A NOTE SAYIN' THE SPIRIT DID IT!
BUT, SUPPOSE THE COPS STOP LOOKIN' FOR HIM?
I'LL SEE THAT THEY WON'T.. I'M GONNA KILL COMMISSIONER DOLAN HAHA! THAT IS, THE SPIRIT WILL!
MEANWHILE, TO MAKE MATTERS MORE COMPLICATED...WE FIND FINNEGAN AND "DEMON" ENTERING WILDWOOD CEMETERY......
ARE Y' SURE Y'HEARD DOLAN SAY THE SPIRIT HIDES OUT HERE?
UGH.
...B..B..BATTLEFIELDS NEVER S..SCARE ME AS MUCH AS C..CEMETERIES ..THERE'S SOMETHING.. HEY, KID!
WHO, ME? YASSUH!
NOW, QUIT STALLIN', I KNOW THE SPIRIT LIVES HERE.. WHO IS HE?
THE SPIRIT? ER..AH... HE AM DAID! HE AM A REAL GHOS' SPIRIT!
G..GHOST ??!
YASSUH! HE AM A REAL SPIRIT AN' EVERY NIGHT JES' ABOUT DIS TIME, HE COME THROUGH DAT DOOR AN' IN HIS GHOSTLY VOICE, HE SAY.... "EBONY, WHAT HAPPEN WHILE AH WAS GONE"?
EBONY, WHAT HAPPENED WHILE I WAS GONE?
IT'S HIM!
?!
ONE SIDE, SLOW POKE, LEMME PASS!

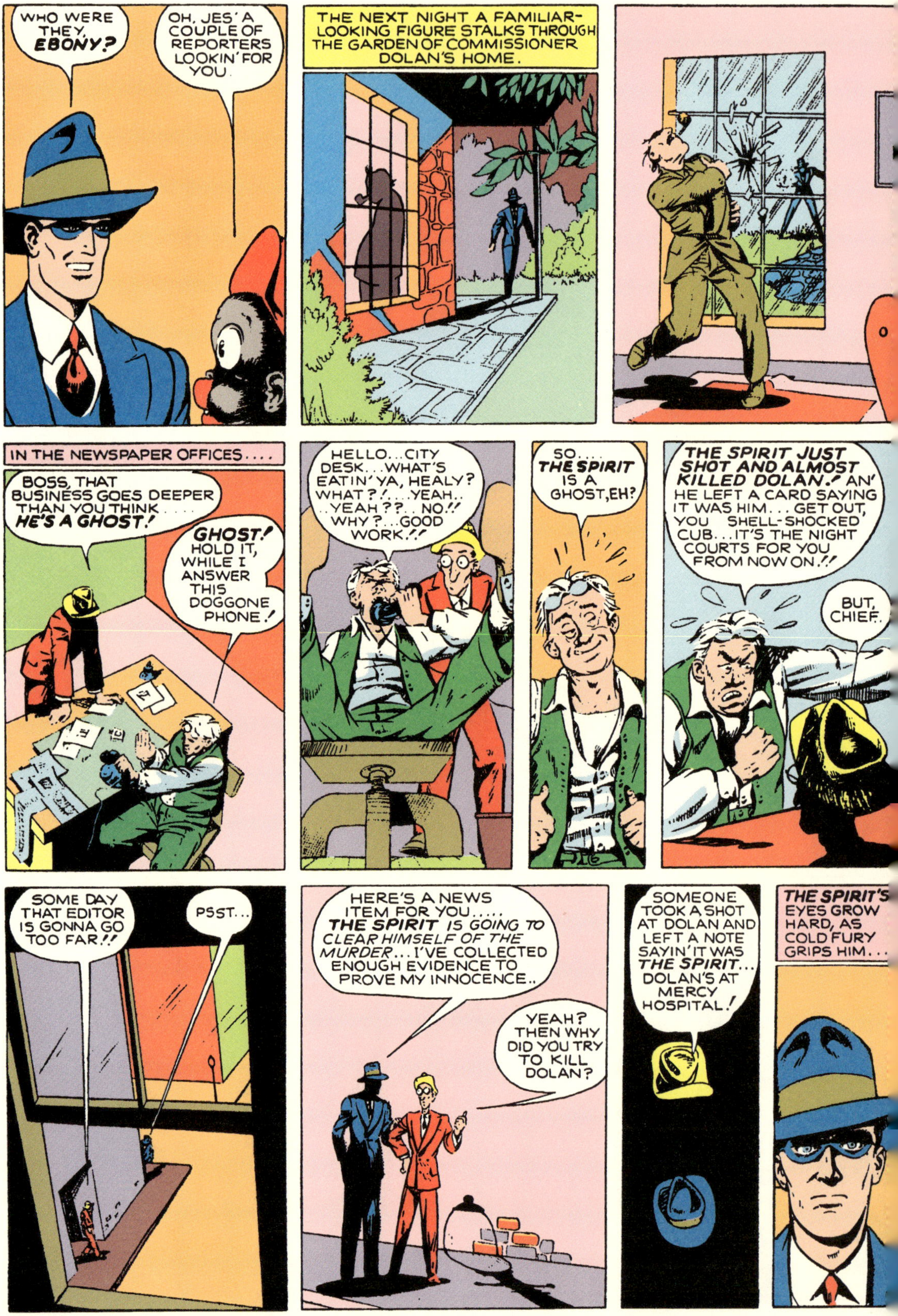
WHO WERE THEY, EBONY?
OH, JES' A COUPLE OF REPORTERS LOOKIN' FOR YOU.
THE NEXT NIGHT A FAMILIAR-LOOKING FIGURE STALKS THROUGH THE GARDEN OF COMMISSIONER DOLAN'S HOME.
IN THE NEWSPAPER OFFICES....
BOSS, THAT BUSINESS GOES DEEPER THAN YOU THINK.... HE'S A GHOST!
GHOST! HOLD IT, WHILE I ANSWER THIS DOGGONE PHONE!
HELLO...CITY DESK...WHAT'S EATIN' YA, HEALY? WHAT?!...YEAH.. ..YEAH??..NO!! WHY?...GOOD WORK!!
SO.... THE SPIRIT IS A GHOST, EH?
THE SPIRIT JUST SHOT AND ALMOST KILLED DOLAN! AN' HE LEFT A CARD SAYING IT WAS HIM... GET OUT, YOU SHELL-SHOCKED CUB...IT'S THE NIGHT COURTS FOR YOU FROM NOW ON!!
BUT, CHIEF.
SOME DAY THAT EDITOR IS GONNA GO TOO FAR!!
PSST...
HERE'S A NEWS ITEM FOR YOU..... THE SPIRIT IS GOING TO CLEAR HIMSELF OF THE MURDER...I'VE COLLECTED ENOUGH EVIDENCE TO PROVE MY INNOCENCE..
YEAH? THEN WHY DID YOU TRY TO KILL DOLAN?
SOMEONE TOOK A SHOT AT DOLAN AND LEFT A NOTE SAYIN' IT WAS THE SPIRIT... DOLAN'S AT MERCY HOSPITAL!
THE SPIRIT'S EYES GROW HARD, AS COLD FURY GRIPS HIM...

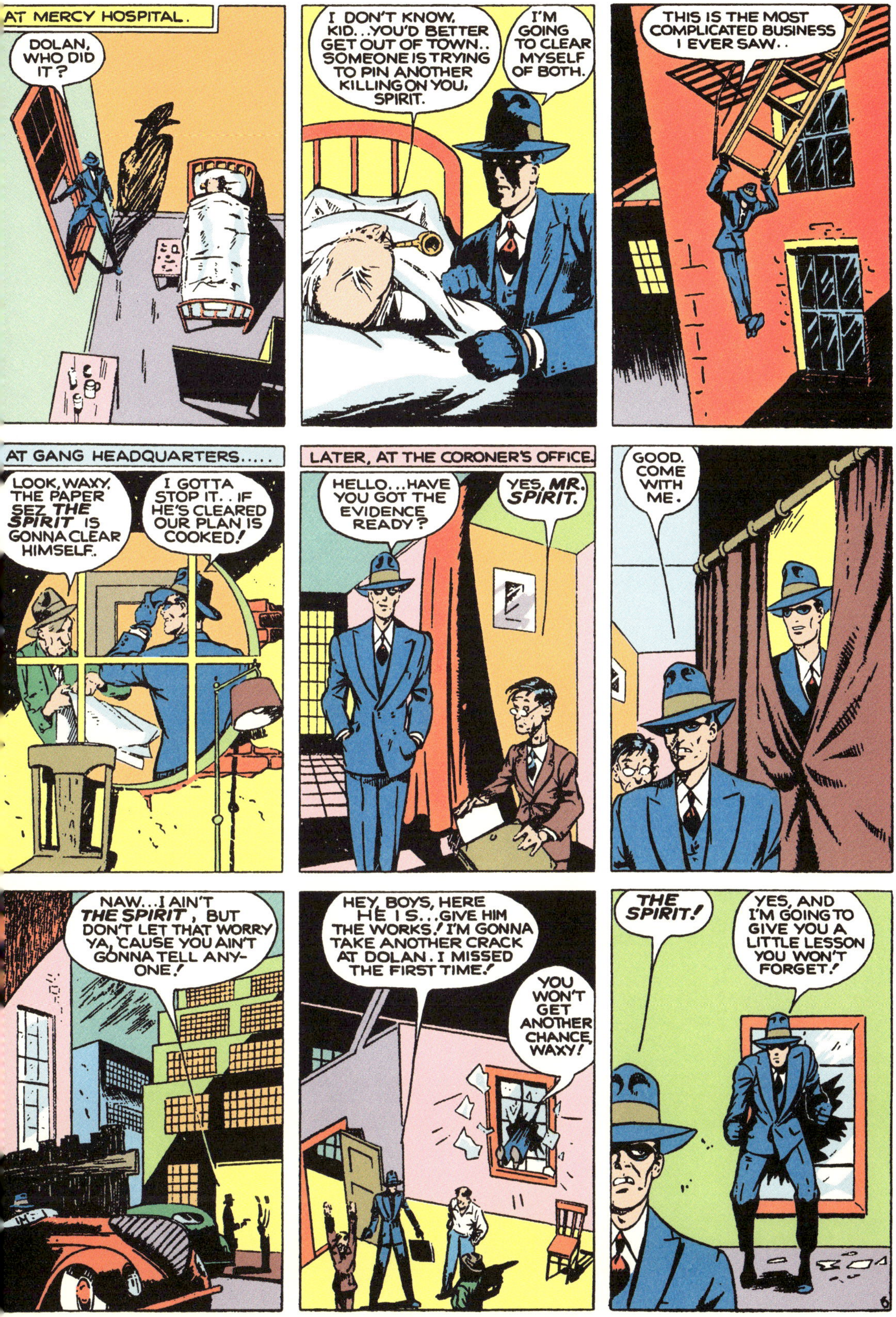

AT MERCY HOSPITAL.
DOLAN, WHO DID IT?
I DON'T KNOW, KID...YOU'D BETTER GET OUT OF TOWN.. SOMEONE IS TRYING TO PIN ANOTHER KILLING ON YOU, SPIRIT.
I'M GOING TO CLEAR MYSELF OF BOTH.
THIS IS THE MOST COMPLICATED BUSINESS I EVER SAW..
AT GANG HEADQUARTERS.....
LOOK, WAXY, THE PAPER SEZ THE SPIRIT IS GONNA CLEAR HIMSELF.
I GOTTA STOP IT.. IF HE'S CLEARED OUR PLAN IS COOKED!
LATER, AT THE CORONER'S OFFICE.
HELLO...HAVE YOU GOT THE EVIDENCE READY?
YES, MR. SPIRIT.
GOOD. COME WITH ME.
NAW...I AIN'T THE SPIRIT, BUT DON'T LET THAT WORRY YA, 'CAUSE YOU AIN'T GONNA TELL ANY-ONE!
HEY, BOYS, HERE HE IS...GIVE HIM THE WORKS! I'M GONNA TAKE ANOTHER CRACK AT DOLAN. I MISSED THE FIRST TIME!
YOU WON'T GET ANOTHER CHANCE, WAXY!
THE SPIRIT!
YES, AND I'M GOING TO GIVE YOU A LITTLE LESSON YOU WON'T FORGET!
6

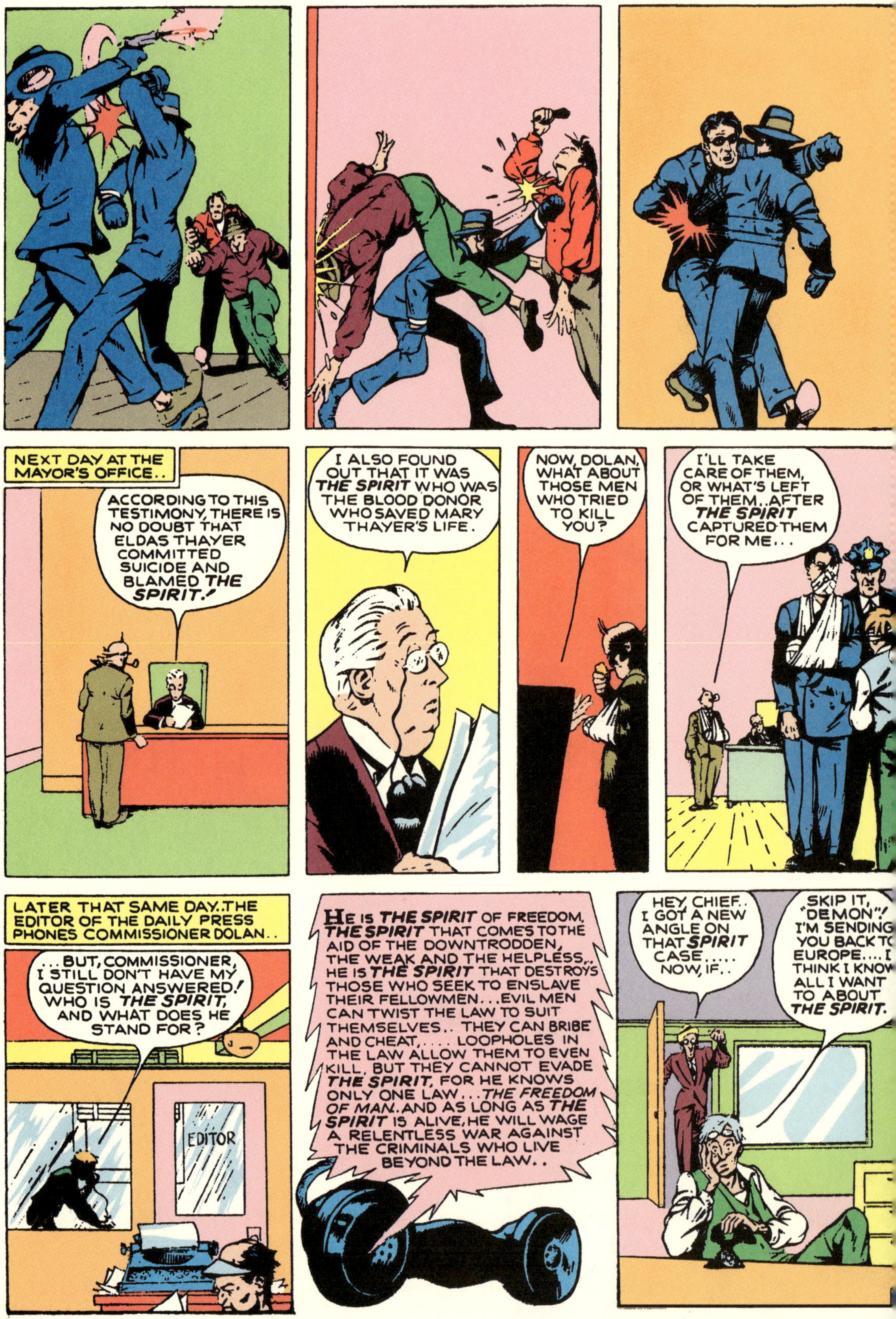
NEXT DAY AT THE MAYOR'S OFFICE..
ACCORDING TO THIS TESTIMONY, THERE IS NO DOUBT THAT ELDAS THAYER COMMITTED SUICIDE AND BLAMED THE SPIRIT!
I ALSO FOUND OUT THAT IT WAS THE SPIRIT WHO WAS THE BLOOD DONOR WHO SAVED MARY THAYER'S LIFE.
NOW, DOLAN, WHAT ABOUT THOSE MEN WHO TRIED TO KILL YOU?
I'LL TAKE CARE OF THEM, OR WHAT'S LEFT OF THEM..AFTER THE SPIRIT CAPTURED THEM FOR ME...
LATER THAT SAME DAY..THE EDITOR OF THE DAILY PRESS PHONES COMMISSIONER DOLAN..
...BUT, COMMISSIONER, I STILL DON'T HAVE MY QUESTION ANSWERED! WHO IS THE SPIRIT, AND WHAT DOES HE STAND FOR?
EDITOR
HE IS THE SPIRIT OF FREEDOM, THE SPIRIT THAT COMES TO THE AID OF THE DOWNTRODDEN, THE WEAK AND THE HELPLESS.. HE IS THE SPIRIT THAT DESTROYS THOSE WHO SEEK TO ENSLAVE THEIR FELLOWMEN...EVIL MEN CAN TWIST THE LAW TO SUIT THEMSELVES.. THEY CAN BRIBE AND CHEAT,.... LOOPHOLES IN THE LAW ALLOW THEM TO EVEN KILL, BUT THEY CANNOT EVADE THE SPIRIT, FOR HE KNOWS ONLY ONE LAW...THE FREEDOM OF MAN. AND AS LONG AS THE SPIRIT IS ALIVE, HE WILL WAGE A RELENTLESS WAR AGAINST THE CRIMINALS WHO LIVE BEYOND THE LAW..
HEY CHIEF.. I GOT A NEW ANGLE ON THAT SPIRIT CASE..... NOW, IF..
SKIP IT, "DEMON"! I'M SENDING YOU BACK TO EUROPE.... I THINK I KNOW ALL I WANT TO ABOUT THE SPIRIT.

COMIC BOOK SECTION

OGRE GORAN

October 20, 1940

3 COMPLETE STORIES

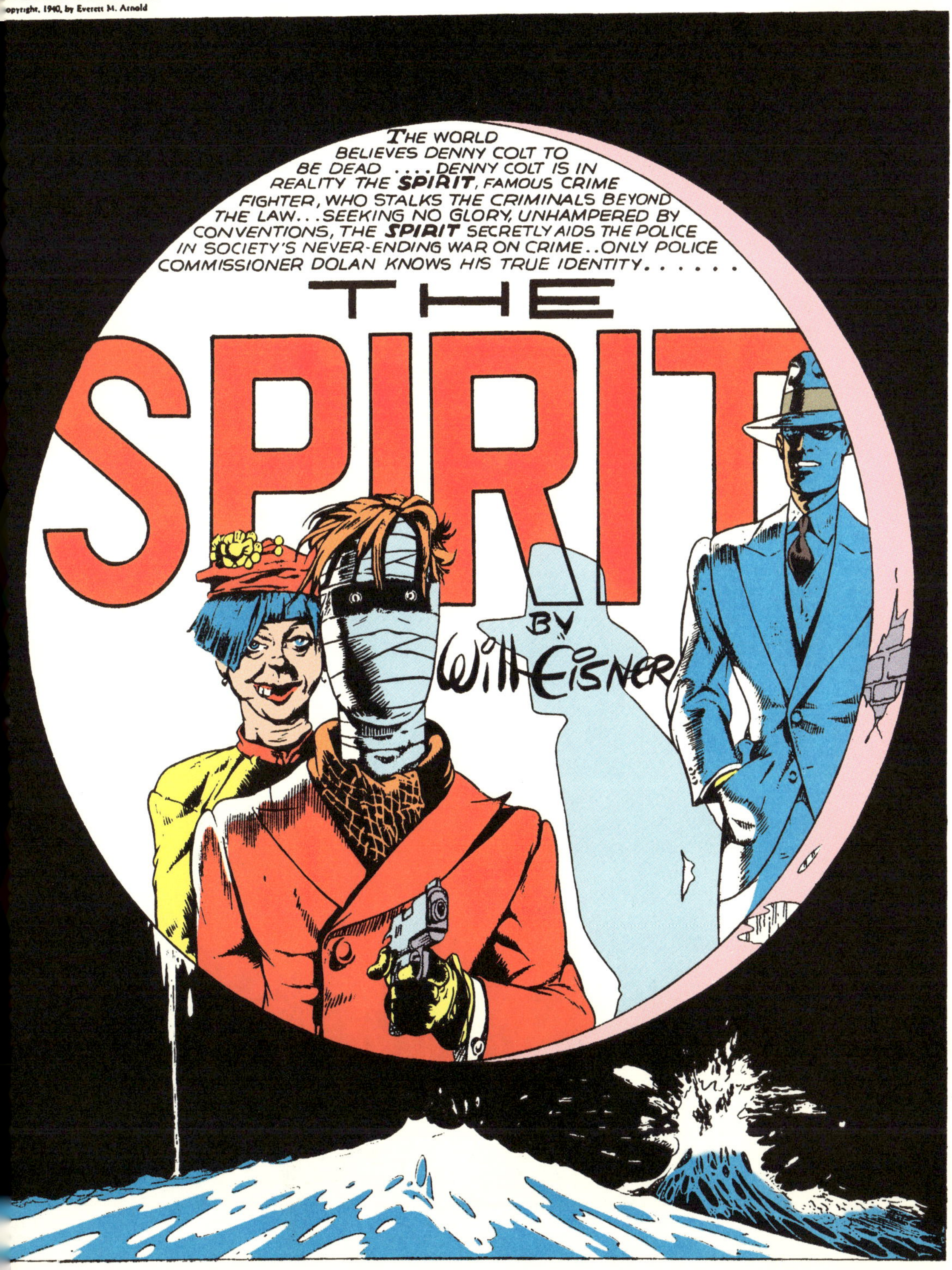
THE WORLD BELIEVES DENNY COLT TO BE DEAD .... DENNY COLT IS IN REALITY THE SPIRIT, FAMOUS CRIME FIGHTER, WHO STALKS THE CRIMINALS BEYOND THE LAW... SEEKING NO GLORY, UNHAMPERED BY CONVENTIONS, THE SPIRIT SECRETLY AIDS THE POLICE IN SOCIETY'S NEVER-ENDING WAR ON CRIME.. ONLY POLICE COMMISSIONER DOLAN KNOWS HIS TRUE IDENTITY......
THE SPIRIT
BY Will Eisner

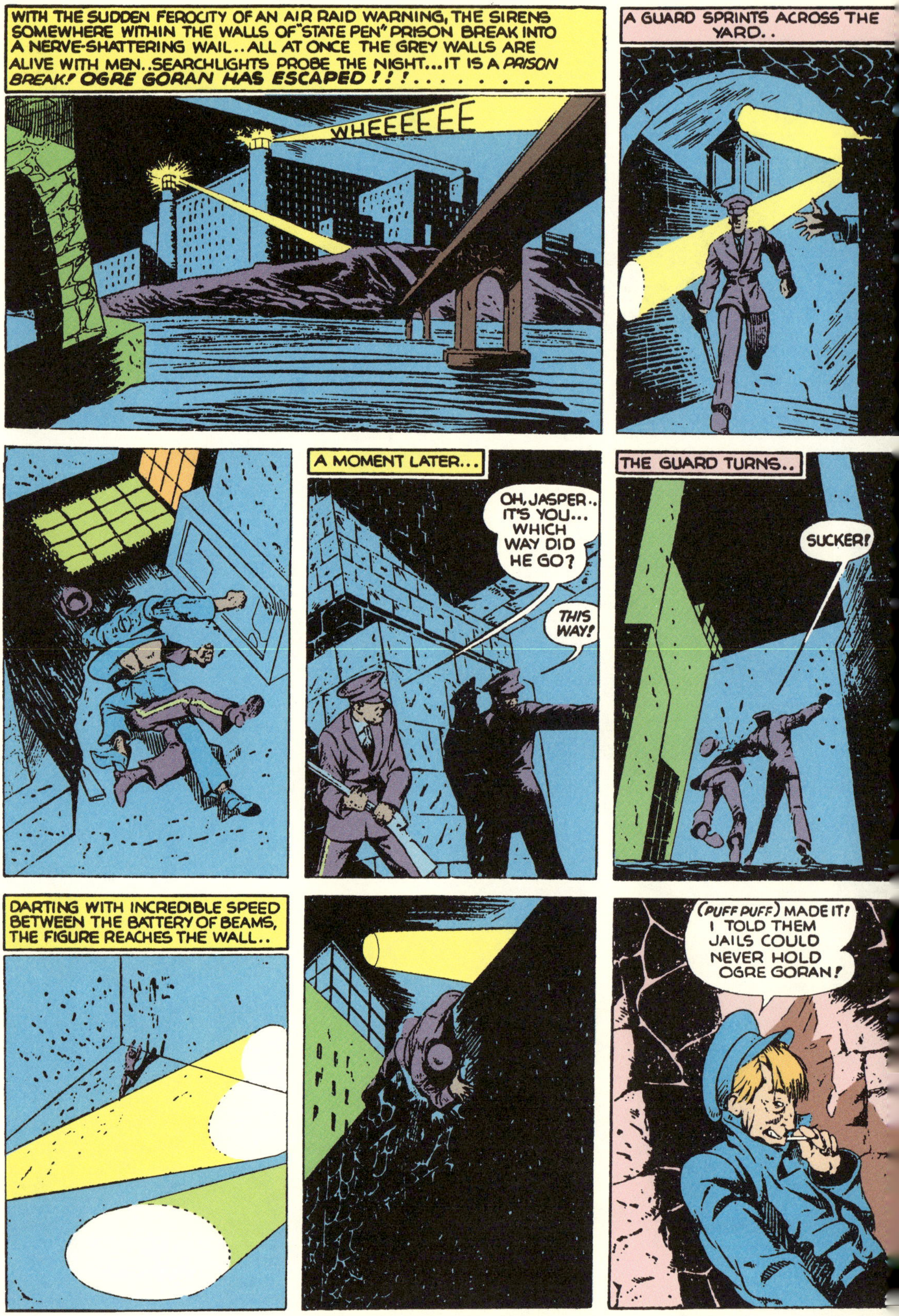
WITH THE SUDDEN FEROCITY OF AN AIR RAID WARNING, THE SIRENS SOMEWHERE WITHIN THE WALLS OF "STATE PEN" PRISON BREAK INTO A NERVE-SHATTERING WAIL..ALL AT ONCE THE GREY WALLS ARE ALIVE WITH MEN..SEARCHLIGHTS PROBE THE NIGHT...IT IS A PRISON BREAK! OGRE GORAN HAS ESCAPED!!!........
WHEEEEEE
A GUARD SPRINTS ACROSS THE YARD..
A MOMENT LATER...
OH, JASPER.. IT'S YOU... WHICH WAY DID HE GO?
THIS WAY!
THE GUARD TURNS..
SUCKER!
DARTING WITH INCREDIBLE SPEED BETWEEN THE BATTERY OF BEAMS, THE FIGURE REACHES THE WALL..
(PUFF PUFF) MADE IT! I TOLD THEM JAILS COULD NEVER HOLD OGRE GORAN!

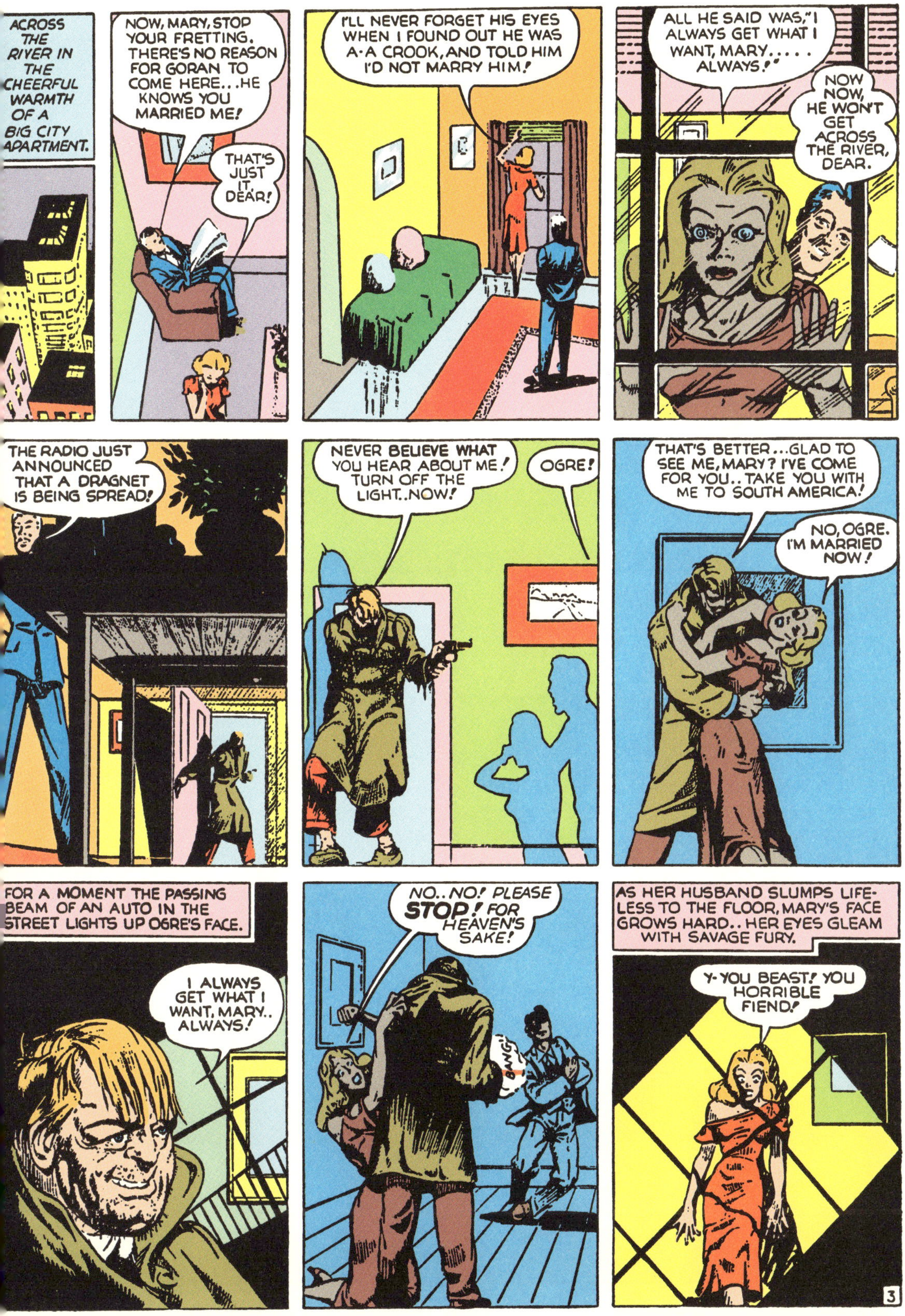

ACROSS THE RIVER IN THE CHEERFUL WARMTH OF A BIG CITY APARTMENT.
NOW, MARY, STOP YOUR FRETTING. THERE'S NO REASON FOR GORAN TO COME HERE...HE KNOWS YOU MARRIED ME!
THAT'S JUST IT, DEAR!
I'LL NEVER FORGET HIS EYES WHEN I FOUND OUT HE WAS A-A CROOK, AND TOLD HIM I'D NOT MARRY HIM!
ALL HE SAID WAS, "I ALWAYS GET WHAT I WANT, MARY..... ALWAYS!"
NOW NOW, HE WON'T GET ACROSS THE RIVER, DEAR.
THE RADIO JUST ANNOUNCED THAT A DRAGNET IS BEING SPREAD!
NEVER BELIEVE WHAT YOU HEAR ABOUT ME! TURN OFF THE LIGHT..NOW!
OGRE!
THAT'S BETTER...GLAD TO SEE ME, MARY? I'VE COME FOR YOU.. TAKE YOU WITH ME TO SOUTH AMERICA!
NO, OGRE. I'M MARRIED NOW!
FOR A MOMENT THE PASSING BEAM OF AN AUTO IN THE STREET LIGHTS UP OGRE'S FACE.
I ALWAYS GET WHAT I WANT, MARY.. ALWAYS!
NO..NO! PLEASE STOP! FOR HEAVEN'S SAKE!
BANG!
AS HER HUSBAND SLUMPS LIFELESS TO THE FLOOR, MARY'S FACE GROWS HARD.. HER EYES GLEAM WITH SAVAGE FURY.
Y-YOU BEAST! YOU HORRIBLE FIEND!
3

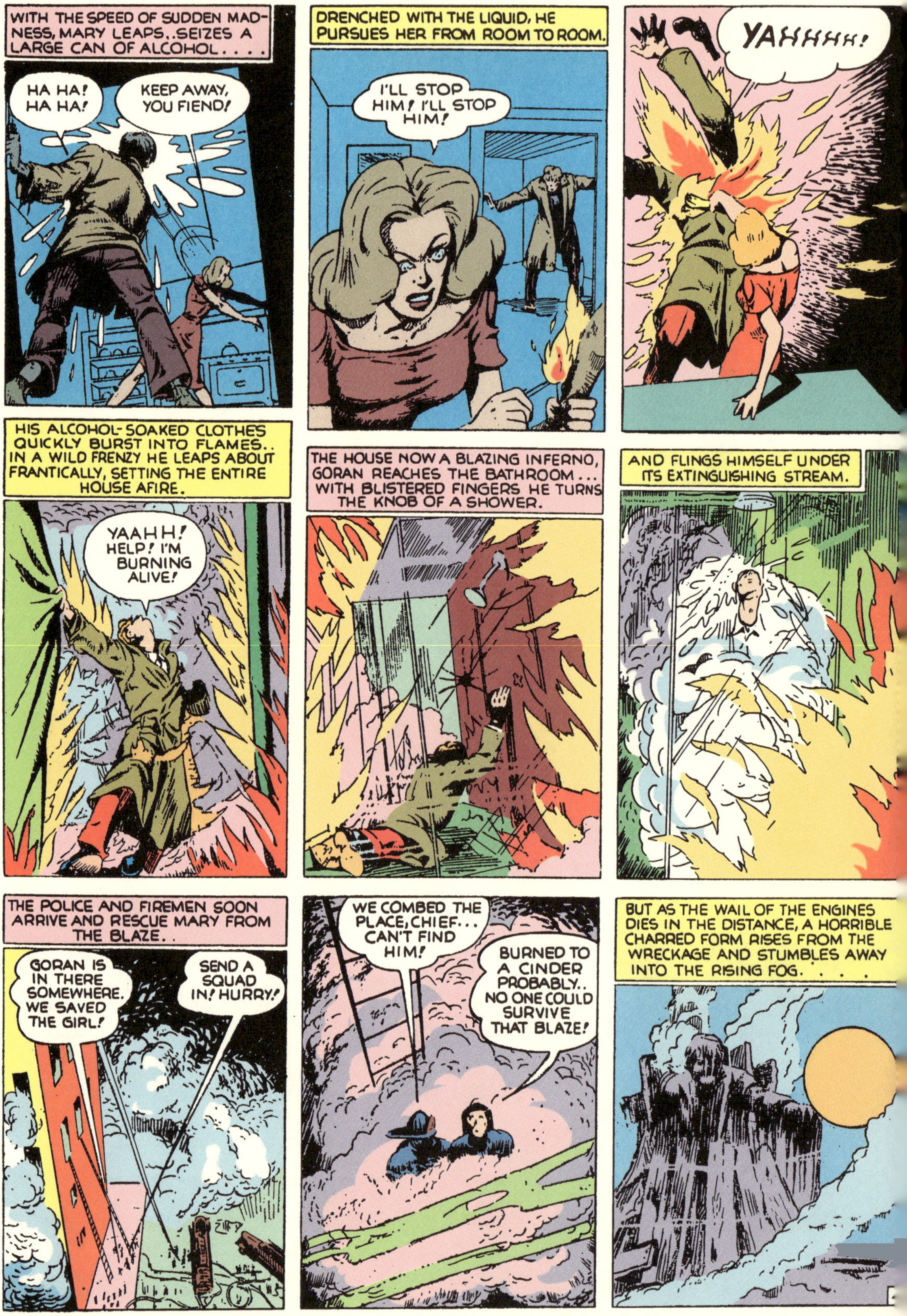
WITH THE SPEED OF SUDDEN MADNESS, MARY LEAPS..SEIZES A LARGE CAN OF ALCOHOL. . . .
HA HA! HA HA!
KEEP AWAY, YOU FIEND!
DRENCHED WITH THE LIQUID, HE PURSUES HER FROM ROOM TO ROOM.
I'LL STOP HIM! I'LL STOP HIM!
YAHHHH!
HIS ALCOHOL-SOAKED CLOTHES QUICKLY BURST INTO FLAMES.. IN A WILD FRENZY HE LEAPS ABOUT FRANTICALLY, SETTING THE ENTIRE HOUSE AFIRE.
YAAHH! HELP! I'M BURNING ALIVE!
THE HOUSE NOW A BLAZING INFERNO, GORAN REACHES THE BATHROOM... WITH BLISTERED FINGERS HE TURNS THE KNOB OF A SHOWER.
AND FLINGS HIMSELF UNDER ITS EXTINGUISHING STREAM.
THE POLICE AND FIREMEN SOON ARRIVE AND RESCUE MARY FROM THE BLAZE. .
GORAN IS IN THERE SOMEWHERE. WE SAVED THE GIRL!
SEND A SQUAD IN! HURRY!
WE COMBED THE PLACE, CHIEF... CAN'T FIND HIM!
BURNED TO A CINDER PROBABLY.. NO ONE COULD SURVIVE THAT BLAZE!
BUT AS THE WAIL OF THE ENGINES DIES IN THE DISTANCE, A HORRIBLE CHARRED FORM RISES FROM THE WRECKAGE AND STUMBLES AWAY INTO THE RISING FOG. . . .

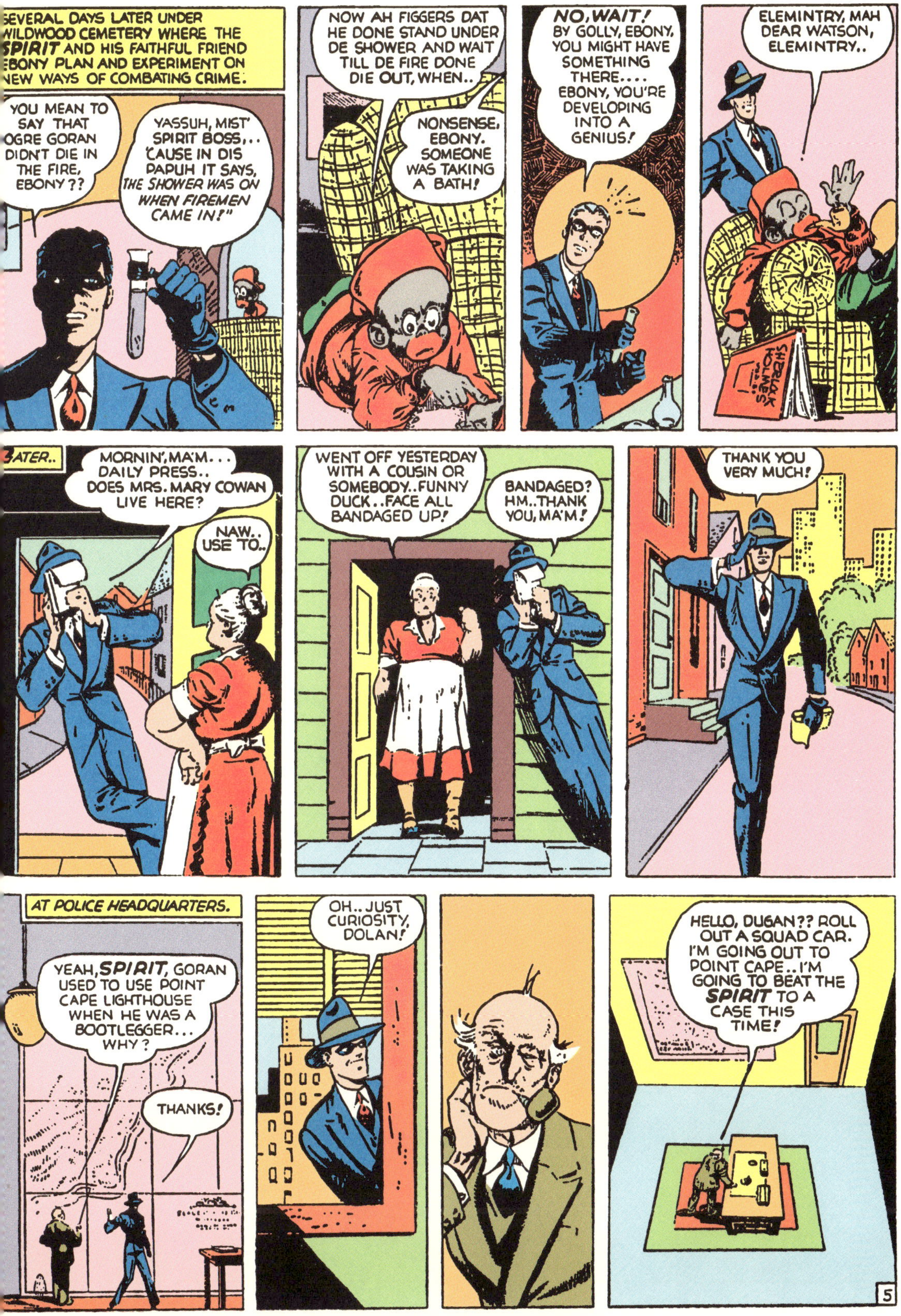
SEVERAL DAYS LATER UNDER WILDWOOD CEMETERY WHERE THE SPIRIT AND HIS FAITHFUL FRIEND EBONY PLAN AND EXPERIMENT ON NEW WAYS OF COMBATING CRIME.
YOU MEAN TO SAY THAT OGRE GORAN DIDN'T DIE IN THE FIRE, EBONY??
YASSUH, MIST' SPIRIT BOSS,.. 'CAUSE IN DIS PAPUH IT SAYS, "THE SHOWER WAS ON WHEN FIREMEN CAME IN!"
NOW AH FIGGERS DAT HE DONE STAND UNDER DE SHOWER AND WAIT TILL DE FIRE DONE DIE OUT, WHEN..
NONSENSE, EBONY. SOMEONE WAS TAKING A BATH!
NO, WAIT! BY GOLLY, EBONY, YOU MIGHT HAVE SOMETHING THERE.... EBONY, YOU'RE DEVELOPING INTO A GENIUS!
ELEMINTRY, MAH DEAR WATSON, ELEMINTRY..
SHERLOCK HOLMES
LATER..
MORNIN', MA'M... DAILY PRESS.. DOES MRS. MARY COWAN LIVE HERE?
NAW.. USE TO..
WENT OFF YESTERDAY WITH A COUSIN OR SOMEBODY..FUNNY DUCK..FACE ALL BANDAGED UP!
BANDAGED? HM..THANK YOU, MA'M!
THANK YOU VERY MUCH!
AT POLICE HEADQUARTERS.
YEAH, SPIRIT, GORAN USED TO USE POINT CAPE LIGHTHOUSE WHEN HE WAS A BOOTLEGGER... WHY?
THANKS!
OH.. JUST CURIOSITY, DOLAN!
HELLO, DUGAN?? ROLL OUT A SQUAD CAR. I'M GOING OUT TO POINT CAPE.. I'M GOING TO BEAT THE SPIRIT TO A CASE THIS TIME!
5

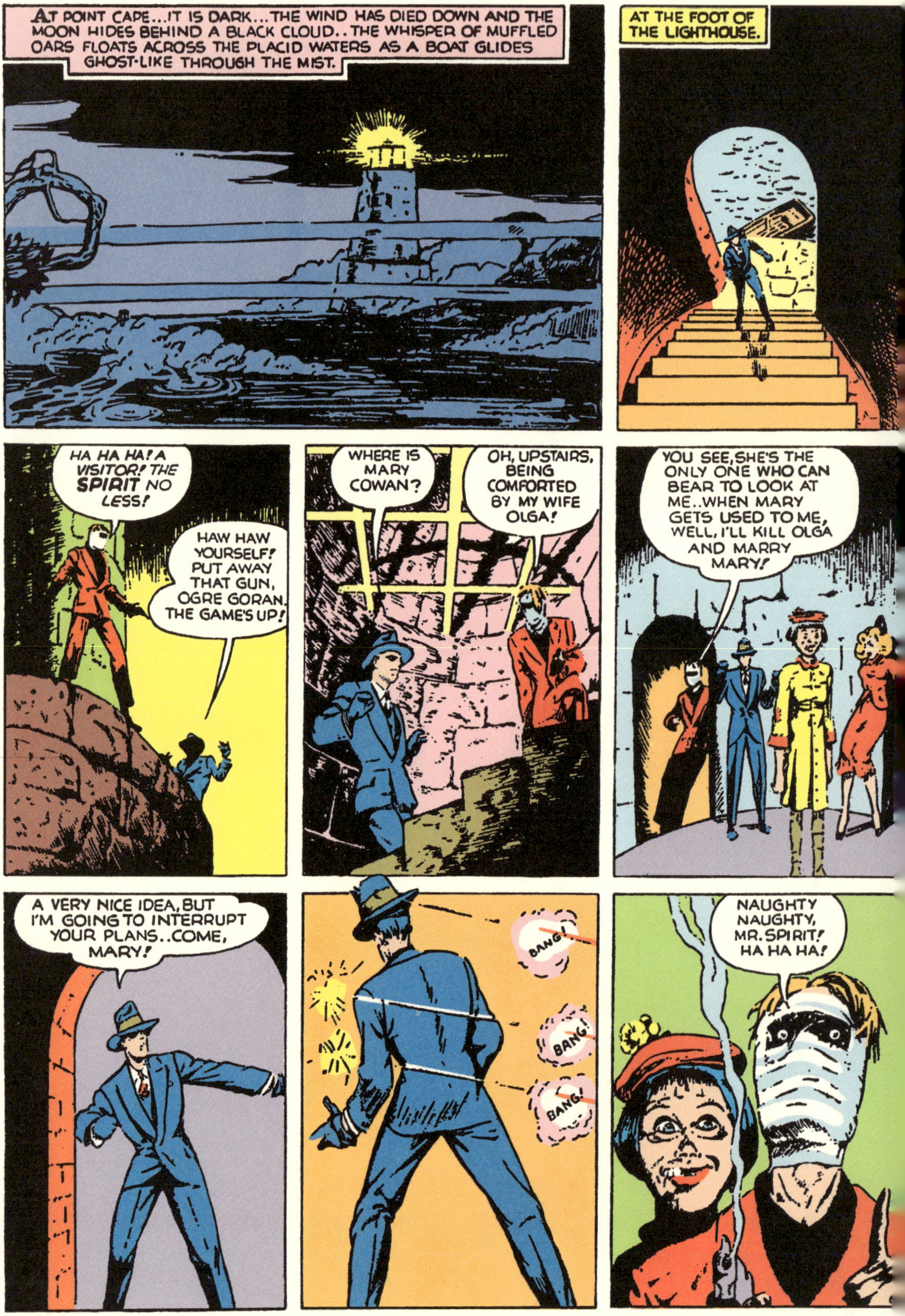
AT POINT CAPE...IT IS DARK...THE WIND HAS DIED DOWN AND THE MOON HIDES BEHIND A BLACK CLOUD..THE WHISPER OF MUFFLED OARS FLOATS ACROSS THE PLACID WATERS AS A BOAT GLIDES GHOST-LIKE THROUGH THE MIST.
AT THE FOOT OF THE LIGHTHOUSE.
HA HA HA! A VISITOR! THE SPIRIT NO LESS!
HAW HAW YOURSELF! PUT AWAY THAT GUN, OGRE GORAN. THE GAME'S UP!
WHERE IS MARY COWAN?
OH, UPSTAIRS, BEING COMFORTED BY MY WIFE OLGA!
YOU SEE, SHE'S THE ONLY ONE WHO CAN BEAR TO LOOK AT ME..WHEN MARY GETS USED TO ME, WELL, I'LL KILL OLGA AND MARRY MARY!
A VERY NICE IDEA, BUT I'M GOING TO INTERRUPT YOUR PLANS..COME, MARY!
BANG!
BANG!
BANG!
NAUGHTY NAUGHTY, MR. SPIRIT! HA HA HA!

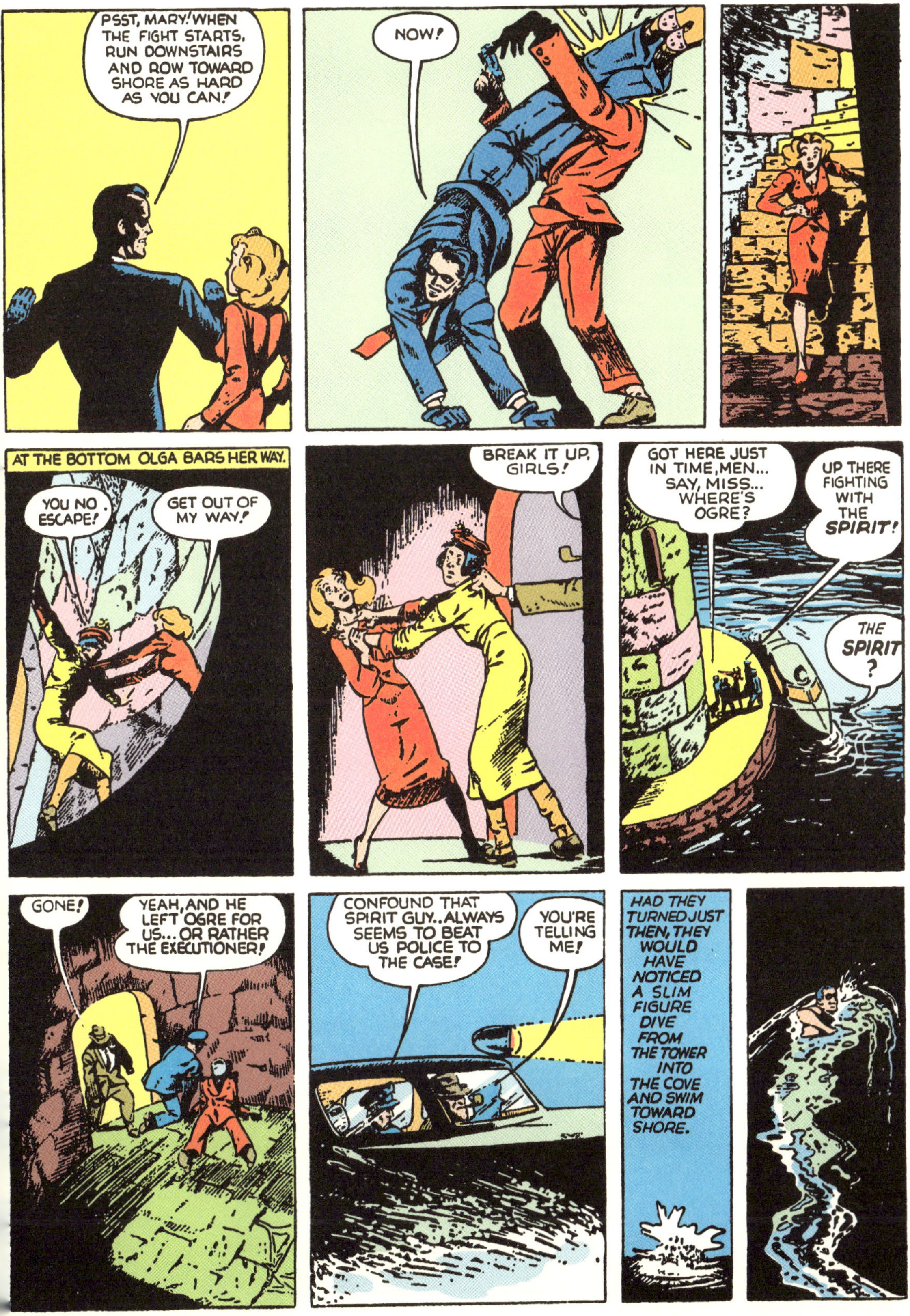
PSST, MARY! WHEN THE FIGHT STARTS, RUN DOWNSTAIRS AND ROW TOWARD SHORE AS HARD AS YOU CAN!
NOW!
AT THE BOTTOM OLGA BARS HER WAY.
YOU NO ESCAPE!
GET OUT OF MY WAY!
BREAK IT UP, GIRLS!
GOT HERE JUST IN TIME, MEN... SAY, MISS... WHERE'S OGRE?
UP THERE FIGHTING WITH THE SPIRIT!
THE SPIRIT?
GONE!
YEAH, AND HE LEFT OGRE FOR US... OR RATHER THE EXECUTIONER!
CONFOUND THAT SPIRIT GUY.. ALWAYS SEEMS TO BEAT US POLICE TO THE CASE!
YOU'RE TELLING ME!
HAD THEY TURNED JUST THEN, THEY WOULD HAVE NOTICED A SLIM FIGURE DIVE FROM THE TOWER INTO THE COVE AND SWIM TOWARD SHORE.

CONSCRIPTION BILL SIGNED

October 27, 1940

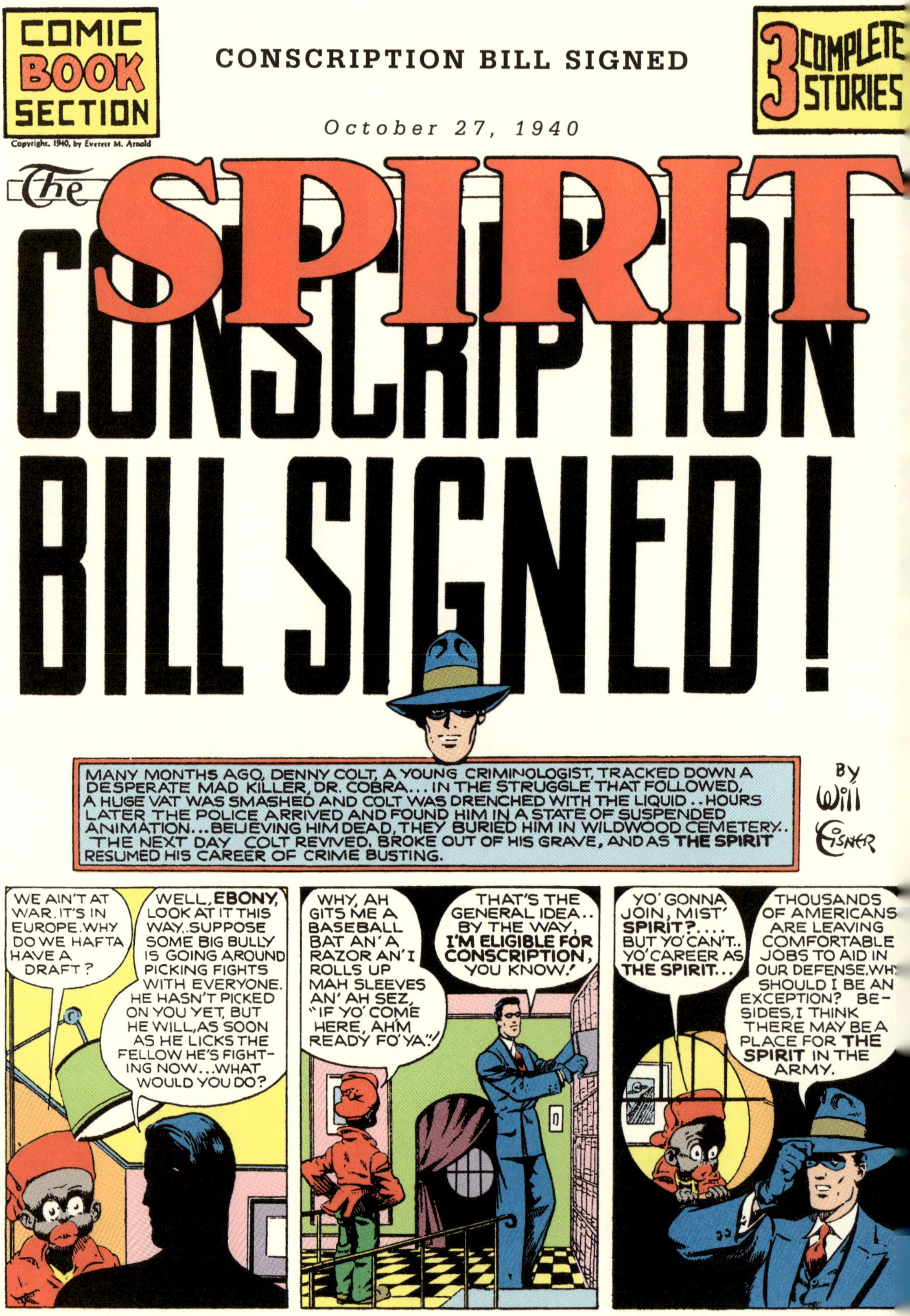

COMIC BOOK SECTION
Copyright, 1940, by Everett M. Arnold
3 COMPLETE STORIES
The SPIRIT
CONSCRIPTION BILL SIGNED !
MANY MONTHS AGO, DENNY COLT, A YOUNG CRIMINOLOGIST, TRACKED DOWN A DESPERATE MAD KILLER, DR. COBRA... IN THE STRUGGLE THAT FOLLOWED, A HUGE VAT WAS SMASHED AND COLT WAS DRENCHED WITH THE LIQUID..HOURS LATER THE POLICE ARRIVED AND FOUND HIM IN A STATE OF SUSPENDED ANIMATION...BELIEVING HIM DEAD, THEY BURIED HIM IN WILDWOOD CEMETERY.. THE NEXT DAY COLT REVIVED, BROKE OUT OF HIS GRAVE, AND AS THE SPIRIT RESUMED HIS CAREER OF CRIME BUSTING.
By Will Eisner
WE AIN'T AT WAR. IT'S IN EUROPE. WHY DO WE HAFTA HAVE A DRAFT?
WELL, EBONY, LOOK AT IT THIS WAY..SUPPOSE SOME BIG BULLY IS GOING AROUND PICKING FIGHTS WITH EVERYONE. HE HASN'T PICKED ON YOU YET, BUT HE WILL, AS SOON AS HE LICKS THE FELLOW HE'S FIGHTING NOW...WHAT WOULD YOU DO?
WHY, AH GITS ME A BASEBALL BAT AN' A RAZOR AN' I ROLLS UP MAH SLEEVES AN' AH SEZ, "IF YO' COME HERE, AH'M READY FO' YA"!
THAT'S THE GENERAL IDEA.. BY THE WAY, I'M ELIGIBLE FOR CONSCRIPTION, YOU KNOW!
YO' GONNA JOIN, MIST' SPIRIT?.... BUT YO' CAN'T.. YO' CAREER AS THE SPIRIT...
THOUSANDS OF AMERICANS ARE LEAVING COMFORTABLE JOBS TO AID IN OUR DEFENSE. WHY SHOULD I BE AN EXCEPTION? BESIDES, I THINK THERE MAY BE A PLACE FOR THE SPIRIT IN THE ARMY.

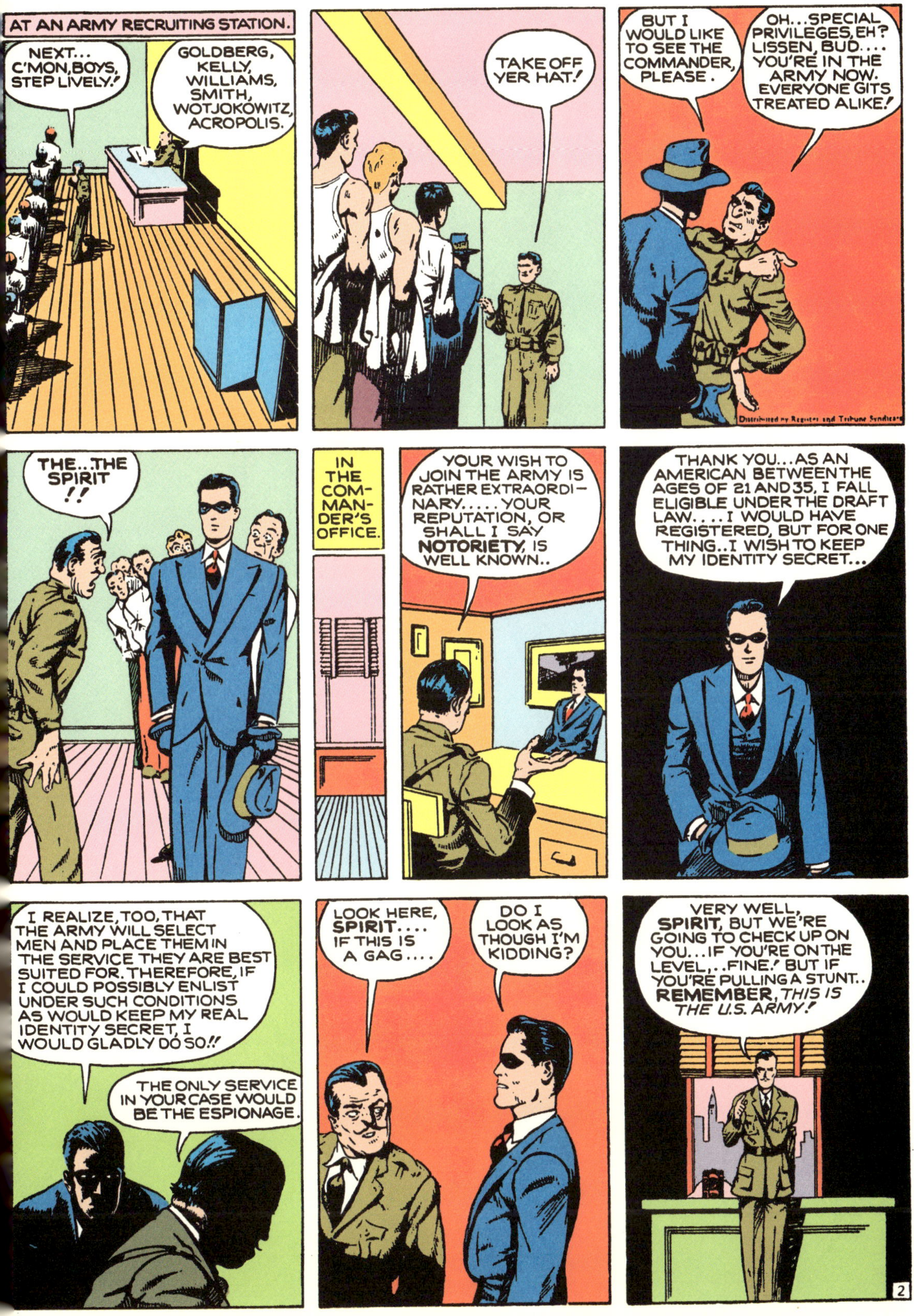
AT AN ARMY RECRUITING STATION.
NEXT... C'MON, BOYS, STEP LIVELY!
GOLDBERG, KELLY, WILLIAMS, SMITH, WOTJOKOWITZ, ACROPOLIS.
TAKE OFF YER HAT!
BUT I WOULD LIKE TO SEE THE COMMANDER, PLEASE.
OH...SPECIAL PRIVILEGES, EH? LISSEN, BUD.... YOU'RE IN THE ARMY NOW. EVERYONE GITS TREATED ALIKE!
THE..THE SPIRIT!!
IN THE COMMANDER'S OFFICE.
YOUR WISH TO JOIN THE ARMY IS RATHER EXTRAORDINARY..... YOUR REPUTATION, OR SHALL I SAY NOTORIETY, IS WELL KNOWN..
THANK YOU...AS AN AMERICAN BETWEEN THE AGES OF 21 AND 35, I FALL ELIGIBLE UNDER THE DRAFT LAW....I WOULD HAVE REGISTERED, BUT FOR ONE THING..I WISH TO KEEP MY IDENTITY SECRET...
I REALIZE, TOO, THAT THE ARMY WILL SELECT MEN AND PLACE THEM IN THE SERVICE THEY ARE BEST SUITED FOR. THEREFORE, IF I COULD POSSIBLY ENLIST UNDER SUCH CONDITIONS AS WOULD KEEP MY REAL IDENTITY SECRET, I WOULD GLADLY DO SO!!
THE ONLY SERVICE IN YOUR CASE WOULD BE THE ESPIONAGE.
LOOK HERE, SPIRIT.... IF THIS IS A GAG....
DO I LOOK AS THOUGH I'M KIDDING?
VERY WELL, SPIRIT, BUT WE'RE GOING TO CHECK UP ON YOU...IF YOU'RE ON THE LEVEL,..FINE! BUT IF YOU'RE PULLING A STUNT.. REMEMBER, THIS IS THE U.S. ARMY!
2

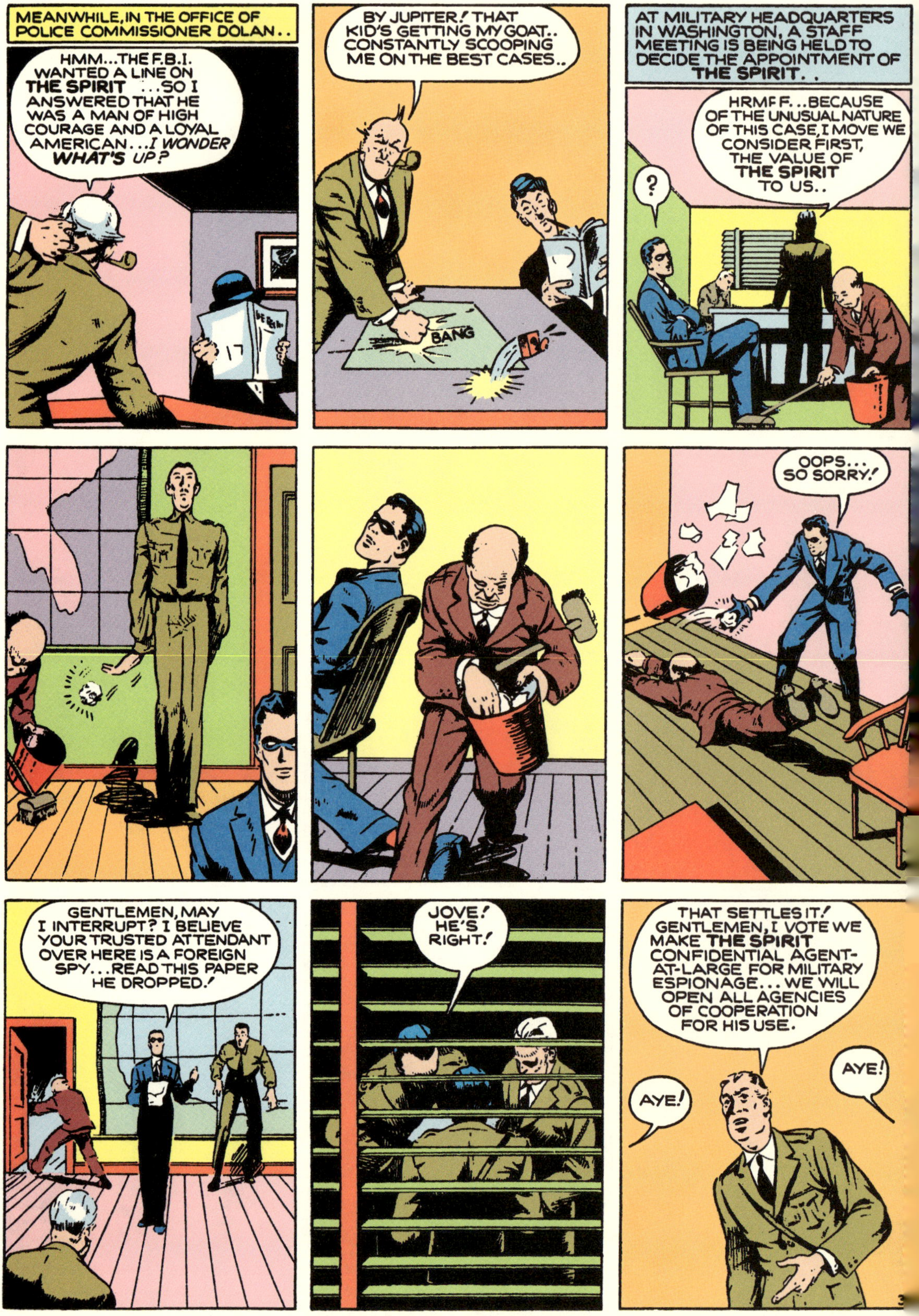

MEANWHILE, IN THE OFFICE OF POLICE COMMISSIONER DOLAN..
HMM...THE F.B.I. WANTED A LINE ON THE SPIRIT ...SO I ANSWERED THAT HE WAS A MAN OF HIGH COURAGE AND A LOYAL AMERICAN...I WONDER WHAT'S UP?
BY JUPITER! THAT KID'S GETTING MY GOAT.. CONSTANTLY SCOOPING ME ON THE BEST CASES..
BANG
AT MILITARY HEADQUARTERS IN WASHINGTON, A STAFF MEETING IS BEING HELD TO DECIDE THE APPOINTMENT OF THE SPIRIT. .
?
HRMFF...BECAUSE OF THE UNUSUAL NATURE OF THIS CASE, I MOVE WE CONSIDER FIRST, THE VALUE OF THE SPIRIT TO US..
OOPS... SO SORRY!
GENTLEMEN, MAY I INTERRUPT? I BELIEVE YOUR TRUSTED ATTENDANT OVER HERE IS A FOREIGN SPY...READ THIS PAPER HE DROPPED!
JOVE! HE'S RIGHT!
THAT SETTLES IT! GENTLEMEN, I VOTE WE MAKE THE SPIRIT CONFIDENTIAL AGENT-AT-LARGE FOR MILITARY ESPIONAGE... WE WILL OPEN ALL AGENCIES OF COOPERATION FOR HIS USE.
AYE!
AYE!

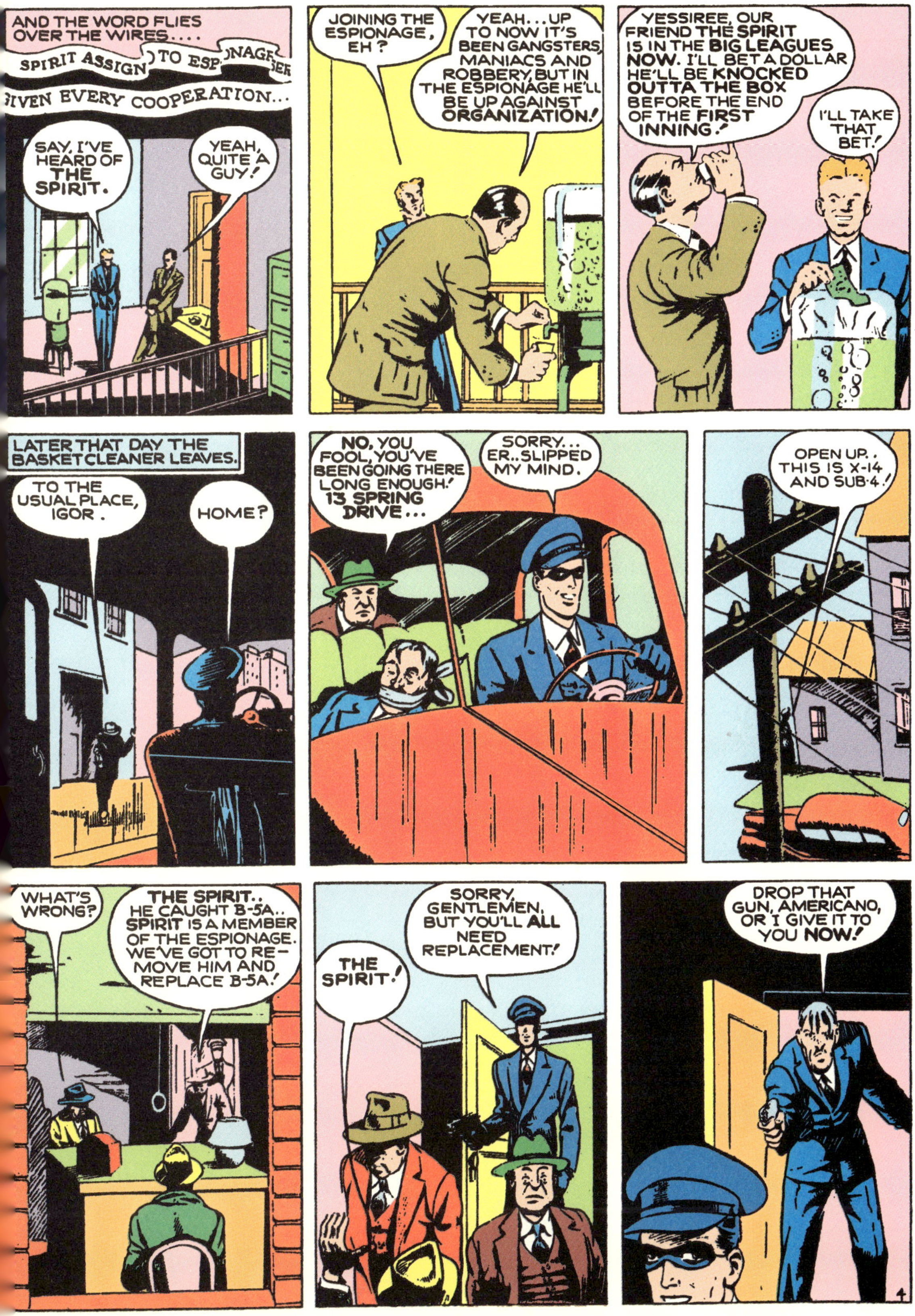
AND THE WORD FLIES OVER THE WIRES....
SAY, I'VE HEARD OF THE SPIRIT.
YEAH, QUITE A GUY!
JOINING THE ESPIONAGE, EH?
YEAH...UP TO NOW IT'S BEEN GANGSTERS, MANIACS AND ROBBERY, BUT IN THE ESPIONAGE HE'LL BE UP AGAINST ORGANIZATION!
YESSIREE, OUR FRIEND THE SPIRIT IS IN THE BIG LEAGUES NOW. I'LL BET A DOLLAR HE'LL BE KNOCKED OUTTA THE BOX BEFORE THE END OF THE FIRST INNING.
I'LL TAKE THAT BET!
LATER THAT DAY THE BASKET CLEANER LEAVES.
TO THE USUAL PLACE, IGOR.
HOME?
NO, YOU FOOL, YOU'VE BEEN GOING THERE LONG ENOUGH! 13 SPRING DRIVE...
SORRY... ER..SLIPPED MY MIND.
OPEN UP.. THIS IS X-14 AND SUB-4!
WHAT'S WRONG?
THE SPIRIT.. HE CAUGHT B-5A.. SPIRIT IS A MEMBER OF THE ESPIONAGE. WE'VE GOT TO REMOVE HIM AND REPLACE B-5A!
THE SPIRIT!
SORRY, GENTLEMEN, BUT YOU'LL ALL NEED REPLACEMENT!
DROP THAT GUN, AMERICANO, OR I GIVE IT TO YOU NOW!
4

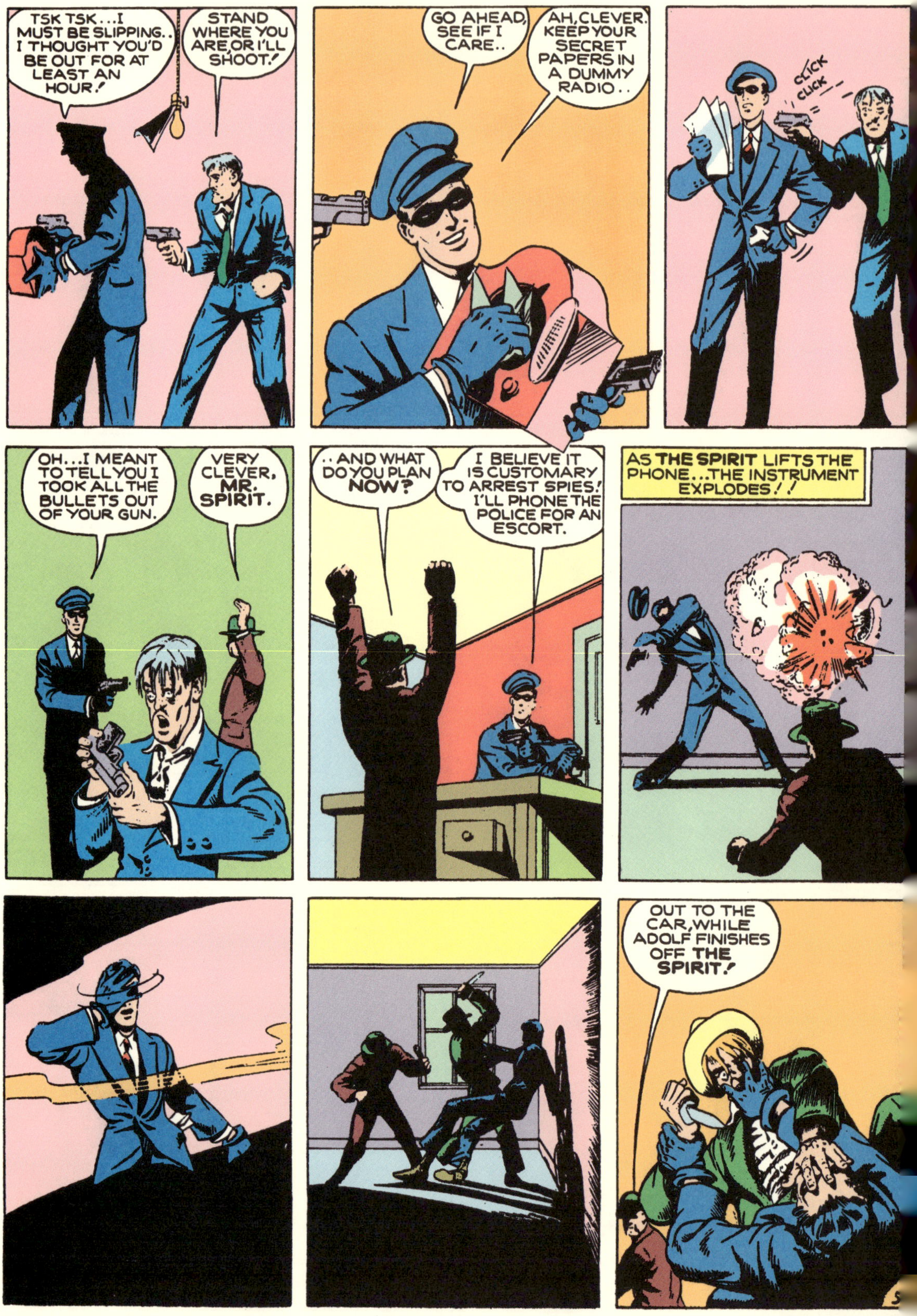
TSK TSK...I MUST BE SLIPPING.. I THOUGHT YOU'D BE OUT FOR AT LEAST AN HOUR!
STAND WHERE YOU ARE, OR I'LL SHOOT!
GO AHEAD, SEE IF I CARE..
AH, CLEVER. KEEP YOUR SECRET PAPERS IN A DUMMY RADIO..
CLICK CLICK
OH...I MEANT TO TELL YOU I TOOK ALL THE BULLETS OUT OF YOUR GUN.
VERY CLEVER, MR. SPIRIT.
..AND WHAT DO YOU PLAN NOW?
I BELIEVE IT IS CUSTOMARY TO ARREST SPIES! I'LL PHONE THE POLICE FOR AN ESCORT.
AS THE SPIRIT LIFTS THE PHONE...THE INSTRUMENT EXPLODES!!
OUT TO THE CAR, WHILE ADOLF FINISHES OFF THE SPIRIT!

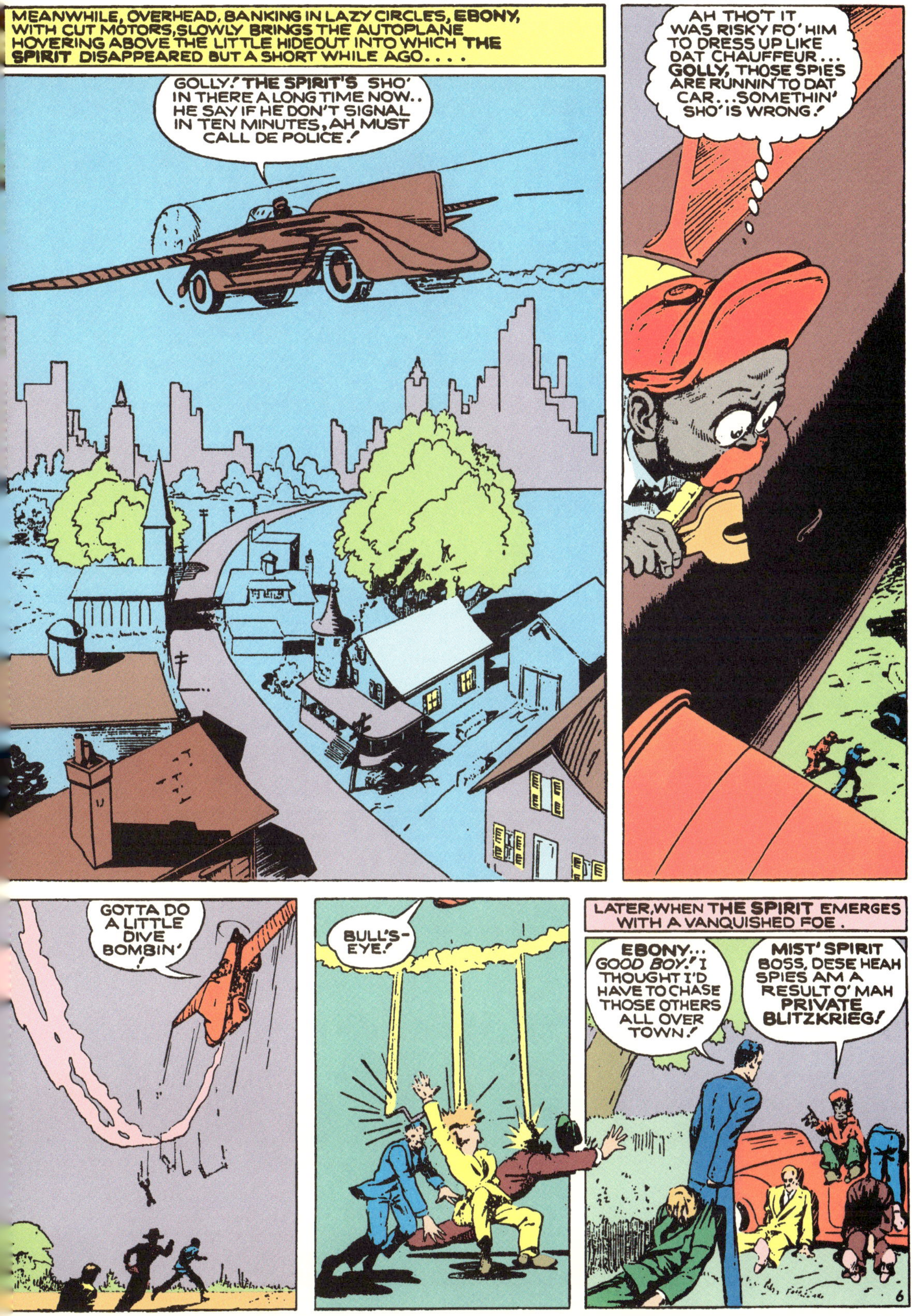
MEANWHILE, OVERHEAD, BANKING IN LAZY CIRCLES, EBONY, WITH CUT MOTORS, SLOWLY BRINGS THE AUTOPLANE HOVERING ABOVE THE LITTLE HIDEOUT INTO WHICH THE SPIRIT DISAPPEARED BUT A SHORT WHILE AGO....
GOLLY! THE SPIRIT'S SHO' IN THERE A LONG TIME NOW.. HE SAY IF HE DON'T SIGNAL IN TEN MINUTES, AH MUST CALL DE POLICE!
AH THO'T IT WAS RISKY FO' HIM TO DRESS UP LIKE DAT CHAUFFEUR... GOLLY, THOSE SPIES ARE RUNNIN' TO DAT CAR... SOMETHIN' SHO' IS WRONG!
GOTTA DO A LITTLE DIVE BOMBIN'!
BULL'S-EYE!
LATER, WHEN THE SPIRIT EMERGES WITH A VANQUISHED FOE.
EBONY... GOOD BOY! I THOUGHT I'D HAVE TO CHASE THOSE OTHERS ALL OVER TOWN!
MIST' SPIRIT BOSS, DESE HEAH SPIES AM A RESULT O' MAH PRIVATE BLITZKRIEG!
6

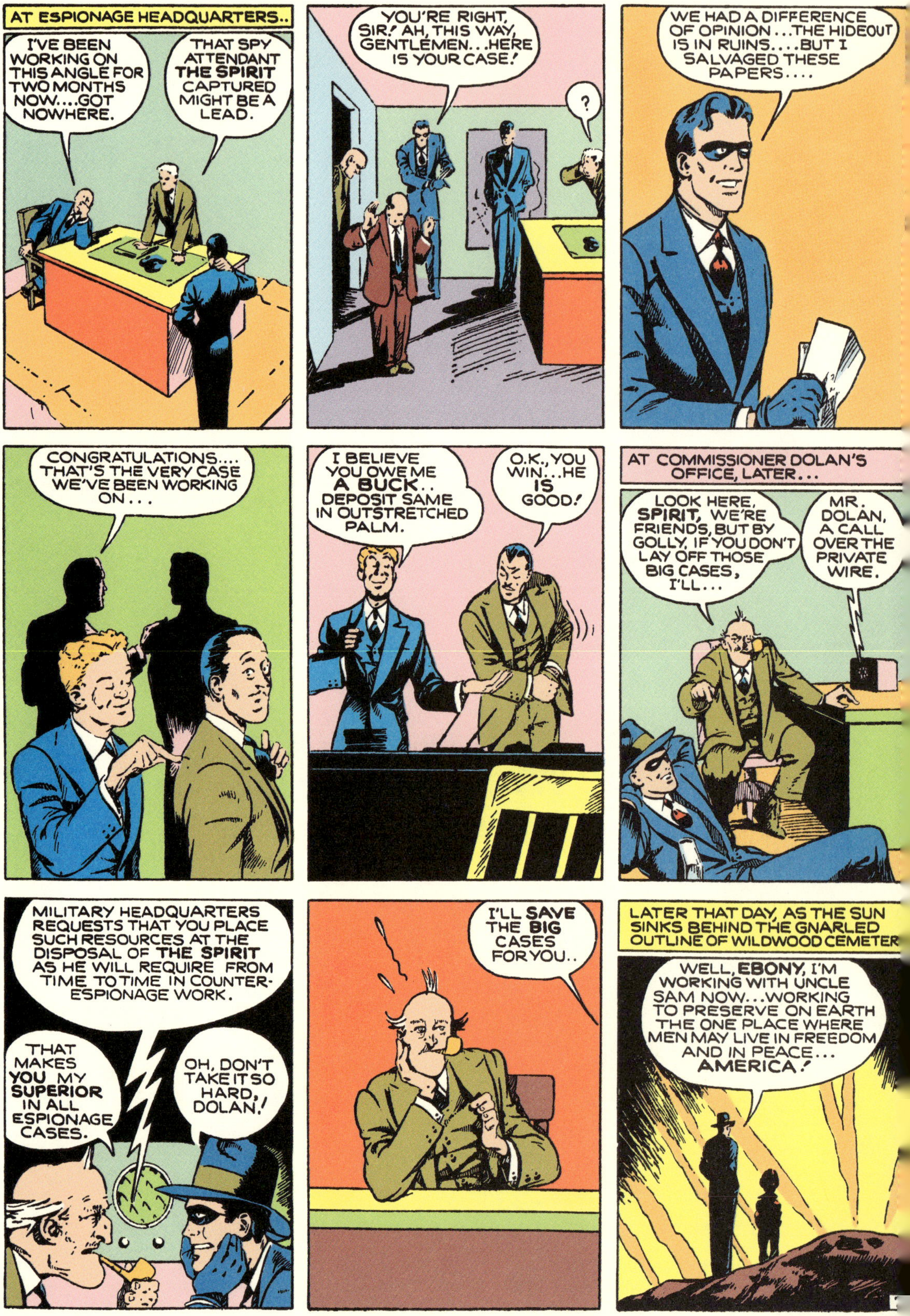
AT ESPIONAGE HEADQUARTERS..
I'VE BEEN WORKING ON THIS ANGLE FOR TWO MONTHS NOW....GOT NOWHERE.
THAT SPY ATTENDANT THE SPIRIT CAPTURED MIGHT BE A LEAD.
YOU'RE RIGHT, SIR! AH, THIS WAY, GENTLEMEN...HERE IS YOUR CASE!
?
WE HAD A DIFFERENCE OF OPINION...THE HIDEOUT IS IN RUINS....BUT I SALVAGED THESE PAPERS....
CONGRATULATIONS.... THAT'S THE VERY CASE WE'VE BEEN WORKING ON...
I BELIEVE YOU OWE ME A BUCK.. DEPOSIT SAME IN OUTSTRETCHED PALM.
O.K., YOU WIN...HE IS GOOD!
AT COMMISSIONER DOLAN'S OFFICE, LATER...
LOOK HERE, SPIRIT, WE'RE FRIENDS, BUT BY GOLLY, IF YOU DON'T LAY OFF THOSE BIG CASES, I'LL...
MR. DOLAN, A CALL OVER THE PRIVATE WIRE.
MILITARY HEADQUARTERS REQUESTS THAT YOU PLACE SUCH RESOURCES AT THE DISPOSAL OF THE SPIRIT AS HE WILL REQUIRE FROM TIME TO TIME IN COUNTER-ESPIONAGE WORK.
THAT MAKES YOU MY SUPERIOR IN ALL ESPIONAGE CASES.
OH, DON'T TAKE IT SO HARD, DOLAN!
I'LL SAVE THE BIG CASES FOR YOU..
LATER THAT DAY, AS THE SUN SINKS BEHIND THE GNARLED OUTLINE OF WILDWOOD CEMETER
WELL, EBONY, I'M WORKING WITH UNCLE SAM NOW...WORKING TO PRESERVE ON EARTH THE ONE PLACE WHERE MEN MAY LIVE IN FREEDOM AND IN PEACE... AMERICA!

COMIC BOOK SECTION

THE MANLY ART OF SELF DEFENSE

November 3, 1940

3 COMPLETE STORIES

THE SPIRIT
BY Will Eisner
The MANLY ART of SELF DEFENSE
THE SPIRIT, IN REALITY DENNY COLT, LONG BELIEVED DEAD, DEVOTES HIS LIFE TO THE TRACKING DOWN OF CRIMINALS WHO ESCAPE BEYOND THE REACHES OF THE LAW.. FROM UNDERGROUND IN WILDWOOD CEMETERY, HE FIGHTS THE FORCES OF EVIL.

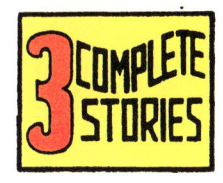

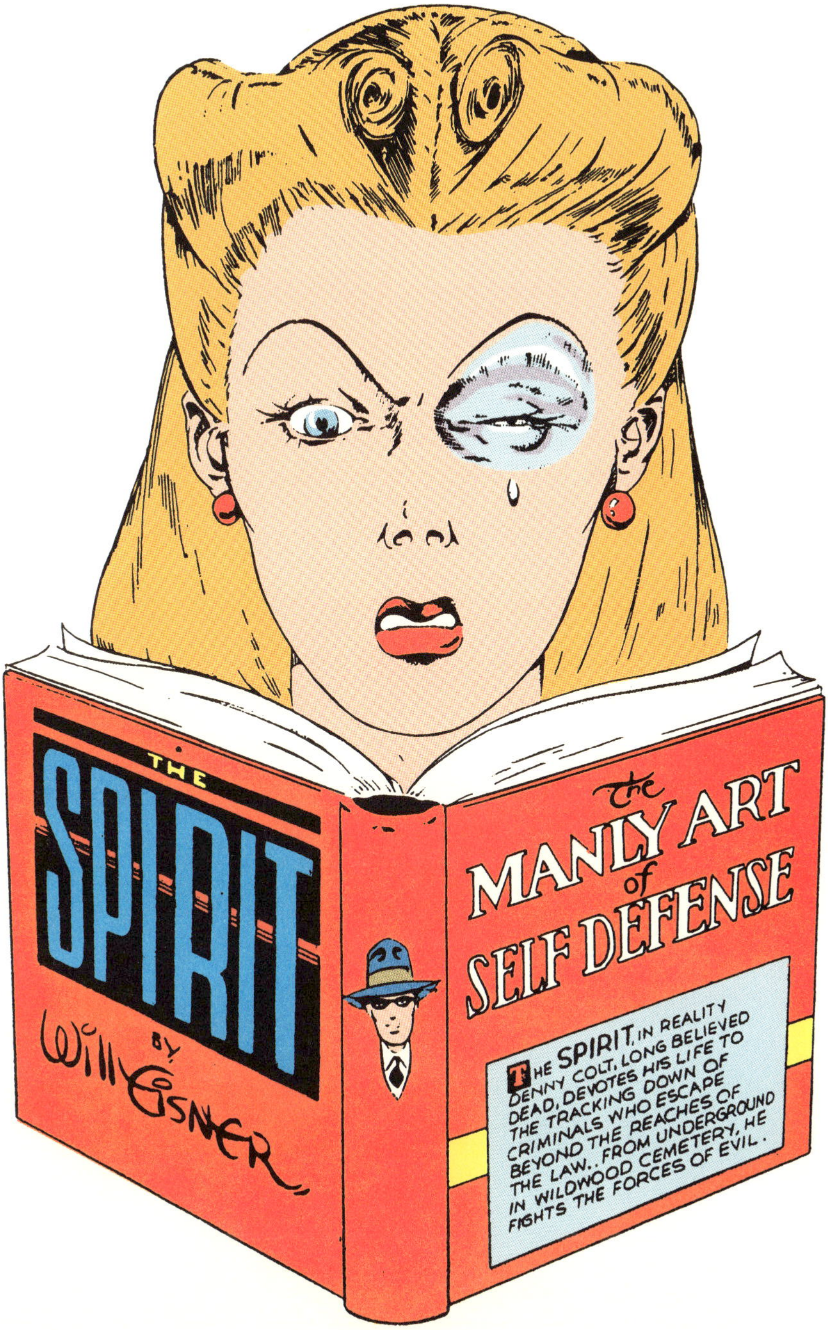

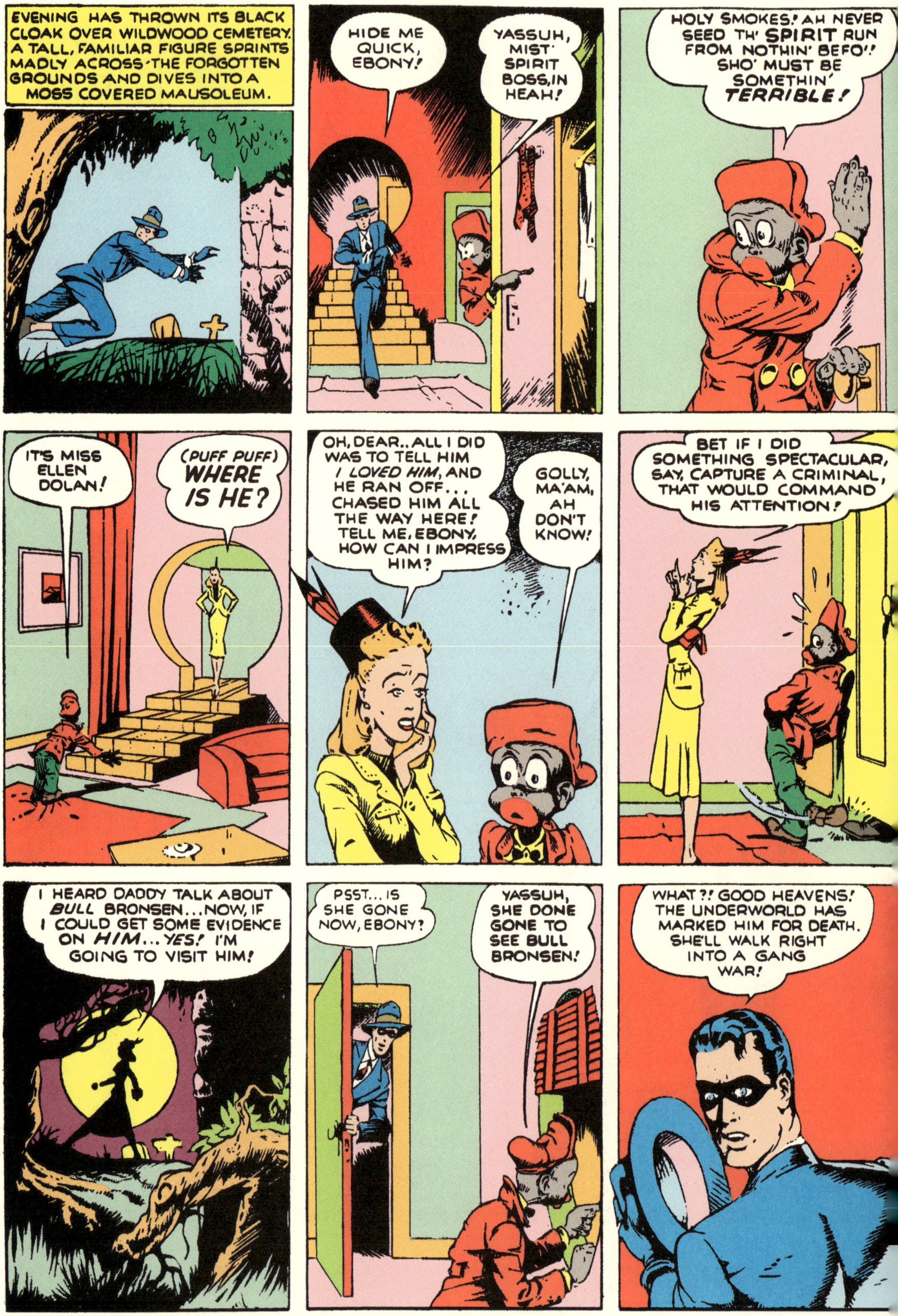
EVENING HAS THROWN ITS BLACK CLOAK OVER WILDWOOD CEMETERY. A TALL, FAMILIAR FIGURE SPRINTS MADLY ACROSS THE FORGOTTEN GROUNDS AND DIVES INTO A MOSS COVERED MAUSOLEUM.
HIDE ME QUICK, EBONY!
YASSUH, MIST' SPIRIT BOSS, IN HEAH!
HOLY SMOKES! AH NEVER SEED TH' SPIRIT RUN FROM NOTHIN' BEFO'! SHO' MUST BE SOMETHIN' TERRIBLE!
IT'S MISS ELLEN DOLAN!
(PUFF PUFF) WHERE IS HE?
OH, DEAR.. ALL I DID WAS TO TELL HIM I LOVED HIM, AND HE RAN OFF... CHASED HIM ALL THE WAY HERE! TELL ME, EBONY, HOW CAN I IMPRESS HIM?
GOLLY, MA'AM, AH DON'T KNOW!
BET IF I DID SOMETHING SPECTACULAR, SAY, CAPTURE A CRIMINAL, THAT WOULD COMMAND HIS ATTENTION!
I HEARD DADDY TALK ABOUT BULL BRONSEN... NOW, IF I COULD GET SOME EVIDENCE ON HIM... YES! I'M GOING TO VISIT HIM!
PSST... IS SHE GONE NOW, EBONY?
YASSUH, SHE DONE GONE TO SEE BULL BRONSEN!
WHAT?! GOOD HEAVENS! THE UNDERWORLD HAS MARKED HIM FOR DEATH. SHE'LL WALK RIGHT INTO A GANG WAR!

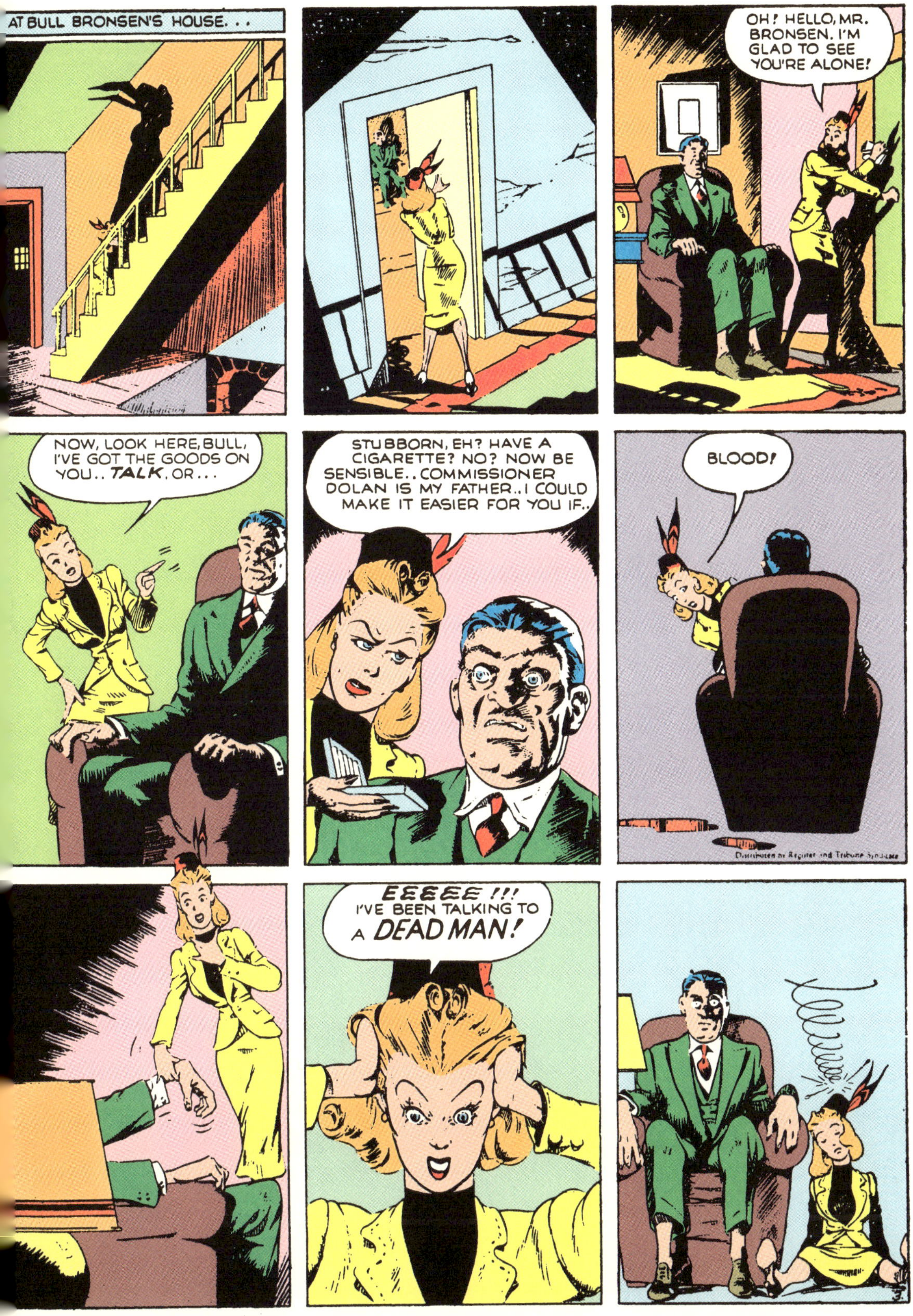
AT BULL BRONSEN'S HOUSE. . .
OH! HELLO, MR. BRONSEN. I'M GLAD TO SEE YOU'RE ALONE!
NOW, LOOK HERE, BULL, I'VE GOT THE GOODS ON YOU.. TALK, OR...
STUBBORN, EH? HAVE A CIGARETTE? NO? NOW BE SENSIBLE.. COMMISSIONER DOLAN IS MY FATHER.. I COULD MAKE IT EASIER FOR YOU IF..
BLOOD!
Distributed by Register and Tribune Syndicate
EEEEE!!!
I'VE BEEN TALKING TO A DEAD MAN!

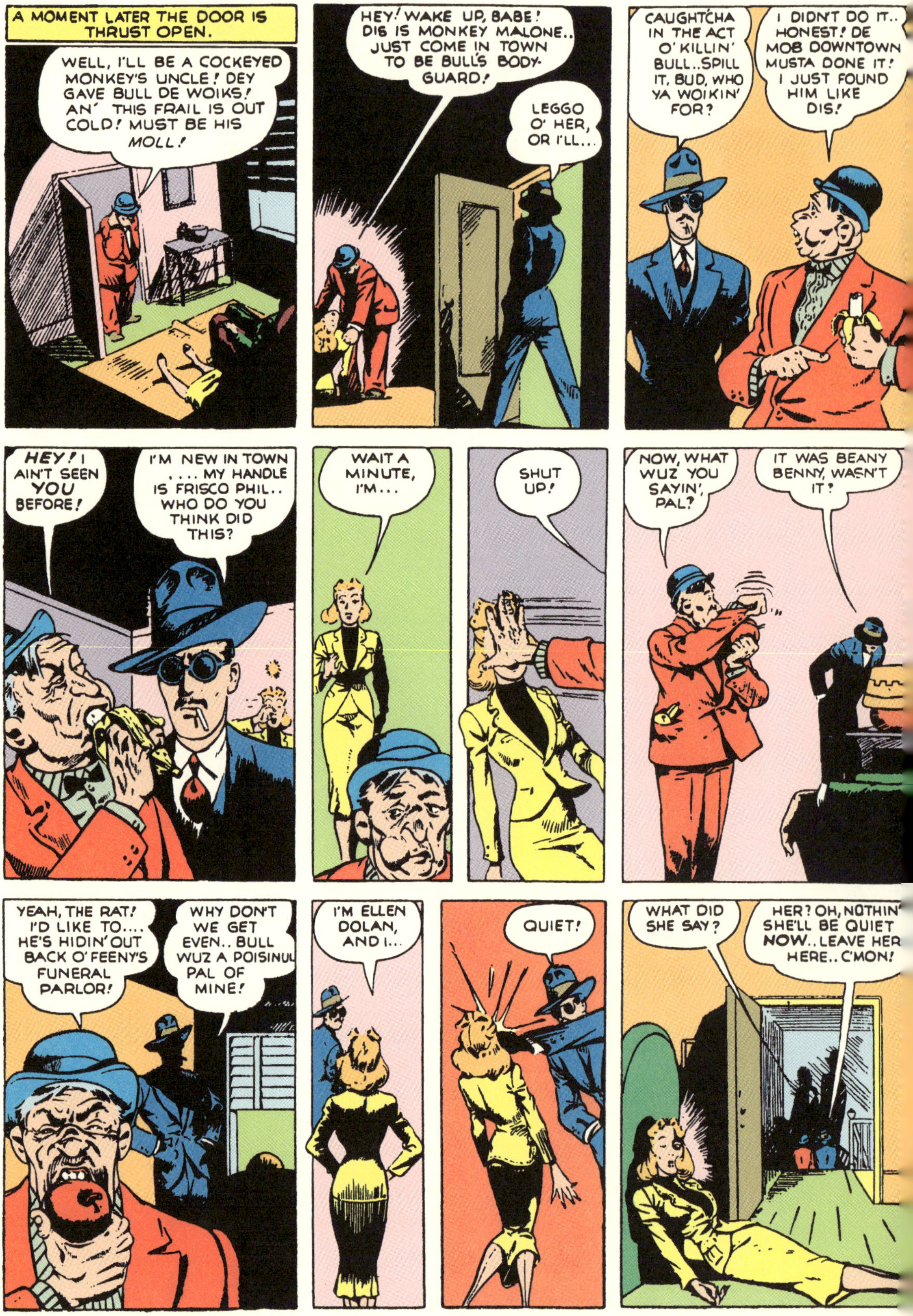
A MOMENT LATER THE DOOR IS THRUST OPEN.
WELL, I'LL BE A COCKEYED MONKEY'S UNCLE! DEY GAVE BULL DE WOIKS! AN' THIS FRAIL IS OUT COLD! MUST BE HIS MOLL!
HEY! WAKE UP, BABE! DIS IS MONKEY MALONE.. JUST COME IN TOWN TO BE BULL'S BODY-GUARD!
LEGGO O' HER, OR I'LL...
CAUGHTCHA IN THE ACT O' KILLIN' BULL..SPILL IT, BUD, WHO YA WOIKIN' FOR?
I DIDN'T DO IT.. HONEST! DE MOB DOWNTOWN MUSTA DONE IT! I JUST FOUND HIM LIKE DIS!
HEY! I AIN'T SEEN YOU BEFORE!
I'M NEW IN TOWN .... MY HANDLE IS FRISCO PHIL.. WHO DO YOU THINK DID THIS?
WAIT A MINUTE, I'M...
SHUT UP!
NOW, WHAT WUZ YOU SAYIN', PAL?
IT WAS BEANY BENNY, WASN'T IT?
YEAH, THE RAT! I'D LIKE TO.... HE'S HIDIN' OUT BACK O'FEENY'S FUNERAL PARLOR!
WHY DON'T WE GET EVEN.. BULL WUZ A POISINUL PAL OF MINE!
I'M ELLEN DOLAN, AND I...
QUIET!
WHAT DID SHE SAY?
HER? OH, NOTHIN' SHE'LL BE QUIET NOW.. LEAVE HER HERE.. C'MON!

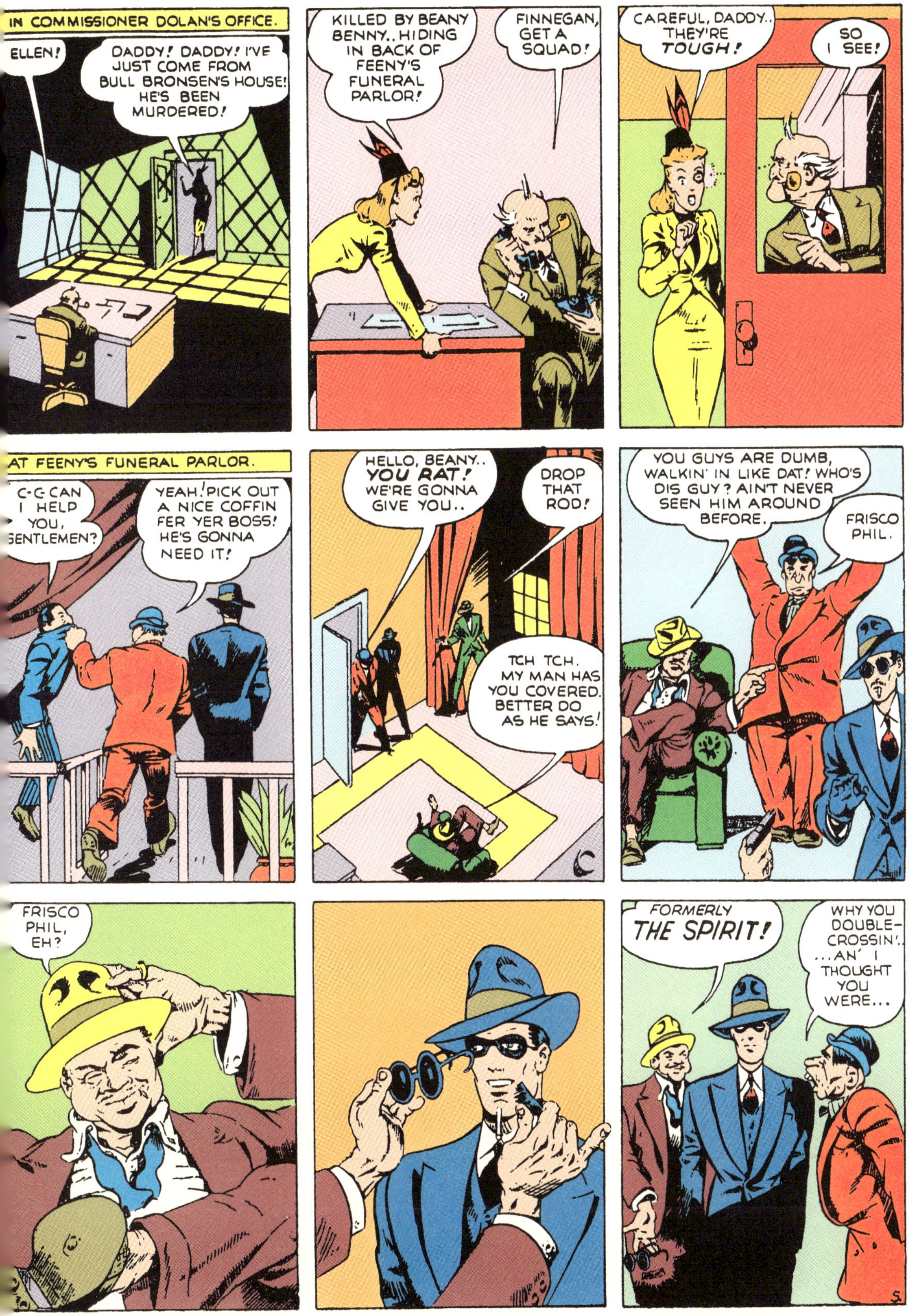
IN COMMISSIONER DOLAN'S OFFICE.
ELLEN!
DADDY! DADDY! I'VE JUST COME FROM BULL BRONSEN'S HOUSE! HE'S BEEN MURDERED!
KILLED BY BEANY BENNY.. HIDING IN BACK OF FEENY'S FUNERAL PARLOR!
FINNEGAN, GET A SQUAD!
CAREFUL, DADDY.. THEY'RE TOUGH!
SO I SEE!
AT FEENY'S FUNERAL PARLOR.
C-C-CAN I HELP YOU, GENTLEMEN?
YEAH! PICK OUT A NICE COFFIN FER YER BOSS! HE'S GONNA NEED IT!
HELLO, BEANY.. YOU RAT! WE'RE GONNA GIVE YOU..
DROP THAT ROD!
TCH TCH. MY MAN HAS YOU COVERED. BETTER DO AS HE SAYS!
YOU GUYS ARE DUMB, WALKIN' IN LIKE DAT! WHO'S DIS GUY? AIN'T NEVER SEEN HIM AROUND BEFORE.
FRISCO PHIL.
FRISCO PHIL, EH?
FORMERLY THE SPIRIT!
WHY YOU DOUBLE-CROSSIN'.. ...AN' I THOUGHT YOU WERE...

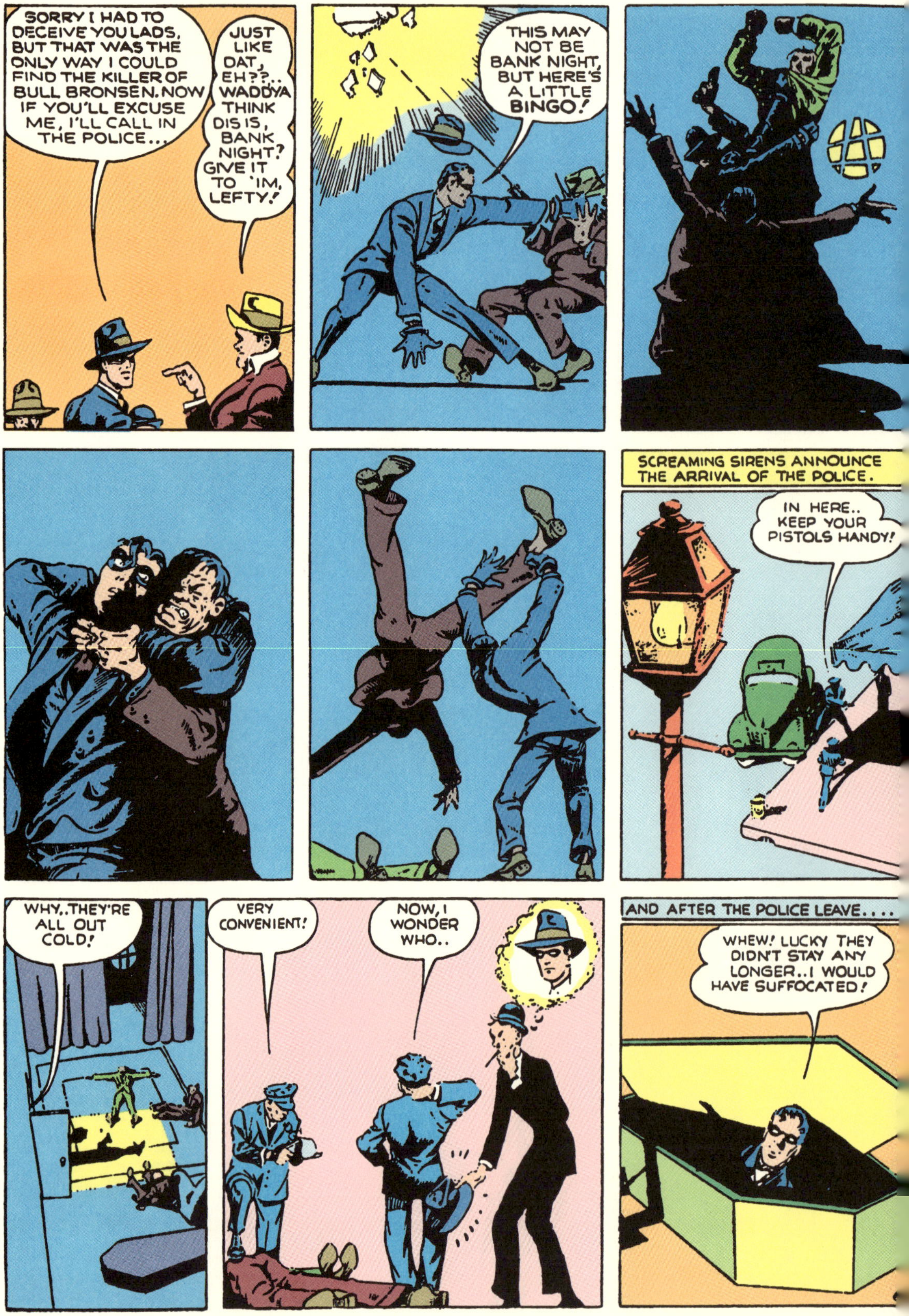
SORRY I HAD TO DECEIVE YOU LADS, BUT THAT WAS THE ONLY WAY I COULD FIND THE KILLER OF BULL BRONSEN. NOW IF YOU'LL EXCUSE ME, I'LL CALL IN THE POLICE...
JUST LIKE DAT, EH??.. WADDYA THINK DIS IS, BANK NIGHT? GIVE IT TO 'IM, LEFTY!
THIS MAY NOT BE BANK NIGHT, BUT HERE'S A LITTLE BINGO!
SCREAMING SIRENS ANNOUNCE THE ARRIVAL OF THE POLICE.
IN HERE.. KEEP YOUR PISTOLS HANDY!
WHY,.THEY'RE ALL OUT COLD!
VERY CONVENIENT!
NOW, I WONDER WHO..
AND AFTER THE POLICE LEAVE....
WHEW! LUCKY THEY DIDN'T STAY ANY LONGER..I WOULD HAVE SUFFOCATED!

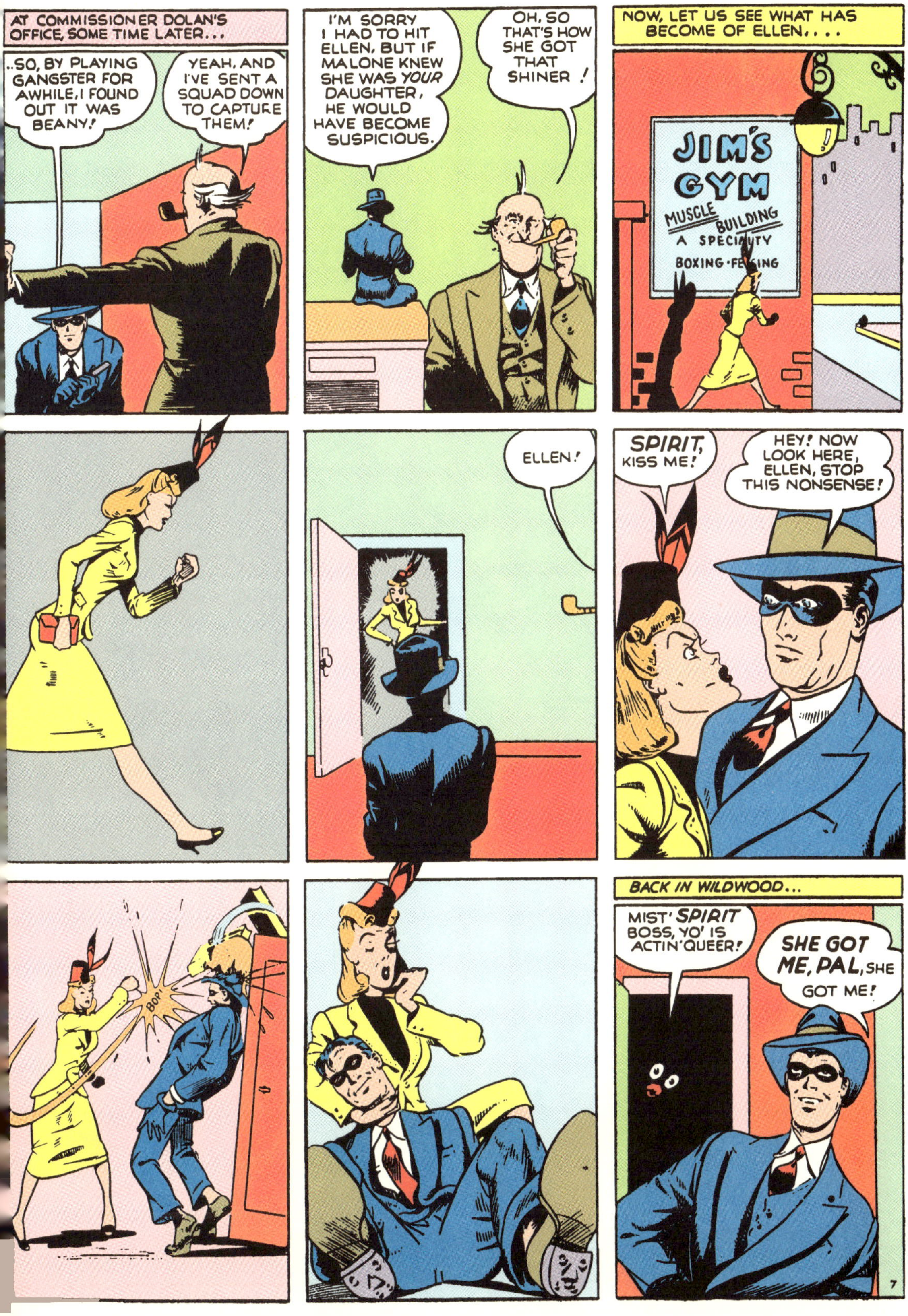
AT COMMISSIONER DOLAN'S OFFICE, SOME TIME LATER...
..SO, BY PLAYING GANGSTER FOR AWHILE, I FOUND OUT IT WAS BEANY!
YEAH, AND I'VE SENT A SQUAD DOWN TO CAPTURE THEM!
I'M SORRY I HAD TO HIT ELLEN, BUT IF MALONE KNEW SHE WAS YOUR DAUGHTER, HE WOULD HAVE BECOME SUSPICIOUS.
OH, SO THAT'S HOW SHE GOT THAT SHINER!
NOW, LET US SEE WHAT HAS BECOME OF ELLEN....
JIM'S GYM
MUSCLE BUILDING A SPECIALTY
BOXING·FENCING
ELLEN!
SPIRIT, KISS ME!
HEY! NOW LOOK HERE, ELLEN, STOP THIS NONSENSE!
BOP!
BACK IN WILDWOOD...
MIST' SPIRIT BOSS, YO' IS ACTIN' QUEER!
SHE GOT ME, PAL, SHE GOT ME!
7

THE KISS OF DEATH

November 10, 1940

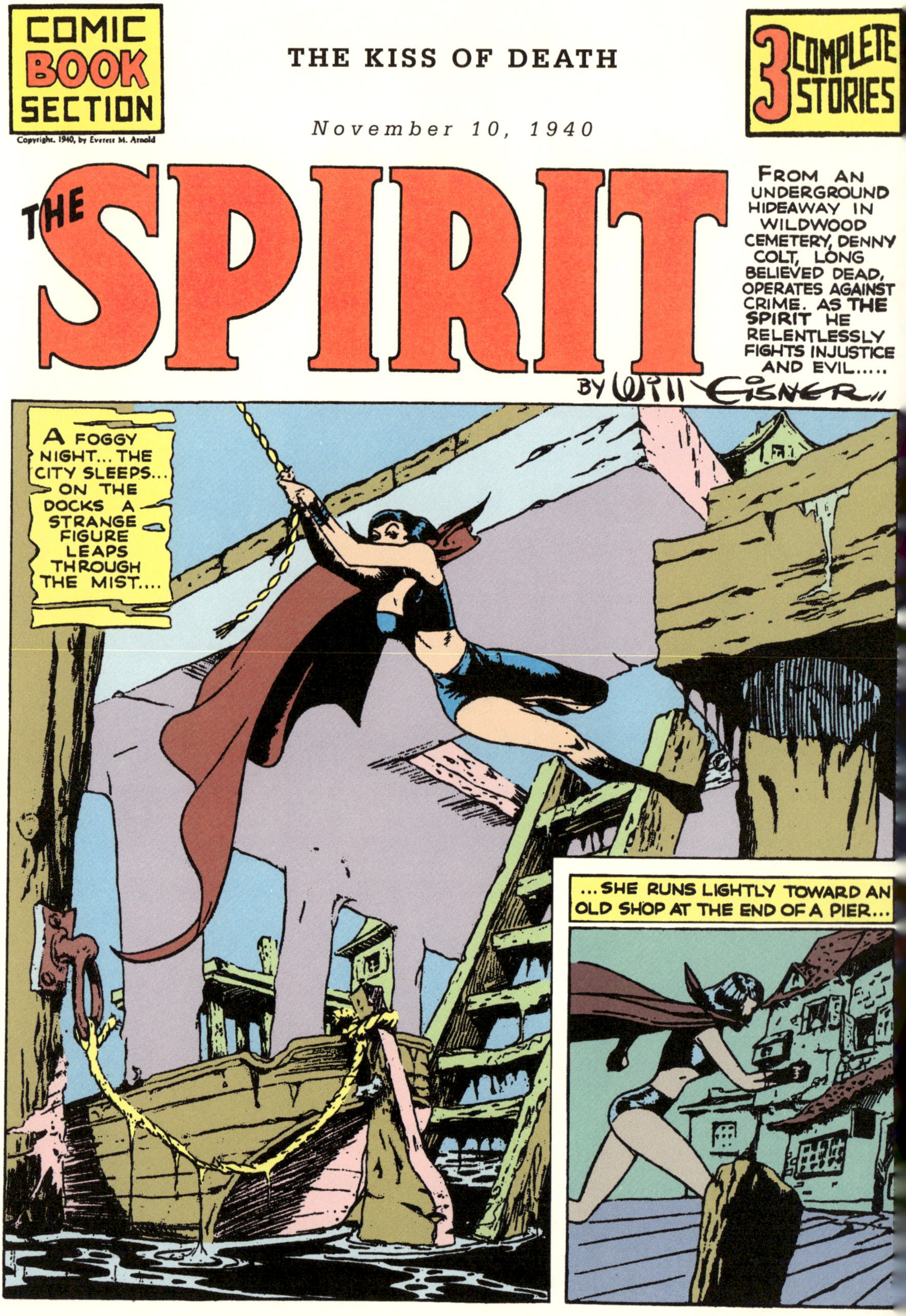
COMIC BOOK SECTION
Copyright, 1940, by Everett M. Arnold
3 COMPLETE STORIES
THE SPIRIT
FROM AN UNDERGROUND HIDEAWAY IN WILDWOOD CEMETERY, DENNY COLT, LONG BELIEVED DEAD, OPERATES AGAINST CRIME. AS THE SPIRIT HE RELENTLESSLY FIGHTS INJUSTICE AND EVIL.....
BY Will Eisner
A FOGGY NIGHT... THE CITY SLEEPS... ON THE DOCKS A STRANGE FIGURE LEAPS THROUGH THE MIST....
...SHE RUNS LIGHTLY TOWARD AN OLD SHOP AT THE END OF A PIER...

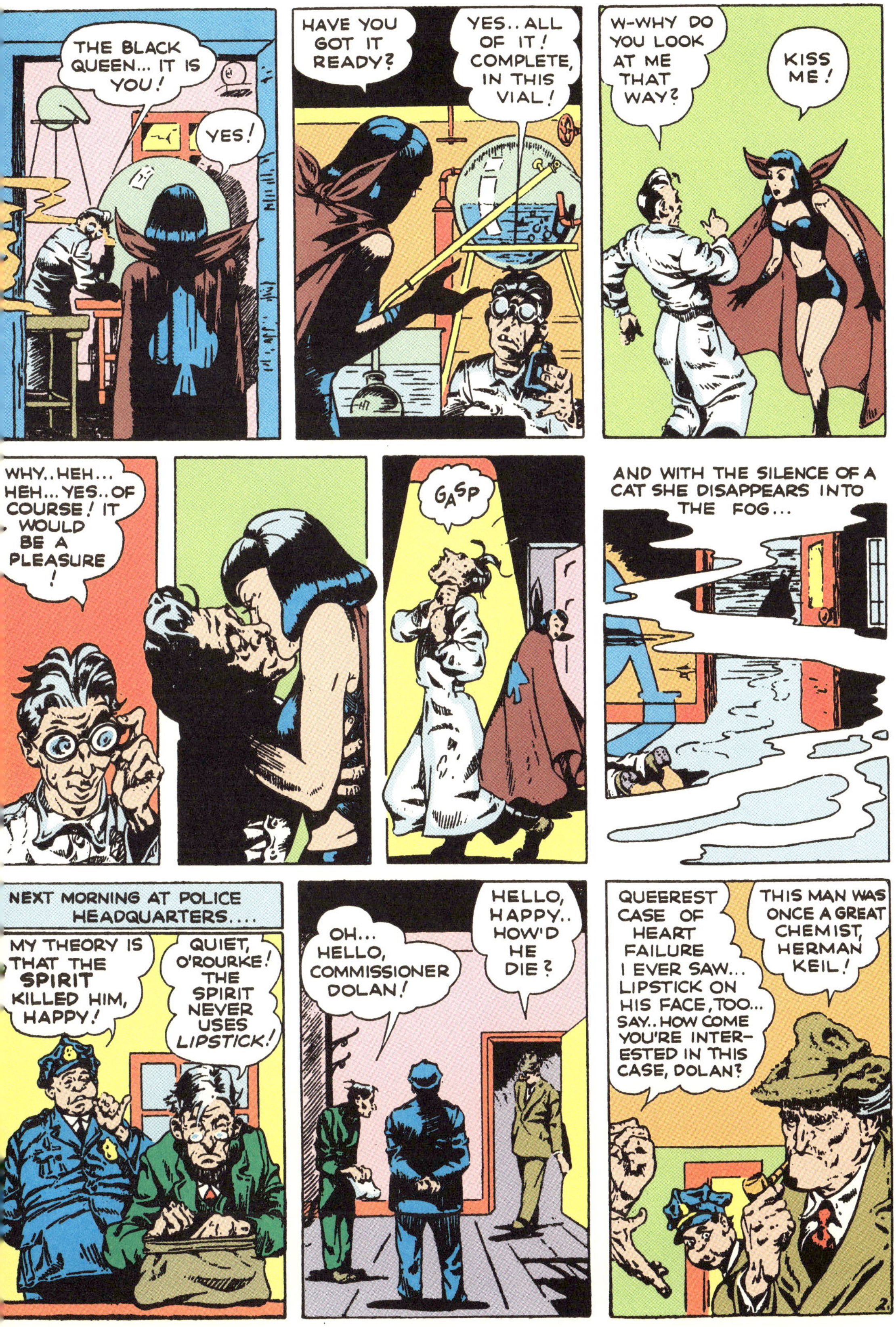
THE BLACK QUEEN... IT IS YOU!
YES!
HAVE YOU GOT IT READY?
YES.. ALL OF IT! COMPLETE, IN THIS VIAL!
W-WHY DO YOU LOOK AT ME THAT WAY?
KISS ME!
WHY.. HEH... HEH... YES.. OF COURSE! IT WOULD BE A PLEASURE!
GASP
AND WITH THE SILENCE OF A CAT SHE DISAPPEARS INTO THE FOG...
NEXT MORNING AT POLICE HEADQUARTERS....
MY THEORY IS THAT THE SPIRIT KILLED HIM, HAPPY!
QUIET, O'ROURKE! THE SPIRIT NEVER USES LIPSTICK!
OH... HELLO, COMMISSIONER DOLAN!
HELLO, HAPPY.. HOW'D HE DIE?
QUEEREST CASE OF HEART FAILURE I EVER SAW... LIPSTICK ON HIS FACE, TOO... SAY.. HOW COME YOU'RE INTERESTED IN THIS CASE, DOLAN?
THIS MAN WAS ONCE A GREAT CHEMIST, HERMAN KEIL!

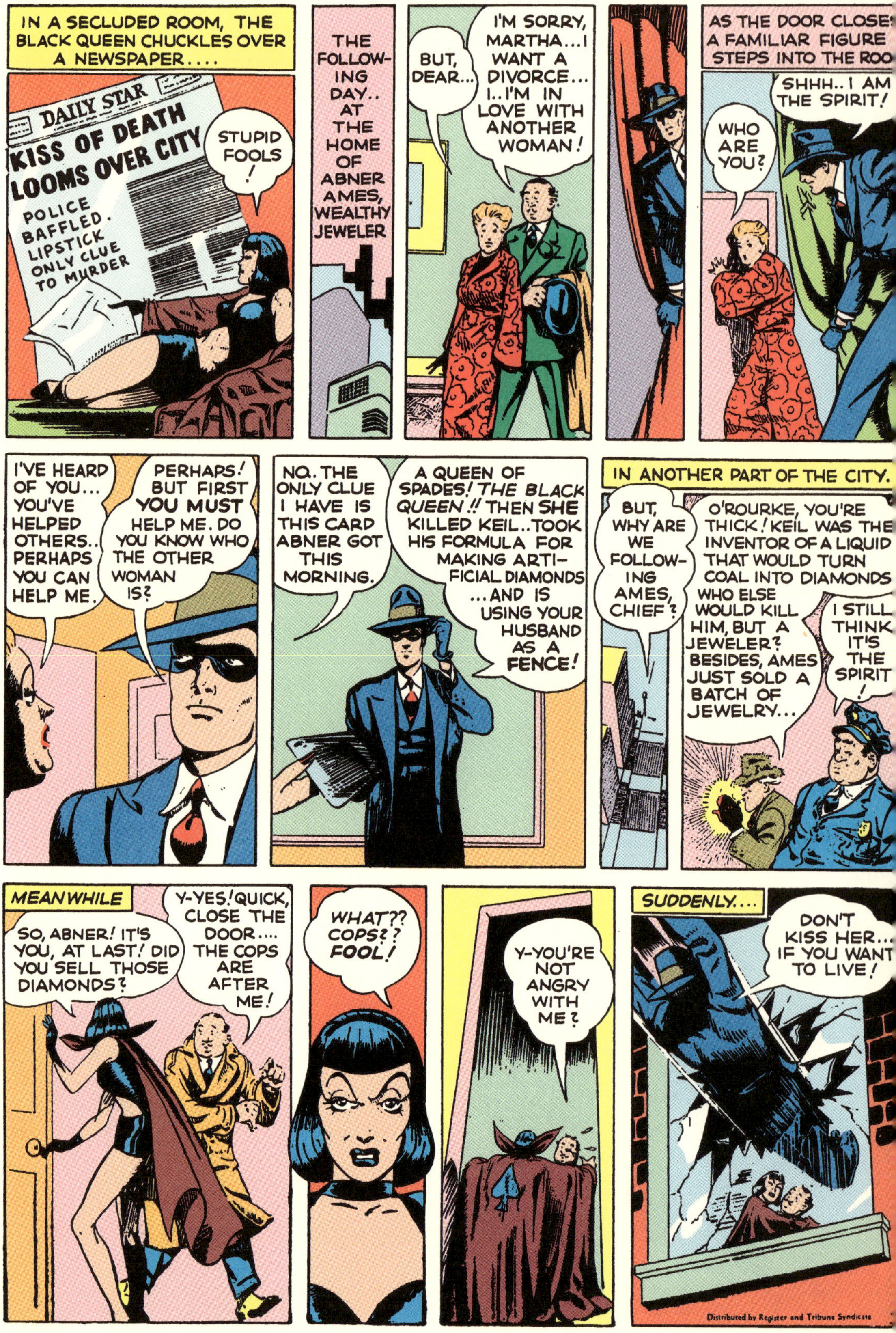
IN A SECLUDED ROOM, THE BLACK QUEEN CHUCKLES OVER A NEWSPAPER....
DAILY STAR
KISS OF DEATH LOOMS OVER CITY
POLICE BAFFLED. LIPSTICK ONLY CLUE TO MURDER
STUPID FOOLS!
THE FOLLOWING DAY.. AT THE HOME OF ABNER AMES, WEALTHY JEWELER
BUT, DEAR...
I'M SORRY, MARTHA...I WANT A DIVORCE... I..I'M IN LOVE WITH ANOTHER WOMAN!
AS THE DOOR CLOSES A FAMILIAR FIGURE STEPS INTO THE ROO
SHHH..I AM THE SPIRIT!
WHO ARE YOU?
I'VE HEARD OF YOU... YOU'VE HELPED OTHERS.. PERHAPS YOU CAN HELP ME.
PERHAPS! BUT FIRST YOU MUST HELP ME. DO YOU KNOW WHO THE OTHER WOMAN IS?
NO..THE ONLY CLUE I HAVE IS THIS CARD ABNER GOT THIS MORNING.
A QUEEN OF SPADES! THE BLACK QUEEN!! THEN SHE KILLED KEIL..TOOK HIS FORMULA FOR MAKING ARTIFICIAL DIAMONDS ...AND IS USING YOUR HUSBAND AS A FENCE!
IN ANOTHER PART OF THE CITY.
BUT, WHY ARE WE FOLLOWING AMES, CHIEF?
O'ROURKE, YOU'RE THICK! KEIL WAS THE INVENTOR OF A LIQUID THAT WOULD TURN COAL INTO DIAMONDS WHO ELSE WOULD KILL HIM, BUT A JEWELER? BESIDES, AMES JUST SOLD A BATCH OF JEWELRY...
I STILL THINK IT'S THE SPIRIT!
MEANWHILE
SO, ABNER! IT'S YOU, AT LAST! DID YOU SELL THOSE DIAMONDS?
Y-YES! QUICK, CLOSE THE DOOR.... THE COPS ARE AFTER ME!
WHAT?? COPS?? FOOL!
Y-YOU'RE NOT ANGRY WITH ME?
SUDDENLY....
DON'T KISS HER... IF YOU WANT TO LIVE!
Distributed by Register and Tribune Syndicate

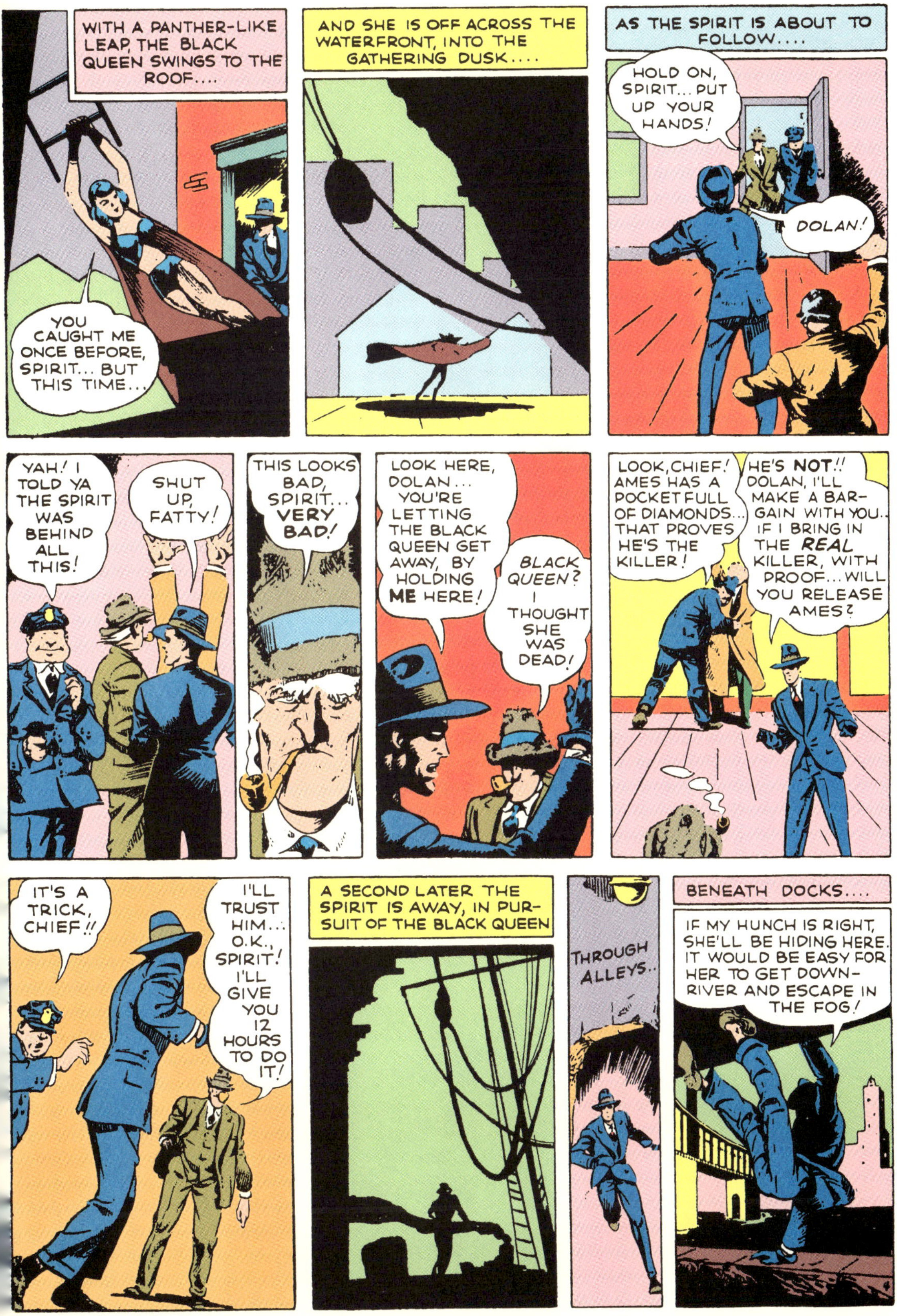
WITH A PANTHER-LIKE LEAP, THE BLACK QUEEN SWINGS TO THE ROOF....
YOU CAUGHT ME ONCE BEFORE, SPIRIT... BUT THIS TIME...
AND SHE IS OFF ACROSS THE WATERFRONT, INTO THE GATHERING DUSK....
AS THE SPIRIT IS ABOUT TO FOLLOW....
HOLD ON, SPIRIT... PUT UP YOUR HANDS!
DOLAN!
YAH! I TOLD YA THE SPIRIT WAS BEHIND ALL THIS!
SHUT UP, FATTY!
THIS LOOKS BAD, SPIRIT... VERY BAD!
LOOK HERE, DOLAN... YOU'RE LETTING THE BLACK QUEEN GET AWAY, BY HOLDING ME HERE!
BLACK QUEEN? I THOUGHT SHE WAS DEAD!
LOOK, CHIEF! AMES HAS A POCKETFULL OF DIAMONDS... THAT PROVES HE'S THE KILLER!
HE'S NOT!! DOLAN, I'LL MAKE A BAR-GAIN WITH YOU.. IF I BRING IN THE REAL KILLER, WITH PROOF... WILL YOU RELEASE AMES?
IT'S A TRICK, CHIEF!!
I'LL TRUST HIM... O.K., SPIRIT! I'LL GIVE YOU 12 HOURS TO DO IT!
A SECOND LATER THE SPIRIT IS AWAY, IN PURSUIT OF THE BLACK QUEEN
THROUGH ALLEYS..
BENEATH DOCKS....
IF MY HUNCH IS RIGHT, SHE'LL BE HIDING HERE. IT WOULD BE EASY FOR HER TO GET DOWN-RIVER AND ESCAPE IN THE FOG!

I WAS RIGHT!
BANG
GAINING A MOMENT'S ADVANTAGE, THE BLACK QUEEN HEADS ACROSS THE RIVER IN A POWER BOAT....
SHE'S CIRCLING TOWARD THE BRIDGE... IF I CAN BEAT HER TO IT....
HA-HA!!
SHE'S ABANDONED THE BOAT... ESCAPED ME!
I CAN PICK HIM OFF LIKE A RABBIT FROM HERE!
OH-OH... SHE'S ON THE SCAFFOLD!
FROM HIS POCKET, THE SPIRIT REMOVES COMPACT RUBBER SHOES....
THESE VACUUM CUP BOTTOMS WILL HELP ME GET UP!
...AND WITH THE EASE OF A FLY, THE SPIRIT WALKS UP THE SIDE OF THE BRIDGE....
5.

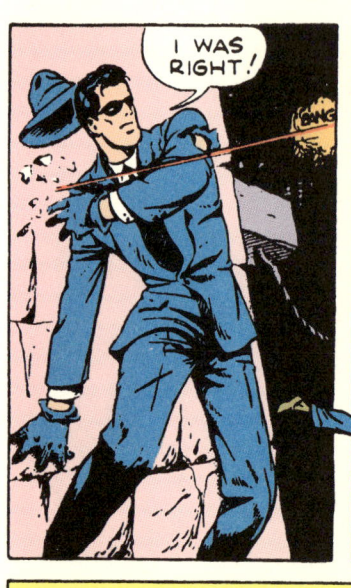

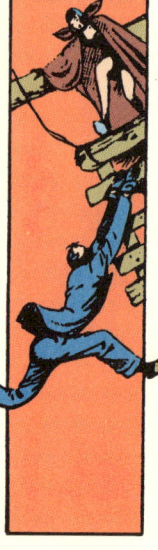

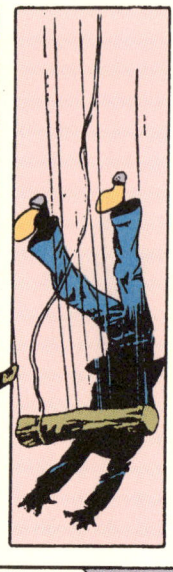

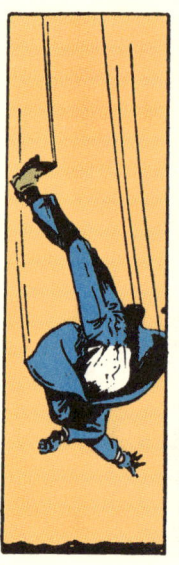

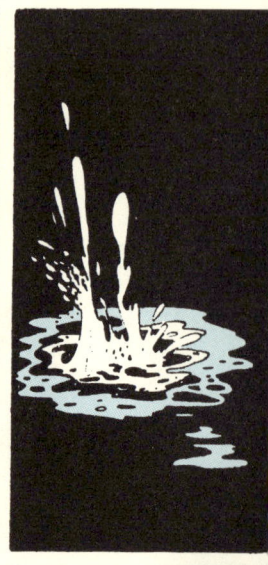

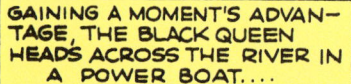

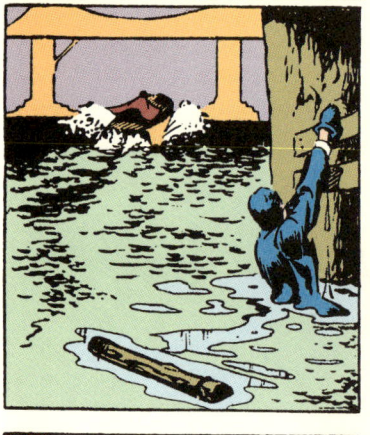

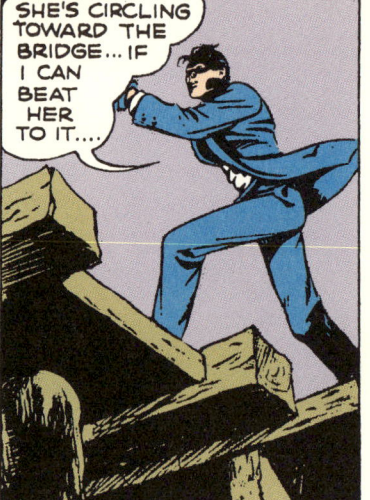

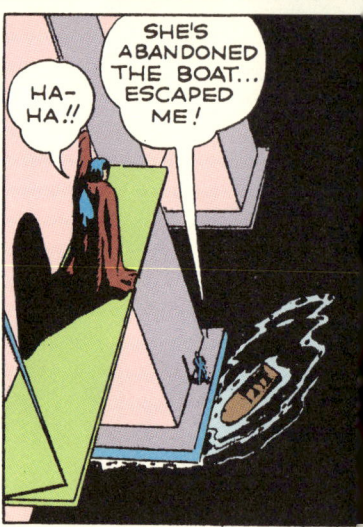

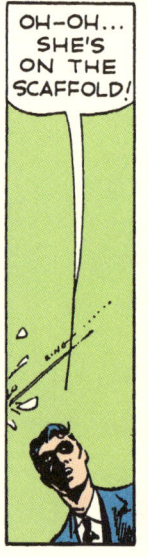

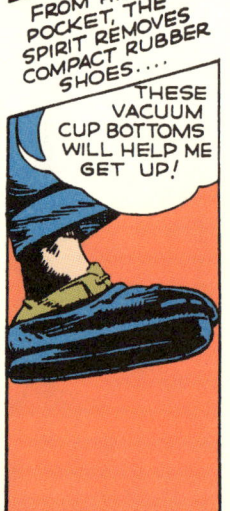

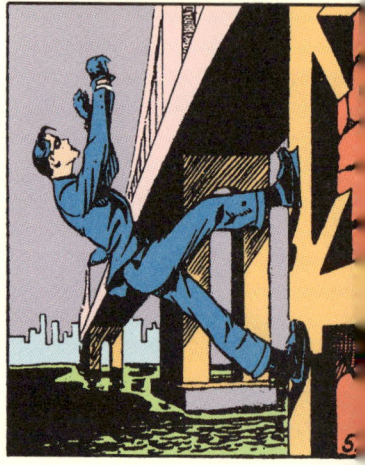

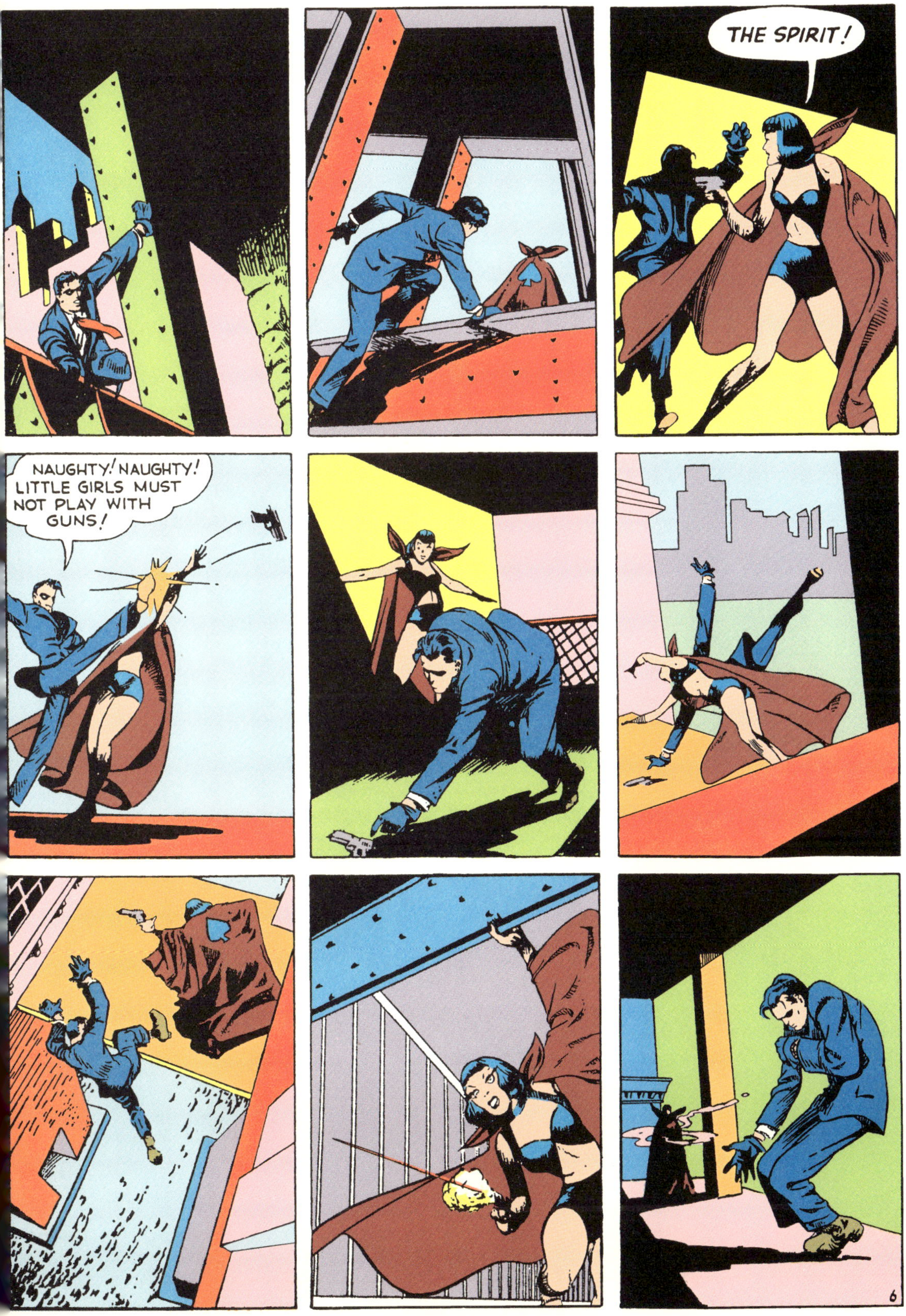
THE SPIRIT!
NAUGHTY! NAUGHTY! LITTLE GIRLS MUST NOT PLAY WITH GUNS!
6

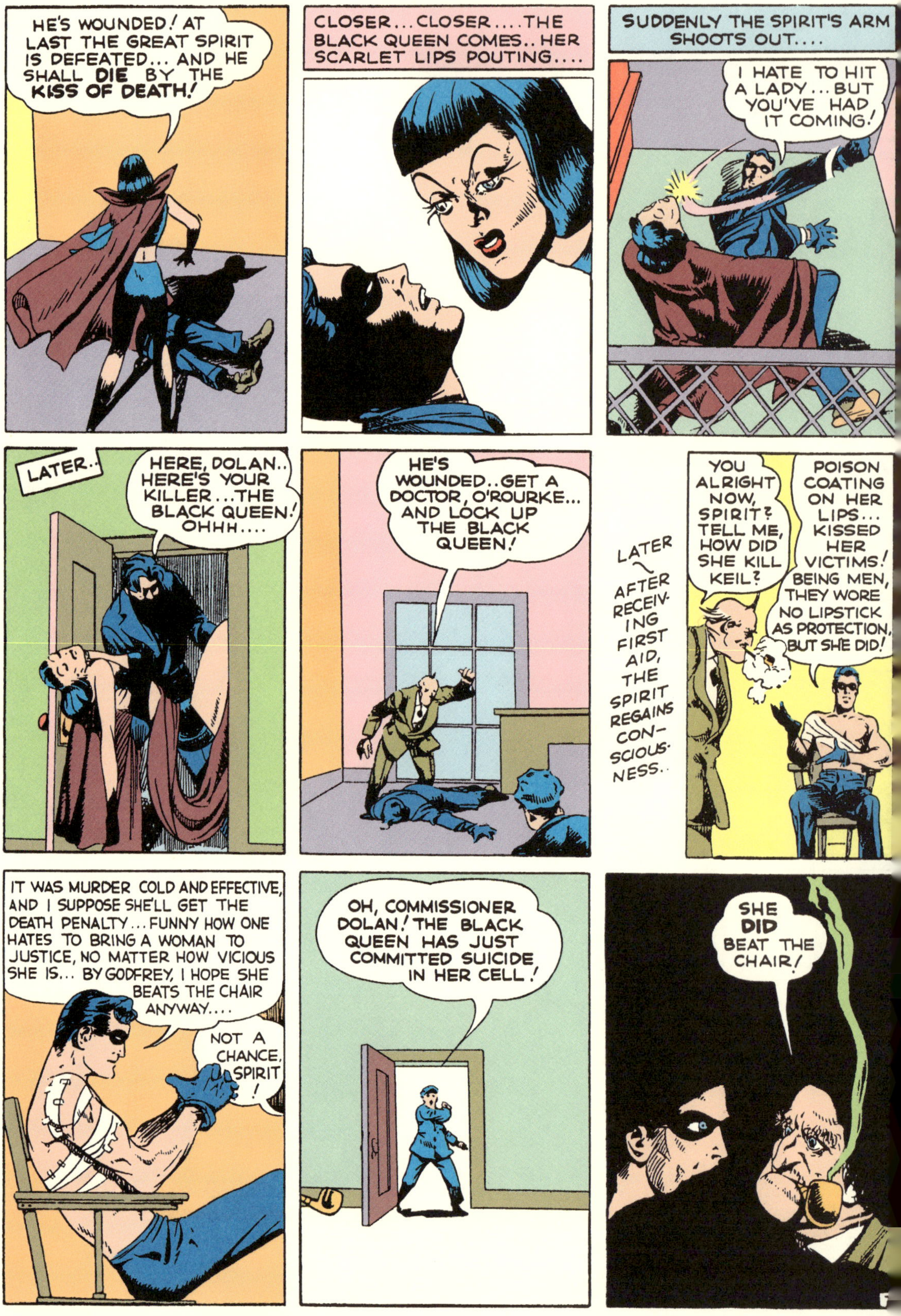

HE'S WOUNDED! AT LAST THE GREAT SPIRIT IS DEFEATED... AND HE SHALL DIE BY THE KISS OF DEATH!
CLOSER...CLOSER....THE BLACK QUEEN COMES..HER SCARLET LIPS POUTING....
SUDDENLY THE SPIRIT'S ARM SHOOTS OUT....
I HATE TO HIT A LADY...BUT YOU'VE HAD IT COMING!
LATER..
HERE, DOLAN.. HERE'S YOUR KILLER...THE BLACK QUEEN! OHHH....
HE'S WOUNDED..GET A DOCTOR, O'ROURKE... AND LOCK UP THE BLACK QUEEN!
LATER ~ AFTER RECEIVING FIRST AID, THE SPIRIT REGAINS CONSCIOUSNESS..
YOU ALRIGHT NOW, SPIRIT? TELL ME, HOW DID SHE KILL KEIL?
POISON COATING ON HER LIPS... KISSED HER VICTIMS! BEING MEN, THEY WORE NO LIPSTICK AS PROTECTION, BUT SHE DID!
IT WAS MURDER COLD AND EFFECTIVE, AND I SUPPOSE SHE'LL GET THE DEATH PENALTY... FUNNY HOW ONE HATES TO BRING A WOMAN TO JUSTICE, NO MATTER HOW VICIOUS SHE IS... BY GODFREY, I HOPE SHE BEATS THE CHAIR ANYWAY....
NOT A CHANCE, SPIRIT!
OH, COMMISSIONER DOLAN! THE BLACK QUEEN HAS JUST COMMITTED SUICIDE IN HER CELL!
SHE DID BEAT THE CHAIR!

COMIC BOOK SECTION

DR. PRINCE VON KALM

3 COMPLETE STORIES

November 17, 1940

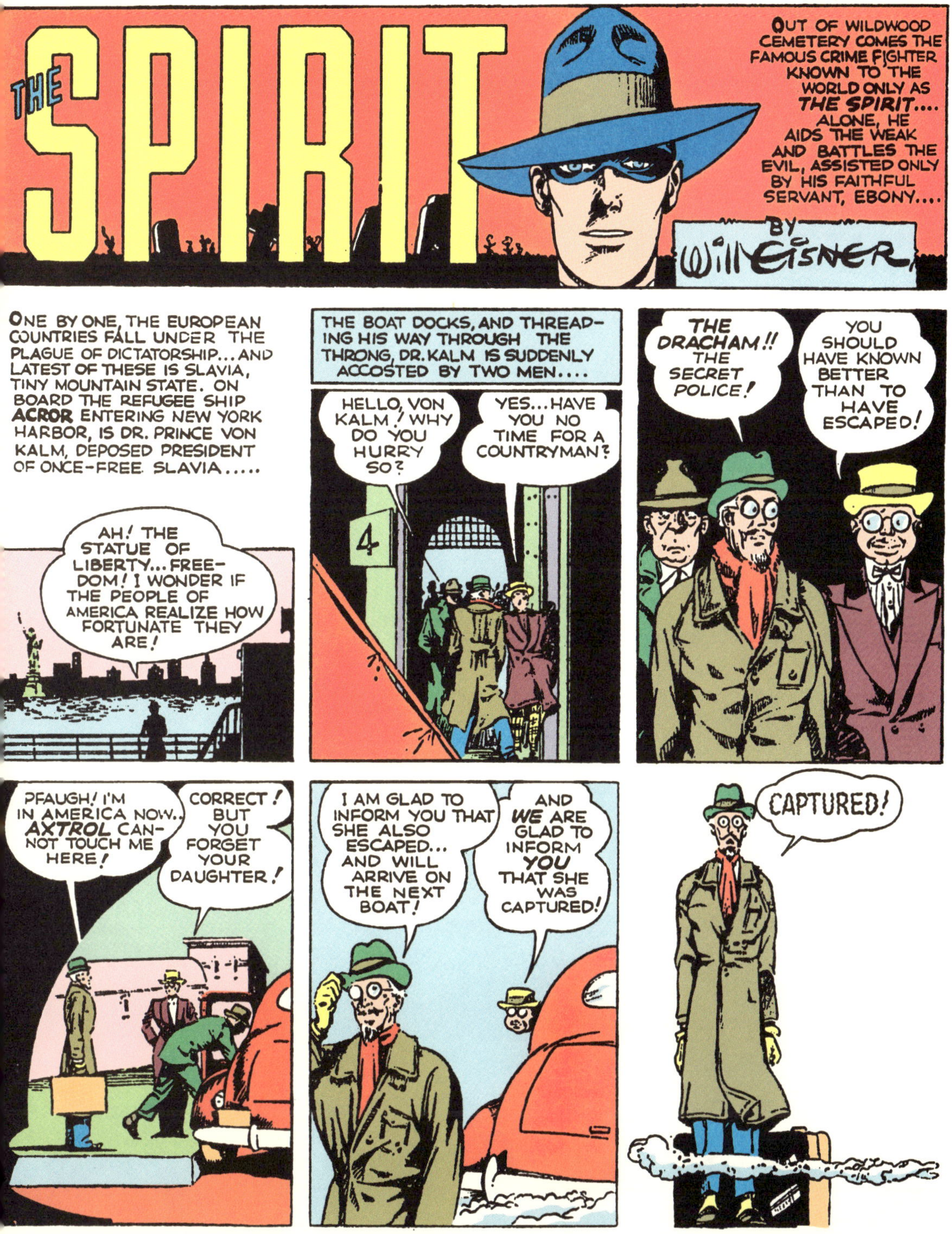
THE SPIRIT
OUT OF WILDWOOD CEMETERY COMES THE FAMOUS CRIME FIGHTER KNOWN TO THE WORLD ONLY AS THE SPIRIT.... ALONE, HE AIDS THE WEAK AND BATTLES THE EVIL, ASSISTED ONLY BY HIS FAITHFUL SERVANT, EBONY....
BY Will Eisner
ONE BY ONE, THE EUROPEAN COUNTRIES FALL UNDER THE PLAGUE OF DICTATORSHIP... AND LATEST OF THESE IS SLAVIA, TINY MOUNTAIN STATE. ON BOARD THE REFUGEE SHIP ACROR ENTERING NEW YORK HARBOR, IS DR. PRINCE VON KALM, DEPOSED PRESIDENT OF ONCE-FREE SLAVIA.....
AH! THE STATUE OF LIBERTY... FREE-DOM! I WONDER IF THE PEOPLE OF AMERICA REALIZE HOW FORTUNATE THEY ARE!
THE BOAT DOCKS, AND THREADING HIS WAY THROUGH THE THRONG, DR. KALM IS SUDDENLY ACCOSTED BY TWO MEN....
HELLO, VON KALM! WHY DO YOU HURRY SO?
YES... HAVE YOU NO TIME FOR A COUNTRYMAN?
4
THE DRACHAM!! THE SECRET POLICE!
YOU SHOULD HAVE KNOWN BETTER THAN TO HAVE ESCAPED!
PFAUGH! I'M IN AMERICA NOW.. AXTROL CAN-NOT TOUCH ME HERE!
CORRECT! BUT YOU FORGET YOUR DAUGHTER!
I AM GLAD TO INFORM YOU THAT SHE ALSO ESCAPED... AND WILL ARRIVE ON THE NEXT BOAT!
AND WE ARE GLAD TO INFORM YOU THAT SHE WAS CAPTURED!
CAPTURED!

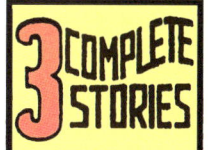

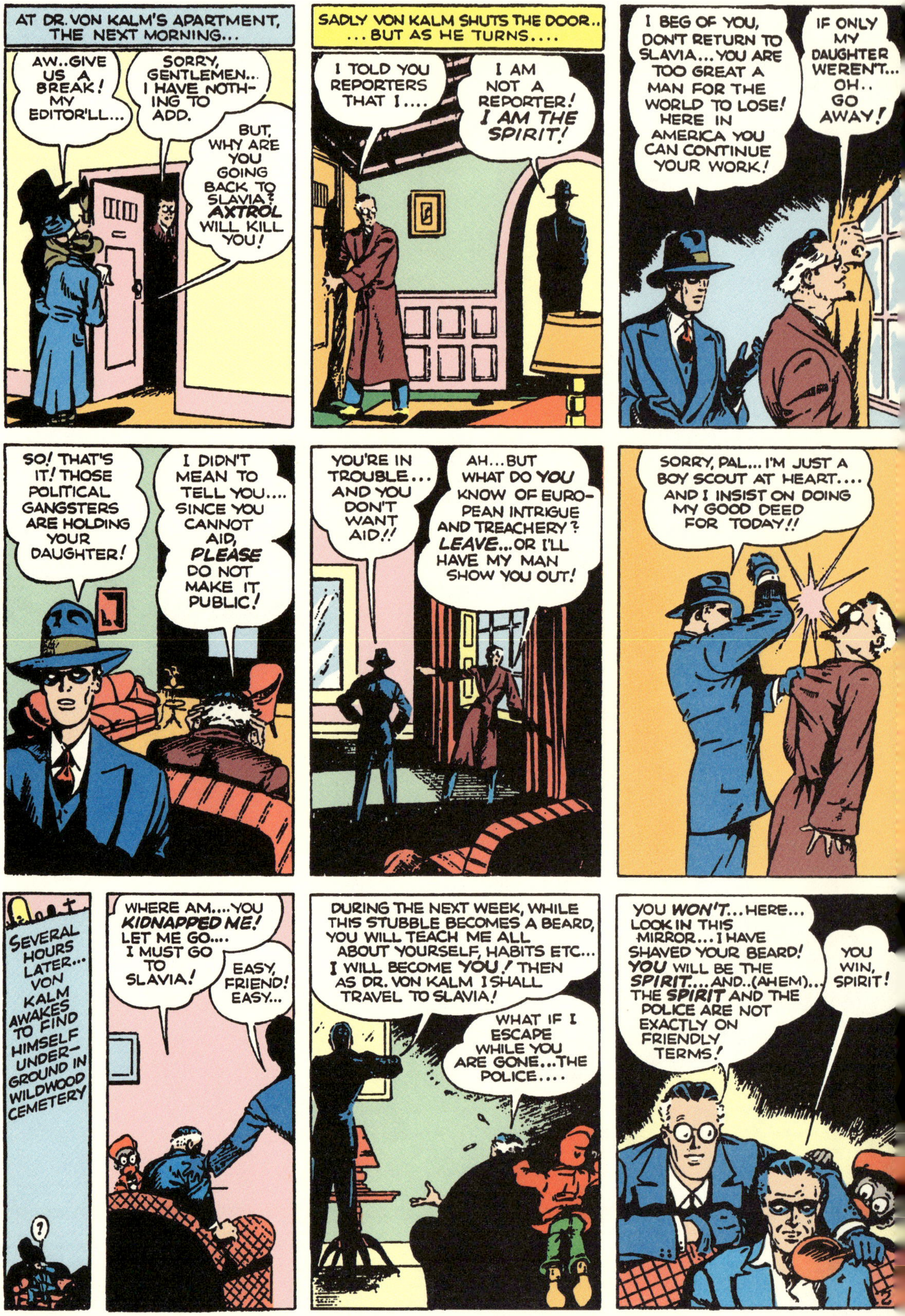
AT DR. VON KALM'S APARTMENT, THE NEXT MORNING...
AW..GIVE US A BREAK! MY EDITOR'LL...
SORRY, GENTLEMEN... I HAVE NOTHING TO ADD.
BUT, WHY ARE YOU GOING BACK TO SLAVIA? AXTROL WILL KILL YOU!
SADLY VON KALM SHUTS THE DOOR.. ...BUT AS HE TURNS....
I TOLD YOU REPORTERS THAT I....
I AM NOT A REPORTER! I AM THE SPIRIT!
I BEG OF YOU, DON'T RETURN TO SLAVIA...YOU ARE TOO GREAT A MAN FOR THE WORLD TO LOSE! HERE IN AMERICA YOU CAN CONTINUE YOUR WORK!
IF ONLY MY DAUGHTER WEREN'T... OH.. GO AWAY!
SO! THAT'S IT! THOSE POLITICAL GANGSTERS ARE HOLDING YOUR DAUGHTER!
I DIDN'T MEAN TO TELL YOU.... SINCE YOU CANNOT AID, PLEASE DO NOT MAKE IT PUBLIC!
YOU'RE IN TROUBLE... AND YOU DON'T WANT AID!!
AH...BUT WHAT DO YOU KNOW OF EUROPEAN INTRIGUE AND TREACHERY? LEAVE...OR I'LL HAVE MY MAN SHOW YOU OUT!
SORRY, PAL... I'M JUST A BOY SCOUT AT HEART.... AND I INSIST ON DOING MY GOOD DEED FOR TODAY!!
SEVERAL HOURS LATER... VON KALM AWAKES TO FIND HIMSELF UNDERGROUND IN WILDWOOD CEMETERY
?
WHERE AM....YOU KIDNAPPED ME! LET ME GO.... I MUST GO TO SLAVIA!
EASY, FRIEND! EASY...
DURING THE NEXT WEEK, WHILE THIS STUBBLE BECOMES A BEARD, YOU WILL TEACH ME ALL ABOUT YOURSELF, HABITS ETC... I WILL BECOME YOU! THEN AS DR. VON KALM I SHALL TRAVEL TO SLAVIA!
WHAT IF I ESCAPE WHILE YOU ARE GONE...THE POLICE....
YOU WON'T...HERE... LOOK IN THIS MIRROR...I HAVE SHAVED YOUR BEARD! YOU WILL BE THE SPIRIT....AND..(AHEM)... THE SPIRIT AND THE POLICE ARE NOT EXACTLY ON FRIENDLY TERMS!
YOU WIN, SPIRIT!

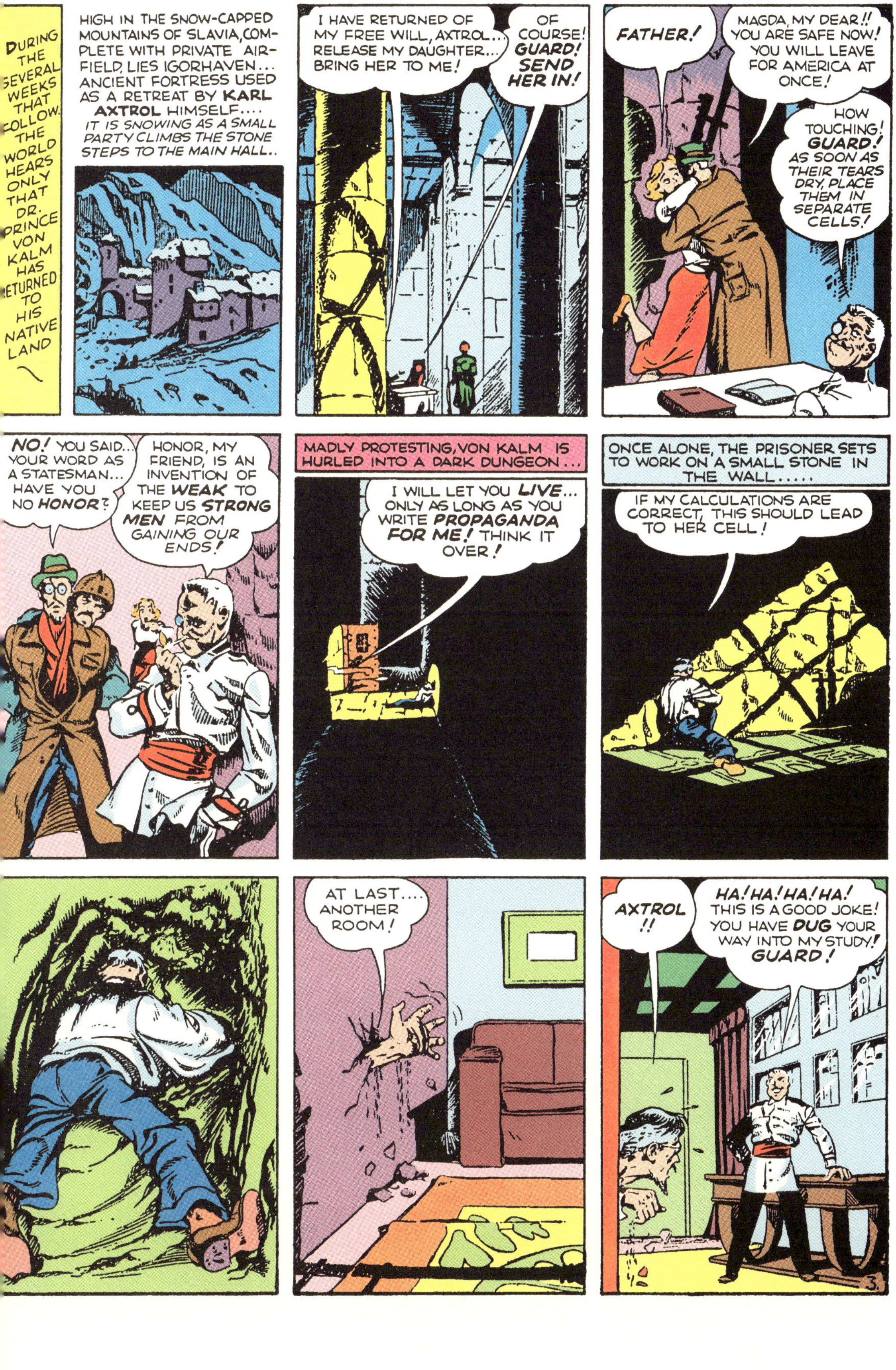
DURING THE SEVERAL WEEKS THAT FOLLOW, THE WORLD HEARS ONLY THAT DR. PRINCE VON KALM HAS RETURNED TO HIS NATIVE LAND
HIGH IN THE SNOW-CAPPED MOUNTAINS OF SLAVIA, COMPLETE WITH PRIVATE AIR-FIELD, LIES IGORHAVEN... ANCIENT FORTRESS USED AS A RETREAT BY KARL AXTROL HIMSELF....
IT IS SNOWING AS A SMALL PARTY CLIMBS THE STONE STEPS TO THE MAIN HALL..
I HAVE RETURNED OF MY FREE WILL, AXTROL... RELEASE MY DAUGHTER... BRING HER TO ME!
OF COURSE! GUARD! SEND HER IN!
FATHER!
MAGDA, MY DEAR!! YOU ARE SAFE NOW! YOU WILL LEAVE FOR AMERICA AT ONCE!
HOW TOUCHING! GUARD! AS SOON AS THEIR TEARS DRY, PLACE THEM IN SEPARATE CELLS!
NO! YOU SAID... YOUR WORD AS A STATESMAN... HAVE YOU NO HONOR?
HONOR, MY FRIEND, IS AN INVENTION OF THE WEAK TO KEEP US STRONG MEN FROM GAINING OUR ENDS!
MADLY PROTESTING, VON KALM IS HURLED INTO A DARK DUNGEON...
I WILL LET YOU LIVE... ONLY AS LONG AS YOU WRITE PROPAGANDA FOR ME! THINK IT OVER!
ONCE ALONE, THE PRISONER SETS TO WORK ON A SMALL STONE IN THE WALL.....
IF MY CALCULATIONS ARE CORRECT, THIS SHOULD LEAD TO HER CELL!
AT LAST.... ANOTHER ROOM!
AXTROL!!
HA! HA! HA! HA! THIS IS A GOOD JOKE! YOU HAVE DUG YOUR WAY INTO MY STUDY! GUARD!
3.

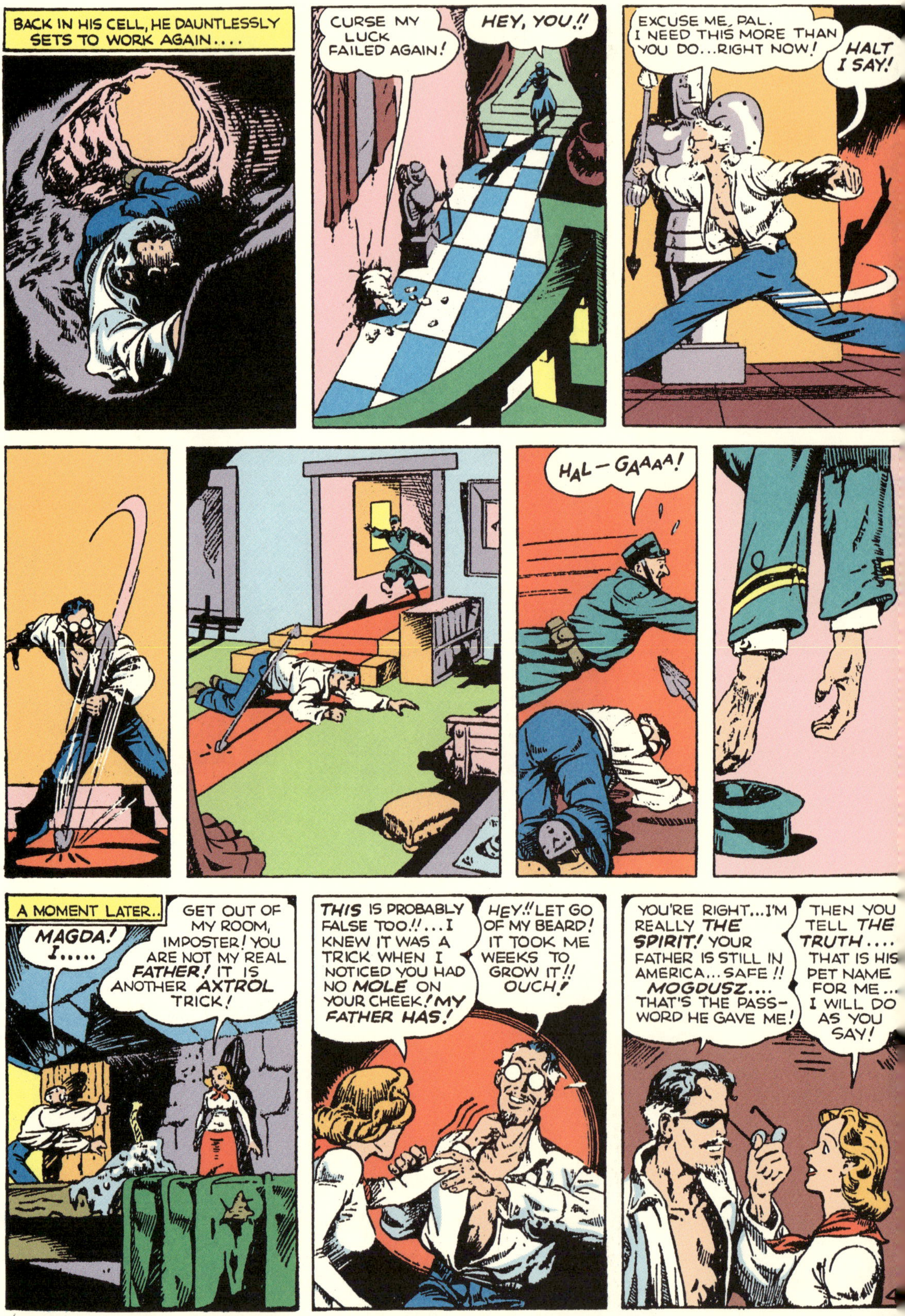
BACK IN HIS CELL, HE DAUNTLESSLY SETS TO WORK AGAIN....
CURSE MY LUCK FAILED AGAIN!
HEY, YOU!!
EXCUSE ME, PAL. I NEED THIS MORE THAN YOU DO...RIGHT NOW!
HALT I SAY!
HAL-GAAAA!
A MOMENT LATER..
MAGDA! I.....
GET OUT OF MY ROOM, IMPOSTER! YOU ARE NOT MY REAL FATHER! IT IS ANOTHER AXTROL TRICK!
THIS IS PROBABLY FALSE TOO!!...I KNEW IT WAS A TRICK WHEN I NOTICED YOU HAD NO MOLE ON YOUR CHEEK! MY FATHER HAS!
HEY!! LET GO OF MY BEARD! IT TOOK ME WEEKS TO GROW IT!! OUCH!
YOU'RE RIGHT...I'M REALLY THE SPIRIT! YOUR FATHER IS STILL IN AMERICA...SAFE!! MOGDUSZ.... THAT'S THE PASSWORD HE GAVE ME!
THEN YOU TELL THE TRUTH.... THAT IS HIS PET NAME FOR ME... I WILL DO AS YOU SAY!

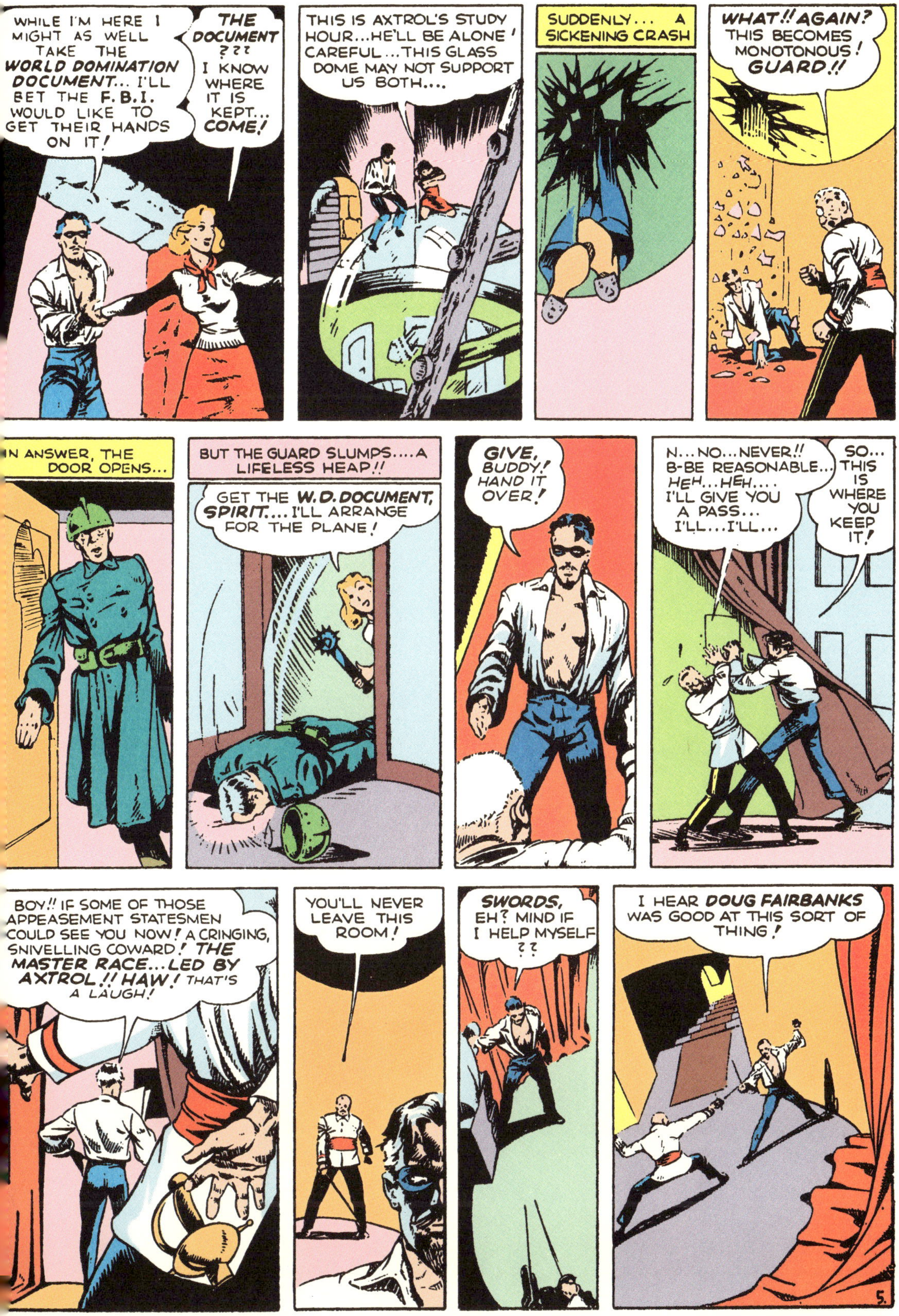
WHILE I'M HERE I MIGHT AS WELL TAKE THE WORLD DOMINATION DOCUMENT... I'LL BET THE F.B.I. WOULD LIKE TO GET THEIR HANDS ON IT!
THE DOCUMENT ??? I KNOW WHERE IT IS KEPT... COME!
THIS IS AXTROL'S STUDY HOUR...HE'LL BE ALONE! CAREFUL...THIS GLASS DOME MAY NOT SUPPORT US BOTH....
SUDDENLY... A SICKENING CRASH
WHAT!! AGAIN? THIS BECOMES MONOTONOUS! GUARD!!
IN ANSWER, THE DOOR OPENS...
BUT THE GUARD SLUMPS....A LIFELESS HEAP!!
GET THE W.D. DOCUMENT, SPIRIT....I'LL ARRANGE FOR THE PLANE!
GIVE, BUDDY! HAND IT OVER!
N...NO...NEVER!! B-BE REASONABLE... HEH...HEH.... I'LL GIVE YOU A PASS... I'LL...I'LL...
SO... THIS IS WHERE YOU KEEP IT!
BOY!! IF SOME OF THOSE APPEASEMENT STATESMEN COULD SEE YOU NOW! A CRINGING, SNIVELLING COWARD! THE MASTER RACE...LED BY AXTROL!! HAW! THAT'S A LAUGH!
YOU'LL NEVER LEAVE THIS ROOM!
SWORDS, EH? MIND IF I HELP MYSELF ??
I HEAR DOUG FAIRBANKS WAS GOOD AT THIS SORT OF THING!
5.

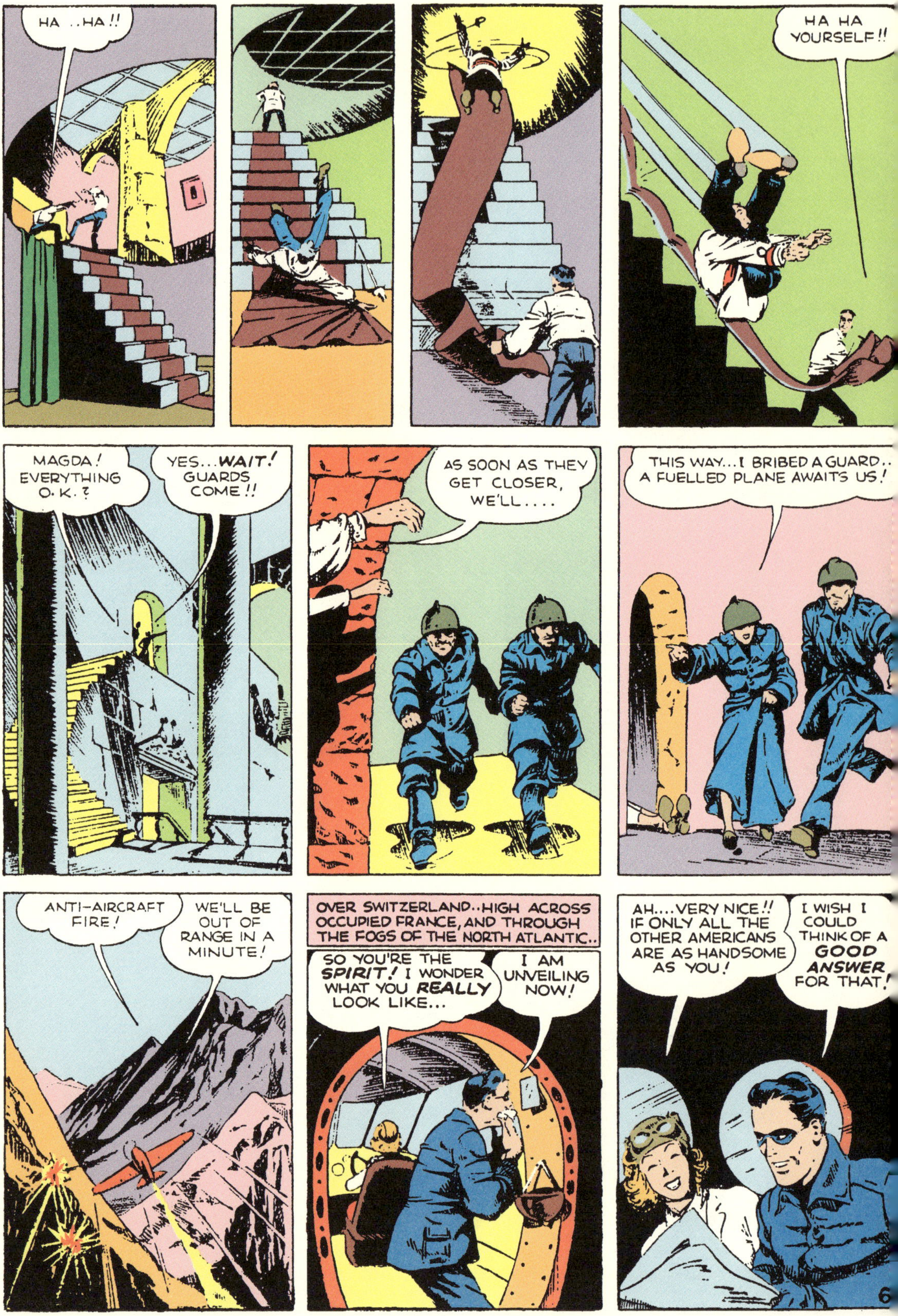
HA ..HA!!
HA HA YOURSELF!!
MAGDA! EVERYTHING O.K.?
YES...WAIT! GUARDS COME!!
AS SOON AS THEY GET CLOSER, WE'LL....
THIS WAY...I BRIBED A GUARD.. A FUELLED PLANE AWAITS US!
ANTI-AIRCRAFT FIRE!
WE'LL BE OUT OF RANGE IN A MINUTE!
OVER SWITZERLAND..HIGH ACROSS OCCUPIED FRANCE, AND THROUGH THE FOGS OF THE NORTH ATLANTIC..
SO YOU'RE THE SPIRIT! I WONDER WHAT YOU REALLY LOOK LIKE...
I AM UNVEILING NOW!
AH....VERY NICE!! IF ONLY ALL THE OTHER AMERICANS ARE AS HANDSOME AS YOU!
I WISH I COULD THINK OF A GOOD ANSWER FOR THAT!
6

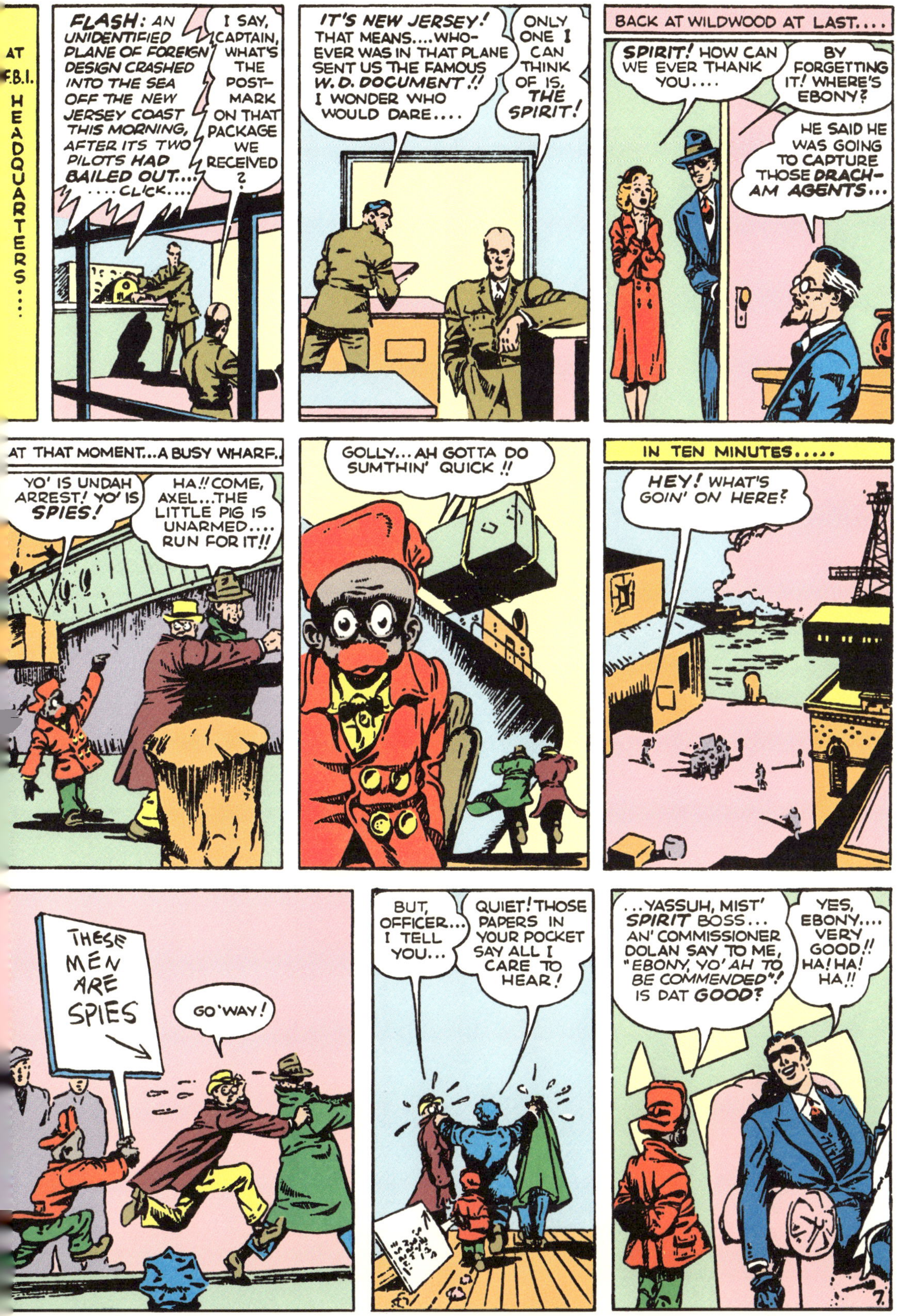
AT F.B.I. HEADQUARTERS...
FLASH: AN UNIDENTIFIED PLANE OF FOREIGN DESIGN CRASHED INTO THE SEA OFF THE NEW JERSEY COAST THIS MORNING, AFTER ITS TWO PILOTS HAD BAILED OUT.... ....CLICK....
I SAY, CAPTAIN, WHAT'S THE POST-MARK ON THAT PACKAGE WE RECEIVED?
IT'S NEW JERSEY! THAT MEANS....WHO-EVER WAS IN THAT PLANE SENT US THE FAMOUS W.D. DOCUMENT!! I WONDER WHO WOULD DARE....
ONLY ONE I CAN THINK OF IS, THE SPIRIT!
BACK AT WILDWOOD AT LAST....
SPIRIT! HOW CAN WE EVER THANK YOU....
BY FORGETTING IT! WHERE'S EBONY?
HE SAID HE WAS GOING TO CAPTURE THOSE DRACH-AM AGENTS...
AT THAT MOMENT...A BUSY WHARF..
YO' IS UNDAH ARREST! YO' IS SPIES!
HA!! COME, AXEL...THE LITTLE PIG IS UNARMED.... RUN FOR IT!!
GOLLY...AH GOTTA DO SUMTHIN' QUICK!!
IN TEN MINUTES.....
HEY! WHAT'S GOIN' ON HERE?
THESE MEN ARE SPIES
GO 'WAY!
BUT, OFFICER... I TELL YOU...
QUIET! THOSE PAPERS IN YOUR POCKET SAY ALL I CARE TO HEAR!
...YASSUH, MIST' SPIRIT BOSS... AN' COMMISSIONER DOLAN SAY TO ME, "EBONY, YO' AH TO BE COMMENDED"! IS DAT GOOD?
YES, EBONY.... VERY GOOD!! HA! HA! HA!!
7.

THE KIDNAPPING OF EBONY

November 24, 1940

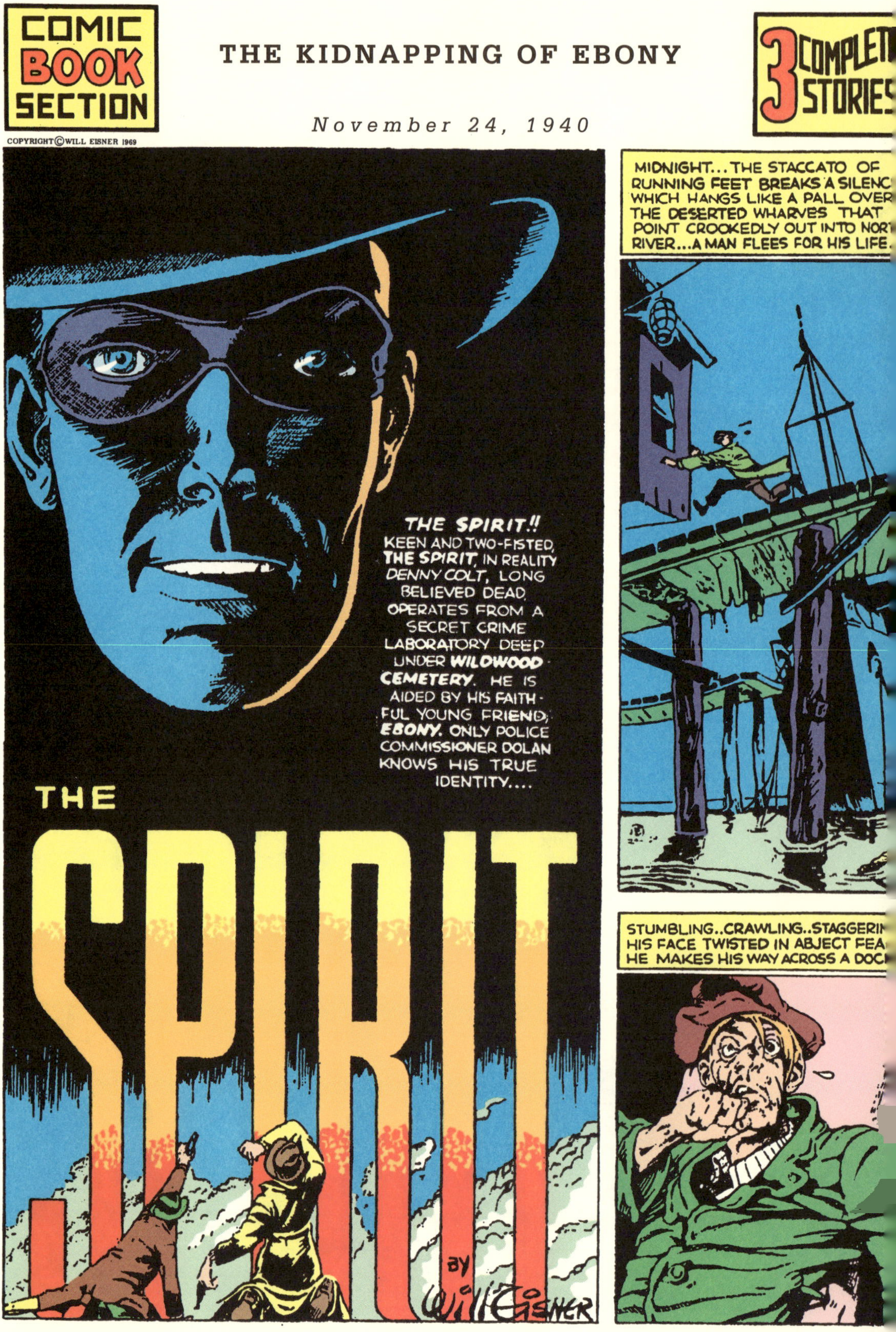
COMIC BOOK SECTION
COPYRIGHT © WILL EISNER 1969
3 COMPLETE STORIES
THE SPIRIT!! KEEN AND TWO-FISTED, THE SPIRIT, IN REALITY DENNY COLT, LONG BELIEVED DEAD, OPERATES FROM A SECRET CRIME LABORATORY DEEP UNDER WILDWOOD CEMETERY. HE IS AIDED BY HIS FAITHFUL YOUNG FRIEND, EBONY. ONLY POLICE COMMISSIONER DOLAN KNOWS HIS TRUE IDENTITY....
THE SPIRIT
BY WILL EISNER
MIDNIGHT... THE STACCATO OF RUNNING FEET BREAKS A SILENC WHICH HANGS LIKE A PALL OVER THE DESERTED WHARVES THAT POINT CROOKEDLY OUT INTO NORT RIVER... A MAN FLEES FOR HIS LIFE.
STUMBLING..CRAWLING..STAGGERIN HIS FACE TWISTED IN ABJECT FEA HE MAKES HIS WAY ACROSS A DOC

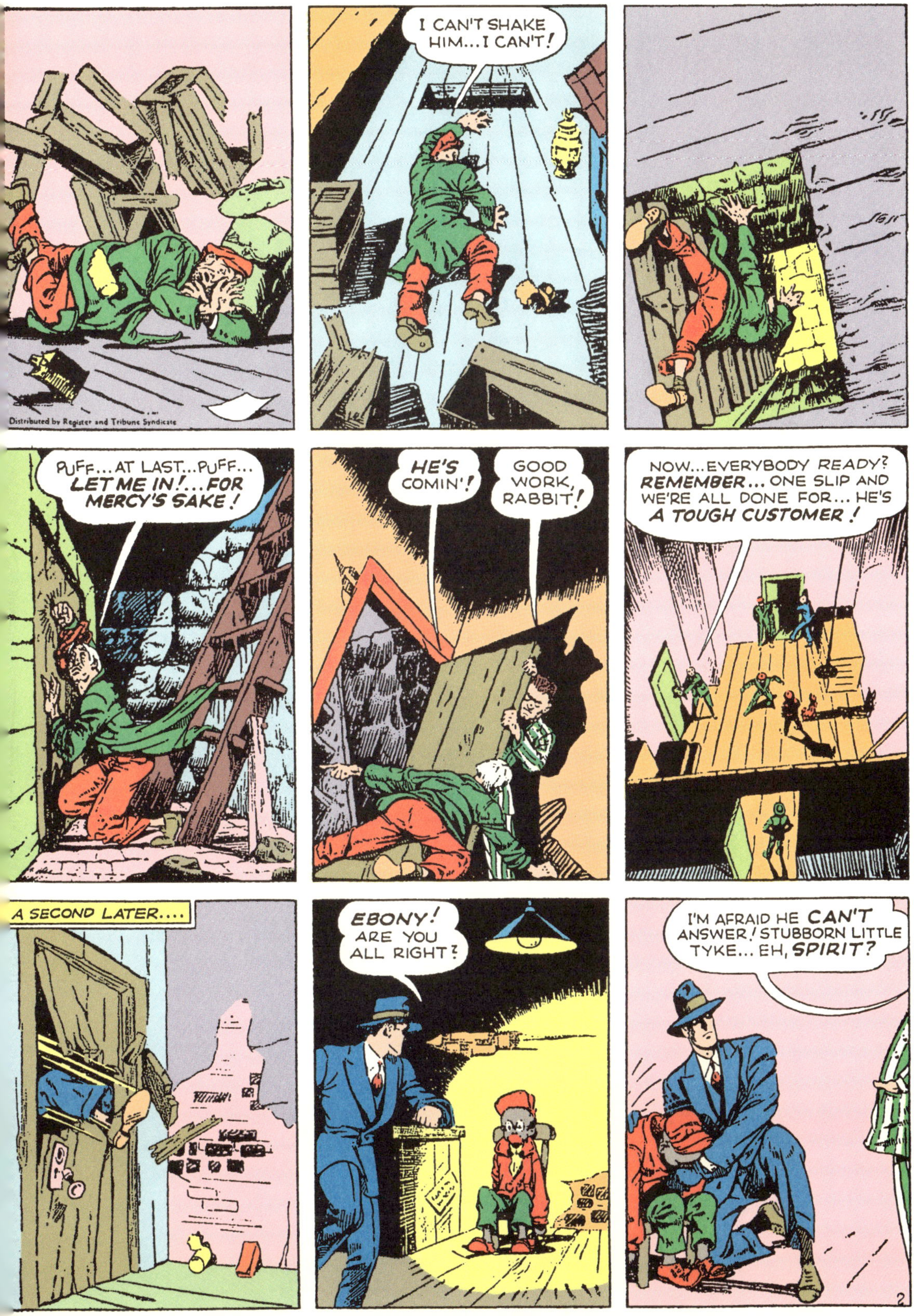
Distributed by Register and Tribune Syndicate
I CAN'T SHAKE HIM... I CAN'T!
PUFF... AT LAST... PUFF... LET ME IN!... FOR MERCY'S SAKE!
HE'S COMIN'!
GOOD WORK, RABBIT!
NOW... EVERYBODY READY? REMEMBER... ONE SLIP AND WE'RE ALL DONE FOR... HE'S A TOUGH CUSTOMER!
A SECOND LATER....
EBONY! ARE YOU ALL RIGHT?
I'M AFRAID HE CAN'T ANSWER! STUBBORN LITTLE TYKE... EH, SPIRIT?
2

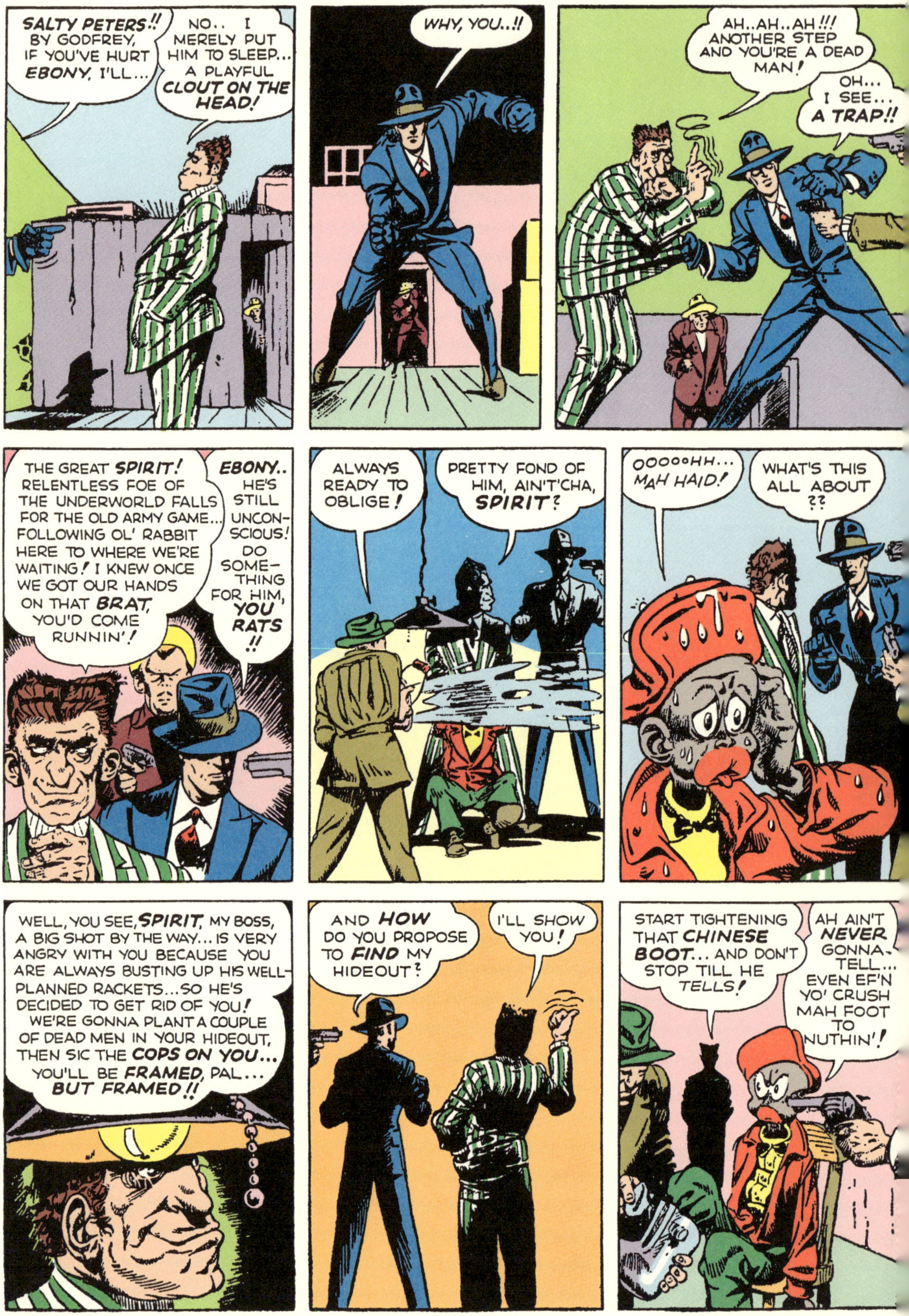
SALTY PETERS!! BY GODFREY, IF YOU'VE HURT EBONY, I'LL...
NO.. I MERELY PUT HIM TO SLEEP... A PLAYFUL CLOUT ON THE HEAD!
WHY, YOU..!!
AH..AH..AH!!! ANOTHER STEP AND YOU'RE A DEAD MAN!
OH... I SEE... A TRAP!!
THE GREAT SPIRIT! RELENTLESS FOE OF THE UNDERWORLD FALLS FOR THE OLD ARMY GAME... FOLLOWING OL' RABBIT HERE TO WHERE WE'RE WAITING! I KNEW ONCE WE GOT OUR HANDS ON THAT BRAT, YOU'D COME RUNNIN'!
EBONY.. HE'S STILL UNCONSCIOUS! DO SOMETHING FOR HIM, YOU RATS!!
ALWAYS READY TO OBLIGE!
PRETTY FOND OF HIM, AIN'T'CHA, SPIRIT?
OOOOOHH... MAH HAID!
WHAT'S THIS ALL ABOUT??
WELL, YOU SEE, SPIRIT, MY BOSS, A BIG SHOT BY THE WAY... IS VERY ANGRY WITH YOU BECAUSE YOU ARE ALWAYS BUSTING UP HIS WELL-PLANNED RACKETS... SO HE'S DECIDED TO GET RID OF YOU! WE'RE GONNA PLANT A COUPLE OF DEAD MEN IN YOUR HIDEOUT, THEN SIC THE COPS ON YOU... YOU'LL BE FRAMED, PAL... BUT FRAMED!!
AND HOW DO YOU PROPOSE TO FIND MY HIDEOUT?
I'LL SHOW YOU!
START TIGHTENING THAT CHINESE BOOT... AND DON'T STOP TILL HE TELLS!
AH AIN'T NEVER GONNA TELL... EVEN EF'N YO' CRUSH MAH FOOT TO NUTHIN'!

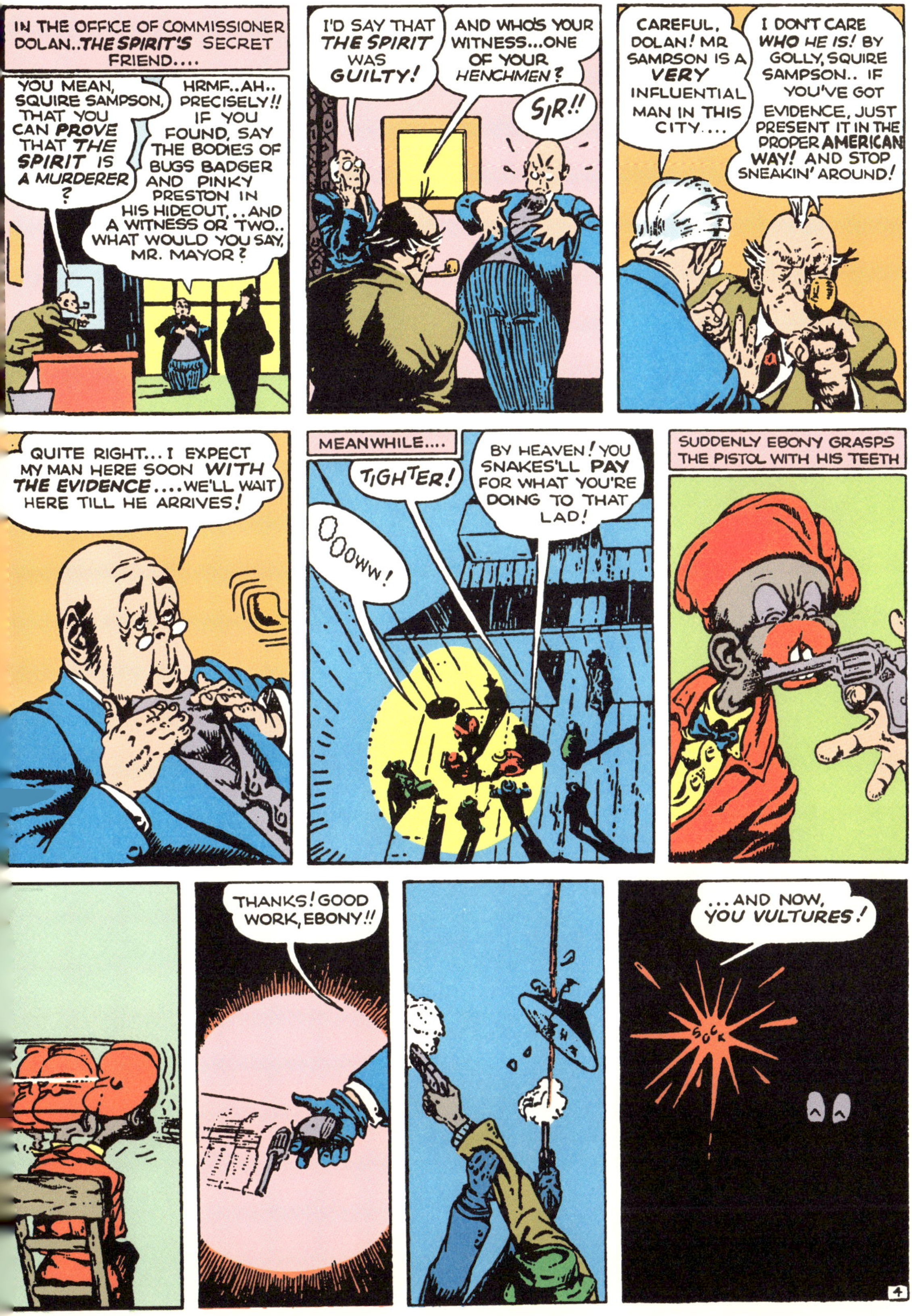
IN THE OFFICE OF COMMISSIONER DOLAN..THE SPIRIT'S SECRET FRIEND....
YOU MEAN, SQUIRE SAMPSON, THAT YOU CAN PROVE THAT THE SPIRIT IS A MURDERER?
HRMF..AH.. PRECISELY!! IF YOU FOUND, SAY THE BODIES OF BUGS BADGER AND PINKY PRESTON IN HIS HIDEOUT,..AND A WITNESS OR TWO.. WHAT WOULD YOU SAY, MR. MAYOR?
I'D SAY THAT THE SPIRIT WAS GUILTY!
AND WHO'S YOUR WITNESS...ONE OF YOUR HENCHMEN?
SIR!!
CAREFUL, DOLAN! MR SAMPSON IS A VERY INFLUENTIAL MAN IN THIS CITY....
I DON'T CARE WHO HE IS! BY GOLLY, SQUIRE SAMPSON.. IF YOU'VE GOT EVIDENCE, JUST PRESENT IT IN THE PROPER AMERICAN WAY! AND STOP SNEAKIN' AROUND!
QUITE RIGHT... I EXPECT MY MAN HERE SOON WITH THE EVIDENCE....WE'LL WAIT HERE TILL HE ARRIVES!
MEANWHILE....
TIGHTER!
BY HEAVEN! YOU SNAKES'LL PAY FOR WHAT YOU'RE DOING TO THAT LAD!
OOOWW!
SUDDENLY EBONY GRASPS THE PISTOL WITH HIS TEETH
THANKS! GOOD WORK, EBONY!!
...AND NOW, YOU VULTURES!
SOCK
4

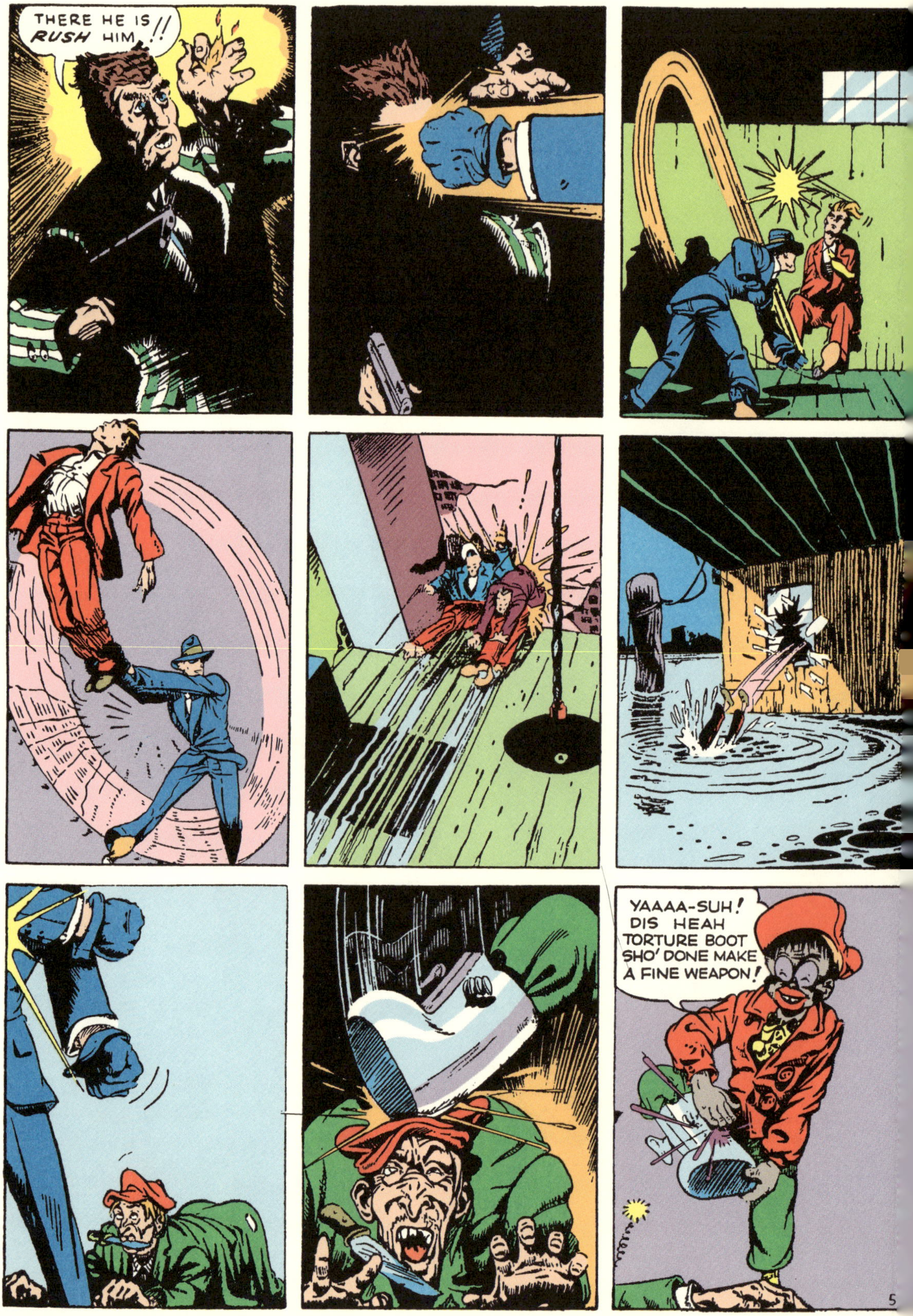
THERE HE IS RUSH HIM!!
YAAAA-SUH! DIS HEAH TORTURE BOOT SHO' DONE MAKE A FINE WEAPON!
5

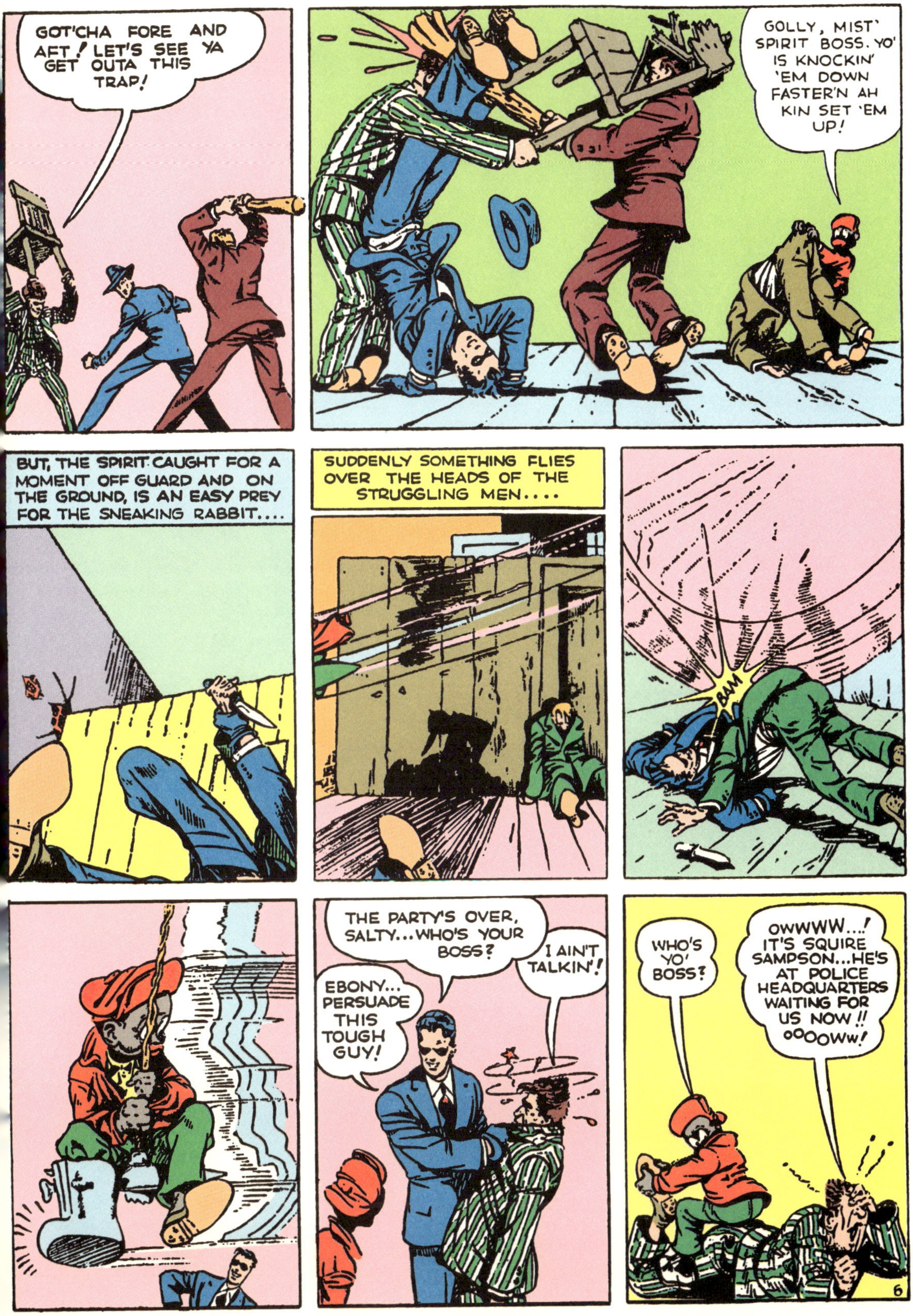
GOT'CHA FORE AND AFT! LET'S SEE YA GET OUTA THIS TRAP!
GOLLY, MIST' SPIRIT BOSS. YO' IS KNOCKIN' 'EM DOWN FASTER'N AH KIN SET 'EM UP!
BUT, THE SPIRIT CAUGHT FOR A MOMENT OFF GUARD AND ON THE GROUND, IS AN EASY PREY FOR THE SNEAKING RABBIT....
SUDDENLY SOMETHING FLIES OVER THE HEADS OF THE STRUGGLING MEN....
BAM
THE PARTY'S OVER, SALTY...WHO'S YOUR BOSS?
I AIN'T TALKIN'!
EBONY... PERSUADE THIS TOUGH GUY!
WHO'S YO' BOSS?
OWWWW...! IT'S SQUIRE SAMPSON...HE'S AT POLICE HEADQUARTERS WAITING FOR US NOW!! OOOOWW!
6

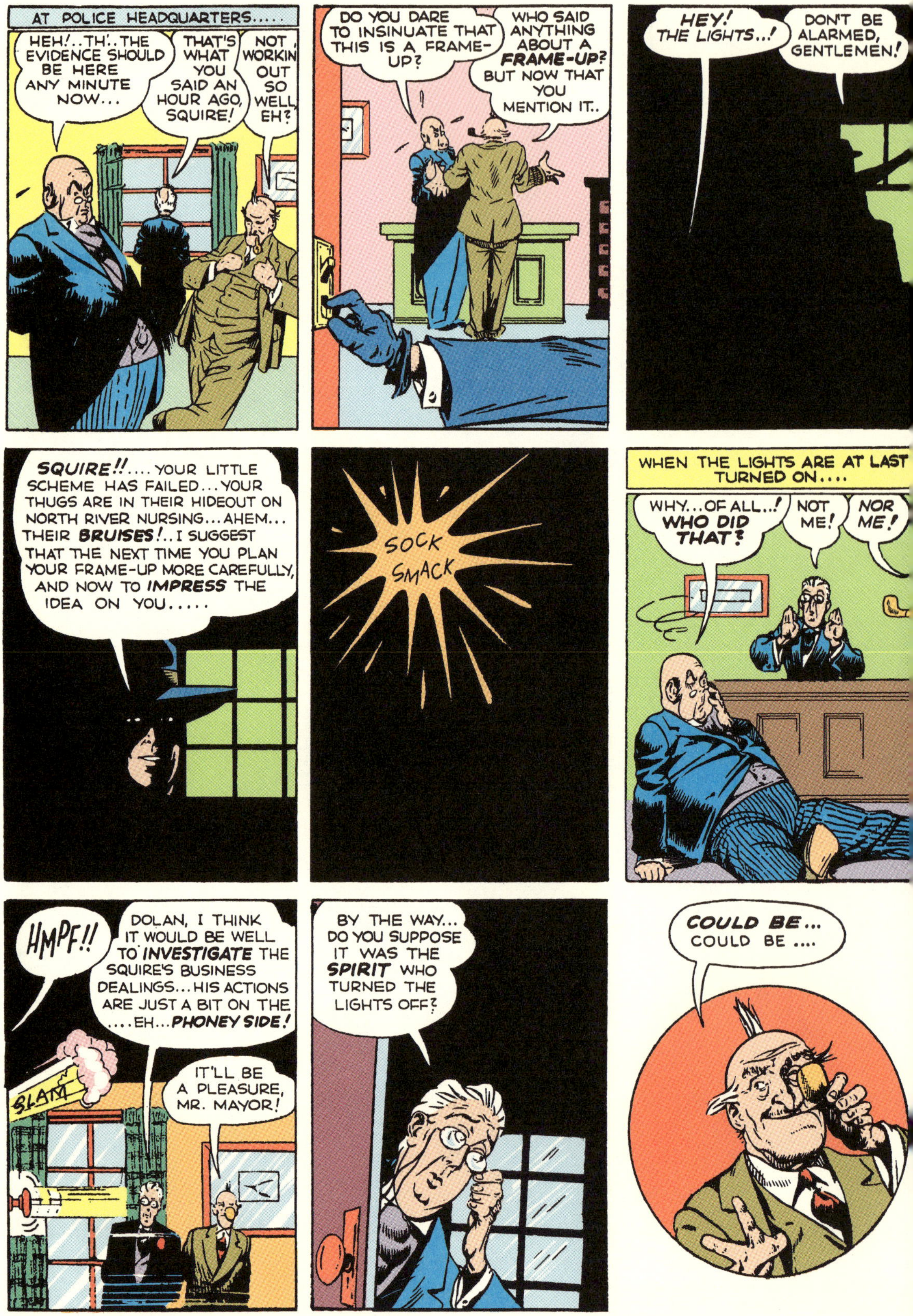
AT POLICE HEADQUARTERS.....
HEH!..TH!..THE EVIDENCE SHOULD BE HERE ANY MINUTE NOW...
THAT'S WHAT YOU SAID AN HOUR AGO, SQUIRE!
NOT WORKIN OUT SO WELL, EH?
DO YOU DARE TO INSINUATE THAT THIS IS A FRAME-UP?
WHO SAID ANYTHING ABOUT A FRAME-UP? BUT NOW THAT YOU MENTION IT..
HEY! THE LIGHTS...!
DON'T BE ALARMED, GENTLEMEN!
SQUIRE!!.... YOUR LITTLE SCHEME HAS FAILED... YOUR THUGS ARE IN THEIR HIDEOUT ON NORTH RIVER NURSING...AHEM... THEIR BRUISES!.. I SUGGEST THAT THE NEXT TIME YOU PLAN YOUR FRAME-UP MORE CAREFULLY, AND NOW TO IMPRESS THE IDEA ON YOU.....
SOCK
SMACK
WHEN THE LIGHTS ARE AT LAST TURNED ON....
WHY...OF ALL..! WHO DID THAT?
NOT ME!
NOR ME!
HMPF!!
SLAM
DOLAN, I THINK IT WOULD BE WELL TO INVESTIGATE THE SQUIRE'S BUSINESS DEALINGS... HIS ACTIONS ARE JUST A BIT ON THE ....EH... PHONEY SIDE!
IT'LL BE A PLEASURE, MR. MAYOR!
BY THE WAY... DO YOU SUPPOSE IT WAS THE SPIRIT WHO TURNED THE LIGHTS OFF?
COULD BE... COULD BE ....

COMIC BOOK SECTION

3 COMPLETE STORIES

THE PROM

December 1, 1940

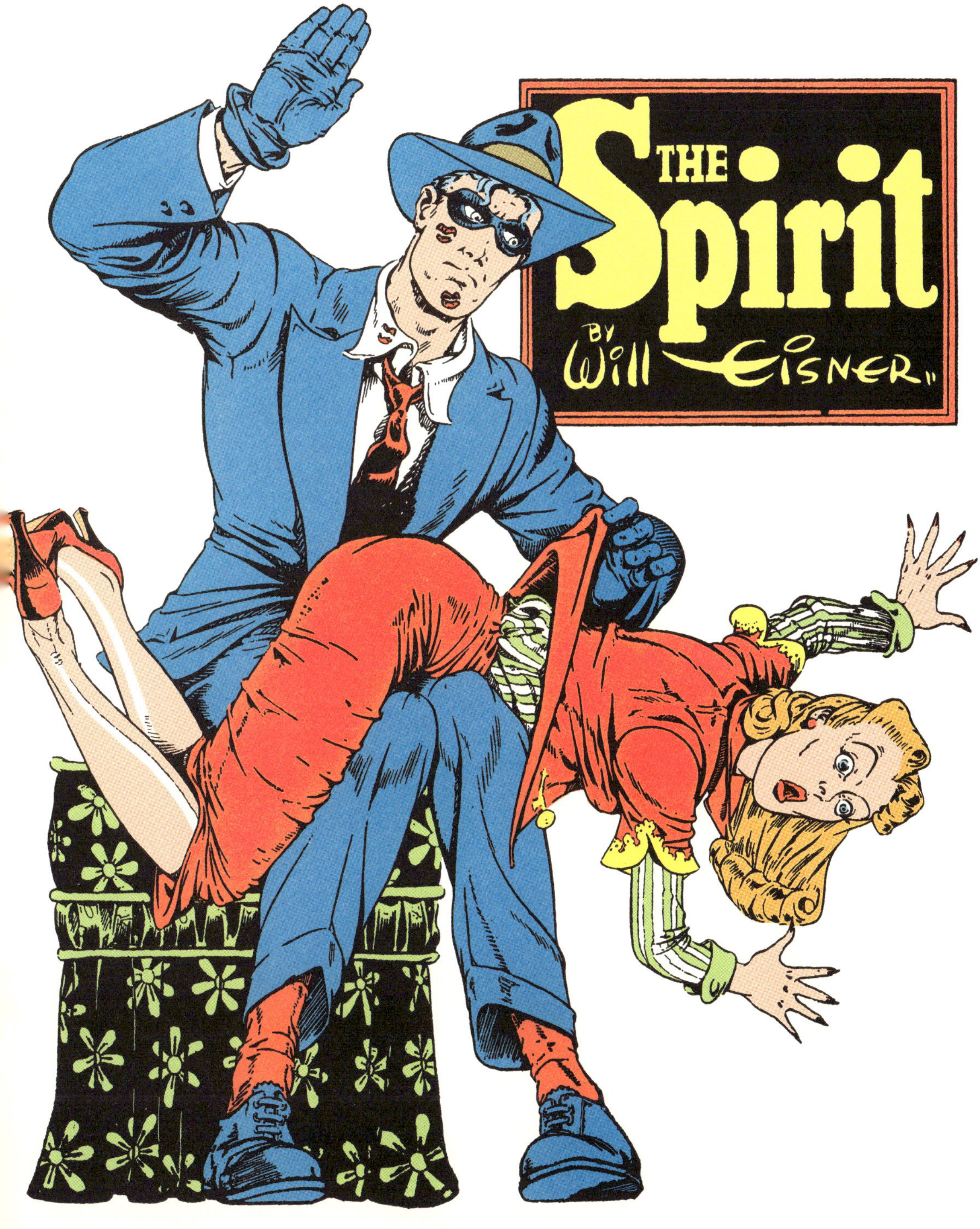
THE Spirit
BY Will Eisner

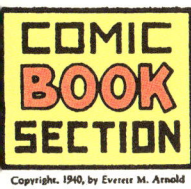

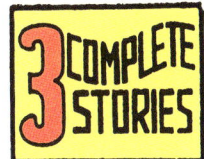

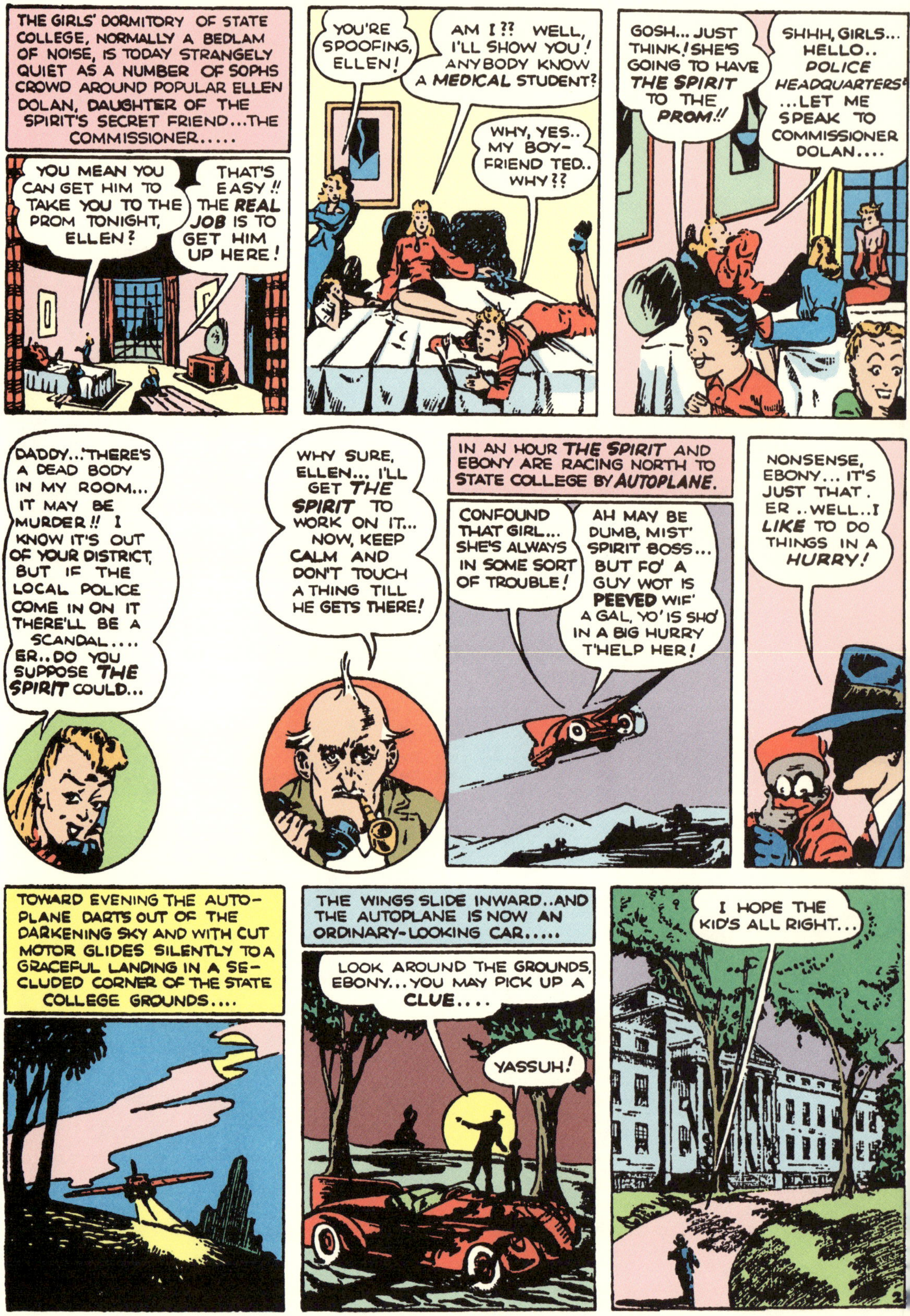
THE GIRLS' DORMITORY OF STATE COLLEGE, NORMALLY A BEDLAM OF NOISE, IS TODAY STRANGELY QUIET AS A NUMBER OF SOPHS CROWD AROUND POPULAR ELLEN DOLAN, DAUGHTER OF THE SPIRIT'S SECRET FRIEND...THE COMMISSIONER.....
YOU MEAN YOU CAN GET HIM TO TAKE YOU TO THE PROM TONIGHT, ELLEN?
THAT'S EASY!! THE REAL JOB IS TO GET HIM UP HERE!
YOU'RE SPOOFING, ELLEN!
AM I?? WELL, I'LL SHOW YOU! ANYBODY KNOW A MEDICAL STUDENT?
WHY, YES.. MY BOY-FRIEND TED.. WHY??
GOSH... JUST THINK! SHE'S GOING TO HAVE THE SPIRIT TO THE PROM!!
SHHH, GIRLS... HELLO.. POLICE HEADQUARTERS? ...LET ME SPEAK TO COMMISSIONER DOLAN....
DADDY..."THERE'S A DEAD BODY IN MY ROOM... IT MAY BE MURDER!! I KNOW IT'S OUT OF YOUR DISTRICT, BUT IF THE LOCAL POLICE COME IN ON IT THERE'LL BE A SCANDAL.... ER.. DO YOU SUPPOSE THE SPIRIT COULD...
WHY SURE, ELLEN... I'LL GET THE SPIRIT TO WORK ON IT... NOW, KEEP CALM AND DON'T TOUCH A THING TILL HE GETS THERE!
IN AN HOUR THE SPIRIT AND EBONY ARE RACING NORTH TO STATE COLLEGE BY AUTOPLANE.
CONFOUND THAT GIRL... SHE'S ALWAYS IN SOME SORT OF TROUBLE!
AH MAY BE DUMB, MIST' SPIRIT BOSS... BUT FO' A GUY WOT IS PEEVED WIF' A GAL, YO' IS SHO' IN A BIG HURRY T'HELP HER!
NONSENSE, EBONY... IT'S JUST THAT. ER ..WELL..I LIKE TO DO THINGS IN A HURRY!
TOWARD EVENING THE AUTO-PLANE DARTS OUT OF THE DARKENING SKY AND WITH CUT MOTOR GLIDES SILENTLY TO A GRACEFUL LANDING IN A SE-CLUDED CORNER OF THE STATE COLLEGE GROUNDS....
THE WINGS SLIDE INWARD..AND THE AUTOPLANE IS NOW AN ORDINARY-LOOKING CAR.....
LOOK AROUND THE GROUNDS, EBONY... YOU MAY PICK UP A CLUE....
YASSUH!
I HOPE THE KID'S ALL RIGHT...

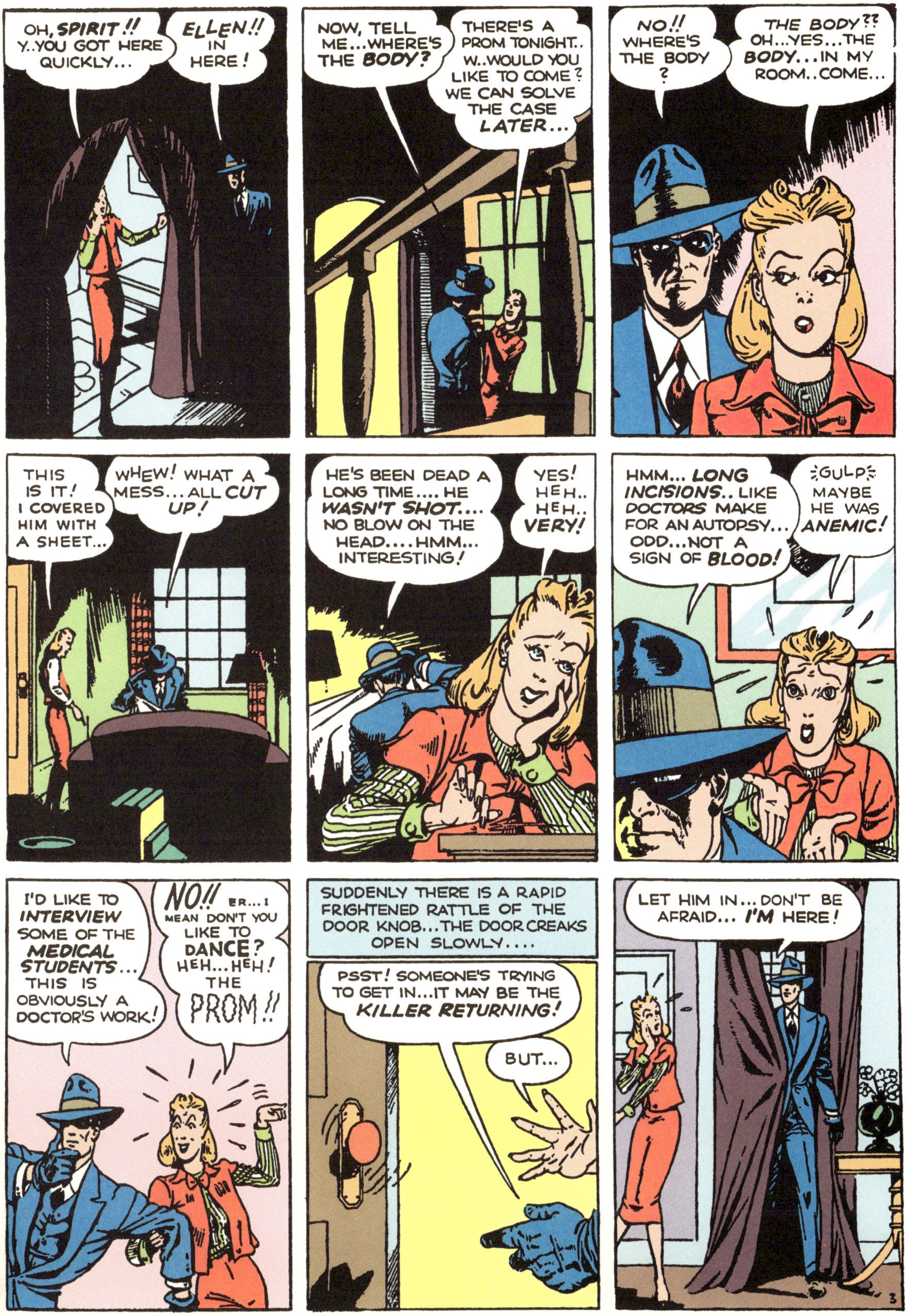
OH, SPIRIT!! Y..YOU GOT HERE QUICKLY...
ELLEN!! IN HERE!
NOW, TELL ME...WHERE'S THE BODY?
THERE'S A PROM TONIGHT.. W..WOULD YOU LIKE TO COME? WE CAN SOLVE THE CASE LATER...
NO!! WHERE'S THE BODY?
THE BODY?? OH...YES...THE BODY...IN MY ROOM..COME...
THIS IS IT! I COVERED HIM WITH A SHEET...
WHEW! WHAT A MESS...ALL CUT UP!
HE'S BEEN DEAD A LONG TIME.... HE WASN'T SHOT.... NO BLOW ON THE HEAD....HMM... INTERESTING!
YES! HEH.. HEH.. VERY!
HMM... LONG INCISIONS.. LIKE DOCTORS MAKE FOR AN AUTOPSY... ODD...NOT A SIGN OF BLOOD!
GULP MAYBE HE WAS ANEMIC!
I'D LIKE TO INTERVIEW SOME OF THE MEDICAL STUDENTS... THIS IS OBVIOUSLY A DOCTOR'S WORK!
NO!! ER...I MEAN DON'T YOU LIKE TO DANCE? HEH...HEH! THE PROM!!
SUDDENLY THERE IS A RAPID FRIGHTENED RATTLE OF THE DOOR KNOB...THE DOOR CREAKS OPEN SLOWLY....
PSST! SOMEONE'S TRYING TO GET IN...IT MAY BE THE KILLER RETURNING!
BUT...
LET HIM IN...DON'T BE AFRAID... I'M HERE!
3

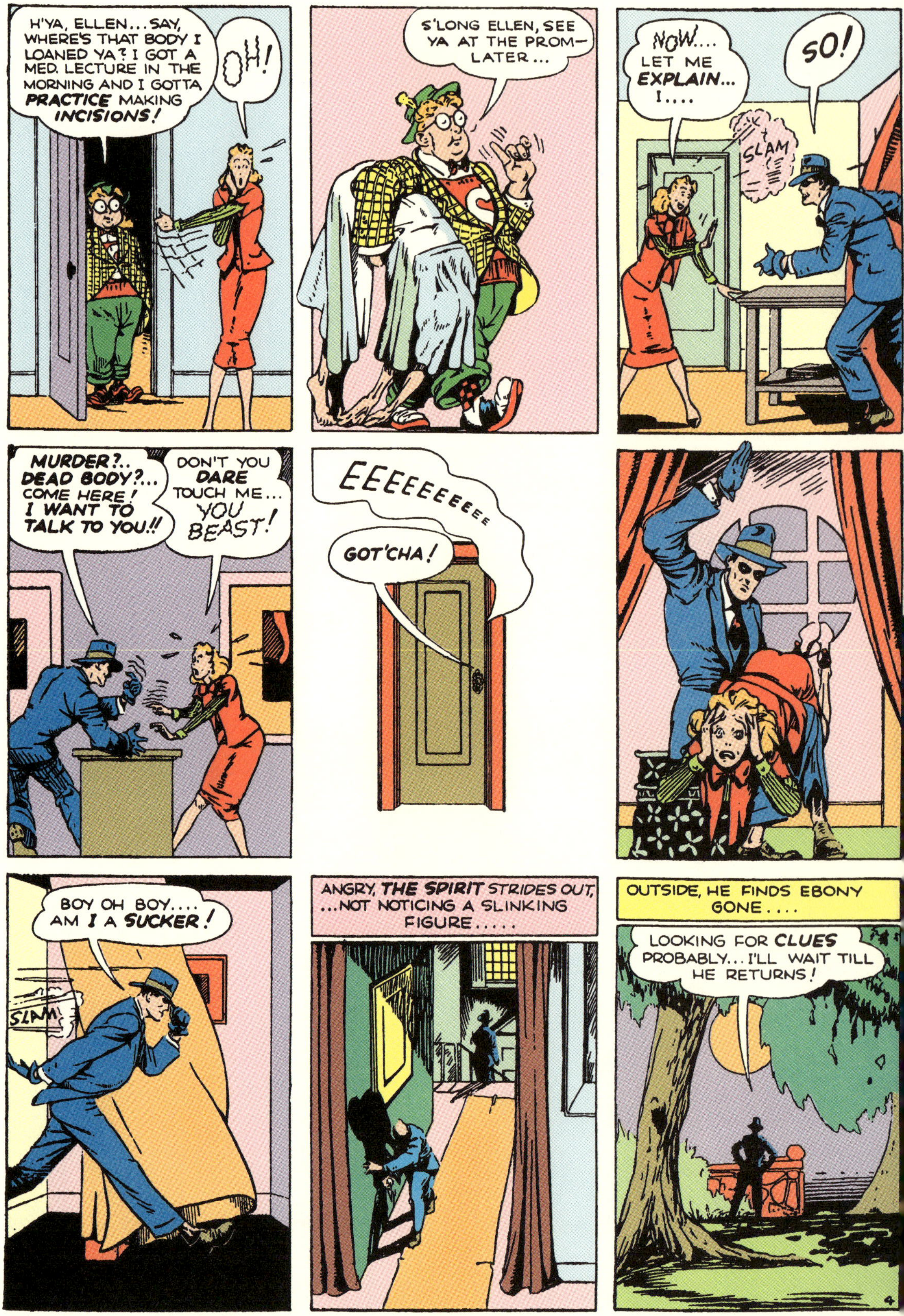

H'YA, ELLEN... SAY, WHERE'S THAT BODY I LOANED YA? I GOT A MED. LECTURE IN THE MORNING AND I GOTTA PRACTICE MAKING INCISIONS!
OH!
S'LONG ELLEN, SEE YA AT THE PROM— LATER...
NOW.... LET ME EXPLAIN... I....
SLAM
SO!
MURDER?.. DEAD BODY?... COME HERE! I WANT TO TALK TO YOU!!
DON'T YOU DARE TOUCH ME... YOU BEAST!
EEEEEEEEeeee
GOT'CHA!
BOY OH BOY.... AM I A SUCKER!
SLAM
ANGRY, THE SPIRIT STRIDES OUT, ...NOT NOTICING A SLINKING FIGURE.....
OUTSIDE, HE FINDS EBONY GONE....
LOOKING FOR CLUES PROBABLY... I'LL WAIT TILL HE RETURNS!
4

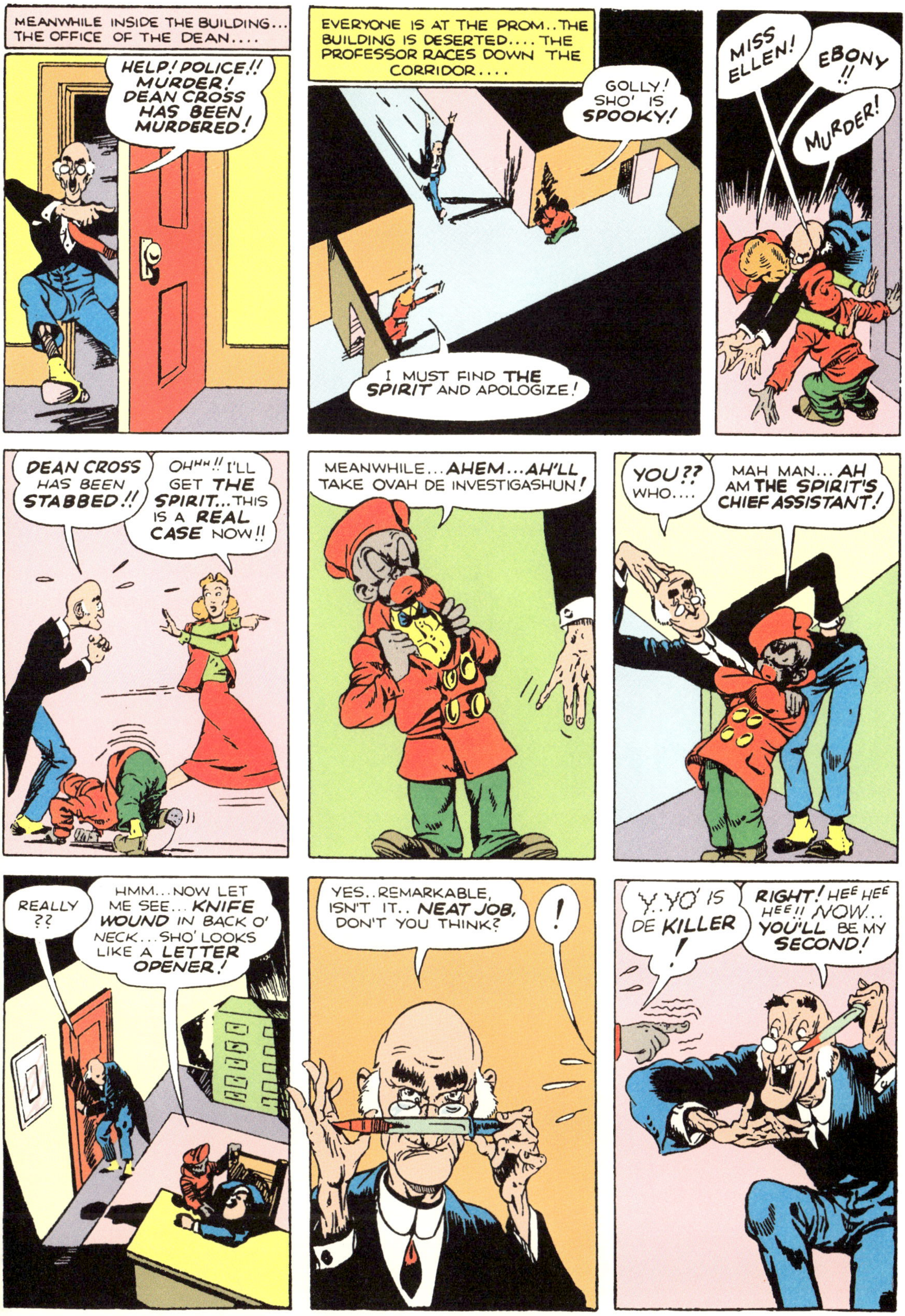
MEANWHILE INSIDE THE BUILDING... THE OFFICE OF THE DEAN....
HELP! POLICE!! MURDER! DEAN CROSS HAS BEEN MURDERED!
EVERYONE IS AT THE PROM..THE BUILDING IS DESERTED.... THE PROFESSOR RACES DOWN THE CORRIDOR....
GOLLY! SHO' IS SPOOKY!
I MUST FIND THE SPIRIT AND APOLOGIZE!
MISS ELLEN!
EBONY !!
MURDER!
DEAN CROSS HAS BEEN STABBED!!
OHHH!! I'LL GET THE SPIRIT...THIS IS A REAL CASE NOW!!
MEANWHILE...AHEM...AH'LL TAKE OVAH DE INVESTIGASHUN!
YOU?? WHO....
MAH MAN... AH AM THE SPIRIT'S CHIEF ASSISTANT!
REALLY ??
HMM...NOW LET ME SEE...KNIFE WOUND IN BACK O' NECK...SHO' LOOKS LIKE A LETTER OPENER!
YES..REMARKABLE, ISN'T IT.. NEAT JOB, DON'T YOU THINK?
!
Y..YO' IS DE KILLER !
RIGHT! HEE HEE HEE!! NOW... YOU'LL BE MY SECOND!

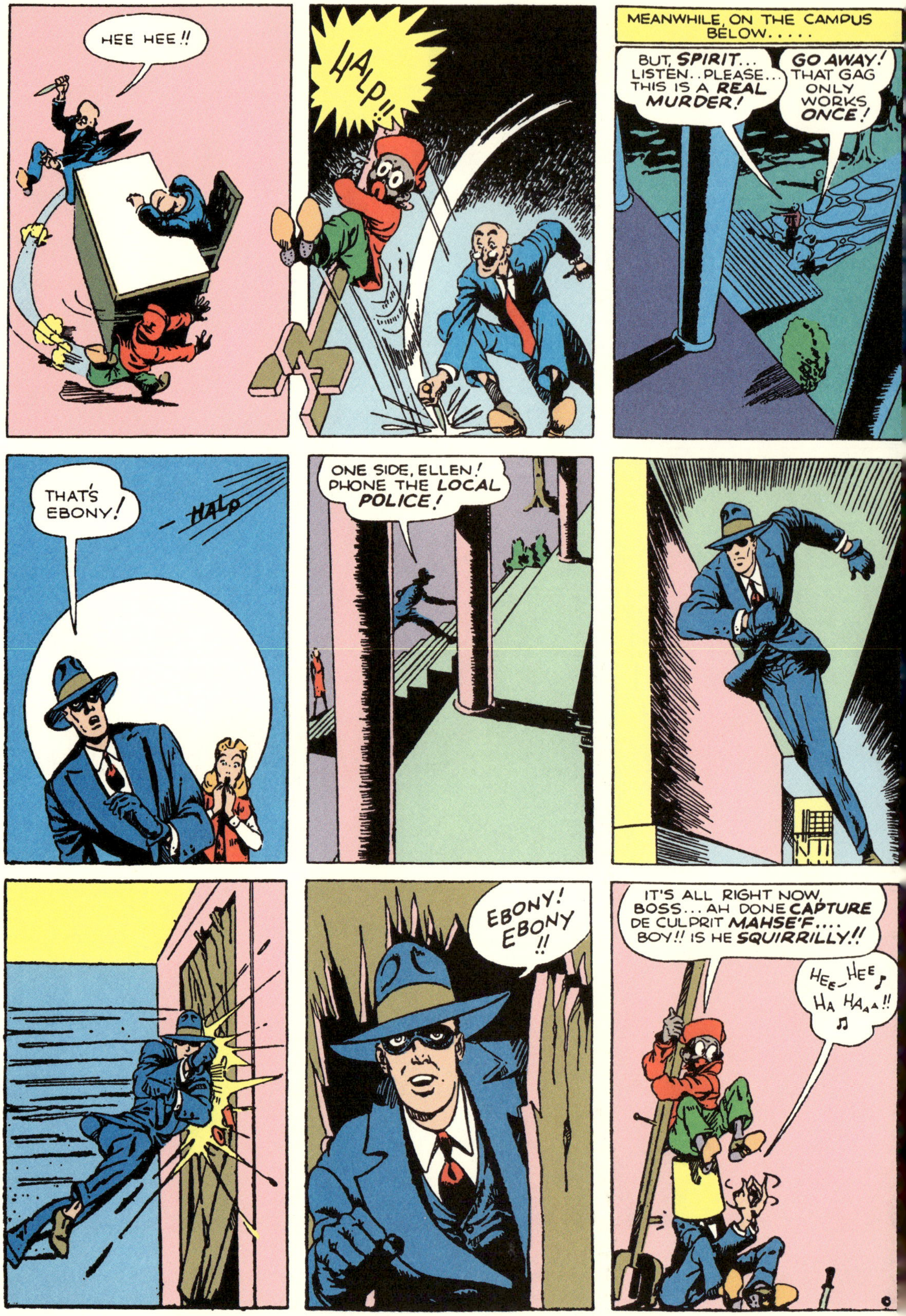
HEE HEE!!
HALP!!
MEANWHILE, ON THE CAMPUS BELOW.....
BUT, SPIRIT... LISTEN.. PLEASE... THIS IS A REAL MURDER!
GO AWAY! THAT GAG ONLY WORKS ONCE!
THAT'S EBONY!
HALP
ONE SIDE, ELLEN! PHONE THE LOCAL POLICE!
EBONY! EBONY!!
IT'S ALL RIGHT NOW, BOSS... AH DONE CAPTURE DE CULPRIT MAHSE'F.... BOY!! IS HE SQUIRRILLY!!
HEE-HEE, HA HAAA!!

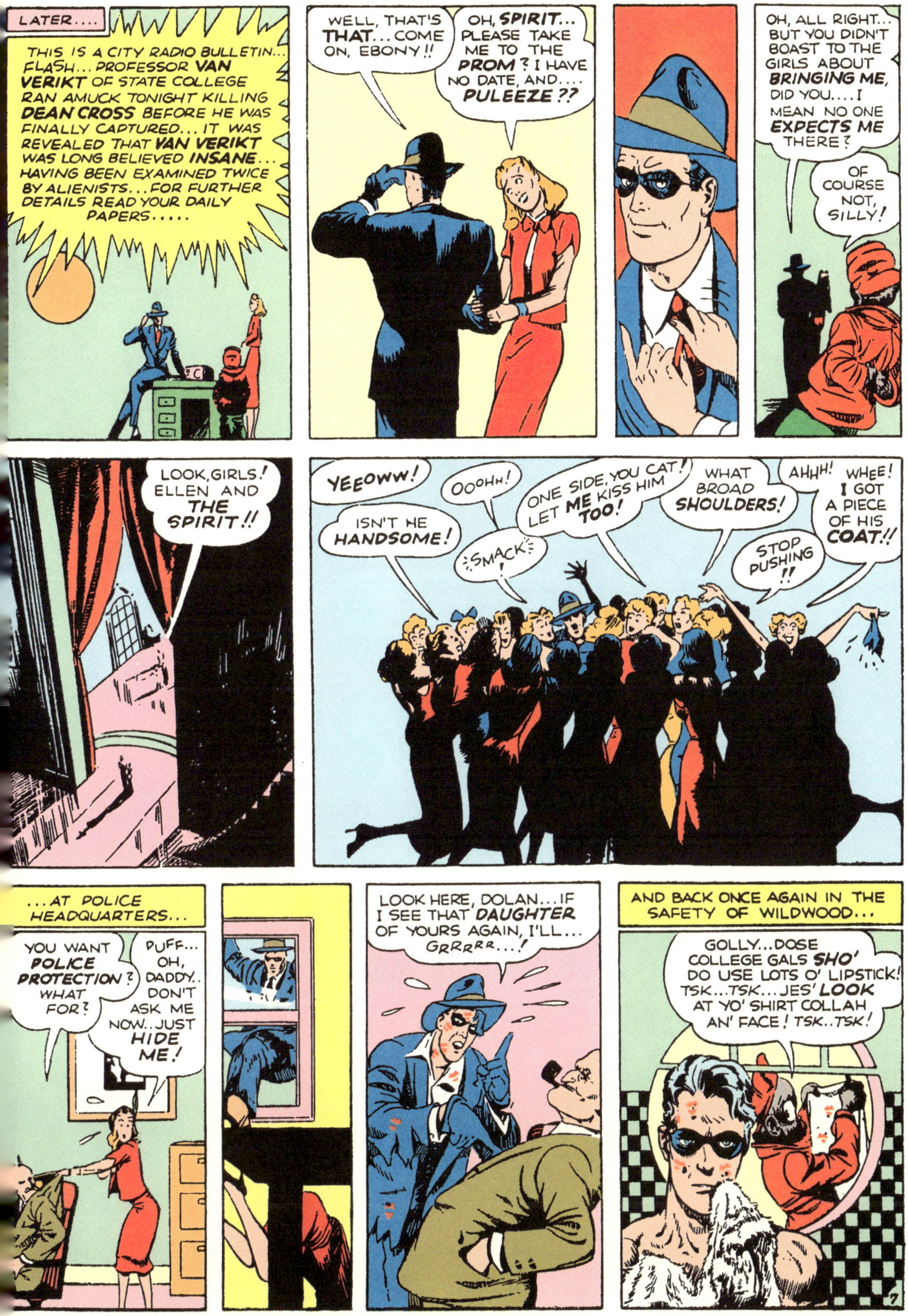
LATER....
THIS IS A CITY RADIO BULLETIN... FLASH... PROFESSOR VAN VERIKT OF STATE COLLEGE RAN AMUCK TONIGHT KILLING DEAN CROSS BEFORE HE WAS FINALLY CAPTURED... IT WAS REVEALED THAT VAN VERIKT WAS LONG BELIEVED INSANE... HAVING BEEN EXAMINED TWICE BY ALIENISTS... FOR FURTHER DETAILS READ YOUR DAILY PAPERS.....
WELL, THAT'S THAT... COME ON, EBONY!!
OH, SPIRIT... PLEASE TAKE ME TO THE PROM? I HAVE NO DATE, AND.... PULEEZE??
OH, ALL RIGHT... BUT YOU DIDN'T BOAST TO THE GIRLS ABOUT BRINGING ME, DID YOU.... I MEAN NO ONE EXPECTS ME THERE?
OF COURSE NOT, SILLY!
LOOK, GIRLS! ELLEN AND THE SPIRIT!!
YEEOWW!
ISN'T HE HANDSOME!
OOOHH!
SMACK
ONE SIDE, YOU CAT! LET ME KISS HIM TOO!
WHAT BROAD SHOULDERS!
AHHH!
WHEE! I GOT A PIECE OF HIS COAT!!
STOP PUSHING!!
...AT POLICE HEADQUARTERS...
YOU WANT POLICE PROTECTION? WHAT FOR?
PUFF... OH, DADDY.. DON'T ASK ME NOW.. JUST HIDE ME!
LOOK HERE, DOLAN... IF I SEE THAT DAUGHTER OF YOURS AGAIN, I'LL... GRRRRR...!
AND BACK ONCE AGAIN IN THE SAFETY OF WILDWOOD...
GOLLY... DOSE COLLEGE GALS SHO' DO USE LOTS O' LIPSTICK! TSK... TSK... JES' LOOK AT YO' SHIRT COLLAH AN' FACE! TSK.. TSK!
7

COMIC BOOK SECTION

COPYRIGHT © WILL EISNER 1969

THE HAUNTED HOUSE

December 8, 1940

3 COMPLETE STORIES

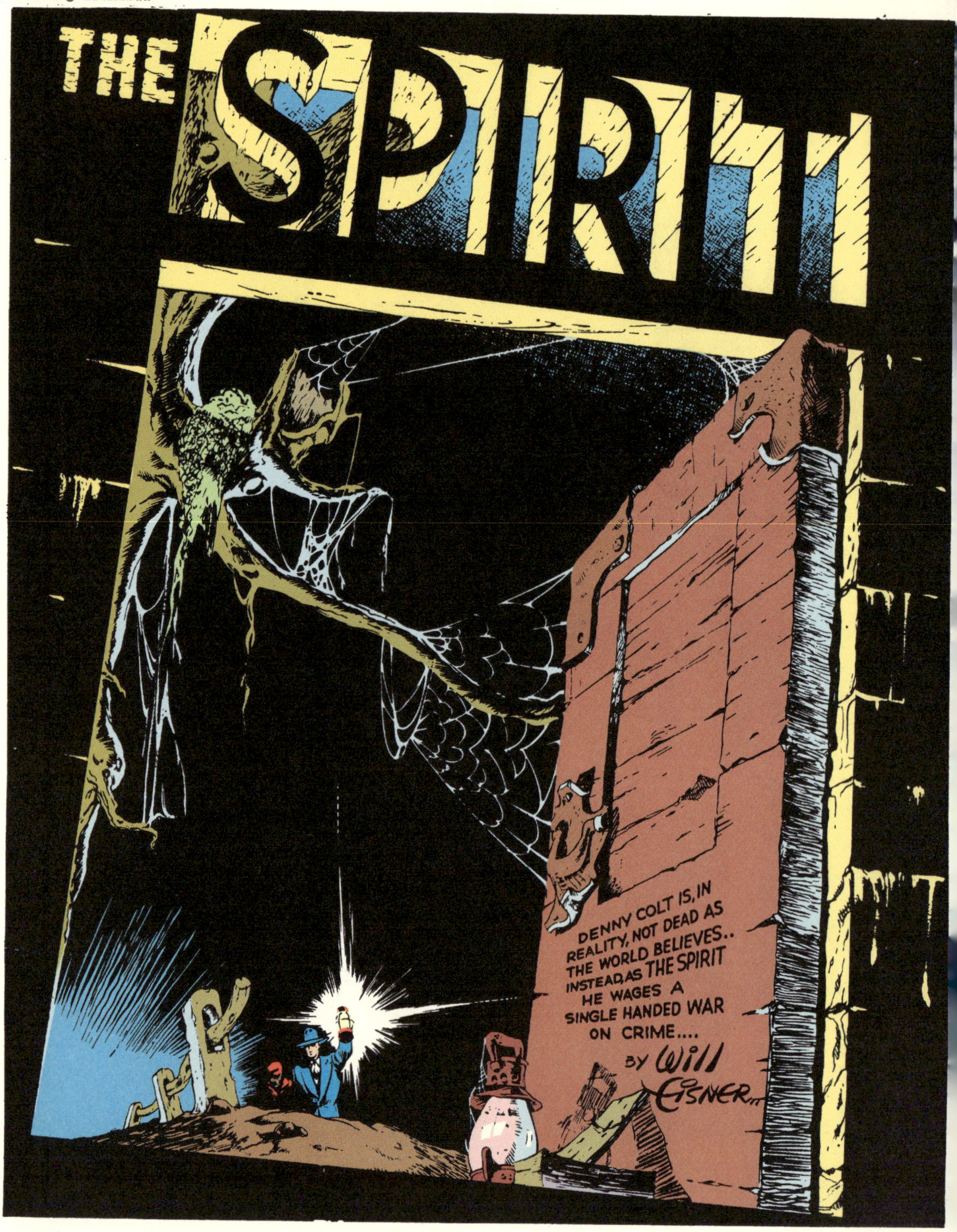

THE SPIRIT
DENNY COLT IS, IN REALITY, NOT DEAD AS THE WORLD BELIEVES.. INSTEAD, AS THE SPIRIT HE WAGES A SINGLE HANDED WAR ON CRIME....
BY WILL EISNER...

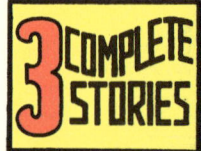

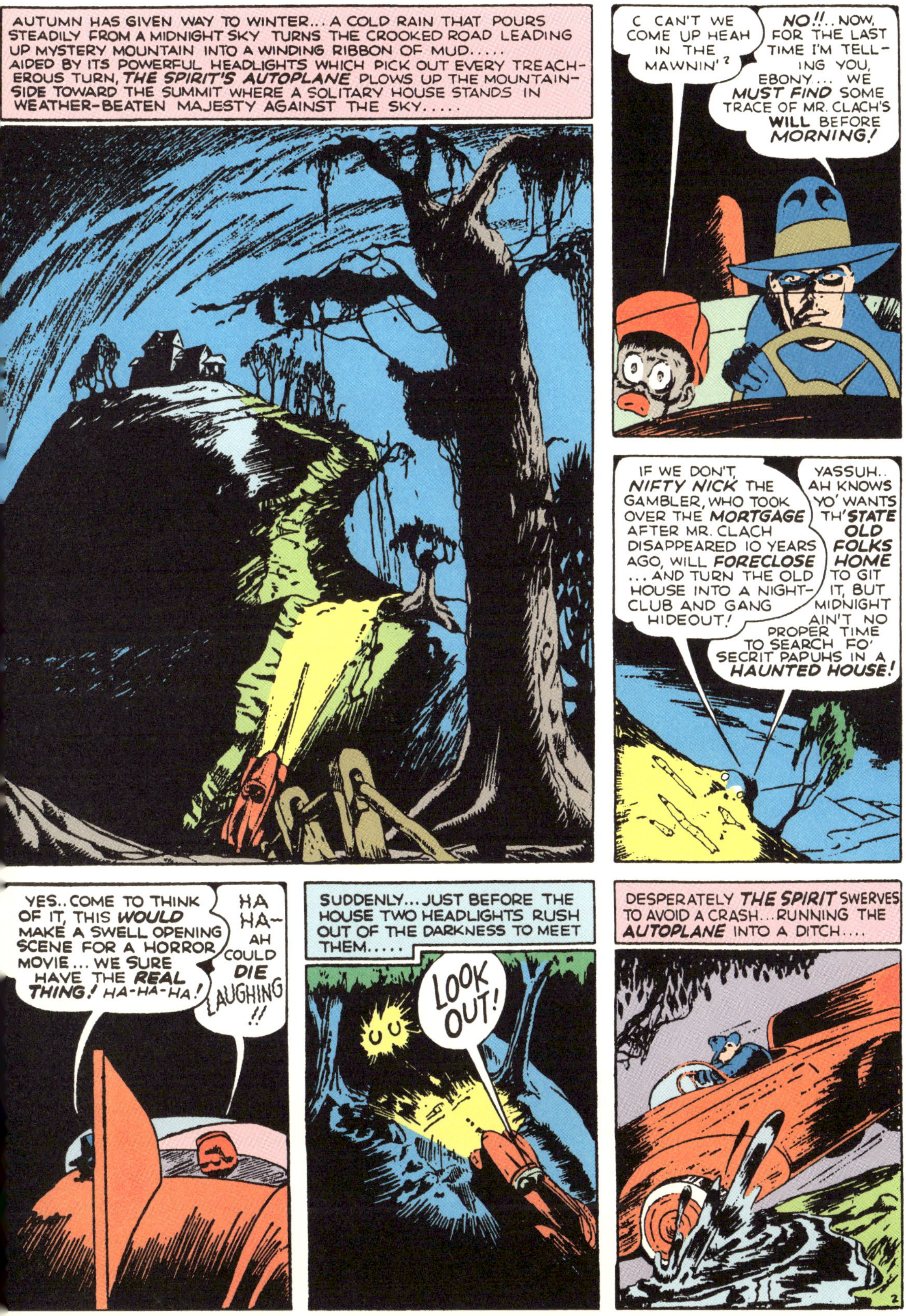

AUTUMN HAS GIVEN WAY TO WINTER... A COLD RAIN THAT POURS STEADILY FROM A MIDNIGHT SKY TURNS THE CROOKED ROAD LEADING UP MYSTERY MOUNTAIN INTO A WINDING RIBBON OF MUD..... AIDED BY ITS POWERFUL HEADLIGHTS WHICH PICK OUT EVERY TREACHEROUS TURN, THE SPIRIT'S AUTOPLANE PLOWS UP THE MOUNTAINSIDE TOWARD THE SUMMIT WHERE A SOLITARY HOUSE STANDS IN WEATHER-BEATEN MAJESTY AGAINST THE SKY.....
C CAN'T WE COME UP HEAH IN THE MAWNIN'?
NO!!.. NOW, FOR THE LAST TIME I'M TELLING YOU, EBONY... WE MUST FIND SOME TRACE OF MR. CLACH'S WILL BEFORE MORNING!
IF WE DON'T, NIFTY NICK THE GAMBLER, WHO TOOK OVER THE MORTGAGE AFTER MR. CLACH DISAPPEARED 10 YEARS AGO, WILL FORECLOSE ... AND TURN THE OLD HOUSE INTO A NIGHT-CLUB AND GANG HIDEOUT!
YASSUH.. AH KNOWS YO' WANTS TH' STATE OLD FOLKS HOME TO GIT IT, BUT MIDNIGHT AIN'T NO PROPER TIME TO SEARCH FO' SECRIT PAPUHS IN A HAUNTED HOUSE!
YES.. COME TO THINK OF IT, THIS WOULD MAKE A SWELL OPENING SCENE FOR A HORROR MOVIE... WE SURE HAVE THE REAL THING! HA-HA-HA!
HA HA-AH COULD DIE LAUGHING!!
SUDDENLY... JUST BEFORE THE HOUSE TWO HEADLIGHTS RUSH OUT OF THE DARKNESS TO MEET THEM.....
LOOK OUT!
DESPERATELY THE SPIRIT SWERVES TO AVOID A CRASH... RUNNING THE AUTOPLANE INTO A DITCH....
2

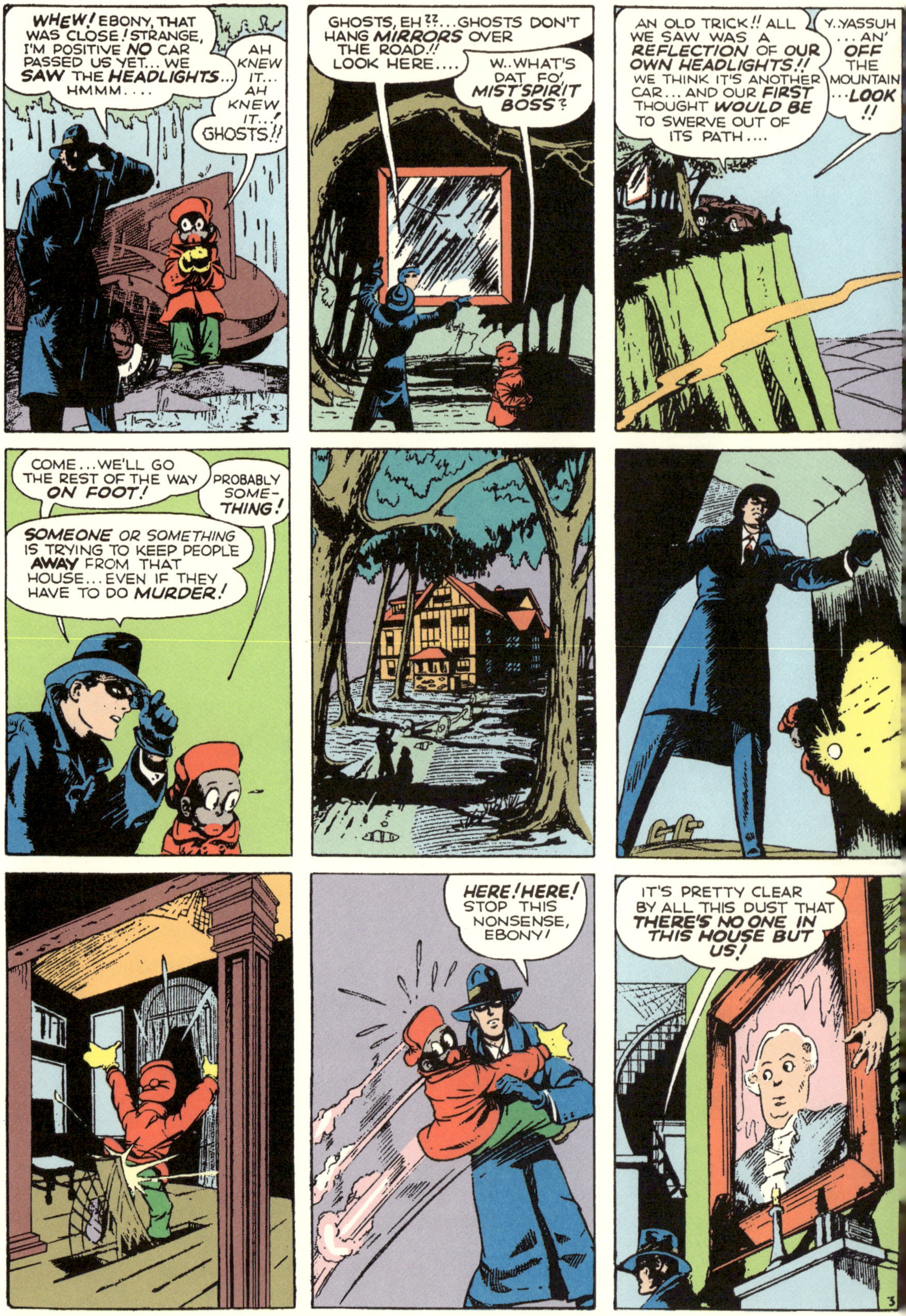
WHEW! EBONY, THAT WAS CLOSE! STRANGE, I'M POSITIVE NO CAR PASSED US YET... WE SAW THE HEADLIGHTS... HMMM....
AH KNEW IT... AH KNEW IT...! GHOSTS!!
GHOSTS, EH ??... GHOSTS DON'T HANG MIRRORS OVER THE ROAD!! LOOK HERE....
W..WHAT'S DAT FO', MIST'SPIR'T BOSS?
AN OLD TRICK!! ALL WE SAW WAS A REFLECTION OF OUR OWN HEADLIGHTS!! WE THINK IT'S ANOTHER CAR... AND OUR FIRST THOUGHT WOULD BE TO SWERVE OUT OF ITS PATH....
Y..YASSUH ... AN' OFF THE MOUNTAIN ...LOOK !!
COME... WE'LL GO THE REST OF THE WAY ON FOOT!
PROBABLY SOME-THING!
SOMEONE OR SOMETHING IS TRYING TO KEEP PEOPLE AWAY FROM THAT HOUSE... EVEN IF THEY HAVE TO DO MURDER!
HERE! HERE! STOP THIS NONSENSE, EBONY!
IT'S PRETTY CLEAR BY ALL THIS DUST THAT THERE'S NO ONE IN THIS HOUSE BUT US!
3

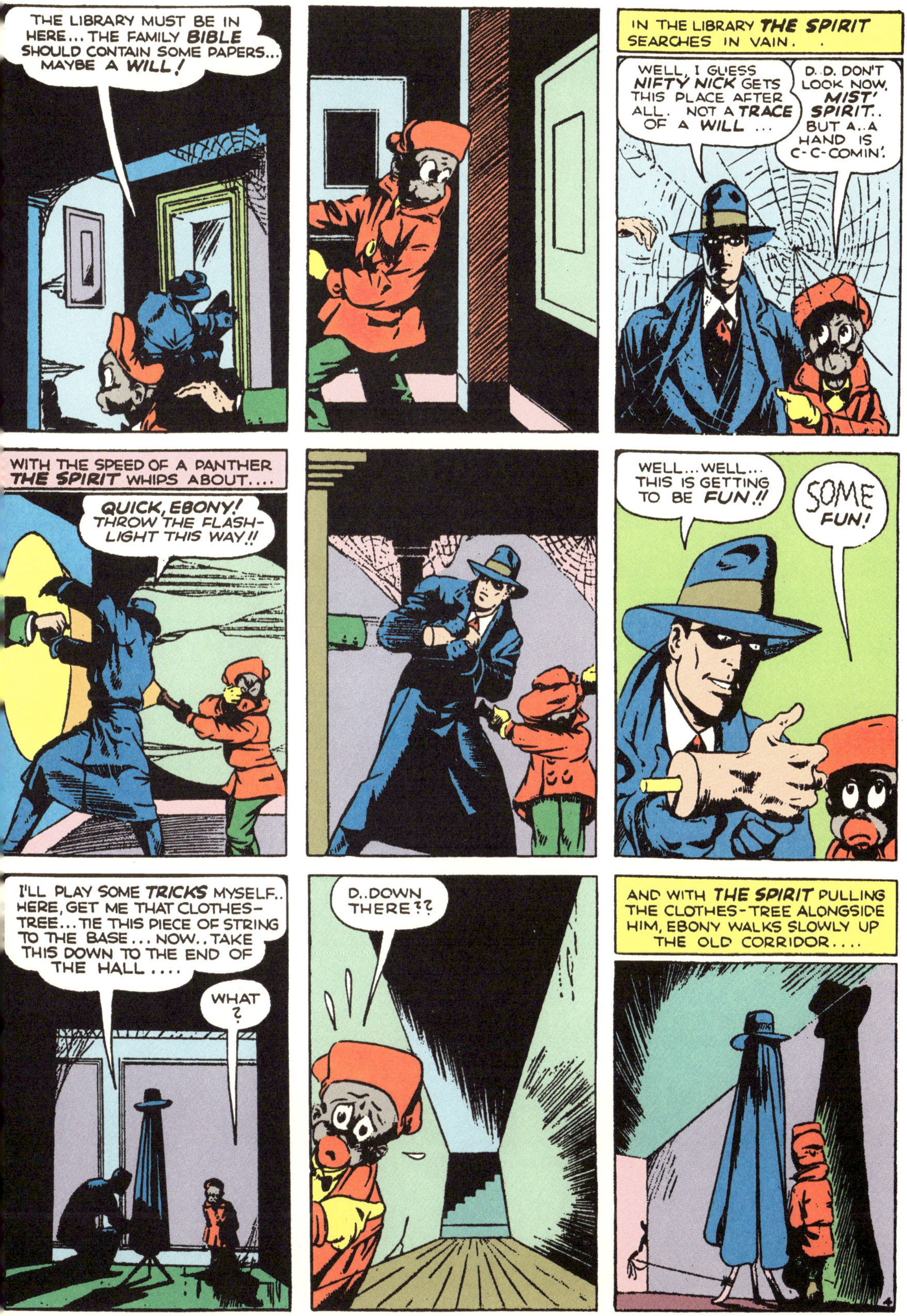
THE LIBRARY MUST BE IN HERE... THE FAMILY BIBLE SHOULD CONTAIN SOME PAPERS... MAYBE A WILL!
IN THE LIBRARY THE SPIRIT SEARCHES IN VAIN.
WELL, I GUESS NIFTY NICK GETS THIS PLACE AFTER ALL. NOT A TRACE OF A WILL ...
D..D. DON'T LOOK NOW, MIST' SPIRIT.. BUT A..A HAND IS C-C-COMIN'.
WITH THE SPEED OF A PANTHER THE SPIRIT WHIPS ABOUT....
QUICK, EBONY! THROW THE FLASH-LIGHT THIS WAY!!
WELL... WELL... THIS IS GETTING TO BE FUN!!
SOME FUN!
I'LL PLAY SOME TRICKS MYSELF.. HERE, GET ME THAT CLOTHES-TREE... TIE THIS PIECE OF STRING TO THE BASE... NOW.. TAKE THIS DOWN TO THE END OF THE HALL....
WHAT ?
D..DOWN THERE??
AND WITH THE SPIRIT PULLING THE CLOTHES-TREE ALONGSIDE HIM, EBONY WALKS SLOWLY UP THE OLD CORRIDOR....
4

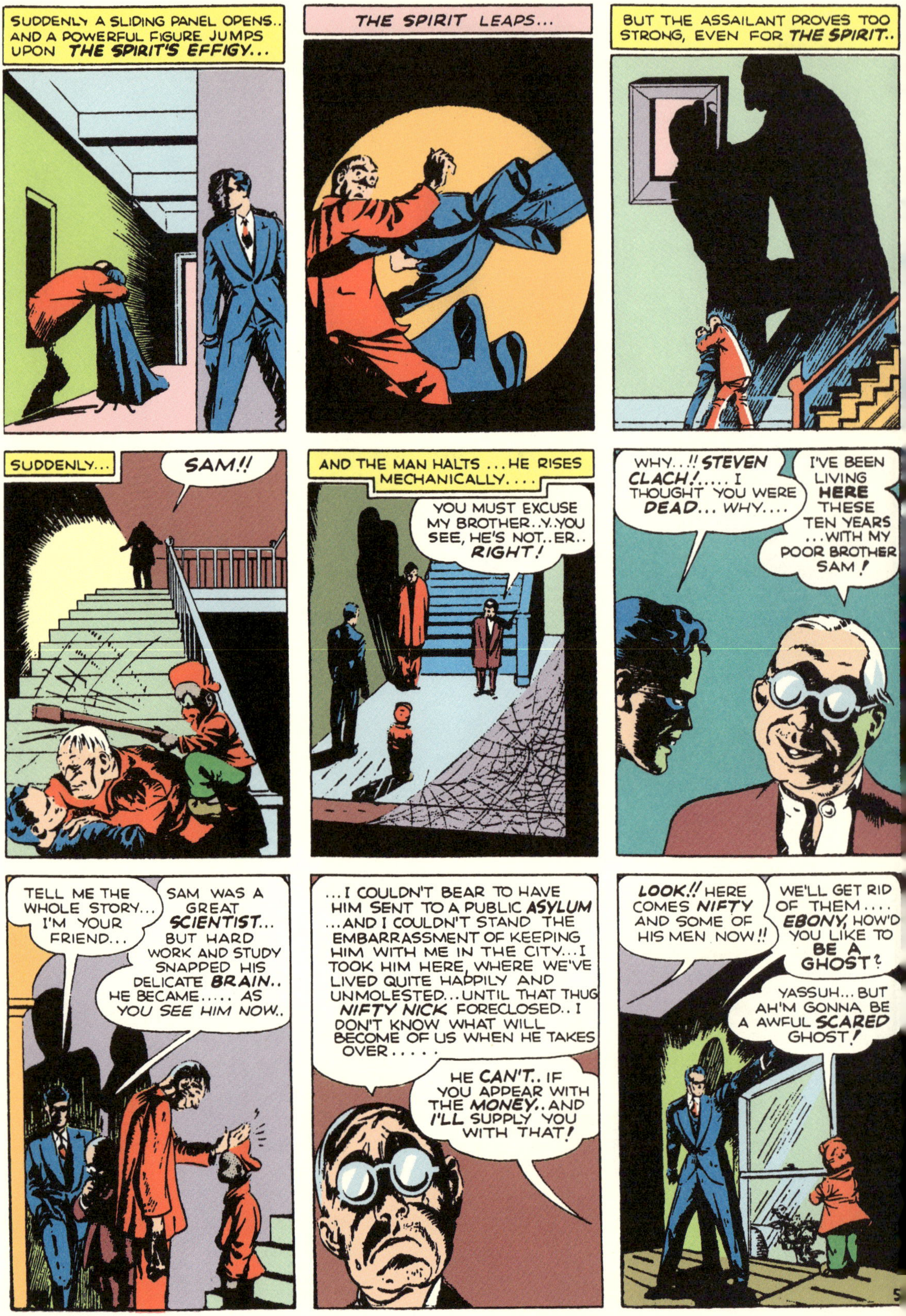

SUDDENLY A SLIDING PANEL OPENS.. AND A POWERFUL FIGURE JUMPS UPON THE SPIRIT'S EFFIGY...
THE SPIRIT LEAPS...
BUT THE ASSAILANT PROVES TOO STRONG, EVEN FOR THE SPIRIT..
SUDDENLY...
SAM!!
AND THE MAN HALTS ...HE RISES MECHANICALLY....
YOU MUST EXCUSE MY BROTHER..Y..YOU SEE, HE'S NOT..ER.. RIGHT!
WHY...!! STEVEN CLACH!..... I THOUGHT YOU WERE DEAD... WHY....
I'VE BEEN LIVING HERE THESE TEN YEARS ...WITH MY POOR BROTHER SAM!
TELL ME THE WHOLE STORY... I'M YOUR FRIEND...
SAM WAS A GREAT SCIENTIST... BUT HARD WORK AND STUDY SNAPPED HIS DELICATE BRAIN.. HE BECAME..... AS YOU SEE HIM NOW..
...I COULDN'T BEAR TO HAVE HIM SENT TO A PUBLIC ASYLUM ...AND I COULDN'T STAND THE EMBARRASSMENT OF KEEPING HIM WITH ME IN THE CITY...I TOOK HIM HERE, WHERE WE'VE LIVED QUITE HAPPILY AND UNMOLESTED...UNTIL THAT THUG NIFTY NICK FORECLOSED.. I DON'T KNOW WHAT WILL BECOME OF US WHEN HE TAKES OVER.....
HE CAN'T.. IF YOU APPEAR WITH THE MONEY..AND I'LL SUPPLY YOU WITH THAT!
LOOK!! HERE COMES NIFTY AND SOME OF HIS MEN NOW!!
WE'LL GET RID OF THEM.... EBONY, HOW'D YOU LIKE TO BE A GHOST?
YASSUH... BUT AH'M GONNA BE A AWFUL SCARED GHOST!
5

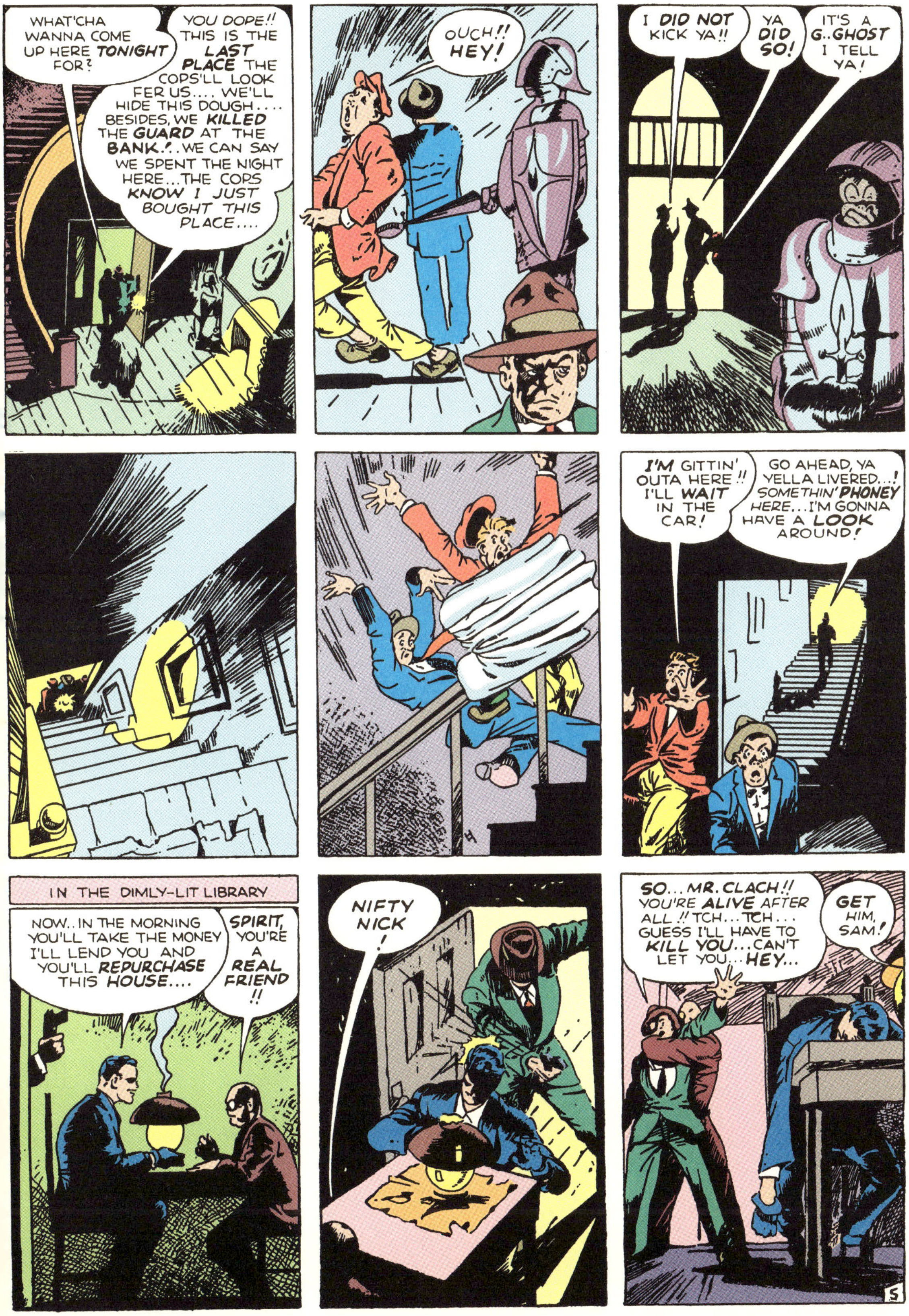
WHAT'CHA WANNA COME UP HERE TONIGHT FOR?
YOU DOPE!! THIS IS THE LAST PLACE THE COPS'LL LOOK FER US.... WE'LL HIDE THIS DOUGH.... BESIDES, WE KILLED THE GUARD AT THE BANK!..WE CAN SAY WE SPENT THE NIGHT HERE...THE COPS KNOW I JUST BOUGHT THIS PLACE....
OUCH!! HEY!
I DID NOT KICK YA!!
YA DID SO!
IT'S A G..GHOST I TELL YA!
I'M GITTIN' OUTA HERE!! I'LL WAIT IN THE CAR!
GO AHEAD, YA YELLA LIVERED...! SOMETHIN' PHONEY HERE...I'M GONNA HAVE A LOOK AROUND!
IN THE DIMLY-LIT LIBRARY
NOW..IN THE MORNING YOU'LL TAKE THE MONEY I'LL LEND YOU AND YOU'LL REPURCHASE THIS HOUSE....
SPIRIT, YOU'RE A REAL FRIEND!!
NIFTY NICK!
SO...MR. CLACH!! YOU'RE ALIVE AFTER ALL!! TCH...TCH... GUESS I'LL HAVE TO KILL YOU...CAN'T LET YOU...HEY...
GET HIM, SAM!
5

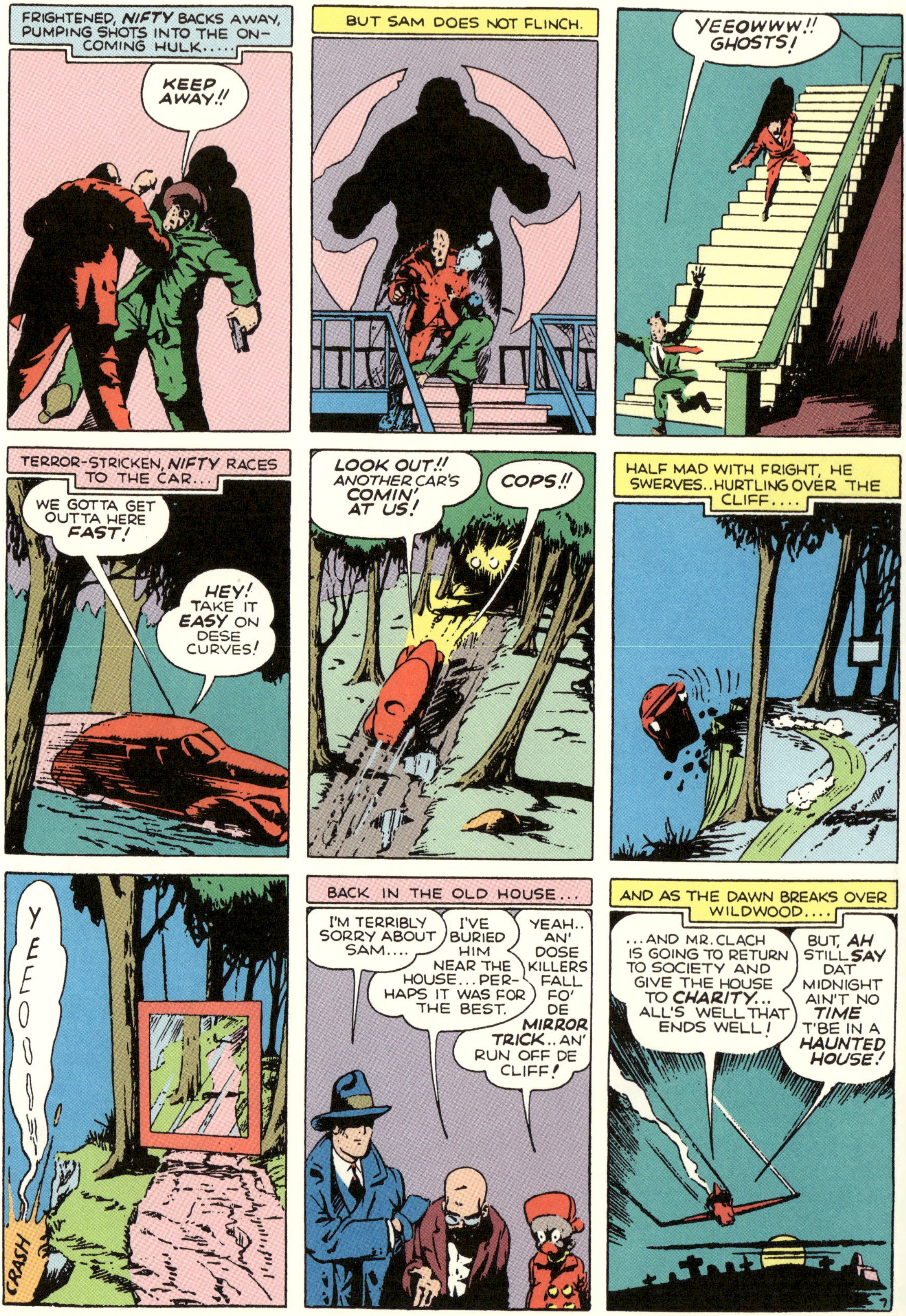
FRIGHTENED, NIFTY BACKS AWAY, PUMPING SHOTS INTO THE ON-COMING HULK.....
KEEP AWAY!!
BUT SAM DOES NOT FLINCH.
YEEOWWW!! GHOSTS!
TERROR-STRICKEN, NIFTY RACES TO THE CAR...
WE GOTTA GET OUTTA HERE FAST!
HEY! TAKE IT EASY ON DESE CURVES!
LOOK OUT!! ANOTHER CAR'S COMIN' AT US!
COPS!!
HALF MAD WITH FRIGHT, HE SWERVES..HURTLING OVER THE CLIFF....
YEEOOOW
CRASH
BACK IN THE OLD HOUSE...
I'M TERRIBLY SORRY ABOUT SAM....
I'VE BURIED HIM NEAR THE HOUSE...PER-HAPS IT WAS FOR THE BEST.
YEAH.. AN' DOSE KILLERS FALL FO' DE MIRROR TRICK..AN' RUN OFF DE CLIFF!
AND AS THE DAWN BREAKS OVER WILDWOOD....
...AND MR. CLACH IS GOING TO RETURN TO SOCIETY AND GIVE THE HOUSE TO CHARITY... ALL'S WELL THAT ENDS WELL!
BUT, AH STILL SAY DAT MIDNIGHT AIN'T NO TIME T'BE IN A HAUNTED HOUSE!

COMIC BOOK SECTION

SLIM PICKINS

3 COMPLETE STORIES

December 15, 1940

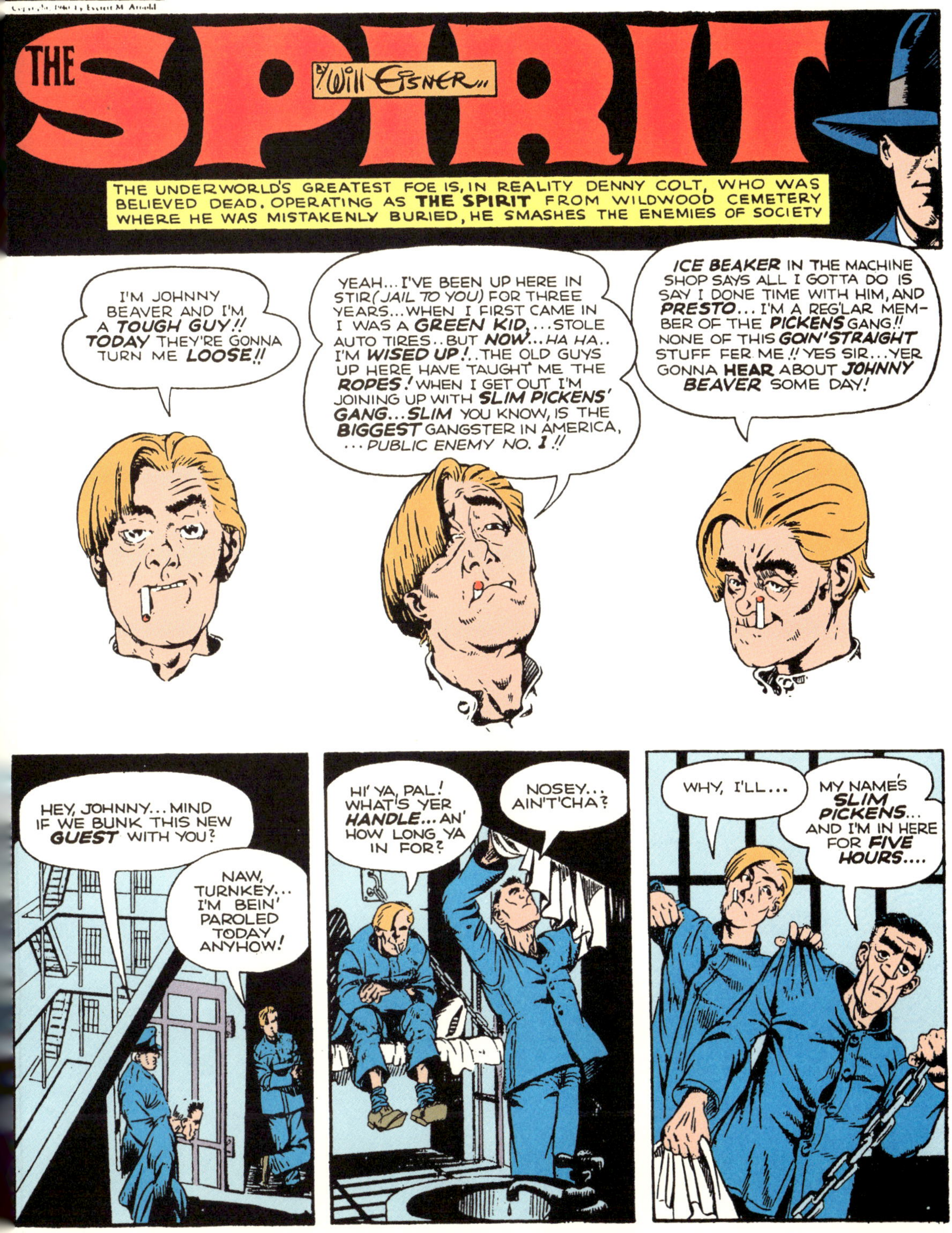

THE SPIRIT
By Will Eisner
THE UNDERWORLD'S GREATEST FOE IS, IN REALITY DENNY COLT, WHO WAS BELIEVED DEAD. OPERATING AS THE SPIRIT FROM WILDWOOD CEMETERY WHERE HE WAS MISTAKENLY BURIED, HE SMASHES THE ENEMIES OF SOCIETY
I'M JOHNNY BEAVER AND I'M A TOUGH GUY!! TODAY THEY'RE GONNA TURN ME LOOSE!!
YEAH... I'VE BEEN UP HERE IN STIR (JAIL TO YOU) FOR THREE YEARS... WHEN I FIRST CAME IN I WAS A GREEN KID, ... STOLE AUTO TIRES.. BUT NOW... HA HA.. I'M WISED UP!..THE OLD GUYS UP HERE HAVE TAUGHT ME THE ROPES! WHEN I GET OUT I'M JOINING UP WITH SLIM PICKENS' GANG... SLIM YOU KNOW, IS THE BIGGEST GANGSTER IN AMERICA, ... PUBLIC ENEMY NO. 1!!
ICE BEAKER IN THE MACHINE SHOP SAYS ALL I GOTTA DO IS SAY I DONE TIME WITH HIM, AND PRESTO... I'M A REG'LAR MEMBER OF THE PICKENS GANG!! NONE OF THIS GOIN' STRAIGHT STUFF FER ME!! YES SIR... YER GONNA HEAR ABOUT JOHNNY BEAVER SOME DAY!
HEY, JOHNNY... MIND IF WE BUNK THIS NEW GUEST WITH YOU?
NAW, TURNKEY... I'M BEIN' PAROLED TODAY ANYHOW!
HI' YA, PAL! WHAT'S YER HANDLE... AN' HOW LONG YA IN FOR?
NOSEY... AIN'T'CHA?
WHY, I'LL...
MY NAME'S SLIM PICKENS... AND I'M IN HERE FOR FIVE HOURS....

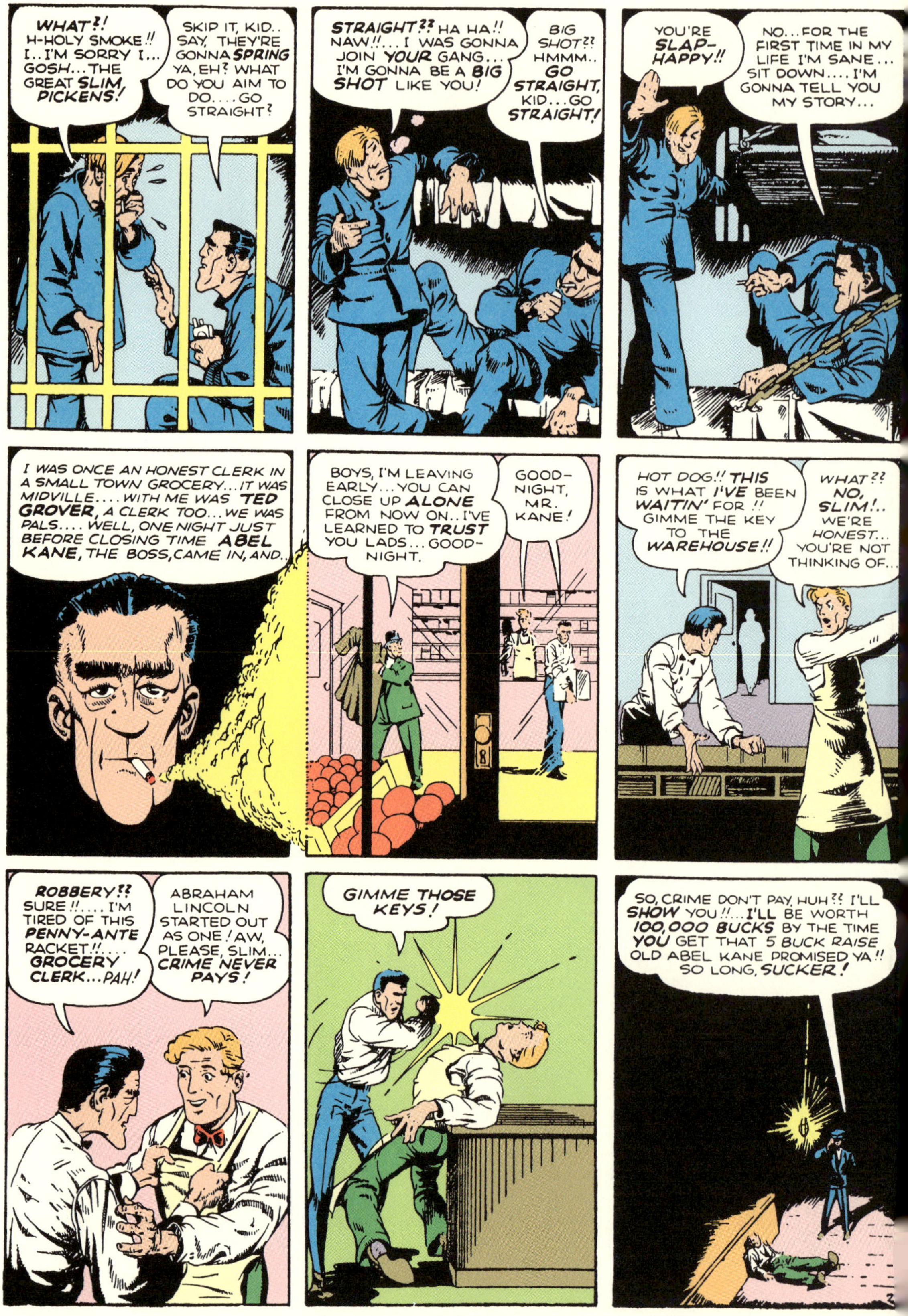
WHAT?! H-HOLY SMOKE!! I..I'M SORRY I... GOSH...THE GREAT SLIM PICKENS!
SKIP IT, KID.. SAY, THEY'RE GONNA SPRING YA, EH? WHAT DO YOU AIM TO DO....GO STRAIGHT?
STRAIGHT?? HA HA!! NAW!!... I WAS GONNA JOIN YOUR GANG... I'M GONNA BE A BIG SHOT LIKE YOU!
BIG SHOT?? HMMM.. GO STRAIGHT, KID...GO STRAIGHT!
YOU'RE SLAP-HAPPY!!
NO...FOR THE FIRST TIME IN MY LIFE I'M SANE... SIT DOWN....I'M GONNA TELL YOU MY STORY...
I WAS ONCE AN HONEST CLERK IN A SMALL TOWN GROCERY...IT WAS MIDVILLE....WITH ME WAS TED GROVER, A CLERK TOO...WE WAS PALS....WELL, ONE NIGHT JUST BEFORE CLOSING TIME ABEL KANE, THE BOSS, CAME IN, AND..
BOYS, I'M LEAVING EARLY...YOU CAN CLOSE UP ALONE FROM NOW ON..I'VE LEARNED TO TRUST YOU LADS...GOOD-NIGHT.
GOOD-NIGHT, MR. KANE!
HOT DOG!! THIS IS WHAT I'VE BEEN WAITIN' FOR!! GIMME THE KEY TO THE WAREHOUSE!!
WHAT?? NO, SLIM!.. WE'RE HONEST... YOU'RE NOT THINKING OF...
ROBBERY!? SURE!!....I'M TIRED OF THIS PENNY-ANTE RACKET!!.... GROCERY CLERK...PAH!
ABRAHAM LINCOLN STARTED OUT AS ONE! AW, PLEASE, SLIM... CRIME NEVER PAYS!
GIMME THOSE KEYS!
SO, CRIME DON'T PAY, HUH?? I'LL SHOW YOU!!...I'LL BE WORTH 100,000 BUCKS BY THE TIME YOU GET THAT 5 BUCK RAISE OLD ABEL KANE PROMISED YA!! SO LONG, SUCKER!

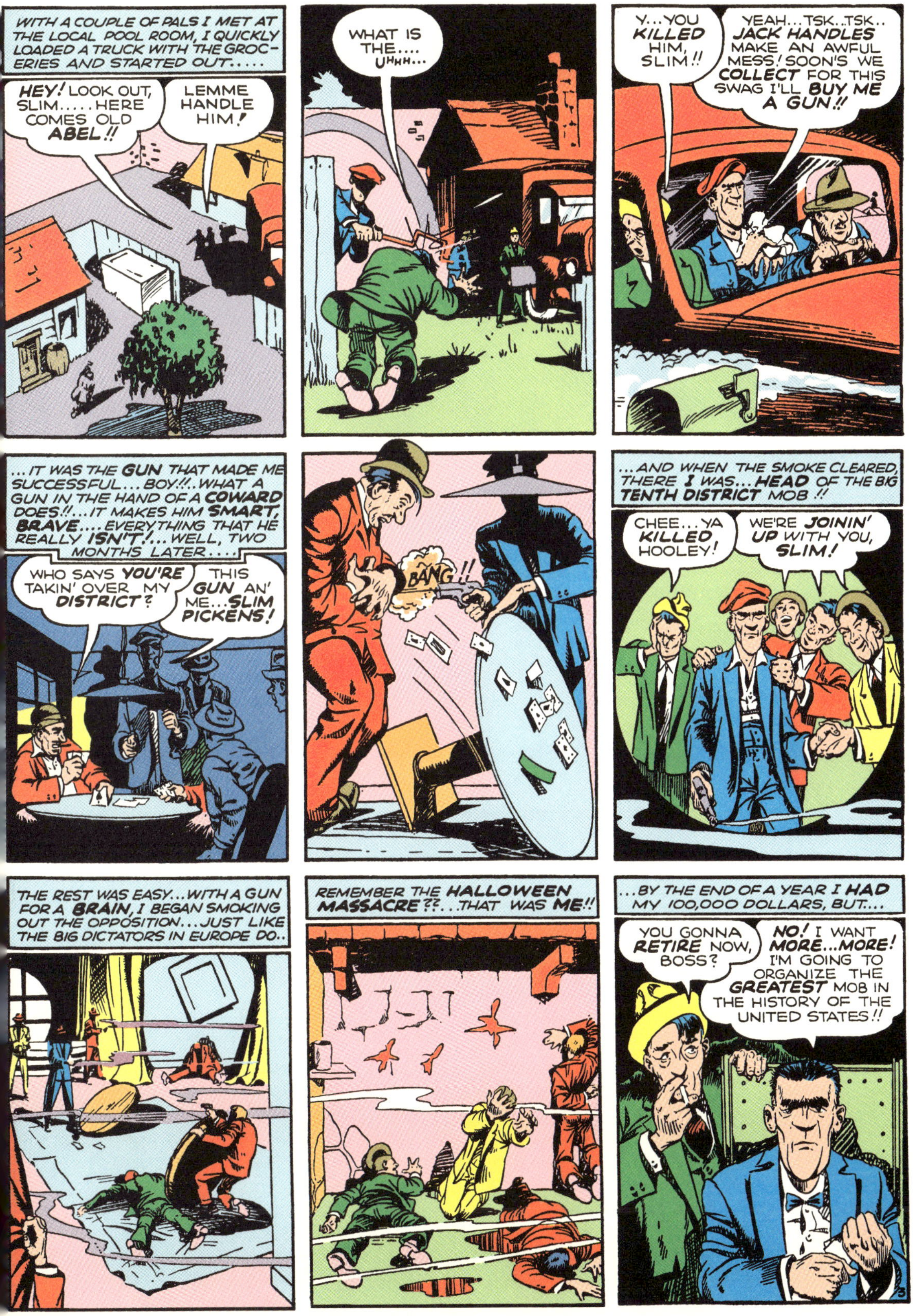

WITH A COUPLE OF PALS I MET AT THE LOCAL POOL ROOM, I QUICKLY LOADED A TRUCK WITH THE GROCERIES AND STARTED OUT.....
HEY! LOOK OUT, SLIM..... HERE COMES OLD ABEL!!
LEMME HANDLE HIM!
WHAT IS THE.... UHHH...
Y...YOU KILLED HIM, SLIM!!
YEAH...TSK..TSK.. JACK HANDLES MAKE AN AWFUL MESS! SOON'S WE COLLECT FOR THIS SWAG I'LL BUY ME A GUN!!
...IT WAS THE GUN THAT MADE ME SUCCESSFUL.... BOY!!..WHAT A GUN IN THE HAND OF A COWARD DOES!!...IT MAKES HIM SMART, BRAVE.... EVERYTHING THAT HE REALLY ISN'T!...WELL, TWO MONTHS LATER....
WHO SAYS YOU'RE TAKIN' OVER MY DISTRICT?
THIS GUN AN' ME...SLIM PICKENS!
BANG!!
...AND WHEN THE SMOKE CLEARED, THERE I WAS...HEAD OF THE BIG TENTH DISTRICT MOB!!
CHEE...YA KILLED HOOLEY!
WE'RE JOININ' UP WITH YOU, SLIM!
THE REST WAS EASY...WITH A GUN FOR A BRAIN, I BEGAN SMOKING OUT THE OPPOSITION...JUST LIKE THE BIG DICTATORS IN EUROPE DO..
REMEMBER THE HALLOWEEN MASSACRE??...THAT WAS ME!!
...BY THE END OF A YEAR I HAD MY 100,000 DOLLARS, BUT....
YOU GONNA RETIRE NOW, BOSS?
NO! I WANT MORE...MORE! I'M GOING TO ORGANIZE THE GREATEST MOB IN THE HISTORY OF THE UNITED STATES!!
3

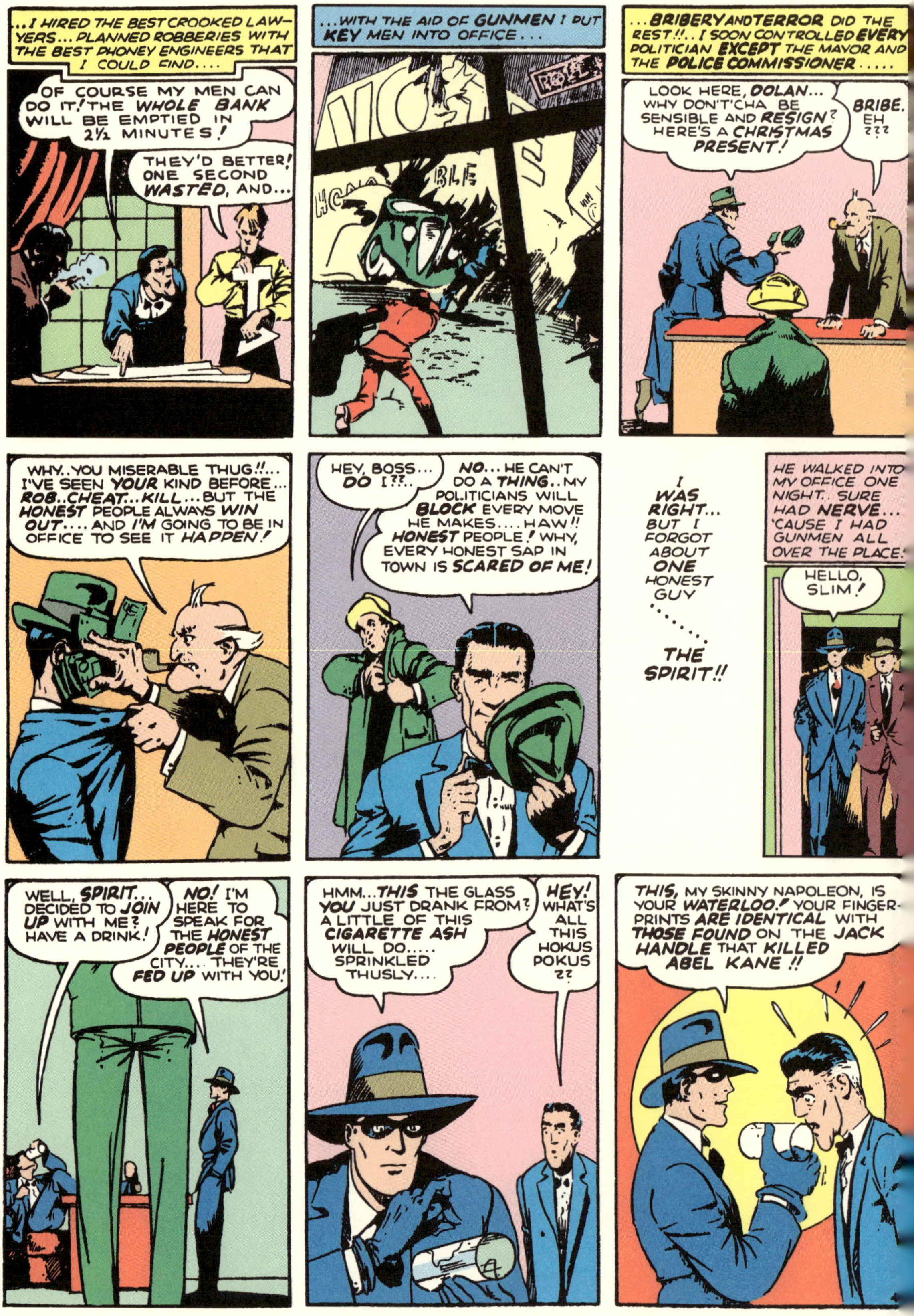
...I HIRED THE BEST CROOKED LAWYERS... PLANNED ROBBERIES WITH THE BEST PHONEY ENGINEERS THAT I COULD FIND....
OF COURSE MY MEN CAN DO IT! THE WHOLE BANK WILL BE EMPTIED IN 2½ MINUTES!
THEY'D BETTER! ONE SECOND WASTED, AND...
...WITH THE AID OF GUNMEN I PUT KEY MEN INTO OFFICE...
...BRIBERY AND TERROR DID THE REST!!..I SOON CONTROLLED EVERY POLITICIAN EXCEPT THE MAYOR AND THE POLICE COMMISSIONER.....
LOOK HERE, DOLAN... WHY DON'T'CHA BE SENSIBLE AND RESIGN? HERE'S A CHRISTMAS PRESENT!
BRIBE. EH ???
WHY..YOU MISERABLE THUG!!... I'VE SEEN YOUR KIND BEFORE... ROB..CHEAT...KILL...BUT THE HONEST PEOPLE ALWAYS WIN OUT.... AND I'M GOING TO BE IN OFFICE TO SEE IT HAPPEN!
HEY, BOSS... DO I ??..
NO... HE CAN'T DO A THING..MY POLITICIANS WILL BLOCK EVERY MOVE HE MAKES.... HAW!! HONEST PEOPLE! WHY, EVERY HONEST SAP IN TOWN IS SCARED OF ME!
I WAS RIGHT... BUT I FORGOT ABOUT ONE HONEST GUY .... THE SPIRIT!!
HE WALKED INTO MY OFFICE ONE NIGHT.. SURE HAD NERVE... 'CAUSE I HAD GUNMEN ALL OVER THE PLACE!
HELLO, SLIM!
WELL, SPIRIT... DECIDED TO JOIN UP WITH ME? HAVE A DRINK!
NO! I'M HERE TO SPEAK FOR THE HONEST PEOPLE OF THE CITY.... THEY'RE FED UP WITH YOU!
HMM...THIS THE GLASS YOU JUST DRANK FROM? A LITTLE OF THIS CIGARETTE ASH WILL DO..... SPRINKLED THUSLY....
HEY! WHAT'S ALL THIS HOKUS POKUS ??
THIS, MY SKINNY NAPOLEON, IS YOUR WATERLOO! YOUR FINGER-PRINTS ARE IDENTICAL WITH THOSE FOUND ON THE JACK HANDLE THAT KILLED ABEL KANE !!

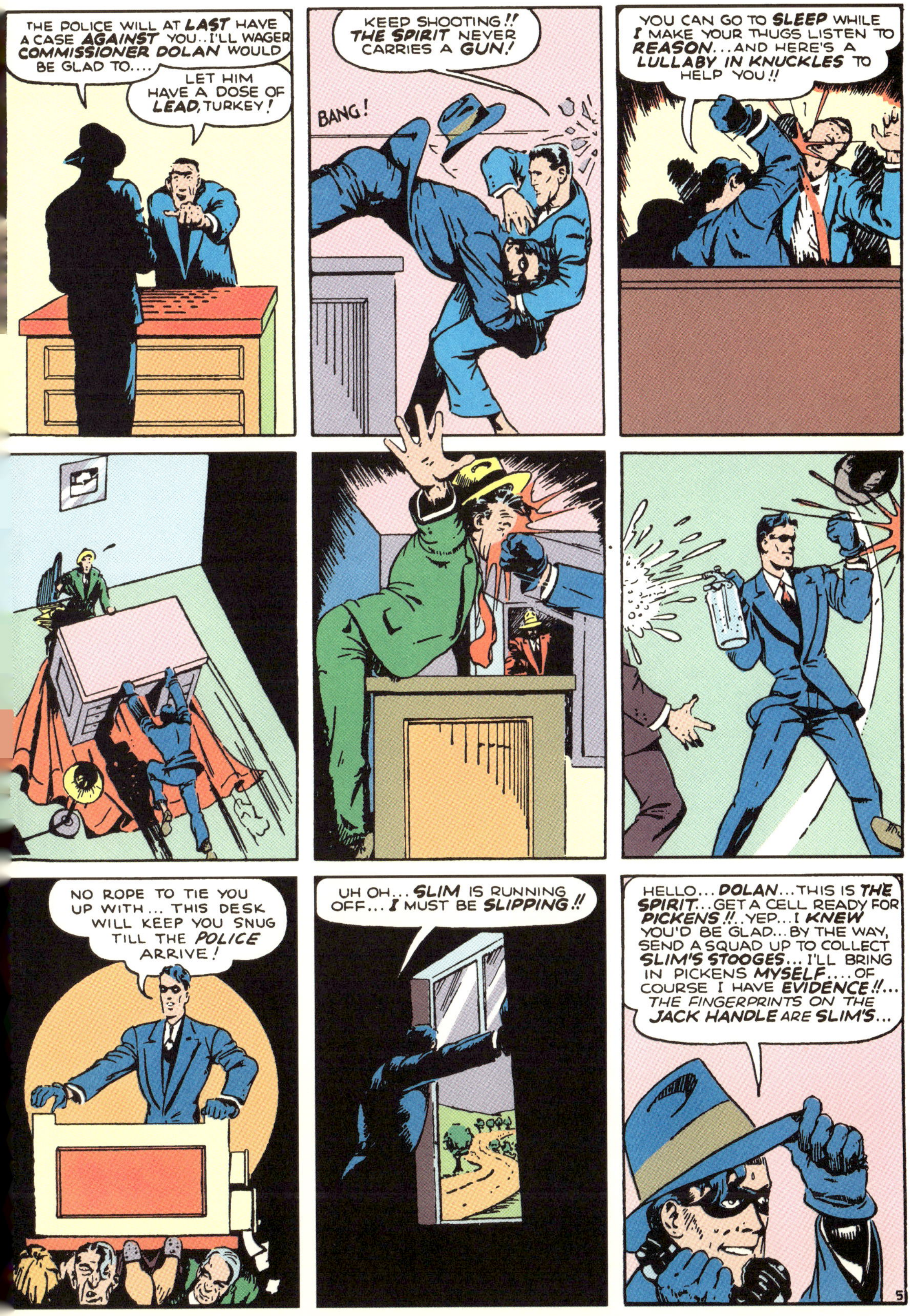
THE POLICE WILL AT LAST HAVE A CASE AGAINST YOU..I'LL WAGER COMMISSIONER DOLAN WOULD BE GLAD TO....
LET HIM HAVE A DOSE OF LEAD, TURKEY!
KEEP SHOOTING!! THE SPIRIT NEVER CARRIES A GUN!
BANG!
YOU CAN GO TO SLEEP WHILE I MAKE YOUR THUGS LISTEN TO REASON...AND HERE'S A LULLABY IN KNUCKLES TO HELP YOU!!
NO ROPE TO TIE YOU UP WITH... THIS DESK WILL KEEP YOU SNUG TILL THE POLICE ARRIVE!
UH OH... SLIM IS RUNNING OFF... I MUST BE SLIPPING!!
HELLO... DOLAN... THIS IS THE SPIRIT...GET A CELL READY FOR PICKENS!!..YEP...I KNEW YOU'D BE GLAD... BY THE WAY, SEND A SQUAD UP TO COLLECT SLIM'S STOOGES... I'LL BRING IN PICKENS MYSELF.... OF COURSE I HAVE EVIDENCE!!... THE FINGERPRINTS ON THE JACK HANDLE ARE SLIM'S...
5

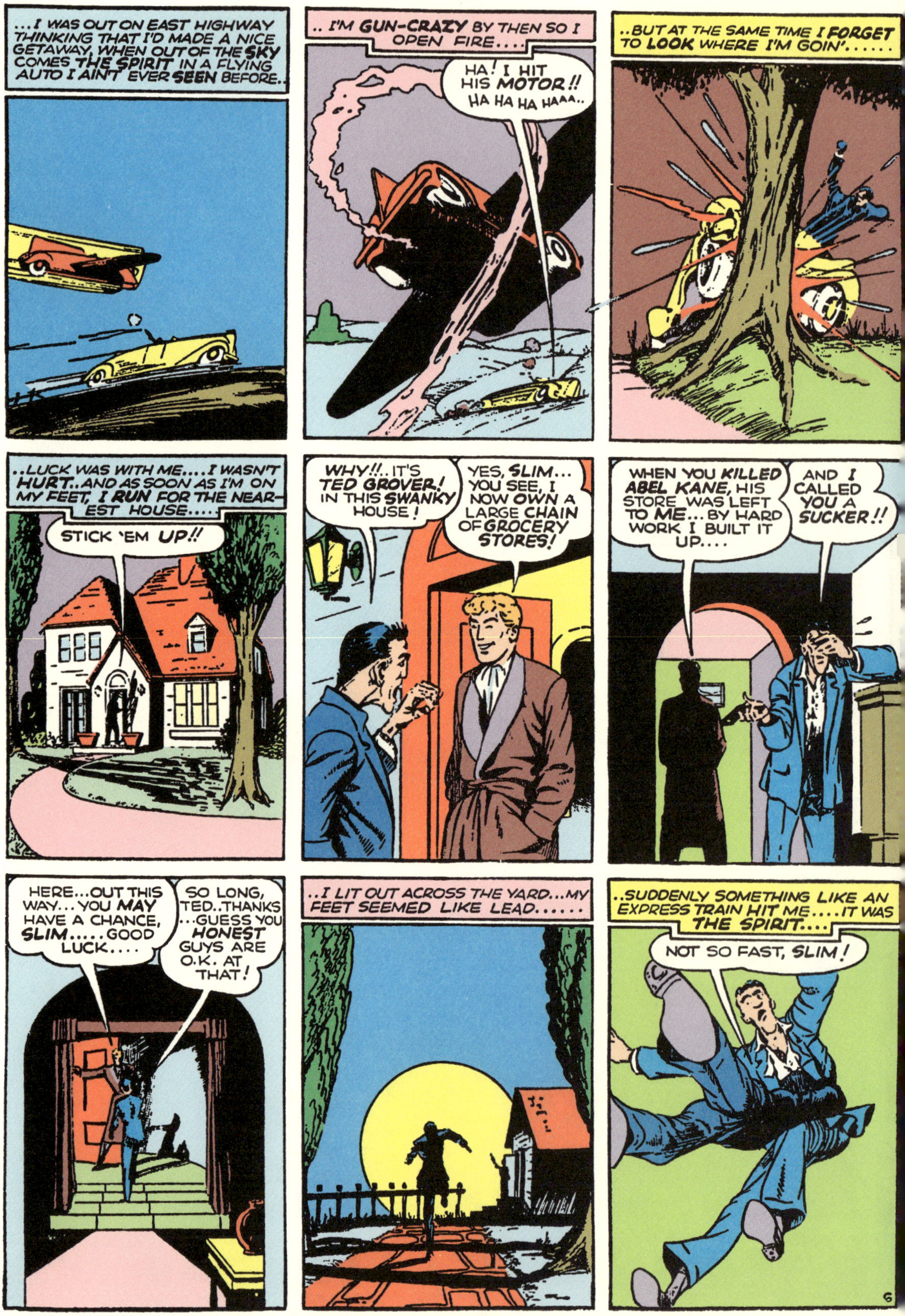
...I WAS OUT ON EAST HIGHWAY THINKING THAT I'D MADE A NICE GETAWAY, WHEN OUT OF THE SKY COMES THE SPIRIT IN A FLYING AUTO I AIN'T EVER SEEN BEFORE..
.. I'M GUN-CRAZY BY THEN SO I OPEN FIRE....
HA! I HIT HIS MOTOR!! HA HA HA HAAA..
..BUT AT THE SAME TIME I FORGET TO LOOK WHERE I'M GOIN'......
..LUCK WAS WITH ME....I WASN'T HURT..AND AS SOON AS I'M ON MY FEET, I RUN FOR THE NEAREST HOUSE....
STICK 'EM UP!!
WHY!!.. IT'S TED GROVER! IN THIS SWANKY HOUSE!
YES, SLIM... YOU SEE, I NOW OWN A LARGE CHAIN OF GROCERY STORES!
WHEN YOU KILLED ABEL KANE, HIS STORE WAS LEFT TO ME... BY HARD WORK I BUILT IT UP....
AND I CALLED YOU A SUCKER!!
HERE...OUT THIS WAY... YOU MAY HAVE A CHANCE, SLIM.....GOOD LUCK....
SO LONG, TED..THANKS ...GUESS YOU HONEST GUYS ARE O.K. AT THAT!
..I LIT OUT ACROSS THE YARD...MY FEET SEEMED LIKE LEAD......
..SUDDENLY SOMETHING LIKE AN EXPRESS TRAIN HIT ME....IT WAS THE SPIRIT....
NOT SO FAST, SLIM!
6

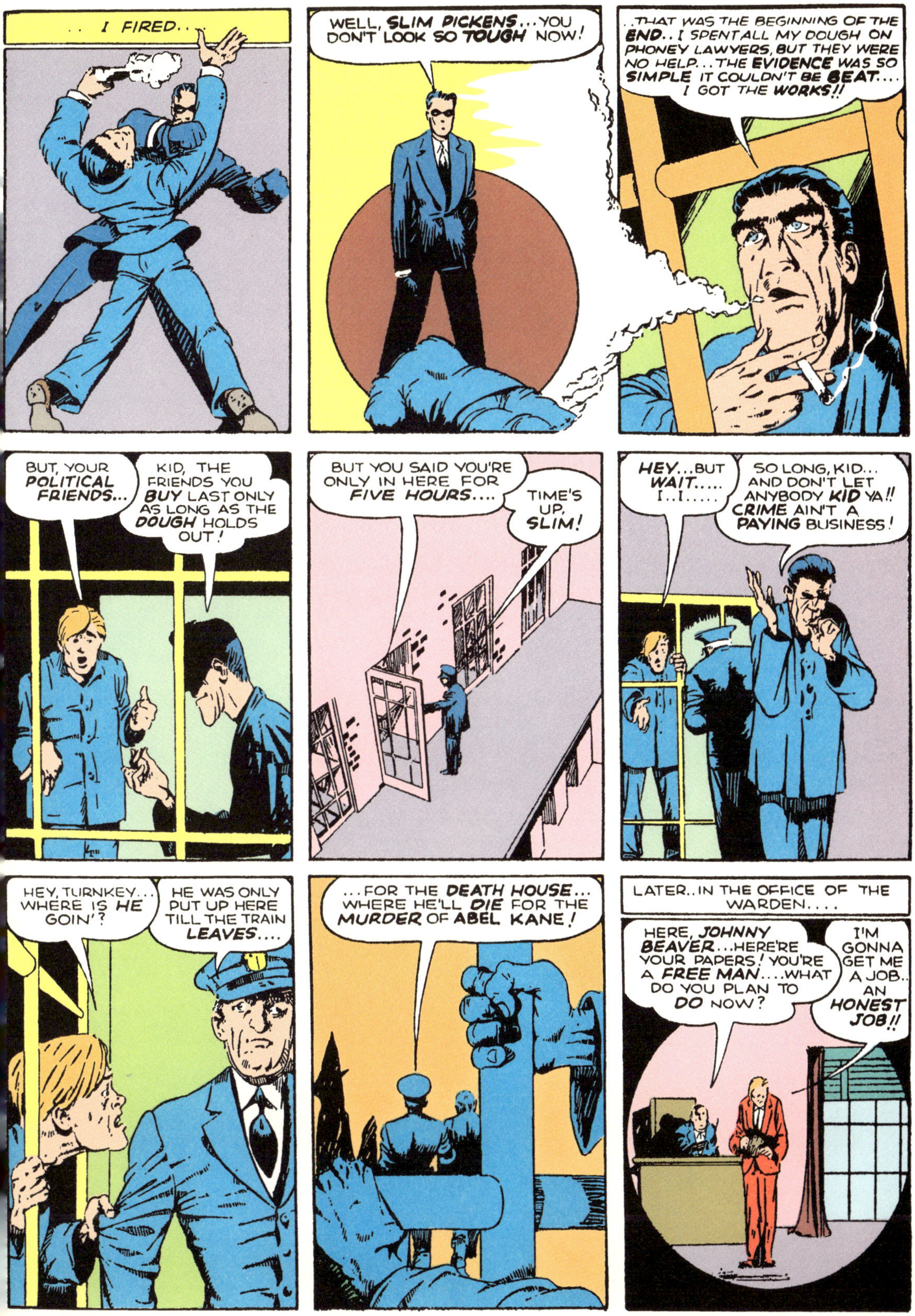

.. I FIRED...
WELL, SLIM PICKENS...YOU DON'T LOOK SO TOUGH NOW!
..THAT WAS THE BEGINNING OF THE END..I SPENT ALL MY DOUGH ON PHONEY LAWYERS, BUT THEY WERE NO HELP...THE EVIDENCE WAS SO SIMPLE IT COULDN'T BE BEAT.... I GOT THE WORKS!!
BUT, YOUR POLITICAL FRIENDS...
KID, THE FRIENDS YOU BUY LAST ONLY AS LONG AS THE DOUGH HOLDS OUT!
BUT YOU SAID YOU'RE ONLY IN HERE FOR FIVE HOURS....
TIME'S UP, SLIM!
HEY...BUT WAIT..... I..I.....
SO LONG, KID... AND DON'T LET ANYBODY KID YA!! CRIME AIN'T A PAYING BUSINESS!
HEY, TURNKEY... WHERE IS HE GOIN'?
HE WAS ONLY PUT UP HERE TILL THE TRAIN LEAVES....
...FOR THE DEATH HOUSE... WHERE HE'LL DIE FOR THE MURDER OF ABEL KANE!
LATER..IN THE OFFICE OF THE WARDEN....
HERE, JOHNNY BEAVER...HERE'RE YOUR PAPERS! YOU'RE A FREE MAN....WHAT DO YOU PLAN TO DO NOW?
I'M GONNA GET ME A JOB.. AN HONEST JOB!!

COMIC BOOK SECTION

Copyright, 1940, by Everett M. Arnold

THE CHRISTMAS SPIRIT OF 1940: BLACK HENREY AND SIMPLE SIMON

December 22, 1940

3 COMPLETE STORIES

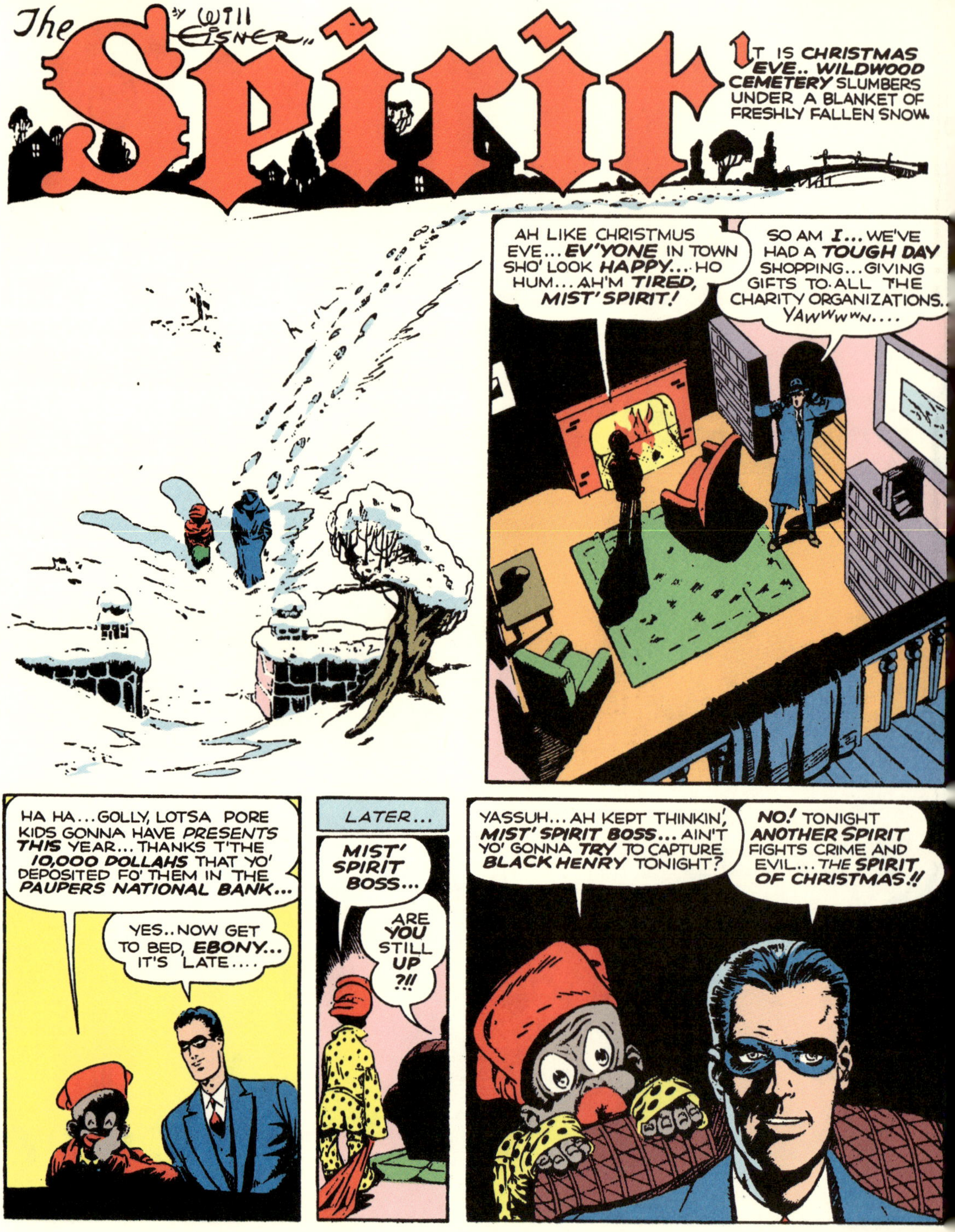

The Spirit
by Will Eisner
IT IS CHRISTMAS EVE.. WILDWOOD CEMETERY SLUMBERS UNDER A BLANKET OF FRESHLY FALLEN SNOW.
AH LIKE CHRISTMUS EVE... EV'YONE IN TOWN SHO' LOOK HAPPY... HO HUM... AH'M TIRED, MIST' SPIRIT!
SO AM I... WE'VE HAD A TOUGH DAY SHOPPING... GIVING GIFTS TO ALL THE CHARITY ORGANIZATIONS.. YAWWWWN....
HA HA... GOLLY, LOTSA PORE KIDS GONNA HAVE PRESENTS THIS YEAR... THANKS T'THE 10,000 DOLLAHS THAT YO' DEPOSITED FO' THEM IN THE PAUPERS NATIONAL BANK...
YES.. NOW GET TO BED, EBONY... IT'S LATE....
LATER...
MIST' SPIRIT BOSS...
ARE YOU STILL UP ?!!
YASSUH... AH KEPT THINKIN', MIST' SPIRIT BOSS... AIN'T YO' GONNA TRY TO CAPTURE BLACK HENRY TONIGHT?
NO! TONIGHT ANOTHER SPIRIT FIGHTS CRIME AND EVIL... THE SPIRIT OF CHRISTMAS!!

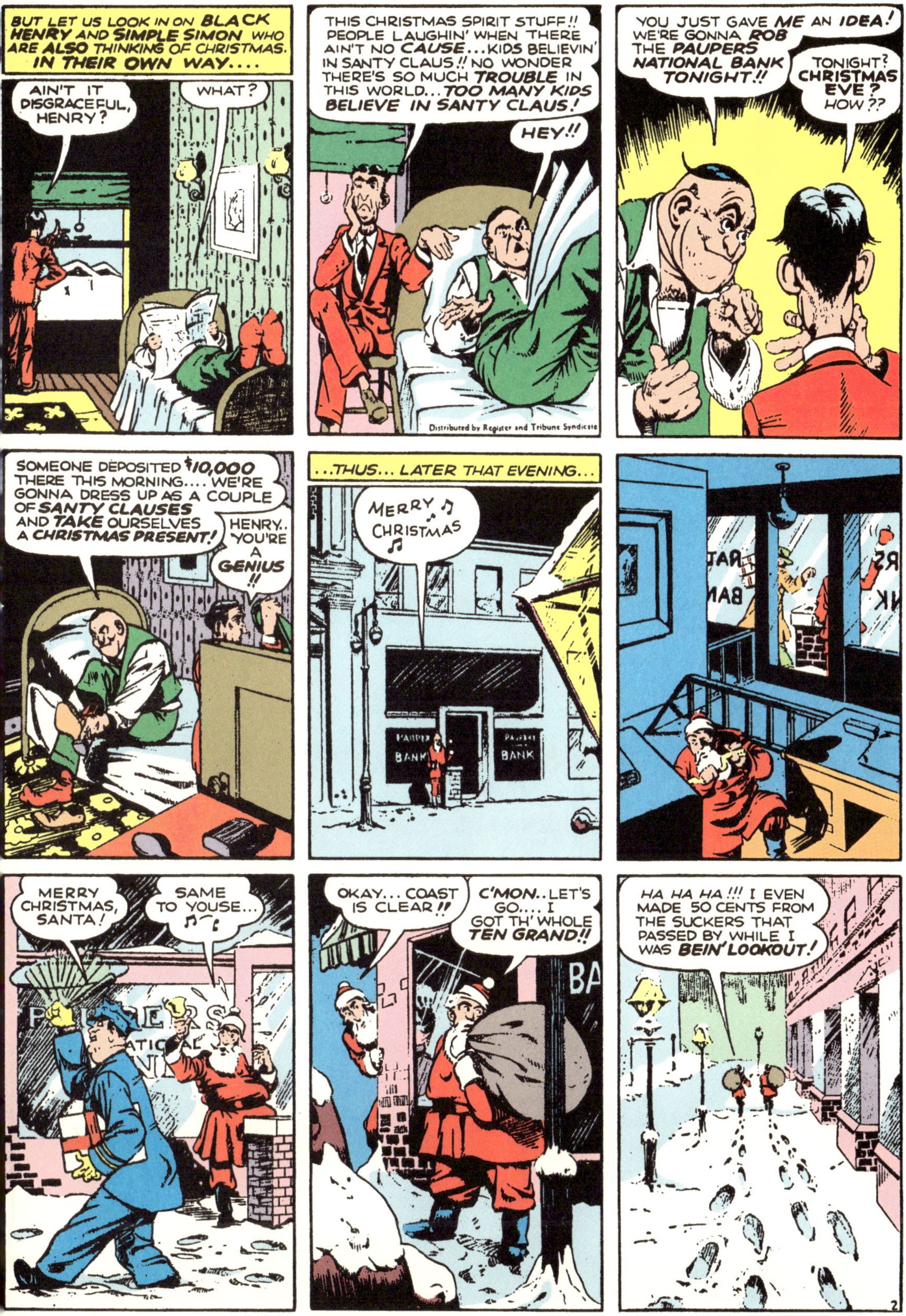
BUT LET US LOOK IN ON BLACK HENRY AND SIMPLE SIMON WHO ARE ALSO THINKING OF CHRISTMAS. IN THEIR OWN WAY....
AIN'T IT DISGRACEFUL, HENRY?
WHAT?
THIS CHRISTMAS SPIRIT STUFF!! PEOPLE LAUGHIN' WHEN THERE AIN'T NO CAUSE...KIDS BELIEVIN' IN SANTY CLAUS!! NO WONDER THERE'S SO MUCH TROUBLE IN THIS WORLD...TOO MANY KIDS BELIEVE IN SANTY CLAUS!
HEY!!
Distributed by Register and Tribune Syndicate
YOU JUST GAVE ME AN IDEA! WE'RE GONNA ROB THE PAUPERS NATIONAL BANK TONIGHT!!
TONIGHT? CHRISTMAS EVE? HOW??
SOMEONE DEPOSITED $10,000 THERE THIS MORNING.... WE'RE GONNA DRESS UP AS A COUPLE OF SANTY CLAUSES AND TAKE OURSELVES A CHRISTMAS PRESENT!
HENRY.. YOU'RE A GENIUS!!
...THUS... LATER THAT EVENING...
MERRY CHRISTMAS
BANK
BANK
MERRY CHRISTMAS, SANTA!
SAME TO YOUSE...
OKAY... COAST IS CLEAR!!
C'MON.. LET'S GO.... I GOT TH' WHOLE TEN GRAND!!
HA HA HA!!! I EVEN MADE 50 CENTS FROM THE SUCKERS THAT PASSED BY WHILE I WAS BEIN' LOOKOUT!
2

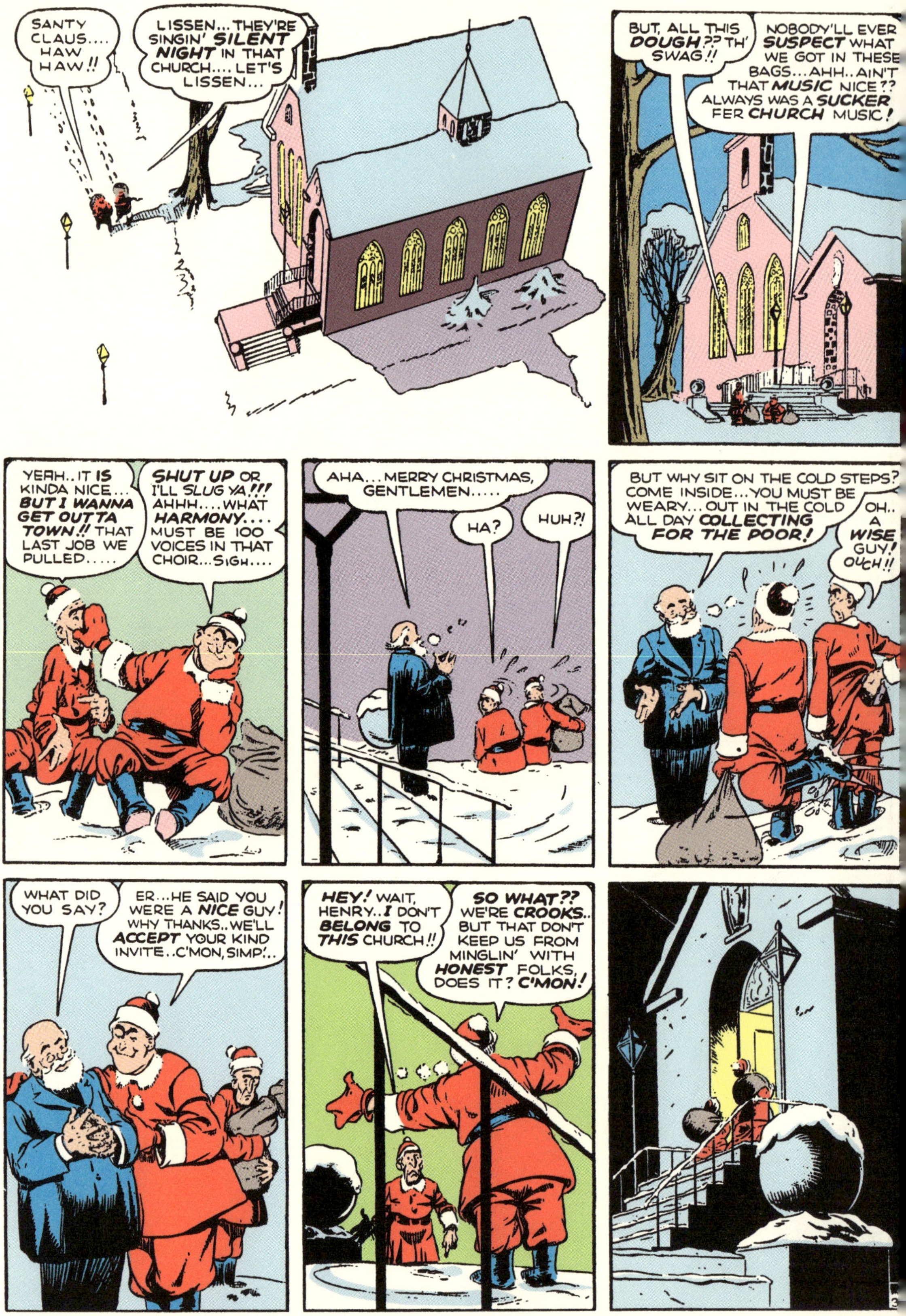

SANTY CLAUS.... HAW HAW!!
LISSEN... THEY'RE SINGIN' SILENT NIGHT IN THAT CHURCH.... LET'S LISSEN...
BUT, ALL THIS DOUGH?? TH' SWAG!!
NOBODY'LL EVER SUSPECT WHAT WE GOT IN THESE BAGS... AHH.. AIN'T THAT MUSIC NICE?? ALWAYS WAS A SUCKER FER CHURCH MUSIC!
YEAH.. IT IS KINDA NICE... BUT I WANNA GET OUTTA TOWN!! THAT LAST JOB WE PULLED.....
SHUT UP OR I'LL SLUG YA!!! AHHH.... WHAT HARMONY.... MUST BE 100 VOICES IN THAT CHOIR... SIGH....
AHA... MERRY CHRISTMAS, GENTLEMEN.....
HA?
HUH?!
BUT WHY SIT ON THE COLD STEPS? COME INSIDE... YOU MUST BE WEARY... OUT IN THE COLD ALL DAY COLLECTING FOR THE POOR!
OH.. A WISE GUY! OUCH!!
WHAT DID YOU SAY?
ER... HE SAID YOU WERE A NICE GUY! WHY THANKS.. WE'LL ACCEPT YOUR KIND INVITE.. C'MON, SIMP!..
HEY! WAIT, HENRY.. I DON'T BELONG TO THIS CHURCH!!
SO WHAT?? WE'RE CROOKS.. BUT THAT DON'T KEEP US FROM MINGLIN' WITH HONEST FOLKS, DOES IT? C'MON!

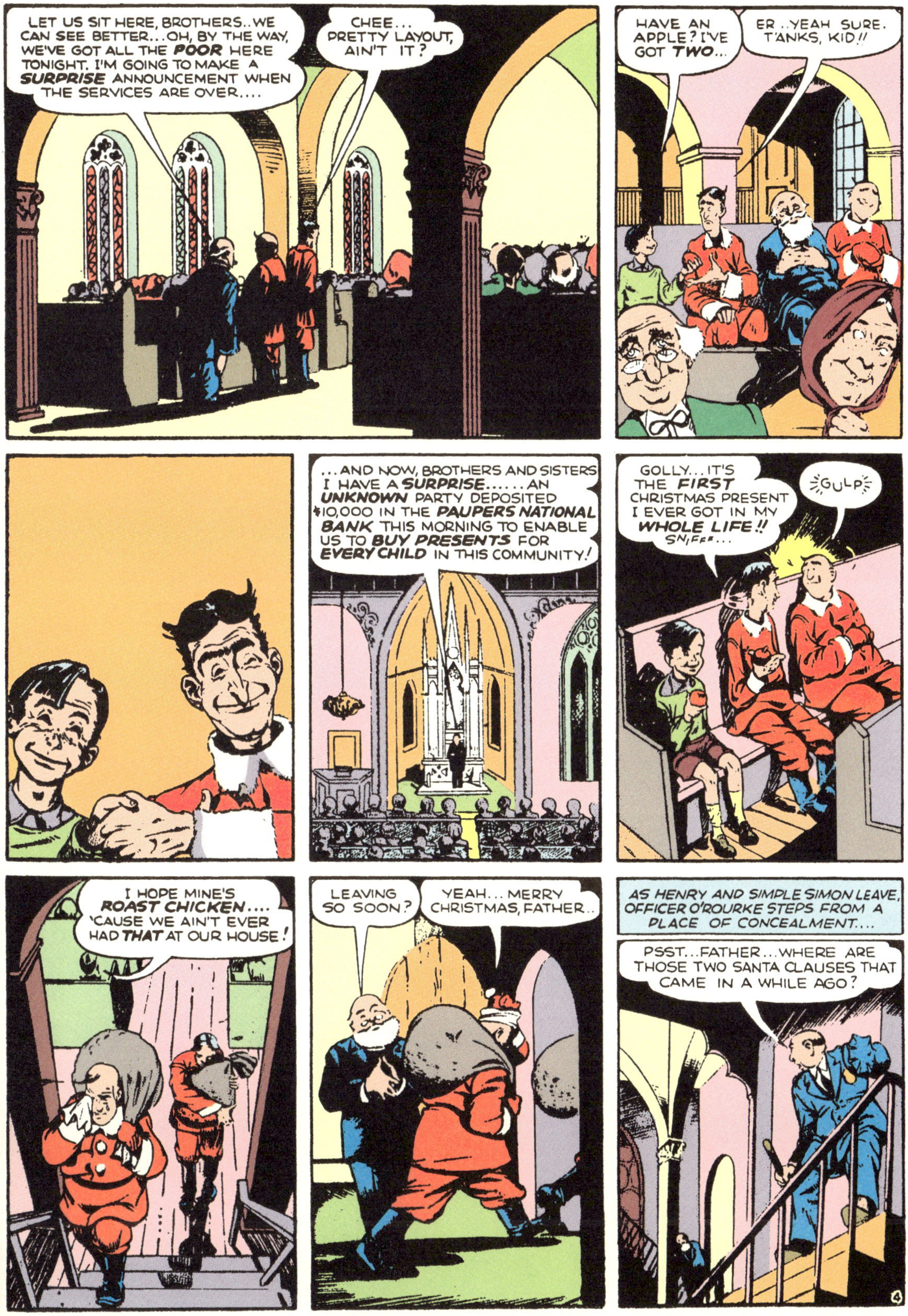
LET US SIT HERE, BROTHERS..WE CAN SEE BETTER...OH, BY THE WAY, WE'VE GOT ALL THE POOR HERE TONIGHT. I'M GOING TO MAKE A SURPRISE ANNOUNCEMENT WHEN THE SERVICES ARE OVER....
CHEE... PRETTY LAYOUT, AIN'T IT?
HAVE AN APPLE? I'VE GOT TWO...
ER..YEAH SURE. T'ANKS, KID!!
...AND NOW, BROTHERS AND SISTERS I HAVE A SURPRISE......AN UNKNOWN PARTY DEPOSITED $10,000 IN THE PAUPERS NATIONAL BANK THIS MORNING TO ENABLE US TO BUY PRESENTS FOR EVERY CHILD IN THIS COMMUNITY!
GOLLY...IT'S THE FIRST CHRISTMAS PRESENT I EVER GOT IN MY WHOLE LIFE!! SNIFFF...
GULP
I HOPE MINE'S ROAST CHICKEN.... 'CAUSE WE AIN'T EVER HAD THAT AT OUR HOUSE!
LEAVING SO SOON?
YEAH... MERRY CHRISTMAS, FATHER..
AS HENRY AND SIMPLE SIMON LEAVE, OFFICER O'ROURKE STEPS FROM A PLACE OF CONCEALMENT....
PSST...FATHER...WHERE ARE THOSE TWO SANTA CLAUSES THAT CAME IN A WHILE AGO?
4

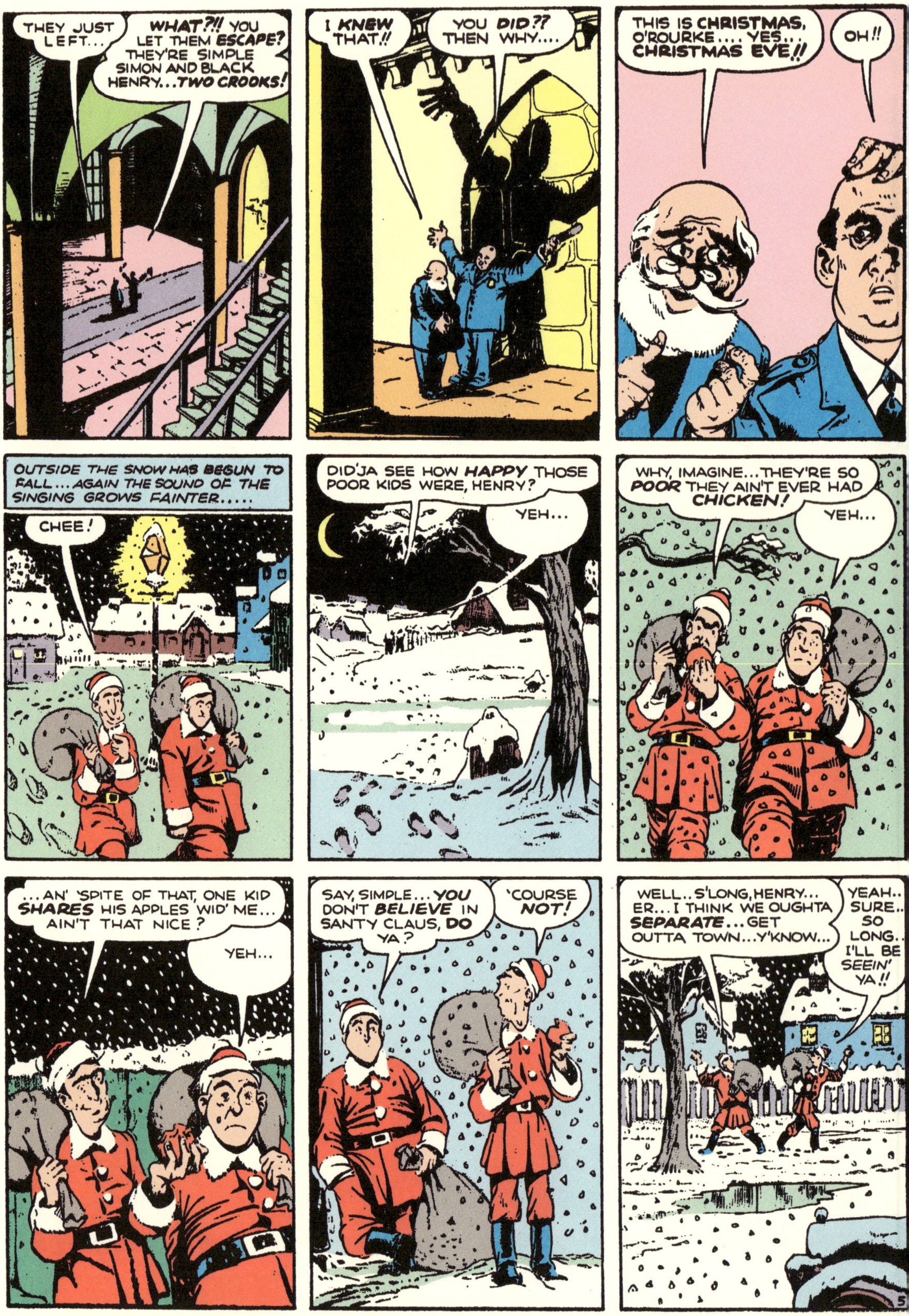
THEY JUST LEFT...
WHAT?!! YOU LET THEM ESCAPE? THEY'RE SIMPLE SIMON AND BLACK HENRY...TWO CROOKS!
I KNEW THAT!!
YOU DID?? THEN WHY....
THIS IS CHRISTMAS, O'ROURKE.... YES... CHRISTMAS EVE!!
OH!!
OUTSIDE THE SNOW HAS BEGUN TO FALL... AGAIN THE SOUND OF THE SINGING GROWS FAINTER.....
CHEE!
DID'JA SEE HOW HAPPY THOSE POOR KIDS WERE, HENRY?
YEH...
WHY, IMAGINE...THEY'RE SO POOR THEY AIN'T EVER HAD CHICKEN!
YEH...
...AN' 'SPITE OF THAT, ONE KID SHARES HIS APPLES 'WID' ME... AIN'T THAT NICE?
YEH...
SAY, SIMPLE... YOU DON'T BELIEVE IN SANTY CLAUS, DO YA?
'COURSE NOT!
WELL.. S'LONG, HENRY... ER... I THINK WE OUGHTA SEPARATE... GET OUTTA TOWN...Y'KNOW...
YEAH.. SURE.. SO LONG.. I'LL BE SEEIN' YA!!
5

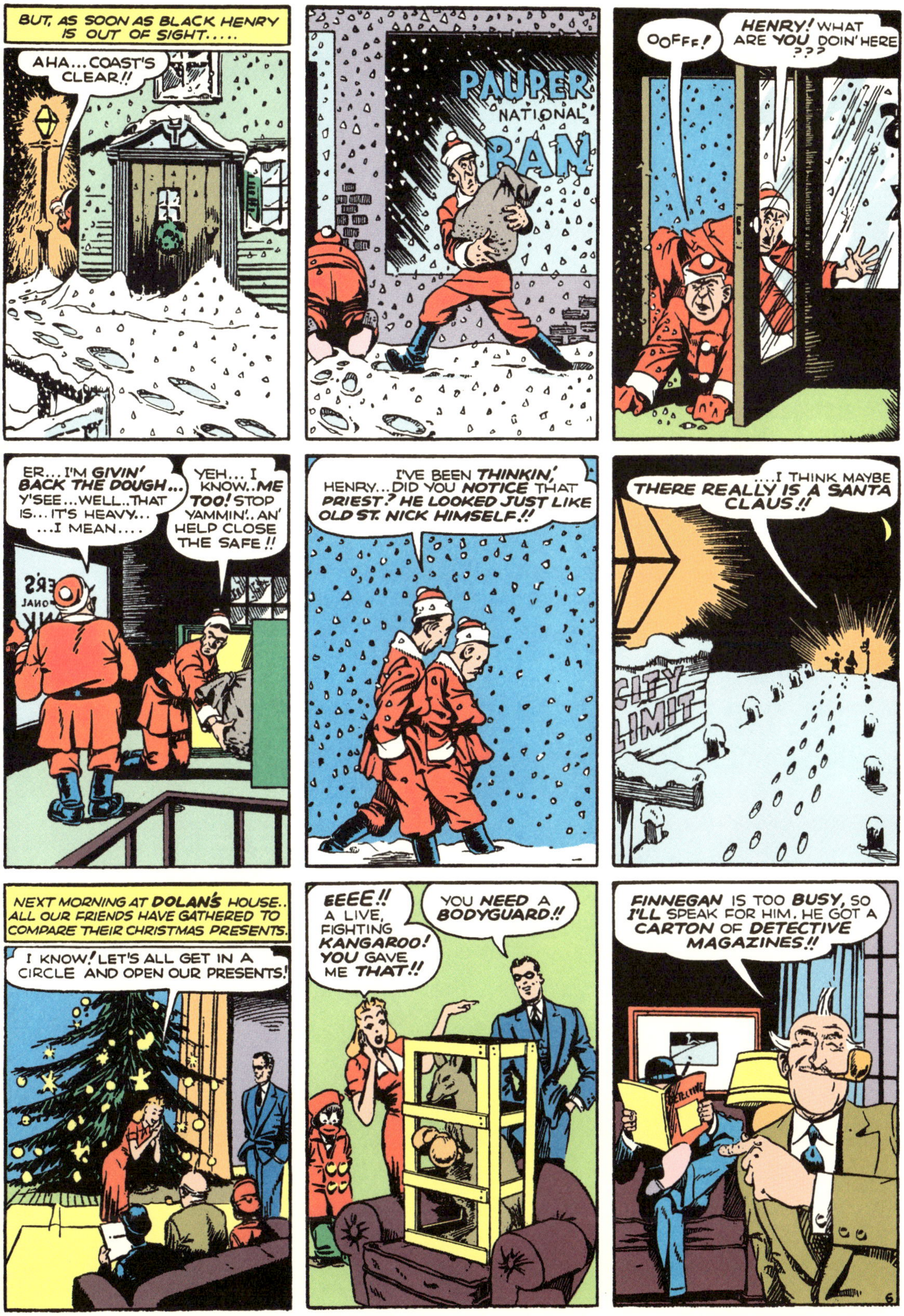
BUT, AS SOON AS BLACK HENRY IS OUT OF SIGHT.....
AHA... COAST'S CLEAR!!
PAUPER NATIONAL BAN
OOFFF!
HENRY! WHAT ARE YOU DOIN' HERE ???
ER... I'M GIVIN' BACK THE DOUGH... Y'SEE...WELL...THAT IS... IT'S HEAVY... ...I MEAN....
YEH... I KNOW..ME TOO! STOP YAMMIN'.. AN' HELP CLOSE THE SAFE!!
I'VE BEEN THINKIN', HENRY...DID YOU NOTICE THAT PRIEST? HE LOOKED JUST LIKE OLD ST. NICK HIMSELF!!
....I THINK MAYBE THERE REALLY IS A SANTA CLAUS!!
CITY LIMIT
NEXT MORNING AT DOLAN'S HOUSE.. ALL OUR FRIENDS HAVE GATHERED TO COMPARE THEIR CHRISTMAS PRESENTS.
I KNOW! LET'S ALL GET IN A CIRCLE AND OPEN OUR PRESENTS!
EEEE!! A LIVE, FIGHTING KANGAROO! YOU GAVE ME THAT!!
YOU NEED A BODYGUARD!!
FINNEGAN IS TOO BUSY, SO I'LL SPEAK FOR HIM. HE GOT A CARTON OF DETECTIVE MAGAZINES!!
DETECTIVE
6

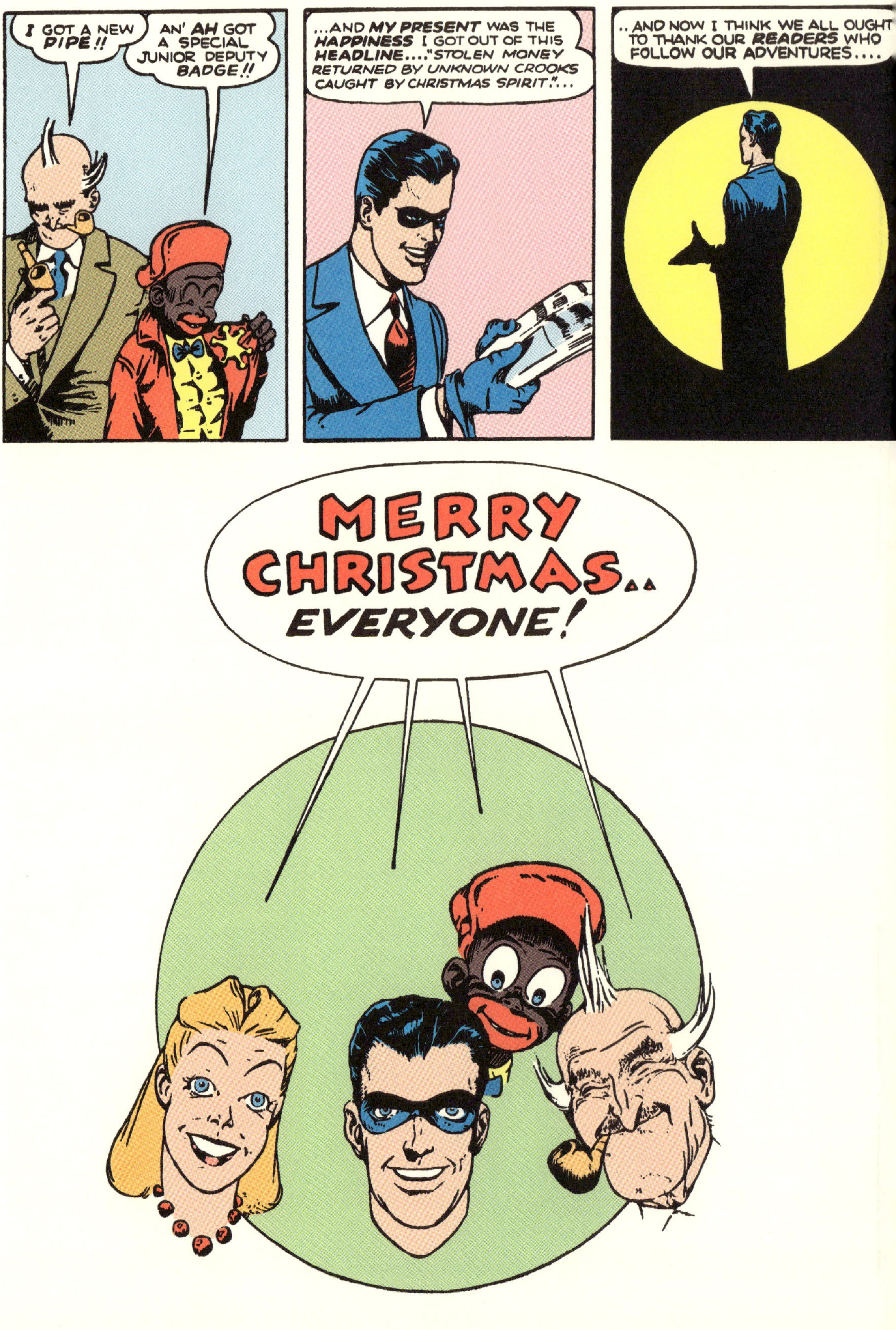
I GOT A NEW PIPE!!
AN' AH GOT A SPECIAL JUNIOR DEPUTY BADGE!!
...AND MY PRESENT WAS THE HAPPINESS I GOT OUT OF THIS HEADLINE...."STOLEN MONEY RETURNED BY UNKNOWN CROOKS CAUGHT BY CHRISTMAS SPIRIT."...
..AND NOW I THINK WE ALL OUGHT TO THANK OUR READERS WHO FOLLOW OUR ADVENTURES....
MERRY CHRISTMAS.. EVERYONE!

COMIC BOOK SECTION

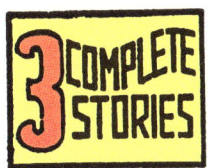

THE LEADER

December 29, 1940

3 COMPLETE STORIES

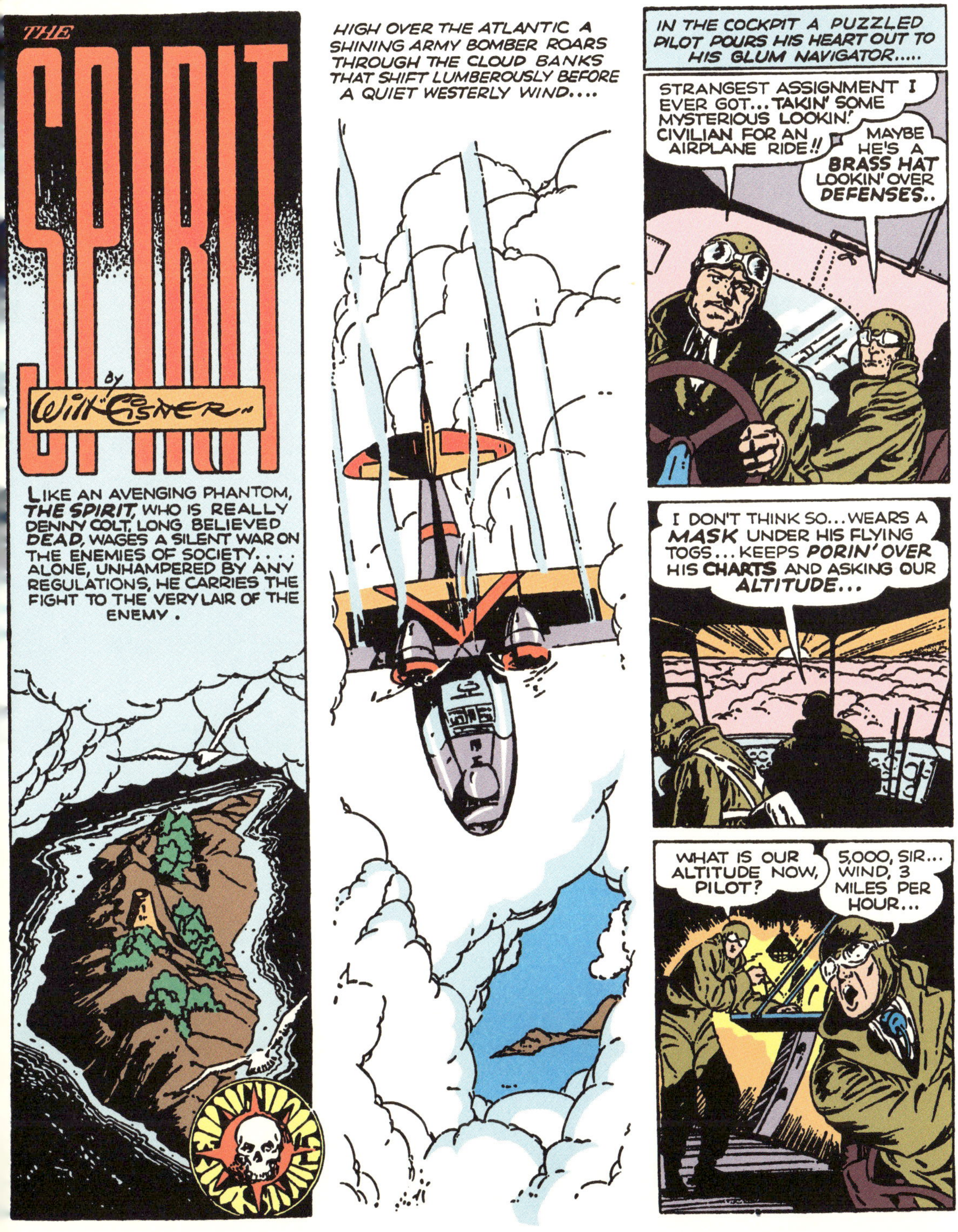

THE SPIRIT
by Will Eisner
LIKE AN AVENGING PHANTOM, THE SPIRIT, WHO IS REALLY DENNY COLT, LONG BELIEVED DEAD, WAGES A SILENT WAR ON THE ENEMIES OF SOCIETY.... ALONE, UNHAMPERED BY ANY REGULATIONS, HE CARRIES THE FIGHT TO THE VERY LAIR OF THE ENEMY.
HIGH OVER THE ATLANTIC A SHINING ARMY BOMBER ROARS THROUGH THE CLOUD BANKS THAT SHIFT LUMBEROUSLY BEFORE A QUIET WESTERLY WIND....
IN THE COCKPIT A PUZZLED PILOT POURS HIS HEART OUT TO HIS GLUM NAVIGATOR.....
STRANGEST ASSIGNMENT I EVER GOT... TAKIN' SOME MYSTERIOUS LOOKIN' CIVILIAN FOR AN AIRPLANE RIDE!!
MAYBE HE'S A BRASS HAT LOOKIN' OVER DEFENSES..
I DON'T THINK SO... WEARS A MASK UNDER HIS FLYING TOGS... KEEPS PORIN' OVER HIS CHARTS AND ASKING OUR ALTITUDE...
WHAT IS OUR ALTITUDE NOW, PILOT?
5,000, SIR... WIND, 3 MILES PER HOUR...

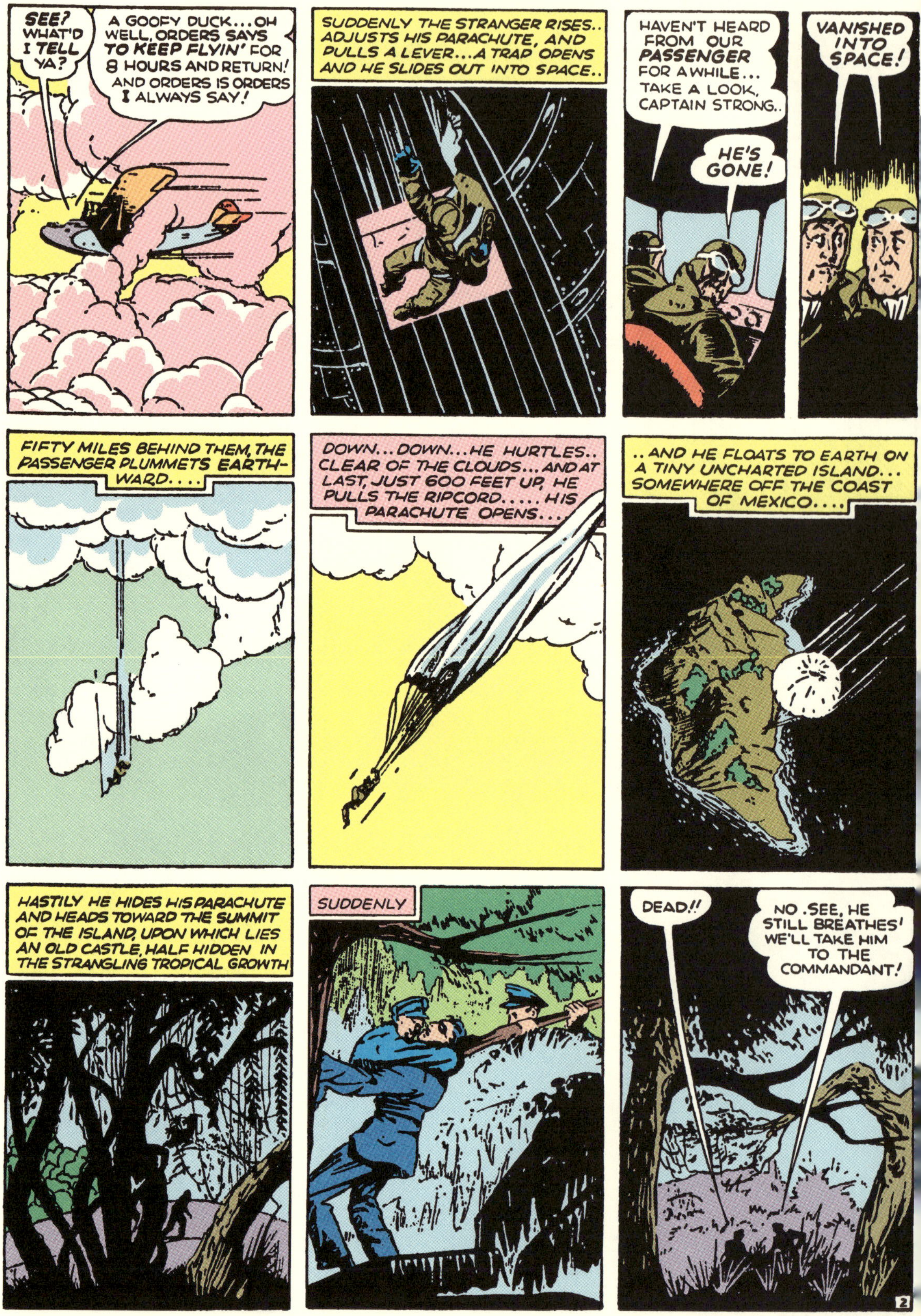
SEE? WHAT'D I TELL YA?
A GOOFY DUCK...OH WELL, ORDERS SAYS TO KEEP FLYIN' FOR 8 HOURS AND RETURN! AND ORDERS IS ORDERS I ALWAYS SAY!
SUDDENLY THE STRANGER RISES.. ADJUSTS HIS PARACHUTE, AND PULLS A LEVER...A TRAP OPENS AND HE SLIDES OUT INTO SPACE..
HAVEN'T HEARD FROM OUR PASSENGER FOR A WHILE... TAKE A LOOK, CAPTAIN STRONG..
HE'S GONE!
VANISHED INTO SPACE!
FIFTY MILES BEHIND THEM, THE PASSENGER PLUMMETS EARTHWARD...
DOWN...DOWN...HE HURTLES.. CLEAR OF THE CLOUDS...AND AT LAST, JUST 600 FEET UP, HE PULLS THE RIPCORD..... HIS PARACHUTE OPENS....
..AND HE FLOATS TO EARTH ON A TINY UNCHARTED ISLAND... SOMEWHERE OFF THE COAST OF MEXICO....
HASTILY HE HIDES HIS PARACHUTE AND HEADS TOWARD THE SUMMIT OF THE ISLAND, UPON WHICH LIES AN OLD CASTLE, HALF HIDDEN IN THE STRANGLING TROPICAL GROWTH
SUDDENLY
DEAD!!
NO .SEE, HE STILL BREATHES! WE'LL TAKE HIM TO THE COMMANDANT!
2

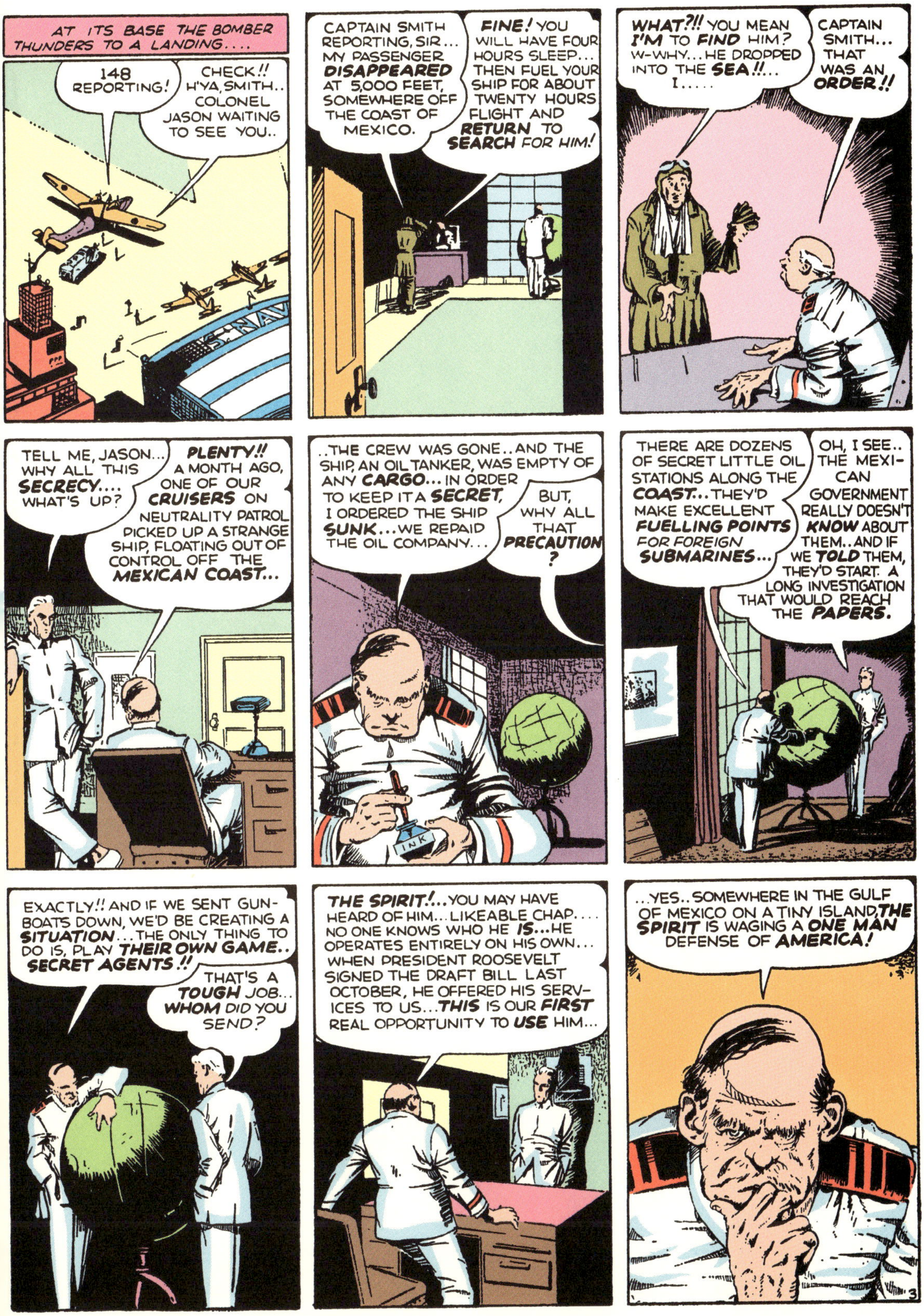
AT ITS BASE THE BOMBER THUNDERS TO A LANDING....
148 REPORTING!
CHECK!! H'YA, SMITH.. COLONEL JASON WAITING TO SEE YOU..
CAPTAIN SMITH REPORTING, SIR... MY PASSENGER DISAPPEARED AT 5,000 FEET, SOMEWHERE OFF THE COAST OF MEXICO.
FINE! YOU WILL HAVE FOUR HOURS SLEEP... THEN FUEL YOUR SHIP FOR ABOUT TWENTY HOURS FLIGHT AND RETURN TO SEARCH FOR HIM!
WHAT?!! YOU MEAN I'M TO FIND HIM? W-WHY... HE DROPPED INTO THE SEA!!... I.....
CAPTAIN SMITH... THAT WAS AN ORDER!!
TELL ME, JASON... WHY ALL THIS SECRECY.... WHAT'S UP?
PLENTY!! A MONTH AGO, ONE OF OUR CRUISERS ON NEUTRALITY PATROL PICKED UP A STRANGE SHIP, FLOATING OUT OF CONTROL OFF THE MEXICAN COAST...
..THE CREW WAS GONE.. AND THE SHIP, AN OIL TANKER, WAS EMPTY OF ANY CARGO... IN ORDER TO KEEP IT A SECRET, I ORDERED THE SHIP SUNK... WE REPAID THE OIL COMPANY...
BUT, WHY ALL THAT PRECAUTION ?
INK
THERE ARE DOZENS OF SECRET LITTLE OIL STATIONS ALONG THE COAST... THEY'D MAKE EXCELLENT FUELLING POINTS FOR FOREIGN SUBMARINES...
OH, I SEE.. THE MEXI-CAN GOVERNMENT REALLY DOESN'T KNOW ABOUT THEM.. AND IF WE TOLD THEM, THEY'D START A LONG INVESTIGATION THAT WOULD REACH THE PAPERS.
EXACTLY!! AND IF WE SENT GUN-BOATS DOWN, WE'D BE CREATING A SITUATION... THE ONLY THING TO DO IS, PLAY THEIR OWN GAME.. SECRET AGENTS!!
THAT'S A TOUGH JOB... WHOM DID YOU SEND?
THE SPIRIT!... YOU MAY HAVE HEARD OF HIM... LIKEABLE CHAP.... NO ONE KNOWS WHO HE IS... HE OPERATES ENTIRELY ON HIS OWN... WHEN PRESIDENT ROOSEVELT SIGNED THE DRAFT BILL LAST OCTOBER, HE OFFERED HIS SERV-ICES TO US... THIS IS OUR FIRST REAL OPPORTUNITY TO USE HIM...
...YES.. SOMEWHERE IN THE GULF OF MEXICO ON A TINY ISLAND, THE SPIRIT IS WAGING A ONE MAN DEFENSE OF AMERICA!
3

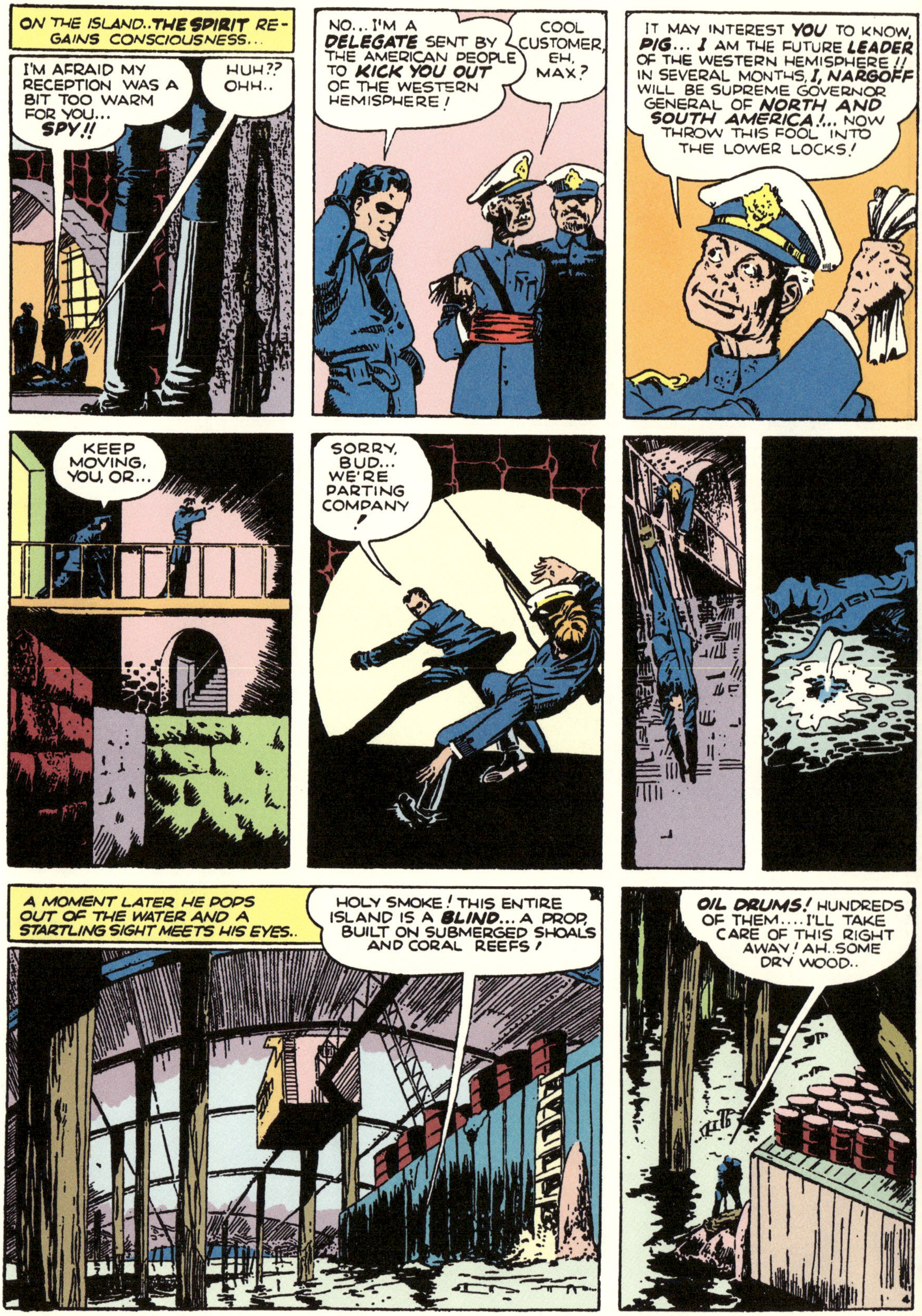
ON THE ISLAND.. THE SPIRIT RE-GAINS CONSCIOUSNESS...
I'M AFRAID MY RECEPTION WAS A BIT TOO WARM FOR YOU... SPY!!
HUH?? OHH..
NO... I'M A DELEGATE SENT BY THE AMERICAN PEOPLE TO KICK YOU OUT OF THE WESTERN HEMISPHERE!
COOL CUSTOMER, EH, MAX?
IT MAY INTEREST YOU TO KNOW, PIG... I AM THE FUTURE LEADER OF THE WESTERN HEMISPHERE!! IN SEVERAL MONTHS, I, NARGOFF WILL BE SUPREME GOVERNOR GENERAL OF NORTH AND SOUTH AMERICA!... NOW THROW THIS FOOL INTO THE LOWER LOCKS!
KEEP MOVING, YOU, OR...
SORRY, BUD... WE'RE PARTING COMPANY!
A MOMENT LATER HE POPS OUT OF THE WATER AND A STARTLING SIGHT MEETS HIS EYES..
HOLY SMOKE! THIS ENTIRE ISLAND IS A BLIND... A PROP, BUILT ON SUBMERGED SHOALS AND CORAL REEFS!
OIL DRUMS! HUNDREDS OF THEM.... I'LL TAKE CARE OF THIS RIGHT AWAY! AH.. SOME DRY WOOD..

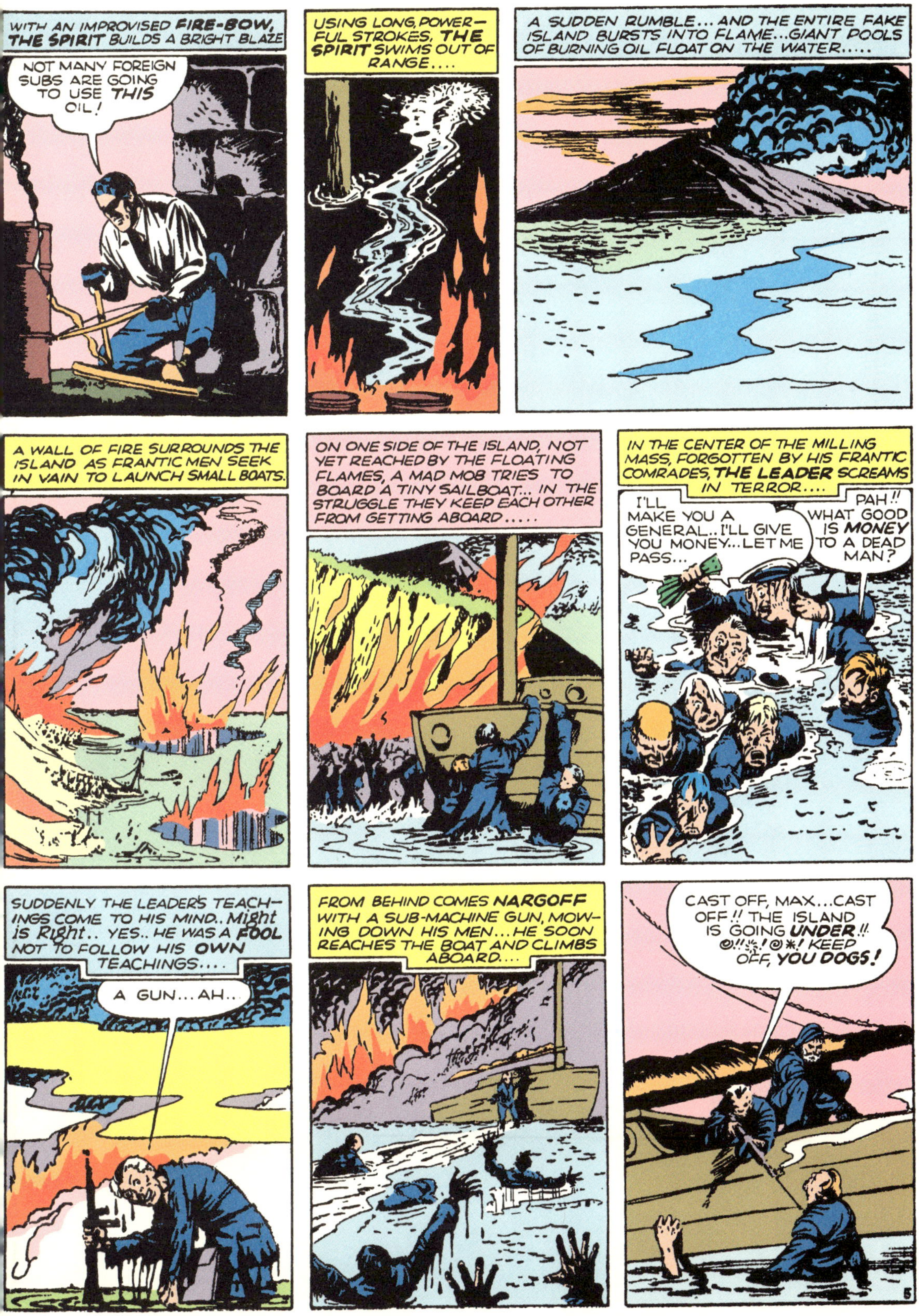
WITH AN IMPROVISED FIRE-BOW, THE SPIRIT BUILDS A BRIGHT BLAZE
NOT MANY FOREIGN SUBS ARE GOING TO USE THIS OIL!
USING LONG, POWERFUL STROKES, THE SPIRIT SWIMS OUT OF RANGE....
A SUDDEN RUMBLE... AND THE ENTIRE FAKE ISLAND BURSTS INTO FLAME...GIANT POOLS OF BURNING OIL FLOAT ON THE WATER.....
A WALL OF FIRE SURROUNDS THE ISLAND AS FRANTIC MEN SEEK IN VAIN TO LAUNCH SMALL BOATS.
ON ONE SIDE OF THE ISLAND, NOT YET REACHED BY THE FLOATING FLAMES, A MAD MOB TRIES TO BOARD A TINY SAILBOAT... IN THE STRUGGLE THEY KEEP EACH OTHER FROM GETTING ABOARD.....
IN THE CENTER OF THE MILLING MASS, FORGOTTEN BY HIS FRANTIC COMRADES, THE LEADER SCREAMS IN TERROR....
I'LL MAKE YOU A GENERAL.. I'LL GIVE YOU MONEY... LET ME PASS...
PAH!! WHAT GOOD IS MONEY TO A DEAD MAN?
SUDDENLY THE LEADER'S TEACHINGS COME TO HIS MIND.. Might is Right.. YES.. HE WAS A FOOL NOT TO FOLLOW HIS OWN TEACHINGS....
A GUN... AH..
FROM BEHIND COMES NARGOFF WITH A SUB-MACHINE GUN, MOWING DOWN HIS MEN... HE SOON REACHES THE BOAT AND CLIMBS ABOARD....
CAST OFF, MAX...CAST OFF!! THE ISLAND IS GOING UNDER!! @!!*!@*! KEEP OFF, YOU DOGS!
5

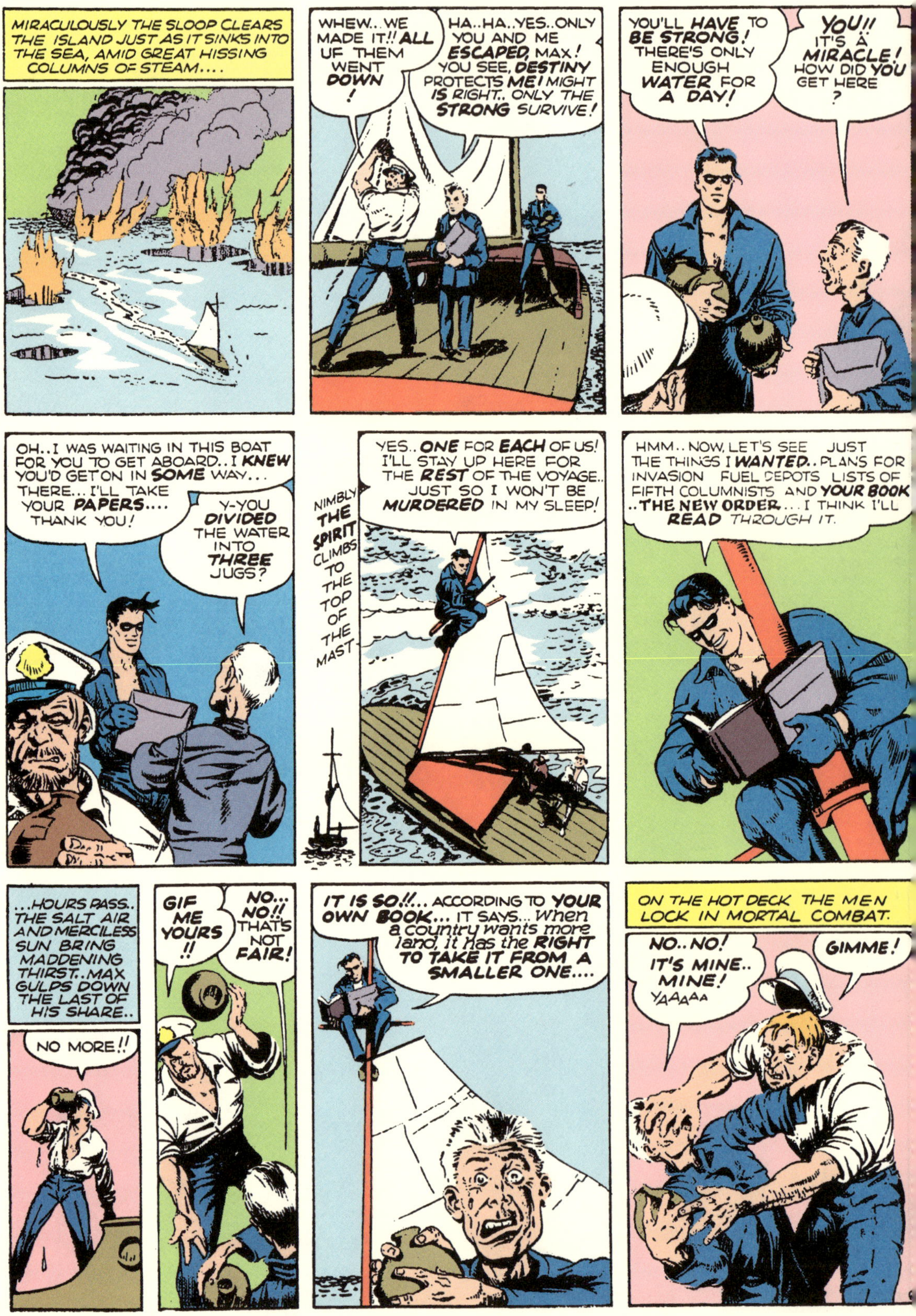

MIRACULOUSLY THE SLOOP CLEARS THE ISLAND JUST AS IT SINKS INTO THE SEA, AMID GREAT HISSING COLUMNS OF STEAM....
WHEW...WE MADE IT!! ALL OF THEM WENT DOWN!
HA..HA..YES..ONLY YOU AND ME ESCAPED, MAX! YOU SEE, DESTINY PROTECTS ME! MIGHT IS RIGHT.. ONLY THE STRONG SURVIVE!
YOU'LL HAVE TO BE STRONG! THERE'S ONLY ENOUGH WATER FOR A DAY!
YOU!! IT'S A MIRACLE! HOW DID YOU GET HERE?
OH..I WAS WAITING IN THIS BOAT FOR YOU TO GET ABOARD..I KNEW YOU'D GET ON IN SOME WAY... THERE...I'LL TAKE YOUR PAPERS.... THANK YOU!
Y-YOU DIVIDED THE WATER INTO THREE JUGS?
NIMBLY THE SPIRIT CLIMBS TO THE TOP OF THE MAST
YES..ONE FOR EACH OF US! I'LL STAY UP HERE FOR THE REST OF THE VOYAGE.. JUST SO I WON'T BE MURDERED IN MY SLEEP!
HMM..NOW, LET'S SEE JUST THE THINGS I WANTED..PLANS FOR INVASION FUEL DEPOTS LISTS OF FIFTH COLUMNISTS AND YOUR BOOK ..THE NEW ORDER...I THINK I'LL READ THROUGH IT.
...HOURS PASS.. THE SALT AIR AND MERCILESS SUN BRING MADDENING THIRST..MAX GULPS DOWN THE LAST OF HIS SHARE..
NO MORE!!
GIF ME YOURS!!
NO... NO!! THAT'S NOT FAIR!
IT IS SO!!... ACCORDING TO YOUR OWN BOOK... IT SAYS... When a country wants more land, it has the RIGHT TO TAKE IT FROM A SMALLER ONE....
ON THE HOT DECK THE MEN LOCK IN MORTAL COMBAT.
NO..NO! IT'S MINE.. MINE! YAAAAA
GIMME!

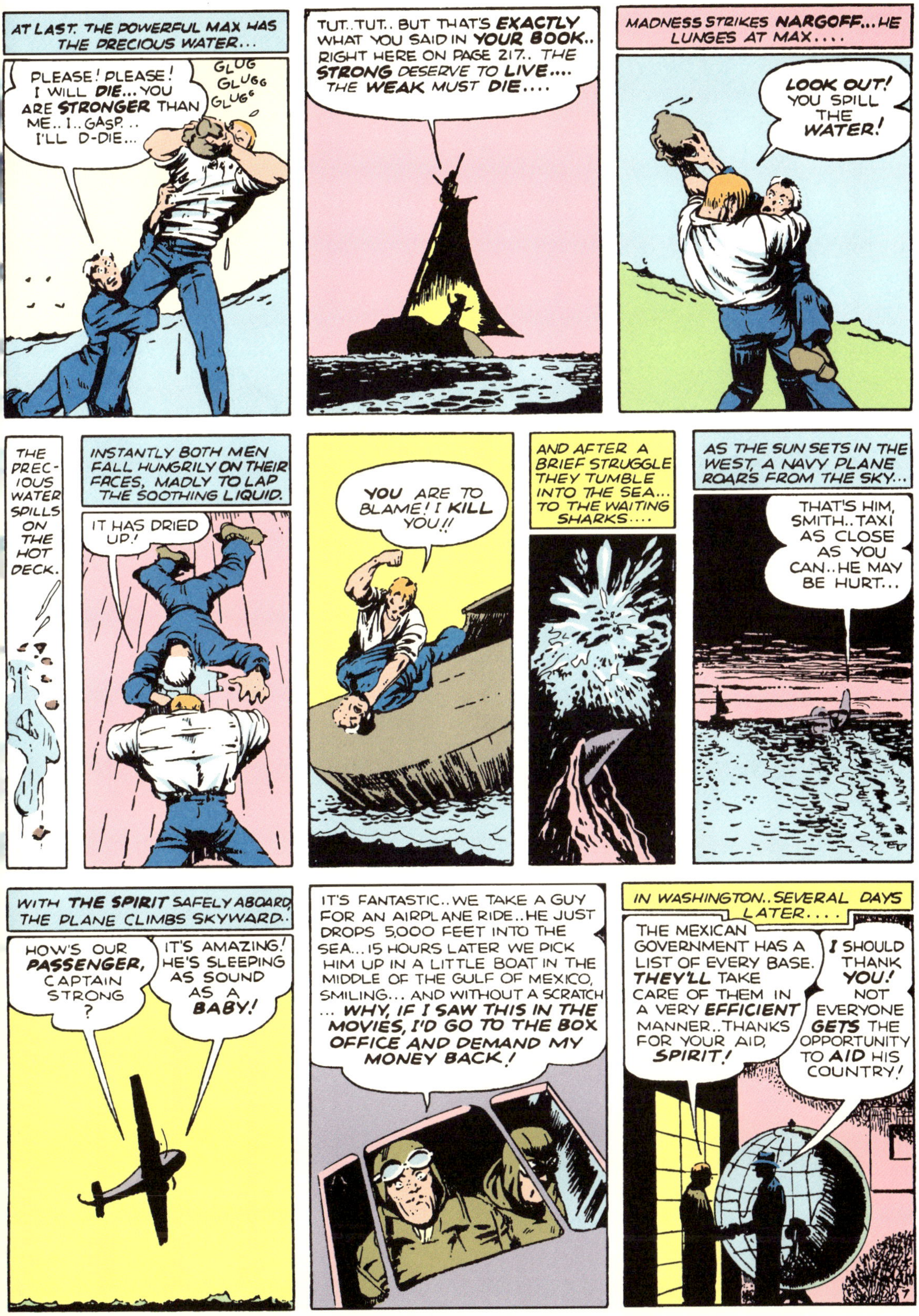
AT LAST. THE POWERFUL MAX HAS THE PRECIOUS WATER...
PLEASE! PLEASE! I WILL DIE... YOU ARE STRONGER THAN ME.. I.. GASP.. I'LL D-DIE...
GLUG GLUGG GLUGG
TUT..TUT.. BUT THAT'S EXACTLY WHAT YOU SAID IN YOUR BOOK.. RIGHT HERE ON PAGE 217.. THE STRONG DESERVE TO LIVE.... THE WEAK MUST DIE....
MADNESS STRIKES NARGOFF... HE LUNGES AT MAX....
LOOK OUT! YOU SPILL THE WATER!
THE PRECIOUS WATER SPILLS ON THE HOT DECK.
INSTANTLY BOTH MEN FALL HUNGRILY ON THEIR FACES, MADLY TO LAP THE SOOTHING LIQUID.
IT HAS DRIED UP!
YOU ARE TO BLAME! I KILL YOU!!
AND AFTER A BRIEF STRUGGLE THEY TUMBLE INTO THE SEA... TO THE WAITING SHARKS....
AS THE SUN SETS IN THE WEST, A NAVY PLANE ROARS FROM THE SKY...
THAT'S HIM, SMITH.. TAXI AS CLOSE AS YOU CAN.. HE MAY BE HURT...
WITH THE SPIRIT SAFELY ABOARD, THE PLANE CLIMBS SKYWARD.
HOW'S OUR PASSENGER, CAPTAIN STRONG ?
IT'S AMAZING! HE'S SLEEPING AS SOUND AS A BABY!
IT'S FANTASTIC.. WE TAKE A GUY FOR AN AIRPLANE RIDE.. HE JUST DROPS 5,000 FEET INTO THE SEA... 15 HOURS LATER WE PICK HIM UP IN A LITTLE BOAT IN THE MIDDLE OF THE GULF OF MEXICO, SMILING... AND WITHOUT A SCRATCH ... WHY, IF I SAW THIS IN THE MOVIES, I'D GO TO THE BOX OFFICE AND DEMAND MY MONEY BACK!
IN WASHINGTON.. SEVERAL DAYS LATER....
THE MEXICAN GOVERNMENT HAS A LIST OF EVERY BASE. THEY'LL TAKE CARE OF THEM IN A VERY EFFICIENT MANNER.. THANKS FOR YOUR AID, SPIRIT!
I SHOULD THANK YOU! NOT EVERYONE GETS THE OPPORTUNITY TO AID HIS COUNTRY!
7

THE WILL EISNER LIBRARY

The Building
City People Notebook
A Contract With God
The Dreamer
Dropsie Avenue: The Neighborhood
Family Matter
Invisible People
A Life Force
Life on Another Planet
New York, the Big City
To the Heart of the Storm
Will Eisner Reader

WILL EISNER'S THE SPIRIT ARCHIVES

Will Eisner's The Spirit
collected in chronological order
in full-color, hardcover editions.

THE DC ARCHIVE EDITIONS

Re-presenting historic comics characters and their stories as they were originally seen.

ALL STAR COMICS ARCHIVES
Volumes 1 - 5
(featuring the adventures of the JUSTICE SOCIETY OF AMERICA)

BATMAN ARCHIVES
Volumes 1 - 4
(The Dark Knight's early adventures from DETECTIVE COMICS)

BATMAN, THE DARK KNIGHT ARCHIVES
Volumes 1 - 2
(The Dark Knight's early adventures from BATMAN)

GOLDEN AGE FLASH ARCHIVES
Volume 1
(The original Scarlet Speedster's adventures from FLASH COMICS)

GOLDEN AGE GREEN LANTERN ARCHIVES
Volume 1
(The adventures of Alan Scott, the original Emerald Gladiator, from ALL-AMERICAN COMICS and the GREEN LANTERN quarterly)

PLASTIC MAN ARCHIVES
Volume 1
(Jack Cole's classic stories from POLICE COMICS)

SHAZAM! ARCHIVES
Volumes 1 - 2
(Captain Marvel's adventures from WHIZ COMICS, CAPTAIN MARVEL ADVENTURES and SPECIAL EDITION COMICS)

GOLDEN AGE STARMAN ARCHIVES
Volume 1
(The Man of Night's earliest adventures from ADVENTURE COMICS)

SUPERMAN ARCHIVES
Volumes 1 - 5
(The Man of Steel's early adventures from SUPERMAN)

SUPERMAN: THE ACTION COMICS ARCHIVES
Volumes 1 - 2
(The Man of Steel's early adventures from ACTION COMICS)

WONDER WOMAN ARCHIVES
Volumes 1 - 2
(The Amazing Amazon's adventures from SENSATION COMICS and WONDER WOMAN)

WORLD'S FINEST COMICS ARCHIVES
Volume 1
(the original team-up tales starring Batman, Superman and Robin)